*Lebanese Blonde*

SWEETWATER FICTION: ORIGINALS

# Lebanese Blonde

A NOVEL

BY

## Joseph Geha

THE UNIVERSITY OF MICHIGAN PRESS
ANN ARBOR

Copyright © by the University of Michigan 2012
All rights reserved

Published in the United States of America by
The University of Michigan Press
Manufactured in the United States of America
⊛ Printed on acid-free paper

2015   2014   2013   2012      4   3   2   1

A CIP catalog record for this book is available from the British Library.

Library of Congress Cataloging-in-Publication Data

Geha, Joseph.
    Lebanese blonde : a novel / by Joseph Geha.
        p.      cm. — (Sweetwater fiction: originals)
        ISBN 978-0-472-11845-8 (cloth : acid-free paper)
        ISBN 978-0-472-02862-7 (e-book)
    I. Title.
    PS3557.E3544L43      2012
    813'.54—dc23                          2012005032

*to Genny and Al*
*in memory of our parents*
*Carmen and Elias*
*and*
*to our cousins Kathy and Mike*
*in memory of their parents*
*Edna and Fred*

# PART ONE

# I

*Before we know it*, that was how Uncle Yousef liked to begin his funeral homilies, with an American phrase he'd adopted to mean *Once upon a time*. *"Before we know it, the ship stop in New York Harbor,"* he would announce to the congregation, *"an' we step down on Ellis Island."* Yousef's voice was high-pitched, and he sprayed his esses—*ssshtep, Ellisssh*. Children in the congregation tittered to see the spit fly, lifting their faces as they followed its arc up into the ceiling lights and then down again toward the casket positioned directly beneath the pulpit between a double row of candlestands. The casket was kept open during the homily, awaiting the final administering of ashes and holy water.

*"He first come here,"* Yousef continued, pointing down at the silk-covered face, *"the same year McKinley was shot."* Or, *"She come the year before McKinley died."* Or two years after. An assassination, rather than the turning of a century, was the hallmark by which an entire generation had signaled its arrival. Settling into America, they grew old with the century. And as they grew old and began to die off, one by one, Yousef spoke at their funerals. Archdeacon of St. Elias Church, educated in the seminaries of Antioch and Damascus, and so almost a priest, he would recount in the formal intonations of High Arabic, how, *before we know it*, ticket agents were riding up Mount Lebanon on donkeyback, sent by steamship companies that needed people to fill their steerage holds. In village after village, from the Biqaa Valley in the north down to the mouth of the Litani River, they announced cheap passage—*Just imagine it, America!*—to a place where one found gold lying in the streets. At the beginning only a

few bought tickets. Those few, anticipating the crash of the silk industry, and understanding that nothing would be left for them after that, not even the work their fathers had done all their lives long, said to one another, *Yallah! Let's go!* So they went, the trickle before the flood. For those who remained, mail began to arrive from America; there were letters to be read aloud by those who could read, and there was something else in the envelopes. American dollars. *W'Allah!*—they had indeed struck gold!

Here Yousef liked to pause, briefly raising both hands to his shoulders as if in benediction, his tiny frame so compressed by age he could barely see over the pulpit's lectern. *"So, the rest of us packed up what we could not sell off, and we followed."* But unlike the many others who came in the great migrations, who also marked their arrival by the shooting of McKinley, the *ibn Arab* from Syria and the Lebanese littoral were not escaping the oppression of unfair regimes. The old folks laughed out loud to hear their grandchildren assume as much. For the Christians, anyway—and the first waves were nearly all Christians from the Mountain—for them the treatment by the Hamidian Turks had been not nearly as repressive as to their Muslim countrymen. All this was before the First World War, of course, and the Great Famine that followed it.

They never came here to stay. Yousef stressed this. They came here to take the gold back with them and live out their days like pashas in the most beautiful mountains of the most beautiful country in all the world. *"But,"* he would add, *"the first step away takes you all the way away."* So that in the end, who remembers the old country? He pondered his own question. Over the years Yousef's eyebrows and mustache had remained black while the hair of his head had turned iron gray. For fun some called him Professor because his bushy hair was reminiscent of a comic popular on the *Ed Sullivan Show*. Also, because of his tendency to hold forth whenever he had an audience, the way his homilies often drifted off on tangents of their own.

*"Forget the old country!"* You rolled up your sleeves instead. You learned the money first, then the language. Books and schools were for your children, not for you. *"America grasps you by the ankles of your children!"* Here Yousef would fall silent, wait for the high, piping echo of his own voice to fade. That trip back to the old country you were planning to take in five years? *"Before you know it, ten years. Before you know it, fifteen!"* Before you knew it, a two-week charter tour in the summer, ex-

4

cursion fare, after your children had sold the store. With luck, you would make it back in time to die in the shadow of Mount Suneen, under the grape arbor of the village where your family name was born. *"But even that is not the end!"* No, in the end your children will send for your body, have it boxed up and brought back to America to be buried. Your dust, now American dust.

Because the *ibn Arab* sometimes got carried away at graveside services, Samir Tammouz's job, once he'd parked the hearse, was to position himself directly behind the immediate family, smelling salts in his pocket, hands at his sides, ready to catch fainters or, if needed, to grab and hold back those who might try to throw themselves onto the descending coffin. But today a sudden cloudburst kept anything like that from happening.

One minute Sam was standing there, his thoughts adrift in Uncle Yousef's homily—What year *was* it McKinley got shot, anyway? 1900? 1902?—and the next minute the sky opened up. It took everyone by surprise—thaw or no thaw, this was still January, still Toledo, Ohio—soaking the mourners even as they rushed to huddle under the canopy tent. And throughout the downpour, Yousef continued on in that high, piping voice of his, from invocation to blessing, one prayer after the next after the next. Not hurrying, not slurring a single syllable. Greek, Syriac, English. By the time he finally ended the service, closing the prayer book with a damp thump, his bushy hair lay matted flat and dripping over his ears.

After Sam dropped the hearse off back at Tammouz & Sons, all he could think about was going home and getting out of his wet clothes. He didn't even touch the lunch his mother had laid out for him, her eggplant *menazlit* with chickpeas and cinnamon tomato sauce; instead, shedding shoes and tie and suit coat, he made straight for the bathroom. There he stood under the shower until finally Mama began rapping on the bathroom door to remind him not to use up all the hot water. When he stepped out, he heard her on the phone in the kitchen. She was speaking Arabic, and he stopped toweling off to listen. It was the funeral home, he could tell by her subdued tone. A moment later, he heard the approach of her slippers on the hall linoleum.

*"Yallah!"* she called out to him, *Get going!* She rattled the doorknob. Good thing he'd remembered to lock it.

"What is it?"

His cousin Aboodeh was on the phone, she said. They needed him back at the funeral home.

"When?"

"Ride now. *Yallah!*"

"But what for?"

"Jeem Weel-zoun," she said, pronouncing *Jim Wilson* as if it were an Arabic name. "He's waitin' for you ride now at the airport." Then, adding another "*Yallah!*" she rattled the doorknob again.

"All right, okay. Tell Bud I'm getting dressed!"

Sam listened for the flap-flap of her slippers before dashing across the hall to his bedroom. His work suit was wet, so his dark sport coat would have to do. Tammouz & Sons insisted on the professional look, even for a Jim Wilson. The funeral home was only a few blocks from here, and the usual routine was for Sam to walk there, take one of the hearses and go pick up Aboodeh, whose new house was all the way over on the East Side. From there it was a straight shot up I-75 to Detroit Metro, where Passenger Jim Wilson would be waiting for them. At the cargo dock. In a hermetically sealed metal box.

He was choosing a necktie when Mama let out a sudden invocation to the Holy Trinity, "*Ism il Ab, ou'l Ibn, ou'l Roh il Idous . . . !*" her voice elevated, meant for him to hear. She was losing the last of her patience. He'd screwed up at work a couple times, nothing serious, and she'd been waiting for the other shoe to drop ever since. He patted down his tie and smiled. As if you could get fired from your own family!

In Little Syria there were plenty of women—Aunt Libby for one—who had come to America believing that over here you roll up your sleeves and work elbow to elbow with the men. But there were also a few like Mama who, in their heart of hearts, never really left the remote hill villages where they had been born. Married off as children practically, to men twice their age, these had become widows in their forties. In their fifties they were like old people who had to be driven to the store, whose mail had to be read to them, notices from the city translated, their bills paid, their own checks written out for them above the large childish loops of their illiterate signatures. As their neighborhoods began to dissolve and their families dispersed into the Greater America beyond Little Syria, the lives of these women became increasingly difficult. To meet their simplest needs, they had to navigate daily the guilty waters between gratitude and

6

resentment. And because they had learned to do so little for themselves, many of them remained, for their children, impossible to leave. Every one of these households had at least one grown, unmarried child.

When Sam was down at the curb, pulling on his overcoat and waiting for a break in traffic, he had the feeling that she was up there in the living room's bay window, ready to lean forward in her chair any minute now and start tapping the pane with her wedding ring.

As he stepped down from the curb, the sudden bray of a siren sent him right back up again. A fire truck lumbered around the corner, so close he could feel the heat of its engine. Then another fire truck, and then a third. Behind him he could hear the carryout's display windows vibrating. There must be a really big one somewhere. Neighborhood businesses had seen a rash of fires lately. Aboodeh said it was most likely arson for insurance, or as he liked to call it, "Syrian Lightning." Typical Aboodeh, with his pinky ring and his imported leather sports jacket: You don't have to be in the know, just sound as if you are.

The wail of the sirens stretched and faded until it was hard to tell whether they were coming or going. Leaning out to see, Sam turned and caught sight of his reflection in the carryout's display window. Something about the face caused him to stop short and take another look.

He hadn't *always* looked so much like her, had he? And yet those cheeks, puffy beneath the eyes, were definitely hers. So were those double worry creases between the eyebrows. He'd heard that such things happened. Married couples beginning to look alike, people who lived together. Even dogs and their masters! Why couldn't Baba have stayed alive a little longer, at least until his son's features had become more fixed? Sam tried jutting his chin out, like Baba's. Narrowing one eye.

But then, sure enough, from the bay window above the carryout, here came the tapping of Mama's wedding ring against the glass. Rapid and insistent, it pierced even the traffic noise. He stepped out to the curb, turned and looked up at her and struck a pose: hands out at his sides, palms up, in Baba's gesture of exasperation. *Yoh! What else?*

He could read her response through the window. *Hiz Teezak!* her lips were saying. *Shake your ass! Yallah! Get a move on! Yallah! Yallah!*

The rain returned, appearing now as an icy, drizzly mist. Sam buttoned the neck of his overcoat. At least Tammouz & Sons wasn't far. Turning the corner off Erie, he could see it already. A funeral home on a dark winter day, you'd think it would look spooky, but all that had been remodeled out of it years ago. Old advertising photos showed a turreted Victorian with ocular attic windows and a stone half-fence in front, topped by iron spikes. Exactly the kind of place you'd choose, Aboodeh liked to say, if you're a Jaycee scouting out a site for next Halloween's haunted house. But back in the sixties, when Aunt Libby had the remodeling done, black was out. Funeral homes had started to brighten up and modernize, replacing velvet drapes with miniblinds and refinishing dark woodwork in stains of blonde. Some places had even begun featuring pastel-colored hearses. The clergy, too, were beginning to look on the bright side. Latin Rite priests started celebrating funeral masses in white vestments, upbeat folk guitar solos replaced the *Dies Irae*. Nowadays at Tammouz & Sons, with the turrets blocked over and the fish-scale shingles on the upper stories sheathed in white aluminum siding, most people wouldn't know what the place really was, if not for the sign set low in the front lawn, its neon outline of a clock above the motto . . . *In Time of Need*.

The office where Aunt Libby ran Tammouz Enterprises was situated off the back hallway, and the keys to the hearses and company limos were hung on a pegboard just outside her door. Sam followed the brick walk that curved between the side of the house and the monument display, slabs of marble and polished granite set up to resemble a family plot, iron fence and all. One of Sam's first jobs had been to weed and hand clip between each and every headstone. One summer, crawling on his knees with the clippers, he'd come up with the idea of finishing off the weeds once and for all by sprinkling around the headstones some leftover glutaraldehyde that he'd found in a metal drum outside the prep-room door. It killed the weeds all right—and every other living thing in a ten-foot radius: grass, bushes, marigolds, a pair of saplings all the way on the other side of the driveway.

An accident, but it immediately became a family story, told for laughs: the time Sammy used embalming fluid as a weed killer. He was still a kid, with hardly any English yet, and already he knew what "fuck-up" meant. Worse, it was a reputation he was beginning to earn. At the funeral home, he was always bumping into stacks of folding chairs or accidentally knocking over rings of wreath wire or fake-marble flower stands. Every closet and hallway and stairwell was kept so cluttered with junk—with votive racks, collapsible biers, urns, candelabras, with pairs of "Praying Hands" in molded Styrofoam—that the whole house was an accident waiting to happen. A bull in a china shop, Sam had overheard Aunt Libby say of him once. She didn't think Sam knew enough English to understand, but he got the gist.

His struggles with English were such that the nuns had repeated him in third grade, and again in fourth. Eventually though, he did adjust, graduating high school the June before last, class of '73. And with honors, too. Not bad, but then again, he was twenty years old at the time!

And so sick of school that he opted to join one of the family businesses, even if it meant he had to start at the bottom. Which was exactly where Aunt Libby had put him. Unfortunately, the bottom was where his tendency toward clumsiness showed itself most starkly. And his absent-mindedness, too. Like the time last fall when he ran out of gas driving the hearse in a funeral procession. It had been his responsibility to keep the tank full, and he *thought* he'd checked it a day or two before, but he couldn't be sure. Either way, it was a sight that nobody in Little Syria would ever forget, a Tammouz & Sons funeral cortege kept waiting in the rain while a handful of mud-splashed mourners pushed the hearse uphill toward a Sunoco station.

Sam wiped his wet shoes on the doormat outside the service entry. It was dark stepping inside. The blinds were drawn, and the air heavy with flowers and cigarettes. Down the hall Aunt Libby's office door was cracked open, emitting a shaft of smoky light. He could hear staticky voices from her police band radio. She always kept the scanner on, a remnant from the old days when Tammouz & Sons operated an ambulance service. He pulled the door shut behind him, turned and felt his shoe strike against something. A wooden folding chair appeared out of the dimness tipping toward him. Quickly, he reached out and gingerly leaned it back, resting against the stack of chairs behind it.

With all the remodeling you'd think somebody would have thought of providing more storage space. For years Uncle Waxy, Aboodeh's father, came back from his morticians' conventions in Las Vegas saying that the one thing Tammouz & Sons really needed was to do exactly that, expand the casket selection room, build some storage sheds out back. But for years business had been shrinking rather than growing. Back in its heyday Tammouz & Sons had served entire generations as a kind of refuge, a place in America where they could do their mourning unashamedly in their own old country language and in their own old country way. But nowadays all that was coming to an end as the *ibn Arab* followed their children out into Greater America, where grandchildren phoned long-distance to make the arrangements. Just like Uncle Yousef said in his homilies.

Sam picked up a rattan wreath from the floor, where somebody could trip over it, and tossed it onto the stack of folding chairs. It slid right off and onto the floor again. To hell with it. He left it there and continued down the hall. Libby's office had been purposely situated in back where her cigarette smoke and the adding machine's clack-and-whir wouldn't disrupt the tranquility of the viewing parlors at the front of the house. Also up front, just off the main entrance, was her brother Waxy's reception office with its upholstered chairs and leather-topped desk for receiving clients and taking information. On the wall behind Waxy's desk hung a pair of icons in gold leaf: one showing St. Michael defeating the dragon, and the other a dark-lidded Mater Dolorosa shedding silver tears. The only thing on the wall in Libby's office was a calendar, and not a Tammouz & Sons religious calendar either, but one from Raceway Park, with the picture of a different horse for every month.

Sam crossed the shaft of light slicing out of Libby's doorway. Glancing over the pegboard, he decided on the new cream-colored hearse—it had hardly been driven yet—and he was reaching up for the keys when he heard his aunt's voice call out, "Hello? S'at you?"

He opened his mouth but stopped short, hearing the electric crackle of his uncle's voice. While Libby continued speaking into the intercom— something about the paperwork for a county indigent case—Sam quietly lifted the keys from the pegboard and made his way toward the service entry, remembering just in time to step over the rattan wreath.

First, before anything else, he checked the gas gauge. It was full, of course. As it should be. As he knew it would be. That's the problem with a reputation, you begin to doubt yourself. He started the engine. It caught, idling so quietly that he had to glance at the dash lights to make sure it hadn't died. He adjusted the mirrors, found and switched on the heat. Then, he sat back a moment just to breathe in the new car smell. The smell of confidence, it made him feel, well . . . *American*. He flipped down the sun visor—it was covered in soft stitched leather, just like the seats—and straightened his necktie knot in the vanity mirror.

Checking for traffic, he slowly backed out of the driveway, careful that the rear end didn't dip and scrape against the asphalt the way the older hearses always did. But of course it didn't, the suspension was brand-new, like floating on air.

Aboodeh's new house was over in East Toledo, across the Maumee. The quickest way there would be to take the Cherry Street Bridge. Normally, a Jim Wilson was a three-man job—one to drive and two to lug the box through airport inspection and down off the loading dock. Lately, though, Tammouz & Sons had been operating shorthanded, and Sam and Aboodeh had had to manage on their own. With the neighborhood changing, there just wasn't enough business to justify even taking on *part*-timers. It was no secret that Libby was keeping Tammouz & Sons going only until her brother felt ready to retire. Aboodeh, too, had seen the writing on the wall. After years of apprenticing to his father, he'd begun attending a series of motivational seminars that went by the acronym DATA, for DAre To Act, where the organizers evangelized salesmanship and brought members up to the podium to give testimony to their business successes, all accompanied by much cheering and clapping. So far, though, none of what Aboodeh called his "venture opportunities" had paid off. His latest, having to do with importing souvenirs out of Beirut, didn't look to Sam to be any more promising, either. "Good luck with that," he'd tell Aboodeh. If Aboodeh ever asked.

Suddenly, an icy gust clattered against the windshield. The rain had returned with a vengeance. Searching for the wiper switch, Sam was only vaguely aware that the hearse seemed to be increasing speed down the hump of the bridge on its descent into Front Street. He lifted his foot from the gas pedal and touched the brake. A light tap, but instantly he felt the rear wheels fishtail sideways. Freezing rain. Oh, shit! When he braked he couldn't steer, when he steered, he couldn't brake. Helpless, he felt the hearse take him on a slow sideways slide toward the curb. Why had he chosen to take the new one? Wasn't Aunt Libby upset enough with him already? The right front tire bumped gently against the curb, and the hearse swung about. Then, a long, slow grind of metal on metal as the entire length of the passenger side scraped against a light pole. The side-view mirror popped up and off and landed on the hood. In it, Sam saw a slowly spinning pickup truck. Then he heard a single, surprisingly loud bang, and the next thing he knew he was on his left side, cheek pressed against the door glass, and the glass moving under him. *Still sliding!* a part of him remarked. *Is that possible?* Then, even as bright pain ran all down his side, that same, logical portion of his mind calmly concluded: *And now, this is death.*

But no, it wasn't. He could hear a siren wailing, constant and loud, right above his head, and he realized that somehow he was lying on his back in an ambulance. And feeling sleepy, very sleepy, despite the pain shooting through his thigh. It had all happened so quickly. He wanted to explain this to the fireman crouched next to him in the ambulance, but the siren was inches from his face, and he could hardly think, much less hear his own voice. *So fast,* he began, then realized he was speaking in Arabic. He tried again, searching for the words in English.

"Shhh . . . ," the fireman's voice cut through the sound of the siren, "*shhh.*" He had wide, staring eyes, as if he too had just had a close call, and he kept trying to put something over Sam's face. Whatever it was, it smelled of rubber and cool air, and it was making a hissing sound. Or maybe that was the fireman.

"*Shhh, shhh . . .*"

"It happened before I knew it!" There, he got it out. But in English it came out sounding like a lie. Just like a lie. The fireman, smiling now and shaking his head, he didn't believe it either.

"*Shhh, now, shhh . . . !*"

~

FIVE SISTERS, COUNT THEM . . .

Kaan makaan. *When he tells his story, if he tells his story, this is how he will begin it, the way* hakawati, *the itinerant storytellers begin, with* Kaan makaan, *the Arabic* Once upon a time, *which means* Perhaps this happened thus, perhaps it did not. *How else to relate his departure out of the Syrian Desert, how he traveled west until he reached the green world? It is all* kaan makaan. *Like memory itself.*

*The memory of his childhood is a blur. His own age he cannot recount, neither the day nor the year of it. Born to desert herders, poorest of the* filaheen, *to a forgotten name.* W'lah, *his father calls him, as if summoning a servant, one more worthless than the white dust beneath their feet. He is not taught to read—can the dust beneath one's feet be instructed?—nor to reckon numbers beyond his five sisters, one for each finger of his mother's hand. He recalls his mother's tattooed hand reaching to light a kerosene lamp. Her hands shredding meat from roasted bones, showing him how it is done. Waving him off, away from the fire, off to fetch her twigs of thyme. Her fingers stripping the leaves from the thyme, rubbing the leaves between her palms. Her eyes closing to smell her own hands.*

*He remembers the early-morning sun already hot, the yelping of wild dogs. And the long-eared goats, the judas dyed red-orange for easier spotting; the sounds of bleating, the sad heave of the donkey; and the smells—orange blossom water, anise and mastic, dung and the burnt-oil bite of his father's rifle. The flies everywhere. The white dust everywhere, on everything; and kneeling in the white dust his sisters, capturing scorpions for the game they called barbout. Five sisters, in the wilderness of the desert where every daughter is a burden. Before they reached womanhood, their father sold them off, far beyond the mountains to the west, each after the other,* filaheen *girls to keep house for the matrons of Damascus or Beirut, to cook, to clean and mend clothes and watch over infants. In return a lump-sum price is paid through a broker. It is abandonment, and it is legal.*

*Their brother counts them on his fingers: one, Hasna, the first to be sent away, bleating like an animal; then two, Reema, gone; three, Fadwa; four, Suha; finally even Baseema, the simple, the always-smiling Baseema, five.*

*Five times he pleads as an elder brother ought, protests with anger and with tears, cursing his father, and then cursing his suffering mother, too, for the silence of her suffering, and five times he is punished, bent over a water trough—almost a grown man by the time his last sister is taken away—to be given lashes with a goat's tether. Afterward, when he is caught trying to pilfer money from his father's satchel—they are paper bills, called piastres; he does not know their worth, but surely there must be enough left to buy back at least Baseema, who has been sold to a toothless old man—his father punishes him for the thief he has become. In fury, his father uses the stock of the rifle to beat him, then takes the goat tether*

13

*and ties him by the ankles to the water trough. He leaves him that way, bleeding from the head, one eye swollen and closed. An entire day. An entire night. It is dawn again before he has worked both legs free.*

*He flees west, traveling on foot and by night, despite the throbbing of his head, despite how the vision in his right eye blurs so that he must keep it half-closed. By the second morning he has reached the gardens bordering Damascus, watered by the River Barada. In the Hamadiyeh souq his hunger is such that he tries to steal food. The approach of soldiers' boots chases him away, their rhythmic scrape-and-stamp.*

*That night he crosses the Barada River, knee-deep now in the dry season. Driven by hunger he climbs goat paths up and up, toward distant thin plumes of cooking fires, far up into the wilderness of the Antilebanon where he leaves the goat paths, pushing through dense scrub to follow the waft and trace of hot dripping fat.*

# 2

The unmistakable aroma of cooked-to-death green beans wafted in through the hospital ventilation system, and then a hint of . . . what? Meatloaf? Maybe. Sam turned to ask Aboodeh, but then thought better of it. Aboodeh probably hadn't been in a hospital for more than a couple minutes at a time, not even when his kids were born. It's different if you're a patient. Sam had been hospitalized before, right here at Mercy. It was when he was in high school, after Aboodeh had told him that he wouldn't catch a cold all winter long if he took two aspirins with a tall glass of orange juice every single night before bed. It worked—from September to April, not even a sniffle. Then, in early May, he was rushed to Mercy with a bleeding ulcer. Aboodeh's fault, in a way, but somehow the whole thing ended up as yet another Sammy-the-screw-up story. All that hadn't happened so long ago that the rhythms of this place weren't still fresh in his memory: those long spaces between visiting hours, the TV soap operas and months-old magazines, and how you begin smelling food long before you hear tray carts rattling off the elevators down the hall. Here at Mercy the aromas came up through the air ducts, floor by floor from the basement kitchens.

He closed his eyes. Strange how he could get so hungry doing nothing but lying in bed all day. Stranger still, he actually *liked* the meals here—Jell-O desserts and all. Compared to what he'd been raised on, the blandness of hospital rice seemed such a novelty. And Cream of Wheat for breakfast! The nurse with the trays couldn't believe that he actually liked Cream of Wheat. She probably wasn't a nurse, but he called them all "Nurse" anyway, even the candy-striper who earnestly passed out magazines. There was one really cute blonde in particular, a physical therapist who assisted him in hobbling up to the solarium and back, whose hair gave off a slight vanilla scent as she leaned in close to help him keep the crutch pads correctly tucked against his ribs.

Nope, hospital life wasn't at all bad. He closed his eyes. Soon, after maybe only a minute, he sensed that Aboodeh had stepped up close to the bed and was staring at him.

"You's awake?"

It wasn't his cousin who'd spoken but Aboodeh's father, Uncle Waxy, and at his side, there was Aunt Libby, too.

Sam reached for the little trapeze suspended above his bed. "Where'd Aboodeh go?" He tried to pull himself up.

"He left a half hour ago," Libby said. "You were sleeping when we got here, so after a while, we had him take your mother home." She cranked the bed up a little and helped reposition his pillows.

"Thanks, Auntie. Wow, those pills must've really kicked in."

"Looka dat han'some face!" Waxy exclaimed. "Not puffy no more. Healin' up good, *hamdillah!*" His words always had a slight after-wheeze to them, as if leaking air. "Howza leg, *habibi?* She's feelin' better?" The breath itself smelled of the clove ointment he used to dose a bad tooth.

"My hip doesn't hurt half as bad as my armpits. The physical therapists got me practicing with crutches already."

"And I'll tell you why," Libby said. "Nowadays they don't want people lying around in the hospital. Not good for you." She looked at him a long moment, as if there was something more. Sam waited. This wasn't like Libby, she usually had no trouble speaking her mind. "You okay, *habibi?*" she said. "I mean, you feeling comfortable?"

"Yeah. Those pain pills, they do the trick, all right."

She gave him an admonishing look. "Well don't get liking them too much."

"Don't worry, Auntie. I don't think they're all that strong, even."

Libby nodded briefly, then sighed. She wasn't here to talk about pills. "You gave us a scare," she said, finally. "Your mama, all of us. You know we love you, right, *habibi?*"

"Look, you guys," Sam said, "I want you both to know I'm really sorry about the new hearse. Really, *really* sorry."

16

Libby looked away, then began rummaging in her purse for cigarettes. Never married, she was in her early sixties, almost ten years older than his mother, but what a difference. Aunt Libby not only spoke English without the slightest accent, she was also first in the family to finish grade school, first to join the armed forces—the WAACs—where she'd spent the Second World War learning accounting and bookkeeping. By the look of her, the war must have been the time of her life. Why else would a woman in 1975 keep her eyebrows plucked to perfectly arched pencil lines and her graying hair pinned into a crowning pouf roll? She favored tailored outfits with padded shoulders, and even her lipstick she applied Betty Boop style, lapping over the lip line and rising to two little points beneath the nose. Which, being a Tammouz nose, was considerable.

"And because we love you . . . ," she lit the cigarette before continuing, her voice full of smoke, ". . . we're worried *sick* about you."

"I don't want you to worry, Auntie."

"Too late," she said, the cigarette bobbing as she spoke. "We're your blood. It's our *business* to worry." She looked to her brother for agreement. Always a formal dresser, at work and away, he'd come to Saturday-afternoon visiting hours in one of his expensive, quietly conservative black suits, looking just like the mortician he was.

"You betcha!"

"I want you guys to know that soon as I'm out of here I intend to pay for the repairs."

"What repairs?" Libby glanced about, careful with the ash on her cigarette. "It was a total loss."

"You's lucky t'be 'live!" Waxy said.

Sam found an ashtray in the bedside drawer. "Then I'll just pay whatever it costs to replace it."

Libby smiled. "Oh, you just will? And how're you gonna just do that?"

"With my Khaleel money."

His aunt and uncle exchanged glances. Years ago Khaleel, Aboodeh's older brother, had died in an auto accident. There was some insurance money, which Uncle Waxy and his wife Nejla, in their grief, refused to touch. Eventually Libby used it to establish a pair of college trust funds, one for Aboodeh, the other for Sam. "No, *habibi,*" Libby said. "That money's for college."

"But it's mine if I need it, right? After all, Aboodeh isn't using his

Khaleel money for college. He 's always investing in those business deals of his."

"Aboodeh, he's using his money to make money," Waxy said. "You's the one need it, d'college, not you cousin."

"If you start spending down your Khaleel money now," Libby added, "you watch how fast it'll go." She shook her head. "You forget about paying us back, that's what insurance is for. No, that's not what we're worried about."

What then? Uncle Waxy cleared his throat, but said nothing. Were they waiting for Sam to ask? He could guess: his wrecking the new hearse was the last straw, and now they wanted this bull out of their china shop. But because they loved him, they worried. Worrying is supposed to be bad for you, you being the worrier. Headaches, ulcers, heart attacks, skin rashes. But does anybody ever think about how dangerous worry is to the one being worried *about?* After years and years and *years* of worrying, most people are willing to see you done for—married off, or secure in some miserable dead-end job, or dead, even *dead*—just so they can finally stop *worrying* about you.

"The docs," Waxy spoke up finally, but again had to clear his throat. There was something wet in there, and it made Sam want to clear his own throat just to hear it. "The docs, they says you gonna be okay. 'Nudder week, they gonna let you outta here." He turned to his sister, who gave him a nod of encouragement. "What we askin' you, *habibi,*" he continued, "is what you gonna do *after* they let you outta here."

"Yeah," Sam shrugged. "I mean, I think about that, too. But it'll be a while yet before I can even walk." His hip injury was essentially a dislocation, and he would have to depend on crutches for a month or more. "But I can promise you one thing."

They waited, silent.

"I won't let you down again. So you don't have to worry about me. I'm serious." He waited, but neither of them would look him in the eye. "I mean it. I swear to God."

"*Hoost, habibi,*" Libby said.

*Habibi,* they kept calling him, Arabic for *sweetheart.* Softening him up. For what, exactly? Sam's best guess was college. They'd made such a big deal last year about his high test scores.

From down the hall came a familiar bump-and-clatter, lunch carts being unloaded off the elevators. "We should let you eat." Libby crushed out her cigarette and turned to her brother. But neither of them made a move to leave.

They'd come determined to settle the matter here and now. And they probably didn't much care how: college, the army, going door-to-door selling thimbles and thread. Because to them, simply the act of setting out was what mattered. That first step that takes you away. *Harakit barrakit*, in Arabic, *Moving and shaking brings luck*. And frankly, how else could they see it? They, their whole generation, had been thrown into adulthood while they were still children. Sam's father was only thirteen and alone when he first came to America, a stowaway. By the time Baba was twenty-three, Sam's age right now, he'd not only started his own business, he'd saved enough money to bring his brother and sister over from the old country. Only when Baba was much older, well into his forties, did he return to the old country. Wearing a fine hat, and his pockets full of Yankee dollars, he had himself brokered an arranged marriage so he could start life all over again. His brother Waxy, too, had married late; Sam and his cousin Aboodeh both grew up the children of old parents.

"Okay, *habibi*," Waxy said. "Lissen'a me a sec. I hadda idea here." Raising a forefinger, he tapped his temple.

"What is it, Uncle?"

"You cousin Aboodeh, did y'know he startin' up 'nudder import deal?"

"Yeah, I knew."

"Perty soon you gonna be up an' walkin' again, yeah?"

"Yeah."

Waxy glanced at Libby, then back at Sam and threw open his arms. "Whaddya say?" He was beaming, as if he couldn't contain his joy.

"About what?"

"Y'wanna go in wid'im?"

"Me? With Aboodeh?" He looked to Aunt Libby. "Doing what?"

She hesitated. But Waxy didn't. "You'd help him out. Like, I dunno. Like a . . . a assistant!"

"I don't know the first thing about business."

"You don't have to," Libby chimed in, finally. "Sammy, *habibi*, your uncle's right. And what your cousin told me he needs right now is somebody he knows. Somebody he can trust. A cousin."

"Aboodeh said that?" He didn't want to imply his aunt was lying, but he really doubted those were Aboodeh's words.

Libby held up one hand as if taking an oath. "From his own lips."

"I don't know, Auntie, I wasn't expecting this. I'm not even sure what exactly he's importing."

"Some nice souvenirs from the old country. Brass trays, those little *derbekee* drums. Worry beads."

"Tourist shit," Waxy added, as if to specify. "He's buyin' it cheap outta Beirut."

"And Aboodeh wants me in on this?"

"More than wants you," Libby smiled. "He needs you." Then she added, her smile turning grim, "He needs our backing, and that means he needs you."

"*Khallas!*" Waxy exclaimed, brushing the palms of his hands together, *Finished!* They'd said what they'd come here to say, and now the matter was settled. They were handing him over to Aboodeh. The bull was out of their china shop and, quick as a wink, they'd shut the door behind it. *Khallas! The end!*

At home, Sam worked his hip cautiously, the way the physical therapist had shown him, first stretching through a series of leg lifts, afterward biking at a slow pedal with the exercycle's resistance tension dialed low. Five miles of that, it took a while. The radio helped, and so did marking each day's progress on a map that he'd thumbtacked to the wall, an insert from an old *National Geographic* depicting the ancient Mediterranean. After each workout, he used a red felt-tipped pen to add another dot, representing five miles. Just off crutches, he'd started in Phoenicia, the Lebanon of antiquity, and followed an imaginary route west and then north along the Syrian shore. That was in the middle of February. Now, nearly a month later, he was rounding the coast of Phrygia, making for Troy and the Dardanelles. His plan was to circle half the Mediterranean, Athens, Rome, down the boot to Sicily, then Carthage, Alexandria, across Sinai, and north again through Philistia, past Judah and Israel, all the way back home to Phoenicia.

The physical therapist had said to take it easy, and he did. He wasn't sweating, not even breathing hard as the numbers on the handlebar odometer neared today's five-mile increment. Just the same, he needed to wash up before Aboodeh dropped by. Apparently an unexpected development had occurred in the import venture—"a wrinkle," he'd called it—that Sam probably ought to be "filled in" about. Must be some wrinkle, Sam thought, because so far he hadn't been "filled in" about anything *else* concerning the venture. For weeks now, his cousin had either sidestepped or completely brushed aside Sam's questions, advising him that, "for the time being," it was best that he focus instead on healing and getting back on his feet. In other words, don't butt in where you're not wanted. Nor, for his part, did Sam care to go where he wasn't welcome. Aboodeh was six years his senior, so this was nothing new between them.

Sam slowed his pedaling, then ceased entirely, forearms resting on the handlebars. Whenever Aboodeh stopped by they usually ended up across the street at the Yankee Cafe for coffee or something to eat. After breakfast there the other day, he'd checked the schedule taped to the cash register and noticed that the new blonde waitress was working the evening shift all week. So, although he'd already shaved this morning, for tonight he'd probably need a quick once-over. Reaching to switch off the radio, he leaned back a little more to catch a glimpse of himself in the mirror above the sink. The men in his family all had that blue-green tinge no matter how close the shave. "An' somma d'women, too," Uncle Waxy liked to add, not entirely joking. During his apprenticeship in Chicago, Uncle Waxy had learned to apply cosmetics on all the different skin types. That was back in the twenties, and he claimed to have advised Al Capone himself to use talc on his left cheek and along the side of his jaw because an olive complexion, more than any other skin type, shows scars so readily.

Dismounting, Sam had to be careful not to bump his head. The space for the exercycle was an alcove with a low, stepped ceiling, the upper side of which formed the staircase leading to the front door of Mama's apartment. He'd had a couple close calls on those stairs when he was fresh out of the hospital. Climbing stairs was never a problem, just position the crutch tips, press with the forearms, hop-and-lift. But descending them, the sense of steepness an inch from his toes unnerved him, looking down into the empty depth in front of him. He sometimes felt as if his center of gravity had shifted; his weight-bearing leg sometimes refused to let go, or else his arms seized up to keep from pushing too hard on the crutch handles and flying out into thin air. After a couple of close calls, Libby had his things moved from Mama's down to here. Since Tammouz Realty owned the entire building, she provided the place rent-free. Then again, what *could* she charge for a place so small, so rudimentary, that the realty couldn't even list it as an efficiency? Originally a part of the store's back room, its door opened onto the alley. There was no kitchen, only a hot plate, but the other essentials were there: commode, shower head piped in over a corner drain in the cement floor, next to a galvanized metal sink. By adding a cot-sized bed, a card table, the exercycle, Sam had made a place of his own. His first. Mama may be just upstairs, and behind the wall the store that Baba's old stock boy, Gene Moon, now managed. But back here was his alone. For the first time in his life, Samir Tammouz had a door he could go in or out of as he alone decided.

His cousin Aboodeh saw it all differently, of course. When he came by to help with the moving, he'd given the place a slow once-over, and declared it "Totally a shithole." And over the past few weeks, the more Sam tried to make the space livable—a portable TV, snap-on lampshades for the two ceiling fixtures, an old Turkish rug of his father's to cover the cold cement—the broader Aboodeh's joking became: "So now it's a *carpeted* shithole!" As usual with his cousin, Sam only shrugged. Aboodeh had a wife and two noisy kids at home, and his mockery bore more than a trace of envy.

All the more reason for his crowing. When things were going his way, he liked to vocalize a low, husky singsong that, for the sake of rhyme, used his true name, Abdullah, of which "Aboodeh" is a common diminutive, and he whisper-sang it like the crowing of a hoarse rooster:

*I'm Abdoolah the Cool-ah,*
*The women's rul-ah,*
*Downtown money spend-ah,*
*Woman's body bend-ah,*
*The men's threat*
*And the ladies' pet!*

Aboodeh wore pointy Italian shoes and suits in those new polyester blends that held pleats so sharp you could cut a finger on them. He liked jewelry, too, favoring yellow gold—ID bracelet, neck chain. His gift to himself last Christmas was a chunky gold pinky ring.

The building's hot water boiler, situated between the store and the little apartment, kept the place so warm that Sam used the back wall to hang his wash. He had finished dressing and was draping his bath towel on the clothesline when he heard behind him the sound of Aboodeh's pinky ring tapping—*tik! tik! tik!*—on the steamed-over glass of the alley window.

Limping a little, he unlocked the double bolts and stepped back as his cousin threw open the door and strode past him, heel plates clicking on the cement threshold. "It's like a Turkish bath in here!" Aboodeh announced. He paused to loosen his necktie and glance about. "Still a shithole, though." He was quite a bit shorter than Sam, and heavier, too, with big shoulders and a thick neck that, along with wide sideburns trimmed stylishly to the jawline, gave him a sloping, bullet-headed look. Especially now as he bent over, making a little show of nosing about the place. He lifted a copy of *Playboy* from the TV tray next to Sam's bed, flipped it open and quickly examined the centerfold. "*Real* blonde," he said, appreciatively. "So, that's what you do around here all day," he dropped the magazine onto the bed. "Jerk off and ride that bike?" Crossing over to the alcove, he bent down to examine the map taped to the wall in front of the exercycle. "Put in your time today?" He traced the red line with his fingertip.

"Five miles."

"Five? It's gonna take you forever to go all the way around." As he spoke he reached into the pocket of his leather sports jacket. He took something out and casually held the hand behind his back.

"I'm only going halfway around," Sam explained. "I'm turning south at Italy, then across Africa and up again."

"What happens when you hit water?"

Sam shrugged. "I don't know, pretend there's a bridge?"

"Pretend." Aboodeh smiled and shook his head. Then he brought his hand around and held out what looked like a small booklet. "Anyway, happy birthday."

"It's not my birthday."

"So *pretend* it's your birthday. Here, take it."

It was a brochure from a travel bureau. Titled "Paris of the Middle East," it opened like a map, revealing glossy photos of Beirut—sidewalk cafes, casinos, beaches, snowy ski lifts. Sam looked up, puzzled. "What is this?"

"I told you something came up about our venture. A wrinkle."

"Our?"

"Let's sit down a minute, okay?"

After they were settled in, facing one another across Sam's card table, Aboodeh remained silent a moment before bluntly announcing that in a few weeks he needed to make a trip to Beirut. "Personally tie up some loose ends."

Sam knew there had to be more. "So?"

"So . . ." Taking a cigar from the breast pocket of his leather jacket, Aboodeh made a big deal out of unwrapping it from its cellophane, patting his pockets for a match. Then he put the cigar down and smiled at Sam.

"What?"

"So, how would you like to come along? You and me, end of April!"

"You serious?"

"Look, I'm still just getting my ducks in a row," Aboodeh began, his voice turned shy by cautious enthusiasm, "but swear to God, Sammy, it already looks like this thing is gonna fly. I mean really, *really* take off." He waited, but Sam had nothing to say. Aboodeh looked hurt. "It's not like we're putting you on a chain gang. I've heard you talk about how you'd like to go back, see what it's like there as a grown-up. So now's your chance." It was true, but how did Aboodeh know? Sam would never mention such a thing to his cousin, how he sometimes found himself thinking—well not exactly, not consciously anyway, more like daydreaming—about what if he went back to the old country and discovered that for once in his life he actually felt as if he fit in, and the problem all along, all his growing up, had been America? "Think of it," Aboodeh was saying, "six weeks from now you'll be in Beirut, the fucking Las Vegas of the Middle East! You'll have money in your pocket and a place to stay, free of charge, courtesy of Salma's cousins."

"*What* cousins?" Salma was Aboodeh's wife.

Aboodeh paused briefly to compose his thoughts, then launched into a rehearsed sales pitch about how his import venture was now incorporating—his word—the services of a couple of Salma's cousins back in the old country. They worked at Beirut Airport, these cousins, and they'd agreed to handle the supply end, along with all the warehousing and shipping. Stateside, Aboodeh would function as a middleman, accepting shipment and transporting the goods on to their distributor up in Detroit.

"They have names, Salma's cousins?"

"Mutraneh. Phares and Nabil Mutraneh." Aboodeh leaned in across the table. "Now, here's the really sweet part: the Mutranehs are being supplied by cousins of *theirs* who'll be our wholesalers."

"How's that the really sweet part?"

"Cousins, dealing with cousins?" Aboodeh said. "It means we'll be able to deal directly." He picked up the cigar and stuck it in his mouth, unlit.

"So, these wholesaler cousins of Salma's cousins, they're wholesalers of—*what* exactly?"

"Locally created artifacts."

"And who'd you say you're selling all these *artifacts* to?"

"I didn't say. Don't go running ahead of me." He tamped the cigar on the table as if it were a cigarette. "*We* don't sell *any*thing. The distributor's already in place. Up in Detroit." He held up a hand before Sam could interrupt. "Up there," he pointed to the ceiling, "there happens to be *the* perfect market for our product." He brought the finger down, aiming it like a pistol at Sam. "Detroit's got the fastest-growing Arabic-speaking population outside the Middle East." He paused a moment to let that fact sink in before dropping his thumb like a hammer. "Pow! And every last one of them's hungry for a taste of home, a souvenir of the old country!"

"So why do you want me?"

Aboodeh sat back. "I don't."

"That's what I thought."

Aboodeh sighed, then swept the air clear with his hand. "Look. The bottom line is this: I need you because I need Tammouz & Sons. If I don't bring you in Libby won't let me use the funeral home as a sponsoring business."

"I don't get it. What does a mortuary have to do with importing, anyway?"

Aboodeh smiled patiently. "Funeral homes are licensed carriers."

"So?"

"So, when you're just starting out, it's easier if you don't have to reinvent the wheel. I mean, the framework's already in place—insurance, pre-certified lines of credit, shipping licenses. If we're lucky maybe even a built-in shelter against tariff charges." He paused to smile conspiratorially, as if Sam were following. Knowing all along that he couldn't possibly be. "When you get down to it, business is business, and everybody—wholesalers, customs officials, distributors—they all prefer dealing with a ready-made, established business. Matter of fact, using the funeral home as a springboard is what got Salma's cousins to sign on."

"Aunt Libby okayed this?"

"No risk to her." He reminded Sam that Libby had been allowing the mortuary to operate in the red—the only satellite business out of all the Tammouz Enterprises that wasn't making money—so that every morning her brother Waxy had a reason to get out of bed. And for the tax write-off, of course. "Bringing *you* in was her idea. She said if she's going to help me out, then I'd have to help you out. Take you along, get your feet wet in that big world out there."

Sam picked up the glossy brochure.

"I *need* you, Sammy." Aboodeh shook his head. "I need this one to work. Look, I admit that so far my record hasn't been all that great. But I'm convinced that this one's gonna take off and fly. I'm betting everything it will."

"What everything? Your Khaleel money?"

"There isn't much left of that. I took a second mortgage out on my house."

"You did?" Sam let out a low whistle.

"Salma signed on. I told you, my suppliers in the old country are her cousins. Her *first* cousins. Like you and me." Gazing up at the ceiling, he recalled aloud the Arabic adage, *"My brother and me against my cousin, my cousin and me against the world."* He leaned forward again, hands flat on the table. "Come on, Sammy, I need my cousin. I'll deal with the airline, you find your passport, make sure it's up to date."

"I gotta think it over."

"Think it over in Beirut." Aboodeh plucked the brochure out of Sam's hands. "Aw, come on, Cuz, didn't you ever for once in your life want to just push your luck and see where it takes you? Put some *real* miles on that map of yours?" He spread the brochure open on the table. "Jesus, I can't believe I actually have to talk you into a month in Beirut."

"A month?"

"Longer if you like it there."

"Um," Sam began, then looked down, shrugged.

"What?"

"Since Libby and Waxy made me a part of this venture, aren't I supposed to be getting some kind of pay, or expenses? Or something? I mean, now that I'm walking, I'm gonna need some, you know, walking-around money."

With a glance that said I knew this was coming, Aboodeh pulled a roll of bills from his trousers pocket—he called it carrying his money "raw"— and peeled off two tens. "Here, and when you need some more, just tell me. I'll get you on a regular payroll, but not till this thing gets going."

Sam looked suspiciously at the money in his hand. "C'mon, Bud," he said, "is it really just tourist shit you're importing?"

"We," Aboodeh corrected him, "*we*. And yeah," he grinned sheepishly, "to start." Then, not grinning, he added, "But eventually, maybe finer stuff."

"Like . . . ?"

"Jewelry, maybe. Rings, cufflinks, those bangle bracelets the women wear. All hand crafted. And maybe spices, too, different coffees. And who knows? Maybe gold."

"Gold?"

"Gold is cheap over there."

"How can that be? Isn't the price of gold . . . the price of gold? How can it be cheaper one place from another?"

"Well," Aboodeh smiled mysteriously, " it's complicated."

Sam gave his cousin a level look. "Is there a chance we can get into trouble here?"

"Trouble?" Aboodeh laughed. "Sammy, you're twenty-three years old. You don't have a girlfriend. You don't have a car. You ride a bike that goes *no*where. You don't even have a *job* yet. Guy like you, I think you could *use* a little trouble!"

BOU'MISHMISH

*A young man must eat, even though he lacks money, lacks identity papers, lacks the ability to read the simplest signpost. His hunger directs him out* of the wilderness toward a foothill town where the cries of market-day vendors summon him, the single word "Pomegranates!" in a high dying wail—"Sweet like roses! Good for the newly weaned baby!"—until another rises, overlapping the first: "Wa-alnuts! They have a white heart! Apricots from Damascus! Dimpled like a baby's hands!"

The apricots are sweet. He has one in his mouth and is stuffing two more into his shirt when a voice shouts, "Thief!" and hands grasp him from behind and pull him down onto the paving stones.

The vendors hand him over to the only law in this remote hill region, a pair of armed men who keep their faces hidden behind colored scarves. They handcuff his wrists and cover his head with a cotton sack and lead him, shuffling like a blind man, away from the town. There is a gap of light beneath his chin. Peering down to keep from stumbling, he sees with his good eye that they are ascending a foot path through mountain scrub.

After a time he hears the approach of other voices. Young-sounding, joshing one another like boys. He is made to sit on the bare ground and the sack is yanked from his head. They are a dozen or so seated around a small fire, all armed with pistols and shotguns. And like the first two, they also have scarves pulled up over their noses. Some wear blue denim trousers, others the baggy, old-fashioned sharwaali of the Mountain people. They quiet down as they squat on the ground in a half-circle facing him. And wait. One keeps a kid goat on a tether. It bleats pitiably as they wait. Soon, one after another they reach into their pockets and take out pistachios and green almonds. They crack the nuts and use two fingers to insert the meat beneath the flaps of their scarves. They toss the shells into the fire. One of them places a lighted coal atop a brass nargileh waterpipe. The coal flares and the water in the jar beneath bubbles. The smoke is tobacco mixed with hashish. The bleating goat reminds him of the home he left for this, and the sound of the cracking shells makes his mouth water. He swallows. Their scarves wag side to side as they chew. He is a young man, too. He, too, must eat. Let them do what they will—cut off his hand for a thief, cut off his head, even. He holds up his head, looks into their eyes and asks what it is they are waiting for.

The one with the goat shrugs, as if the answer is obvious. He lifts his scarf enough to suck deeply on the tube of a water pipe that has been passed to him. He holds the smoke a moment or two before replying that they have sent for their sheikh shebaab.

Even a herder from the Eastern Desert has heard how every mountain district has an old man leading his own private force of young toughs.

When their sheikh shebaab arrives, the young men touch their foreheads in a show of respect. He too wears a scarf. It is silky looking, and pink, like something taken from a woman. He wears it tucked into the neck of his military jacket. Squatting by the fire, he pulls down the scarf and smiles. His mustache is white in the growing dusk, his teeth square and yellow. "Do you know who we are?" he asks.

"Who has not heard of the Old Man of the Mountain? And the hashishsheen who do his bidding?"

This makes the sheikh shebaab laugh. "These assassins of mine, they accuse you of theft. Bou'mishmish, they call you, lover of apricots." He glances back toward his men, a signal to pull down their scarves as well. Men? They are boys, their upper lips still downy. "Tell me, Bou'mishmish, do you confess it?"

Bou'mishmish, better than the name his father gave him. So be it, then. Bou'mishmish raises his chin. "W'Allah, I do confess it."

The sheikh's face darkens. Swiftly, he raises the back of his hand, a master's threat. "Shall I punish you? Shall I give you a second dead eye? Tell me why I should hold back!"

Bou'mishmish keeps his head up. "I was hungry," he says, the simplest defense, and incontestable.

Slowly, the sheikh lowers his hand. "For food, then?" He stands, knees crackling, and turns toward the half-circle of faces, firelit now. "You are the thieves!" he shouts, and the boys flinch. "Not this one. You steal my sustenance by bringing me—what? Another mouth to feed?"

He unclips a military flashlight from his belt and holds it while one of his boys unlocks the handcuffs. By flashlight, Bou'mishmish devours what they bring him to eat—bread and white cheese and dry lemon sausage.

The mountain stars gleam and flicker behind the old man's head as he watches Bou'mishmish eat.

"Ya Sheikh," Bou'mishmish says, "make me one of yours."

"Can you shoot, with a dead eye such as you have?"

29

Bou'mishmish lifts his chin, the upward nod that means no.

The sheikh sighs, his voice a weary father's voice, "No. I thought not. Can you read, then? Or go into the city squares and tell me what you have overheard in Engleez or in Frenshowi?"

Bou'mishmish lifts his chin. "No."

"Can you count, even?"

"Only my five sisters."

"Have you learned nothing, then?" Still shaking his head, the sheikh steps away into the dark.

"That goat." Bou'mishmish points to it and explains, his voice trembling, how he could gut and skin it, the words coming out of him urgently as he recalls the work of his mother's hands, how she used to steep the butchered meat in vinegar overnight. Next day he would slice pockets in the meat and stuff them with garlic and thyme and, well, pistachios and . . . and apricots, and then sew up the pockets and encase it all in salt and, and then heap hot coals over the salt. "Does the thyme plant grow in these mountains?" Bou'mishmish asks a young man squatting near him.

The young man is about to answer when they are startled by a pistol shot and the goat begins a frantic thrashing. The sheikh fires a second bullet, and then a third, until the thrashing stops.

# 3

The hood vent over the Yankee Cafe's fry station was beginning to vibrate again, an intermittent buzz and rattle that got everything on the wall behind it vibrating as well, the suspended pans and ladles, the clock, the magnetized sign announcing:

*The Yankee Cafe*
*Just Like Home*
*You Don't Always Get What You Want . . .*

Seated on a counter stool next to his cousin, Sam was looking at what he wanted. The new waitress worked the row of booths with a carafe in each hand, decaf and regular, trying to keep up with the sudden rush, slowing down only when she paused to pour. As she poured, she frowned in concentration. Even frowning, she had a pretty face, heart shaped with an angular little chin. Her hair was long and blonde, and what she didn't tuck under the hairnet she had tied into a thick, shiny ponytail that quivered with the dip-and-bob rhythm of topping coffee mugs.

"Probably married," Sam said. "Probably has two kids and a dog."

"One kid," Aboodeh said. "No dog."

"You talked to her?"

"Who can resist Abdoolah the Coolah?" He tugged a paper napkin from the dispenser and placed it under his mug. "Oh, and she's got no husband, either."

"You just came out and asked her?"

"I keep telling you, Sammy. You gotta get 'em laughing, that's the key."

Outside, the wind picked up, gusting noisily against the plate glass. They both spun around on their stools to look. It was springtime by the calendar, mid-April, but the radio said it might snow by morning. In a couple weeks they'd be in Beirut, where it was warm all year round. Sam turned back. The new waitress was working her way up the counter toward them again.

Get them laughing. Yeah. Easy for Aboodeh to say.

"Top you gentlemen off?" Up close, her uniform's stiff pink fabric made a rustling noise. *Nikki* it said on her plastic nametag.

Soon the rush began to ebb as customers with places to go pushed away coffee cups and counted out tips in nickels and dimes. In a matter of minutes the place had quieted enough for the fry cook to light a cigarette as he scraped the griddle top with a spatula. Sam watched Nikki lift a tray of dirty dishes and carry it into the back room. Only a second or two later, she stepped out again. Her face was flushed, and she stood looking nervously about as if she didn't know what to do next. Then she turned her attention up the counter, and Sam looked down. Had she sensed him watching her? He studied the steam rising from the surface of his coffee.

"You're not taking off yet, are you?" With the fan noise Sam hadn't heard her come up. She was addressing his cousin.

"Why, what's up?" Aboodeh asked.

She made a face, curling down the corners of her mouth. "Didn't you say you work for the same people that own this place?"

"Yep," Aboodeh replied. "Tammouz Enterprises."

"Okay, then. I was wondering if you would—" She glanced toward the fry cook then leaned in, elbows on the counter. "If you're not doing anything right now, would you mind doing me a quick favor? Since we both work for the same people and all?"

"Depends on the favor," Aboodeh said.

"I was just in the back room?" She kept her voice low, but not so they couldn't hear her. "And there's this *mouse*. It's dead. In a trap and everything? And it's been there all day."

"You're in luck," Aboodeh said. "This big guy here, he's the man you need." He reached up and clapped Sam on the shoulder. "My cousin Sammy not only works for Tammouz, too, he specializes in maintenance jobs."

"Really?" Nikki turned her attention now to Sam. Her eyes were a deep brown. Like dark chocolate.

"I do repair work, too."

"You do?" She looked interested.

"Yeah," Sam said. "Pretty much." It was true, in a way. While he was assigned to Tammouz Realty, he'd learned a fair amount watching and assisting the maintenance repairmen. He actually liked using tools. "So, this mouse, it's been there all day, huh?"

"Ever since I punched in. I thought somebody'd get rid of it by now, but some people." She glanced meaningfully in the direction of the fry cook.

"Not a problem." Sam was already on his feet.

"It's back there under the sinks," Nikki said, her voice thickening with gratitude and relief. "The two double sinks? Just past the restroom? You'll see it."

Sam was conscious of her eyes still on him as he rounded the counter, and he liked the feeling. Her hero.

In the back room, he squatted for a look under the double sinks and immediately stood back up again. All day? Jesus, more like all month! The damned thing had *mold* on it! He found a scorched oven mitt which he used to pick up and carry the mouse, trap and all, out to the alley. Afterward he felt he had to wash his hands anyway. The dispenser above the sinks was out of towels, of course.

Wiping his hands on his jeans, he stepped out of the back room to see Nikki laughing and shaking her head in disbelief at something Aboodeh was telling her. "Aw, come on!" she protested. "Honest?"

"Honest to God," Aboodeh insisted. "Tell her, Sammy."

"Tell her what?" He straddled his stool and sat down.

"What're we supposed to do when we accidentally drop a piece of bread." He flicked Sam a play-along wink. "We gotta pick it up right away and . . . ?"

"Kiss it."

Nikki smiled suspiciously.

"No, really," Aboodeh said, all wide-eyed innocence. "You can't *make* this stuff up!" And he went on about more superstitions: flipping an overturned slipper so it doesn't face God; not going directly home after being out in the world so the *djinn* and *afareet* don't learn where you live.

"The who?" She wasn't quite laughing, yet. So he began telling her about the sliver of the True Cross his father wore on a string around his neck when a pair of customers came in, Toledo Edison linemen in yellow hard hats. They took stools at the other end of the counter, and she reached for the carafes on the coffee station behind her.

"Easy, sweetheart," Aboodeh cautioned. "If you spill any it's seven years bad luck, y'know!"

"That's for *mirrors!*" she laughed, moving on to the linemen's booth.

"Hold on a sec," Aboodeh protested. "We haven't even told you about the Evil Eye yet!" He waited until she was beyond hearing before he turned back to Sam. "You know what?" he said. "Couple times there I thought she might be giving you the eye."

"Aw, bullshit."

"No, seriously." Aboodeh turned to watch her a moment. "She's got great hair. But with those brown, brown eyes, a guy can't really tell. Only one way to find out for sure."

"Find out what?"

He winked. "Whether or not she's a *real* blonde."

Luck is made by stirring things up, *harakit barrakit*. Sam decided to bide his time and let a few days go by before returning to the Yankee, choosing the quietest part of the graveyard shift, that dead hour between the last of the bar crowd and the beginning of breakfast rush.

"You're up late tonight," she said, pouring his coffee.

"Or early. I just might be getting an early start."

"There I go," she said, shaking her head, "jumping to conclusions." She turned to replace the coffee carafe but changed her mind and poured herself a mug as well. After all, they were alone in the place, this being the middle of the week, and she the only waitress on duty. A minute ago even the fry cook had lit a cigarette and stepped into the back room.

"It's supposed to get cold again," she said. "And I thought Michigan weather was bad."

"You heard of April in Paris? Well, welcome to April in Toledo."

"I think it actually wants to *snow* again."

"Speaking of Paris, they say it's like Paris where I'm going," Sam said, and when she cocked her head questioningly, he added, "Beirut. In Lebanon."

"Really?"

"Yeah. Thought you knew. My cousin and me, we'll be gone a month. At least a month. Maybe longer."

She smiled a polite, lucky-you smile. "So, the weather's nice there now?" she asked.

"Like southern California."

"Halfway around the world," she said wistfully. Perching her elbows on the countertop, she cupped her cheeks in her hands, a pose that can make an already pretty face look striking.

"Not for me, it isn't." He looked down to sip his coffee. "For me, right *here's* the other side of the world. I was born over there."

She brightened. "Ah-*ha!* I *thought* I heard an accent!" But she must have read something in his expression and quickly added, "I mean, just a little? A touch?"

"Yeah," Sam shrugged. "I don't know why, but sometimes it's more noticeable than others." He wondered whether she was aware of the fry station's wavy-mirrored wall tiles directly behind her, and how, when she leaned on the counter like that, canting her body at a slight angle, they caught a wavy reflection of her sweet, out-thrust bottom. Was she shifting ever so slightly side to side like that on purpose?

"Uh-oh," she said, glancing up at the plate glass windows. She put down her coffee mug and stepped back. "Don't say I didn't tell you so."

He turned to look. Huge, April-wet snowflakes were dropping through the streetlamp's arc, plopping heavily onto the windshields of the cars parked along the curb. "They must be big as half-dollars," he said.

"I *hate* driving in snow."

"It's too warm out to stick."

"It better not." If it did accumulate, she swore she had half a mind to call her son, Deano, in sick from school tomorrow. The only thing holding her back was that he'd missed so many days already that the school was threatening to hold him back another year. "Punishing a kid for allergy attacks." She shook her head slowly.

Sam, too, shook his head. "What grade's he in?"

Dean was *supposed* to be in fifth grade, she explained, but had been kept back in fourth. "He's highly allergic. Highly." The school district, however, didn't make allowances for that. "He inherited the allergies from me."

She must have had him young, Sam thought. "I got held back in fourth grade, too," he said.

"Really?"

"Because of my English. When I first came to America."

She was looking beyond him, out at the snow, so he turned and watched with her. Hypnotic, how steadily it fell. Into the arc of light, out of it again, appearing and disappearing. "I used to have a house in Michigan," she said. "There was a kitchen window that got broken. The whole bottom pane knocked out? This one time, right before Deano and me moved away, we sat on the floor with a blanket around us and watched the snowflakes come floating in. They were moving, like, in slow motion until, all at once, they lifted up over the heat duct and . . . poof! Gone before they could even touch down. It was beautiful."

For a time the only sound was a faint buzzing from the menu board's neon border. Finishing the last of her coffee, Nikki locked her fingers around the empty mug and looked up directly into his eyes. Was she waiting for him to say something? The moment grew awkward, and she laughed. "More coffee?" she asked.

"Please."

Watching her turn to reach for the carafe on the coffee station behind her, he caught the wiggling reflection of her face in the wavy-mirrored tiles, looking back at him.

"Where in Michigan?" he asked as she finished pouring. "Your house with the broken window."

"Up in Ann Arbor."

"A house in Ann Arbor?" He put down his mug.

She thought a moment, touching her hairnet. "Lost it in the divorce."

"In Ann Arbor?"

"Hey, plenty of working stiffs live in Ann Arbor. Leonard used to say that college professors need their cars fixed, too, like anybody else. Besides, it wasn't a mansion or anything. Only two bedrooms. Only one bath. No basement even, just a crawl. But still," she raised one hand as if testifying, "it was *my* dream come true." Lowering her hand, she placed it on the counter, resting so close to his that all he had to do to touch it was slide his own hand over ever so slightly.

"So, what happened with the house? I mean, how did your ex end up with it?"

"I let him have it, that's how." Since the decision to break up was mutual, Leonard had convinced her to share the same lawyer, claiming it would save them both money. "Sure, what did I care? All I wanted was Deano and me out, O-U-T." She chuckled. "And out is *all* I got."

"Well, you got Dean, too. At least you got custody."

"Oh, it was never a *custody* battle." Leonard, she explained, was not Deano's father. He'd talked about adopting, but never got around to it. "Typical."

She didn't polish her nails, in fact she had them cut short and square, probably a necessity, working the way she did. He was looking down at her hand when it moved, rose up to find a strand of hair that had escaped the hairnet. "What did you do, scrimp and save, so you can vacation in Beirut?" she asked, tucking the tendril back behind her ear.

"It's not a vacation, it's a business trip. I'm going there with my cousin Bud."

"Oh, him?" She rolled her eyes.

"You know what he calls himself, don't you? Abdoolah the Coolah."

She laughed. Finally. "You work for him?"

"For the family, really. We're both with Tammouz Enterprises, which includes the funeral home and the realty company. They own this place, too. In fact, the Yankee is probably the only business of Tammouz Enterprises I *haven't* worked for." Sam forced a smile. *"So far."*

"You work at the funeral home?" She seemed hesitant. "Doing what?"

"Whatever they need me for. Removals, landscaping, driving."

"Didn't you say once you were in maintenance? Repairs and stuff?"

"Yeah. Fix a leaky faucet, sweat pipes. Glaze a broken window so the snow doesn't blow in." He shrugged. "I'm kind of handy, I suppose. They say I'm the only one in my family who knows which end of a pliers to use."

That got . . . not quite a laugh. But close.

"I'm sort of on call for everything and anything. I've had days where I have to leave a repair job undone and drive up to Detroit Metro to pick up a Jim Wilson, make the drop-off, and then rush straight back to pick up another one. Meanwhile the first job's still sitting there, tools all over the place, waiting for me to finish up. Let me tell you, it can get hectic."

"Pick up Jim *who* did you say?"

"Not who, what. A Jim Wilson's a what." He explained that the name

37

was a code-term used by the funeral industry for a body in transport. "If you go up to the airlines desk and ask for Mr. Jim Wilson, whoever's at the desk will know you're there to pick up a dead guy. No whispering or acting hush-hush. If the passengers overhear, they'll think this Jim Wilson is just some guy with a ticket. Which he is . . ." Sam paused briefly the way Aboodeh did, telling this same joke, ". . . except, of course, he's traveling in *baggage* class."

She didn't laugh, instead gave him a slow, wide-eyed look. "So do you *like* it, working with dead people?"

He shrugged for effect. "You get used to it. Unless you're like my uncle Waxy and you end up sort of devoted to the profession. But I don't think even Uncle Waxy *likes* it."

"So, what's the business thing you two're going to do in Beirut? Is it the same line of work?" Her hand was back on the counter again, inches from his.

"No, that's an import venture. Gold. Jewelry."

"Gold? Gee, no kidding."

She was looking into his eyes, and he was looking right back as he lifted his hand and placed it gently over hers. Her skin felt cool.

Immediately, she gave him a sharp look and pulled her hand back.

He masked his embarrassment awkwardly, with a fixed grin.

Nikki began to glance busily about. "Well," she said, picking up their mugs and the coffee carafe, "I guess I'd better get back to the ol' grind." She turned away, then stopped short and turned back. "How old *are* you, anyway?"

"Me?" He cleared his throat. Tall for his age, he always got away with adding an extra year or two. Or three, since Nikki herself looked to be mid-twenties. "Twenty-six," he replied, surprised that his voice could come out as clear and strong as it did. If only he could stop grinning.

"Really?"

"Well, almost. In a few weeks."

She was at the center sink now, setting the mugs in to soak. "Then you'll be having your birthday over there?"

"Over where?" He could feel the grin stiffen on his face.

"In Beirut." She laughed. "Remember?"

"Yeah. I guess." He stood up and placed money next to his empty coffee mug, then some extra for the tip. She didn't really care one way or the other, she was friendly because she was a waitress. A waitress is *supposed* to be friendly. She was doing her *job*. And her feet were killing her, that's the reason why she liked to lean on the counter; that little sway was from shifting her weight from one tired foot to the other. And now, looking into those wavy-mirrored tiles at the distortion of his own stiff, self-deluding grin, he realized that, in a way, she had done him a favor. If he'd been at all hesitant before about going away, then she'd just made it all that much easier.

## MARONITE, SUNNI, MELKITE, DRUZE

*The delicate savor of the goat surprises even Bou'mishmish; he did not know he could cook until, w'Allah, he cooked, but this earns him only a single day. When the last of the kid-goat is finished, its bones picked clean and sucked of their marrow, he asks again,* "Let me join your men." *The sheikh cuts the air with a single wag of his finger: no. Bou'mishmish is sent on his way. It is for your own good, the sheikh tells him.* "Ya musq'een," *he calls him,* O poor fellow, "there is trouble following us."

"What trouble?"

"Ya musq'een," *the old man replies,* "how could you travel into the center of it and not know?" *For months now, he explains, militias from the Mountain to the Shouf have been aligning themselves according to sects—the Sunni, the Shi'ites, the Maronites and Melkites, the Druze and the Greek Orthodox.* "You say you have come thus far to escape your father? W'Allah, you have not yet traveled far enough."

"How far must I go, then?"

*The old man smiles, one eye half-closing for a joke.* "That red star rising from the Mountain, we call that one the Armpit of the Giant. Certainly that would be far enough."

*But Bou'mishmish's face remains serious, his manner earnest.* Where? *he asks, searching the sky.*

*The sheikh's smile vanishes. He is taken aback—has he discovered a simpleton?* "Hear me, ya musq'een, you know the saying, 'Harakit barrakit'?"

"Everyone knows it, ya sheikh."

39

"Explain it, then, lest I take you for a simpleton."

"The saying says this: To stir up brings luck."

"Ma'aloum!" The sheikh smiles. Truly taught! "Therefore, I instruct you: Stir yourself. Go from here and learn Engleez."

"Engleez?"

"America will be far enough away. Were I a young man I would go there again and stir up my luck once more. Tell me, what have I returned to here but the trouble that is coming?" He places a hand over his heart. "W'Allah, were I not as a father to these, I would go back there with you."

"But how can one learn Engleez, one who cannot read even?"

The sheikh swings his arm in a wide, all-encompassing arc. "Where I first learned it, here, in the Mountain. The monasteries all around harbor learned ones. And in the restaurants of Beirut even the cooks must learn Engleez and Frenchowi both. But do not linger, neither in the monasteries nor in Beirut. Learn what English you can, I instruct you, and book passage to America."

"How can one who cannot read or write book passage?"

"With money, Bou'mishmish. Surely, even a musq'een such as yourself sees the world, how it is. How it makes thieves of us all. How one must take food from another's mouth to put into one's own."

"I do see it."

"W'Allah, it is the world, Bou'mishmish."

"W'Allah, it is."

"Therefore, I instruct you: steal."

*Because* kibbeh neyeh *is eaten raw, he is instructed, the first step in its preparation is to scrub all the utensils, and he does this, starting with his hands. He washes down the marble-topped work table next, then soaks the knives and the bowls in soapy water. He takes the tea kettle out back and pours steaming water over the stone mortar and pestle, just as he has been instructed.*

"After the water it cools a little," the kitchen monk says in English, offering him some clean rags, "soak it out with these. These are named: rags. Say 'rags.'"

"Rags." *A transient earning his keep, he does not shy from hard work. He takes the strips of frayed black muslin.* "Rags." *The kitchen monk* insists on cleanliness, on following recipes and seeing what the recipes are truly showing us.

"Truly showing?" He understands so little whenever they practice English.

"Yes. Because the God he talks to us in the recipes," the monk says. A short man, too wide for his height, and in a too-tight apron. Black sleeves rolled almost to the shoulders, flour dusting his greasy black beard. And a talker. He drops the English and goes on to explain in Arabic. "Often in Scripture, when God passes down wisdom to the beni Adam, to human beings, it is in a recipe. Look in the Holy Texts: bleed the animal just so; take meat from the shoulder; be sure that the ram is free of blemish; seal the ark with pitch mixed from thus and such—"

"But those are not recipes!"

"You're instructed to take thus and so, then add to it such and such." The monk blesses himself, his face smiling within its oval of black muslin. "Deuteronomy and Leviticus and, yes, even Proverbs—if those are not recipe books, then what are they?"

Onions. Cinnamon. Burghul wheat.

"Are you not Christian?"

Bent over the stone mortar, he makes no reply, instead keeps at his work, month after month of pounding onions and lamb together for the kibbeh neyeh. Cinnamon. Burghul wheat.

"Muslim?" the monk persists. "One or the other, God bless you, I am only curious."

The pestle's wooden handle has grown slippery with grease.

"Which are you? Yahood, perhaps, a Jew?"

He rises with effort, knees crackling, and carries the pestle inside to rinse it under the pantry pump. The monk follows him.

"Are you Druze, then? Perhaps a Yazid?"

He drops the pestle into a soapy bath and swings the door shut. He reaches under the sink for the cloth sack he has kept stashed there, removes his jacket from the peg next to the door and wraps it around the cloth sack. The he opens the door again.

"A simple question, nothing more. What are you—this or that?"

Without a word, he steps around the monk and out the doorway. There *is nothing that belongs to him back there on his cot in the dormer, not a hat for his head even, so he hefts his jacket under one arm and continues on out the front gate, out beyond where the monk can follow him—"No need to feel offense! Everyone is something!"—and turns down the goat path toward the town below.*

*The town is large enough to be divided into two districts, one for Muslims and the other for Christians. The sight of a passing funeral procession tells him he has entered on the Muslim side: here the mourners go forth on foot, the relatives carrying blue handkerchiefs to twirl above their heads. They follow after the bier because it is taught,* ma'aloom, *that angels walk before it. In the Christian district, if a young man dies unmarried, the mourners sometimes pause outside the church to celebrate a mock wedding ceremony in his honor, even to the dancing of wedding dances. In both districts the dead are simply washed and wrapped in linen, big toes tied together, and put to rest within a single day. If those too are not recipes, what are they?*

*There might be work here if he wants it, here or nearby in the Bardoni resorts of Zahleh. After all these months, the monk's recipes have become his own now, and any number of restaurants would be happy for a trained kitchen worker. But there are even more restaurants in Beirut, where one must learn more than a smattering of English to work in them, where there is also an airport and a harbor, offices where the papers necessary for booking passage can be bought or bribed or, if need be, stolen.*

*When the funeral procession has passed, he continues on through the town, following the jitney road that passes up through the Antilebanon and down to the seacoast and Beirut. The mountain air grows cooler with such steep progress. He puts on his jacket and slings the cloth sack over his shoulder, clanking with a silver ladle, with a clutch of silver forks, and the kitchen monk's silver rosary cross.*

# 4

At first all Sam could see were lines of white waves crawling beneath the flap of the 747's wing. Then, pressing his face to the window, he watched a beach appear, dotted with bright umbrellas, a cluster of high-rise buildings in the near distance—Beirut!—and then the surprise of the airplane's own shadow, a quick dark speck sliding across the beach and up the faces of those buildings. He was here, back again where he came from. And so quickly. Half a world, but it had taken little more than half a day.

On line at customs, Aboodeh found his wife's cousins, the Mutraneh brothers, Nabil and Phares, both wearing identical red Middle East Airlines blazers and neckties. They looked to be in their mid-thirties, Sam thought, and with their identical haircuts and neatly trimmed mustaches, they might even be twins. Nabil, however, did seem to display more of a take-charge manner; as a shipping manager for MEA, his ID badge was gold embossed, unlike the plain laminated tag pinned to Phares's breast pocket, and he presented it with quiet authority as he ushered Sam and Aboodeh to the front of the customs and passport queues.

From the airport, they were driven into the city's Ashrafiyeh district, to an apartment provided by cousins of the Mutranehs who'd left for an early season in the mountains. The rooms were large with high ceilings, the furniture heavy and ornately carved. Each dining room chair looked like something a bishop would sit in. Every window was floor length and had louvered shutters that opened onto balconies. The floors were polished slabs of veined green marble.

Early next morning the Mutraneh brothers returned to take them on a day trip that would combine a little sightseeing along with some business appointments they'd arranged for this new joint venture with their *Amerkani* cousins. From his backseat window Sam watched the hot, sun-soaked streets of Beirut slide by—the taxicabs were all diesel-belching Mercedes—and in no time at all they were high in the chill mountain air. How small the country of his birth was, its borders in any direction no more than a couple hours by car. On the flight over Sam had had plenty of time to think about possibly staying here longer than a month. Maybe much longer. Why not? Nobody knew him here. He could be like the opposite of the immigrants that Uncle Yousef preached about in his funeral homilies. It would be a fresh start, all right, but in the *old* world. At the same time, of course, he had prepared himself for disappointment, too, understanding that his childhood memories of golden sunlight and jasmine nights might belong to some vaster-than-real dreamscape of childhood remembered. And yet, now that he was here, he couldn't deny that the April sun really did seem to give everything a honey-gold cast, and that the Chiclets boys who appeared at stoplights peddling gum and cigarettes and sprigs of flowering jasmine had eyes and hair like the eyes and hair of his own little cousins back in Toledo. Nor could he deny the strong sense he kept getting of his father's presence. He heard Baba's voice in the passing shouts of cabbies and doormen, his familiar posture in the shopkeepers who stood watching the street with hands clasped behind their arched backs. They wore mustaches, many of them exactly like Baba's thick iron-colored brush that hid his upper lip. "A kiss without a mustache is like soup without salt," he used to say to the female customers in his store. *Baba.* Sam stroked his upper lip; he could easily start his own mustache. Come to think of it, he hadn't shaved since leaving the States. What the hell, he already *had* started it! He sat back against the cab's leather seat and watched the red-tiled roofs of the mountain villages flick by. Off to the right, dark clouds were promising rain. He smiled. Let it rain. Let it hail and storm. He was home.

They turned away from the weather, following a northern route that circled out of the Beirut foothills toward the famed grotto caves at Jeita. There, crouched in hired boats, they wove between the illuminated stalagmites and stalactites. Next, the Mutranehs took them east into the Antilebanon to Zahleh, with its famous Bardoni restaurants, called casinos.

Here, high above the Biqaa, Sam had been born, and his father, too. Up out of the lozenge-shaped central plaza, he walked the very streets that Baba had walked, more like narrow alleyways than streets, and some not even that, simply stone staircases gouged into the mountainside.

Acting as guides, the brothers spoke an English that sounded almost British, clipped, with broad *a*'s, and with Sam they used only English. Yet they spoke Arabic to his American-born cousin as if *he* were the native. True, Sam's Arabic sounded rusty, and Aboodeh did speak it fluently. But the Mutraneh brothers were mistaken if they thought that not speaking a language fluently meant you couldn't understand it. During the long car rides that weekend the conversation often turned to business matters, and whenever it did, the Mutranehs switched to Arabic. They didn't need to, Sam couldn't have been less interested. He gazed out the car window, half-listening to them go on about the near-success of this deal or that deal—in Arabic, *mashrou*. Did they think he didn't know *mashrou*?

There were relatives to meet with in Zahleh, and after a huge outdoor luncheon in honor of the *Amerkani* cousins, Sam and Aboodeh were driven to nearby Baalbek to see the Roman temples. Outside the ruins Sam saw men carrying automatic rifles with orange-colored stocks and long ammunition clips. The men didn't look like soldiers, strolling hatless in the hot sun, sweating through their suit coats beneath the canvas straps of the weapons. Among the crowds of tourists stepping down from buses, some were speaking German or French or Japanese, but the majority appeared to be, like Sam and Aboodeh, Lebanese émigrés, visiting from America. And they all seemed oblivious to the men with weapons who stood apart from them. They simply went on buying souvenirs, photographing the giant pillars of Jupiter, the wide steps of the temple of Bacchus. The men carrying weapons would smile and wag a forefinger in admonishment should a camera point their way.

Next morning, while Phares took Aboodeh off to a business meeting in Beirut's banking district, Sam was taken in Nabil's Peugeot for a tour south along the coast highway to see the ruins of a crusader castle at Sidon and then to Sur, the ancient island city of Tyre which Alexander the Great had transformed into a peninsula, dumping rubble into the sea so he could bring his siege engines up to its walls and conquer it. On the way back, Nabil insisted they stop for supper at a seaside restaurant where the fish was so fresh it wasn't even caught until *after* you ordered it. Out back along the shore, fishermen stood waiting with their poles.

"The place is famous," Nabil claimed, "a favorite of the French actress Brigitte Bardot." He winked and added, "I saw her here myself once."

The restaurant turned out to be a surprisingly small place, only three little tables, and although the fish was indeed fresh—Nabil pointed out the window at the fishermen with their long poles—Sam didn't see any French actresses. Nor any other customers, for that matter.

Back in Beirut, they met up with Aboodeh and finished the long day browsing the tourist *souqs* surrounding Martyr's Square. That night, when the two of them were alone in the Ashrafiyeh apartment, Aboodeh sat Sam down to talk business. But first he paused to remove his watch and set it on the coffee table between them, a gesture that no doubt came from his DATA seminars: my time is your time. He began by explaining that setting up an import business was an expensive enterprise.

Sam agreed, cautiously.

Aboodeh cleared his throat. "On the other hand," he went on, "the spices and the other stuff we saw in the bazaars just now? They're practically *giving* it away. Do you realize that with four Lebanese pounds to the dollar, our money has *four times* the buying power over here? This thing I'm setting up, Sam, it just might pay off really, *really* big."

"Honestly, Bud? Now that you ask, I gotta say I don't see how. I mean, yeah, you might unload some stuff, imported spices and coffees maybe, but selling brass drums and worry beads to the *ibn Arab* up in Dearborn and Detroit? That's like trying to sell refrigerators to Eskimos."

"I told you before, we're not selling. We're just the middle men." He paused, reached across the coffee table and touched Sam's sleeve. "I need you, Cuz." He thought a second. "Remember on the plane coming over? You mentioned something about what it'd be like to stay over here longer, maybe even make a fresh start?"

"Yeah."

"Well, whaddya say?" Aboodeh sat back. "You really want to do it?"

"You serious?"

"Are *you?* With the exchange rate at four Lebanese pounds to the dollar, you could live here like a king!"

"Guy's gotta speak French and English *and* Arabic just to sell shoes around here."

"The Arabic'll come back. You watch."

"Come back? The last three days I've had to say almost everything in English. And you know why? Because it's the only way anybody understands me. There's even times my Arabic goes away *completely*—I can't think of a single word. Back in Zahleh the other day I was telling the Mutraneh women about my mother? How she's starting to get some white in her hair now? And they started laughing because what I told them was she's got *eggs* in her hair!"

"Okay, so what." Aboodeh made a sweep of his hand as if clearing away a cobweb between them. "No big deal." Being able to speak the language wasn't all that important. It could always come later. "Just listen a minute," he said. "I'm not talking about you selling shoes over here. You won't need a job. You can live off the proceeds from your investment."

"What investment?"

"In the venture I'm putting together. It's gonna take off like a rocket, Sammy, but you can't make a dime unless you invest. Think a minute, four Lebanese pounds to the dollar. It'll be like *quadrupling* your money! And the more you put into it the more you'll take out. Think of it. An apartment with a balcony facing the sea. A life with money and something else—respect."

"For being an investor?"

"For being a success. Everybody respects success."

"Look, Bud, I can see *you* ending up as some sort of Beirut playboy," Sam tried a chuckle, "but *me?*"

"Why not you? Twenty-three years old, you don't even know who you are yet. So who's to say how you'll end up?"

"But what—what do *I* have to invest?"

Aboodeh looked down at the coffee table, as if something in its wood-grain pattern had caught his interest. When he looked up again, he stared Sam straight in the eye. "You can invest the same thing I've invested," he said evenly.

Sam pushed back his chair. "But my Khaleel money isn't even really mine. It's for college."

"College." Aboodeh's voice turned flat, bored with patience. "C'mon, Sam. We'll be a team, my cousin and me against the world."

"How come you're so sure it's going to be a success?" Sam dropped his gaze, lest Aboodeh find incertitude in his face, and shook his head no. All along it had been for this his cousin had wanted him to come along, and this alone, for his Khaleel money.

Aboodeh glared, unblinking, allowing a silence to develop. Then he picked up his watch from the coffee table and slid it back on. "Okay then,

*Sammy,*" he said. He pronounced the name as if addressing a child, as if embarrassed at having attempted to talk man-to-man with a boy. "Since that's how it is, then I'll have to do some traveling around without you, try and scrounge up some other support before we go back."

Left to his own devices, Sam tried to make the best of things. After all, why should he feel guilty? It wasn't his fault that Aboodeh had gone and banked everything he had—whatever remained of his share of the Khaleel money, and his house. Probably his marriage, too, putting all his eggs into one basket like that. Besides, Aboodeh had set him free, in a way, so why shouldn't he go off to wander now and explore on his own? He could do what he felt like doing, maybe just go sit at one of the sidewalk cafes in the Hamra District and watch the parade of high-fashion women, the men in their slick summer suits and sunglasses. Back when he and Aboodeh had first arrived at the airport, Nabil Mutraneh had pointed out a sheik in full regalia—*kaffiyeh* and *abaya*—stepping down out of a private jet, and his women following behind, covered head to toe in black. "Soon as they get to their rooms at the St. Georges, it's out with the Paris fashions," Nabil had said. "Tomorrow that same sheik will be at the casinos, talking French and drinking Pernod."

"I'd like to see that," Sam had said.

But now that he was free to go out and see, now, while his cousin traveled back and forth setting up appointments in Sidon, in Baalbek and across the Syrian border in Damascus, Sam found that he preferred sticking around the apartment. For the time being anyway. It was funny, actually: here, in what that glossy brochure of Aboodeh's had called *"the most gastronomically sophisticated city between Paris and Hong Kong,"* he was calling down from his balcony to the passing street vendors, ordering up *falafel* sandwiches. Well, so what. He'd go out when he felt good and ready to go out. Meanwhile, he enjoyed sitting on the balcony, watching the hustle and bustle on the street below; over the roof lines to his right, the edge of the sea seamlessly became the purple horizon. Evenings, he watched villages appear one by one upon the face of the black mountains off to his left, winking pebbly smears of yellow lights.

Eventually, when he did venture out to sit at a restaurant table, he was acutely conscious of the *maitre* casting impatient glances toward this singleton taking up an entire table for four. He ended up eating quickly, downing the last of his drink and getting out of there. More and more he found himself simply walking the streets.

He felt safe enough doing that, people were everywhere on the streets in Beirut. One evening, circling the Bourj Plaza, he came upon what he learned was the *souq il sharameet,* a network of alleyways behind the police station where women's names, all of them French sounding—*Lola, Fifi, Estelle, Louise*—were fancy-scripted in neon above the doorways, and men, hundreds of men, milled quietly, almost soundlessly, up and down the pavement or else stood smoking in clumps at the curb sides in that head-down posture of waiting your turn. Around a corner, Sam caught sight of an image straight off the cover of a cheap paperback: a man, backlit by an open doorway, stood buckling his belt. In the room behind him, a woman wearing a black slip reclined on a bed, her face turned away. The woman was hefty, her back padded with fat, and she was not young. Sam remembered Nabil or Phares saying that the professional prostitutes of the *souq* had been getting older and older since the city stopped issuing new permits. Although Sam had gotten only a quick glimpse before the door swung shut, what he'd seen startled him; that, and the vague stirring that just being here seemed to have aroused in him. Had he let himself get that much alone? A man with a black beard stepped out of a shadow and asked him for a match. Sam pretended not to hear. He quickened his step, looking neither left nor right until he was well beyond the winding alleys of the *souq il sharameet.*

Every other day or so the apartment's heavy, French-style phone would ring, and it would be Aboodeh calling to say he'd be another day in Damascus or a couple more in Baalbek, too busy to talk, sometimes hanging up without even saying goodbye, just a click and a dial tone.

Expanding his walks, Sam soon learned to find the city's different plazas, places where men and women sat together at sidewalk cafes where the heavy aroma of jasmine blossoms mingled with wafts of diesel from the Mercedes taxis. The sunlight had the golden cast of his memories, and the sudden salty gusts of sea air were like something breathed in his childhood. When he stopped for a haircut, the barber knew what to do without any direction; he'd dealt with such curled whorls all his life. And yet, cab drivers addressed him in English before he even opened his mouth. So did barmen and waiters and ticket takers at the museums.

With his mustache fully in now, he looked like any one of them, and yet they all easily took him for a visiting American.

Even on the beach, they knew him for a Yankee. Stepping out onto the Riviera Beach was like entering one of those early Technicolor movies that had been retouched with a heavy hand: too-blue sky, too-white sand, the stripes of the canvas beach chairs almost painful in their contrasting red-and-green brilliance. But before he could utter a word, an attendant carrying a folded beach chair under one arm ushered Sam out onto the sand. Setting up the chair, he asked Sam, in English, if this was close enough to the water and whether he would also like a gin and tonic.

The beach was crowded. Except for a few couples scattered about, lying side by side, the majority seemed to be families with children. In the babble around him, he heard mostly French, and some German, but not one word of Arabic. And for that matter no English either. Every ten minutes or so an airliner rumbled in low from the west, its following shadow a quick dark slap across the beach. Sam reckoned that the Beirut Chamber of Commerce, or whatever they called it here, must have charted this landing approach. Just two weeks ago, he himself had arrived in one of those planes, his own face pressed to the window for a glimpse of the marvelous beach below. And now here he was, on that very beach, gazing up at the descending planes.

Finishing his drink, he rolled a towel for a pillow and closed his eyes to the sun. Minutes later, when he opened them again, he noticed a young woman sunbathing a few yards away. She lay on her stomach, chin resting on her crossed arms, and she appeared to be studying him. Or possibly not. She had on sunglasses, so he really couldn't see her eyes. He waited, but after she still had not turned away her gaze, he forced himself to do what he would normally never do: turning his head a little, he stared right back at her. A jot of alertness came to her face, almost a smile, and he saw that she was very pretty. Barely suppressing his own smile, he lay back and pretended to doze. Out of the corner of one eye he watched her change position. Her hair was sun-streaked blonde, and her bikini was made of a stretchy green material, cut European-skimpy so that as she shifted over and to one side, he caught a delicious glimpse of the tan line at the tops of her breasts.

She was making room for someone, a man who was joining her. Of course. Setting down a bottle of tanning lotion, the man stretched out, blocking her from Sam's view. His haircut was expensive looking, touches of white feathered elegantly over gray. He was trim, well-built even, but too old for the jockstrap of a swimsuit he was wearing. Certainly too old to be her boyfriend or husband. Could he be her father? No, not by the way he was reaching over now to stroke lotion onto her tanned back.

"Yeah, I'll say it wasn't her father," Aboodeh said. They were having *maza* appetizers at a sidewalk cafe, and he was lighting a cigar, which he'd gotten only half lit before he began laughing himself into a coughing fit. "Her . . . father!"

The cigar was celebratory. Aboodeh's business meetings had succeeded, and Sam sensed some diminishing of the disapproval he'd felt directed at him for the past two weeks. He touched his mustache lightly, with his fingertips. "I don't see what's so funny."

"And I wouldn't be laughing if you did," Aboodeh said. "That wasn't her boyfriend wiping lotion on her back. And you can bet he was no *husband,* either." He took the cigar out of his mouth. "Dumbshit, that was a *hooker* making eyes at you."

"A hooker?"

Aboodeh tore off a piece of flat bread and used it to scoop up some *baba ghanouj.* "Yep. A genuine, first-class Beirut hooker." He popped the bread into his mouth, leaning forward so as not to drip on his necktie.

"I thought she looked kind of American, actually."

Aboodeh stopped chewing. "Blonde?"

Sam nodded. He didn't understand how his cousin could stand to eat and smoke at the same time.

"Could be . . ." Aboodeh chewed thoughtfully. Then he began nodding his head, as if in agreement. "Yeah. I mean, it's possible. Could be the guy was getting blonded." He pressed thumb to fingertips in the sign for patience and swallowed before continuing. "Something they do here. Phares told me about it." He picked up the cigar and sat back from the table. "Blonding's sort of a *mashrou.*" He glanced over in a quick aside. "You know what *that* means, right?"

"Yeah, I know. A scam."

"Scam? Where'd you hear that? Uh-uh, *mashrou's* like a business deal. But shrewd." Aboodeh placed the cigar in the ashtray and leaned in close. "You want to know how things work in this part of the world? Listen and learn. According to Phares, the way blonding works, you find a young woman who isn't Lebanese to work for you. An American exchange student, say, would be really good. But a *blonde* American exchange student would be perfect." The blonder the better, as Phares had explained it. "Even if she has to peroxide it." It was no secret that men over here were especially attracted to blondes. Posters at the airport. Billboards all over Beirut. For that matter, pretty much all over the Arab world, according to Phares. Here, in the land of olive skin and almond eyes, where there were born and bred some of the most beautiful brunettes on the planet, the men wanted blondes. Aboodeh shrugged. "Go figure."

"But *American* blondes?"

"According to Phares? Guys here have their pick of Lebanese women. Being an American makes you more adventurous, more open-minded."

"For what?"

"For making drug connections." Aboodeh gave Sam a sharp look. "Yeah, that's right, Cuz." He leaned forward, smiling to explain that not only did Lebanon produce the finest hashish on the planet—"On. The. *Planet.*"—but Beirut Harbor also happened to be *the* primary poppy conduit between Kabul and Marseilles. A whole other world of wealth, privilege, adventure. And to play in that world, you first had to find a willing blonde to dress up sexy and show off with at the nightspots, the casinos. "You introduce her around."

"To drug dealers."

Aboodeh smiled. "To playboys." He sat back and went on to lay it out as Phares had laid it out to him, how the first-born son always inherits the family business, along with the headaches, the long hours at the office, and how this leaves his younger brothers nothing to do except to become playboys. Roulette, polo, yachts, beautiful women. And drugs. Which are seen as very chic, very hip, with an aura of adventure, even danger. "So there you are in the casino, you and your blonde, and you get her to go up to one of these bored playboys and flirt with him a little, gain his trust, offer to introduce him to her American girlfriends—"

"Sleep with him?"

"Or not. Phares says that it's usually enough if she just lets him play the big shot and show her off at the night spots. Then, out of gratitude to *you* for introducing them, he connects you with his drug supplier. The blonde serves as the go-between. You get a guaranteed first-class product, and she gets a first-class ticket to the playboy world."

"Phares seems to know a lot about big-time drug dealers and playboys," Sam said. "So how come he and his brother are so interested in joining a nickel-and-dime venture that imports, what, tourist shit?"

Aboodeh stared at him, piping a thin stream of smoke out the side of his mouth.

"It's not artifacts at all. Is it?"

"Good morning, Cuz!"

"Huh?"

"Sounds like you finally woke up."

"It's not jewelry, either, is it? Or gold?"

Aboodeh shook his head no. Then he leaned in close. "Okay, listen. We *are* importing artifacts and . . . and what you like to call tourist shit. But only on paper."

"Really?"

"Really. I was going to hold off telling you all this until after you'd invested. In some businesses, things need to operate on a need-to-know basis. You know what that means?"

"Sure."

"It means you don't know what you don't need to know. Until such time as you need to know it." Sitting back, Aboodeh reached into his jacket pocket. "And it looks like now's the time." With that, he took his hand out of his pocket and showed Sam a foil-wrapped cube.

"Jesus, Bud! Is that what I think it is?"

Aboodeh chuckled as he peeled back the foil. "See how light colored it is? It's called Lebanese Blonde. It's the smoothest, best-grade hashish in the world. In. The. World. And they grow it right here at Baalbek."

"Baalbek?" Sam wasn't sure he'd heard correctly. Baalbek lay to the north of Beirut, up where they'd seen the famous Roman ruins, the temples of Jupiter and Dionysus and . . . and slowly, it dawned on him. "You mean where we saw all those guys in suit coats walking around carrying tommy guns?"

"Those were AK-47s, actually." They carry guns, he explained, because not far from the ruins stand the ancient hashish fields of the northern Biqaa Valley where hashish has been cultivated for thousands of years. In ancient times overseers shaved the bodies of slaves and marched them naked through the crop. Afterward, other slaves would take scraping hooks and skive the resin off their bare skin. "Nowadays they use leather aprons."

"Where'd you hear that?"

"I didn't hear it. I saw it. I *watched* them do it."

"Right. I suppose those guys with the guns let you right in."

"They let Phares Mutraneh right in. And I was with Phares."

"Where was I?"

"In Tyre and Sidon, eating at jet-set fish bistros," Aboodeh said, then quickly dismissed his own mockery with a little wave; he was too wrapped up in showing off the beauty of his venture. "The Mutranehs have Baalbek connections who showed me how it's done, how they press the Lebanese Blonde into these one-kilo bricks. Now, the cost might fluctuate some, but I'm figuring around four hundred dollars American per kilo."

Sam said he didn't even know what a kilo was.

Aboodeh shrugged. "Two pounds, and change. Which our distributors divide up and re-wrap. He placed the cube in Sam's hand.

"You trust these people?"

"They're not just people. They're Salma's people. Cousins, like us."

Sam looked at the cube. "But you can't just send it air mail, Aboodeh. They've got *dogs* now. Special trained. They've got x-ray machines."

"Which is why the Mutranehs adopted my plan in the first place." Aboodeh's voice grew cocky. "Our method of transport is foolproof, and it's already in place."

"Bud, you could go to jail for this. For *years.* Shit, *I* could go to jail for just sitting here with this in my hand." He waited a moment. "Tell me I'm wrong."

All confidence, Aboodeh took his time before responding. He tore off another strip of bread, folded it into a scoop.

"No, wait." Sam stood up and carefully placed the foil cube on the table next to the bread. "Don't tell me." He wiped his fingertips on a napkin. "I don't want to know."

## Uncle Sam's

*The forks and ladle are only plated. In the silversmith's souq off Martyrs' Square they give him very little for the whole bagful. Like him, they are thieves, too. But the rosary cross is what one of them calls fine sterling.*

"See the little mark on the back?" he says, pointing it out. "Feel the heaviness?" He is a more clever thief than the rest, exclaiming outright what he is thinking: that the man who brings in this much can bring in more. "You show promise." A Syrian by his accent, he is called Zeid. He speaks a formal Arabic, and Bou'mishmish soon finds himself struggling to keep in step with it.

"Promise? In what, say you?"

"In picking pockets, I say. Most would argue that success resides in the practice of nimble fingers. In this I differ with most. It is good to be nimble and swift, yes, but even better, I say, is to be trusted. Success resides in trust. I saw that you know how to present a trustful face." Zeid holds out a package of cigarettes. English Dunhills. "Have one. See? This cigarette says to the pigeon: I am your friend. If you smoke my cigarette, you are indebted to trust me just a little more than you had only a moment ago." He pauses, adds, "But we will have to do something about that eye. Maybe sunglasses. Teyib?" he adds, an interjection which can mean All right or Understood.

Bou'mishmish understands, all right. "Teyib," he replies.

In a room behind the stall Zeid has fava beans soaking in a kettle. Seeing this, Bou'mishmish bids his host wait, to have another cigarette before lighting the gas ring. Then he dashes out. The cigarette dangling in Zeid's lips is half finished when he returns. Hidden in his cloth sack are packets of ground cumin and coriander that he'd lifted from the spice stalls. He shakes hot chilies from his shirt cuffs. Out of his jacket pocket he makes a dried onion seem to appear in his hand. Nudging Zeid to sit back down, he drizzles olive oil to warm in the kettle. "Trust me," he says, chopping the onion into the kettle. He adds the peppers.

"And here I was going to instruct you?" Zeid laughs.

"Teyib," Zeid says, a word which also means tasty. He puts out his bowl for more. "Where did you learn such cookery?"

"In the mountain monasteries," Bou'mishmish replies. "I cooked in return for instruction in English. And for what little I can read."

"Teyib," Zeid says, which also means I see. Then he chuckles, "But tell me, did these monks accept Bou'mishmish as your true name, Lover of Apricots?"

"They did not question it."

"Monks in their cloisters, they are not the world. Take this instruction from me, and find another name. Teyib?"

"Teyib."

"Very well, Teyib it is then. A good name.

Day and night the instruction continues, moving across the city from district to district, from the central plaza called Bourj to the Corniche with its hotels, from the Plage to the fancy shops and restaurants of the Hamra. It ends abruptly and unexpectedly in the souq il sharameet, the prostitute district. "I bring you here for two reasons," Zeid says. "The second reason needs no explaining," he gives a knowing wink, "but the first is to show you a place filled with pigeons." He points them out, the loner, the drunk, the trusting foreigner. But he gets scarcely beyond the approach to trust—Got a match? and The coffee's on me, I insist!— when Zeid is suddenly clapped on both shoulders by a pair of armed men who lead him away into the crowd. Next day Bou'mishmish learns that it was the Police du Moeurs who arrested Zeid. On what charge? The single word, loti, explains it all, and in a whisper. Sodomite, a sinner after the sin of Lot. Later Teyib—now no longer calling himself Bou'mishmish— learns too that Zeid's stall in the silver souq has been boarded up. But loosely enough that one can easily squeeze in and out. A place to stay and look for work. But to find decent work in Beirut, honest or dishonest, one needs to know French and English—at least something of each.

He takes temporary jobs at hard labor, one day road repair, another day riding in the back of a refrigerated truck unloading deliveries of meat. Work that only a donkey would do, but each day it is only for a day. And easier than thieving every day. His coworkers are donkeys, like himself, and speak no English. Rather than try improving their Arabic even, they prefer to babble away in their own tongues—Urdu and Dinka and Filipino Spanish. All day they deliver chickens by the crate, pork to the Christian Ashrafiyeh district, whole and half-carcasses of lamb to the hotels of the Corniche and the fine restaurants of the Hamra district. In the Hamra, across from the American University of Beirut, is a little cafe restaurant called Uncle Sam's where AUB students sit practicing English with one another. Many of them wear neatly trimmed little beards. Evenings when his job ends, he takes his pay and returns to Uncle Sam's to watch how the students switch from Arabic to English and back again, how they while away their study time dropping piastres into a jukebox to hear the rock and roll of the Amerkani. How they drink Pepsi-Cola and nibble potato chips fried in lamb grease. How they eat the beef of the Amerkani, patties made from oatmeal mixed in with the gristly haunches of worked-to-death plough oxen that he himself unloaded that very morning. All the while he sits with sugared coffee and listens. Talk of politics, this sect and that sect, being saddled by the French with the burden of a confessional government. The Palestinians growing bolder. The quarrels among the ruling zuama families. He understands enough to see that the sheikh shebaab was right, that trouble is indeed coming.

But this is no way to learn a language. And neither is walking the wide boulevards past the hotels Phoenicia Intercontinental and the St. Georges, pretending to look for work just to listen to the talk in English and French.

There in the hotel district he finds a position as kitchen helper in the Kit Kat Club, built up over the water's edge where diners sit listening to the Mediterranean crash against the concrete embankment below. He is instructed how to address the American customers, the men by adding an honorific to their first names: Mr. Michael, Mr. William; the women more elaborately and, no matter their heritage, always in French: Madame, Mademoiselle; and the older men Khawaja, as if they are lords. And in a way they are. Money makes them so. To them a stack of liras, four to the American dollar, is like a handful of rags. (Even thinking this, he is careful not to roll the r.) Filthy rich, they say. Dirt cheap, they say. Have a nice day. Stroking his chin, the stubbly beginnings of a beard, he parrots them, then asks, Teyib? They laugh to hear that Teyib is also his name, and they leave him enormous tips. They want to practice their Arabic, these Amerkani visiting the homeland of their parents' generation, but he keeps switching them back to English. And as for Teyib, yes, he likes the sound of it.

British English, he learns, is close to but not the same as American English. It is American he wants to practice. It will take time—months, maybe years. No matter, he understands patience. In America, he is told, grown men chew gum. He buys packets in different flavors from the Chiclets boys who roam the plazas. He tries the different flavors, the mint

*and the fruit, but none are as tasty to him as the rosy mastic. At a kiosk
outside the Hotel St. Georges, he buys a pair of sunglasses, dark green. In
the kiosk's little mirror the dead eye does not show at all.*

*Chewing, walking the streets, Teyib starts smoking Zeid's Dunhill
cigarettes. "Got a match?" one might ask a stranger in English. Or, "Have
one of mine." The smoke makes him dizzy and he tries to appear to smoke,
taking it in, holding it in his mouth, then blowing it out. Hello. Try one of
mine? Need a light? Good. Now trust me just a little more.*

# 5

Next morning, while Aboodeh slept in, Sam took a cab to a sidewalk cafe that he'd discovered on one of his walks in the Hamra district, a place popular for serving American-style breakfasts. He sat in the shade and ordered flapjacks with his eggs. Sipping coffee, watching the shops across the street open for the day, he decided that if Beirut had a "Little America," then this neighborhood had to be the center of it; the American Consulate compound was just down the block, the seaside campus of the American University a little farther up and across the boulevard. Around the corner there was even an American-style student hangout, a hamburger joint called Uncle Sam's.

Waiting for his meal, he glanced through one of the English-language newspapers and imagined himself living here, free, completely on his own. An apartment in this very district, maybe, with a balcony overlooking one of these shaded side streets. Tastefully decorated, sophisticated. For sure none of those brass trays and figurines he saw for sale in the *souqs*. What did Aboodeh take him for, thinking he'd actually believe that a fortune could be made on importing cheap souvenirs? But the other thing, *that* might actually work.

"With your investment we can get up and running in a matter of weeks," Aboodeh had said yesterday. "Without it, I'll have to keep scrounging for . . . for I don't know how long." He'd sighed, given his head a slow, sad shake. "Sammy, I have this image of you in my mind, representing our operations over here. Having coffee at a sidewalk cafe, money in your pockets. People treating you like a man of respect."

Sam shrugged. His cousin was wearing him down. "You make it sound nice and all, but what if, I don't know, what if I end up not fitting in over here?" He'd been afraid to admit as much, but there, he'd said it.

"Staying here was *your* idea, Sammy, not mine. If you want to stay and make a fresh start, you can. Or not." The important thing was the large, steady return Sam would be getting on his investment dollar. "I could set it up so you'd be a subinvestor, like a subcontractor. That way, you'd be an anonymous investor, and I'd assume all the risk. How much sweeter can I make it for you?"

And that was how Aboodeh had left it. "It's in your court," he'd said. All Sam had to do was say the word.

When his meal arrived, Sam discovered that the syrup tasted more of rose water than maple. But the eggs were perfect overeasy, and the bacon crisp, hickory smoked. Chewing contentedly, he closed his eyes. And immediately sensed someone close by his table. It wasn't the *garçon,* but a stranger, a passerby from the street. The man was standing politely to one side, as if waiting to be noticed. He wore sunglasses and a neatly trimmed beard, unusual for most Beirutis, except here near the university, and he was holding an unlit cigarette to his lips.

"Mister, please the match, please?"

The man's English was so heavily accented that Sam instinctively chose Arabic to explain that he didn't smoke. *"Ma'b dakhen, annah."*

At that the man smiled sadly, heaving a sigh of good-natured disappointment. But he didn't leave, instead remained standing right there next to the table. Looking down at Sam's plate. He was small-built, even skinny, and probably hungry. Probably ashamed to ask. Sam didn't know how to ask either.

Again, the man sighed, thrusting his hands deep into his jacket pockets. The jacket looked too big for him, and Sam remembered thinking that with its suede elbow patches, it belonged with a pipe more than a cigarette. Just then the man's eyebrows lifted in surprise, *"Shu?"* and his hand withdrew a book of matches from the pocket. "Ri-aght *here* the match!" Chuckling at his own absentmindedness, he lit his cigarette. Then, just stood there holding the extinguished match as if not knowing what to do with it. So Sam slid the ashtray across the table and invited him, in English, to sit down if he'd like.

Yes, the man did indeed like. Although English was clearly a burden to him, it was a burden he seemed determined to carry. Looking to Sam for guidance as he struggled for the words he wanted, he eventually got across that he'd suspected from the start that Sam wasn't from around here.

"That's true," Sam said. He touched his mustache, then lowered his hand. Exaggerating a smile, he asked whether the man was a *taleb,* over at AUB, a *student.*

The man seemed puzzled. Sitting back, he drew lightly on his cigarette and immediately blew the smoke out again, like someone pretending to smoke. Then—"Ah!"—he brightened. "Because this?" he asked, indicating his beard. He was a student, yes. Then, pressing palm to breast with a little bow, the man clarified further that he was a student who was *not* in school. All the more reason, therefore, to "make practice English."

And what practice he got, launching into a string of questions, each on the heels of the last. Sam had barely replied that he'd come from Toledo in Ohio before the man was asking how much an automobile costs in Ohio. And whether Ohio is nearby to Nashville City. "Last week I meet here two folks from Nashville City," the man explained, pronouncing the word *folks* as if it were two syllables, *foc-us.* But when Sam tried to correct him, it came out two *fucks* from Nashville, so he let it go and backed off completely. It should have been pleasant, this friendly chat beneath the hanging bougainvillea, a sea breeze fluttering the tablecloths, but instead the talk was so confusing, even dizzying, that afterward Sam couldn't remember whether or not the man had even given his name. Only the barrage of nonstop questions, and the strain of piecing out that impossibly heavy accent. Has Toledo subway trains? And in the same breath practically, How do you like to eat in Ohio, the lamb or only the beef? And, he asked, what of the currency exchange rate; did "Mr. Sam" exchange his dollars here or at the airport?

After ten minutes, the man lit up another cigarette, and Sam had had enough. Reaching into his jacket pocket, he took out his wallet and signaled the *garçon.* If this guy was hitting him up for meal money, he needed to learn to just straight-out ask for it.

But then the man took his own wallet out and offered to pay the check. The offer was a customary gesture, and of course Sam couldn't allow it. Besides, he was pretty sure the wallet was empty. The little guy insisted—again with hand to breast and the little bow—that at least he be allowed to do his new young friend from Ohio a favor. *Ya sheb,* he called Sam, *Young fellow.* Eyeing Sam's wallet, he noted that it contained American greenbacks. By lucky chance, he knew of an Armenian exchange counter close by here, just up the corner. The Armenians, if you are their friend—as the man, with a nod and a wink, now announced himself to be—will pay out five, sometimes as much as *six lira libanaise.* Tourists do not know this, not even most Beirutis.

Sam understood. "Sure," he said, and took a ten out of his wallet. The guy could be hungry or pulling a scam, or both. Or maybe there really *was* an exchange counter around the corner. What did I care? he imagined telling Aboodeh later. He handed over the ten; worth every dime just to be done with the little guy and his chatter.

The man examined the bill, then frowned and shook his head. No, perhaps Sam didn't understand how advantageous such rates were. Surely, he would want to exchange more than this?

Sam stood up, looming over the table. "That's it," he said and put his wallet away. Enough to eat off for a month.

The little guy got the point all right. He tucked the bill in his jacket pocket. Then, as if suddenly seized with gratitude, he rested his cigarette in the ashtray, then reached out to embrace his newfound American friend.

Well, Sam knew that over here men did that sort of thing. Some of them even walked around holding hands with each other. So, okay, he returned the hug, went ahead and let the man backslap him like a long-lost cousin. Up close, his hair smelled of cooking.

When the man stepped back, his sunglasses were askew from the hug. Straightening them on his nose, he urged Sam to sit now and finish his coffee; he would return in just one minute. He raised a forefinger to indicate just one, then turned and started quickly up the block. Sam watched him go, watched him vanish around the corner. He chuckled to himself. Wouldn't it be funny if there actually *was* an Armenian exchange around the corner, and the guy *did* return with six pounds to the dollar? Later, thinking back on this moment, he would conclude that it must have been the cigarettes that got him doubting his own cynicism. The man had left not only a half-full package of Dunhills on the table, but a newly lit cigarette in the ashtray as well. Staring down as if mesmerized by its stream of smoke, he had an odd sense that this was indeed a temporary absence, and that the guy would certainly return to finish his cigarette. And when he did, wouldn't *that* be a story to tell Aboodeh, how, all on his own, he'd run into a guy who got him a better exchange rate than even the Mutranehs could. Ha!

As the cigarette ash lengthened, the *maitre* brought Sam's change back on a little saucer. He asked if there would be anything more, and Sam thanked him and told him no. And that was all it took, a brief exchange with another person, to break the spell. Suddenly Sam was on his feet, ashamed that he'd let himself sit there and play along. What was he thinking? He wasn't thinking. And now he just wanted to put down a tip for the *garçon* and go, just get the hell away from the sight of that smoldering cigarette, but when he reached for his wallet, he discovered that it too had vanished.

He didn't even have carfare. He considered asking the *maitre* to let him use the phone to call Aboodeh but instead asked him for walking directions back to Ashrafiyeh.

Making his way through a crowded stretch of Rue Clemenceau, he felt scorn in the casual side glances of passersby, heard it outright in laughter coming from a side street. Car horns honked at him while he was still crossing in the zebra-walks. Just trying to disappear, he found himself in everybody's way. People elbowed him aside or impatiently stepped around him. Where did he come from, this looming, plodding hulk? Where did he think he was going?

In Martyr's Square there was a demonstration going on, people angrily chanting, waving placards and Cedar flags. Instead of circling around the mob, Sam shouldered his way through the very center of it. And sure enough, one man did take offense—not even a man, a teenaged boy—and he struck Sam on the side of the mouth with his fist. It hurt, but it was only a glancing blow, and Sam felt he deserved much, much more.

"Did you look in your luggage?" Aboodeh asked. "In your dirty laundry? Maybe your wallet fell out there?"

"I looked. I looked everywhere." Sam noticed Nabil and Phares Mutraneh exchange glances. They'd all eaten supper together, and Sam had found them having Arabic coffee on the balcony.

"Maybe it fell out when you tripped and busted your lip?"

Sam touched the bruise at the side of his mouth. No, he explained, that had happened after he realized he'd misplaced the wallet. "Last I remember having it was this morning when I paid the cab driver who took me out to the Hamra." His lip hurt and he had a headache. He wanted this day to end so he could just lie down. "There wasn't all that much money in the wallet, anyway."

"How much?"

"Oh, fifty. Maybe a little more. And everything else I can replace after we get back, my driver's license, my social security card. Right now all I really need is a new debarkation card."

"You had your debarkation card in your *wallet?*" Aboodeh's eyes widened in exasperation. "Jesus Christ, Sammy, didn't I tell you to keep all those papers together with your passport?"

"I guess I just never took it out of my wallet after customs."

"There's a whole *industry* over here," Aboodeh said, "deals in nothing but counterfeiting identity papers."

Sam turned to Nabil Mutraneh. "A new card shouldn't be a *huge* problem, should it?"

Nabil frowned, "Not 'uge," he said, and scratched his ear. "But this I will have to see to myself in person." There were people he knew through his airline job. But he couldn't say for sure how long it would take to have a replacement card issued. Not with all the unrest lately.

The demonstration in Martyr's Square was only the tip of an iceberg, according to the English-language newspapers. Reports were that a bus filled with Palestinian refugees had been fired upon after a traffic accident high up on one of the mountain highways. Twenty-six people were shot and killed. Over the weekend a demonstration in Tripoli had turned into a riot. Last night the BBC Radio reported another series of riots suddenly erupting to the south, in Sur and Sidon.

"Probably tribal," Aboodeh had said, but Nabil had disagreed. No, it was something far bigger, he suspected.

Next day, however, in his office at the airport, his brother wasn't so sure. "*Inshallah* it can be contained and dealt with quickly," Phares said, but he was not optimistic, and the sooner Sam's new debarkation card could be processed the better.

"If these troubles increase, however," Phares turned to Aboodeh, "my brother and I feel that, for our thing to succeed, a liaison may prove more necessary than ever. Someone of our choosing, however, to be our representative in America."

"In America?" Although Aboodeh was trying to smile, Sam saw that he hadn't been expecting this.

"It is not our decision alone," Nabil chimed in. "Our venture is a joint effort, and the suppliers from Baalbek insist that we have someone who can keep an eye on your end of the operation." Nabil leaned forward in his chair, low and tense, arms down on his knees. "This liaison person, should we need to send him for an extended stay, he will need to be formally sponsored. Easier for everyone if we call him a cousin, yes?"

"Who did you have in mind," Aboodeh asked, "this 'cousin' that Baalbek wants sent over? Anybody I've met?"

Nabil glanced at his brother and laughed. "Even *we* don't know him yet!" He held up a hand and waved Aboodeh's concern away. "Please remember, this is all maybe, maybe not." He laughed again. "Think of it as an option we must keep open."

"All right," Aboodeh said, "all right," beginning to sound more like himself. "And you know what else? I wouldn't worry too much about the political situation." He turned to Sam. "You watch."

"Why's that?" Sam asked.

"Because around here, Sammy, whenever something political like this pops up they skip the police and go straight to the army—right, guys? They come down on it with both feet."

"Our army?" Phares said, then clicked his tongue for no. "No, not the army, " he said. "More likely the Phalange or the Marada."

"The *who* or the *who?*" Sam asked later, while they were alone on their balcony.

His cousin rolled the ash off his cigar and shrugged. "Search me."

"You know something else I don't get?" Sam scooted his chair closer. "About the Mutranehs sending some guy over to keep an eye on things? You're married to their cousin. That practically makes you *their* cousin. Don't they trust you?"

"It's not just the Mutranehs. They're middlemen, same as us. We're accountable to them, and they're accountable to their wholesale suppliers up north in Baalbek. It's Baalbek." He ran a hand through his hair. "And it's not for sure, anyway. Me, I wouldn't be surprised if they end up not sending anybody at all. There's a lot of bluffing goes into business negotiations."

"But what if they do send somebody?"

"Well, it's an added expense, totally unnecessary, but okay, fine. We got nothing to hide." Aboodeh drew on the cigar but it had gone out. "Meanwhile, you better hope Nabil's connections don't take too long to replace that card you lost. Otherwise I might have to leave you here." Aboodeh struck a match, looked over at Sam, and immediately shook it out, laughing. "Jesus, you look like you just saw a ghost!"

As it happened, Nabil's airline connections turned out to be as slow to act as they were ineffectual. After nearly a week of call-backs and wait-and-sees and even a bribe or two that went nowhere, the Mutraneh brothers began pushing for Aboodeh to return alone, with Sam following as soon as the papers cleared. Thank God Aboodeh resisted the idea.

At night Sam lay awake in bed, listening to the faint tik-tik-tik of the ceiling fan. What was in his head all those weeks ago, imagining he could start over here? He didn't belong here. Maybe once upon a time he did, but not anymore. And something else: wouldn't staying here amount to an unraveling of all his father had worked so hard to do, bringing him to America?

On a Monday morning Sam gathered his resolve, along with his passport and airline information, and on his own took a service cab across town to the American embassy, out in the Hamra district. He went there fully expecting to face the wall of impassive bureaucratese he'd heard so much about, but he was also prepared to breach that wall with reason and persistence. And if that failed he was prepared to plead, to get on his knees if he had to. He was an American citizen—they *had* to let him back in!

Outside the gates of the embassy compound a demonstration was taking place. Sam couldn't make out the crowd's repetitive chants, but they sounded increasingly insistent and angry. At a checkpoint outside the gate a pair of marines in combat fatigues checked his passport and directed him inside to an office complex. After waiting for the charge d'affaires, he was shuttled to the receptionist for the consular officers, where Sam confessed he had no appointment, hadn't known he needed one. The receptionist had a kind face, but she seemed beleaguered, and her assistant explained that everything was running late and that for days now even those with appointments had had to wait.

Late that afternoon, after having spent the entire day either filling out forms or idly reading back issues of *Time Magazine,* Sam stepped outside the compound gate to find the street quiet now and people in yellow armbands picking up litter from the demonstration. All day he had spoken to nobody beyond two receptionists and one pink-faced marine guard standing silently alert in a khaki shirt and blue slacks with a red stripe who, with a curt nod, had directed Sam to the men's room.

Next day he did get in to speak with one of the consular officers, a man who frowned and shook his head as he paged through the forms Sam had filled out the day before. "So you were born here, then?" he said with a faint southern drawl. "And that's why no birth certificate?"

"Yes, up in the mountains the Christians just use baptismal records. My dad and mom brought me to America when I was little."

"How little? Do you have a naturalization certificate?"

"Yes. But it's back home. Why?"

The man didn't respond right away. He leaned back, his head nearly touching the large American flag behind his desk. His hair was lank, the color of wet straw. And his eyes so blue nobody would ever doubt where he belonged. "You have it but you didn't happen to travel with it?"

"Did I need to?" Sam felt his right arm tingle and want to tremble. "I mean, you have my passport."

"And, under normal circumstances, that would be enough. But if you haven't noticed, circumstances here haven't been very normal lately. With the political situation turning unstable, there's been a rash of incidents involving counterfeited documents. Especially *American* documents. No, Mr. Tammouz, I'm afraid you'll need to wire home for proof of naturalization." The man was businesslike, trying to sound neutral, but there was no denying the suspicion in his voice as he went on to explain the process and that one of the receptionists outside could help with the first step, namely sending the wire. The reply might take as much as a week, and until then there was nothing else to be done.

Over the next few days, while Sam sat clenched and waiting, the Mutranehs grew more and more restless for Aboodeh to leave. And just thinking about his cousin leaving him here was enough to get Sam's arm to begin trembling. It was from fear, only that, and he knew it. He would take a slow breath, and it would stop. But when he looked, it would be trembling again.

There was another demonstration on the day Sam was summoned to the embassy to receive his newly issued travel papers. Again, he couldn't make out what the crowd outside was saying, but they were yelling their heads off to say it. He didn't care. His documents were in order.

The consular officer glanced briefly toward the window and the sound of chanting, then turned back to finish stamping Sam's papers spread out on his desk. "Not a problem," he said when Sam thanked him. He leaned his elbows on the desk and with a practiced smile—the smile you make at a child who should have known better—he went on to explain that attending to such details was part of the embassy's mission, and "the least we could do for," he paused here and winked, "one of our own."

*One of our own.* No sweeter words. But why the wink? And at the office door, the man's handshake was limp and abrupt, done with Sam as soon as they'd touched.

Belted in now and half-dozing while the plane waited on the tarmac, Sam dismissed thoughts of the consular officer and of himself stumbling through the crowd, his mouth bleeding, alone in a foreign country with no money, no papers, plucked like a pigeon. No. He forced himself to think instead about how lucky he and Aboodeh had been to catch an earlier flight.

Lucky? Aboodeh had shrugged at the very idea of luck. He'd been confident from the start that, for one thing, the embassy would expedite Sam's papers. For another, that they'd catch this earlier flight. As if he'd simply known things would work out. Earlier today, while waiting in line to board, Aboodeh had seemed unruffled by the sight of armed guards all over the airport. Maybe because, Sam wondered, with the civil unrest spreading, the venture was already dead in the water anyway? "Not at all," his cousin had replied. On the contrary, the distraction might actually help provide cover. No, the only thing that worried Aboodeh now was whether those newly recruited investors he'd managed to scrounge up would be enough. Then he shrugged a tired little smile that seemed to ask, yet again, whether Sam would reconsider.

Sam had tried to smile back. He was exhausted. They both were. His cousin didn't look like Abdoolah the Coolah anymore, not with his business suit all rumpled, the knot of his necktie slack and tugged askew.

Even the pinkie ring looked sad, a dull gold flicker as he'd turned to show Sam the way out toward the boarding stairs. And yet as they approached the boarding line, Aboodeh had managed to square his shoulders and lift his chin. A man walking in the world. Sam followed him, out into the sunlight. The line moved swiftly across the tarmac, but in fits of lurch and stop, lurch and stop. Sam kept close to Aboodeh, who now and again glanced over his shoulder to check on him. *His cousin, looking out for him.* Suddenly, Sam stopped cold, swept up by a crazy surge of gratitude. *His cousin was taking him home.*

Now that they were settled in and waiting, Sam turned to Aboodeh. He spoke before he knew it and without knowing why. "You can count on me, too, Bud," he heard himself say.

Aboodeh, paging through the airline magazine, was only half-listening. "For what?"

"For my Khaleel money. I'm in." He meant it. Only now, hearing himself, did he believe he meant it. And he was glad. Because here next to him was his cousin who had watched out for him, and who needed him.

The jet engines revved to a scream, and the great thrust pressed Sam back in his seat. Soon they were off the ground and in a steady climb. More than glad, he was relieved. The earth swooped to one side as the jetliner banked low over the St. Georges Hotel and the Riviera Beach beside it. Gazing out the window, he imagined the tiny faces down there looking up from their drinks, from the shade of their beach umbrellas. Americans going home, they would be thinking. Going back where they came from.

He touched his mustache. He wanted it off. It didn't belong in America. If he could, he'd shave it off right here on the plane.

UNITED STATES OF AMERICA

*On a side wall in Uncle Sam's there is a map of the United States with flagged pins in every major city. Teyib memorizes their names as one of the kitchen workers reads them off for him: Chicago, Los Angeles, Pittsburgh, Providence. Our people are there and there in America. And there, and there. Dozens of tiny flags pierce tiny Detroit. Dozens more sprinkle down the Great Lake's littoral coast through Toledo and Cleveland.*

*Zeid's friends—loti like Zeid himself, sodomites who shadow their*

*eyelids with kohl—know people who know people who trace the wallet's
documents to connections in Baalbek; the debarkation card alone is
basis enough to forge the rest; retaining the naturalization number is
all it takes, after replacing the name and signature of Samir Tammouz,
American citizen. By necessity the destination must remain as on the
original: City of Detroit, State of Michigan, United States of America.
But once inside America, Zeid's people had assured him, the disappearing
will be nothing. Zeid himself had gone there. In America, Zeid said once,
anyone can disappear. Loti, sinners of Lot's sin, they knew how to color
the hair yellow for America.*

# PART TWO

# 6

Nobody had seen it coming, not on this side of the world, anyway. And even after that April bus accident up on the Mountain erupted in gunfire, even then, nobody recognized what it truly was, the beginning of Lebanon's fifteen-year war against itself. The news media reported a series of car bombs in the mostly Muslim Hamra district, calling them acts of simple gangsterism, and for a time afterward—despite sporadic outbreaks of looting and small-arms skirmishes between factions nobody had ever heard of (one of them a roaming band wearing pink scarves over their fatigue jackets)—Radio Beirut continued to repeat assurances that there was nothing to fear, even while it announced an early closing to the summer tourist season.

"Pink!" Sam had shown Aboodeh the newspaper. "Why would they wear pink?"

Aboodeh pushed the newspaper away. "Don't believe everything you read, Sammy. I don't listen to any of that negative shit anymore."

"When you said that the unrest over there might actually help us by giving the venture some, you know, cover, that made sense to me. But how can we ship anything from over there with a full-blown civil war going on?"

"It's not a war."

"Not yet, maybe—"

"Even if it does turn into a war, and it won't, delivery will be the least of our problems."

"The delivery—that's something else I don't get."

"You'll know when you need to know. In the meantime, just take my word for it—cousin to cousin—and stop asking so many questions. And besides, Sammy, Beirut's a world-class banking center. World. Class. If there's one thing these people know, it's *business*. Businessmen run the government. And businessmen won't *let* it turn into a war."

Sure enough, by the end of May 1975, a cease-fire had been announced. Prime Minister Karami, a Sunni Muslim, and President Franjieh, a Maronite Catholic, shook hands on it. But then, in June, more street fighting erupted, and the casualty list grew in a matter of days from an estimated 300 dead and injured to 650, including women and children killed in cross-fire. There were claims that the violence had been exactly timed to ruin the tourist season and drive the economy to crisis. In July, a U.S. Army colonel was abducted, and throughout the summer, reports of kidnappings grew, sniper killings, neighborhood sieges; and along with all this the interruptions of electricity, shortages of food, medicine and water. By August Price Waterhouse had left Beirut, and Ampex closed its offices.

In autumn, during the Muslim feast Eid al-Fitr—a rocket exploded outside a Muslim bakery, leaving twelve dead and wounding twenty more. Another missile hit a group of children playing in a suburban Beirut street. Reporting that five little ones died while several more lost arms or legs to razor-sharp fragments, the Radio Lebanon announcer interrupted the news copy he was delivering to cry out, "Murderers! Your rockets are hitting women and children, the innocent ones! You are all murderers!"

In America, Middle Eastern immigrant organizations began work along with the Red Cross and the Red Crescent to establish delivery of relief supplies and to sponsor out refugees. By October, the debate on whether Lebanon—despite the combined efforts of Assad of Syria, Karami and Yassir Arafat—could be saved from civil war had become mostly a matter of semantics. On the radio a news panel featuring government experts and foreign correspondents agreed that the level of violence was now such that for all intents and purposes a civil war in Lebanon had begun, one of their number declaring it an "Irish-style sectarian war of attrition."

On the ceiling above him Sam could hear his mother's footsteps crossing the kitchen floor, the familiar slip-slap of her house slippers. Bicycling in a full sweat down the boot of Italy, he reached over the handlebars to the shelf above and switched off the radio. No wonder Aboodeh had told him to quit listening to news from the old country. It seemed like every bulletin on the BBC opened with "In the latest round of bloodshed . . . ," followed by the awful tallies: "Fifty killed, over two hundred wounded . . ."; "Dozens feared dead, hundreds injured . . ." The newscasters rattled off the numbers as if they were ball scores. Like Aboodeh said, how many reports of bombings and kidnappings and casualty lists can you listen to before you start tuning it out? Sam wiped his face with his tee-shirt and pedaled on in silence.

A rumbling noise in the alley caused him to stop and listen. At first he could hardly hear anything beyond his own rapid breathing. Then there it was again, a sound like thunder. He dismounted carefully—his hip was sometimes trembly right after exercise—and went to the window. Only the wind. An empty garbage can had blown over and was rolling back and forth across the alley stones. For days now the air had been warm and unstable, more like summer than early October. In the narrow patch of sky above the alley, he could see low clouds scudding by. Another storm. No weather to be flying in. Or driving in, either. He'd be fighting the wheel the whole way up to the airport.

A couple weeks back, around the end of September, the Mutranehs had notified Aboodeh by wire that a representative—actually, they'd called him a "cousin"—would be arriving after all, flying in to Detroit Metropolitan. Aboodeh was surprised; he'd figured that, given the political situation, the paperwork alone would have discouraged their sending anyone at all. "But go figure, our State Department actually went and *eased up* on the red tape. For *humanitarian* reasons."

Just before the last telephone blackout, Phares had managed to rattle off a series of possible flights that this "cousin" might be arriving on. The connection was staticky, and Phares had sounded impatient to hang up. No, he didn't have the exact flight numbers because as yet there *were* none. "The man, this cousin, will most likely be traveling under our name," he'd said, his voice awash in static. Why all the uncertainty? "Because," Phares replied, "everything here is uncertain! Our suppliers in Baalbek might have to send him on a flight out of Damascus."

"Damascus?"

"Beirut Airport is shut down for the time being."

Soon after, so too was the phone service. Twice already Aboodeh and Sam had driven up to Detroit to meet flights originating out of Damascus, only to find no "cousin" looking for them, no one at all traveling under the Mutraneh name. Tonight a third Damascus flight was arriving. Sam lifted the exercycle and placed it out of the way in a corner next to the shower stall. If this turned out to be the night, then he'd carry it upstairs later. He'd already moved out the rest of his things, kept the place swept and clean for a week now. The sheets on the little bed were brand-new from Sears, never used.

Apparently, it had been Aboodeh's plan all along that, if this "cousin" ever did get sent over, he would be given Sam's apartment. "C'mon, Sammy, don't look so surprised. We've got to provide the guy a place to stay."

"So, meanwhile, what am *I* supposed to do, move back upstairs with my mother?"

Aboodeh's expression said it all. *Where else?* A temporary arrangement, his cousin hastened to add. Temporary, like Aboodeh's return to apprenticing for his father, and Sam's driving hearses again.

The wind made a humming noise in the door. A loose seal, it had annoyed Sam for weeks. Funny, now he was going to miss the sound of it. Using the red felt pen, he marked the map: a sixteenth of an inch closer to Naples. Then he unpinned it from the wall, folded it and set it on the exercycle's seat. He had time yet to go upstairs for a shave and a shower. Aboodeh would be waiting for him at the funeral home. "Dress nice," his cousin had said. "This is business. When this guy shows up, we want him to see we're serious businessmen."

The service stairs leading to the basement were carpeted for silence. And, like most other utility areas at Tammouz & Sons, piled with stored junk. Sam had to pick his way down through stacks of wicker flower baskets, votive stands, wire wreaths, shoeboxes filled with holy cards.

The preparation room had been situated downstairs since Waxy first took over the business and had the cellar next to it dug out and enlarged for a casket selection room and the installation of a small freight elevator. The work had all been done back in the sixties, along with the other remodeling. The remodelers' final touches—knotty pine walls, a checkerboard floor of red-and-gray linoleum, the high-set windows with their pleated half curtains—gave the basement the look and feel of a rumpus room, of overnights at friends' houses, teen parties with a make-out pit off the furnace room. But here the glass behind the half curtains was frosted to discourage the curiosity of neighborhood children, and next to the furnace were the double doors to the prep room. These were lightweight, sheathed in metal so you could bang them open with a cart. A taped-on sign warned of just that (STEP BACK), and one of the doors had a small round Plexiglas window.

Through the window Sam could see Aboodeh hunched over the guttered table, and Uncle Waxy at his shoulder, guiding him. They were working on one end of what appeared to be a heap of blue toweling, out of which a pair of legs extended naked onto the cold enamel surface. The feet were angled in toward one another. The county ID tag attached to the big toe meant this was most likely an indigent case. As the *ibn Arab* moved out of the neighborhood, Tammouz & Sons had come to accept more and more indigents, mostly street people from near downtown, which county welfare paid for.

Aboodeh looked to be suturing the incision points, which meant they were almost finished with the prep. It was close work, and as Uncle Waxy repositioned an overhead worklight, Sam watched how its beam threw the shadow of Aboodeh's arm against the wall, dipping then tugging up and back, dipping and tugging. The room's floor and walls were tiled in white ceramic. That and the yellow-green overhead lights often gave visitors the impression of a surgery. But on closer examination that image would soon disintegrate. After all, those were hardware-store bolt cutters in the tray there with the hemostats and aneurysm hooks. And sticking out of a box filled with suture kits, that was an ordinary kitchen turkey baster; the box itself was a fisherman's tacklebox, its top tray filled with dime-store cosmetics. Uncle Waxy's profession was one of expediency. When hypodermic needles were needed to inject Perma-Glo dye beneath the eyelids, that's what he used; when a form was required for keeping the hands cupped naturally, restfully, he snipped tennis balls in half and dotted them with Crazy-Glue. Prep room workers wore black rubber aprons and gloves made of heavy-gauge neoprene, reminding Sam more of photo developers than surgeons.

He pushed the doors open and, even with the exhaust fan going full tilt, was met by the familiar smells of formaldehyde and disinfectant. And something else he'd noticed before in here; not a smell so much as a change in humidity, a dank feel he'd come to associate with the presence of a newly washed naked body. Or not *quite* naked. Wet toweling covered the head and groin, showing matted chest hair and skin that looked greenish-white under the surgical lights.

Aboodeh looked up then glanced over at the wall clock. "Time to go already?" he asked, hopefully.

Sam shrugged. Actually they had plenty of time. Aboodeh had told him to come by early.

"We ain' finished up yet, Sammy," Waxy said over his shoulder. "G'wan back outta the way," he added, then turned his attention back to Aboodeh and the body.

The body. Waxy always insisted on his workers referring to it that way, as the *body*. Never the *corpse*, or *cadaver*, or even *remains*. And never, ever, *stiff*, which was what the removal men, out of Waxy's hearing, usually called them. After all, that's how the removal men sometimes found them. The worst rigor Sam personally had seen was the one they called the Thinker. He had been found sitting on a sofa in front of his TV, leaned forward with an elbow on one knee, fist under chin in the posture of Rodin's famous statue. And stiff as a statue. Sam had been called in on that one. The removal men needed extra muscle to shove and heave the Thinker through a series of narrow doorways and around two stairwell landings. But rigor mortis was temporary. After a few hours in the cold room even the stiffest body would go limp again. When it did, the limpness seemed at times to create an appearance of passivity, Sam thought, even meekness; like this one, the way its head beneath the toweling kept dipping with each jab and tug of Aboodeh's needle, in what looked like timid little nods of submission.

While Aboodeh sutured the carotid incision, Waxy hovered close at his elbow, uttering throaty grunts of guidance, "*Ih . . . ih . . . ih . . . ih . . .*" It was quick but careful work. Sam watched how his cousin's heavy, muscular neck bent down to the effort of it, how reluctantly those thick shoulders stooped, shifting their bulk like some slow dumb animal, a bull or a donkey, being prodded *ih . . . ih* this way and *ih . . . ih* that way.

At one point, Uncle Waxy stepped back and nearly bumped into Sam. "Whad is it I'm just tellin' you, Sammy?" The clove breath from his tooth medicine pierced even the prep room smells.

"Sorry, Uncle." He circled around to the side counter. Watching a prep up close was a bit like watching a game of pool: the more you tried to get out of the shooter's way the more you ended up right back in it.

While they were finishing, Sam pulled a pair of rubber gloves from the wall dispenser and pitched in to help clean up and put away the equipment. He filled two sinks with disinfectant and a third with rinse water. Aboodeh, over by the other end of the counter, began arranging jars of Perma-Glo so they could be stored according to tint. Tammouz & Sons served a clientele that came primarily from Little Syria, so the prep room was kept stocked with an array of specially mixed batches in deepening shades of olive.

"Psst! Sammy!" Down the counter, Aboodeh was waving something. He held it still a moment, a small blue jar. "Cavicel!" he mouthed. Then, glancing around to check that his father had his back turned, he wound back as if to toss it.

Yeah, right. Sam showed him a bored, knock-it-off smile. He knew his cousin was only screwing around, that he'd never actually risk *throwing* it. But he got set anyway. Just in case. Cavicel, a concentrated embalming emulsion, wasn't dangerous in itself. In fact, prep workers kept jars of it handy as a kill-anything disinfectant. The problem was getting it wet. Its label warned that mixing with water will cause an intensely pungent odor. A reaction so intense and so fast, prep room workers who'd experienced it claimed that exhaust fans were useless; a Cavicel accident was always a house-clearing event. Which was why, as his cousin began to cock his arm back, Sam began to frantically shake his head no. For crying out loud, he was standing right over one of the floor drains! The *sinks* were right behind him! Besides, catching was a talent that Sam lacked, as Aboodeh very well knew . . . But the thing was already airborne, lobbed toward him in a high lazy arc. Sam snapped both hands out, and to his surprise not only grasped the thing out of the air but, after briefly fumbling it on his fingertips, even managed to hold on to it.

And, of course, it wasn't Cavicel, after all. Of course not. Just an empty jar of Perma-Glo. Even so, Sam couldn't deny the satisfaction he felt at catching it. If you're a male in America, not being able to catch somehow diminishes you. In the movies, the hero always catches the car keys or the coin, and always one-handed. It's in the comedies where you find a grown man on his hands and knees trying to find where the dime rolled to.

Sam tossed the jar back to his cousin, just as Uncle Waxy turned back around.

"Sammy! What're yous, ten years old?" Looking up, he called out, "Ya Rasheed!" addressing his dead brother. "What'm I suppose t'do wid this kid a yous?"

*Wrong direction, Uncle,* Sam thought. If the nuns at school had been right about anything, then the soul of Sam's father had to be somewhere *down* there, because Baba had been a *welad bendouq.* Everyone in Little Syria used to call him that—meaning *rascal*—even to his face, smiling and wagging their heads in admiration at this *billy-the-kid* who didn't give a damn what anybody else thought, who went right ahead and did what he wanted to do, when he wanted to do it. And if you didn't like it, he'd tell you—in English and in Arabic—to go straight to hell. *Djhunnum il Hamra* in Arabic. That was a *welad bendouq.*

Upstairs, waiting for Aboodeh to wash up and get his raincoat, Sam sat in his uncle's office, in the high-backed desk chair between the icons, listening to the wind. The icon on one side was the Virgin in tears, St. Michael on the other, thrusting his spear to prod the dragon down under the flaming grates of hell.

Yes, grates. When Sam was just learning English, he'd misunderstood and thought the nuns were talking about those sewer openings in the street. And it remained *grates* even after he learned better. The image remained fixed in his imagination, Baba on tiptoes amid the burning coals of *Djhunnum,* a *welad bendouq* in a white grocer's apron, stretching his scalded arms up through the slots of an enormous sewer grate.

The wind gusted heavily, making the office windows shudder. No night to be driving up to Detroit Metro. Or flying, either. They said the weather system was approaching from the northwest, out of Canada, so if the guy was coming in tonight, by now he would be in the teeth of it, starting his final descent. Welcome to America.

Turbulence

*There will be no accident. The sudden falling is each time followed by a sudden catching, and he is safe. No matter that each time this happens Teyib must hold the razor away from his chin and stiffen the grip of the other hand on the edge of the tiny aluminum sink. The stewardess,* speaking in English, calls it turbulence. Only turbulence. Again he feels it, the abrupt drop and the buckling of his knees beneath him. He has never flown before but turbulence is nothing to fear. He is safe. It is autumn here on the other side of the world, the season for storms. They say that here the leaves turn colors before they fall.

Thus they call it fall, but they mean the leaves that fall in the season of il khareef. Saying fall on an airplane does not bring bad luck. Even so, better to say autumn. Better, here on this side of the world, to say October, and not tishreen al awal. Watching his lips, he pronounces it carefully in the mirror: Ok-a-tow-a-bur.

The stewardess knocks on the door. She wants him to come back to his seat because of the turbulence. His chin feels cool where the little beard had been. Giving the mustache a final careful trim, he mulls over the word. Tur-bul-enz. Will he ever need such a word again?

"Sir?" The stewardess calls in English. "Sir?" She is growing upset and begins knocking with insistence. "Sir!"

He rinses the last of the lather from his face. "Patience!" he calls back to her in Arabic, Sabr! and waits for another sinking turbulence to pass before he slaps his face with aftershave. The mustache is a thin stubble now. It forms a straight line when he smiles, and how can he not smile? With the beard gone, the hair streaked with peroxide bleach, he must smile as if to a stranger, give himself the stranger's half-bow greeting. "Meen haddertakh, inteh?" he asks his reflection. And who do we have here? He laughs. Yes, you there with the little mustache and the yellow forelock, do we know you?

He feels the plane's descent. Nothing to fear. There will be no accident. Ever since an hour ago when the captain announced, "We are over the U.S." he'd begun to feel America's luck reach up to envelop him. They will be landing soon, and his American sponsor will be pleased to greet someone well-groomed. He unwraps a new shirt, bright blue, shiny like polished silk.

He is still buttoning the cuffs as he unlocks the door, and the stewardess immediately yanks it open. Her eyes are fierce with authority. She reminds him of an angry bird, chattering lockstep down the aisle after him to his seat, speaking English so quickly now that he can catch nothing but the single word "turbulence!" She sees to it that he rebuckles his seatbelt, warns him to keep it buckled from now on. He turns to

his seatmate, a red-faced British woman who had boarded the plane at
Heathrow, and offers her a package of Chiclet gum. She doesn't reply, only
takes a sniff of his aftershave and looks away, blinking.

It is familiar to him, this turbulence, like the soaring in dreams, the
sudden sinking and the upward sweep that catches you. He somehow
enjoys it. Glancing over, he has to smile at how the hands of the British
woman grip the armrests each time the turbulence drops then lurches the
plane up again, safe.

"Bit of a close shave, that," the red-faced woman says quietly, her voice
trembling.

"Thank you," he replies, and touches his chin.

Outside the oval window the storm clouds are dispersing and behind
them the sun is rising. Gazing downward, he watches a city passing below,
its lights winking out as the sun approaches. So far below it's hard to tell
what colors the trees have changed to. He pops two Chiclets in his mouth
and chews them vigorously until the pressure, like a growing fullness in
his bad ear, pops and begins to subside. Bad ear. Bad eye. He is coming to
America not quite whole.

All at once the wings tremble, and there is an odd, backward sensation
of the plane dropping tail first. This is new! he thinks. Next to him, the
red-faced woman lets out a yelp. He smiles, offers her the Chiclets box.
"Turbulence," he says to comfort her. "Only turbulence."

Moments later, looking down upon America he begins to laugh.
Turbulence—why be concerned that he will ever learn such a word?
W'Allah, he has learned it already!

# 7

The man waiting for them at the airport customs office didn't look anything like what the two of them had expected. Instead of some professional type in a business suit, the little guy bobbing nervously behind
the shoulder of the customs officer was dressed as if he'd just stepped
out of a disco club—platform shoes, flamenco-snug trousers, a glossy
go-go shirt, electric blue, with collar points that extended over the lapels
of his fitted jacket. And his hair! Blonde-tipped and streaked dark on the
sides, it looked as if somebody'd dunked the top of his head in a pan of
bleach. One of his eyes had an off-cast to it, wanting to look elsewhere
on its own. His eyebrows were black, and so was his small, pencil-line
mustache.

Sam tried to catch Aboodeh's eye, but the customs officer had directed the little guy their way, and he was approaching quickly, arms out
wide and a big smile. They greeted him with the traditional embrace,
each in turn touching right cheek, left cheek, right again, Lebanese style.
He smelled like a barber shop. Lilac Vegetal.

In age he appeared to be somewhere between Sam and Aboodeh,
maybe thirty, and he spoke a labored, schoolroom English; when he listened to their names, it was with head atilt, favoring one ear. "Mr. Abdullah?" he repeated their names as if they were questions, "Mr. Samir?"
Tagging on the *mister* was an old country show of respect.

Aboodeh waved away the formality, suggesting the man not call him
Abdullah but by the name's common diminutive. "I'm Aboodeh, okay?"

"Mr. *Aboodeh*," the man silently mouthed, then repeated it aloud,

"Mr. Aboodeh?" and rocked back a little as if unused to standing in platform shoes.

"Hey, relax," Aboodeh said. "And drop the *mister*, too. Think of us as cousins. Which we are . . . sort of." He turned to Sam. "Right?"

"Right." Sam put out his hand. Cousin or no, couldn't they have found somebody with better English? "Me, too. I'm just Sam."

The man hesitated before reaching up to take the hand, and when he did he kept his gaze averted as if suddenly stricken by shyness. "Jussam," he muttered in the direction of Sam's shoes.

"No." Sam smiled. "Just . . . ," he began and waited for the man to look up at him, "Sam."

"Sam!" the man said, pleased with himself. Then he lifted his eyebrows in a frank, searching expression. Even his slight cock-eye seemed to focus in. What was he looking for?

Sam chuckled. "What?"

"Teyib?" the man said. His Adam's apple bobbed. "Teyib?" he repeated.

Was he posing a question? "I don't understand," Sam said. Neither did Aboodeh. They both knew what *teyib* meant, of course, the word itself. In the old country people used *teyib*, literally meaning *tasty*, the way Americans used *okay*. But okay what? "What's *teyib*?" Sam asked.

"Maybe that's his real name," Aboodeh said. "Teyib's your nickname?"

Looking more confused than ever, the little guy screwed his face up but nodded yes anyway, too quickly, too enthusiastically. He wanted to please.

"That's probably it," Sam said. "Do they call you that back home?"

"*Parrrdon?*" the man asked, rolling the *r* like a Frenchman. Was he hard of hearing, too?

"Okay, okay," Aboodeh said. "Teyib it is." He motioned Sam to pick up the suitcase. "C'mon, then, *Teyib*," he said.

The man tilted his head as if maybe he *was* a little deaf.

Sam reached out his free hand and guided him by the elbow. The suitcase was small, made of laminated cardboard, and light as a feather. Probably the rest of the luggage was being shipped over.

As they passed through the automatic doors to the parking lot, the man gave a startled little jump back: doors that anticipate your approach! Leading the way, Aboodeh explained that the apartment they'd arranged for him was in back of a carryout store.

*"Pardon?"* Teyib asked, raising his voice.

Sam lagged behind a step, then put a finger up to his ear so Aboodeh could see: A little deaf, maybe?

Aboodeh tapped his temple: Or a little slow.

Rain and wind buffeted their car the whole way back from Detroit Metro. Turning off Telegraph Road, Sam wove through the five-fingers intersection and was about to take Manhattan Boulevard North when Aboodeh suggested a detour to show their guest more of the city. The whole way down from the airport, Sam had kept glancing up at the guy in the rearview mirror. He couldn't help it. There was definitely something familiar about this Teyib, but it wasn't the name or those clothes. And it definitely wasn't that blonde-tipped hair. What then? Probably just the greenhorn way he clutched his bag with both arms, sitting back there, eyes hardly daring to glance out at this new vastness he'd been set down in the middle of.

"This is called the downtown,," Aboodeh said as they turned onto Adams. "Like you have the Bourj."

Teyib acknowledged this information with a grunt, chewed his gum a moment, then asked, *"Il allam, feinuin?"* wanting to know where all the people were.

"Because rain," Aboodeh replied over his shoulder in foreign-speak. "Everybody get wet—yes?" Newcomers arrived expecting to see street life, plazas, *souqs* filled with people. "But you here, in America now. In America we don't get wet walking the street. We drive the car!" He mimed a steering wheel and said, *"Sierrah!"* Arabic for *car.*

"Automobile!" Teyib said, pronouncing it *otto-mobeel,* like a Frenchman.

"Yes! And someday soon you drive *otto-mobeel* too. Just like Sam." He gave a little snort in Sam's direction. "Except faster, I hope."

Sam smiled at his cousin and lifted his middle finger from the wheel. He'd always been a cautious driver—even more so since his accident— but Aboodeh wasn't permitted to drive any of the company cars. He had a lead foot, and last year, after four speeding tickets in as many months, Tammouz Enterprises almost had its entire fleet insurance suspended.

Leaving downtown they headed out toward the North End. Summit Street's warehouses gave way to blocks of abandoned commercial buildings, and then to the duplexes and cyclone-fenced empty lots that bordered Little Syria. Sam had been an eight-year-old child when he first came here. Only now, an adult, did he realize how forlorn these deserted American streets must look to a newcomer: the puddles and the litter, the bent patches of weeds dripping into the alley entryways. He remembered how, years ago, Baba had tried to ease Mama's homesickness and stop her crying. *Yes, I took you from your home,* he'd agreed, *but look around you!* Many of the families were moving out, but the specialty shops were still there back then—in the fifties—and the Eastern Rite churches, so the North End could still be called Little Syria. *Don't you see,* Baba exclaimed, *how your home is already here waiting for you!* But all Mama ever saw was that her parents had handed her off to an old man newly returned from America wearing a fine hat, his pockets sagging with Yankee dollars.

In the backseat, Teyib started on a new piece of gum. The rosewater smell reminded Sam of Beirut and the Chiclets boys selling packets of mastic beneath the statues at Martyr's Plaza. Teyib was chewing softly, or trying to, close-mouthed. But in the car's hush, even this was audible, rhythmically blending into the shh-shh the Lincoln's tires were making on the wet macadam. And then came another sound: a slow, bubbly gurgle. At first Sam thought it was Aboodeh's stomach, or his own. But the next one definitely came from in back. "Teyib," he said, addressing the rearview mirror, "did you eat anything on the plane?"

Silence.

"The Yankee's on our way," Aboodeh said. "Let's introduce him to an all-American burger-and-fries."

As they crossed Cherry, Teyib glanced back at the street sign. "Cherr-rry," he read aloud, rolling the *r*'s. "Ss-tuh. Dot."

"Street," Sam explained. "S T is short for *street.*"

Teyib made no reply, his jaw mechanically working the gum as he continued to gaze out the side window. A few minutes later he whispered to himself, "Ches'at-nut Ss-tuh. Dot."

"Was that you?" Aboodeh asked as Teyib's stomach made the noise again, a rumbling drop and rise.

The man smiled shyly. "Only turbulence," he said.

Business was slow, they practically had the place to themselves. Nikki set down the hamburger platter in front of Teyib and returned with a carafe of coffee. "Top that for you, honey?" she asked.

86

The poor guy, mouth full and chewing, looked up at her with such a perplexed expression on his face that she had to smile as she poured.

She stepped over to Aboodeh next. Then she came to Sam. He didn't acknowledge her, simply put a hand over his cup. "Not even a warm-up?" she asked. He turned to show her that, yes, he could look her in the face. He even forced a little smile as he shook his head no. She wore her pink waitress apron cinched snug at the waist, and the three of them watched her walk all the way back to the coffee machine. The way she walked, she knew they were watching.

Aboodeh nudged Teyib. "It's *nice* in America, eh Cuz?"

*"Pardon?"*

Down at the far end of the counter Nikki had begun refilling salt shakers and napkin dispensers. If she sensed someone staring at her, it was probably a feeling that good-looking women were used to. Sam spun slowly on the counter stool, putting his back to her before she could glance up and catch him. While he hadn't been unfriendly in the weeks he'd been back from the old country, he'd kept his distance.

"Her name's Nikki," Aboodeh said. Then he chuckled. "But you don't wanna know what I call her for short!" He laughed again, trying to get the guy to laugh. "Okay, okay. You wanna know?"

"C'mon, Bud," Sam said, "knock it off, will ya?"

"I call her"—Aboodeh paused for effect—"Nik." He smiled because in the old country *nik* was street language for *fuck*. "Get it? Nik? Nik-Nik-Nik!"

As they pulled into the driveway, there was Aboodeh's wife standing in the front window with the baby perched on her thrust hip. Sam threw the car into park and fluttered the fingers of his wheel hand in a little wave that she saw but declined to acknowledge. Salma scared him a little. "She pissed off?"

Aboodeh rested one hand on the door latch but made no further move to step out. "She's always pissed off." Turning to the backseat, he repeated the arrangements for Teyib's first week: a welcoming dinner at Aunt Shofia's this Sunday; some time midweek going up to Detroit to meet with their import distributor; but before any of that, first thing tomorrow, in fact, they had to take Teyib out shopping for some decent clothes. He took his hand off the door latch and sat back. "Let's see, am I forgetting anything?"

"We've been over it twice already." Sam saw that the toddlers, Tonia and Little Khaleel, had appeared at the window, peering over the sill. "She's waiting."

"Let her wait," Aboodeh said. "It's good for her." He opened his door, finally, but paused to turn and give Teyib a thumbs-up before stepping out.

Pulling away, Sam glanced up into the rearview, and there was Aboodeh, still trudging toward his front door, head down, sidestepping the tricycles and wagons left scattered on the walk. A modest three-bedroom ranch, mortgaged to the hilt. "Just a couple blocks down, a couple more over and we're home," he said, then corrected himself. *"You're* home."

The gum chewing stopped. "'Ome?" he said, mulling over the word.

*"Beitak,"* Sam said, trying it in Arabic.

The man sounded surprised. *"Beiti?"*

"That's right, *your* home. Behind my father's old store. See up ahead? The green awning?" A carryout now, it had been a butcher shop when his father ran it, the letters TAMMOUZ & SON MKT still faintly visible across the awning fringe, white on green. Above the awning were the windows of the apartment where Sam had grown up. The bay window was Mama's, where she sometimes sat for hours in that familiar posture of old country widows, one hand under the chin, the other grasping a rosary. Turning into the alley, he followed its sharp curve and parked opposite the store's cement loading stoop. Two side-by-side doors shared the stoop: the left one opened to the carryout's backroom, the right to the little apartment that, until now, had been his. "This is it," he said and shut off the engine.

No response.

*"W'silnah,"* Sam said in Arabic, *We've arrived.*

Teyib still didn't move. So Sam slid out from behind the wheel, went around and opened the car door for him. That, the little guy understood. He stepped out. Tomorrow, Sam explained, he and Aboodeh would be picking him up to do some clothes shopping. "But for now, though," he said, handing him the suitcase, "you can rest up."

He motioned Teyib to follow him across the alley stones, up onto the stoop to the right-hand door, where he demonstrated how to release the dual deadbolts, first the upper, then the lower. "Same key for both locks," he said. Then he stepped aside and offered the key. Teyib didn't make a move to take it. He just stood there wide-eyed, holding the cheap suitcase clutched to his chest. You'd think he was about to be marooned. *"Beit Teyib,"* Sam said, as if making an announcement. *House of Teyib,* unnecessarily formal, but this felt like a formal moment. He reached over and tucked the key in the man's jacket pocket. Then he pushed open the door and invited him in, Arabic-style. *"T'fedall!"*

The place was stuffy from being closed up, and, as usual, far too warm. But otherwise it looked all right, swept and neatened, just as Sam had left it. "Now you see why we always called it the *little* apartment."

Teyib didn't get the humor, nor did he seem disheartened by the smallness of the place. Curious, even starting to smile a little, he walked in and directly up to the cheap partition screen Sam was using to hide the alcove. He rose onto his toes to peer over it.

*"Shu haad?"* He'd discovered the stationary exercycle.

"Yeah, right," Sam said. "I still need to move that upstairs."

Teyib seemed bemused by the machine, smiling and frowning at the same time. Running his hand over the sturdy tube frame. Handlebars with plastic grips. It had pedals and a chain. But only *one* wheel? Rotating his hand, he asked Sam in pantomime: How can it go?

"Watch, I'll show you." Sam swung a leg over the saddle, and Teyib stepped back out of the way. "Don't worry, it's not going to run you over." Sam began to pedal, slowly at first, then a little faster, raising his voice above the noise of the chain and the whirring tire. "It's for exercise. You can make it harder to pedal if you want. Watch." He demonstrated by reaching beneath the handlebars and tightening the tension on a small hard rubber wheel positioned to press down atop the tire. Now Sam had to nearly stand in the pedals just to keep speed. "Have to exercise . . . my . . . hip. Every . . . day. Doctor said." The little wheel began to give off a hot rubber smell. Sam stopped pedaling and sat, resting his arms on the handlebars. "Whew!" He smiled. "Want to try?"

Smiling, Teyib begged off, giving the bike the old country gesture of dismissal, a single backhanded wave upward.

"Well, I'll stop by tomorrow and get this out of your way. All right?"

Teyib didn't reply. He had seated himself on the low, cot-sized bed and was taking in the alley view of the only window. His window now. His bed. His mirror. Sam always had to bend down to see himself in it. Among Americans he was average for a man, a touch under six feet. But there was no denying the Tammouz nose, the whorled black hair. His eyebrows came from his mother's side, the way they circumflexed above the nose. Don Ameche, Uncle Yousef liked to joke. But he'd grown to be taller than any of the uncles. Now, as he bent down to look in the mirror, his heart sank at the sight of himself. Big galoot on a tiny bike. He quickly got off the thing.

Teyib was back by the window again. He seemed to have forgotten all about his fear of being deserted. Turning in a long slow look about the place, *his* place now, he sighed like someone who had things to do. He was ready to be left alone.

"Okay, then," Sam said, extending his hand, "welcome."

Teyib took the hand in a too-firm grip, then too quickly let it go. He followed Sam to the door.

Out on the stoop Sam turned. "Remember now, I'll be right upstairs if you need me." He pointed past Teyib to where the alcove's sloped ceiling was formed by the staircase above it. "Those are my stairs going up. You just knock, and I'll hear you loud and clear." Teyib smiled at that. And held the smile, his weak eye wanting to drift, to look at other things. He was impatient to be alone. And why not? Here he was, in America, holding the door to his own place.

Sam stepped down off the loading stoop and across the alley stones. When he turned again to wave, he watched the door closing after him. His own door. He knew every creak and slam of that door. How strange to stand here and look at it from the outside. To hear from the outside those double locks click home.

BEIT TEYIB

*He can't help laughing. As soon as the door is closed, as soon as he has thrown both bolts into place and listened to Cousin Samir's footsteps diminish on the alley stones, the laughter rises from his belly. Beit Teyib? He can hold back no longer, free now to laugh out loud.*

*But his laugh sounds strange in here. Flattened by the curtainless walls, it echoes back at him from the left. The hearing in his right ear keeps wavering, sometimes filling with pressure to a high thin hissing that abruptly gives way to nothing. To simple, utter soundlessness.* Oreille de Beirut. *The French doctor had seen so many cases, he'd given it a name,* Beiruti ear.

*He sits on the little bed, waits for it to pass.*

*Above his head, the alcove's sloped ceiling begins trembling to a slow trudge, Cousin Samir's heavy feet ascending the stairs. Each footstep sends down a sprinkle of plaster. Teyib feels a sour rising from his gut. His first meal in America, and it does not want to stay down. The meat was all grease. It needed cumin. It needed parsley, too, and the onions ground right into it, like a proper* kifta. *He tries to belch, but tastes only rising acid, and he swallows against it.*

*Now, as for the automobile, that he liked. Truly an American automobile. Long, black, and bearing the name Lincoln, after the five-dollar president. So powerful beneath him, it could fly if only this Cousin Samir would have let it.* Teer, teer! *the Damascene song comes to him,* Fly, fly! O automobile, O swift one . . . *And now that he's thought of the song it remains in his head,* "Ya auto-mo-beel, ya gameel, ma ahlak . . ."

*Cousin Samir kept lifting his eyes to the rearview mirror, and still he had recognized nothing. Why? Because a clean shave? Because a little yellow in the hair? So simple. That, and a practiced calmness to the eyes, the way Zeid had shown him. So simple, he must laugh.*

*But not too much laughter, Zeid had warned.*

*At the airport in America he had been sent into one slow line after another, carrying his papers in both hands like a supplicant. Officials in uniforms had licked their thumbs and shuffled through his documents, hands working like casino dealers. Here, as in Beirut, they looked you in the eye before stamping your papers and again after. He tried to keep his face open, his expression calm. All of America waited for him beyond a low wooden railing, but he let them see nothing, those men in buttoned uniforms. Show them openness, he thought. Show them nothing. He watched them inspect his suitcase, close and seal it with stickers, set it down beyond the wooden railing. And like that his suitcase was in America—like that!*

*It took all he had to suppress his joy. To smile as he himself passed through the low gate of that wooden railing to join his suitcase in America!*

*Then to disappear. But how? He has to laugh, for Zeid's forgers must* have worked a miracle with the papers. At the airport it was as if his arrival had been expected, a cousin greeted by cousins. In America, Zeid had instructed him, there is a saying for what must be hidden: Under the nose, *the Amerkani say. Until you have your foothold, stay* under the nose, *where nothing can be seen. Keep your eyes filled with a show of wonder. But not too much wonder. Answer laughter with laughter. But not too much. When your time comes to go into America, go. Disappear.*

Ya auto-mo-beel!

Next to the bed the ancient wallpaper is peeling, revealing the plaster behind it. The wallpaper is patterned with bouquets of faded flowers. A design, only that, yet something about it troubles him. Unfolding across the wall, one flower burst after the other, each identical, like an urgent repetition. He peels back a loosened corner. The plaster beneath, already cracked, crumbles easily with just a gentle scraping of his fingernail. The urgency is his stomach, sickened by the airplane and the meal afterward. He catches the dust in his palm and licks it.

Above him, the ascending footsteps stop abruptly, shuffle, then begin to descend again. He remains still, quiets his breathing as he listens. The hesitant tread of someone who has forgotten something. Or remembered something. Maybe a face he's seen before? Teyib feels a sudden chill. But then the footsteps begin once more to ascend the stairs. He waits, perfectly still, as they step up over his head, up and up, fading. Gone.

He sighs. Breaks a small piece of plaster from the wall. Crushes it in his palm. W'Allah!—his second meal in America! The old timers tell stories of what they were forced to eat during the Turkish Famine. Chewing, he begins to feel better, cleansed after so much grease. His teeth are gritty, though. He places a mastic in his mouth, chews it for the saliva. This new home of his is stifling hot. The back window facing the alleyway is painted shut. He can open the door, but he doesn't like sitting in a room with a door ajar, much less a weed-choked door that opens to a row of trash bins, all smelling of mouse . . . or worse. The rats in Beirut had become bold during his last weeks there. No, far better to endure the heat.

His eye falls on the bicycle of the single wheel. A purposeless thing, its metal tubing gray with plaster powder. He dusts off the map lying on the shelf next to it and unfolds it. A wiggling red line, but is it leaving Zahleh in the Mountain, or is it just arriving there? Or both, perhaps, a purposeless back-and-forth? On the partition wall, a red pen hangs from a

*string. He refolds the map and puts it back where he'd found it. Soon all*
*these things will be out of here.*

*Then this truly will be* beit Teyib, *his own house.*

*Teyib unbuckles his trousers and belches. Finally.*

Beit Teyib. *A little bed, a card table, even a Western toilet. But for*
*a kitchen there is only a sink and a hot plate. Not even an icebox. So,*
*how can this be a house? He steps out of his trousers. What is a house*
*without the smell of food in it? Certainly not a* beit, *a proper house. And*
*yet, he is lucky. This is America, and they had greeted him as if cousin to*
*cousin, giving him his own house here where he can hide under the nose,*
*where—w'Allah!—where even this Samir looks into his face and does not*
*see him. He belches again. The relief! How can he not laugh?*

# 8

"Tee? Zee? You get it?" Aboodeh nudged Teyib with his elbow. "Toledo Zoo? TZ?" He laughed encouragingly. "Look over there." He pointed to the zoo's entry gates, the monogram letters *TZ* fashioned into their wrought-iron design.

Sam rolled his eyes. "He's not gonna get it, Bud." It was a children's joke straight out of Little Syria, *teezee* meaning *my ass* in Arabic.

The sun was warm as they stepped up out of the underground walkway from the parking lot to the zoo's admissions gate, and what had begun as a cold autumn day was turning into Indian summer. "How's that for perfect timing?" Aboodeh said, smiling up into the warmth.

They made the usual zoo circuit—elephants, polar bears, monkeys, big cats. Aboodeh called out to one of the camels, summoning it in Arabic— *T'ah la houn!*—and damn if the animal didn't stand up and walk directly to the fence! The sun grew even warmer as the afternoon progressed, and Sam took off his bomber jacket and carried it slung over one shoulder. Watching him, Teyib did the same with his own cotton jacket. But not Aboodeh. He'd shown up this morning in a new, trim-fitting leather car coat that came with a matching dutchboy cap. Bulky his whole life, Aboodeh liked to dress as if he were built lean; probably another "positive structuring" tactic from his DATA motivational seminars. To make the inner man successful, you must first change the outer man: in other words, *dress* skinny, and soon you'll *be* skinny. But the car coat was cut to a V style that would make you look sleek only if you were sleek to start with.

Its leather, tanned a deep reddish cordovan, was stretched tight over the wide back so that Sam, glimpsing Aboodeh in his side-vision, kept picturing a flayed side of beef.

At the great ape house, Sam hung back, held by the stare of Togo the silverback male. But after a moment, the gorilla spun around on its knuckles, and abruptly sat down, its muscular shoulders pressed against the thick glass. It remained that way, waiting to be left alone. Sam didn't move. Finally, the animal turned its head to glower at him over one shoulder, and in that instant Sam saw what it was that had caught his eye, a similarity between the ape's flat, jaw-thrusted frown and the memory of Baba's face. Absent the Tammouz nose, of course. But that heavy brow was remarkably like his father's, and those small, deep-set eyes, the way their troubled, disappointed gaze seemed to sharpen on him, as if expecting something. *Shu, Baba? What?*

Togo only sneered and turned away again.

*G'wan, scram, That's what.*

He found Aboodeh and Teyib waiting for him near the exit gates, close by the Elephant House. Aboodeh was saying something about blondes, but Teyib either wasn't listening, or else was interrupting Aboodeh on purpose. Speaking Arabic, he turned the conversation to the elephants, how he loved them, even the fresh smell of their dung. "It reminds one of steamed vegetables—no?"

Sam started to ask what was going on, but Aboodeh held up a hand. Looking Teyib straight in the eye, he spoke slowly, distinctly. "Blonde," Aboodeh said, "you understand?" He repeated, "Blonde?" and when that didn't click, he specified by adding, *"Lebanese . . .* blonde."

There was something about the earnest, clueless stare of Teyib's eyes that made Sam think the man might actually break down and cry as he looked questioningly at the two of them. Finally, Aboodeh made a wave of disgust toward the exit turnstile.

Watching Teyib pass through, Sam leaned in toward his cousin. "It's like he doesn't know a thing."

"Maybe he doesn't. Or maybe he's too cagey to let on. Ever notice how he hangs back from everything? Like he's listening, but not too hard? And all the time looking around, taking everything in when he thinks nobody's watching. Well, *I've* been watching."

"Watching *what?*"

"How he doesn't drink, for one thing. And how he doesn't smoke. Everybody from the old country smokes! But not him."

Sam laughed. "He does chew gum, though." He gave his cousin a playful cuff on the shoulder. "C'mon, Aboodeh."

"And that's something else, too. I don't think I've ever seen the guy laugh. At Aunt Shofia's, after dinner, when Uncle Yousef and Uncle Boutros were going back and forth with the Arabic insults and everybody's practically falling out of their chairs? I looked over at him and, swear to God, he looked like he was going to bust out crying." Aboodeh glanced beyond the exit turnstile, where Teyib stood waiting for them. "He's nothing like what I expected."

"But there *is* something familiar about him, too, don't you think?"

"You kidding? Not at all. Matter of fact, I'm beginning to wonder if the Mutranehs might've sent us the wrong guy by mistake."

"Easy enough to check out, I guess."

Aboodeh shook his head. "Phone lines over there have been scrambled for days now."

"The war." Sam nodded in sad agreement. "Sounds like it's spreading."

"It's not a *war.*" Aboodeh stepped back. His DATA training had taught him to avoid negative energy the way old-timers avoided the evil eye.

"Well, that's what they're calling it in the news."

"The news." Aboodeh lifted his leather cap and swiped a forefinger around its inner band. "As if the *news* knows anything about anything."

Last Sunday the zoo, this Sunday the Toledo Museum of Art. Sam kept the motor running while they waited in the alley. Teyib had come out dressed for the museum in a suit and tie, and Aboodeh had sent him back, directing him to change into one of the new slacks and sports shirt outfits they'd bought him.

All week Aboodeh had remained preoccupied with Teyib, pronouncing his name sarcastically, as if it were some kind of joke. And just as he'd suspected, when he finally did get through to the Mutranehs, they'd never even heard the name. Teyib, they agreed, was indeed unusual, and very likely an alias. At any rate, they certainly hadn't sent him. But Phares and Nabil both had been informed that someone might be sent from their Baalbek suppliers. At any rate, they planned to check into it as soon as the fighting up north subsided. Meanwhile, their advice was to keep the man occupied and don't let on.

"So, at least the phone lines are clear again," Sam said.

"Not only that, but the airport's up and running, too. Call came in from the Jim Wilson desk at Detroit Metro. There's a delivery already on its way out of Beirut."

"That's good news, right? I mean if they're shipping bodies, then they can start shipping import goods too."

"The Jim Wilson's arriving day after tomorrow." Aboodeh glanced over at Teyib's door. "What say we take our little buddy to the airport with us? Show him the ropes?"

"Sure. Why not?" After all, a Jim Wilson was best handled as a three-man job, one to stay with the hearse at the airline's loading dock, two to go in and cart out the box. "Who is it? Somebody from the neighborhood?"

"Remember Eliyeh Djuheh? From the furniture commercials?"

"Ahab the A-rab? Jesus, I thought he died years ago," Sam said. "He was ancient when I was a kid."

"Always told people he wanted to go back for one last look at Mount Suneen." Aboodeh laughed. "Well, goes to show, some guys oughta be careful what they wish for."

When Teyib reappeared he was wearing an outfit Aboodeh had bought for him last week: knit shirt, cranberry slacks with matching white belt and shoes. There was even a pair of crossed golf clubs stitched over the breast of the shirt. Sam didn't know what look his cousin had in mind for the poor guy—businessman on his day off?

"That's better," Aboodeh said, watching Teyib climb into the backseat. Turning back, he showed Sam a sly smile, one eye almost closed to a wink.

"What?"

Aboodeh didn't reply, but a few minutes later, he directed a turn onto Collingwood, saying he wanted to show Teyib the cathedral.

"That's not on our way to the museum."

"Sure it is. Now, step on it."

When the Holy Rosary Cathedral's twin romanesque towers appeared above the surrounding rooftops, Aboodeh twisted in his seat to look back at Teyib. Just as they were passing the front entrance with its enormous, two-story-tall wooden doors, he announced, "Church!" And made the sign of the cross. He did this slowly, deliberately, the way the nuns in grammar school had insisted it be done when passing by a Catholic church. Then he turned and signaled Sam with his eyes to follow suit. Sam blinked. A quick nudge and a frown insisted, *Do it! Now!*

So, okay, what the hell. Sam raised his right hand from the wheel and, thumb pressing two fingertips, crossed himself rapidly, forehead-breast-bone-right-shoulder-left-shoulder. A person could tell whether someone was Eastern or Latin Rite by the way they crossed themselves. In the West it's open hand, and you cross by touching left shoulder first, then right; in the East it's thumb and two fingers joined—the Trinity—and from right shoulder to left. Could *that* be what his cousin wanted to find out? But Aboodeh was looking out the corner of his eye toward the backseat. Sam glanced up into the rearview in time to see that, sure enough, now Teyib had begun crossing himself as well. But as if unfamiliar with the gesture, touching his forehead twice then his breast in rapid succession, almost like a . . . Sam exchanged glances with Aboodeh. Like a *salaam.*

"So, what do *you* say it is?" Aboodeh asked, his voice a respectful whisper. The sculpture was huge, reaching almost to the ceiling of the art museum's Grand Foyer, a construction of metal strips welded into a tight arc. Sam had to lean back so that his eye could follow its steeply rising curve.

Teyib, standing between them, also leaned back. He took a backward step, then another, craning to see the top of the thing.

"Like a bird's wing, maybe?" Aboodeh suggested. He was impatient to resolve the puzzle and move on. "Well, it's a bird," he decided. There. End of story. Now, taking Teyib by the elbow, he ushered him off in the direction of the Grand Gallery. The little guy looked uncomfortable walking in his new white-belt-white-shoes outfit, especially the cut of those low-riser slacks, so tight in the rear.

In the Grand Gallery, the three of them soon took up the pace of the crowd, a steady, respectful flow interrupted by occasional brief pauses at one ornately framed painting after another. Each doorway opened onto a new gallery and a new era, sun-dappled picnics shadowed by lurking fauns, still-lifes with ants crawling on the grapes, a bright landscape that faced you directly into a white sun.

Soon Aboodeh had had enough and was ready for coffee and a snack.

He was motioning Sam to hurry it up, when a man's voice knifed through the murmurs and hushed footfalls. "Good grief!" the voice declared. "Will you look at *that!*"

Sam turned to look. Everyone in the Modern Gallery turned. *That,* they all saw, was a large canvas consisting of three thick black strokes against a stark white background. The paint looked as if it had been applied hastily and with something like a mop. A newly acquired Motherwell, Sam recognized it from a recent Sunday *Blade* feature story.

The man was shaking his head in dismay. "I coulda done that myself," he said, "with my *eyes* shut!" At first he seemed to be addressing his wife, a grayish woman shrinking next to him, but then he turned to the crowd, chin up and smiling, as if expecting applause for his frank appraisal. He shifted his weight from one foot to the other, then tugged his belt up. A white belt. And matching white shoes. He was wearing an outfit just like Teyib's. Even to the cranberry slacks. No wonder the man's eye fell on Teyib. "Right, Sport?" he asked.

Teyib cocked his head toward his right ear as if he hadn't quite heard. Then he smiled and extended the gesture, touching hand to forehead in a brief salute.

Beaming, the man turned back to his wife. *See?*

Aboodeh glanced at his watch. "C'mon, Sport," he muttered, motioning Teyib toward the museum coffee shop.

"Sbort?" Teyib asked when they were seated.

"*Sp*-ort," Sam said. "*Spuh- spuh-,*" stressing the *p*, sound which does not exist in Arabic, then looked about to see if people were watching. The museum coffee shop—tiny, glass-topped tables beneath Cinzano umbrellas—was situated along an open walkway beneath a bank of skylight windows. You were supposed to feel like you were in an outdoor European cafe. Sam lowered his voice. "A sport is like baseball or hockey, see?"

Teyib seemed to turn in on himself while he translated. "Football?" he asked, finally.

"He probably means soccer," Sam said. "That's what they call soccer over there."

"No shit?" Aboodeh knitted his brows in fake sincerity. "Hey, thanks for telling me." He turned back to Teyib. "You follow soccer?"

"Me?" Teyib lifted his chin and clicked his tongue—"*Tch!*"—for *No.*

"You follow any sports at all?"

"Really, no," he said, then added, "Thank you, no," as if turning down an offer.

"Y'know, here in America," Aboodeh glanced over at Sam, "sports are very big."

"Very big," Sam agreed.

Teyib nodded solemnly. Wide-eyed. Determined.

"And each sport has its season," Sam added. As if he knew the first thing about sports, any sport. But he recognized in Teyib the clueless, desperately eager look of his own face, and it felt good for a change, being the one in the know. Acting like it, anyway. "There's baseball season, football season, basketball, hockey. In America, sports go the whole year round."

"Pretty soon it'll be the World Series," Aboodeh said. "That's baseball."

"Baseball, now there's your all-American game," Sam said.

"*All*-American?" Teyib asked.

"Yeah, all-American," Aboodeh said.

Teyib mouthed the term silently—*all-American*—as if it were a solemn promise. Then he sat back, smiling at Aboodeh, and at Sam. And then, oddly, at something beyond Sam. Sam turned. Nikki was approaching their table. The last person he expected to see here.

"Hey, another art lover!" Aboodeh called out. Sam was a little taken aback by how good she looked in a miniskirt. And that powder-blue sweater. Until now he'd never seen her in anything other than a waitress uniform.

Teyib leapt to his feet. "Hi," Nikki said, extending her hand. He took it in both of his . . . and held on as if he didn't quite know what to do with it. Shake it? Kiss it? He did both, first pumping away two-handed like an eager salesman, then bending from the waist to place a chaste, dry peck upon the top of her wrist.

Wide-eyed, Nikki smiled and turned to share her amusement with Sam. Teyib pulled out a chair for her and waited.

As soon as she was seated, Aboodeh scooted in close and rested his arm on the back of her chair. Her hair hung down in a thick ponytail, and she had to lift it free from him.

Sam looked away. "C'mon, Teyib," he said, "I'll show you the Egyptian room. They have a real mummy there." He stood, and Nikki immediately turned to him.

"Wait, Sammy," she said. "Can you wait just a minute?" She got up, extricating herself from Aboodeh's arm, and stepped around the table. "Can I talk to you a minute?" He followed her through the entry arch, out into the hallway. "I don't want you to get the wrong idea," she said. Her voice was soft, almost a whisper. "The only reason I came here today was I knew *you'd* be here."

"Me?" He looked down at her hand on his arm.

"Something came up I need to talk to you about. Can we talk a minute?"

"Sure." Through the entry arch he saw Aboodeh smirking and trying to catch his eye. "What happened? Did something happen?"

"No, no. I just need to ask you something." She glanced back through the arch to see what he was looking at. "C'mon." She led him around a corner and down a tapestried hallway into the Cloister Gallery. Dimly lit to depict a monastery courtyard at dusk, the Cloister was nearly empty.

Behind Nikki was a carved altarpiece of a beheaded saint holding his own head in his hands like a cantaloupe. The head, its face bearing a dead, wall-eyed expression, wore a bishop's miter. "Y'know, this room is kind of creepy," Sam said.

Nikki began a slow, meditative pace around the colonnade. "I haven't seen you around the Yankee for a while," she said, "so I didn't want to just call on the phone." She stopped and looked into his eyes. "It's a favor, Sammy. I need to ask you face to face, in person." Quickly, she went on. "Remember my home, the house I told you about that time, that I lost in the divorce?"

"Yeah, up in Ann Arbor."

She nodded. "Seems a couple months back my ex decided to just walk away from his job and leave town." She smiled grimly. "He didn't *tell* anybody, of course." She'd first heard of it when the loan officer from the bank called to inform her that the property had been inspected for repossession and, during the process of the usual paper search, it was discovered that her ex-husband had neglected to have her name removed from the house documents.

"You saying the house is legally yours?" Sam asked.

"I wish. No, it's just a technicality." But the bank *had* presented her with an offer of sorts. Rather than assume the default, their loan office preferred to see the place occupied and, frankly, making money for the bank. So, since her name was already on the deed, perhaps she would be interested in assuming the payments—"*Adjusted* payments!"—after fixing the place up, of course.

"Fixing it up?"

"Clean-up mostly, I think. Stuff that Deano and me, we could do ourselves. But there's other work, too. Leonard never did take care of things around the house, and they told me there's a few repairs that need to be done. Not a lot, I don't think. Just enough to get the place back up to code."

"Like what?"

"I don't know." She sighed. "I *wouldn't* know. That's why I thought of you, Sammy. That time when you told me you did repair work for your aunt's realty company?" She stopped and put her hand on his arm. "What I was hoping was maybe you could go up there with me and take a look?"

"Me?" He shook his head. "Geez, I don't know . . ."

Nikki withdrew her hand from his arm. "Well, I guess you can't say I didn't try," she said. "That's what I do best, isn't it? Just try and try . . ." She fell silent. She wasn't crying, but looked like she wanted to. It was something Sam had noticed before, working funerals, how sorrow can turn an already pretty woman even prettier. He was used to seeing Nikki under the stark, unforgiving fluorescents of the Yankee, pouring coffee, rolling her eyes at the fry cook. Not like this.

"All I mean is," he shrugged, "it's not like I'm an expert, or anything." Again, he shrugged. "But okay. I suppose I could at least take a look."

Just the catch of her breath and its release, like a sigh of relief, seemed to promise levels of gratitude he could only imagine. "My shift ends early on Saturday?" She said it like a question.

"Okay, sure. Saturday. We'll take a look, see if it's worth the effort."

"Worth the effort?" she said. "Your own home? Sammy," she shook her head and smiled.

"Just Sam."

"Sam. Don't you know, Sam? Your own home? That's *everything*. It's the American *dream!*"

HOOKERS

*Chewing his mastic-flavored gum two pieces at a time, Teyib recounts aloud to himself the street names and their order, fixing them in his* memory—*Mulberry, Superior, Ash, Huron, Locust, back around to Erie, Galena and Buckeye and Champlain . . .*

The American streets are emptier than he ever could have thought. How different from the old country, where you awaken to people's voices, the muazeen's call to prayer when the sky is still dark, and with dawn the cries of vendors. All day the chatter, the dice clattering on the backgammon boards, the bubbling of the water pipes, and voices in the streets talking, shouting. Here, even the automobiles are quiet.

On weekend drives the cousins Aboodeh and Samir take him to the museum, and if not there then back again to the zoo, or to a park called Oak Openings, or for a drive along the River Maumee. He prefers drives within the city. The countryside here is empty of people, field after field, and so are the enormous parks, their lonely woods. They stop to watch a group of deer cross the road, putting Teyib in mind of his father's flocks grazing in the empty barriyeh wilderness. "Poor things," he says. "Who herds them here in America?"

"The deer?" Cousin Samir asks, looking at him with growing curiosity. "In America nobody herds deer. These are not like sheep."

Teyib wants to end the matter so that Samir will turn away his face and stop staring at him.

"Did you always have just the mustache?" Samir asks. "Did you ever wear a beard as well?"

"A beard? Me! Why do you ask this?"

"No reason. Probably just the look of your face right now."

On weekdays, and then only at the noon hour, Teyib does see people walking the downtown streets. The American faces fascinate him—clerks, shoppers, noon-hour workers taking their lunch on benches in the sun, all of them good-looking people. Not like in the Bourj Plaza. Here he sees no leprosy at all, not even the leonine look that indicates its onset; nor is there any face, not a single one, with the scars of smallpox.

Many men wear mustaches, but none wear them trimmed small and narrow like his. Here, they prefer thick and droopy down the sides of the mouth, the fashion they call cheeto bandito, with long sideburns.

Downtown at night, the only faces are of those going in or coming out of the bars along Monroe and Madison: the Scenic, whose men, their eyelids darkened like women, must surely be the loti of America; and the Zanzibar, whose black sharameet stand outside on the pavement and stare at him shamelessly until he must cross the street. In the old country there are sharameet, too, but here none of them appeal to Teyib, neither the sood Zenji nor the white. Here they are called hookers. The word alone frightens him.

In his home a little shaving mirror hangs on a pipe that rises out of the shower's cement floor. This morning he stares into it through the steam and, before he knows it, he has shaven away the little mustache.

The carryout closes weeknights at eight, and there are no ahwa coffeehouses here in the near-downtown, no neighbors to make noise, no voices, no footsteps even. Escaping the silence, Teyib decides to step out beyond the neighborhood, out where the houses look closed at night, with shades drawn and their large pull-down doors facing the street. At first he thinks that the doors open to attached family shops that are shut just now, probably for some American holy day. He is amazed that everyone in America has shops. When Cousin Aboodeh hears this ("You mean garages?") he laughs until his heavy shoulders shake.

"Everybody in America has cars," Cousin Aboodeh says. "But first things first. You save up for a television first."

Walking at night, Teyib is approached by a young man wearing an expensive-looking overcoat He is of the darkest of the zenj, his skin black enough to be called Sood. Corralling Teyib toward a lamppost, the man reveals a display of jeweled watches kept hidden beneath his coat sleeve. He is selling them.

Teyib lifts his chin sharply and clicks his tongue—tch! But the peddler doesn't understand no; he keeps pleading and calling Teyib his man.

"My man," the zenji says, his voice thinning to a whine, "this one has seventeen jewels. And this one here, this one here's Swiss made! C'mon, my man."

Teyib tries to step around but the man puts forth his hand, fingers out-stretched, and the fingers are laden with rings, both men's and women's.

"Got solid silver sterling, got solid gold sterling, too."

Teyib does not want a ring or a watch, but he does not want trouble, ei-ther. He feels the threat of physical danger, a familiar tensing that he hasn't felt in the weeks since coming to America. His head clears. He stands still, *stops chewing his gum and changes the set of his face, readying himself for anything. Live, die. One or the other. Right here and right now.*

*The man notices that something has changed. "Easy. Take it easy. Hey, look what I got here for my man." He holds out a small plastic box the size of a cigarette package, clicks a dial along its side. A little voice comes from an ear piece at the end of a pink wire. It is a miniature radio. The man raises it to Teyib's ear. A voice rises from thrill to thrill above the noise of an excited crowd. It is announcing American baseball.*

*"How much?" Teyib asks.*

# 9

Sam was driving the hearse back from Detroit Metro, and just as the car behind him pulled out to pass, he glanced over in time to catch the front-seat passenger making the sign of the cross.

"Think you can pick it up a little?" Aboodeh said. Sam had chosen Telegraph Road instead of the interstate. A slower route, sure, with a lot of two-lane stretches between Detroit and Toledo, but with far less truck traffic to deal with. Besides, now that they'd met the plane and picked up the Jim Wilson, what was the big hurry?

"Ball two," Teyib said. Seated in back on the fold-down jumpseat, he was idly fingering the dial on a little transistor radio. Oblivious to everything except the baseball game in his ear. Every now and then, a barely audible "Stee-rike two!" came out of him, or "High and inside," in a quiet, breathy little voice. Imitating the sportscaster.

He didn't have a lot of room back there, and had to keep one arm braced between himself and the long Ziegler box that kept sliding up against him. The box, standard equipment for transport of Jim Wilsons, was sheathed in zinc and reinforced for overseas shipping. Its lid had been soldered shut all around with a heavy leaden bead, the required hermetic seal. There were stickers on the lid in Arabic and French, and it had a stamped manifest attached to its side with postal tape, like any ordinary warehouse delivery.

Sam loosened his necktie. He didn't want Nikki to see him dressed like a mortician. Some people are more sensitive than others to what's known in the profession as "the contamination of death," and he figured

Nikki for one of them. Thinking ahead, he'd set aside a clean pair of jeans and a workshirt at his tool shop in the funeral home's garage. As soon as he was finished with the Jim Wilson, she and Deano were picking him up, and the three of them were heading to Ann Arbor.

"Foul ball," Teyib muttered.

Sam glanced up at the mirror. Although transporting a Jim Wilson involved some heavy lifting, Uncle Waxy insisted that his workers dress like professional representatives of the funeral home. White shirt, dark coat, tie. But the closest Teyib had to a white shirt was a pale salmon, a color so flesh-like that from a distance it looked like he had no shirt on at all. And Teyib may as well have been shirtless for all the customs people back at the airport had cared. They'd rushed through the paperwork—hurriedly examining the embassy seal and checking the transit permit against the transit labels—before simply waving the box on through. Glad to have the thing off their hands. Then to go and wash those hands and remove the contamination of death. Professional look, what a laugh. A guy could pick up a Jim Wilson in bathing trunks!

According to Uncle Waxy, the contamination of death affected all kinds of people you'd never think it would. He claimed to have known hospital workers—nurses, orderlies—who would dodge having to prepare a body by simply shutting the door and letting the next shift discover the death. Even some doctors, once they're out of medical school, will avoid touching a dead body. There were *morticians,* Waxy said, who ran the business from their offices and contracted out the hands-on work. But the worst case that Sam or any of them had ever heard of had been right in the family. Aunt Olga, Uncle Waxy's sister-in-law who lived in Louisiana and every Christmas came north to visit. (Or "naw'th," as she drawled it out; how odd to hear her chatter away in her Baton Rouge dialect, then smoothly slip into Damascene Arabic!) Aunt Olga seemed normal in every respect, but if somebody mentioned death, or flashed even a memorial card in front of her, she'd start turning pale. The phobia worsened in her old age, eventually taking her to where she refused to sit on a sofa if she suspected that someone who'd died had previously sat on it.

One of life's ironies, of course, was being the way Aunt Olga was and having your only sister marry a mortician. It was because of Aunt Olga that Waxy and Nejla, years before, had bought and moved into the bungalow across the parking lot from Tammouz & Sons. Aunt Olga died in that bungalow on a visit north, New Year's Day, 1971.

Sam parked at the rear of the funeral home, backing up to the small, hydraulically operated service elevator that off-loaded one floor below, directly opposite the prep room. Aboodeh unlocked doors and cleared the way, leaving Sam and Teyib to do the heavy lifting.

"Remember to use your knees when you set it down," Sam said.

"Neez?" Teyib asked, his voice straining. The Ziegler box wasn't just heavy; this one had no handles, only the sharp zinc edges.

"Yeah, knees. You know, *il rikub?* "

"To hell with it," Aboodeh said. "Just hurry!"

After they got the Ziegler box down to the prep room and positioned on sawhorses, Aboodeh removed the green vinyl envelope taped to the lid. He broke its plastic seal, peeked in at the photo and transport documents inside before handing the envelope over to Sam. Then he snapped on rubber gloves, took up a hammer and a heavy, wide-bladed screwdriver and began tap-tapping at the lead bead. Sam and Teyib backed out of the way. The air escaping from the gap smelled sweetish at first, but soon took on an acrid, chemical tang.

Aboodeh paused, sniffed. "Who ordered sardines? You, Sammy?"

"Not me." Sam switched on one of the two exhaust fans. "Must be your breath."

Once the lid was free, Aboodeh motioned Teyib to take one end and help Sam lift it away. Inside, the body lay zipped into a black vinyl bag. Aboodeh took hold of the zipper ring, gave Teyib a wink—"Ready for this, Sport?"—and unzipped the bag down far enough to expose the head and chest. The face was covered with what looked like a dusty white washcloth. The chest hair, matted and white, was even whiter from the formaldehyde powder that had been sprinkled into the bag.

Aboodeh took a corner of the washcloth, waited a beat, and with a magician's flourish, yanked it away. "Ta-DAH!"

White male. Old. Eye sockets like black caves. But close enough in resemblance to the document photo to satisfy the required identification matchup. More than close enough, Sam thought. No mistaking that nose, those large bucky front teeth with a glint of gold bridgework on one side. Any Toledoan with a TV set could have identified that face. Back when Eliyeh Djuheh ran a chain of furniture outlets, he'd appeared in a series of locally produced commercials costumed as "the Sheik of Araby" in full Bedouin garb. Or, for a living room sale he might be "Al E. Baba" in baggy *sharwaali* trousers and a tasseled *tarbouche* fez, invoking *Open Sesame!* as a sleeper sofa magically unfolded. The background song of all his commercials was "Ahab the A-rab." The going-out-of-business sales he ran pretty much annually were a local joke, and while some in the Little Syria community saw him as an embarrassment, others gave him credit for taking a song whose function, if not intent, was ridicule, and turning it into money. A real success story, Eliyeh Djuheh. Having shoveled gold from America's streets, he'd managed to return to the old country in time to die in the shadow of Mount Suneen, a rich man, and full of years.

"You two get the shoulder end," Aboodeh said. He positioned himself at the feet. Seeing Teyib hesitate, Sam reached over and zippered the bag shut.

Aboodeh gave a three-count, and they hefted the bag up and over to the guttered table.

"Now the lid," Aboodeh said. "We need to set the lid up on the counter."

"Up there?" Sam asked. "What for?"

"Because that's where I want it."

Teyib helped lift the Ziegler's lid, flipping its slightly domed top upside-down on the counter. Then, brushing the flats of his hands together, he gave Aboodeh a questioning nod toward the double doors.

"You want to leave? Now?" Aboodeh crossed his arms over his chest, bemused and a little surprised. "You sure?"

"We're done, aren't we?" Sam glanced at his watch. Nikki's shift would be ending soon. "What else did you want us for, Bud?"

"What, you got a hot date?"

"Maybe."

Teyib shifted his weight from one foot to the other. It was clear that all he wanted was to get out of the prep room.

"Okay, go ahead and go," Aboodeh sighed, "both of you," but he placed a hand on Sam's shoulder and kept it there.

With a grateful half-bow, Teyib turned to leave. He wiped his hands on his suit coat before touching the double doors, then wiped them again after he pushed them open.

Aboodeh didn't take his hand from Sam's shoulder until the doors finished swinging. "Fucking guy looked scared," he said. "Can't believe he actually took *off.*"

"Why not?" Sam shrugged. It was simple. "Contamination of death," he said.

"Maybe." Aboodeh shook his head. "But I get the feeling like this guy doesn't have a clue."

"So?" Sam checked the time. "Neither do I."

"Yeah, you." Aboodeh chuckled. "But you, Cuz, at least *you* I can trust." He thought a moment. "Listen. Next week we're meeting with our distributors up in Detroit. Let's let *them* have a look and see what they make of Teyib, or whatever his name really is."

"I don't think there's anything to worry about. But, okay, whatever."

"Until then, we need to keep him occupied. But not here at the funeral home."

"How about the carryout? Gene Moon can always use help."

Aboodeh thought it over a second, gave the nod. "Yeah. Good enough. Until this gets cleared up, we'll just put an apron on the guy."

"So." Sam glanced down at his watch. "Okay, then?"

"Yeah," Aboodeh laughed, "okay. You go meet that hot date. I got stuff to finish up here."


Flashlight. Measuring tape. Wire strippers? Maybe. Sam scanned the pegboard. Pipe wrench? Probably. Cramped into a corner of the L-shaped garage, the maintenance tool shop was a mess, the workbench overflowing with all manner of odds-and-ends leftovers from former repair projects—clamps and washers, faucet springs, pieces of copper tubing. Things that guys who fix things might find useful again someday. He'd even stored his crutches here, suspended above the pipe wrenches and the hacksaw blades. Because you never know.

Drain snake? Maybe. Voltage meter, for sure. He latched shut the toolbox and hefted it outside to Nikki's rust-colored Ford Galaxie. She gave him a little wave from behind the wheel. Folding down the passenger seat, he saw that her son was sitting in back. "Oh?" He gave the kid a smile. "Hi there."

The boy looked up from a little handheld pinball game. Interrupted, he didn't return the smile, instead met Sam's eyes with a blank stare and asked, "Wha-at?" He didn't look to be a teenager quite yet, but his voice already had that bored flatness.

Nikki turned and gave him a stern look. "C'mon, Deano, what did I tell you?"

Apparently the boy didn't remember. "Wha-at?" he asked again.

Sam set the toolbox on the floor, flipped the seatback upright, and got in next to Nikki. "So it's Dean-*oh*," he said. "What's that, a nickname for Dean?"

Behind them the boy exhaled a slow, wet snortle, but otherwise didn't reply. Nikki gave Sam a raised-eyebrow look, grownup to grownup, and pulled away from the curb. She was dressed for housework, jeans and a chambray shirt. The bandanna holding back her hair was dark blue, and by contrast made her forehead look even whiter. "This is Sam," she said.

"I *know*," Deano replied.

"It's his sinuses," she explained. "The antihistamines haven't kicked in yet."

Sam had seen the boy before in the Yankee, sipping Cokes while he waited for his mother to finish a shift. He was thin like Nikki, small shouldered and blonde, but he must have gotten those blue eyes and that high dolphin-domed forehead from Daddy. Whoever *he* was. "When I was a kid, younger than you," Sam said, "I wanted my nickname to be Ike."

That seemed to surprise Nikki. "Did you say Ike?" she asked. "As in *Ei*senhower?"

"Yeah, as in *I like Ike*." He explained that he'd first seen the phrase back when he was newly arrived in America, on one of the old campaign buttons his cousin Khaleel collected. The face of the smiling American named Ike had seemed kindly, and people liked him. Khaleel died not long after that. He had quite a collection, buttons going back to the thirties.

"Thanks for doing this," Nikki said.

"Haven't done anything yet."

"Still, you coming along like this. I appreciate it. We both do." From the back there came the spring-release sound of Deano's little pinball gadget followed by the rattle of a bb ricocheting off hard plastic.

"So, this house up in Ann Arbor. You say the bank's going to let you take over payment if you bring it up to code?"

"Better than that," she said, so pleased she was smiling to herself. "*Adjusted* payments!"

"Well, that sounds like some deal."

"Really? Do you really think so?"

"Well, yeah," Sam said. For a moment he considered voicing the opinion that if a bank *could* have unloaded a property as is, it would have; instead he added, "Depending on the condition of the place, of course."

For some reason, that made her sigh. "Thing is," she began, then paused, waiting for a bb to roll down a plastic chute, "the loan officer said that Leonard had neglected the place."

"Neglected?"

"Sounds like he went and trashed a few things before he took off." She touched her bandanna. "Typical. I don't know how bad, though."

In back two bbs bounced and rattled home in rapid succession—*ding! ding!*

"Well, I guess we'll see when we get there." Sam tried to sound hopeful. "One thing at a time."

And one thing he noticed, after they reached Ann Arbor, passed through and drove on beyond it, was that the house wasn't exactly *in* Ann Arbor but more like, as Nikki put it, "in sort of a suburb." Another thing was that her "sort of a suburb" turned out to be a good five miles *beyond* the Ann Arbor city limits, on a country road so deep into a cornfield that its last half-mile wasn't even paved. But then, why should he be surprised? Nikki and Leonard owning a house in *Ann Arbor?* What was he expecting, some professor's mock-Tudor on Faculty Row? He closed his vent against the road dust catching up to them as Nikki slowed to a stop. "This is like the middle of nowhere," he said. "What'll you do out here, you and Deano all alone?"

Nikki turned to him. "It's not the middle of nowhere," she said, mildly annoyed. "And there's plenty of waitress work in a college town." She glanced back at Deano, who was asleep in the backseat; apparently, the antihistamines had finally kicked in. "Besides, I don't expect to be alone for long." She pushed the gearshift into *park*. "That's never really been a problem for me."

From the outside, the property looked simply run-down, an abandoned house at the edge of a weedy lot. Paint peeling, a cracked front window, porch steps needing repair. It was inside that the real damage revealed itself. The minute Sam stepped into the front door he could see that Leonard hadn't "neglected" the place so much as tried to *destroy* it.

All the rear windows broken out, holes gouged in the walls. Ceiling in one bedroom stained with a sooty deposit from some sort of oil fire. In the bathroom, it looked as if he'd taken a hammer to the commode.

"Well," Sam said, "at least somebody thought enough to turn off the water."

"More like Leonard just didn't pay the utility bill."

"Lucky he didn't." Wall tiles had been pulled down, and the floor was littered with charred paper—another fire?—and ceramic shards from the toilet bowl. The jagged stump remained bolted to the floor. "Still, just from what was in the refill tank, I wouldn't want to guess at the kind of water damage we'll find under those floorboards."

Deano was looking into the bathtub. It was an old cast-iron model, practically indestructible. As a finishing touch, Leonard must have poured something corrosive in there to see if he could pit out the enamel.

"Looks like he poured some here in the washbasin too," Nikki said. She was at the medicine cabinet mirror, tucking escaped strands of hair back under the blue bandanna. The mirror was the only *un*damaged thing in the entire bathroom.

But for a guy like Leonard, Sam figured, what's another seven years bad luck? "Was your ex superstitious?" he asked.

"Superstitious? Leonard?" She looked at him, chin up. Her jawline, prominent anyway, looked naked and sharp and seemed to jut out at him. "Why do you ask that?" She was seething.

"Nothing. Just wondering what the guy was like."

"What the guy was like?" Her eyes widened. "What the guy was *like?*" She held out her hands, palms up. "Like this." Her gesture took in the bathroom, the whole house. "*This* is what he was like."

For some reason, her exasperation got a chuckle out of Deano. He observed that "Uncle" Leonard may as well have burned the place to the ground.

Wrong thing to say. His mother, looking stricken now as well as angry, told him he didn't have to be here if he didn't want to. She took a cigarette from her shirt pocket and began rifling through the kitchen drawers, looking for matches. Sam didn't know she smoked.

"But I do have to be here," Deano protested. "I *always* have to!"

Nikki slammed a drawer shut and spun around. "You wanna leave? Then leave, get outta my sight!" The boy's chin trembled with rage, but his eyes remained cool. He tried to suck air through his congested nose, finally opened his mouth with an audible little gasp. Then he turned and left, slamming doors behind him. After a moment, the car door slammed as well. Through the kitchen window, Sam could see the boy in the backseat. He appeared to be simply sitting there, staring ahead.

Nikki was leaning over the stove top, trying to light the cigarette off it. The gas ring kept sparking, but wouldn't flame. "He wants to pout, let him pout."

"He did have a point, though," Sam shrugged. "His 'Uncle' Leonard really could have burned this whole place down."

"Oh, totally," Nikki agreed. "He *totally* could have burned it down. And he would've, too, except—" Her jeans were tight-fitting, and bent over that way, she held her rear end cocked like a pool player's. "Except that he probably couldn't find any *fucking* matches either."

"I didn't know you smoked."

"This isn't gonna happen," she said, giving up. "He must've done something to the propane line." She turned to Sam. "I don't even *smell* gas. Do you?" She was holding the cigarette pinched between her thumb and forefinger, like a joint. "Okay. What do you think?" She slipped the joint—now he could see its pointy end—into her shirt pocket. "About the house, I mean. Just tell me."

"I gotta be honest. Right?" He waited, but she didn't reply right away, instead continued to look up at him, wide-eyed. She wasn't going to make this easy. Suddenly he felt very tired.

"Just *tell* me," she hissed.

Something in her voice—defiance, stubbornness—dared him to do his worst because she was determined to hear only what she wanted to hear anyway. "Okay," he sighed. "I'm no expert, okay? I can do *some* things. I've worked on basic wiring—*simple* basic wiring. Some plumbing. But I gotta say, a lot of what I'm seeing here, Nikki, it's beyond me. Way beyond what I know how to do."

"Like what?"

"Like what? Well, like the propane, for one thing. I've never connected gas lines before. Never even *seen* it done. I wouldn't know how to *begin* looking for a leak. And there probably *is* a leak somewhere. But where? In the line? In the connections? In the tank outside? And even if I did find it—"

She put a hand out between them. "You're telling me you won't even try? Is that what you're saying?"

"I'm saying I could blow us up."

"Okay, then, say we forget that part of it." She swatted that idea away with her hand. "Forget the propane part."

"It's not just the gas, Nikki. Look, some things I *know* I can fix. I've installed new commodes in the rentals. Helped do it, anyway. But if there's serious water damage, well, you need a contractor to look at something like that." She drew a sharp breath, and he waited for her to say something, but she remained silent. He tried a different tack. "I mean, look at it the way the bank does. If you walked away today, I wouldn't be surprised if they sent in bulldozers to finish what Leonard started. Because right now, this lot has to be worth more to them than a house in *this* condition."

"But the bank told me that if I occupied and, you know, made it livable . . ." She swayed a little and reached back, touched the kitchen counter behind her. "The loan officer called it a sweet deal."

"Sweet for *him*. Think about it. Why should the bank sink its resources into repairing the place when it could get you to sink yours?"

"Well, what then? Just give up?"

She wasn't just pleading with him. There was something else now in the narrowing of her eyes, and it came to him that she'd brought him here expecting that once he saw this place he would love it. No wonder she looked heartbroken. This was her dream home that she'd brought him to, and here he was, almost as bad as Leonard, pissing all over it. "All right, Nikki," he said.

"All right what?" She took a step closer and looked up into his face. Her expectant posture, the hopeful lift of her eyebrows, everything about her seemed to promise gratitude, rewards he'd only dreamed of, if only he'd tell her what she wanted to hear. So he did.

"All right," he said. "Sure. I mean, I'll do what I can do."

"Bet I know how he broke it," Deano said during the drive back.

"Broke what?" Sam asked.

"The toilet bowl. Leonard told me he learned how when he was in Alcatraz."

"Alcatraz?" Nikki said. She looked away from the road long enough to send Deano an icy glance. "Leonard was never in Alcatraz," she said. "Or *any* prison." She tucked a loose strand of hair behind her ear. "Maybe the School for Boys. Or Juveniles, or whatever they call it. But not *prison.*"

"All I know is that's what he told me," Deano said.

"See why I had to get Deano away from him?" Nikki said, her eyes on the road. "He was a terrible influence."

"It's real easy," Deano said. "What you do, " he leaned forward, clutching the back of the front seat, so that Sam could feel the words on the side of his neck, "you save up a bunch of toilet paper? And you stuff it all down inside that hole at the bottom of the toilet bowl."

"In the trap?"

"The hole," Dean said. "You know, the *hole*. Where all the you-know-what goes down?"

"Yeah, it's called the trap."

"Anyway, what you do is, you keep stuffing paper down there until all the water gets soaked up. Okay?"

"Yeah."

"Then, you take newspaper you've been saving up—magazines, pages out of books—anything you can scrounge that'll burn, okay?"

"Okay." The kid had it down like some recipe.

"And you bunch up all the magazines and paper in a big pile until the toilet bowl's full. Then, you just . . . light it with a match."

"But what about the water?"

"The toilet paper that's *underneath* already soaked it up." There was a hint of disdain in his voice, as if forced to explain the obvious. "If you put in enough toilet paper, the top part'll stay dry. See?"

"Oh, I see, all right." He could see that Little Deano wanted to try out this little recipe himself someday.

"Okay, then. So you keep throwing on more newspapers and magazines and keep getting the bowl hotter and hotter and hotter. When the whatchamacallit's, the white part's really hot—"

"The porcelain?"

"Yeah, when the porcelain's really, *really* hot, everybody stands back . . . except one guy, and he's *ready* to jump back. And then . . . ." Here Deano paused for effect. "The last thing, what this one guy does just before he jumps back, he *flushes* the toilet. Cold water gushes in, hits the red-hot porcelain and—ka-*BOOM!"*

Nikki flinched so violently that Sam almost reached for the wheel.

## PATIENCE

*The first morning sound from the street is of Teyib himself, cranking down the store's green awning. Then the sound his broom makes sweeping the pavement in front of the store. Sweeping, he will sometimes look up and catch sight of* Im Samir *sitting in the bay window upstairs, praying her beads as she looks down on the deserted sidewalks below. Each time he sees her he waves, and although she has grown impatient with waving back, he doesn't know how to stop without seeming to offend.* Im Samir, *he addresses her out of respect, Cousin Samir's mother. And because he pities her. How it must pain her that it is Mr. Gene, an* Amerkani, *who runs her dead husband's store instead of her son, Cousin Samir. The leftovers that she sends downstairs comprise the only food Teyib has found truly worth eating in America. In the old country it is said that a cook of such talent has secrets. Someday he will summon the courage to ask* Im Samir *if he can watch how she makes the cinnamon sauce for her eggplant with pine nuts.*

*What Mr. Gene Moon gives him to do is not work so much as it is a show of work—sweep the store's two narrow aisles, sort the soda pop bottles, deliver a cartload of groceries, crank down the awning. Whatever it is, he does not demand it. A good-natured man, he prefers to ask, as if an idea has just occurred to him. "Teyib, why don't you go on down to the Yankee and bring us some burgers for lunch?" Always hungry, Gene Moon is so thin he wraps his apron strings back around his waist and knots them in front. He was a coal miner before coming to Toledo, and his skinny arms are as strong as coiled cables. After lunch Teyib watches him go off behind the beer coolers, there to stand and rock on his heels for minutes at a time, smiling to himself, thinking that Teyib cannot hear the quiet farts he is passing.*

*Whenever there are customers, Mr. Gene works the cash register.*

*When there are no customers, he stands with the newspaper spread
open on the counter, laughing out loud at a section called funny pages.
Sometimes he calls Teyib to come look. He taps his finger from one little
picture panel to the next, trying to explain what is funny. Teyib has seen
funnies before, but these are in English. So, when he laughs, it is only out
of consideration.*

*Gene Moon tries to explain the neighborhood to Teyib, the order of the
surrounding streets and their names. He traces the different bus routes,
where to wait for which, how much to pay.*

*The North End is an old neighborhood, Mr. Gene explains, and
the curbs are set high the way they are to make it easier for a rider to
dismount a horse. There are stretches of Champlain Street near the
Buckeye Brewery where you can still see creosote-soaked wooden paving
blocks from the last century. In some places Teyib has to watch out for
trolley tracks left over from olden days; the gap alongside each rail is wide
enough to swallow a shoe.*

*He goes forth with the radio in his left ear, listening to whatever game
is being broadcast; anything, so long as there is a voice talking, talking,
talking, the harsh chomp and bite of its English so full of slang he gives up
trying to understand it. No matter. The important thing is that the voice is
always there, always saying something even when the crowd noise swells—*
High fly ball to center field! Estevez is under it . . . and it bounces out of
the pocket!

*With his right ear Teyib listens to the counter girl in the Yankee Cafe,
humming as she folds silverware into paper napkins. Her name is Nikki,
but Gene Moon says to call waitresses* honey *or* dear.

*More coffee?*

Please, honey.

*How about more apple pie?*

Thank you, dear.

*He loves to look at the back of the counter girl's neck when her blonde
hair is pulled up and to one side, showing that place where the skull and
neck join. In Beirut there were women who would pin their hair up like
that for him, let him kiss them there. He hasn't thought about them in so
long, and now just look at how he is staring! This may be a good sign, he
tells himself.* Sabr, he tells himself, patience.

# IO

Sam smelled spiced bread and knew that it was Monday, Mama's baking day. But what time Monday? The clock ticked away on the night-
stand, only inches from his pillow, that same round-faced wind-up clock
whose double bells had jangled him awake all through high school; he
didn't feel like turning his head to look at it. And here he was again, back
in his old room, watching how the windowshade pulsed, alternately darkening then glowing with the motion of the clouds. Before he knew it he
was dreaming.

And on crutches again. Descending the stairway to his father's store,
back when it was still a butcher shop, the familiar smells rising to meet
him, sawdust and raw meat. He sets the crutch tips down a tread, careful
that the rubber caps are firmly planted. Then, shifting the weight of his
whole body up into his stiffening arms, he lifts his good leg and lowers it
to the next tread. Stops still a moment, his shadow looming before him
down the long stairwell wall, and waits out the brief, light-headed sensation of continuing on even though he's stopped still. And there, having
made one step, his shadow moves again. Slowly, carefully, he presses the
crutch caps down onto the next tread. Far below he can hear his father
at the wooden block, the rhythmic skree and ring of knife edge against
sharpening steel, and he feels again the sense that this is indeed a dream
and that he has dreamed it before. Again, too, the urgency and the hope
that this time the dream will last long enough for him to reach the bottom
of the stairs before his father puts down his knife and disappears. *Baba!*
he calls to him, but his sleep voice comes out so small it sounds like a

baby-whimper. He presses down onto the crutches, hands and armpits, pushes from the forearms. Hurrying, knowing it is wrong to hurry even as he feels his arms begin to betray him, their strength increasing with every pump of the crutches, until easily, far too easily he vaults out, out over the dark stairwell, soaring until . . . with a sudden lurch, he awakens to find himself still here in his old bed, and the smell of baking bread.

Monday.

"What smells so great, Ma?" Showered and dressed, Sam stood in the kitchen doorway and made a show of inhaling appreciatively. "Is that *zaatar?*"

His mother, refusing to be so easily disarmed, made no reply. Still, he could tell she was pleased, lips pressed tight, suppressing the urge to smile. Apparently, the *tlamit zaatar* had turned out well. Hands clasped, she stood to one side like a deep-bosomed waiter, and watched his face as he surveyed the breakfast feast she'd laid out for him: olives and pickled turnips, wilted chard in lemon and olive oil, quince preserves, cold fava beans with chopped onion and coriander, two different dishes of *jibni* cheese, one soft and milky, the other pungent and crumbly.

He sat at the table, careful where he rested his elbows, and Mama immediately set before him a dish of pureed eggplant, then a small bowl filled with briny olives. The table was starting to look like one of those *mazas* people order in Middle Eastern restaurants. Something was up with her. Sam turned to her, but she was in motion again, hastening from fridge to stove. "Were you up all night cooking, Ma?"

She replied in Arabic with the hope that *My Heart*—meaning Sam— had slept well. But the tone of her voice belied the words, and he saw now that what he'd first seen as eagerness was actually anger, a whole night of holding it back. Suddenly, she stepped in close, and he flinched, thinking for an instant that she might actually lash out and slap without warning, the way she used to do when he was little. Instead she banged down in front of him a saucer of *bizri*, the little fishes that you crisp whole and eat like french fries, dipping them in sesame-lemon sauce.

"Wow, when'd you make *these*, Ma?" He tucked a corner of a towel into his shirt collar.

But she was at the fridge again, shuttling things from the back to the front, from one shelf to the other, until, dizzy from all that bending over, she came to the table and sat down. She closed her eyes. It wasn't good for her to bend over that way, not with her blood pressure and her heft.

"This is plenty for me right here, Ma."

When she opened her eyes, her gaze settled on the window above the sink. On the familiar vista of flat roofs beyond flat roofs, all tarred black so that sunlight made the air above them wiggle and dance like a mirage.

"What is it, Ma?"

"*Fee shemis,*" she replied in Arabic, *There is sun,* as if this were a shocking revelation.

"Yeah," he said, pinching the pit out of an olive. "Not like they forecast on TV, huh?"

Mama's face brightened. "Then, *w'Allah,*" she said, "it is miracle from Her. *She* did this."

His mother's chin-up posture should have clued him, the defiance in her voice. Instead, he stepped right into it. "She?" he asked. "She who?"

Her face softened, then beamed into a smile that could only be described as beatific, but when she spoke her voice was still firm. "So that I can keep my promise to *Her,*" she said. "I promise I go to Her before the winter begin."

"You mean Carey?" He should have guessed. Of course she meant Carey. The shrine of Our Lady of Consolation in Carey, Ohio, where the families made annual pilgrimages. A statue there supposedly performed healing miracles, and among the banks of votive lights at the statue's feet was a candle Mama had dedicated to Baba's memory. Encased in red glass, it needed renewing every year. Sometimes just the thought of its flame guttering out could make her frantic with urgency. From Toledo the drive to Carey amounted to little more than an hour and change—but you couldn't just drive down, light a candle and drive back. No, there were services to attend, mass, benediction, and there were *zoueidehs* of food you had to bring along and eat. A pilgrimage to Carey usually killed an entire day.

"Bless Your hands," Mama said, turning in her chair to directly address a picture of the Virgin taped to the wall above the kitchen table. It was an illustration cut out from the funeral home calendar. Mama used to save favorites from past months—the Sacred Heart, Our Lady of Fatima, the Good Shepherd. They were in every room except the bathroom.

"Problem is, I can't take you today, Ma. I have work. With Aboodeh."

She put down her coffee cup and eyed him suspiciously. *"Heydeh,"* she said, meaning Aboodeh, *That one.*

"He needs me to drive him to Detroit." Aboodeh had arranged a meeting with the distributors. "Ma, it's *business,*" Sam said, as if this were a magic word. Which, among the *ibn Arab,* it was. In America *business* trumped everything, even the Church. Still, it wasn't easy, watching her hopes sink, the droop of her round, cheeky face. She had double worry creases between the eyes, just like his. "I wish you would've let me know earlier." She looked away. "Listen, Ma. I *will* take you to Carey. I promise. I can't today. But soon. Before it gets to be winter. And you won't have to cook a feast just to soften me up. Okay?"

She didn't reply. Why should she? The *maza* spoke for her, the goat cheese and pickled eggplant, the *zaytoun* and *bizri* and quince jam. The fresh-baked *tlamit zaatar* releasing steam as it accused him: *A mother puts this effort out for you, and all she asks is such a small favor in return.* Mama. Her strongest arguments were wordless.

Teyib had the radio earpiece twisted firmly in like a hearing aid, and still the miniaturized baseball chatter leaked out, carrying all the way to the front seat. He has to be a *little* deaf, Sam thought, and was about to suggest that Teyib turn it down some when Aboodeh looked up from the notepad in his hand. "Take the next exit," he said.

"You sure?"

"No, but take it anyway."

They were trying to find the apartment house that their distributor, Larry Morton, had moved to. Given the nature of what he distributed, he couldn't risk staying in one place too long, and Aboodeh hadn't been to the new place yet.

The ramp bottomed into a T intersection. "Which way?"

"Left?" Aboodeh consulted the notepad. "Yeah. Left."

In the backseat, Teyib echoed the sportscaster softly, "Ball three," like a sleep-talker.

Best to bring him along to meet their distributors, Aboodeh had reasoned, just in case Teyib really was representing the people in Baalbek. This way he could report back that he'd seen it for himself, a network in place and operational.

"But what if he isn't an agent?"

"Then for all he knows, we brought him along on a trip to Detroit, and I stopped off to unload some of my old eight-tracks." Before they'd left this morning, Aboodeh had filled a gym bag from a crate-load of old-fashioned eight-track tapes he kept stored in the basement at Tammouz & Sons. He'd ended up stuck with them after a previous venture had gone belly-up. Typical Aboodeh timing, signing off on a huge shipment weeks before the entire auto industry announced it was switching to cassette-type players as standard equipment.

The left turn had put them onto a main artery which soon narrowed into a one-way street lined with crowded-together apartment buildings. Some appeared vacant, others had all the window glass removed or knocked out, as if waiting for the wrecking ball. "Hard to believe Larry Moe'n Curly would move out here."

"We're not there yet," Aboodeh said. "And I don't want him to hear you calling him that."

"Hey, it's not like *I* gave him the nickname." According to local legend, Larry Morton lived in a threesome arrangement, with two beautiful hippie "wives" who waited on him hand and foot.

Aboodeh thought a moment. "You know what? I don't want you saying anything at all when we get there."

"Fine." Sam shrugged. "Whatever. It's just hard to imagine somebody like Larry Morton collecting vintage tapes."

"How would you know? He's got the money, so why not? You'd be surprised the things people with money collect. And if he likes these," Aboodeh nudged the gym bag with his toe, "he might take the rest off my hands. Anything wrong with trying to make back some of my investment?" They drove on in silence, only the faint, mile-a-minute chatter trickling out of Teyib's earpiece.

"Is it true," Sam mused after a while, "about the two wives?"

"The fuck should I know?" Aboodeh looked up from the notepad. "I can't even figure out where he lives."

Taking a turn indicated on the directions, they entered a deserted-looking business district where the storefronts were either boarded up or wrapped in chain-link fencing. Increasingly, there appeared gaps between many of the buildings, muddy lots showing the fire-blackened remnants of brick foundations. Such emptiness in the middle of a huge city, it surprised Sam. The riots had been so long ago that he figured this would have all been rebuilt by now. When they stopped for a red light, Teyib sat forward on the jumpseat, staring at everything, mouth open with puzzlement.

"Shades of Beirut, eh, Sport?" Aboodeh said.

Soon, the neighborhood changed again, seemed to repair itself as they continued on into a residential district. Another left turn, and there was the address on the notepad. Larry Morton's place turned out to be a three-story Victorian on a gentrified, tree-lined side street off Outer Drive. "You sure this is it?" Sam said. "With the spear-point fence?" It looked more like a funeral home than Tammouz & Sons.

Aboodeh glanced at the notepad one last time before snapping it shut. "I'm sure," he said. Hefting the gym bag, he stepped out, then took Sam aside. "Before we go in, I meant what I said about keeping your mouth shut. It might be kind of a freaky scene in there, so unless you're spoken to, I don't want to hear you saying anything. Not word one. You hear me?"

Sam took a step back. Something was up, all right, he wasn't stupid. But not until this minute had he figured out what it was. "This isn't legal, is it," he said. Not a question, a simple statement of fact.

"What?" Aboodeh looked surprised. And caught.

"Those tapes in there," Sam indicated the gym bag, "they're bootlegs, aren't they?"

Aboodeh's look of surprise melted into a sheepish grin, and he dipped his head. "Well, not *all* of them."

"I *knew* it!"

"So, okay," Aboodeh said and gave the gym bag a little shake.

"And what about me, walking in dressed up like this," Sam indicated the turtleneck and bomber jacket that Aboodeh had told him to wear today, "keeping my mouth shut and all. What am I supposed to be, the muscle?"

"Sammy," Aboodeh looked disappointed, "you're the cousin. *My* cousin. That's why you're here."

"I *am* your cousin. Which is why you should've told me."

"You're right. I'm sorry." Aboodeh reached up to touch Sam's shoulder. "C'mon, Cuz." He turned to Teyib. "You too."

The unmistakable fragrance of sandalwood incense greeted them as they started up the carpeted porch steps. Sam nudged Aboodeh. "Smells like a church on Easter." His cousin frowned and touched a finger to his lips. The lights were on inside, although it was the middle of the morning, and the beveled glass panels surrounding the door threw little rainbow bars on the porch carpet. The doorbell chimed a slow Westminster measure.

A woman came to the door and let them in. She was young, thin-built, and judging by her hair which she wore scrunched and sprayed into a white-girl version of an Afro, Sam figured she might be Curly. Nobody called her that—nobody called anybody anything. There were no introductions, she simply greeted Aboodeh with a perfunctory hug, patting the back of his jacket. As they followed her inside, Sam's eyes began to water from an overpowering mix of fragrances—sandalwood incense, marijuana and, more pungent than anything that Uncle Waxy kept stored in the prep room, the piercing tang of patchouli. Apparently, stoking the incense was the responsibility of the other wife—Moe? From the doorway Sam could see her on her knees, feeding little cones of incense to a series of brass pagoda-looking things that sat on an end table. Her hair was short, like a boy's, but her blouse was made of a gauzy, see-through material, and she was clearly no boy.

Larry was waiting for them in the dining room, Moe said and gave Aboodeh a sideways nod toward the music, indicating he should lead the way. Curly accompanied Teyib, taking him by the elbow, and Moe fell in step beside Sam. Ushered along, he felt the flat of her hand between his shoulders. Supposedly friendly, it didn't quite feel that way. The music was a whiny sitar backed by a psychedelic mix of whispers and tinkling bells. She did a strange thing as they paused at the arched entry to the dining room—or what would have been a dining room had there been a table instead of a shag carpet strewn with pillows and sofa cushions and pads of yellowing foam rubber. In taking her hand from the back of his bomber jacket, Moe first let it slide down from shoulder to waist in a lingering, ticklish diagonal that ended with a quick thump on the belt line. Had he just been patted down?

Larry Morton was sitting cross-legged on a throw cushion, the mouthpiece of a waterpipe clenched in his teeth. He looked like a sultan, a hippie sultan, in jeans and a fringed leather vest. Moe and Curly arranged themselves on either side of him like harem girls in a movie poster. Something about the waterpipe struck Sam as odd, and not that it appeared to be burning marijuana instead of tobacco. He'd been around *nargilehs* all his life, but this was the first one he'd seen that had dark green liquid bubbling away in its water bowl.

"Creme de menthe," Larry Morton said, reading Sam's look. "Cuts the harshness." He invited them all to sit, indicating the pillows with a regal sweep of his hand. He had the coloring of a sultan, too, dark eyes, olive skin, and hair so black that, judging by the gray-flecked mustache, Sam figured it for a dye-job.

Aboodeh squatted down awkwardly, keeping the gym bag between his knees. He took a puff, held it briefly. "Does turn it smooth," he agreed, exhaling. "Smooth as glass."

Larry Morton liked that. "Smooth as glass-sss!" he echoed, turning from side to side to exchange looks with Moe and Curly. "Here," he offered Sam the tube, "you try it."

Aboodeh put out one hand. "No," he said. "He's gotta drive."

Larry Morton had nothing to say to that, simply turned to Teyib and offered him the waterpipe instead. Teyib touched his heart as if to politely decline, but then seemed to change his mind. Placing the carved wooden mouthpiece to his lips, he took a long, deep draw, causing the creme de menthe to bubble furiously.

"So you come to us all the way from Beirut?" Larry Morton asked, smiling.

Holding in the smoke, Teyib nodded.

"And no trouble getting through? With the war, I mean? Your transit papers—"

"What war?" Aboodeh said, alerted. "Think he'd make it through if what's going on is a *war*? Nah. It'll all blow over in a month, two months. You'll see."

"So you came to work with them," Larry Morton was asking Teyib, "in the business?"

Sam gazed about at the dizzying patterns of the Indian prints that had been tacked up over the windows in place of curtains; at posters of Jimi Hendrix and Mao and the Doors, most of them with inflated psychedelic letters all tangled together and impossible to read. One wall was decorated with mirrors and pieces of mirrors, like a mosaic.

At one point Larry Morton opened his mouth to say something but suddenly frowned, as if whatever it was had disappeared—*poof!*—out of his brain. He remained like that a moment, mouth open, brow furled in amazement. The waterpipe tube dangled listlessly in his fingers. Finally, Teyib reached over and took it from him. He puffed quickly to get the tiny coal going again. Holding in the smoke, he passed the tube back again.

Then Larry Morton's face *unfrowned*. Wherever he'd been, he was back, and now he seemed to take a new, if listless, interest in Aboodeh's gym bag. "You brought me something?"

"Solid gold," Aboodeh said, "through and through." He didn't sound very stoned. He'd put on his salesman's voice.

"Gold? *Blonde,* you mean."

"Exactly what I mean. Blonde beats gold every time."

Aboodeh nudged Sam on the foot with the gym bag, indicating that he slide it over to Larry Morton. "Have a look yourself," he said, giving Larry Morton his salesman's wink. "All solid *blonde* hits here."

The slow, lingering way Larry Morton unzipped the bag gave Sam the sense of watching a slow-motion sequence. Larry Morton's hand slowly reaching in, slowly taking out an eight-track cartridge. *Anka Plays Vegas,* still in its black plastic case.

Larry Morton was frowning again. Puzzled. But then he sniffed the eight-track case, and his face lit up. *"Blonden* oldies!" That didn't sound right. He giggled. "Blonden goldies?" He snapped open *Anka Plays Vegas* and let out a staccato laugh. The sound of it spooked Sam.

There was no eight-track tape inside. Instead, the case was tightly packed with amber-colored cubes, wrapped in cellophane. Sam closed his eyes. Opened them again. *Of course.*

"Lebanese Blonde," Aboodeh said.

"Signed, sealed and delivered." Larry Morton zipped the gym bag shut and motioned for Curly to take it away.

*"Hermetically* sealed," Aboodeh smiled.

"Right."

"The liqueur might shave the edge off," Aboodeh continued, his voice rising to a salesman's pitch, "but that's because Acapulco Gold's got an edge. So does Jamaican Red. Even Beirut White'll give you some edge." He paused to toke the waterpipe. "But Lebanese Blonde blows them *all* away. There's no edge to take off!"

Larry Morton didn't appear to be listening. He seemed instead to have taken a new interest in Teyib. Leaning forward on his cushion, he began staring at him, hard. Teyib, straightening his back, returned his own flat, steady gaze. Something had changed. Maybe it was the way the weak eye slowly locked in with its mate that caused Sam to feel the need to get ready, that something was about to happen. He waited while the stereo speakers tossed whispered half-sung words and tinkling little one-note sounds all around the room. Then Larry Morton grimaced. He motioned to Curly. "Get them outta here," he whispered. Immediately, she stood up and brought Aboodeh a paper A&P bag, its top rolled down like a large sack lunch.

Sam laughed, a loud guffaw that exploded out of him before he knew it was coming. He felt another rising in his chest and he tried to cover it with a cough. All the dope in the air, this had to be some sort of contact high he was having. It had bothered him when he'd heard Aboodeh say *hermetically sealed*, but before he could understand why, they were all on their feet. Himself included. When had he stood up?

The Detroit-Toledo expressway was choked with rush-hour traffic, the lanes all reduced to stop and crawl, stop and crawl. Sam turned on the headlights. How short the days were getting already. From the backseat, Teyib's stomach emitted a long, comic gurgle. He lay stretched out, hands folded across his chest like a dead man. Larry Morton's dope must have agreed with him. And with Aboodeh, too. His face, lit by the brake-lights of the car ahead, showed a flushed but placid smile as he nodded in and out of a doze.

Sam felt alert, though. More than that, impatient. Like edging onto the shoulder and just giving it the gas. He couldn't wait to drop Teyib off. Then, after they were alone, he'd yank his cousin out of the passenger seat and shake him awake, keep on shaking him until he spilled everything.

It was full dark by the time they reached Teyib's. It seemed to take him forever to unlock his own door. He kept stopping, removing the key, looking at it and reinserting it. Sam was ready to get out and help him when he heard the double locks spring open. But Teyib didn't go in. He turned instead, belched loudly, then lurched off the stoop and onto the alley stones where he waited, bent over and gagging. Aboodeh sat up to look, but Sam turned away. Bad enough hearing the liquid splatter of it. He waited until Teyib had finished and waved them on. Slapping it into reverse, Sam backed up, stopped with a jerk, turned and spun out of there, the rear wheels spitting alley stones.

"Whoa, Cowboy!" Aboodeh sat up straighter as the Lincoln squealed a sharp right onto Michigan. "Hey, you okay?" he asked, sounding both cautious and amused. And still, Sam said nothing, not a word. He hooked a sharp left onto Jefferson, heading across Erie and straight for the Maumee River. Across St. Clair, Superior—making the lights—Summit, all the way down to Water Street.

"The fuck you going?" Aboodeh said.

Bouncing across Water Street's wavy brick pavement, Sam slammed on the brakes and, with nothing but river ahead, screeched to a stop. A ways down the concrete embankment two carp fishermen turned to look. A pair of shadows, the only light their lantern and, behind them, the twilight glow of downtown. Sam switched off the engine. "Don't think I don't know what's going on." He took a moment to breathe. "And don't act like you're stoned out of your mind, either."

"But I *am* stoned. Jesus, that was strong shit. I bet Larry laced it with something."

"We weren't going up there to have Teyib meet with Larry Morton, were we?"

"You asking me or telling me?" Aboodeh's face showed a spaced-out, vacant smile.

"And those tapes—"

"Hey, I'm starvin', Marvin. You?"

"The hashish, *our* hashish, was delivered and you don't even let me know? And telling Larry Morton it came *hermetically* sealed, what the fuck was that about?"

"I think you know, Sammy."

"That it came in . . . It was delivered in . . ."

"In . . . ?" Aboodeh nodded encouragement.

"The Jim Wilson . . . ?"

"See? You told me back in Beirut that you didn't want to know, and now you went and figured it out all on your own." He tapped a forefinger to the side of Sam's head. "Right. In. There."

Sam slapped the hand away. "Jesus Christ, Bud! You got the *family* involved! Your dad, Aunt Libby!" Sam thought a moment. "Oh Christ, do *they* know?"

"Of course not. But we needed the funeral home." Aboodeh's voice steadied, reaching for his salesman's rhythm. "That's the part of the venture that attracted the Mutranehs from the start. And don't get your shorts in a bunch over involving the family. The way this thing's set up, it's foolproof."

"Nothing's foolproof, Bud."

"Well, *this* is. Tell me, Sammy, what is it that all the old people say when they go back to visit Lebanon? All they want is to die in the shadow of Mount Suneen—right?"

Reluctantly, Sam nodded. Old guys with bad tickers, they did travel back, more and more of them every year, and every year a few did end up dying over there.

"And almost always, the bodies are shipped back to the States for burial in the family plot—right?" Aboodeh didn't wait for a response. He was so proud of himself he was beaming. "The paperwork between embassies is expedited," he shook his head, "no, practically *pre*-expedited, because all they really verify is that transport has been arranged with a bona fide funeral home. Which is us. See, this sort of thing doesn't really pay unless you deal in volume. And that's the beauty of it. We *can* deal in volume—fifty, sixty kilos at a throw."

"But how?"

"Remember my dad's stories about the old days in Chicago, how they built caskets with false bottoms big enough to hold two, three cases of bootleg they'd bring down from Canada?"

"You're telling me they built a false bottom into Eliyeh Djuheh's Ziegler box?"

"Close," Aboodeh chuckled, deciding not to make it a guessing game. "Not the bottom, the *top*." He could see that Sam wasn't getting it. "False top. Inside the lid? There's this tin sheathing that just peels back." He went on about how he had shown the Mutranehs how each Ziegler box's domed lid contained a void large enough to stuff in a minimum of fifty kilos. On each shipment, the Mutranehs would personally lock the box then have it soldered shut with a lead bead—the hermetic seal required by international law—before sending it on to the airport under embassy authorization. "And that's another beauty of this deal: here it's coming on 1976, and only two mortuaries in all of Beirut embalm for transport. And the Mutranehs linked us up with both of them. All we do on this side, we show up at the airport to pick up a Jim Wilson. And because Tammouz & Sons is a bonded carrier, legally authorized for final customs clearance, there's no dogs, Sammy. No x-rays. No special detecting machines. No *nothing*."

Sam felt a flush spread through him, and he closed his eyes. His palms were sweating. He was afraid, certainly that, but there was something else, too; a thought, full blown: *Might work? It's* already *working!* "You got me into this!" He trembled his jaw, consciously trying to induce in himself the outrage he thought he ought to feel, the alarm. "This isn't Dare to Act or some pyramid scheme! We can go to prison. For years!"

Aboodeh's mouth formed a weary grin. He shifted in his seat and looked Sam full in the face. "In America alone, the airlines handle over seventy thousand Jim Wilsons a year. Every. Single. Year." His smile vanished. "That's a haystack. And this right here," he reached into his pocket, took out a cellophane-wrapped cube of Lebanese Blonde and placed it in Sam's hand, "this is a needle."

*It actually* is *working.* Sam tried to force the thought away but he couldn't. It sat there in the palm of his hand like a truth, a matter of cold fact. *Someday, somehow, at least* one *of Aboodeh's deals has to work . . . and this was it.*

"That's right," Aboodeh said, as if Sam had spoken his thoughts aloud. Unrolling the A&P sack at his feet, he took out a stack of bills, peeled off six one-hundreds and placed them in Sam's hand, on top of the cube of hash. "Your share of the first delivery," he said, and closed Sam's fingers over all of it. "It's nice in America, eh Cuz? Well, take this hash to your girlfriend's tonight and you'll really see how nice it feels."

Yes, this was no dream. His eyes were open. And, yes, he was in Nikki's apartment, in her bed. The TV was still going, a low background mutter. Here on the pillow next to him lay Nikki herself, her slow sleep-breaths tickling the hairs of his shoulder. The red lipstick he'd watched her put on smudged now, her lips pursed in dream, puffy like raspberries you just want to lean over and nibble on. But not right now. Now, he settled back under the covers as gently as he could so as not to disturb her, content to simply lie back on the pillows, Nikki's pillows, and gaze about . . . Nikki's bedroom. Lit only by the flickering of the television, it looked just as he'd imagined it, like a bedroom you see on television. None of the crucifixes with palm fronds that he'd grown up with, framed holy cards of Blessed Charbal of Lebanon, the dizzy-patterned rugs Baba had brought over from the old country, worn through and ragged. No, here it was all wall-to-wall shag carpeting. A matching dresser and bedside table, made of plain maple. Maple headboard, too. In the dresser's mirror he could see part of the long, narrow painting above the headboard. A foggy cityscape, it was probably painted by machines on an assembly line, surely something he wasn't supposed to like. And yet he did. Was he still stoned? If so, would he be asking himself whether he was stoned? It was too complicated. But either way, he enjoyed resting his gaze on those tall geometric shapes suggesting skyscrapers, the geometric rows within them like little windows glowing through streaks of mist.

It was beyond him why she'd ever want to move out of here and into that falling-down wreck of a place in Michigan. Earlier tonight when they'd sat at the kitchen table together, and he'd offered to take a few weekends and go up there with her to do what repairs he could, she'd quickly put her elbows up on the table and covered her face with her hands. "No, no, no, Sammy," she'd said, cutting short his attempts to explain how this was the best he could do right now. Her tears, she explained, were because she was *happy*. She was *grateful*.

Then she took his hand and led him into the hall, pausing to look in on Deano and give him permission to stay up and watch all the TV he wanted as long as he stayed in his room.

"Deano has his own TV?"

"Just a small one," she said.

Sam waited until she'd closed her bedroom door before he took the cellophane-wrapped cube out of his pocket and showed it to her. *Oh, yeah.* She opened a dresser drawer and took out a little brass pipe and a lighter. Then she turned on her own bedroom TV. "For sound," she said. Johnny Carson, in a cape and a huge swami turban, held an envelope pressed to his forehead.

How could the Carson show still be on? Time was crawling. He didn't know why, but right now that was funny. Laughing, he felt Nikki rustle the sheets, then the warm silken slide of her body against his.

"What?" She started to laugh along, but tentatively, without knowing why. "What, Sammy?"

He didn't know what. Whatever it was he'd been thinking didn't seem funny at all anymore. Not at all. Looking down, he saw that she was smiling up at him. Why?

"What's so funny?" he asked.

"That's what I was asking *you! You* were the one who started it."

"I was?" Sam tried to trace back the line of his thoughts. No good.

Whatever it was was gone. "Wow. I really must be wasted." He lay back and closed his eyes. This Lebanese Blonde stuff really was potent. Nikki was talking again. Had been talking. For how long he couldn't say. He tried to pay attention.

"The back porch is a mess," she was saying. "The support posts are all rotting out. There's an old wringer washing machine back there, Sammy? I don't know what's keeping it from falling through the floorboards." For a moment the television's flickering gave him the impression that she was alternately kinking one eyebrow then the other. She looked crazy. "Anyway, I don't think it'd be worth, you know, trying to salvage it or anything."

"The porch, you mean, not the washing machine."

"That's right, Sammy, the porch. Now, you just stay with me. Are you with me?"

"I think so."

"Well, I was thinking a deck. You know, tear out the whole thing, the whole back porch, and put in a deck. Right off the kitchen door. Can you picture it?" She propped herself on an elbow, and his eye went right to her breasts slung snugly in her white satin slip.

"I think so." He could hear a piano repeating chords and, farther off, what sounded like gunshots.

"Sammy?"

"What?"

"Are you with me?"

"I'm listening." Nikki's TV had somebody singing now, a woman in an evening gown leaning on a piano, so the gunshots had to be something from Deano's room. His little TV.

"A deck, remember?"

"A deck?" Sam cleared his throat. *Deck?* What was she talking about?

"It wouldn't take long, Sammy." She slid up against him, nuzzling her cheek into his shoulder. "You know, a picnic table, one of those barbecue grills, we could set up a hammock."

"Hammock," Sam said.

"For me," she said.

"For you? What about me?"

"In an apron," she said.

"An apron?"

"Yeah, with *Kiss the Cook* across on the front of it."

133

Nikki's eyes flashed in the television light as she rose up and straddled him. Her kisses tasted like raspberry candy.

Above their breathing he heard a television voice announce the sign off of another broadcast day. Voices began singing, "America the Beautiful," whole choirs of them. Nikki's lips traveled up the side of his neck to his ear. He pulled down the narrow satin straps of her slip, and she helped, bending one elbow through then the other.

Beyond the wall he could hear faint gunshots over action music, Deano's station still on the air, but in here, in this bedroom, it was all spacious skies, all amber waves of grain as Nikki's hair tumbled over him. His heart pounded and swelled as she leaned down over him. *America—* he loved this song. *Loved it.* Her hair engulfed him

~

## Oreille de Beirut

*There are times he will turn the radio up so loud that the high thin noise of it pierces his ear like a needle. Sometimes he will change ears because of the pain. The right, partially deafened anyway, tends to bleed. A 60 percent loss the doctors in Beirut had told him at the AUB hospital. It was the car that had done it, the one on Rue Zokak El Hamra, as he was carrying flour to the restaurant. In two months' time he had seen with his own eyes two cars go up, and he had remained unscratched; this one he only heard. It happened more than two city blocks away, and it wasn't the explosion itself but its echo that had deafened him. He was walking next to a flat concrete wall, the flour sack on his left shoulder. The explosion, off to his left, caused him to stop short. An instant later the echo struck from the right, knocking him off his feet in a white cloud of flour. He was sheltered from the metal fragments by a building, a hospice for wounded children run by the Lazarine Nuns.*

*"Oreille de Beirut," the doctor smiled sadly, addressing the medical students in French. Beiruti ear. "This baker was lucky," meaning Teyib, "that he has not been deafened completely. More and more," he explained, "Beirut has been teaching us an interesting lesson about echoes: namely, that because such echoes seemingly bring the subject closer to the sound, they can have the same otological effect as an explosion going off only a*

*few meters' distance from the ear." Then the doctor turned to the nurse who stood at his elbow with a notepad and spoke in Arabic: "Idneyt Beirut. Estimated loss: right side, negligible; left side, 60 percent."*

*Sixty percent, and lately there are days it seems like more. In Toledo, walking down Monroe Street and up Erie to the bus stop, there are whole days he can turn up the radio in his left ear, close his eyes, and there is only the radio. He misses the Monroe Street bus that way. He hears nothing, opening his eyes only because he feels the hot blast of its exhaust pass over him.*

*Late some nights WJR in Detroit rebroadcasts entire Tigers games, one after the other. Teyib falls asleep as a new one begins, O-ho say can you-ou see-ee wavering in and out of the static. Before dawn he awakens to the bottom of the eighth and an intermittent hissing in his ear; yawning makes it go away. He twists out the earpiece, leaves it dangling off the pillow by its cord. Reaching up, he pulls on the light string and settles back again to gaze sleepily at the wall beside his cot, at wallpaper patterns of identical flower bursts. They must have once been red, but are now faded to pale almost colorless flesh tones.*

*Then suddenly, and with startling clarity, the fleshy colors coalesce before his very eyes until the flower bursts have become clusters of faces, puffy-cheeked little children. The little children are pressing pink petal hands to the sides of their open mouths, and all their mouths are screaming. Teyib turns quickly away. He blinks. These are only the pictures of flowers, he assures himself, flowers and nothing more. He gets up, eyes averted from the wallpaper, and uses the toilet. Returning to bed, he glances at the wall, quickly. Once. Again. Then, squeezing his eyes shut, he feels around blindly for the light string.*

*These are only the pictures of flowers, he tells himself, flowers and nothing more. Each morning he reassures himself as he washes and dresses, using his key to enter through the back of the carryout, where he works each day for Mr. Gene. Each night, preparing for bed, he fixes his gaze downward, away from the wallpaper. And lies fretful, barely able to sleep. Before the third night of this, he gives in. Using a length of twine, he takes a rough measurement of the wall next to his bed. Then, reluctantly, he unlocks the back room and through it enters the store. He hopes no permission is*

135

*needed for what he is about to do because he would not be able to explain it, neither in English nor in Arabic. There is a tool drawer in the wall behind the meat case. He takes from it a hammer and a handful of tacks. The store's giant spools of wrapping paper are kept here, too, on wooden dowels.*

*Later, when the job is finished, the wrinkled brown sheets look something like curtains that have been gathered at the top and tacked in bunches. The entire wall alongside his bed is covered. At last, he can close his eyes and sleep.*

# PART THREE

# II

Uncle Waxy dressed formally every day, ready to meet clients at any hour, but for the dentist, he'd really outdone himself. Freshly shaved and cologned, he'd put on a three-piece suit. His necktie was plain, muted, and his thick silk shirt had a collar that shone as white and stiff as a priest's. Going to the dentist? He looked ready to meet his Maker.

"Honest, you won't feel a thing," Sam said, trying to sound reassuring as he opened the car door. He could see his uncle was in pain just from the way he sat, the fingertips of one hand protectively touching his jaw as he stared straight ahead through the windshield, waiting for Sam to close the door. "Dr. Lamb'll shoot you up with Novocain, probably give you some of that laughing gas, too, and before you know it, it'll all be over."

Waxy took a cigar from his suit coat pocket and unwrapped it. Apparently the discomfort of smoking with a bad tooth didn't outweigh the discomfort of not smoking at all. "Mos' people dey look an' dey can see trouble comin' from a mile away. But you ask 'em about it, an' dey don't know dey seeing it. How come? I'm tellin' you it's because dey don't *wanna* see it." He was speaking now with a kind of urgency: somebody had to wise this kid up, and since Sam's father was gone, the task had fallen to him. He lit the cigar, drawing in short, rapid drags that made the flame of the lighter flare up two, three, four times. Satisfied that it was lit, he pulled the cigar from his mouth with a wet sound. ""Let's say dis," he began, suddenly reignited. "Let's say you gonna get into some kinda trouble."

"Okay, like what?"

"Don' matter! I'm tellin' you listen to inside of you head. Just before the trouble come, inside a you head come a voice talking to you." Waxy exaggerated a breathy whisper. "'Hsst!' the voice he says. 'Hey you, whad-dya think you doin', anyway? Look out! Here comes trouble!'"

The cigar was getting juicy, and something from the *Hsst!* had flecked Sam's ear. He wiped it with his sleeve. "Maybe so, Uncle." But there had been no warning the time Sam totaled the new hearse, no little voice when his wallet got lifted in the old country. "Maybe for some people."

"Whad, you t'ink I'm talkin' *some* people? No!" Suddenly he winced, and puffed out his cheek. The tooth again. *"Yechrib beitak!"* he said, fi-nally, *Confusion on your house!* The mildest of Arabic curses, a cry of exasperation more than anything else.

"We're almost downtown, Uncle." Sam cracked a window to let out the smoke.

Waxy didn't respond. Just sat there giving the road ahead his deter-mined stare. After a few blocks, he took his hand away from his jaw and relaxed. Then he put the cigar back in his mouth. It looked tasty, a dark chocolate brown. Waxy's regular supply of Cubans was smuggled in from Windsor to Detroit beneath the Ambassador Bridge. Same exact route as during Prohibition when Waxy helped smuggle liquor in false-bottomed caskets.

"Y'know, Uncle, I really don't think Dr. Lamb is going to appreciate the smell of that cigar on your breath."

That got a smile out of him. "Good," Waxy said. "Serve him right." The way Uncle Waxy smoked, he held the cigar dead center in his pursed lips. When he smiled, it pointed up.

"Seventy-six years," Uncle Waxy bragged to the dentist, "an' every toot' my own."

Dr. Lamb smiled appreciatively as he reached past Sam to clip the x-ray films to the lightboard. But the smile quickly vanished, and he gave out a low whistle. He couldn't believe what he was looking at—an im-pacted wisdom tooth? In a man *Waxy's* age? He propped the old man's mouth open with a rubber dam and took another look.

Tall and burly, Lamb had black hair curling out the V of his shirt, but his forearms were completely hairless. Waxy glanced fearfully at the dentist's arm and spoke to Sam with his eyes: *See that?* The overhead lights shone on Lamb's forearm as if it were polished wood. Sam winked his assurance; he'd heard of surgeons who shaved their arms for hygienic purposes, so why not dentists? When the rubber dam was removed, Waxy spat into the little sink at his shoulder and asked, with a child's quaver to his voice, "Whad about de pain, Doctor?"

Dr. Lamb explained that pain indicates trouble, and that this was the sort of trouble one shouldn't allow to fester. He spoke as if to a child, and like a child, Waxy sat there, eyes widening as he listened. "What most concerns us right now," Lamb said, glancing over his shoulder to include Sam, "is the risk of infection spreading to surrounding tissue." He patted Waxy on the arm. "And we don't want that to happen, do we?"

Afterward, Sam would wonder whether his uncle's had sensed a warning that day as they led him out of the treatment cubicle and down the hall into another room where a registered nurse prepared hookups to pressurized tanks of gas and oxygen. Maybe he had. Abdullah "Waxy" Tammouz, seventy-six years old and the very picture of health, back straight, every tooth his own, hearing a voice in the anesthesia's hiss, a whisper saying, *Hsst—hey you! Look out!*

In the waiting room, Sam's thoughts weren't even on the magazine he was paging through, instead kept gravitating from Nikki to the import venture, and back again. Sure, there were still silences when he and Nikki weren't talking about her house, but that would take care of itself with time. It had been two weeks since the last Jim Wilson arrived, and already there was word that Beirut airport had been reopened and another Jim Wilson was being prepped for shipping. Aboodeh was excited. And so too, Sam supposed, was he. In a way. Also scared. That sinking-elevator sensation down deep in his stomach.

"Mr. Tammouz?"

Sam looked up to see that the receptionist had stepped into the waiting room to summon him. She was pretty, and he was pleased to put down the magazine and follow her. By her starched, strictly business manner, his first thought was that this probably had something to do with insurance or billing information.

"He's being closely monitored." The woman spoke without turning, and it took Sam a moment to realize that she was addressing him. Her hair was a dark chestnut with streaks that flared gold as he followed her beneath the hallway's overhead spots.

"I see," Sam said. Although he didn't.

"Actually, these things happen more often than you think. You just don't hear about them because almost always . . ." she stopped now, turned and smiled, ". . . they turn out perfectly fine." She hadn't led him to the billing desk. They were standing at the open door of a treatment cubicle.

"Perfectly fine?" he asked . . . and only then did it dawn on him that something had gone wrong. He stepped past her into the cubicle.

Dr. Lamb was in there, bent over Waxy. "We're just monitoring Uncle," he said without looking up.

Two nurses hurried in, wheeling an IV unit. As they crowded over Waxy, Sam stepped back out of their way, almost into the hall. In all the commotion he had caught only a glimpse of his uncle: the lights were an intense greenish yellow, giving his face a fluorescent glow. Waxy's mouth was propped so wide Sam could see the bloody cotton wad all the way in back where the tooth had been extracted. Mouth gaping like that, his uncle didn't look anaesthetized, he looked startled to death.

"Call to him, say his name." One of the nurses began pinching Waxy's earlobe, hard.

Sam bent down to the ear, the hair tufting out of it, and he spoke over the nurse's whitened fingertips, "Uncle? Uncle Waxy?"

Nothing. But Lamb told him to keep trying, and he did, "Waxy? Uncle Waxy?" right up until the ambulance arrived, and even then Sam kept it up, "Uncle? Uncle?" crouch-stepping alongside as they wheeled Waxy out a back doorway to the parking lot.

Stooped next to him during the ambulance ride, Sam thought to try Arabic, calling out his uncle's name. "Abdullah? *Ya Abdullah?*" He saw an eyelid flutter, or thought he did, and searched his mind for something else in Arabic. Nothing came. *Nothing!* Christ, Sam didn't speak *English* until he was eight! Before that he used to *think* in Arabic! His *dreams* were in Arabic! But still nothing. And the harder he scoured his mind the more his native tongue receded from him. Or maybe it was speech itself. He tried to think, but how could you think anything with a siren screaming right over your head? He crouched there mute, watching a look like surprise grow rigid on Waxy's face as the ambulance wailed up Madison toward Mercy Hospital. A bluish tinge was showing around his uncle's eyes, around his mouth and lips, too.

Arabic. Why hadn't his mother insisted that Sam continue to speak

Arabic at home? And then he found himself naming the dishes his mother cooked, whispering them into his uncle's ear—*Warak inib, koosa bi joze, kibbeh bil saniyeh, riz ma'loub* and *rizb haleeb.* His uncle's eyelids moved, fluttered open. Gave Sam a puzzled glance, then closed again. Something, at least! An Arabic saying came to him, and he began to repeat it as readily as it had sprung into his mind: *"Inshallah tisl'm, inshallah tisl'm."* The words were vaguely familiar, and they *had* to be more meaningful, anyway, than *squash stuffed with walnuts,* so he repeated them over and over into his uncle's ear, *inshallah tisl'm, inshallah tisl'm.* The words seemed to have the quality of a blessing, and he kept on repeating them until he realized with a start that they *were* a blessing, and that where he'd heard people say *inshallah tisl'm* was at the funeral home. What he was repeating into his uncle's ear was the standard blessing the *ibn Arab* used at wakes and funerals, the greeting in time of death.

Aboodeh was the one who knew Arabic, who spoke it like a native; *he* should have been in that ambulance with Waxy. *He* should have been the one down here signing medical releases for his own father, insurance forms and God knows what else Sam was giving them permission to do.

Pen in hand, he watched them wheel his uncle out of the emergency room and onto an elevator. An intern—or maybe just a medical student, he looked to be Sam's age—stopped briefly to explain that the patient had been stabilized and now was being taken upstairs to the intensive care unit.

Sam signed the forms, then followed the admittance clerk's directions down a corridor to the pay phones.

He dialed Tammouz & Sons. When the phone rang past the customary four rings, he realized that not only wasn't Aboodeh at work, he apparently hadn't thought to switch to the answering service before leaving the reception desk unmanned. Sam hung up, retrieved his dime, and tried Aunt Libby's home number. No luck there, either. Nor had he really expected any. It was past three o'clock, and by now she was probably placing her first bet at Raceway Park. So who else? Not Waxy's wife, Aunt Nejla; she was practically an invalid. And he sure wasn't about to try Aboodeh's house. Salma wouldn't know where to find him. *Abdoolah the Coolah.* She made a point of not knowing some things.

Which left Aunt Afifie. Not really a relative, not even a Tammouz, she was called Auntie out of respect for her age and her standing among the families. She was a gossip, though. Calling her would be like calling the newspapers, but what else could he do? She was his last resort.

Her line was busy, as usual. So, also as usual, he had to claim an emergency so the operator would break in. Nearly deaf, Aunt Afifie relied on an old-fashioned hearing aid; a wire ran from her ear to some mysterious heavy lump of a listening device she kept nestled deep within the cloth of her bosom. Using the phone, she had to hold the receiver upside down, the talking end at her mouth and the listening end pressed between her breasts. And that's how she'd sit for hours on end, making her daily round of calls. Word would reach Aboodeh, all right, but only after it had reached most of what was left of North Toledo's Little Syria first.

The ICU visitors' lounge was in the hospital's old wing, at the end of a dim corridor. Behind its frosted glass doors, though, the lounge itself appeared to have been recently remodeled. All primary colors and hard plastic furniture, it put Sam in mind of some fast-food place, a Big Boy's or a Denny's. There were even those stamped tin throw-away ashtrays scattered about.

The room seemed larger for being nearly vacant. The TV, tuned to a whisper, was showing an old cowboy movie in black-and-white. The room had newly installed floor-to-ceiling windows, tinted blue, and the light passing through them felt somehow cool, like blue fluorescence.

The muffled TV gunshots continued—*Pfh! Pfh!*—like the mouth-sounds children make playing cowboy. The old Mystic Theater on Bush, a supermarket now, used to show films back-to-back every Saturday afternoon: Rocky Lane, the Durango Kid with his kerchief mask, Lash LaRue. Sam loved them all, but none more than Hopalong Cassidy. Probably because Hoppy was old, with white hair like Baba. And, like Baba who paid bums to do odd jobs around the store, hauling and sweeping, Hoppy had Gabby Hayes to get supplies or tie up the bad guys for him. As a side-kick, Gabby not only resembled the bums who hung out all along the bar district of Summit and Cherry, but being toothless, he spoke English like them, too, muttering and wheezing, spit flying whenever he got worked up.

During those first months in America Baba had insisted that Mama take Sam to the Mystic every single Saturday afternoon to learn English.

Baba himself had no patience for the movies, finding the experience too trifling and passive for grown men.

Mama went reluctantly. The rapid-fire cowboy slang gave her such headaches. And all those cows mooing and milling about. She regularly confused the bad guys with the good guys, and she yelped with alarm whenever the cowboys slapped leather and the lead started to fly.

Born in Damascus, and a Christian, she had heard the stories of the *Sit Sineen* massacres just across the border, as a child had beheld with her own eyes the violence of the Druze revolt and the French bombardments; so nothing Sam said could persuade her that the bullets up there on the screen were fake, that nobody was really dying. Sometimes she rose out of her seat and made her way amid the gunfire up the Mystic's long center aisle to wait for him in the lobby.

Baba died in this very hospital, just upstairs. Now, standing here at the visitors' lounge windows, the television whispering at his back, Sam looked out in the direction of the store, somewhere deep in the North End, and imagined Mama in her bay window, her own television whispering English at her; she who never learned English, who never learned to do the bills, the shopping, the driving around; who couldn't answer a phone. What else had Sam expected from a father with hair as white as Hopalong Cassidy's? He'd somehow always known that someday Baba would be leaving her to him.

An orderly found Sam in the lounge and handed over to him a sealed plastic bag the size of a small pillow. In it were Uncle Waxy's personal things, his gold-framed reading glasses, his wallet, fountain pen, keys. And something else. Sam had to smile. Waxy's *djrab il khirdee*. He'd never seen it off him. An old country holdover from the days before men wore European trousers, the *djrab il khirdee* was like a secret pocket you wore under your shirt. It looked like a wad of bandages taped tightly into the shape of a small banana, and had a braided string looping out from either end so that it could be slung over the shoulder, with the packet itself nestled in the armpit. Only the real old-timers used to wear them, usually to hide away something of value or luck—money, a talisman, an important document. Uncle Waxy's *djrab il khirdee* concealed a sliver of the True Cross upon which Jesus Christ had been crucified. Or so said the Turk who sold it to him in Beirut Harbor as he and his sister Libby were boarding a ship for America. Within the *djrab il khirdee*, Waxy claimed, lay all his luck in America. Which was why Sam would have to get it back on him before he woke up.

A laminated list of rules above the doors to the intensive care unit stated that visitors were allowed in only on the hour, and then for no more than ten minutes at a time. The nurse on duty was busy, repeatedly leaving and returning to her desk, so Sam didn't have to wait long for a chance to quietly sneak inside. Baba would have been proud.

Waxy had oxygen tubing taped to his nose; they'd had to shave away part of his mustache to do it. His frown was gone, pulled up into what looked like a perplexed, closed-eyed shrug, seeming to say: *What-can-a-person-do?*

Sam knew that the *djrab il khirdee* was worn under the left armpit, close to the heart, but his uncle's whole left side was hooked up with tubes and monitor wires. For the time being it would have to go on the right.

He took some white adhesive tape from a tray next to the bed and tore off a short strip. Wrapping it around the *djrab il khirdee*, he took his uncle's gold ballpoint pen out of the plastic bag and wrote on the tape: DO NOT REMOVE!!!, darkening the exclamation points for emphasis. He lifted his uncle's arm and carefully looped the *drab il khirdee*'s string over the shoulder, then tucked the True Cross, or whatever it really was, up into the armpit. Bending low over his uncle, Sam spoke quietly into his ear. He asked him, in English, to come back to us, and not to die.

From the doorway, he turned for what he feared might be his last view of his uncle. Waxy's expression remained unchanged, shoulders hunched in a seeming shrug. But now, oddly enough, Sam was put in mind of an old-time comedian, like one he'd seen on TV, the deadpan way he delivered a punch line then looked down at his cigar with exactly that same drawn-out shrug, waiting for the audience to catch on.

EVAPORATED

*When the tears begin, Teyib is at work in the back room of the carryout, sorting soda pop empties into their crates. Pepsi-Cola, Faygo, Hires Root*

*Beer, Vernors Ginger Ale—and out of nowhere his chest heaves, and he is sobbing. For days afterward the sobbing recurs, on and off, bursting out of him, and Mr. Gene is puzzled. It must be homesickness, Mr. Gene decides, finally, and naming it is as much a relief to Teyib as it is to the customers who are starting to feel embarrassed for him, this blubbering that comes on unawares, that he must suppress and swallow and which finally sends him choking out the back and to his room like a schoolgirl. A single room and a door he can lock, and only the mice and cockroaches to be disturbed by the weeping that ambushes him during his most ordinary daily tasks, toothbrush or toilet paper in hand. Homesickness, Mr. Gene assures the customers. Some get it bad.*

*The Cincinnati Reds, the radio announcer says, are facing sixty-eight games at home this year. Little better than a .500 club on the road, at an earlier exhibition game they stole eleven bases from the Pittsburgh Pirates.*

*What do you know? a fellow announcer exclaims.*

*Last year Cincinnati won the World Series against the Boston Red Sox.*

*Boston last took the championship, the first announcer says, in 1918 with Babe Ruth pitching.*

*What do you know?*

*What the first announcer knows is that Highland Appliance in West Toledo is having a price-slashing sale on portable televisions. They are called teefees for short, and some of the models come with living color.*

*It'll make the Series jump right out atcha!*

*The teefee that Teyib buys is not only a color set, it also comes equipped with one of the new hand-held devices for remote control. He sets the machine on a cinder block which he has to move next to the bed to be near the room's one working electrical outlet. Since his bed is along the same wall he angles the block a little so that the entry door can be cleared.*

*Next, he makes room for the stuffed armchair that he salvaged from one of the alley trash bins, adjusting its position for glare from the overhead bulb and reflections from the window. Finally, he settles himself into the armchair, opens a Budweiser and puts his feet up on a crate, just like the pictures in the funny papers of Americans watching teefee. He presses the button on the remote control device, and the first sounds to*

*come out, before even the picture tube has warmed up, are unmistakable:
an Uzi, judging by the low-caliber sound of its rapid bursts. Or possibly its
American-made counterpart, the Ingram. Teyib fumbles with the remote
control device, looking for the off button, but succeeds only in muting the
sound. The tears begin of their own accord, and the first images he sees on
his teefee are the blurred moving rainbows of colors.*

*In silence the picture snaps to a man running down a city street. The
man is afraid. This is only a television program, Teyib reminds himself.
The clerk had certainly been right about what he called the black matrix
screen—the colors jump right out at you. Abruptly, the man drops like a
top-heavy sack of flour. Only a television program, Teyib reminds himself,
but the actor too must have seen such a thing before. Because the body
does not fall backward, arms in the air as in cowboy movies, but forward,
in a top-heavy crump; the weight of the human head and chest does
this, especially in children. Teyib reminds himself to take a sip of his
Budweiser.*

*Only when he thinks for sure that the tears will begin again does he
switch the station. His hand feels stiff, his fingers tingly as if threatening
not to press the buttons. And so changing channels on the remote control
becomes an effort.*

*Channel 13 has a police program. Just a glimpse of the holstered pistol
at the detective's armpit is enough to make Teyib continue pressing the
channel button:*

*. . . doctors in an operating theater . . .*

*. . . a slow scan of time and temperature . . .*

*. . . a rock-and-roll show . . .*

*For minutes Teyib stares at the buttocks of dancing women in full
color and through the bright clarity of his tears. He turns off the mute
button and raises the volume because his left ear is acting up. The women,
maneuvering to face the camera, grind their teeth in sexual smiles that
say* Shu b'himni annah? Shu b'himni annah? *What do I care? What do I
care?*

*On Channel 11 there is a program in which a man named Mr. Roger
speaks calmly and so slowly that Teyib does not even have to strain his
good ear toward the set. Mr. Roger speaks caringly, too, and just to Teyib,
until the tears subside. Then, in the middle of speaking just to Teyib,
Mr. Roger begins singing, breaking into song exactly as Teyib has seen*

148

*announcers do on television programs in the old country. Only when the camera follows a talking trolley car to a land of puppets does Teyib realize that this is a program for children, the poor things. Sobbing anew, he finds the off button.*

*The next day is a Saturday, and Mr. Gene closes early so that he can make it to visiting hours at the hospital. Tucking in a newly ironed shirt, he gives Teyib the rest of the day off. Because it is morning still, and a Saturday, there is nothing else on the teefee except cartoon programs. But such colors!*

*And the faces! Some he recognizes from movie houses in the Bourj Plaza in Beirut, Popeye and Mighty Mouse and Woody Woodpecker, and all of them can speak English now. Learning English himself, he mouths the salesman's words: The colors jump right out atcha!*

*In the afternoon there is a baseball game coming atcha from the state called Sunny Florida. He watches all three and a half hours of it, and when it ends he switches to Channel 13 and finds another game just beginning.*

*Evaporated. During the second ball game there is a news brief, and all evening afterward Teyib has been walking to rid his mind of it, images of buildings that he himself once stood before shattered, the car that caused it evaporated—the American newsman speaking from Beirut had used that word, evaporated—and leaving a crater in the pavement. Evaporated. On teefee, the crater was strewn with all the different colors of shredded clothing.*

# 12

Aboodeh was there suddenly, the way people in dreams sometimes appear out of nowhere. Sam flinched at the sound of footsteps down the hall. His cousin wore shoes with metal heel guards, and that resolute click-click pace could belong to nobody else. He got up from his chair to see.

Aboodeh was all the way down by the elevators, but approaching fast, head down, his leather car coat slung thumb-hooked over one shoulder. Behind him, in the knot of people collecting at the elevator doors, Aunt Nejla stood leaning on her cane. She had been sickly for as long as Sam could remember, and she was supported now by several women from the neighborhood, all of them yammering away in mile-a-minute Arabic.

Aboodeh's face was flushed red, his mouth tight. Sam started to explain how sorry he was about calling Aunt Afifie, but Aboodeh didn't let him finish. He took Sam by the neck, pulled him down and kissed him, a scratchy, loud kiss next to the ear. "Thanks, Cuz," he said, his voice husky. "You talk to the doctor yet?"

"No, not yet. You?"

Aboodeh nodded. "Downstairs. An intern, I think. He says Dad had some sort of reaction to the anesthetic. Put him under too deep. Something to do with not enough oxygen in the mix."

"A coma?"

"He didn't say coma. Kept calling it an insult."

Others were approaching now, the two Abdu sisters, arm in arm, leading the way. Widows whose children had grown and moved on, the Abdu sisters lived together and shared a dramatic interest in the tribulations of others. You could count on seeing them at the first sign of illness—before the ambulance, before the priest even. Now, gaping into one patient doorway after another, they kept up a string of Arabic ejaculations at the sights they beheld, *Ya dilli annah!* and *Harram! Harram il shoum! Ism il saleeb!* Meanwhile, the elevator doors kept opening and the hallway began filling up. Uncle Toufiq, both Uncle Georges, and here too came Aunt Dorah, who prided herself on what she saw as her uncanny ability to perceive what was going on in other people's minds by reading coffee grounds. Sam pretended not to catch her knowing smile (oh, she'd seen this coming, all right!), instead looked past her toward the elevators, where Uncle Yousef was just now stepping out. The families claimed him as their aged patriarch. From down the hall Sam could hear Aunt Afifie's deaf-loud voice ringing above the rest.

Suddenly, Aunt Libby emerged from the crowd, one arm pumping in her determined, WAAC-sergeant stride right up to the nurse's window. Watching her, Aboodeh shook his jacket out and put it on. Then he thrust one hand into a side pocket and began nervously jingling his keys. "We don't even know his condition yet," he said. "It might not even be all that serious, but look at her. She's been itching to shut the place down for good, and now she's got all the excuse she needs." He took the car keys from his pocket and thrust them onto Sam. "Here. My car's downstairs in the emergency lot. You can pick the Lincoln up later. For now, get over to the office and cover the phones. A new delivery's been shipped out of Beirut."

"When?"

"I don't know when. A day, maybe two days ago. So it could come in any time. The Jim Wilson desk at Detroit Metro said they'd call and let us know as soon as it arrives."

Sam looked down at the keys in his hand. He'd wanted to stay and hear what the doctor had to say. "How about if I wait just until . . . ," he hesitated, afraid of setting Aboodeh off. But his cousin wasn't even listening. He was looking past him, his face tightening into a phony smile.

Sam felt a shove from behind as Aunt Libby nudged past him and cornered his cousin between the corridor wall and a cart of dirty lunch trays. "Auntie," Aboodeh said, "I was just now sending Sammy back to cover the phones so you could come out here."

"The phones?" She raised her penciled eyebrows. She didn't care about *phones.* "I heard you talked to a doctor."

There was a commotion at the elevators as even more people arrived. Aunt Anissa and her sister Roufa, leaning on her arm. Another elevator opened, and here came Uncle Alex, his wife, Shofia, on one arm and on the other, stepping out into the hallway, Sam's mother.

Christ almighty, Sam thought, are they letting *everybody* up here?

Sam was getting his mother a chair and a sip of water when a doctor arrived, asking for Waxy's wife. He was so soft-spoken that Sam had to step in close to hear what he was telling Aboodeh, who then turned aside and translated for his mother. Although Aunt Nejla had been in America many years, speaking English had always been a struggle for her, and after the death of Khaleel, her elder son, she gave it up entirely.

"Unfortunately, one of our problems," the doctor was saying, "is that whatever depresses pain also depresses breathing . . ." He paused and gave Aboodeh the go-ahead.

Aboodeh turned to his mother, thought a moment, then took a stab at it in Arabic. Aunt Nejla nodded. But too quickly, and it was clear she wasn't getting it. With effort, one hand on her cane and the other on her son's arm, she rose from her chair and asked something in Arabic. "She wants to know about all the tubes and wires," Aboodeh said. "So many of them. All that equipment scared her when they took her in to see him. She wants to know if they hurt."

The doctor addressed Aunt Nejla directly. "He needs them. The tubes. The wires. Tell her he can't feel them."

Sam took a step closer, and just like that, the doctor turned—*Dr. Warren* was stitched onto the breast pocket of his white coat—and began to address him. "Along with oxygen," he informed Sam, "he's also getting intravenous steroids for swelling and diuretics to remove fluids."

Sam nodded. Mama, next to him now, was also nodding. Christ. He didn't envy Aboodeh, who had begun abbreviating his translations. Finally, as the doctor went on about the consequences that can be expected from an anoxic insult, *"Medical learnedness,"* was all Aboodeh was saying in Arabic, and *"More medical learnedness."* Sam was embarrassed. You don't need to know another language to recognize something being repeated that way.

Dr. Warren must have caught on. He cut short his explanation and simply smiled encouragement at Aunt Nejla. "We're doing everything we can, Mrs. Tammouz," he said, his voice soft.

Aunt Nejla rested her head on Aboodeh's shoulder, and he comforted her. He was a good son. It was easy to be a good son to a mother like that. Aunt Nejla had a kindly smile, wide-eyed and sweet. She wasn't all there, of course. Hadn't been since Khaleel died. In all that sweetness, there was really nobody home. Watching them shuffle their way back to the lounge, Sam almost felt sorry for his cousin, having now to bear the whole weight of the family on his shoulders. And Khaleel, his elder brother, so gone away and free.

A Jim Wilson might best be a three-man job, but two could manage it well enough. Sam left the hearse, its hazard lights blinking, at the Northwest Orient loading dock and followed after Aboodeh, who was pushing the wheeled pallet up the dock ramp toward the customs office. Inside, all they had to do was flash their laminated ID cards, which they wore on lanyards over their neckties, and the customs officer let them through.

Sam had expected to feel nervous, knowing what the Ziegler box had hidden in its domed lid. But this felt more like giddiness or exhilaration, even, as if he might forget himself and laugh out loud. Hard not to, seeing how easily the transport papers had been approved and stamped, and what a cursory scan customs had given the Ziegler box before releasing it to Aboodeh. My God, they were getting away with it! In no time at all, they were doing sixty down Telegraph Road, Sam wisecracking about the customs agents and the baggage handlers, how they were probably still scrubbing the contamination of death off their hands.

Aboodeh wasn't laughing. He'd been quiet on the ride up, too. "What is it, Bud?"

"I got a call this morning from Mickey Shaloub."

"Yeah?" Mickey was the lawyer for Tammouz Enterprises. Nothing unusual there.

"Libby wants him to start procedures for shutting down the funeral home."

"Because of your dad?"

Aboodeh didn't reply. Fixing his gaze out the side window, he began to twist his pinky ring.

After a minute, Sam reached over and gave his cousin a nudge. "Y'know, Bud, I bet Libby probably just means to close down *temporarily*. For the time being. Until we know more about your dad's situation."

Aboodeh showed him a look of amused contempt.

"Doesn't she know," Sam continued anyway, "that our entire import business is tied in with the funeral home? She's the one who gave us the green light to do it."

Aboodeh shook his head. "Not anymore. Not with the political situation over there. The way Libby sees it, you don't do importing out of a country at war." He sighed and returned to twisting his ring. "And even if she does shut down temporarily, we're still shit out of luck."

"Not necessarily," Sam said. "For years now the funeral home's been nothing but a tax write-off—right? I mean, everybody knows the only reason Libby keeps it open is so your dad can have something to get out of bed for in the morning."

"So?"

"So who's to say he won't pull out of this? *We* don't know. And if he does recover, he's gonna need something to do. Something to get out of bed for every morning." His cousin tried to look skeptical, but Sam could see he liked where this was going. "So if Libby closes down *permanently*," Sam went on, "isn't that like saying he won't make it?"

Aboodeh sat forward. "It's like *asking* for bad luck."

"Exactly. You might want to bring that up at the meeting with her and Mickey Shaloub. Then just sort of explain how she doesn't have to close down completely. Just taper down. Any calls we get we'll send on to Abele's or Doyle's, or whichever mortuary's next on the rotation. But we keep the office open, man the phones. And as for any Jim Wilsons that come in, just tell her that you and me, we can handle those ourselves."

"That way, when Dad's recovered and ready to work again—"

"The place'll be ready for him."

"What else I'll do, I'll talk to Mickey ahead of time, get him to back me up."

"Will he do that?"

"For me, he will." Aboodeh sighed deeply and smiled. Just like that, his mood had lifted.

Only after they got the Ziegler box down the service elevator and into the prep room did Sam notice that all but one of the tickets and transport labels affixed to its side were in Arabic. "There's just this one in French," he said. "You think customs had any idea what they were stamping?"

"Sure they had an idea," Aboodeh said, taking a pair of latex gloves from the wall dispenser. "The *wrong* idea!" He chose a spot along the hermetic seal and asked for the hammer and screwdriver.

Instead, Sam pulled away the green vinyl envelope taped to the side of the box. "Look at this," he said. The envelope's plastic seal had been broken, the flap folded back. The papers inside were stamped and initialed. "But these're all in Arabic, too. And look, this isn't even an American passport."

"Doesn't have to be."

"And look, the ID photo's missing. Just a glue spot." Sam dropped the vinyl envelope onto the guttered table. "What are we supposed to do?"

"We can start with you handing me that hammer and screwdriver."

When he was ready, Aboodeh bent down to push the edge of the large screwdriver into the soldered bead. He hesitated briefly before swinging out sideways and giving the screwdriver a sharp whack. Trapped air hissed out, and Sam immediately winced at the familiar, astringent bite of powdered formalin, like something tasted more than smelled. Sam flipped on the exhaust fan. Whoever prepped this Jim Wilson must have used whole handfuls of the stuff.

"Really amateur," Aboodeh said as they lifted away the heavy lid. "They got it all over everything." Aboodeh brushed his gloved hands together. "Just look at that!" Sam had to step back as formalin clouded the air between them, like chalkboard dust off clapped erasers, before floating toward the exhaust fan. Inside the Ziegler box, the black rubber body bag looked dusty-white. The teeth of its long zipper were encrusted with the stuff.

"Do you think they used so much on purpose?"

Aboodeh made a wry frown. "What for?"

"The hash in the lid. In case customs used sniffer dogs."

"With a hermetic seal?" Aboodeh shook his head. "Sammy, they used so much of this shit because they're amateurs. Because over there nobody hardly ever embalms." He took pliers and a tinsnips down from the pegboard above the counter. "Now," he handed the pliers to Sam, "you said something about hash in the lid?" He chuckled. "I'll clip, you pull it back. But easy, try and keep the lid from rocking. I don't want to lose a finger. When we come to something, just hand me the pliers and I'll take it from there."

They started in on a corner of the lid's inner zinc lining and soon revealed the beginning of a shallow cavity. It looked to deepen as the top of the lid rounded toward the center. Aboodeh directed Sam to hold the lid steady while he used the pliers to widen the opening. "Okay, Sammy, let's see what forty kilos looks like." Smiling, he set down the pliers and eased his gloved hand into the opening. After a moment, the smile faded, and he plunged deeper, almost to the elbow. He withdrew his hand. Puzzled, he took up the snips again, positioned himself at the lid's opposite corner, and started cutting from that end. Every few inches he paused to tug at the lining. At the halfway point he set down the snips, got heavy-gauge neoprene gloves from a supply drawer and tossed a pair over to Sam. The gloves separated in midair. One Sam caught cross-armed against his chest, like a girl, and the other he had to search under the table for. When they were ready, fingers gripping the tin lining, Aboodeh said, "You pull that way and I'll pull this." They leaned back, grunting with effort, leveraging their weight against one another until, abruptly, the lining gave way with a metallic screech. The entire length of zinc lining had popped out. It quivered in their hands with a rolling sound, like distant thunder. Aboodeh let his end drop, then Sam let go as he turned to the exposed lid cavity. It was empty.

"I don't see anything, Bud."

But Aboodeh was running his hands down into the spaces between the body bag and the Ziegler box's side panels. Then he stopped and looked down. He was white to the elbows with formalin powder. "Okay," he said. "Okay. All this means is," he inhaled sharply, "is for some reason they must've gone and tucked it *under* the body. C'mon." Reaching into the box, he gripped the rubber bag by the shoulders and waited for Sam to get the feet end. "On three. One . . . two . . ." But even as they heaved the body up—*three!*—bringing such nervous force to the effort that they managed to lift it to the guttered table in a single motion, they could see that the Ziegler box itself, like its lid cavity, was empty. Aboodeh began rapping his knuckles along the sides and bottom. A waste of time. The zinc-sheathed plywood couldn't conceal a hollow large enough for even a single layer of foil-wrapped cubes, much less forty bricks.

Sam felt as if he'd been conned again, this time he and his cousin both. "Why would they do this? They're your wife's *cousins*."

Aboodeh wasn't listening. He stood as if stunned, absently running his gloved fingers through his hair.

"Don't do that," Sam said. "You'll get that shit all over your head."

Aboodeh took his hand away, looked at it. He pulled off the neoprene glove and brushed at his hair. His eyes had a wide, panicky look. Then he thought of something. "Wait a second. What if they were in some sort of a hurry and couldn't get a carpenter to do the lid? What if they didn't have time, so they ended up just zipping the bricks in with the body?"

"Maybe," Sam said. "Sure, if they were in a rush!" He grasped the top of the bag with one hand, the zipper ring with the other, then quickly tugged it down to about shoulder height. And immediately leaped back as—"Jesus *Christ!*"—tangled coils of gray hair sprang out at him. He turned to Aboodeh, half expecting to find his cousin laughing. He wasn't. His eyes had that wide look again. "It's a woman," Sam said. Beneath the hair her face was covered with a cloth, but it was clear that this had been a woman, and a fairly old one. A roughly sutured seam began just beneath her collapsed breasts and ran in a line down her small, withered torso, past the navel where the hands had been positioned for modesty's sake, thumbs tied together with twine, over the pubis. Sam took a deep breath. "Guess I thought the documents would be for a man."

"Move aside," Aboodeh said. He had recovered himself. Taking hold of the zipper ring, he finished opening the bag down to the toes. He thrust a gloved hand down and in and began sliding it up and down along the inside of the bag.

"Anything?"

Aboodeh didn't reply. He stepped around the table and rooted with his hand down the other side of the body. Then he spread the bag wide open, top to bottom. Nothing. He leaned both hands on the side of the gut-tered table and hung his head. "They said to expect forty packets. Forty. At least. One kilo each." He pulled his gloves off and slapped them hard against the side of the table. "Forty! Fucking! Kilos!"

Sam knew he ought to wait, give his cousin a second. He looked down at the floor, chewing his lip. "Okay," he said finally, "so, what now?"

"We gotta reach Beirut. We gotta find out what happened." Aboodeh sighed, "Because somebody, *some*where along the line, fucked up."

"You really think that's all it is, just a fuckup?"

"What're you talking about?"

"Aboodeh, what if it's a burn?"

"Burn?" Aboodeh's lip curled in derision. "What comic books you been reading?"

"How do you know it's not? Just because they're Salma's cousins?"

"No, because of *logic*. Think a minute, Sammy. We already transferred the Khaleel money, yours *and* mine. *And* the money from my house. They got it in their hands. All we got. So if this was a *burn*," he paused briefly to let the mockery sink in, "then why go to the trouble of even shipping a body? *Or* the expense? Christ, they can just keep the money and tell us to take a hike." He smiled sourly. "Burn? No, huh-uh. This one, she's the only thing around here getting burned. Soon as I get her to Perrysburg."

"Is that legal?" The crematory that Tammouz & Sons contracted with was in the suburb of Perrysburg, just south of Toledo.

"Long as we're operating a certified funeral home, it is. Hey, all *we* know is that we received a wire from a family in Beirut named Mutraneh telling us to expect arrival of remains." He was right. Lacking further contact, or payment, standard operating procedure called for cremation and storage of the cremains under the sender's name. "So, whose to say this wasn't . . . ," he took a pen from the counter, quickly jotted something on a stringed toe tag, ". . . Marie Mutraneh." He looped the string over the big toe and knotted it.

"But who *was* she? How'd she die?"

"Old age." Aboodeh tossed the pen back onto the counter. "The fuck should I know!"

Sam bent down and lifted the cloth covering the face. Her jaw was tied shut with a heavy cloth that framed her face like a nun's wimple. Formalin dust filled every crease and wrinkle, crazing her face like an old gray bowl. She hadn't died of old age, though. Someone had performed a clumsy plaster repair of some sort of major trauma that went up the side of her jaw to behind one ear. "What happened to her?"

Aboodeh took a quick look. "Car wreck?" He shrugged. "You saw how they drive over there. Most likely, she got in an accident right around the time the shipment was ready to go. One of the Mutranehs got a passport made and went down to the hospital or the morgue or wherever—Beirut's a big city—and it just so happens there's a body that's been on ice a while unclaimed. Probably no ID, which is all the better. In that case Nabil or

Phares just gives it a name, claims it as a cousin. The morgue's happy to be rid of it."

"But it's a female."

"Probably there's no time to change passports. So the picture came unstuck, cheap glue." Aboodeh gave him a flat look. "There's a war. You move stuff out when you can."

Sam held the gaze a moment before turning away. "I don't know, Aboodeh."

"That's right. You don't. But I do. And right now I'm going to need help transferring this body into one of those." Aboodeh nodded toward the cardboard crematory coffins stored nested in a stack beneath the work counter. Aboodeh peeled back the edges of the body bag. "Okay now," he said, "let's lift her up and over." He grasped the ankles, waited for Sam to take hold of the shoulders. "Okay. One, two—"

"Aboodeh, wait."

"Fuck me." Aboodeh set the feet down. "What now?"

"Look at this." Sam pulled aside a handful of the woman's hair to expose the trauma repair. "Right here." With his finger he followed the crudely stitched line up to a small patch of formalin packed thick and white on the upper back of the woman's head. Tilted toward the light the patch looked more like some sort of plug. "Could this be what I think it is?"

"What?"

"You know what."

"*What?*"

Now that he was looking closely, Sam realized that the tiny black flakes around the formalin plug, sprinkling the gray hair, could be dried blood. "A bullet hole."

Aboodeh tried to laugh, but it came out more like a bark. "You trying to scare me, or what?" Sam didn't reply. He simply removed his gloves and set them on the counter. "Listen, Sammy, I apprenticed with my dad four years through high school, and after that I put in almost a year at Columbus toward certification, and I've seen a lot more accidents than *you* have." He bent over the body, as if to reexamine the injury. "*Bullet* hole?" He straightened up and turned halfway around to find Sam backed up to the counter. "You wouldn't know a bullet hole from your *ass*hole." He stepped over to Sam, reaching out as if to give him a playful whack on the shoulder, but Sam sidestepped away and continued backing toward the double doors. "Hey," Aboodeh said, "where do you think you're going?"

"It *is* the war, all right." Sam's eyes were watering from the formalin powder, and he couldn't stop blinking.

"What is?"

Something Uncle Waxy had babbled on about once, lost in one of his fogs, something they used to do during the underworld wars of the early thirties.

"They're dumping bodies!"

"The fuck you talking about?"

"That's what they're doing, isn't it!"

"Hey, Sammy, come back here! Don't you leave me!"

THE LITTLE KITCHEN

*Each morning before sweeping the sidewalk, Teyib lowers the store's awning. As he turns the crank, dew runs down the green canvas and trickles onto his shoulder. The sun rises later now and sets earlier in the evening. W'Allah, everything changes. One morning the awning crackles with frost. In the little radio in his ear, the season changes from baseball to football. Again, the hearing in his ear has been coming and going on him, filling with pressure until the high thin hissing gives way to nothing, a simple, utter soundlessness that bewilders him.*

*He brushes his sweepings into the gutter. Behind the register, Mr. Gene sits reading a newspaper. Teyib hangs the broom on its nail in the back room and takes down the feather duster. A customer comes in, and while Mr. Gene waits on her, Teyib dusts the shelves of cans and bottles. Then the cash register rings, and for another long while the place is quiet again, only the hum of the coolers in back and Mr. Gene rattling the newspaper. Teyib takes the broom down off its nail and begins sweeping the aisles, the radio voice a soft murmur in his ear. "May as well close up early," Mr. Gene says as Teyib sweeps past him. "See if I can still make the afternoon visiting hours at Mercy." Teyib does not understand. Ah muy az way-ul—the man's English seems more heavily accented than Teyib's.*

*Mr. Gene rolls his eyes and laughs. "Aw, cut me some slack, Jack!" he*

*says. But Teyib doesn't understand. The store is empty. Who is Jack? Mister
Gene bursts into laughter. This is only a saying, he explains, like Gimmie
a break or Hep hep me Rhonda. Then, with a good-natured wave toward
the backroom, directs Teyib to go ahead and take the rest of the day off.*

*He pulls the heavy door shut after himself, and immediately the heat
closes in. Cut me some slack, Jack! He begins stripping down to his
underwear. The room is stifling whenever the furnace is lit. Just as he is
reaching up to hang his shirt on a hook in the alcove, there is an abrupt
silence. Teyib stands perfectly still. Feels gingerly for the radio earpiece
dangling at his neck. Finds it, presses it back into his ear with a twist, and
there is the voice again. Relieved, he nods his head in relief and finishes
hanging the shirt.*

    *He stretches out on the narrow bed. After only a few days, the
wrapping paper on the wall next to his face has already begun to sag and
tear, made worse by his repeated need to lift its edge for a quick scan
of the wallpaper pattern, checking to see whether the little faces have
returned to being flowers once again.*

    *He falls asleep only to find himself wide awake a few a minutes later,
drenched in sweat and hungry. But this hot little alcove isn't a proper
home any more than out front is a proper store, not with its beer and wine
and snack foods, its dusty cans and days-old refrigerated bread. There is no
cooking in this house of Teyib, and he has to make do with what he can
find on the shelves out front. In the middle of the night he eats sardines
and smoked oysters and the tiny canned sausages of Vienna. And the
Spam. It is cold food, all of it, and the only aroma in this place is a faint
odor of mouse. That and his feet after he pulls off his socks. Mercy. Me.
What is a house without the smell of food in it? Certainly not a beit, a
proper home.*

*In the middle of the night the Yankee Cafe is crowded with people. Apple
pie and coffee. Bacon and eggs. A teefee hangs in the corner ceiling where
the long counter curves and abuts into the wall, close by the restroom
doors. The picture is poorly tuned so that the announcer's shirt keeps
fading into green, the lines of his mouth purple-tinged. Yet the customers
crane their necks to watch anyway. They cry out as the ball is kicked up,
up into a yellow-green sky. Even the fry cook cries out, watching the game*

*as he works. His cry becomes a cough, then a whole string of coughs,
ragged and wheezing, which he must keep suppressing as he returns to
his work. The man is fast, flipping the burger patties, pressing them down
to sizzle in their own grease. To save effort and time he has put salt and
pepper together in a single metal shaker. Teyib would have added a little
cinnamon as well, a hint of clove. He would have ground onions directly
into the meat, and fresh parsley. And above all, he would have used lamb
instead of beef. The game on the television is the same as the one coming
through the earpiece of Teyib's little radio. The different announcers
confuse him, though, one of them speaking with an accent almost like
Gene Moon's. He turns the radio down.*

*Finishing his coffee, it occurs to him that, like Gene Moon, he himself
ought to go and pay his respects to the Uncle, his benefactor. The cousins,
Aboodeh and Samir, go to the hospital every day, but yesterday they left town
to pick up Mr. Jim Wilson, and Teyib doesn't know whether they are back
yet or not. If he wants to go soon to the hospital, he will have to get there
on his own.*

*Mr. Jim Wilson. Teyib considers the name. So American sounding.*

*The bus route to Mercy Hospital is simple to follow: buy a transfer for a
penny, change lines downtown at the stop across from the Lowe's Valentine
Theater. Even so, he cannot go empty-handed. He must take some gift up
there with him—but what? He looks down into his coffee cup and tries to
think, but all around him the voices are rising along the booths, up and
down the counter, a churning babble of English that rises and ebbs like
the crying of children. Quickly, he shuts his eyes tight and presses the radio
earpiece in deeper. A beer commercial. Yes. He turns up the volume. Budweiser, the King of Beers.*

*When he opens his eyes, he sees the fry cook is bent over and coughing as
if he cannot stop. Both hands to his chest, he sits down on the rubber mat-
ting in front of the grilltop, coughing. The two counter girls show frightened faces to one another. They do not know what to do. The man starts to
get up, and they help him into the back room. Then the blonde one hurries
out to the cafe's only phone, a public wall phone. She leaves the receiver
dangling and rushes back to open the cash register. Teyib watches as she
quickly takes out a dime, and then a five-dollar bill. Her hair is yellow down
her back, and thick. She tucks the bill into the bosom of her uniform with
one hand and slaps the drawer shut with the other.*

*The eggs on the grill begin to curl and smoke. With all the commo-*

*tion, no one pays them any mind. Teyib sees that no one else is going to do anything, so he gets up himself and steps behind the counter. Taking the heavy metal spatula, he scrapes off the charred eggs. He flips the vent fan to high, drowning out the wail of sirens, and moistens a heavy towel for wiping down the grill top. Then he spreads new grease. In the cooler next to the stove, he finds the egg cartons. Behind the eggs are packages of sliced bacon. Someone at the counter speaks up, suggesting he put on an apron lest he spatter the front of his shirt.*

*In the quiet of his home, Teyib takes a can of beer off the windowsill—Budweiser, the King of Beers—and yanks off the tab. The place is a furnace, but the can is cool from the window. His shirt smells of food. Fry grease and butter. Onion. It is in his hair, too, even the hair of his arms. Delicious. The hairs on his knuckles. He sniffs his fingers and tastes them. Lemon.*

He imagines the Uncle's face upon awakening in a hospital room and finding among the flowers and cards on the bedside stand something familiar and heartening. Rishta soup, or better yet shoribit kishk, *the garlic and onion porridge that makes your blood flow again.*

From the Armenian he can purchase the basic ingredient, that blend of crushed wheat and yogurt fermented together, then dried and ground to the powder called kishk.

But roasting lamb shanks? Making marrow broth from the bones and mixing kishk *powder into it with the simmering onions and garlic until it all thickens into a bubbling porridge? All that he cannot do here, not without an oven or a decent pot, with only a hot plate that can barely heat water!*

He takes another sip of beer. The whole village used to make kishk *in the early autumn, spreading the burghul and laban out to dry on the hot flat roofs of their houses. When it came time to grind the mixture into powder, relatives and neighbors gathered with hand grinders to help one another in completing the project quickly. There were songs they sang as they worked, songs just for the making of kishk. All this, of course, before the sheikh shebaab's warning came to be, and the shooting changed everything.*

But, harakit barrakit, *change itself begets change. Returning from hospital visiting hours, Aunt Libby strides into the store and calls Teyib* aside. She has additional work for him, with Gene Moon's permission, of course. Tammouz & Sons must temporarily close down because of her brother's illness, and for the time being she will need a caretaker to keep the place dusted and clean, maybe clear out some of the clutter. There are storage spaces in the basement and up in the attic apartment that haven't been touched in years. She hands Teyib a key to the side door. After finishing his morning routine at Mr. Gene's, she explains, he can work afternoons in the funeral home.

The first afternoon Teyib spends sweeping the upstairs and clearing cardboard boxes out of the upper hallways and off the attic stairs, carrying them down to the basement where he stacks them neatly against a wall. On the second afternoon he begins clearing the entry to the attic apartment where the Uncle and his wife used to live before they had children and bought the house next door. Over the years of neglect this attic apartment has become yet another nook to cram full. Vases, pedestals, ornate candlesticks, cardboard boxes filled with bolts of embroidered cloth. Teyib moves and stacks until he uncovers the apartment's tiny kitchen. It looks untouched since Aunt Nejla last cooked the Uncle's suppers here. The kitchen has a small stovetop and an oven. And look, there are still pans in the cabinets. He tries the oven and realizes that the gas had been disconnected. But the faucets work, sputtering orange rust before running clear. The old, round-topped refrigerator with its door propped open needs only to be plugged in. As for the stove, Teyib has connected gas pipes before; in Beirut he'd kept the bakery ovens going for months by finding and piping into a neighborhood main. Here the hookups already exist; all he needs is a trip to the hardware store. The Adams bus will take him there.

And the Madison bus stops in front of the hospital. When the kishk is ready he will wrap the pot in towels and carry it down to the bus stop.

# 13

Sam took long showers, he scrubbed his face repeatedly, kept blowing his nose after there was nothing left to blow, and still he couldn't get rid of it, that vague whiff of powdered formalin. It couldn't still be in his nostrils, could it, not after, what, three, *four* days now? He sat back, sighed. And in the sigh there it was again, that slight, acrid taste at the back of his mouth. It tainted everything. Even the savory aromas of Sunday lunch rising now from the hospital's ventilation ducts. Roast chicken and giblet gravy . . . buttery potatoes . . . and powdered formalin. He took out a hanky and tried clearing his nose, sniffling and snorting one nostril, then the other.

"What's the matter, Sammy?" Aunt Shofia was sitting across from him. "You catching a cold?" He hadn't even heard her come in.

"I'm just tired, Auntie. I haven't slept much the past couple nights." There had been a crowd up here all morning, but now everyone had gone down to the cafeteria for lunch, leaving Sam to wait in case Dr. Warren came by. The doctor had been a tough man to get hold of the past couple days; they kept missing him on his regular rounds, and the only news anyone got on Waxy's condition came secondhand, through the nurses. But earlier this morning they'd heard Warren's name paged, so at least they knew he was in the building. When Sam was a patient here, it had been the same thing: if you weren't eating or sleeping, you were waiting for the doctor to show up.

"None of us been getting much sleep, *habibi.*" Aunt Shofia shook her head. "What a week."

Not even a whole week. But time enough for word to spread. For people to arrive from Detroit and Cleveland and Pittsburgh, a few setting out from as far away as Chicago and New York. All of them relatives of one sort or another, former North Enders or their offspring who no longer knew their way around the city. Naturally, since Sam was a *sheb,* a *young man* of the family, Libby volunteered him for chauffeuring duties. Some of these so-called relatives Sam had met only once or twice in his life, others were complete strangers, yet he found himself at their beck and call, having to drive them to the hospital for visiting hours, then taking them back across town to Aunt Shofia's house for the suppers that she and Uncle Alex hosted every night, returning afterward to drop them off at the various houses of the families putting them up. And not only the out-of-towners. He had to drive the older folks, too, those who could no longer drive themselves. Every day the crowd in the ICU lounge seemed to grow larger, louder with talk, with people shaking their heads as they remarked to one another what a shame it was that it had to take something like this to bring them all together again. It was funeral visitation talk, Sam had listened to it all his life.

"You been cooped up here long enough," Shofia said, rising to her feet. "Come on, have lunch with us down in the cafeteria."

"You go ahead, Auntie. I don't really have much of an appetite yet. Besides, Aboodeh wanted me to stick around."

Aunt Shofia arched an eyebrow. "Where *is* your cousin anyway? How come he isn't here today?"

"He's up in Detroit. Taking care of some business for the funeral home."

"That one?" She shook her head disapprovingly. "Some *monkey* business, you mean."

Sam smiled obligingly. She had no idea. Because monkey business was exactly what it was, Aboodeh's trying to explain to Larry Morton how the failed delivery was just a glitch, the kind of thing you had to expect in a start-up enterprise. Maybe Larry Morton would go for it, but what Sam had seen with his own two eyes was no glitch. He inhaled sharply at just the thought of it. Formalin.

"Roast turkey?" Shofia sniffed the air. She was a Yakoub by marriage, but her nose was all Tammouz. "Or chicken, maybe?"

"Maybe."

"Well, when your cousin gets back from Detroit, tell him to bring Salma and the kids over to my house tonight. I haven't seen the kids since last Fourth of July." Shofia turned, one hand on the door. "And you too," she added. "Bring your mother."

"I will, Auntie."

"You better have an appetite when you sit down at my table. That's all I can say."

"Don't worry, I will."

Still holding the door, Shofia leaned in, "Oh, and bring—"

"Yes, Auntie, I'll bring Mama."

Shofia raised that eyebrow again. "I was *going* to say why don't you bring your girlfriend, too. Is she your girlfriend, or what, the blondie from the cafe?"

"Maybe."

"Maybe what?"

"Maybe I can bring her, Auntie. She's up in Ann Arbor now. But I'll ask her. I think she'd really like your house."

"Everybody likes my house!" She let go the door. "You take care of that cold." Sam watched till the door softly hissed shut, half expecting it to pop open again.

In the past few days, Aunt Shofia's had become the natural gathering place after visiting hours. On the same side of town as the hospital, her house was one of the largest in a neighborhood of large Victorians. Would Nikki like the place? She'd love it. He was new to America when he first stepped into its foyer, holding his parents' hands. His first impression had been that this must be how the *Amerkani* lived, in houses like this, and understanding that not *Amerkani* but *ibn Arab* lived here—his own cousins, the Yakoubs—he'd felt a surge of hope. In America everything was possible, everything.

Inside the foyer there was a second front door, made of beveled glass set in lead. When Baba pressed a lighted button, there sounded a series of chimes. The woman who answered the door welcomed them in Arabic, *"Ahlan wa sahlan!"* She looked younger than Mama, and heavier, with gold earrings that brushed her cheeks as she bent down to kiss him. *Ahlan wa sahlan*, she repeated *You're among family, and now all's well.* She was a cousin, so he had been instructed to call her *Aunt* Shofia, out of respect.

Seating them in her living room, she brought out thick Turkish coffee for the adults, for Sam sweetened hot water touched with orange blossom oil. He knew to wait, balancing the little demitasse cup in one hand, until their hostess put down the serving things and joined them. They did not take their first sip until she uttered the traditional *"Daime,"* short for *May we always be together like this.*

Returning from the men's room, Sam thought he caught a whiff of something other than formalin. It was familiar, but what? Incense? Down by the nurse's station, he heard a woman describing somebody.

"Short guy," she was saying, "about yay tall? Thick neck, kinda red-faced?"

Sam stopped short in the middle of the hall. That boyish haircut, it was Moe. Standing beside her was a bearded man in a leather vest.

There was a bulletin board close by Sam. He edged over to it and pretended to read the notices: a benefit raffle; a lost set of keys . . .

"His father's in the ICU here," the woman said.

Her clothes reeked of incense, he could smell it all the way to here. The duty nurse was shaking her head no, explaining to Moe how she couldn't bend the rules for her, but all the while her eyes were on the man standing next to Moe. He was about Larry Morton's age, but taller, and more heavily built. Despite the leather vest and the beard, he was no college hippie either. He looked dirty, and his arms were heavily tattooed, like a jailbird's.

"I'm sorry," the nurse said. "And if you're not relatives yourselves, I'm afraid you won't be able to wait up here, either." At this, the man with Moe planted his feet and crossed his tattooed arms across his chest.

For a while none of them moved an inch. Then Moe turned to glance up the hall toward Sam. He froze, sensing her gaze stop and focus in on him. After a moment, he heard the nurse pick up the telephone. That got the two of them moving. When he looked again, they were at the far end of the hall, entering an elevator.

Realizing he'd been holding his breath, Sam released it now in a long slow gasp. He stepped into the visitors' lounge and flopped himself heavily onto the vinyl couch.

A woman's voice cried out, *"There* you are!" Sam shot bolt upright and nearly fell off the couch. It was Nikki. Here? "Nikki!"

"I must've walked up and down this wing ten times already!" She looked like she'd been out in the rain; dark streaks of wet ran down the shoulders of her jeans jacket, and her hair was all tucked up under a damp-looking corduroy cap. Turning to the windows, he saw that a downpour was gusting silently against the heavy glass. He asked the obvious. "You get caught in it?"

"Caught?" Nikki said, tucking a strand of hair back up into the hat. Sam noticed a smear of dried paint on the heel of her hand. Avocado green. "I've been *walking* in it. I'm soaked." She thrust out a foot to show him the sodden cuffs of her bell bottoms. "The lots are full so I had to park all the way down Madison!" Nikki drew a long breath, her eyes widening as she started in on what an ordeal she'd been through cleaning and painting in Ann Arbor, all by herself, except of course for Deano. "We don't even have a working toilet up there. We had to go out in the backyard, in the rain." She looked away and seemed to slump.

"You drove straight here from Michigan?"

No. She'd stopped home first to drop off Deano. Poor kid, sick all weekend. "Then I saw it was close enough to visiting hours so I thought I'd drop by and see how your uncle's doing."

"Really?" Sam tried to look as if he believed her. "That's really nice of you, Nikki," he said, although he guessed the real reason. She dropped by, painting clothes and all, so he could witness her exhaustion after a weekend of trying to do alone what he'd promised to help her with.

"Why don't you sit down? You want coffee?"

She nodded. "So, how *is* he doing?"

"Uncle Waxy? No change. Same old wait-and-see."

"Mm," Nikki said by way of acknowledgment, but her mind already seemed elsewhere.

"You hungry?" Sam asked.

"Cup of coffee'd help."

At the coffee maker, Sam glanced up as a lightning flash lit up the windows. A close one, but no sound had come through the heavy glass, not even a rumble. How long had it been storming like this? He pictured Nikki driving back from Ann Arbor, those paint-spattered knuckles of hers tight on the steering wheel, and he felt guilty for having suspected her motives.

When he returned, carrying two Styrofoam cups, he found her sprawled wearily on one of the vinyl couches. He set both cups on a table near her, and she sat up. Tucking in her feet, she patted the cushion next to her. She didn't touch the coffee, and she didn't speak right away. Simply leaned her head back, eyes half closed, as if to demonstrate again how worn out she was.

"Deano's sick?" Sam asked, trying to sound concerned. "With what?" Getting sick seemed to be a way of life for that kid, especially when there was school the next day.

"Fever. Low grade, but he was feeling fluish the whole time we were up there."

Sam made a little frown. "So, where is he now?"

"Now? He's home. I set him up all comfy in bed."

All comfy. What did she want him to see, chicken soup and Kleenexes and a thermometer in a glass? The kid was in bed, all right, and no doubt playing that bb game and watching television. Deano's TV was a small portable that couldn't have been cheap, designed as it was for the youth market. Wrapped in blue denim, it had a jeans pocket sewn onto the side, with a red bandanna poking out of it. Like somebody's ass.

Nikki sipped her coffee then sighed pointedly. "So," she said, "in case you're interested . . ."

"What?"

"After I finished clearing the downstairs hall, I got all of the back bedroom painted. It turned out nice."

"Avocado green."

"How'd you know?"

"You missed a spot." He took her hand and turned it to the side to show her.

"Hunh." She pulled her hand back. "Well, it wasn't easy. Maybe if I had some real help—" Her voice gave way, and she quavered on the last word. It was a reproach arising from all the loneliness and frustration of the past couple days. Sam understood this and kept silent.

"Fact is, Sammy," she sat up now, "it's not like people here can't get around for two days without you."

"No, the fact is some of them really can't."

"Like who?"

"Like people from out of town, they don't know their way around. Like the cousins from Pittsburgh coming in on the train tonight. And like some of the older people, like my mother, she can't drive, and—"

"All right, all right!" she said, shutting him up. "I know. It's just that I can't stop thinking about all the rent I pay!"

"Rent?" It took Sam a moment to realize she'd struck off in a different direction.

"Every month I may as well *burn* the rent money I pay on that apartment." Nikki shook her head in disgust. "A house is an investment. And the sooner it's fixed and livable, the sooner it'll be a real home again, too. Deano will be in a decent school system."

"Nikki, listen a minute."

She didn't want to listen. "And it'd be great for you too. If you wanted you could even go to school up there. Stay with us and once you establish Michigan residency, you won't even have to pay out-of-state tuition."

"Listen, Nikki, please. I know it sounds great, but you gotta think, too. I mean, for one thing the house isn't even *in* Ann Arbor. Everything will be a commute. Some of it on gravel roads. Think of wintertime." He could see that she'd stopped listening, distracted by a commotion outside the door. A deep voice rumbling something short and stern, followed by a scuffle of footsteps. He got up to see, with Nikki right behind him.

Out in the hall a uniformed security guard was confronting a skinny little guy carrying something in both hands. It was Teyib! And the guard now had him by one elbow and was forcibly escorting him back toward the elevators. They were moving fast, Teyib protesting. The guard's voice was so deep, his replies echoed unintelligibly down the hall.

They'd reached the elevators by the time Sam caught up. Teyib was carrying a cooking pot wrapped in a towel. Whatever it contained had slopped over in a thick steaming liquid. The stuff was the color of oatmeal, and Sam thought he recognized its savory smell, garlic and something tangy. *Kishk* porridge?

"What happened, Officer?"

"Cousin Sam!" Teyib said. "Help me, Rhonda!"

The guard turned to Sam. "This *gentleman*," he may as well have said *fool*, although he sounded exasperated more than offended, "you know him?"

"Yes, officer."

"He a relative to you?"

Sam explained that his cousin was new here, still learning the language.

"Well, you tell your cousin that he can't go into the ICU carryin' that. We have *rules* here. And he sure can't be carrying no pot of *food* in there with him." He paused to sniff appreciatively. "What *is* that, smells so good?"

"*Kishk,*" Teyib said.

"Like a garlic porridge," Sam explained. "Sort of."

"Garlic? Well, you and Rhonda here, you take your cousin back down to the cafeteria with that garlic whatchacallit." The elevator had arrived, and he was holding the door open for the three of them. "And you tell him I don't want the nurses calling me back up here again on his account."

A hot, garlicky-wheat aroma quickly filled the enclosed space of the elevator. Sam breathed it in, shallowly at first, cautiously, but it was just *kishk* he smelled, no trace of formalin. Relieved, he breathed in again, more deeply. Yes. Just *kishk*.

"Whatever that is you got there," Nikki said to Teyib, "it sure does smell good."

Teyib acknowledged this shyly, with a little dip of his head.

"But what for?" Sam asked. He had never seen Teyib so dressed up, in a sports jacket and tie, a white shirt so new the fold-creases stood out. His hair was different, too. He'd had it trimmed to almost a crew cut, buzzing away the last of the blonde tips, and his sideburns were beginning to fill in.

Teyib cast a timid glance down at the pot. "For the Uncle," he said. Standing hunched with the pot in his hands, Teyib looked as if he were trying to make himself smaller by squeezing backward into a corner of the elevator. Still embarrassed, probably, at the commotion he'd just caused.

Sam gave a sad shake of his head, explaining that the only eating that Uncle Waxy would be doing for a while would be through a tube.

Teyib cocked his ear to show he didn't get it. It was then Sam noticed that the little radio button wasn't there. "How come you're not wearing your radio, Teyib?"

Teyib's eyebrows went up in surprise. He lowered his ear and rubbed it against his shoulder. Sam took the pot from him while he searched for the cord. He ran his fingers down one lapel then the other, patted down both jacket pockets. Then he closed his eyes to think a moment.

He opened his eyes and smiled with relief. "*Beh mutbakhi,*" he said, speaking softly to himself, *It's in my kitchen.*

*Muhtbakhi?* Sam couldn't help smiling. A hot plate and a sink and he calls it his *kitchen*? Handing the pot back to Teyib, Sam explained again, this time in hesitant Arabic, that Uncle Waxy wasn't able to eat right now.

"Hey!" Nikki held out one hand. "Somebody mind telling *me* what's being said here?"

In the cafeteria, Aunt Shofia and the others were having lunch over by the windows, where they'd pushed together several tables. Sam didn't notice that Aboodeh was sitting with them until his cousin stood up, angrily threw down his napkin and strode out the double doors. Sam followed him. The others, familiar with Aboodeh's moods, were more interested in the pot Teyib was uncovering.

"You're here," Aboodeh said, "so who's up there with Dad?"

"C'mon, Bud, I haven't been gone five minutes." In the hall, Sam told his cousin about seeing Moe upstairs. He started to ask whether things had gone okay up in Detroit, when his cousin suddenly wheeled about. "Things went fine, as if you give a shit! Real fine and dandy. Larry Morton doesn't want us forgetting about that delivery that never came through.

"What does *he* care?"

"Because he's an investor, just like us."

"Since when?"

"Since the first day I explained to him how my venture would work. Larry Morton was one of the very first people to see the beauty of it." Aboodeh's face darkened. "But now, if we can't find the shipment, he's gonna want us to cover his losses."

"Us? We lost our investment, too!" Sam thought a moment. "He thinks we *stole* it?"

Aboodeh brushed Sam aside as the elevator doors slid open.

Back in the cafeteria, Aunt Shofia was trying to get the recipe out of Teyib. She'd tasted plenty of *kishk* in her time, and she was determined to learn exactly what he put into his. She actually had a ballpoint out and was writing on a paper napkin.

"*A little olive oil, a little butter,*" he was saying in Arabic, "*then you take a small handful of the dried wheat and yogurt to start off. As it heats, stir in just a little broth at a time.*"

"*How much is it little?*" Long in America, Aunt Shofia spoke a broken Arabic.

"*Bes shwey'yeht,*" Teyib answered, *Just a little,* shaping a tiny cup with thumb and four fingers to show her.

Sam began translating for Nikki, but her eyes soon took on a faraway look as she slowly savored a spoonful of *kishk*.

"*Shwey'yeht?*" An out-of-town cousin started laughing. *A little?* "He cooks the way my grandmother cooked," she said, "all in the wrist." She performed a loose-wristed pantomime of tossing things in with both hands, "*Shwey'yeht* this, *shwey'yeht* that."

Teyib brightened and he nodded encouragingly, as if to say, "Yes, exactly!" And he demonstrated how, when he'd got the pot bubbling just so, he crumbled baked *kibbeh* meat into the mix.

"The *kibbeh*, you baked it yourself?"

He nodded.

"Actually," Sam interrupted, in English, "I think he's got some of this confused."

Teyib only smiled, so it was Aunt Shofia who asked, "How so?"

"I used to live where he's living now. The little apartment in back of the store? The place doesn't even *have* a kitchen."

Teyib shook his head. "I make this *beh mutbakhi*," he said, mixing Arabic and English. Amused, he added, "Little *mutbakh*. Up in the stairs."

*Upstairs?* Sam still didn't get it. The little *kitchen* up what stairs?

Teyib seemed pleased to explain that it had been Sam's aunt who had given him the okay to cook up there. "She tell me, 'Okay, guy!'"

Libby? And Sam understood. Aunt Libby must have let him use the attic at Tammouz & Sons. "Oh, *that* little kitchen."

"Well, I don't have a *little* kitchen," Shofia chuckled, putting the recipe in her purse and snapping it shut. "I have a *big* kitchen. And you can come cook in it any time. Tonight if you want."

"Looks like it's still raining a little," Nikki said. She had finished her *kishk* and was putting her cap back on now, tucking her hair up under it. "I had to park way the hell out."

"You want company?" Sam asked. "So we can talk?"

"I suppose. If you think they can spare you."


But Nikki didn't feel like talking. Her weekend of scraping walls and painting had exhausted her, driving in the pouring rain, and with Deano's cold suddenly improved enough that he was able to rise from his sickbed and dash over to a friend's house, now all she really wanted was to get out of her wet things and crawl into bed for a nap. Sam lingered while she showered, unsure whether she wanted him to leave or not. All over the apartment was heaped the debris of her weekend: rolled-up sleeping bags, dirty clothes, Styrofoam coolers, a plastic bucket spattered with paint, avocado green. In the hallway, his feet kicked against a pair of Deano's mud-caked tennis shoes. Michigan mud.

She hadn't even dried off completely when she got into bed, still steamy and moist, her hair wrapped in a towel. Sam sat on the edge of the bed. Then, kicking off his shoes, he stretched out beside her. She muttered something about not starting anything. "Jesus, no, of course not," he said. "I drove all day today, too. Back and forth to the hospital, I mean. Must've been half a dozen times." After a minute he asked, "So when did it start raining?"

Nikki breathed out heavily, but made no reply. She kept her face nuzzled deep into the covers. After a while, he couldn't tell whether she was asleep or not. When he did speak, he kept his voice soft, feigning sleepiness; in fact, he felt wired and had been forcing himself to lie still. "You know something?" he said, and waited. Her breathing was regular, like somebody sleeping. Or pretending to sleep. "Tell you what," he said, keeping his voice pensive, "I had a thought."

"Good," she spoke finally, her voice muffled. "Hang on to it."

"No, seriously. Don't you want to know about what?"

Apparently not. He waited another minute. "I've been thinking about the house in Michigan."

The sleep-breathing stopped. That got her attention.

So he continued, explaining how, yes, he'd promised to help her with the place. To do what he could, anyway. But with him being so busy while Uncle Waxy was in the hospital, he just couldn't say for sure exactly when he'd be able to go back up there again and help.

She was silent. Still listening.

So what he was thinking was maybe, *maybe,* she ought to think about—this wasn't what she wanted to hear, he understood that, but it needed saying anyway—think about doing just enough repairs to, well, sell the place.

Silence.

He took a breath and went on, but had barely gotten into what it might take to show a potential buyer what, well, *potential* the place had—when Nikki rose to one elbow, turned and gave him a steady, he thought at first *sleepy,* look, before abruptly throwing back the covers, a flash of white skin, and marching off to get dressed, her luscious white behind thrust out in anger.

❧

## EAT THE RICH

*Aunt Shofia has a new double-door refrigerator, and Teyib feels he must feign at least some measure of amazement. Especially while Salma, Cousin Aboodeh's wife, is watching him. He opens the door to the freezer and smiles as if surprised by the little light winking on in there. He closes the door and opens the other, glances in. Both doors are thick with shelves. He shakes his head in wonderment. Then he looks over at Cousin Salma and makes the thumbs-up sign he has learned from umpires on television.*

*Shofia's kitchen has been remodeled so that it is like a kitchen on television, everything new. Too new: tugging a chef's knife off the magnetic rack, he finds it too dull even to cut open an eggplant. He takes the sharpening steel and begins to slide the knife against it in quick up-and-down strokes. Cousin Salma cringes at the sound, her porcelain-pretty face smiling and grimacing at the same time. A few seconds, and—"Dakheelak!"—she can bear it no longer. "I beseech you!" she says in Arabic. "Enough!"*

*How to explain? He raises his eyebrows and thinks a moment. Although Cousin Aboodeh's wife is not nearly as new to America as Teyib, she is more reluctant to give up the old ways. He can see sometimes how his attempts at English distress her. Well, okey-dokey then, he will have to explain in Arabic how a dull knife is more dangerous than a sharp one. "The sharp knife keeps to the path it is given," he says. "The dull one turns aside from its path and does harm."*

*Salma sighs impatiently, and like a teenager being lectured she turns away before he finishes explaining. What does she care about knives? The tomatoes and onions for the* suf-souf *salad are already chopped, and now she is "helping" him by overusing the noisy blender machine, turning into a clumpy paste the parsley he himself has hand-picked, washed and dried.*

*No wonder he prefers working alone. Alone, and in his own upstairs kitchen at the funeral home. But Shofia insists that he cook for them here* again tonight, in her new kitchen, and that he have help, especially now that even more relatives from out of town have begun arriving. Every day Cousin Sam drives them to the hospital in shifts, and afterward brings them here for a family meal.

Into the second week now, and still the old man sleeps. Sleep? Yesterday, when Cousin Sam had managed to sneak Teyib in, the Uncle had looked near death. The skin of his forehead was yellow and papery, showing a thick vein that throbbed with his heartbeat. A tube ran from his nose to a machine that breathed with a regular moist sigh that sounded like someone else breathing on the other side of the bed.

Slicing pockets into each of the long thin eggplant wedges, Teyib stuffs them with a mixture of rice, ground chickpeas, chopped mint, cinnamon and walnuts. Then, buttering a casserole pan, he arranges the boats in overlapping chevrons and pours crushed tomatoes over them. Shofia's kitchen has two ovens, gas in the stove and electric in the wall next to the stove. Even so, he prefers the oven he himself reconnected in his own little mutbakh upstairs, this despite the fact that this is the finest kitchen he has seen here in America, and the house itself is a palace. As Alex and Shofia showed him the house for the first time, taking him from room to room, they both seemed astonished by their own success in America. For their sakes he widened his eyes, opening his mouth in a show of awe. No matter that he has seen this and better in the summer villas where the rich go to escape Beirut's heat, taking their favorite cooks with them. No matter that he has worked in kitchens with marble floors and triple arched windows opening to vistas of Mount Suneen itself.

Finally Salma's blender machine stops, and Teyib can once again hear the voices of people collecting in the living room. More of them will be on their way from the hospital, Cousin Sam driving them here in shifts. Soon Boutros will stink up the entire house with his cigar while Old Yousef goes on with stories about how the first ones stepped off their cattle boats and that very day got set up to begin peddling door to door. Still, supper isn't until seven, so Teyib has plenty of time. And he has more parsley, too, which he can take out and chop properly if Salma will only leave him just a minute alone in here.

Salma begins watching an interview program on television as she scoops into a bowl the mess she's made. Yes, a teefee in the kitchen! At least Teyib has the radio which he can press into his ear and turn up. He understands *that the season of baseball has ended and that the season of football has already begun. In Detroit the football team is named the Lions.*

*All day today the television news has been of Beirut. While he pours water off the soaked rice, Cousin Salma cries out "I was there!" and tells him to look when a teefee crew goes into the streets behind Martyr's Plaza, and again when another crew crosses the Green Line check points heading for the coastal road and views of the Pigeon Rocks, and the whole time she keeps calling out to him in Arabic, saying I was there! or Look, see there? I know that place! and You missed it! Why won't you look?*

*He does look. Once. Boys gathering for the camera, making faces and posturing around a Jeep-mounted recoilless rifle. Around their necks holy medals or little silver crosses. Christians. "Tonys," the Christian boys are called, because so many of their generation have been named Anthony. Their tee-shirts have English words on them. Teyib recognizes some as the names of rock-and-roll bands. But a number of others bear the identical depiction of a skull above words that he isn't sure of, a saying of some sort that he has to ask Salma to read. Yes, the saying on the tee-shirts of the Tonys says what he had thought it said, but she, too, is puzzled by it. Eat the Rich, it says.*

# 14

Nikki waited in the car while Sam got out to help the three old women, extending an arm as each extricated herself from the backseat. Then he guided them, one at a time in careful tiny steps, across the slick driveway and up the front porch steps to where Aunt Shofia's son, Little Alex, waited to help them the rest of the way in. A varsity wrestler at Central Catholic, Little Alex wasn't so little anymore.

For Sam this had been yet another afternoon of hurry up and wait: Hurry over to Aunt Afifie's, but wait, has it started sleeting again? She'll want to change into a heavier coat. Hurry now, or we'll miss visiting hours. But wait! Aunt Roufa's not ready; she needs to put on her galoshes. Hurry to Aunt Anissa's, but be patient with her, poor thing, while she turns and crouches, extending her rear to drop it heavily onto the car seat—*ouf!* Now, hurry! *Yallah, yallah!*

One thing he was glad of, at least Nikki could see for herself now what it had been like for him the past couple weeks. When he got back to the car he found her sitting as he'd left her, gazing up at the house. "I told you it was something else," he said. "But wait'll you see the *inside*."

From the driveway, they could already hear Uncle Yousef holding forth in his high, piping voice. "Hope you're ready for this," Sam said.

"I am," she said. Then she squeezed his hand and laughed, "At least I *think* I am!" She'd been warm like this ever since yesterday, when he'd taken her to the Sears store out in Westgate Plaza and told her to pick out a toilet bowl, "Because if I'm gonna spend all next weekend doing repairs up there, that's the *first* thing we're gonna need!" Nikki was stunned. "The *whole* weekend?" It was what she'd been waiting so long to hear. And right there in the bathroom fixtures department, as they stood before an array of commodes displayed in various pastel shades, Nikki had risen to her tiptoes and planted a kiss on his neck, just below the ear.

Sam could feel the warmth of it even now as he led her up Aunt Shofia's front porch steps, into the mingled aromas of toasted pine nuts and eggplant, the bright scent of fresh lemon. But inside the vestibule, wiping the wet from their shoes, there was also now the stinky undercurrent of Uncle Boutros's cigar. Boutros smoked constantly. Even now, *before* supper. Yesterday must have been a Boulos day. Sam explained it to Nikki. Boutros and Boulos—in English Peter and Paul—were brothers who'd kept a feud going for so long now that the families had come to accept that when you invited one, you didn't invite the other. One night Boutros came to Shofia's, the next night Boulos. One night they had the stink of Boutros, who puffed away and said little; next night no smoke, but there was Boulos's loud voice, and his loud opinions that always hung in the air about him, challenging anyone to an argument. The brothers were presented as a caution to quarreling siblings: "You don't want to grow up to be like Boutros and Boulos, do you?

Sam took Nikki's coat and guided her by the elbow, through the foyer and down a step through an arched entryway. He watched her eyes widen as she took in the dining room with its fireplace and crystal chandelier. Now *this* was a *home*. Beneath their feet was one of the rugs Baba himself had brought back from the old country, its curlicue patterns of rich blues and reds.

The kitchen door swung open. "Don't tell me it's started sleeting again!" Aunt Shofia said, propping the kitchen door open with one elbow. Her hands looked oily and she was holding them up like a surgeon. "You parked in back, I hope?" She looked past Sam to Nikki. "Ah, you brought her! *Ahlan wa sahlan!*"

Nikki smiled at Shofia. "I love your home," she said.

As Sam ushered Nikki on toward the living room, he glanced back at Shofia, who winked her approval. He had to smile in agreement; Nikki certainly did look terrific. Her hair was piled up in something like a French twist, and she'd worn a simple pale blue dress which, though tasteful, was made of a clingy knit fabric that couldn't help but show off her figure. Most of the family, if they'd seen her at all, had seen her in the middle of the night shift at the Yankee, wearing her waitress uniform and a hairnet.

The TV was turned up loud for Aunt Afifie—Sam had brought her over earlier, along with Mama—and Uncle Yousef had to raise his voice to talk over it. Because the living room was half again as long as it was wide, conversations usually broke into smaller groups, but when there was really a crowd, like now, its length often had the opposite effect, funneling the noisy attention toward whoever was holding forth. Poor Mama, seated over on the far sofa, had Yousef yammering on one side of her and the TV blaring away on the other. She was already beginning to look stunned. Soon the women and men would separate, sooner if Uncle Boutros relit the cigar whose ash he was examining.

Children played on the back stairway, the carpeted thumps carrying all the way in to here. Aboodeh's kids. Salma wasn't around, probably helping in the kitchen again. Aboodeh was in the living room, slouched in a stuffed chair next to the piano. He looked to be in one of his moods. Probably still waiting to hear from Beirut. Or the hospital. News from neither one had been very good lately. Sam touched Nikki's shoulder.

"Mm?"

"This way." Skirting the archway, he led her down the hall past the kitchen's back door. Sam glimpsed Salma in there and, at the stove, Teyib and Shofia working away in matching frilly aprons.

"*Ya ibn Rasheed!*" Uncle Yousef called out as soon as he spied Sam entering the living room. Calling him *Ibn Rasheed*, the son of his father, was a storyteller's formality. The old man put down his glass of *arrak* and cleared his throat. "Waxy Tammouz," he began, "he come to America only because his elder brother, Rasheed, God give him rest, this boy's *baba*, he got here first. Three years after they shot him, McKinley. Rasheed, when he got to America, he was fourteen years old—the *welad bendouq!*—wearing his father's pants, an' his belt was a piece a rope!"

"Why do you call him that?" a cousin from Cleveland asked.

Yousef replied by asking who else but a *welad bendouq* would run away at fourteen and take with him his father's only pair of trousers!

And in the pocket of those trousers a pouch of gold dinars his father had buried to evade the Turkish tax collectors. A small pouch, but enough to bribe his way aboard ship as a stowaway only minutes before departure from Beirut Harbor. Enough, and more. But that very pocket was picked while the steamship was put in overnight at the port of Marseilles. In the morning Rasheed touched his pocket for the gold, and it was gone—gone!

As the story goes, there was a Frenchman aboard ship, a doctor who'd heard of the boy's plight and took pity on him. He bought Rasheed a meal and a bath, a suit of clothes in the ship's store, including trousers that fit; he did all this, and then he led the boy up from steerage, to make the acquaintance of a tall red-headed woman waiting on an upper deck. She was in her middle years, well-dressed, reserved. The boy had supper alone with her that evening in her first class cabin, and there he remained for the rest of the crossing.

Sam had heard this story as a child. When he was grown he learned that that which had happened to his father had been arranged to happen. And not just to Baba. Many young men from those immigration years would tell a similar story—suddenly finding themselves rendered penniless mid-journey, their pockets picked in a faraway port; then just as suddenly rescued, their only obligation being to provide companionship to some rich woman traveling alone.

That was how Baba avoided processing at Ellis Island. Holding the red-haired woman's hand, he debarked with the other first-class passengers at Battery Park. Nearby on Washington Street was Manhattan's Little Syria. Nearly all the *ibn Arab* stayed a while at the Little Syria near their port of entry before moving on, boarding trains for the Little Syrias of Massachusetts or western New York to find factory work in Syracuse and Utica and Rochester; some traveling eventually to Cleveland's steel mills, to the auto plants of Toledo and Detroit. But factory work meant working for someone else, and they didn't come to America to do that. No, best was to work for yourself, in your own store. *That* was how, Yousef maintained, you shoveled gold from America's streets.

*Ibn Arab* suppliers all over the East and Midwest stood ready to stake the newcomers, sending them out on the road to sell what in those days were called notions and white goods: bolts of cloth, pins and shears and buttons. Some traveled in horse-drawn wagons, others in automobiles, but most went forth on shoe leather, tramping from small town to small town, sleeping in boardinghouses, in barns, under the stars. Learning the money as they went along, and the language after that, door to door to door they unpacked their wicker *kashishis* and let the products sell themselves. *Needles, Missus? Thread?*

After years of peddling, Rasheed Tammouz had mustered savings enough to strike out on his own. He settled first in Chicago, where he opened a small corner grocery. After the First World War, he learned that of all his family only his younger brother, Abdullah, and little sister, Labibeh, had survived the Great War, the famines and the rampant epidemics that had followed it—typhus, typhoid and the Spanish influenza.

Now Yousef pictured for them Abdullah and Labibeh, sent for by their brother, as they stepped off the Ellis Island ferry. Look how they'd grown! His brother was already a young man. Labibeh, not yet a woman, still wearing a floppy child's bow in her hair. Rasheed rushed to embrace the two of them as they stood hand in hand, still trembling from the ordeal of processing, the questions, the physical inspections, and were further shaken by the embrace of this near-stranger of a brother. Behind him loomed the tall buildings of Wall Street. All around was the American harbor, great sweeping bridges, Ellis Island and Bedloes Island with its Liberty statue. Playing host, their brother Rasheed stretched out an arm to take it all in, saying, in English, "It's nice in America, yes?"

Nice in America? After war and famine and pestilence, did young Abdullah find it *nice* in America? Overwhelmed, he began blowing kisses at the Colossus. *"Bless your breasts and your nipples!"* he cried out to her in Arabic. *"Bless the milk that swells them up!"* He began unbuttoning his shirt to show her the *djrab il khirdee* with its piece of the True Cross.

"Abdullah, you're taking things too far!" Rasheed said, and he gave his brother a cigar—stuff your mouth with this. The two of them sat down on a bench and smoked together. Meanwhile Libby, even then with more business sense than her two brothers put together, used hand signals and schoolgirl English to arrange the retrieval of their luggage.

The train that brought them to Chicago was called the Twentieth Century Limited. Next day, seated at a restaurant in the Little Syria at Eighteenth and Michigan, Young Abdullah was surprised to find *koosa* squash here in the very heart of America, and *sishbarrak* dumplings, and fresh lamb for *laham mishwee* and *kibbeh nayeh* even though it wasn't the slaughtering season. He ordered all this and, as an afterthought, grape leaves, too, and *arrak* to drink and—why not?—a *maza* to start off with.

Rasheed shook his head at the wide-eyed waiter. His brother was taking things too far again.

A few years later, when Rasheed moved to Toledo, he brought his sister with him, but Abdullah remained where he was, apprenticed at Sbarbaro Brothers' funeral home. And there, because of his skill with reconstructions in wax—a crushed nose, a missing cheek, a shot-away chin—he earned himself the nickname "Waxy."

One of the cousins from Pittsburgh spoke up. "They say Al Capone gave him that nickname."

Yousef pulled down the corners of his mouth, thought a moment, then shrugged. And got a laugh.

"Did Waxy even *know* Al Capone?" the cousin asked.

*"Kaan ma kaan,"* Yousef replied, the Arabic *Once upon a time* that translates literally to *Perhaps this happened thus, perhaps it did not.* In other words, Maybe, maybe not. But Pittsburgh—Sam didn't know his name—wouldn't let it go.

"So which is it? *Kaan* or *makaan?*"

The Sbarbaro Brothers did have a reputation, Yousef admitted. They were *the* funeral home of choice to the Chicago underworld. And if your business was shady business, the funeral profession would be perfect for keeping people's noses out of your affairs, wouldn't it. A concept not lost on an associate of Capone's who operated the New York mortuary that invented the double-bottomed casket. "Fella named Giuseppe," Yousef added.

"But what about Capone?"

The man was either rude or stupid. Yousef ignored him.

After the Immigration Quota Act of 1924, Waxy began making use of his mortician's access to bring people over on the papers of dead people. The scheme involved the use and reuse of the same documents. Over and over. Three, four, five different people could be processed through on a single set of papers. Because a brother helped his cousin who helped his neighbor, Immigration and Naturalization called it a chain migration. "And without the funeral business, it would have been impossible to smuggle in a single one of them."

"Smuggling, eh?" Sam said, then turned to find Aboodeh glaring at him from across the room.

The children were fed first, afterward ushered into the living room to watch TV. When the adults were seated, Aboodeh chose a place directly across the table from Sam and Nikki. Interesting, Sam thought, how his cousin's mood began to brighten during the meal. There were comments and laughter around the table about how much these meals at Shofia's had improved since Teyib came into her kitchen. Showing Nikki how to fold her flatbread into a scoop for the sauce, Sam caught his cousin openly smiling at her, flirting with her. In front of Salma. In front of Sam. She did look terrific in that knit dress, her small shoulders and the blonde hair, and she responded to Aboodeh's attention by warming up to Sam, leaning in close, touching his hand lingeringly as he passed the bread plate.

Mama noticed too, and she smiled. But it was a hesitant, troubled smile. Did she think here was the love of her son's life? Love? She knew more about food. Her parents had practically sold her to a *welad hendouq*.

After Baba died, Sam, who was eleven at the time, remembered being obsessed with an image of his father's sleeves rolled up, those arms of his reaching out, red and scalded, pleading through the flaming grates of hell. During the visitation at Tammouz & Sons, he'd watched his mother receiving visitors. She sat in the leather widow's chair recounting Baba's story to each of them in turn, a commonplace at wakes and visitations.

It wasn't love. When Sam was still a child, even then he knew it was never love. Arranged marriages sometimes turned to love, yes, but not theirs. All through the visitation Sam had sat watching his mother from across the room, expecting her to get up when this was over and wipe her hands on a dishtowel, another chore done.


They were finishing up, putting coffee on for the dessert, when Little Alex poked his head around the dining room arch and called out, "Beirut's on the news. It just started!"

Everyone immediately got up in a clatter of silverware and chairs and filed into the living room. There on the screen was Martyr's Plaza. The heroic statues were hard to miss despite the rubble and smoke.

"The *Bourj!*" someone called out.

"Where?"

"See? To the right there, up that street would be the silversmith's *souq*. What's left of it."

"We were there—remember?"

"Oh, look, all that's been changed now."

The newsman began his commentary, keeping his statements brief, letting the camera speak for itself. There had been two more car bomb explosions, he said. One in the posh Hamra district, the second here in central Beirut, where the *souqs* all come together. And today was market day. The camera looked up a side street splattered with fruits and vegetables, and came to rest on a group of women alternately weeping then looking up to cry out in grief over what looked like a pile of rags.

"*Udrub!*" A woman here in the living room uttered the word of shared pain, but the rest remained silent. In the silence, Sam thought he heard a thin, barely audible radio voice. It was babbling away in excited bursts. Craning to one side, he followed its sound to Teyib, seated in an armchair that wasn't even facing the TV screen. Head down, apron bunched in both hands, he seemed to be listening for dear life. There had been a penalty on the play, Sam could hear the announcer clearly. Beyond the droning television came the shrill noise of cheers as a field punt sent the ball up, up, up toward the goal posts. And behind it all, a phone ringing.

Aunt Shofia made her way to the telephone table. She listened, plugging one ear. "It's the hospital," she said. "He's awake."

*Yallah!* From the backseat the old women urged Sam to drive faster—*Yallah! Yallah!*—his mother and Aunt Afifie. But not Aunt Nejla, and she *should* have been urging him on. Waxy was her husband, after all. Yet she sat quietly between them, too sweet to say anything about Sam's driving. Luckily, Aunt Libby had convinced them that not everyone should go, that her brother might not be able to handle a crowd, this as she took off for the hospital herself, out the door without waiting around for anybody to put on a coat or find a cane. So now Sam was following after, except that in the time it had taken him and Aboodeh to help the three old women down the porch steps and into the backseat of the Lincoln, Libby had probably reached the hospital already.

"Go for it!" Aboodeh said as a green light ahead changed to yellow. "Go, go, gogogo—yeah!" He was sitting forward, one hand propped on the dash as if ready to leap out at any minute. All the time tapping his fingers against the dashboard in a galloping, hurry-up rhythm, *pa-TA-ta-rum, pa-TA-ta-rum*, his pinky ring flashing under the passing streetlights.

"Would you knock that off?" Sam said. "I'm getting us there as fast as I can."

Aboodeh's response was to turn his face toward his cousin, smile and drum even faster. Lady Luck had returned; his father would recover, the funeral home would resume operating again. *Pa-TA-ta-rum!* They'd find out what had happened to the missing shipment. He couldn't wait to put a call through to Beirut.

"Listen, Bud," Sam began, "what we just saw on TV? Those car bombs? One of them went off in the Hamra district. Close to the American embassy. The announcer said the State Department's already begun tightening travel restrictions to Lebanon."

"So?"

"So? You think something like that isn't going to cause a serious hitch?" In the backseat the women had gone totally silent with listening.

"Not us." Aboodeh waved away the very idea. "It's not in our blood."

"What's that supposed to mean?"

"We're businesspeople. Look at Beirut. Built on international banking. Look at our history. Overseas traders, merchants. Way back before Bible times even."

Sam thought he heard a grunt of approval from the backseat. "So what?" he said.

"So look at the news we're seeing now—and not that State Department crap, I mean news from the street; some poor chump's grocery store gets blown to bits, and two days later, *two days* later, he's selling melons out of a pushcart. *And* he's turning a profit. They're businesspeople over there, Cuz, and businesspeople don't let things stay bad. Not for long, anyway."

"Unless the war itself happens to *be* the business."

"What's that supposed to mean?"

"C'mon, Aboodeh, you don't think *some*body's got to be making money off all this?"

"*Some*body? More than that, a *lot* of somebodies. Sure they are. And a lot of money, too. But that's only for the short run, Sammy. In the long run it's bad for business. *Big* business, that is. Me and the Mutranehs, we discussed all this, and they'll tell you the same thing. Soon as *big* business starts hurting, then the *zuami*, and I'm talking the real movers and shakers, they'll step in and start applying the pressure to cut it off. You watch."

"We are beaceful beobles!" Aunt Afifie couldn't resist adding her two cents. In the rearview Sam could see her adjusting the volume knob on the listening device hanging at her bosom.

"That's right, Auntie," Aboodeh said. "We *are* peaceful people."

But now Sam's mother also piped up, asserting in Arabic that most truly we are a peaceful people, and therefore we can hold our heads up to anyone.

"I suppose so, Ma," Sam said. Aboodeh smirked, gave him a little nudge with his elbow.

The two women began a running commentary while Aunt Nejla, seated between them, nodded in agreement and softly uttered Arabic encouragements: "We are *lawful* beoble . . ."

"*Aeh na'am . . .*"

". . . We are *honorable!* . . ."

"*Ma'aloum . . .*"

". . . We don' do it the shooting and the blowin' up . . ."

"*Mezbout . . .*"

". . . No. This the other beobles do, not us . . ."

"*Haq ma'aqi . . .*"

"Other people?" Sam glanced up into the rearview. "Like who?"

His mother was ready with an answer and she smiled. "*Il Irish,*" she said in Arabic, "they are on *il* CBS every day, *il Irish!* Not us."

"Okay, not us." The traffic lights were all synchronized; Sam found a constant speed and began making them one after the other. A year ago, he might have kept the argument going, convinced that there was no such thing as *us*. But not anymore.

*There is no us,* he used to think, listening to Uncle Yousef go on and on about this small country at the great crossroads of East and West that had been repeatedly invaded over thousands of years by anybody and everybody, from Egyptians to Macedonians, from Mongols to Turks to European Crusaders.

"Australians, too, and the French Senegalese," Yousef would hasten to add, recounting how the people of this small country were once natural sailors and pioneers; how they had founded Carthage and Syracuse, colonies on Malta and the coast of France and Spain and, some claimed, beyond the Mediterranean; how they circled Africa and even touched, Yousef firmly asserted, "the coast of America, two thousand years before Columbus."

*Us who?* Sam had concluded. *No such thing, not after all those years and all that mixing. How could there be an us?*

But visiting the old country last summer had changed his mind. It happened during the time he'd been left alone in Beirut while Aboodeh went off to set up business arrangements with the Mutranehs. Like many of the city's high-rises, the building Sam was staying in had its balconied apartments stacked around the central shaft of an elevator. Ascending in the slow cage elevator, a person could hear everything in the building, and smell everything, too. One evening he was coming up just at suppertime, and the shaft was fragrant with roast lamb, garlic and onion, cinnamon, the unmistakable aroma of toasted pine nuts. As familiar as the aromas of his growing up—but then the voices too began to sound familiar, funneling up the shaft in a noisy accumulation: dinnertime shouting from room to room and down hallways, snaps and retorts and the yammering laughter of a nervous people. Is that what we are then, the thought flashed through his mind, a nervous people? His father had been called that, his father who'd been excused for being an old man, a sick man, finally a rascal who in frustration with age and illness slammed dishes to the floor, who would not let things be but had to snipe and curse and say vicious things until Mama was in tears. He had heard these very same voices in his own house at dinnertime, echoes rising up the shaft all around him, a pleading wife on this floor, a screaming wife on the next floor, another one giving back as good as she was getting, the old familiar curses of blood clot and blindness and fiery *Djhunnum* the Red. And all of it in the same Arabic dialect he had grown up with, the same after all these years, family after family up that slow ascent. Some of the voices were only talking—he knew that—light, affectionate talk amplified by the building's hollow, but even the talkers, even the laughers, seemed to harbor a dangerous urgency, an out-of-breath readiness to explode into shouting. Somewhere below his feet Sam heard something crash sloppily against a wall. He recognized the sound; a food-laden dish.

Not all of us are like that, he reminded himself, and with the very thinking of such a thought—that there were those of another sort, others like Uncle Alex and the Yakoubs who sat to quiet dinners and gave you Arabic blessings instead of these curses resounding up the elevator shaft; others who were kindhearted and patient and more than welcoming, famously hospitable—with the very thinking that not all of us are like that, he began to understand that, yes, there *is* an us. There had to be, or else he would not have recognized it. And he had recognized it again this evening, watching those television children stacked in death against a wall, their dark eyes like the dark eyes of his nephews and nieces, of his own eyes in the old photographs, the whorled curls of their hair like his own hair, the same golden skin, those little teeth that should be smiling. Oh, yes. There *is* an us.

## IN A BLINK

*Salma leaves the teefee on when finally she takes off her apron to join the others in the living room. One news program after another after another. In Beirut . . . In Beirut . . . In Beirut today . . .*

*America will change you, he was told, and Teyib can feel it happening. After Zeid's connections had come through, he had been forced to travel first to Baalbek and then across the mountain and down to Damascus in order collect the last of the duplicate documents waiting for him there. America will change you, Zeid's people had said, handing him the papers.*

*Just seven more weeks to go, the Channel 11 announcer is saying, before America celebrates 1976, her two hundredth anniversary year. The dazzle of fireworks before and after each news broadcast is simply a show of American celebration, as when the ibn Arab fire weapons into the air to express jubilation. Two hundred years. In Damascus, he had stood on the famous street called Straight, the very street traveled upon without interruption for more than five thousand years. What are two hundred years compared to that? A blink? Yes, a blink. But even in a blink things change, himself a blink watching the screen.*

*He shuts off the teefee, and immediately there is a small, excited voice babbling away. A sports announcer. He follows its sound down to the bib of his apron where the little radio ear button hangs from its wire. Maybe someone has made a touchdown. Teyib can't be sure because the announcer's voice, so clear at first, is suddenly swallowed up in a roaring hiss, like the sound of steady rain. There is no storm outside, but the static keeps exploding into abrupt, lightning-like bursts.*

*He sits. Now none of the radio stations will stay put, and he has to keep dialing carefully, ever so carefully back and forth over the voice of the sports announcer, trying to fix onto it. But it is no use. After a moment he loses the station entirely to a peal of thunder so far away there isn't even a flash to it. Or what sounds like thunder. So he contents himself to leave the radio dial alone and listen to the static itself, which sounds like rain.*

# 15

A nurse was waiting for them outside Waxy's door. "You're *Khh*aleel?" she asked, putting extra emphasis on the *Kh* sound.

Baffled, Aboodeh put his hands on his hips. "Khaleel?"

"Yes?" Her voice tended to go up, as if asking a question. "You were the first person he asked to see?" She turned a puzzled smile expectantly to Sam; maybe *he* was *Khh*aleel? The old women were approaching, and to keep Aunt Nejla from having to hear Aboodeh's explanation, Sam moved now to intercept and direct them all into the lounge.

"Confusion is to be expected," the nurse was saying when Sam stepped back into the hall. "Especially the first day or so." She pulled open the door, held it as Sam followed his cousin into the room. And there Waxy lay, still yellow and shrunken, but awake.

Or sort of awake. When Aboodeh called out, "Dad? Dad!" his father opened one eye and gave the room a prolonged squint, waiting. Then, annoyed at not seeing what he'd expected to see, abruptly closed it again. His throat formed a word, breathed it out like a sigh, *"Khaleel?"* After a moment he opened the eye again, awaiting a response.

"Who's gonna tell him?" Sam whispered, realizing even as he spoke that the duty would have to fall to Aboodeh.

"Dad?" They watched the eye flutter and close. Then Aboodeh turned to answer Sam's question. "If this is as awake as he's going to get," he said, "maybe nobody."

Khaleel Tammouz, Waxy's firstborn, was sixteen and just learning to drive when he died in an auto wreck. Although it had happened within weeks of Sam's arrival in America, Sam remembered him clearly because it had been Khaleel who had taken him to a barbershop for his first haircut in America, and right after that to his first movie at the Mystic. Sam remembered Khaleel's curly hair, his two-tone blue summer jacket, and the dozen or so buttons he had pinned to the front of that jacket. While they waited in line, Khaleel had told Sam to go ahead and pick a button out for himself. He chose an American-looking one, its border printed in red, white and blue, emblazoned with the words *I Like Ike* above the likeness of a smiling, grandfatherly man. To show off his English, Sam had read the words aloud, "I like Ikh?" and everyone laughed. Even sad-faced Khaleel. At least Sam would remember his face as sad, his best memory of it coming not so much from life as from the stiffly posed eight-by-ten high school graduation photo that had been displayed atop the closed casket lid. His dark, mournful eyes and girlishly long eyelashes, the hint of a mustache, dark where he'd begun shaving it. His hair black and even more thickly curled than Sam's own, like a helmet of lamb's wool.

Khaleel would become the first person Sam ever knew who died. People spoke of the accident in English, to shield him, but he was able to make out that his cousin had died in a car crash while "joy-riding" with friends. For weeks the older women would bless Sam and Aboodeh in passing, and do so vigorously, slashing crosses above their faces with three fingers joined; now that the twin angels of death had turned their eyes on the family, children were especially vulnerable. Sam felt himself succumbing to the contagion of their fear; how fragile being alive seemed to be now, how abruptly everything could stop, even in happiness. In the middle of a "joy-ride." Whatever *that* was. He asked his father how that could be. Baba, standing in his apron at the display window, was lighting a cigar and did not answer at first. Instead, he continued to gaze out at the homeless *bumiyeh* who loitered in the shade of the store awning, or perched their bony behinds on wall hydrants, passing wine bottles back and forth. Men down on their luck, all of them looking, Baba used to say, as if they'd had the shit kicked out of them. The match had gone out, and he dropped it. Then, he pulled the dead cigar from his mouth and replied, in English, "Shit luck."

By the end of the second day Waxy was awake enough—one eye opening, looking around, closing again—for the doctors to decide to begin the unhooking, the unplugging. If not quite alert, the old man was certainly responding to stimuli—sounds, pinpricks. By the end of the week he had begun sipping liquids and, with the catheter removed, was putting out water on his own. "A good sign, right?" Aboodeh said, nudging Sam with his elbow.

"*Very* good," Dr. Warren assured them all, "the best." Tomorrow, they would be moving him out of the ICU and into one of the recovery wards.

"I can feel it," Aboodeh said, nudging Sam again. "I can feel our luck finally turning." He was like a boy, bubbling with anticipation.

Luck? Libby cast him an impatient look. Luck was for the horses. For the slots. Her brother was still so weak he was barely able to suck ice chips, for Christ's sake, much less eat. And what of those long hypnotic silences he kept drifting in and out of, leaving him scattered, responding only in English, if at all? Even so, the doctors maintained, all this was understandable. Waxy may have lost a little or a lot, time would tell, particularly after he was returned to more familiar surroundings. At Shofia's that night, Aboodeh tapped a wine glass with a spoon and announced that his father was finally well enough to be moved out of intensive care. This was met with sighs of relief and utterances of gratitude to St. Maron, Patron of Lebanon, and to Our Lady of Consolation. But when Aboodeh added that, *inshallah*, his father would be on his feet and back to work again in no time, the response was more muted, given amid shrugs and the exchanges of side-glances.

Next morning, Sam found that because of the hospital's crowded conditions, his uncle had been placed in a makeshift recovery ward at the end of the St. Joseph wing. The space, called a solarium, had windows on three sides, but the effect was anything but sunny. A new wraparound wing under construction just a few yards beyond the windows blocked the view from all three sides and threw everything into permanent shadow. Although it was noontime, Sam couldn't even tell whether the sun was shining. Weeks-old paper pumpkins and curling witches' hats, still taped to the glass, only added to the dreariness.

From the doorway he could see that a TV was on over his uncle's bed, one of those little hospital rentals attached to a ceiling bracket. The volume was turned low, and he looked to be napping. Aboodeh sat next to the bed, paging through a *Newsweek*. On the tray table, lunch dishes awaited picking up. Apparently Waxy had started eating again.

As Sam stepped around the privacy screen, his uncle opened one eye.

Then the other. But there seemed to be no recognition. He didn't even blink. Could he be eyes-open asleep? The old man lay flat on his back, in a flannel *amise nohm* nightshirt that looked too big for him, the v-neck exposing where they'd shaved to attach electrodes.

Aboodeh looked up from the magazine and, seeing that his father was awake, spoke out in a too-hearty voice, as if encouraging a child, "Hey, Dad, look who came to see you!"

Sam sidled around the bed so Waxy wouldn't have to crane his neck. He looked aware now, even alert. Sam bent down and kissed his cheek.

"Tell me, Brother," Waxy spoke in English, and with a hesitant quake to his voice, "where d'you s'pose we are?" He sounded scared, but trying not to show it.

Sam gave Aboodeh a look, which his cousin avoided, turning to the television where the Sunday matinee was just beginning. Sam said, "We're here, Uncle, in the hospital. We're in Mercy Hospital."

Crooking a forefinger, Waxy beckoned him closer. Sam slid the tray table aside and leaned in. Waxy peered into his face a moment, one eye half-closed. "Khaleel?" He whispered the name, then smiled wryly as if he'd caught a trickster at his own game: *Trying to pull my leg again, are you?*

"No, Uncle, I'm Samir."

"Who?"

"Samir. *Ibn* Rasheed."

*"Rasheed?"* Both eyes opened wide with alarm. "The hell you say!"

Again Sam looked over toward his cousin.

"He'll be himself again," Aboodeh said. "Soon as we get him home, in his own room. You'll see. Hardly touched his lunch, but we'll get him eating again, too."

"He's not eating?" The lunch tray looked a good deal more than hardly touched.

"I want to get him out of here as soon as we can. Even the doctors say that getting him back in familiar surroundings would help him recover faster. He needs to get busy *doing* familiar things again."

"Like what? You talking about him working again?" Sam felt uncomfortable discussing Waxy this way, right there in his presence.

"You bet I am. And the sooner the better."

"Dr. *Warren* said that?"

"He didn't have to." He smiled encouragingly. "After all, there's no better cure than getting back to work. Right?"

Sam didn't smile back.

"Ah, you'll see." Aboodeh turned his attention back to the television. "Give Dad a day or two back in the prep room, and you'll see. He'll snap right back to his old self again."

Sam eyed his cousin suspiciously. "How come you're in such a good mood?"

Aboodeh's smile widened; he'd just been waiting to be asked. "The phone lines to Beirut came back up," he replied. "I finally got through to Nabil Mutraneh, and swear-to-God, Sammy, he's more surprised than we were about—" he stopped short, gave a glance toward his father, then continued with a whisper, "—about what happened. You know, to that delivery?"

"Why don't we go downstairs?" Sam said. "We can get some lunch and talk about this down there."

Aboodeh shook his head. "Nothing to talk about. What I just told you is all I know so far. Nabil's looking into it and he'll be calling back, probably early next week." Waxy appeared to be listening, his mouth working silently as if trying to form words. He finally got it out in a whispered rush, "Where are we, Brother?"

This time Aboodeh answered. "Still in Mercy Hospital, Dad. Remember?"

But Waxy seemed to have already drifted off. He made a snuffling sound, maybe a snore. Sam couldn't tell from the eyes; they were either closed or hooded low. "Is he asleep?"

"You tell me."

"He looks it to me. C'mon, Bud, let's get some lunch. Let him sleep."

"Salma gave me lunch before I came over," Aboodeh said. "And then," he indicated the tray table, "then they brought this in . . ."

"*You* ate it?"

"I got bored, sitting here." Aboodeh stood to turn the volume up on the TV. "You want to go down and eat, go ahead."

"Maybe later." Sam took the chair on the other side of the bed. The TV was showing a classic scene, a variation of which, Sam thought, must have appeared in a dozen Second World War–era movies: Iowa farm family just sitting down to Sunday dinner . . . on December the Seventh, 1941. They have no idea what they're in for today, Pa talking about bringing in hay for the livestock while his handsome, draft-age son piles on the mashed potatoes. Soon the radio cuts from the dinner table to a still shot of the family's huge console radio. An authoritative voice announces: *We interrupt this program with a news bulletin. The United States Naval Base at Pearl Harbor, Hawaii, has been attacked from the air by squadrons of Japanese* . . .

Instantly Uncle Waxy lifted himself up onto his elbows, eyes wide in outrage and disbelief. "Dem sonnoma bitches!" he wheezed. "Dey did it *again!*"

Waxy was discharged the week before Thanksgiving. Aboodeh had a rented hospital bed set up for him in the bungalow's little sun parlor, where, separated from the living room by a pair of french doors, he could observe all the comings and goings of the house. But when Sam stopped by, the only thing holding his uncle's interest seemed to be a portable TV sitting atop a dresser at the foot of the bed.

"The doctors said it would help if we left it on a few hours every day," Aboodeh said. "For stimulation." He sat slumped in a stuffed chair, telephone in his lap, receiver pressed to his ear while he waited for the overseas operator to come back on the line. Service to the old country, so recently restored, had been disrupted yet again by an upsurge of violence. Yesterday CBS reported that the fighting in Beirut had reached the hotel district along the *Corniche*.

"Stimulation?" Sam said. "How about if we just talk to him."

"Yeah, well *you* try it. He listens for half a minute—*may*be—and then he drifts right on back to the TV, right while you're still talking. And it's not like he's really paying attention to the TV, either. Look at him. He just stares at it."

"Good color," Sam said. A blonde in a silver evening gown was advertising a silver car. "It looks new."

"It *is* new. Our buddy Teyib brought it over from his place."

"It's his?"

"Says he's too busy to watch it anymore. Look, it comes with one of those remote controls, so you don't even have to get up to change channels. There's a button that turns off just the sound." Aboodeh demonstrated.

Instant silence.

That *is* progress, Sam thought. "What's Teyib so busy doing he can't watch TV?"

"Cooking. He's up there right now," Aboodeh gestured toward the window, "cooking up a storm."

Sam looked out at the funeral home across the parking lot and saw that the window to the attic kitchen was half-open.

"What for?"

"Trying to come up with something Dad'll eat." Aboodeh toyed with the phone receiver, flipping it from one hand to the other. "Dr. Warren said if he doesn't start eating soon they'll have to take him back to the hospital and put a feeding tube in him." He frowned at the receiver. "Thing is, whatever Teyib cooks, he makes enough to feed a whole restaurant."

Waxy chuckled at that, or made a sound like chuckling. His eyes fluttered, wanting to close. Then his mouth formed a grin, his jaw tightened, and he passed a low sputter of gas.

"Farts in his sleep," Aboodeh observed. A moment later, when a voice chirruped out of the telephone receiver in his hands, he nearly dropped the thing but quickly recovered and pressed it to his ear. "Hello? Yes? Yes! Would you say that again?" He waited, "Yes, this is him—" then stopped short, realizing he was talking to a dial tone. "Shit," he muttered to himself. Now he would have to start all over again.

Sam went to the window and stood there, as if interested in its view of the gravel lot separating Waxy's bungalow from the funeral home. The weather was unusually warm for mid-November, and the room felt stuffy. He opened the window. Almost Thanksgiving, but the air rushing in had a wet-earth smell that reminded him more of springtime.

Behind his back he heard a burst of rapid beeping indicating that Aboodeh had regained connection to an overseas operator. Sitting up attentively, his cousin assured the operator that yes, yes, he'd be waiting right here for the call-back. Then he closed his eyes and hung up. There. It was out of his hands now.

"How long will it take?" Sam asked.

Aboodeh didn't answer.

Stupid question. Across the parking lot, the funeral home's attic windows were steamed over. Teyib working away. "Must be sweltering in that little kitchen up there," he said.

"He's been at it all week." Aboodeh angled his jaw sideways and up until his neck released a little crack. "Yesterday Dad didn't eat a thing."

"Nothing at all?"

"Didn't even touch the soup that Teyib made special for him. And you should've tasted that soup."

"Good, huh?"

"*Good?* Teyib made his own stock with onions and lamb bones and spices and I don't know what else, but he kept it simmering for hours. *Hours.* I had to take some stuff out of the basement and you could smell it all the way down to the prep room. The whole house smelled like, I don't know, like somebody lives there."

"Tammouz & Sons, the funeral home that *smells* like home."

"Dad didn't even touch the soup. He took one sniff and he went '*T'fou!*'" Aboodeh made the Arabic dry-spit sound of contempt.

Sam listened to his uncle breathe slowly in and out. Maybe he was asleep, maybe he was listening. Hard telling. "I'm surprised Teyib can cook anything at all in that tiny kitchen."

"Only time he leaves is to go to the grocery store. I don't think there's even a bed up there. At night I think he just flops on the couch."

"Libby lets him stay up there."

"She thinks it's starting to do Dad some good. That '*T'fou*' he made? She told me it's the closest sound to Arabic that's come out of him since the anesthesia."

"Teyib." Sam stood gazing out the window. "I mean, at least he's trying *something.*"

"He's not the only one. Know what *I* do?" Aboodeh lowered his voice. "Every afternoon when we get Dad out of bed, I wheel him over to the windows on this side of the house and leave him turned so that he's facing the funeral home."

"Why?"

"Libby comes in and sees him sitting there, how can she even think of closing the place? Look at him there, just pining to get back to work."

"I don't know, Bud."

"Well, I do. The sooner he's back on his feet the better. For him *and* me. *And* you, too." Aboodeh gave the phone in his hands a brief, impatient shake that made its bell tinkle weakly. "Meanwhile, looks like I'll be spending the whole Thanksgiving weekend waiting around for the overseas operator to call back."

"Maybe the holiday'll work in your favor," Sam said. "The lines on this side might not be as busy."

Aboodeh set the telephone back on the bedside table. "How about you? Bringing your mom over to Shofia's this year? Teyib wants to try stuffing the turkey with pine nuts and cinnamon lamb *heshweh!*"

"I heard. I'm dropping my mom off early so she can help him. She's the only one he likes cooking with." Sam shook his head. "I told her to save me some of that *heshweh.*"

"You're not coming?"

"After I drop Ma off, Nikki and I are heading up to her place in Michigan. She got the whole holiday weekend off, so we figured that'd be the best time to go up and get going on some repairs. Place doesn't even have a working toilet."

"So, she's got you playing house, eh? That's sweet." Aboodeh sat back smiling, head cocked to one side. "Y'know, there's something I always wondered about her." He waited, but Sam didn't take the bait. He continued anyway, "Whether or not she's a *real* blonde."

Sam only smiled. Let Aboodeh picture what he wanted.

Outside, a screen door clapped shut, and they both turned to the window. It was Teyib, leaving by the side door of the funeral home. He had on an apron and he was carrying a towel-draped pot.

Sam held the back door open for him. "Mm," he sniffed, "I smell vanilla. And, what is that, is that orange blossom water? Did you make *rizib haleeb?*"

Teyib gave the tongue-click for no. *"Riz bi laban,"* he replied. "For eat hot, not cold." The apron he had on was one of Aunt Nejla's, eggplants and tomatoes dancing across its bib. He didn't put the tray down in the kitchen, but followed Sam with it into the sunroom.

Waxy opened his eyes.

"What you got?" Aboodeh asked.

"He made your dad rice in hot yogurt."

Teyib placed the pot on Waxy's tray table, then removed the towel and gently wheeled the table around. Moving with the quick efficiency of a nurse, he cranked the bed up a few notches, adjusted the pillows. He tucked a paper napkin into the neck of Waxy's nightshirt, dipped a spoon into the pudding and touched it to the old man's lips. Uncle Waxy looked down at the touch, but he wouldn't open up. So Teyib muttered a soft encouragement in Arabic, *"Akl il anab habbi wa habbi,"* literally *Grapes*

*are eaten one berry at a time,* but really meaning *Baby steps, baby steps*—
a reassurance that Sam remembered from childhood. And as if feeding
a baby, Teyib blew on the spoon before touching it to Waxy's lips. Waxy
looked down at the touch and clamped his lips tight.

"Nice try," Aboodeh said. "But I coulda told you."

Teyib paid no attention. Continuing to weave the spoon back and
forth under Waxy's nose, he started in on a gently coaxing patter, mixing
Arabic and English. "When you are strong," he said, "I myself put you
in the auto-mo-beel and take you on drive to *shim il hawah."* In English,
*smell the air.* Sam thought he saw Waxy smile at that, or want to smile,
one side of his mouth tightening ever so slightly. Teyib saw it, too. "Oh,
not me," Teyib said, switching completely to Arabic. "No, we will ask this
young fellow to drive us," including Sam now in the patter. "Or maybe
this young fellow he will teach *me* to drive!" This young fellow, in Arabic
*hil sheb.*

Such patient, gently urgent tones. There was something familiar here,
and Sam felt a flash of déjà vu. Something about Beirut, maybe? The
word *sheb?* Maybe just fond memories of people in the old country sitting at sidewalk tables, leaning in close to urge one another with endear-
ments—have yet another coffee, another pastry—and, yes, how much
he'd come to actually like Teyib. So odd looking at first, those off-putting
clothes he'd arrived in, his hair dyed ridiculously, and for what? For trying
to fit in in America, for trying too hard. That's all. He looked so much better now. The dyed tips grown out and clipped away. Sideburns growing in.
Beneath the sideburns, some stubble. Too busy cooking to shave.

"Sure smells good," Aboodeh said. Picking up the TV remote, he adjusted the volume as the screen lit up to a montage of bursting fireworks,
something Channel 11 News had adopted as a countdown to 1976, the
upcoming Bicentennial year. "Sammy, go get us a couple bowls, willya?
Looks like he made enough for a small army."

It took Sam a minute or two to find where Aunt Nejla kept her bowls,
and when he returned, Aboodeh turned to him with an index finger
pressed to his lips. "Look," he whispered.

Teyib had done it. Uncle Waxy was eating the rice mixture, and he
seemed to want more. Each time Teyib dipped the spoon and brought it
up again, Waxy was waiting, eyes fixed on Teyib's smiling, talking face.

"Oh, he's a smooth operator, all right," Aboodeh whispered as he took a bowl and spooned into it a sizable helping for himself. "You'd never think it to look at him."

"Yeah," Sam agreed, reaching around Aboodeh to dip his spoon into the pot, "smooth." Then he looked up, blinked, quickly looked down again. He peered around Aboodeh's shoulder. That earnest manner, that leaning in while he kept up the patter. He'd had a full beard then, and sunglasses, and he was talking in this same cajoling way. But it couldn't be . . . *him*? No. Couldn't be. How could it?

"You okay?" Aboodeh asked. "Go down the wrong tube?"

Sam realized he had made a noise, low and throaty, and now he continued it, pretending to be coughing. Pretending he was going into the kitchen for water. There, leaning both hands on Aunt Nejla's sink, staring into the crosshairs of the drain hole, he tried to stop a minute and think. To be reasonable. But what he had thought was déjà vu was already draining away down into that hole, displaced by black hollowness, by shame and anger, and the sense that he'd been made a dupe and a sucker all over again.

～

## Song of Teyib

*"Want to party, Mister? Yes or no—make up your mind!" Her sandals have heels so high and wobbly that the zenji hooker can barely keep her balance as she follows after him, all the time talking. Her hair frizzes out in a fluorescent yellow puff that circles her face, and the sandal straps that transverse up almost to her knees are fashioned from the same tight white plastic as her short-shorts and the little purse hanging from her shoulder. She has crossed the street to approach him, all the time talking, telling him how tired she is of how he walks by her corner night after night only to cross the street right at the last minute. He stops short, and she almost seesaws into him on those heels. But she recovers herself quickly and keeps on coming, backing him into a doorway. She motions for him to take the radio button out of his ear.*

*"How can you hear me with that thing blasting?" Clarence, she*

*informs him, isn't around yet. So how about it, a little party? "Clarence don't have to know."*

*Clarence? What party?*

*French party, she tells him. Then she tells him that he talks funny. Where you from? she asks. Leaning out of the doorway, he points up the block. But she isn't watching. She is still talking, again telling him to never mind about Clarence. Twenty dollars, she says—talking so fast he can barely follow—so she can go home with something for herself tonight. "Twenty's a french."*

*What is she saying? "Français?" he asks.*

*She frowns. "You must be from wa-ay far away. Where you from?"*

*Once more he points it out, up Erie toward the North End.*

*"Like my shoes?" she asks.*

*"Beautiful," he says because she has caught him looking.*

*With that, she reaches down and takes hold of his hand. "It's all right," she says, "lemme have it." She puts his finger in her mouth. "That's french. Understand?"*

*He understands.*

*"Twenty."*

*He shakes his head no, side to side, American style.*

*"Fifteen."*

*No, he shakes his head. Watch. Now he demonstrates. Takes her hand palm up, places his palm down over it, then begins gently humping the heel of his hand into hers. "Yes?" he asks.*

*She understands, but quickly reminds him that Clarence is gone, and without Clarence she has no place for that. No room. Understand? "No bed?"*

*He has a bed. Just up the street. He points.*

*She looks up the street. "Forty dollars," she says.*

*He nods once to show agreement.*

*Staring into his eyes, she opens her white plastic purse and puts her hand into it. "I got a knife in here. I ain't afraid to use it."*

*Again, he nods to show he understands.*

*In his room behind the store, she wants to know what it is that smells so good.*

Lamb shanks, he tells her, in a stew. She is heavy in the thighs and rear, but the rest of her is skinny. He asks if she is hungry.

She shakes her head no. Then she asks, "What you got in this bowl?"

Pomegranate seeds, but he does not know the word in English. He tells her to taste, see if she likes.

"Nice," she says.

He shows her the electric coil, offering to heat up the stew for her, but she declines. Business first, she tells him, holding her hand out for the two twenties which she drops into her white plastic purse. Because he does not want to frighten her, he does not even look to see whether there is indeed a knife in there.

As she undresses, she asks if he wants her to keep the shoes on.

"Beautiful," he tells her.

"What's that mean, you want 'em on?"

He lifts his chin for no, but remembers she is an American. He shakes his head side to side, American-style.

"Make up your mind, honey."

"Yes, dear."

She gives him a look. "Where you say you from?" she asks. "What country?"

She is too thin, but her nakedness is exciting him almost to trembling. "Lebanon," he tells her.

"That's one of them Ay-rab countries? Where there's the war?"

He nods, trembling. "Aeh na'am," he answers in Arabic.

She laughs. "What you say?" But before he can reply, she goes on, "You gonna tell me you one of them oil sheiks?"

He shakes his head no, American style.

"You sure got sheik eyes," she says. "In America we call them bedroom eyes," she says. "Let's see if you're ready," she says and draws him to her. "You ready, sheik? Let's say hi to the little sheik."

When he mounts her she asks, "Lebanon, you say?" And after a minute, "Like in the gospel song?"

And he realizes that a sound like singing is coming out of himself, his own voice rising and rising with the efforts of his body.

"That's right, honey-sheik," she says. "Come to me like the gospel song say. Come to me from Lebanon."

# PART FOUR

# 16

He knew it. He just didn't *know* yet that he knew it. But how could that be? How can you know something *before* you know it? You can't. It doesn't make sense.

Sam put down his tools. He had to stop this, he was giving himself a headache. And his knees were killing him. The work was more slow-going than he'd figured, prying a circle of caulk out of the floor tile with a screwdriver, carefully digging out each chip and shard of broken commode. Slow-going, and mindless. And for background the shrieks and frantic music of Saturday-morning cartoons. Keeping the bathroom door closed didn't help, Deano's TV came through anyway.

He got back on his knees, eased the flat head of the screwdriver into the joint line between caulk and tile.

But if you think about it, déjà vu doesn't make sense either; you haven't actually seen something before, it only *feels* that way.

Same thing yesterday, with Teyib. The thought hadn't completely formed yet in his mind, and already it felt like remembering. The sidewalk cafe. Bougainvillea and the fragrance of jasmine twigs. The cigarettes, the fast talk. Christ, even the accent! Without that trimmed professor's beard, of course, those cheap sunglasses and the hair before he'd blonded it. Stepping off the plane with that ridiculous hair, did he really think it would fool anybody?

Fooled *me*. Sam dropped the screwdriver and sat back on his heels. He was spinning wheels, and the best thing for that was to stop thinking entirely, to pick the screwdriver back up and let the repetitive tedium of the work take over his thoughts. Press the screwdriver into the caulk, jab when it won't give, dig, pry . . . that lying . . . son . . . of a *bitch*. It *was* him. It *had* to be Teyib. *Teyib*—hah! Was that even his name?

"Hey in there," Nikki called from the other side of the door, "how's it going?" Her voice had to compete with Deano's TV, but the falsely upbeat lilt came through just the same.

"Getting there!" He waited. No response. Only a steady string of maniacal, revved-up cartoon noises from Dean's room.

The door opened, and Nikki breathed out a flat, disappointed, "Oh."

He half-turned toward her. "What?" he said, although he knew what; she'd expected more progress by now.

"You sure you got the directions right?" She was giving him a look he was really getting to dislike, her one-eyed half-squint with the opposite eyebrow kinked. "That stuff's taking you so long to dig out, does it *all* have to come out?" She'd changed into work clothes, jeans and a sweatshirt, and had her hair bunched into a thick mass down her back. She carried some old newspapers tucked under one arm.

"Well, we can do it fast, or we can do it right." He gestured toward the new commode, sitting unboxed in the hallway behind her. "I've helped replace those before at our rentals, but never where I had to dig *out* pieces of the old commode first. Okay? Now the manual that comes with it says that if you don't want water damage down the road, then you got to start with a clean, smooth surface for the wax ring to seal against the flange." He was sounding like a prick and he stopped himself. "Sorry," he muttered, "I'm kind of distracted today." He set back to work, prying with the blade of the screwdriver, pressing it down and in, then gently levering another line of caulk up and out. Long slivers of porcelain were stuck to it. He could feel her watching him. Hunching low into his work, he shifted his weight and winced. He sat back on his heels.

"Your knees?"

He nodded. Rose to a squat.

"Here. I brought you these." She'd folded the newspaper into a pad. "See if that helps."

"Good idea. Thanks."

"I'm sorry," she said. "I really do appreciate you giving up your Thanksgiving weekend. All I'm saying is . . . ," she hesitated, her voice tentative, thinking how to put this. "It's just that every time I come up here I look around, and everywhere. . . ." She shook her head. "Who knew we'd find so *much* that needs doing?"

Sam wanted to say: *The bank, that's who!* He kept silent instead, adjusted the newspaper pad, repositioned the screwdriver and resumed prying.

It wasn't until the loud flush of the toilet startled him awake that Sam realized he must have finally fallen asleep. He blinked and sat up. Blinked again. He couldn't see a thing. This afternoon he'd nailed plywood over the broken-out windows, and now the bedroom was utterly dark. He lay back down again, down into the warmth of Nikki's soft breathing. Then he heard the bathroom door creak open followed by footfalls; Deano sleep-lumbering back down the hall. After a moment the boy's bedroom door closed with its own slow squeak. Every single door in this wreck of a house squeaked. Could Nikki blame her ex for rusty hinges, too? Well, why not? Sam pictured Leonard putting down a sledgehammer and, as a sort of finishing touch, taking a stepladder and going around pissing on all the door hinges.

Water filled the tank, diminished, then came to an abrupt stop. The sound of a new toilet working perfectly. He was fully awake now and starting to feel like maybe he needed to go himself. But maybe not. He didn't want to move if he didn't have to. Nikki lay nuzzled up against him, and he felt completely warm for the first time all night.

Some holiday. For Thanksgiving dinner they'd eaten cold sandwiches sitting on the floor with an upturned Styrofoam cooler for a table. Afterward, Nikki spent the entire evening bundled next to Deano in front of that little denim-assed TV, watching *The Wizard of Oz*. A movie about a fever dream. Sam left them to it and went to bed early.

Too early, no wonder he was awake. Wide awake.

Teyib.

And now the name just popping into his head like that, he could feel his teeth starting to clench, his hands to grip the sheets. It wasn't enough that the son of a bitch was a thief, he probably used the money and Sam's debarkation card to have documents forged so he could get away. So he could come to America and smile in his face while he put another one over on him!

"Jesus, Sam, I can practically *hear* you thinking!"

"You're not asleep?" He turned toward her, shifting his weight up on an elbow.

"Ow! Ouch!"

"What is it?"

"My hair, get off it, get off it!"

He rolled aside, lifting his elbow. "Sorry. I thought you were sleeping."

"I was *trying* to."

"Guess I'm not used to it being so dark," he said. Meanwhile, this Japanese futon-thing she'd bought out of a catalog was like sleeping on a towel. He turned over onto his back. His hip was killing him.

He lay a while with his eyes closed. He may even have fallen back asleep. For five minutes, maybe, before Dean's door squealed open again. He listened to the boy's footsteps, then to the sound of his stream, interrupted once when he must have wandered off target. Then the flush. After Dean's door closed again, Sam felt Nikki rustling next to him in the dark. "You asleep?" she asked.

"No."

"I think you got that toilet put in just in time."

"Deano must have finished off that half-gallon of apple cider all by himself."

"And you know something else?" Her voice changed, turning low and throaty. "Not just any guy would have dropped everything and come all the way up here. And on Thanksgiving—" Her breathing caught. Was she crying?

"You okay?" He couldn't see a thing.

"Yes," she said, "I'm fine." After a moment, she sighed. "And I really do appreciate all you did. The windows, the *fuse* box. Jesus, me and anything to do with electricity, forget about it. But that's not all." She touched his chest. "I was thinking today how I really do love having you here." Her hand began to glide over his chest hairs, skimming gently across the slow up and down of his breathing. "I only wish *you* loved being here."

"I'm sorry, Nik. I've had stuff on my mind." The floor was getting harder; was that possible? He leaned forward, hugging his knees.

"What stuff?"

He shrugged; a wasted gesture, she couldn't possibly see a thing in this utter dark. "I told you about the business venture my cousin and me are into."

"Yeah, the importing thing." She lay her cheek on his shoulder and snuggled in. The thick press of her hair felt cool against his chin. The hair itself smelled stale, like oil from the Yankee's deep fryer. Now that the toilet was finished, first thing tomorrow he should try hooking up the shower. "With all the news from Beirut, I can see why you're worried."

"Yeah, but Aboodeh says that won't last long. No, what's on my mind right now, I'm—" he stopped, feeling Nikki's finger to his lips.

"Listen, Sammy. If I were you, I wouldn't trust anything your cousin Bud says all that much."

"Hey, I'm not blind." Sam shifted himself on the futon. If it wasn't his hip it was his tailbone. "I know he's had a poor track record so far. But setbacks are how you get ahead in business. Anyway, he's not the one I'm worried about."

"No? Who, then?"

"Teyib."

"That little guy? The cook?"

He was nodding his head yes, but how could she tell? "Yes," he said. "Teyib. The guy Aboodeh sponsored over as a business partner. He stole somebody's ID papers to get over here. Probably had them counterfeited. I read in *Newsweek* that there's a whole industry over there that deals in fake documents."

"You mean like a spy?"

"No, not *spy*, exactly." She might be mocking him, but he couldn't tell just from her voice. "We sponsored him because our associates over there wanted us to. Like a stipulation we had to agree to. Actually, it was the associates *of* our associates who sent him. We think. The thing is, he might not be the guy he says he is. He might not be connected with the venture at all."

"So who *is* he, then?"

"My opinion?" What the hell, he decided to go ahead. "I think—no, I'm *positive*. He's nothing but some small-time con man who lucked out. He saw an opportunity right there in his hands, a chance to get away, and he took it. *Stole* it."

"Get away? From what?"

"I don't know. The war? I mean, you just say the word 'Beirut' around this guy, and his face goes white as a sheet. Once Aboodeh was joking around and said something about having to send him back there—just jerking him around, y'know?—and the guy actually broke into a sweat. I thought he was gonna have a heart attack."

She was silent; he could feel her thinking. "Well, if that's all he is," she said, finally, "then what d'you care? I mean, what are you, the FBI or something?"

"Huh?"

"What's it to *you* how he got here?"

"He lied, he stole. He conned his way here. You should see how he cons people, talking all kinds of slang lingo when he doesn't even know what he's saying."

"Like what?" He could tell from her voice that she was smiling now.

"You heard him at the hospital that time. 'Cut me some slack, Jack.' 'Help me Rhonda.'"

"Didn't your dad do something like that?" she asked.

"My dad?" He rose up on one elbow. "Something like what?"

"Remember? At your aunt's house the other day, your uncle with the teeny voice? He was telling the story about the first time your dad came to America, how he was alone, just a kid? There was something he did to get over here, something that wasn't on the up and up. That red-headed woman who got him past customs. Didn't he have to lie, or something?"

"Something," Sam said. He didn't want to go into it.

"And there wasn't even a war then, right? But nowadays, cars blowing up all over the place? Checkpoints run by *boys* with machine guns. I mean, Jesus Christ, think about it. You're telling me about *Newsweek*? You know what else *Newsweek* says? There's soldiers over there who wear necklaces made out of human ears. Beirut sounds like hell, Sammy, and you're blaming him for trying to get out of hell any way he can?" She put her hand on his shoulder. "You know, he's not the only one. The house I grew up in, that was hell, too. That was Beirut for me. I even used to look at other people as if I was a foreigner, and I remember thinking that when I got away from there I was going to live like them."

"Cut him slack, huh? Okay, and what else? Trust him? Hand my wallet over to him?"

"Your wallet? What are you *talking* about, your wallet?"

"I'm talking about how he's a con man, Nikki. He's smooth. He's slick. You should have seen him con my uncle—had him eating again before he knew it."

"And that's what, a *bad* thing? Jesus, Sammy, listen to yourself. You know, when I had Deano—and I was still a kid myself—I swore to God I'd get away, the both of us, and someday we'd live a life like other people. So who do I end up marrying? Leonard. May as well have married my father." She fell silent, her breathing loud in the darkness. "Sammy, he's just trying to make it. Like me. Like you. Except you gotta admit you've had more lucky breaks than a lot of us. Which is why you could stand to cut all of us a little more slack"—she paused, let out a sad, breathy chuckle—*"Jack."*

In the week after Thanksgiving, Uncle Waxy awoke with a cold that soon settled in his chest. Between persistent, bark-like coughs, he began to gurgle with every breath. Aunt Nejla, certain she was hearing the death rattle, went upstairs and closed her bedroom door against the sound of it. When the visiting nurse arrived, she took one look at Aboodeh, sitting red-faced with worry at his father's bedside, and asked Sam to take his cousin out into the living room. There, staring at the closed French doors, they sat listening to the nurse's muffled directions, "Breathe out . . . Yes, like that . . . Again . . . And again."

When the sunroom doors opened again, the visiting nurse almost laughed at the look on Aboodeh's face. "Hey, now. You keep on working yourself up like that and I'm going to have the doctor put *you* in the hospital." As for Waxy, she went on to explain that, no, this wasn't the end. But it could be, she warned, if they didn't get the old man upright and out of bed, at least for a little while. "And I mean every day." He had a a a chest cold, she said, and keeping him flat on his back like that, they were just asking for pneumonia.

Next morning, Sam opened the side door of the bungalow and stepped into a piercing, alcohol smell. That, and something burning, too. He heard a commotion of voices—Aunt Nejla, Teyib, Aboodeh—coming from the kitchen, and his first thought was that something had happened to Waxy. He bounded through the kitchen and down the hall and almost ran into Aboodeh. "Shh." His cousin touched a finger to his lips, then pointed.

There, beyond the open French doors to the sunroom, sat Uncle Waxy, legs apart and straddling a kitchen chair, his flannel nightshirt rolled up to his neck. The skin of his back had reddened where six or eight inverted fruit juice glasses stood out. It was cupping—the old country cure-all that Sam had heard of but never actually seen. Teyib stood behind Waxy, administering the treatment. In his hand he held one of Aunt Nejla's blackened shish-kebob skewers which he'd made into a torch by wrapping a wad of alcohol-soaked cotton around its tip. He was removing the glasses from near Waxy's neck, each one lifting off with a sticky *thun-ck* sound, and adding them anew down another row behind the ribs. He did this by sticking the blue flame of the skewer into each glass, burning out its oxygen, then quickly placing the glass on Waxy's back, where it stuck, raising the skin with suction, and giving the old man the look of a porcupine with glassware quills.

"You think that really helps?" Sam whispered to his cousin.

"It's what Dad grew up with." Aboodeh smiled. "And listen to him. He already seems to be breathing easier."

They watched in silence while Teyib finished up, removing the last row of glasses—*thun-ck! thun-ck! thun-ck!* He used a cloth that Nejla handed him to gently swab olive oil over the reddened rings where the cups had been. Waxy's back was nearly hairless except for a ruff of white along the neck and the tops of his shoulders. Probably, Sam thought, his own back would look like that someday. He didn't see the *djrab il khirdee* and was surprised that Waxy had allowed the packet to be taken off him, even for this. Teyib slipped a clean nightshirt over the old man's head and the three of them helped ease him back into his wheelchair. Then, as Teyib leaned over to position Waxy's feet onto the chair's metal rests, Sam glimpsed it, the braided string of the *djrab il khirdee*. He nudged his cousin and, with the slightest flick of an eyebrow, directed his attention to the open neck of Teyib's shirt.

"We need to talk," Aboodeh said. He led Sam down the hall toward the kitchen.

"You think he stole it?" Sam asked.

"A toothpick wrapped in a dirty bandage? Think, willya?" Aboodeh shook his head. "If he stole it, wouldn't he try hiding it?"

"Y'think he conned your dad out of it?"

"Who knows, who cares?" Aboodeh leaned aside for a quick glance down the hall. "Listen, the Mutranehs got through to their Baalbek supplier."

Sam nodded. "And?"

"And this Teyib guy, he's definitely not *their* man either. What they're trying to figure out now—and it's got everybody a little worried—is whether or not he was sent here by one of their competitor suppliers."

"Worried? About what?"

Aboodeh sighed. Did he have to explain *every*thing? "*Somebody* screwed up that last shipment. They swear up and down they took care of their end, and so do the Baalbek people."

"They're lying, Bud. They kept our money and sent nothing."

"I don't think so."

"Why not?"

"For one thing, the Mutranehs are cousins—and the Baalbek suppliers are cousins *of* cousins. For another thing, it's simply not in anybody's interest. Our losses combined are nothing compared to the profit *all* of us could've made." Aboodeh let that sink in before continuing. "So, say they did their part, and we *know* we did ours. It might be the problem is with where the Jim Wilson originated."

"Not Beirut?"

"The Mutranehs said it was flown out of Beirut, but its point of origin might have been somewhere in the Shouf mountains. Thing is, there's a lot of fighting right now up in the Shouf."

"Okay, but what if we find out that Teyib's got nothing to do with that? What if it turns out that all he is is some poor chump in the middle of a war zone who got hold of some papers, identification that he could maybe use to get the hell outta there?"

"Got hold of? How? How's he supposed to get hold of these ID papers in the first place?"

"Who knows? But it *could* happen. Look, he's a con artist so—" Sam stopped short as Teyib approached, carrying the skewers and juice glasses in an open cardboard carton. He opened the side door for him and, with a see-you-later nod to Aboodeh, followed him out and across the parking lot to the funeral home.

He held the door for him there, too, waiting until Teyib had reached the bottom of the service staircase before giving him a stiff shove from behind that sent the box flying out of his hands. The next shove brought him to his knees atop the tumble of skewers and juice glasses and spilled alcohol. Sam's eyes stung, but he could see the little guy trying to get up and he wanted to hit him in the face, knock him out cold, like in the movies, and he tried it, but there was no satisfying fist-on-jaw crack, only a dull thump of flesh on flesh and pain that shot from his wrist up to his elbow. So he used his other hand to shove Teyib back down again. The alcohol must have got in Teyib's eyes, too; he was wiping at them with his sleeve as he turned and began to crawl up the stairs backward on his rear.

"It was you!" Sam hissed. He wanted to shout but Aboodeh was just across the lot. "I know who you are!" Through a blur of tears, he could see Teyib positioning to get up again. "You stay down!" Sam cried just as he felt something large and heavy knock the wind out of him. He back-stepped in a stagger, but whatever it was struck him again, then seized him with an iron grip, pinning him against the wall. He could barely breathe, and he couldn't move his arms at all.

*"You know me?"* Teyib said in Arabic. He slammed a forearm against Sam's throat and slowly pressed. *"You do* not *know me."*

Sam gasped for air. He felt his legs give out, and he was on the floor. He blinked. His eyes cleared. Teyib's face was inches from his own, the flat, dead-eyed look of it that said, *Live or die, right now, your choice.*

MUSQ'EEN

*"Breathe in," Teyib says, then: "Don't hold it in. Breathe out." He is speaking English so there will be no confusion. Cousin Sam has bitten his lip and blood is dripping from it. Teyib takes a cotton ball from the spilled carton and hands it to him. Teyib, too, is bleeding a little, his hand from picking up a broken fruit juice glass, the calf of his leg where the point of a skewer poked into him. The side of his jaw is tender, promising to hurt tomorrow when the swelling comes. "Breathe in again."*

*Cousin Sam breathes in. He is sitting on the stairs, knees up, pressing the cotton ball to his lip. Teyib's eyes keep watering from the spilled alcohol, and there is broken glass on the stairs, but neither of them moves to get up just yet.*

"Your face," Cousin Sam says, gasping out the words, "I thought you were going to kill me."

Teyib makes no reply.

"It was you that day in Beirut," Cousin Sam says. "You had a beard back then, but I know it was you."

"Surely you are thinking of some other musq'een who resembles me."

"Musq'een? You?" Cousin Sam snorts. "A musq'een doesn't make a face like I saw you make."

"That was the face my father taught me."

"Then was he a welad bendouq, too, like my father?"

The term is quaint, old-timer Arabic, and Teyib has to smile: What else can one speak but the dialect of one's arrival? "No," he says. "Something worse."

Cousin Sam turns the cotton ball in his fingers, then presses it back to his lip. "Worse how?" he asks.

So, he tells Cousin Sam about his five sisters, each one as beautiful as the moon. He counts them off on his fingers: one, Hasna, the first to be sent away, bleating like an animal; then two, Reema, gone; three, Fadwa; four, Suha; finally even Baseema, the simple, the always-smiling Baseema, five. And all five sold by their father into servitude. Five times, Teyib explained, he had pleaded as an elder brother ought, and five times his father had punished him, bent him over a water trough and gave him lashes from a goat's tether.

"Where was your mother?"

Teyib remembers watching her cook, how her hands were patterned with henna. That, and the sound of her weeping. "After Baseema, I ran away from their house." He pulls a towel from the carton and wipes the blood from his fingers. "I was alone in the world, like my sisters. Like them, I did that which I had to do."

"Anybody would, I guess." Cousin Sam sighs deeply. His breathing is back to normal now.

"You guess it?"

"I think it."

"If so, then best you forgive that musq'een, whoever he may have been. After all, it probably was not much money in the wallet anyway. Probably the papers that musq'een found within it were of far more value to him . . . whoever he may have been."

*Sam smiles, and fresh blood begins running from his lip.*

*Teyib hands him another cotton ball. "But then you must forgive yourself as well—yes?"*

*"Me? What for?"*

*Teyib shows Cousin Sam a wide-eyed, innocent shrug, as if the answer were obvious. "No deception without an accomplice!" he says, reciting the Arabic adage. "For being accomplice to that* musq'een. *For taking the money from your own pocket and handing it to him . . . whoever he may have been."*

# 17

When Sam walked in with the packages of lamb, he found Teyib at the sink, twisting grape leaves out of their jars and rinsing the brine off them. "The Armenian closed early," Sam said, "and Uncle Alex didn't have any shoulder cuts like you asked for. He gave me these shanks and a leg roast instead. He says if you want loin, though, he expects some later this afternoon."

"Loin?" Teyib laughed and waved off the very idea of such a thing. "It waste the loin," he explained. "The shoulder cut, he's what the grape leaf you wanna have it." He unwrapped a package of shanks. Shook his head. Unwrapped the leg roast. Shook his head again. "Too much lean." Finally, raising his eyebrows high in a what-can-you-do look, he finished clamping the meat grinder to the kitchen counter. When it was secure, he sliced off a wedge of white fat and dropped it into the cast-iron funnel. If only he had a car, he said, muttering under his breath in Arabic, he could drive to Detroit himself and not have to depend on the Armenian.

"You'll need more than a car. You'll need to know how to drive it."

"Someday, you teach me." Teyib thrust an apron at Sam, another of Aunt Nejla's frilly ones, and set him to work cranking the handle while he began trimming the leg roast into chunks. These he pushed into the grinder, fat and lean together, with a wooden pestle. The stuff came out a pink, wormy looking mass, which Teyib tasted raw and decided to run through again for consistency.

Look at him, Sam thought, perfectly happy just to be wearing an apron, cooking grape leaves in return for—what? A little slack. Enough grape leaves to feed an army, it looked like. "How much you making, any-way?" There were two large jars of them on the counter.

"Soon you see," Teyib replied. "Keep it on, your shirt."

Sam looked over the tins of spices set out on the counter next to the grape leaves. "Since there's lamb in the stuffing," he said, "won't we need cinnamon and allspice both?" An obvious question, maybe, but he wanted to show that he knew a thing or two. His mother, after all, was renowned for her stuffed grape leaves.

"Cinnamon yes. But awlspice? No!" Teyib started to make the upward nod for no but quickly caught himself, and shook his head side to side, like an American. "Not for him, the Uncle. *Um Aboodeh,*" he explained, referring to Aunt Nejla traditionally, as *Mother of Aboodeh,* "she tell me he like it the *warak enab* with *haraa.*" Teyib paused. "Hot taste. You know what is it?"

"Yeah, I know *haraa*. Hotness."

"Okay, then. Look. So." He demonstrated for Sam a blending of clove, cinnamon, nutmeg, black pepper and white pepper. Kneading these into the ground lamb, he tasted the mixture, eyes focused off somewhere. "Hotness!" He offered Sam a taste.

"I'll wait till it's cooked."

After rice was added, and a measure of salt, the stuffing was complete. Teyib sat Sam down at the enamel-topped table and showed him how to roll the leaves, vein side up, the ends tucked in just so. Sam's efforts were pathetic, one after the other, but Teyib only laughed. "Now you see why I need t'open the two jar-ez?"

Next day, Waxy refused to taste the grape leaves. All afternoon Aboodeh moped around the reception office at Tammouz & Sons, watching the phones. His father was getting weaker, his face thin and blurry. Mickey Shaloub, the Tammouz lawyer, was supposed to call as soon as he'd fin-ished drawing up some papers that the family would need to sign. Just in case.

As Sam was heading toward the back hallway, carrying a sack of gro-ceries to take up to the attic kitchen, Aboodeh called him into Uncle Waxy's office.

"Put that down and c'mere a minute."

"What is it?" Sam shifted the sack from one arm to the other. "I should get these in the fridge."

Aboodeh put his hands flat on the desk and looked down at them. Silent, except for the dull tap-tap of the pinkie ring on the blotter, waiting while Sam put the groceries down and took a seat.

"What's that I smell?" Sam gave his cousin a puzzled look. "You wearing patchouli?"

"That's incense," Aboodeh said.

"Christ," Sam sat forward. "She was *here?*"

"Her and her buddy," Aboodeh said.

"The guy with the tattoos?"

Aboodeh nodded. "They must've left an hour ago," he said, sniffing the air. "Whew, that shit lingers."

Sam sat forward in the chair. "What did they want?"

"What do you think?" Aboodeh gave out a long slow sigh. "I already told them that we don't know what happened to the last delivery. And the suppliers up in Baalbek don't, either. Somehow, somewhere, things got screwed up. So I told them again."

"What, they think you're lying?"

"Lying or not, Larry Morton doesn't care. Screwed up or not. Either way, he just wants his investment back. And he's right."

"Jesus, Bud." Sam shook his head.

"Somehow I gotta scrape together enough to pay him back."

"How you gonna do that?"

"What do you care?" Aboodeh gave him a level look. "You're either running to the grocery store or else getting your ashes hauled up in Michigan. Cousins! Jesus Christ," his breath caught, "I'm alone in this, aren't I?"

That evening, Aunt Nejla found a pan of baked *kibbeh* on her counter that Teyib had left there. He'd scored the meat into the traditional diamond patterns, browned the top to a perfect crust. But Uncle Waxy refused to even look at it, so she cut a portion for herself and another for Shofia and practically forced Sam to take the rest home for his mother to try.

*Shu ha'ad?* his mother wanted to know. Since when did Nejla Tammouz know to cook anything? And this *kibbeh* looked perfect. Mama served it for supper, and later that night, Sam heard her muttering her amazement to the television as she ate a snack of it, warmed up and dipped in ice-cold tangy yogurt.

For lunch the next day, a Friday, Nejla had Sam take home half of an *al-baqli* salad that Teyib had left on the little table inside her door. He had fixed it tart, with olives and cucumber and . . . purslane? This time of year? In America purslane is a weed that you look for growing around rose plants. Mama devoured the salad, and all that afternoon sat at the window with her rosary, fondly marveling with every lemony belch that reminded her of it.

Waxy had looked at the salad with a flicker of recognition, Nejla later reported, but he wouldn't take even the smallest taste.

Next morning Sam left town for Ann Arbor, where he spent the weekend glazing windows, repairing Nikki's back porch steps and cementing in a newel post for attaching a handrail, all the while waiting for the propane man who never arrived. In bed that night, bundled against the cold, he was too exhausted go into it when Nikki asked about Teyib. "Don't worry, I'm cutting him slack," he mumbled, turning over his pillow. "Plenty of slack. You watch. Before you know it I'm going to be giving him driving lessons."

Over the weekend Teyib had brought Waxy *sheikh il mihshee*, eggplant stuffed with lamb, but in a yogurt rather than a tomato sauce, the way many of the Zahlawis from the Mountain were known to prefer it. Waxy, a Zahlawi from the Mountain, didn't touch it. Instead, all he ate for supper that night was a little bread.

Bread? All right, Teyib figured, bread then, and spent the next two days baking loaves which he flavored, as they used to be flavored when Waxy was a child, with rosewater and traditional *mahlab*, the spice ground from the kernels of black cherries that the Armenian had to special-order from Chicago. This, too, Waxy sniffed at, but he would taste none of it, not even a crumb. And, as usual, Teyib had made enough to feed a restaurant. Nejla divided the loaves up, wrapped them in waxed paper and doled them out to Sam and the others.

Okay, not bread. What then, sweets? Teyib made *knafi bi riz*, almond-flavored rice cakes baked in cream with orange blossom water. He made a honey-lemon *attar* syrup as a topping and flavored it the old-fashioned way, with a boiled geranium leaf. Waxy never touched it. As for Sam, he had to take his belt out a notch. Aunt Nejla, Mama, Aboodeh, they were all feeling the effects of heavy eating. But not Uncle Waxy. He was losing weight. And by the hollow look of Teyib's own face, so was the cook.

Next, Teyib tried *mjedderah*, a lentil-onion pottage drizzled with olive oil. The monk who'd trained him in the old country had claimed it to be a miracle food that had the power to soften a hard heart.

"Where'd the monk get that idea?" Sam couldn't help the sarcasm. Cutting a guy some slack was one thing, but *miracle* food?

"From his Book," Teyib explained. The monk had said that *mjedderah* was the pottage that tempted Essau to trade his birthright to Jacob. "Oldest cooking in the world, the monk he says, before bread even." He showed Sam how to start by browning onions until they were a touch past too dark, then to finish them in three stages, dissolving each stage with broth before finally adding the lentils. Although *mjedderah* goes best with *lifit*, pickled turnips would have taken days to prepare, so Teyib decided to make do with radishes.

At supper Waxy complained that his teeth pained him. He seemed satisfied only to sip a little leftover broth, with a little rice to soak, so Nejla didn't even put out the *mjedderah* for him to try.

But that night, she awoke and went downstairs to find that he'd gotten himself out of bed and wheeled into the kitchen, where she found him, leaning into the light of the open refrigerator. He was using pocket bread to dip out scoops of the *mjedderah* pottage with one hand, and with the other he was pushing aside bottles and jars, noisily searching the refrigerator shelves. *"Shu ha'al ousa?"* he asked when she switched on the overhead light, *What's this story?* His mouth was full and he was chewing around his words, so it took Nejla a moment to realize that he'd spoken to her in Arabic. *"Fein il lifit?"* he was asking her, *Have we no pickled turnips to go with this?*

Teyib took the colander of sliced turnips from Sam and carried it away at arm's length, careful not to splash onto his shirt. He was wearing one of Uncle Waxy's monogrammed shirts, a formal white-on-white, frayed at the collar. Dangling from the collar by its beige wire, ready for use, was the earplug to his little radio. It looked as if the pleated trousers he had on were Waxy's, too. Waxy and Teyib were both little guys—Aboodeh's square beefiness had come from his mother, not his father—and ever since the hospital the only clothes Sam had seen his uncle in were flannel nightshirts that hung so huge on him they probably belonged to Aunt Nejla.

She was in the living room, watching television with his mother. He heard them switching channels, flipping right past a news program that was just then mentioning Lebanon, until they stopped at what sounded like a Lucy rerun. In another minute Mama and Aunt Nejla, as if on cue, were letting out twin peals of laughter. Sam was glad to hear his mother laugh.

Teyib handed him a gray smock—"This keep it offa you shirt, the juice"—and put one on himself. The smocks, starched and neatly folded, had TAMMOUZ & SONS stenciled across the back; Teyib must have taken them from the prep room supply cabinet. They worked at the sink in silence, falling into a smooth, efficient routine of Sam sealing each jar, one by one, after Teyib ever so gently poured into it first vinegar then, every so gently, the beet juice, as dramatic as bright blood.

At every commercial break Mama got up to look in at them from the kitchen doorway. Teyib seemed to know what he was doing. Still, Mama had to say something. "Not too much *khal!*" she warned, meaning vinegar.

During the next commercial, she saw that Teyib was sprinkling pinches of minced dill into each jar. *"Yoh?"* she said, an Arabic expression combining surprise and righteous outrage: she'd caught him at something *we* didn't do.

Teyib smiled, addressing her as *Um Samir* to charm her. "I ask only this," he said in Arabic, "that you try it with the *shabath*. Then, *then,* let me hear you say *Yoh!"*

Mama refused to listen. She narrowed her eyes and tipped her head to one side, like some volunteer from the audience focusing past a magician's patter in order to detect his sleight of hand. Magician, Sam thought, or con artist, same thing. In the next room Aunt Nejla began shrieking with laughter. Apparently the commercial break was over, and Lucy was back to her old tricks again. Mama let go of the kitchen door and returned to the living room, still shaking her head in disapproval.

After the door swung shut, Teyib took a head of garlic from a ceramic jar and began to rub off the papery coat. Then he paused, took out another head of garlic and tossed it over to Sam. Instantly, Sam reached up and, in a snap, caught it. One-handed.

He watched the way Teyib was separating the cloves from the head, and he began to do the same. A light slap with the flat of a knife loosened the jacket; that part was simple enough, but the second, angled slap, the one that sent the slippery clove skittering along the tiles of the counter, that one was harder to get the hang of. In the other room the Lucy show ended, and they heard the familiarly cadenced delivery of the news. It sounded like another "latest round of bloodshed" report. Finished with the garlic, Teyib appeared to be intent now on checking the seal on the jars, trying to screw each lid down even tighter. Sam looked to see whether the radio was back in his ear. It was.

Teyib softened butter in a saucepan and poured olive oil over it. A substitute, he explained to Sam, standing at his elbow. In Mountain cooking, one prefers the taste of *qawahrma*, which comes from the pad of fat beneath the tail of the fat-tailed sheep, which is melted down and clarified. "There is," he sighed in Arabic, "no flavor like it." His gaze took him far away, beyond the windows of the attic kitchen, which were steamed over from his cooking.

"What are you thinking?" Sam asked, his Arabic rusty, but improving with use.

"Nothing, only that this is America. Here, one must mix butter and oil." Teyib began to demonstrate how to crush semolina threads before sprinkling them into the butter and oil. "Stir, lest they burn."

Pouring pine nuts into a dry pan to toast, Teyib said, "If next I show you how I make dough for the *phtire* meat pies, will you return a favor to me?" Looking down, he stirred pine nuts with a wooden spoon and waited.

"What favor?"

"Help me to do something." Teyib pointed the spoon out the kitchen window, toward the L-shaped garage.

In three days the pickling was barely finished when Aboodeh stopped by to pick up a platter of *mjedderah*, ringed with slices of bright red *lifit*. Accompanying him was Mickey Shaloub, carrying papers that needed signing. In the past few days the two had convinced Libby of the need, given her brother Waxy's condition, for Tammouz Enterprises to begin establishing the distribution of some of its holdings—specifically Tammouz & Sons. It didn't take a lot of convincing, what with the new year approaching and the opportunity to avoid a tax carryover into 1976. Libby had considered the mortuary as essentially closed anyway. So, if Waxy's only surviving son wanted the physical property put in his name now, rather than later, why not? It was his due.

"Looks good," Aboodeh said, meaning the platter, then smiled sweetly at Sam in his apron. "So do you, dear."

Teyib missed the sarcasm. Bursting with pride, he beamed over at Sam. "Uncle gonna like it. You take it to him, an' you see." Then his smile weakened. The bread was not as fresh as it should be, he explained in Arabic. He would have baked a new batch himself, maybe some nice *zaatar* bread, but his attic kitchen was lacking in necessary ingredients. If one could drive a car, one could have gone out oneself to fetch the necessary ingredients. In America, a man needs to drive a car. He looked around to see if the others did not agree.

"If it helped get Dad back on his feet, I'd teach you myself," Aboodeh said. "I mean it. I would. If I had the time." Then he looked at Sam in his apron and chuckled. "But Sam here, he's got lots of time."

Before leaving, they all drank shots of *arrak* together, and Mickey Shaloub told one of his mildly off-color jokes. ("You know why is it the woman she havta sit sideways onna horse, dontcha?") Everybody liked him, small-built guy with a big head and a nose that hooked down between his thick-lensed glasses.

Later, Uncle Waxy signed the papers where Mickey showed him, one after the other, pausing only to mash the *mjedderah* onto a fold of bread, using his side teeth to bite into the *lifit*.

IGNITION

*They begin in the parking lot facing the L-shaped garage. "This is called the steering wheel," Cousin Samir says. So Teyib replies, "Il'agalah," to show he is not completely green, that such things are named in Arabic, too. "Here, in the middle of the wheel is the horn."*

"Ikkalaks."

*"Don't honk it so!" Cousin Samir warns. "In America the driver uses the horn only when needed. Now, here is the ignition."*

"Il 'ish'ehl."

*"Yes, put the key into il 'ish'ehl."*

"Il mefteh," *Teyib says, the key, then names the gearshift for him:* il asa il fetehs.

"But before you turn il mefteh, *you must first be sure the car is in P,* for Park."

"B for Bark."

*The fireworks before the noon news is nothing more than a show of American enthusiasm, but the commotion of it sometimes confuses the Uncle, who stirs from his nap and sits up, blinking into the blossoming flashes on the teefee. He seems to think that America's birthday has arrived already, the Fourth of July—except that he keeps calling July by its Syrian name,* Tammouz, *which is the same as his own. Teyib, spoon in hand, reminds him that the month is not July but* Tishreen it-tehni, *November.*

*Teyib decides to use the remote control to mute the fireworks, so when the flashes of fireworks continue to be accompanied by resounding reports—Brrt! Brrt!—he thinks at first it is a problem with the mute button, or perhaps he is hearing things; his ears, after all, are no longer what they used to be, not since Beirut. Then a brrt! without a flash, and he realizes it is the Uncle doing this. The old man is not asleep. His eyes are slitted open and his breath going quickly in and out in little gasps; he is laughing. Then he grows still, clenches his jaw, and releases yet another string of farts, this time a slow, lazy brrrrt! He is growing sleepy. After a minute, his breathing slows, and then he is snoring. Teyib cranks the bed back down to make the old man's nap more comfortable.*

*Asleep and snoring, and yet there is still another passing of gas. Confined to bed, the Uncle can't help himself, it flutters out of him with a sound like faraway gunfire. Teyib recalls how once he had heard the reverse of this, gunfire that sounded exactly like farting. Or rather, its echo did.*

*This happened in the middle of the Ashrafıyeh district of Beirut. Teyib was waiting on the balcony of a large apartment building, along with scores of others on the balconies around him, for fire trucks to come with their ladders. The building's west end had been set afire, no one knew how. None of them had heard an explosion. One minute he was meeting over coffee with Zeid's Baalbek connections—yes, they were telling him, for a price, it was possible; his stolen documents could indeed be duplicated and used to make a passport—and the next minute people were calling out that a fire had broken out. Their voices were loud but calm, even matter-of-fact. The narrow double stairwell down the center of* the building had become a chimney, belching black smoke, so Teyib and his hosts found themselves stranded four stories above the street. People were leaning out on balconies all around, above and below. Only a single ladder truck responded, but there was no panic; the fire was slow, and rescue was simply a question of waiting one's turn. His hosts opened a bottle of wine, a very good Lebanese red, Chateau Musan, a label Teyib recognized from the time he cooked up-mountain in the Bardoni resorts.

For a while they had been hearing gunfire—these days little more than background noise, like traffic—but what had sounded to be many blocks away now seemed to be approaching. As the balcony people waited, they occasionally called out sightings of the gunmen. Only two of them, near as anyone could tell, but who knew what side they were on or what they were shooting at. One looked to be gray-haired beneath his knit watch cap and the other a good deal younger. Teyib's hosts guessed them to be one of the many father-son teams that the Phalange prided themselves on. But, then again, the Druze had father-son teams, too.

The younger gunman had fired several rounds and was reloading when an odd thing happened. The older gunman put down his automatic weapon and fired off a round from a huge high-powered hunting rifle he'd been carrying slung over his shoulder. What was odd was the sound made by this particular rifle. The high-rise apartment buildings, facing the sea in a crescent, formed a canyon for echoes and the echoes of echoes. The hunting rifle's report, because it came from a distance, began with a pop and ended with a clap-like echo. But in the pause between the pop and the clap there came an abrupt ripping sound: brrrt, an over-echo, amplified as it traveled in sequence across the seaward face of the apartment buildings. Then it happened again. And again. The hunting rifle popped, there was a pause, followed by a flatulent brrrt, ending with the faraway clap of the final echo. Exactly the sound of a fart, the kind that escapes unexpectedly, called drahta filtani.

The children, bored with waiting for the slow ladders, were the first to laugh, and soon the adults were laughing, too. Even Teyib, who had been having an entire week of close calls, scared witless three times in as many days, he too began to laugh. What was that old man doing down there with such a big gun, was he hunting elephants? Next to it, the bursts of the son's AK-47 sounded like firecrackers on a short string, and no echo at all that Teyib could make out. But that old cannon! The old man took aim again—at what? Nobody was shooting back, and Teyib could tell it wasn't target practice from the way the two men kept ducking and weaving from doorway to doorway. Possibly they were putting on a show for the people in the balconies. Militia men weren't above showing off with such displays. Not in a country where mail carriers and firemen parade around in their uniforms even on days off, where scout leaders in short pants carry sidearms.

But if this was for the benefit of the crowds, all the two of them got was ridicule. The old man took aim, and his huge rifle could be seen recoiling into his shoulder just before the loud pop. A pause—every ear on the balconies cocked now—then that distorted, comic brrrt, just before the distant afterclap.

In Arabic the singleton fart is called a fus. The silent stinker is fusweh. Drahta is the rapid-fire grouping, like a machine-gun burst. The surprise grouping that shoots out suddenly, before you know it, that is the drahta filtaneh.

The gunfire's echo sounded just like the drahta filtaneh, abrupt and without warning. The two men had to have heard all the laughter, even from several streets away. Most likely, they had no idea what the people were laughing at. The middle echo probably never reached the old man, so cocky in his fatigue trousers and camouflage tee-shirt, showing off the thatch of white hair on his chest. He was still firing—brrrt! brrrt!—when the ladders reached Teyib's balcony.

Each day, Teyib catches a glimpse of the Uncle sitting in his wheelchair in the window of the little bungalow, each day laughing at the sight of the hearse turning slow circles around and around the parking lot, creeping slowly, slowly, down the driveway until—gearshift on R for Reverse—it creeps backward up the drive. All the while Teyib keeps wanting to rest one arm on the doorsill, the way American drivers do, but Cousin Samir is strict about both hands on the wheel. Which is named il 'agalah.

Batih means slow. Slower is batih kama'an.

Il farrahmil is the brake.

# 18

Some people can tell right off that they're having a nightmare, but Sam was never one of them. In his dreams, as in his waking life, he had come to expect to be the *last* one to find out what was going on. Until now, anyway. Now, something had changed, *things* had changed, and he could see this nightmare coming. Even so, he remained calm. Noting that his mouth seemed to be crammed with something ropy and dry and incredibly dense, he decided, calmly, in accordance with nightmare logic, to chew up whatever it was and swallow it away. So he began to chew. And to swallow, and to chew some more. Until he realized that what he was chewing was . . . hair. His jaw dropped. *Nikki's* hair! So, she was here too? He couldn't see her, couldn't even open his eyes. Wait, yes he could. He willed his eyes to open, saw the moonlit window. Was he awake? Not yet, apparently. The hair was still there, and it was moving again, coiling into his mouth, compressing itself down his throat. He knew that taste, a familiar chemical tang. Looking down at himself, cross-eyed, he saw that the hair in his mouth was not blonde, as he'd thought, but iron gray. Caked with formalin powder and flecks of dried blood. He lurched upright in the darkness.

"Mama?" She was outside his door. The room was filled with sunlight. He must have fallen back to sleep.

"Aboodeh, he's onna tele-aphone for you."

Sam threw back the covers. "Tell him just a minute." Pulling on his khakis, he heard Mama convey the message before setting the receiver down and hurrying back to whatever it was she had cooking in the kitchen. She couldn't leave town, not even for a short day trip, without packing enough food to survive a national disaster. All year Sam had been promising to drive her to the shrine at Carey so she could light her annual votive candle for Baba, and now the year was almost over. December had been mild so far, and the forecast looked for it to remain that way through the weekend. He'd parked the limo in the alley last night, gassed and ready to go. Aboodeh was supposed to come along, accompanying his own parents to honor a pledge Aunt Nejla had made to Our Lady during her husband's illness, but as soon as Sam heard his cousin's voice on the receiver—"Sammy?"—he knew somehow that he was bailing out.

"You're not going."

"I can't. There's a—huh?" Aboodeh stopped short. "How'd you know?"

Sam could hear a rhythmic noise on the other end, machinery clattering in the background. "Where are you?"

"Doyle's."

"The crematory?"

"No, the ice cream parlor. They been after me to come over and pick up the box of ashes. From that last Jim Wilson? You remember, the one you *left* me with?"

"So, how come you're not coming with us to Carey?"

"Larry Morton's coming down from Detroit. He wants me to show him around the funeral home. Now that the property's signed over to me, he wants to see for himself how it fits into our setup here."

"Setup? What do you mean?"

"What do *you* mean? Larry Morton needs to see that the venture's still workable and that we can recover his losses. *Our* losses. Jesus Christ, I really *am* all alone in this." Aboodeh exhaled a long, slow sigh into the receiver. It sounded like a blowtorch flaming out. "Sammy. You asked me the other day what you can do to help. So, listen. Right now, today, what I need is for you to go down to Carey with your mom, and take my parents along. Okay? Help them light their candles and all that. Just cover for me while I stay here and show Larry Morton around. Okay, Cuz? Will you do just that much for me?"

"Sure. Of course. But when I get back we need to sit down and talk. I mean, this stuff's really getting to me."

"What now?" Aboodeh was turning impatient again.

"Well," Sam glanced down the hall. He could see Mama working in the kitchen, humming to herself, practically. He lowered his voice. "I'm just—" No, he couldn't tell Aboodeh about the nightmares. "I'm just getting the creeps, is all."

"Welcome to my world," Aboodeh said before he hung up. "Tell you what. While you're over there in Carey lighting candles, maybe you oughta light a couple for us."

When Sam was a kid he used to look forward to the Carey trips. There was a kind of spooky fun to be had there, especially in the basement chapel of the shrine church. The chapel was an eerie, low-ceilinged room where for the suggested donation of a dollar—free, if you were a child—a pilgrim could enter though a curtained doorway and gaze in wonder upon the displays of what the cured had left behind: dozens upon dozens of wicker litters and polio leg braces, wheelchairs, metal canes, bone-handled canes and the white canes of the blind, shoes with thick boxy soles. And crutches, everywhere crutches of all sizes hanging floor-to-ceiling up one side aisle and down the other. Place like that, a kid didn't even need an imagination.

And today, Uncle Waxy even reminded Sam of a kid. They'd dressed him up in a suit and tie for his pilgrimage to Carey, but he'd lost so much weight his clothes swallowed him up. Standing in the sunshine on the side steps of his bungalow, leaning on Teyib for support, he looked like a boy playing dress-up in his father's clothes.

While Sam got out to take Aunt Nejla's arm, Teyib helped ease Waxy into the backseat across from Mama. Nejla paused before getting in and gave the car a blessing, x-ing the air before her—left, right, center. They'd all dressed for church, but carried their overcoats since it was warm in the sun. Perfect driving weather. Teyib placed a Styrofoam cooler in the trunk, then came around and took the passenger seat. It had been Uncle Waxy who'd wanted him to come along to prepare their *zoueideh* lunch in Carey. And maybe get in a little highway driving experience, too. Yes? Maybe?

Maybe. Actually, Sam saw no problem. On the return trip they could take the McCutchenville Pike, a commuter route that would be deserted on a Sunday. So, why not? Teyib had proven to be more than capable behind the wheel. Clearly he'd driven before, back in the old country, and all he really needed to pass his test and eventually, *hopefully,* take over some of the family driving chores was a little more practice.

Travel time to Carey would be a little over an hour, Sam figured. Unfortunately, what he hadn't figured on was a stretch of roadwork on the interstate that quickly bottlenecked traffic heading south out of the city into a bumper-to-bumper crawl. Mama was first to begin complaining. Squeezed into the jumpseat in back, she moaned that the car heater was giving off a "funny" smell; she couldn't get any air. But when Sam opened a window, she felt chilled. Worse, they soon found themselves stuck behind a huge eighteen-wheeler that Sam had failed to pass earlier when he'd had the chance. Now, every time the semi inched ahead, its twin stacks belched out double clouds of black diesel smoke which the limousine's vents sucked right in to the passenger compartment. Mama began fanning herself with a hanky and sighing *Yallah!* under her breath.

"Sorry," Sam said. "No way around."

"No way roun'nid," Aunt Nejla muttered to Waxy, as if needing to translate for her husband.

Mama fanned and sighed until her *yallahs* turned strident, and she let out her most extreme cry of supplication, *"Dakhl baidaat Yessouq!"* invoking the sake of Jesus's testicles.

"I'm doing the best I can, Ma!"

To which Aunt Nejla offered, *"Musq'een,* Sam, he doin' it bes' he can doin' it."

Then Uncle Waxy spoke up. *"Dakhilak,"* he said in Arabic. *Please,* but with the sense of beseeching or making an appeal.

"What is it, Uncle?" Maybe the problem was the morning sun glaring into the backseat. He pulled down the visor. "Better?" he asked.

But Waxy only sighed. *"Dakhilak,"* he said again. *Please.*

"What, Uncle? What is it?"

"Cousin," Teyib said, nudging Sam with his elbow. "Whad he wan', he wanna take a time out," Teyib tapped the flat palm of one hand onto the fingertips of the other, the referee's T sign. "He gotta make a bit stob."

What a production every little thing becomes when you're old, Sam thought, watching Teyib help Waxy up the flagstone path into the Men's. On a parallel path, Mama and Nejla leaned into one another, making their way to the Women's. Afterward, when everyone was back and situated again—Waxy, Nejla, Mama, all oofing and acching their way into their seats—Sam realized that, perversely, now *he* had to go to the bathroom.

"I'll just be a minute."

Mama pronounced an exasperated the Sign of the Cross. *"Ism il Ab ou'l Ibn ou Roh il Idos. Ameen!"*

When he returned a few minutes later, he found Teyib seated behind the wheel. "I don't know," Sam said, shaking his head. "I thought we'd hold off until the trip home."

"Whad for?" Uncle Waxy called from the backseat.

Teyib smiled and gently revved the engine. He'd been waiting for this all week.

Well, what for indeed? Traffic had been light ever since they got off the interstate, and here on this final stretch of two-lane they were only about twenty minutes out of Carey.

*"Yallah!"* Waxy called out.

Sam got in on the passenger side. "Remember now, easy does it."

Teyib nodded solemnly. "Easy duzzint!"

Sam put Teyib through the routine of adjusting the mirrors and doing a head check on both blind spots before shifting into gear. "You know which way you turn?"

"Way? You tell me way."

Simple as that. Teyib gave the steering wheel a one-handed spin, like a cabbie, and steadily accelerated as he eased the limousine onto the highway. The sun was higher now, out of their faces, and Carey was a straight shot down a nearly empty two-lane. Seeing that Teyib was holding it at just under fifty-five, Sam began to relax, loosening his grip on the armrest.

"When you tell me turn," Teyib said, "lemme know which way. *Yameen?"* he suggested in Arabic, and gave the wheel a wiggle to the right. *"Shmael?"* A wiggle to the left.

"Don't do that," Sam said. "You won't be turning at all until we're almost there."

They crested a rise in the road, and Teyib sped up a little on the descent, letting the speedometer needle edge past fifty-five to just under sixty. He kept it there—maybe aware of Sam's scrutiny—until Uncle Waxy called out, *"Yallah!"* and with a sudden whoosh of air the limo took off. Sixty-five. Seventy.

"Hey, whoa—"

*"Hoost!"* Uncle Waxy shushed Sam. Then, to Teyib, *"Yallah, yallah!"*

Sam sat back. Now he got it. They'd grown impatient with his careful driving. While he was in the bathroom they must have conspired against him. His own family.

The limousine passed seventy, zooming into mile after mile of perfectly straight, perfectly empty roadway, lit white in the morning sun. In back Mama began a song, first humming the tune, then singing it outright.

*Ya automobile,*
*ya ghameel,*
*ma ahlaak . . .*

Aunt Nejla knew the song, too, an old-time, old country ode to the wonders of driving—*Oh automobile, oh fine one, how wonderful you are*—and soon Teyib joined in.

*Min warrah sahbaak,*
*annah rakbaak—*
*Teer . . . teer . . .*

Eighty. Eighty-five. Sam felt pressed back against the seat. Telephone poles were flashing by and the wind became a sustained rush. He wanted to shut his eyes but couldn't; they seemed to be hypnotized open by the straight-ahead motion. In the backseat, the women continued piping away like children on a carnival ride. His mother had never driven a car, nor had Aunt Nejla, so neither one of them understood the situation. And Uncle Waxy—who could say what faculties had survived the anesthesia? Faculties or no, he seemed to be having a wonderful time for himself, joining his wet, gargly singing voice to the women's.

*Behind your wheel I master you,*
*I bestride you—*
*Fly . . . fly . . .*

Sam held on, trying not to let himself sink into that same stomach-flipping giddiness of being on crutches, teetering at the top of some dream staircase.

"Teyib, the police're going to stop us!"

He *wanted* to get stopped. But there weren't any cops around. Only distant glints of sunlight striking what might be cars in the far distance. They *were* cars! Sam suddenly slammed both feet hard against the floorboards. That made Teyib smile, but he remained at speed for another second or two before gradually easing off on the gas. Soon they were in the traffic entering Carey, keeping smoothly with the flow of it.

Their first stop in Carey was always a brief visit to the Shrine Park, a couple blocks up the street from the basilica. Dominating the park was an outdoor altar beneath a dome that arched across four tall columns. A via dolorosa encircled the altar, fourteen stone grottoes depicting the Stations of the Cross, from the "Judgment of Pilate" to the "Laying to Rest in the Tomb," all spaced out on a gently curved lane that was paved so that Carey's many invalid pilgrims could be wheeled from station to station. One of Aboodeh's early but unrealized venture ideas, and one that Sam thought might actually have had a chance of succeeding, involved opening an electric golf cart concession at the gates to the Shrine Park.

At the basilica they found an open parking spot right by the side door, marked reserved for clergy. Sam told Teyib to pull into it, then took a magnetic *Tammouz & Sons Funeral Home* sign out of the glovebox and slapped it on the dashboard. Perk of the trade.

Inside, the basilica had been permitted to maintain its Byzantine configuration, which meant it had survived Vatican II still looking the way many pilgrims felt churches were supposed to look, with communion rails in front of altars that faced away from the congregation. Walking in, you could actually hear the old people sighing with relief at just the familiarity of it. The tabernacle, the enormous Gospel book open on its golden stand, the six golden candlesticks.

It was early for the service, so Teyib stayed with Uncle Waxy while Mama and Aunt Nejla proceeded directly to one end of the communion rail, where a small crowd had gathered to light vigil candles before the miraculous statue. Which was in fact *two* statues, one of Our Lady of Consolation, and the other one, called the Infant of Prague, which she held in her arms. Both were small as statues go, a little larger than doll-sized, and the shrine staff dressed them like dolls in matching puffy capes and miniature gold crowns. On Christmas their gowns would be changed to white and gold, but for now, while it was still Advent, they wore purple velvet edged with ermine. According to a poster in the vestibule, the first miracle was recorded here exactly a hundred years ago, at the shrine's consecration in 1875. There had been a thunderstorm, Sam read, and nobody marching in the consecrating procession got wet. Since then, the poster said, there have been numerous other miracles, the evidence of which were on display in the basilica's basement chapel.

Sam hadn't been down there since he was a child, but he could have found it with his eyes shut. While people continued filing in for the devotions service, he got his uncle and the women situated in a pew, then made for the side door that led to the basement chapel.

On the stairs going down, a sign hanging from a velvet rope suggested the donation of a dollar for adults. Sam didn't have any singles. Searching his pockets, he did manage to find a nickel and a quarter. The coins made no sound as he dropped them into the brass box, no doubt cushioned by layers of paper money. He unhooked the velvet rope and continued down the stairs. The entry was low-ceilinged, like a vault, and dimly lit. Through it, he could make out the nave's Crucifixion scene looming and trembling in the flicker of votive candles. The mural had fascinated him as a child. Painted in plaster relief, it gave off a 3-D effect. To one side of the cross an angel stood with a chalice, catching the flow of blood as it spurted from Christ's side, while beneath the cross, more angels were reaching down to grasp the arms of Poor Souls stretched up to them out of Purgatory.

Now that Sam's eyes were adjusting, an old-fashioned high-backed wheelchair took shape out of the gloom, and next to it a man-sized litter made of woven rattan. All along the wall the crutches and canes had begun to appear, the metal leg braces and baskets of eyeglasses, the baby shoes and hearing aids. There was so much more now than he remembered. Some of the stuff was stored behind glass in what looked like long pie safes, some hung suspended from pegs or were stacked right out on open shelves running the length of the chapel's side walls. So many more miracles must have taken place since he was last here. But something else looked different, or maybe as a kid he'd just never noticed before how each piece on display now had a small card or strip of paper attached to it. He bent closer to examine one of them in the candlelight. It looked to be a hastily scribbled message of gratitude to Our Lady of Consolation. So was the next, and the next. One was written in what looked like Arabic script. He considered taking it upstairs for Mama to translate. But then again, she might have written it. He left it where it was.

Mama believed in miracles, in saints who hung their coats on sunbeams and statues that wept blood. And standing here, looking around at all this evidence, he couldn't deny that there had to have been at least some miraculous cures. But why only *some*? Why this one and not that one? Why not Baba? Sam lifted one hand and let it drop. Well, maybe not Baba. He was a *welad bendouq* and maybe didn't deserve a miracle. But Khaleel?

Sam turned and walked back up the side aisle, where a row of wicker baskets occupied an entire shelf. One basket was filled with discarded neck braces, another with orthotic shoe inserts, another held only a single prosthetic arm, elbow to hand. So much clutter, so haphazardly stored, like the attic at Tammouz & Sons. Or even better, like the cramped maintenance shop in the garage behind the funeral home. Even to his crutches stored there.

As he was reaching up to read a card Scotch-taped to a leg brace, his elbow knocked into a metal cane and started it bounce-rolling against the shelves. He reached for it, still holding on to the leg brace, and ended up losing both in a pair of crashes whose echoes resounded off the marble walls. He held his breath, eyes shut, then breathed out as the singing from the basilica above continued uninterrupted . . . *Tantum ergo, sacramentum* . . .

When he opened his eyes, he was looking again at the nave, where angels were reaching down to the tortured souls. Purgatory was temporary, but otherwise exactly like hell. Flames, demons. Poor Souls stretching their scalded arms up through iron grates. One of them a poor balding guy with a white mustache just like Baba's. He'd seen it so many times, coming to Cary year after year, all his growing up.

Sam felt a shiver run through him.

*Baba?*

He felt unsteady on his feet. The mustache, bald, gray-fringed head. Even to the rolled-up sleeves. Those were Baba's arms, too, scalded, reaching up. He back-stepped against a pew and sat down. So this was where the *grates* of hell had come from. Above his head he couldn't hear the priest, only the congregation responding *ora pro nobis* after *ora pro nobis* to the litany of Our Lady. He listened until the organ faded then

238

burst anew into the processional "Holy God We Praise Thy Name." The devotions service was ending. The sound of the congregation shuffling to its feet was like thunder.

He stood up now, too. *Shit luck,* Baba had called it when Khaleel died. Turning to a bank of votive candles near him, Sam leaned over to one candle in particular and blew it out. Watched a moment how the wick smoked. Then, licking thumb and forefinger, slowly pinched out another. Blew out a third just for the hell of it, but blew out the fourth for Baba's sake. Then, for Waxy's son, Khaleel, who died so young, he blew out an entire row, candle after candle after candle.

It was late afternoon by the time they finished eating and started back, the December sun already low in the sky. A short day, and certainly the quickest Carey trip Sam could recall. But he felt within him no sense of hurry, not even as he accelerated to merge onto the highway. Soon a peaceful calm settled over them all, Teyib dozing in the passenger seat, and in back Uncle Waxy and Aunt Nejla and his mother, all of them nodding and heavy-lidded, like children after playtime.

Sam drove with the sun on his left, so low by now that it threw a perfect silhouette of the car against the grassy embankment alongside the right lane.

Back when he was recovering from his car accident, he used to lie in bed and picture himself descending a shadow staircase. Asleep, or dropping off, he observed with dream intensity the very spot where the tip of the shadow crutch touched the shadow tread, felt that instant of stillness just before his shadow self pushed off—*Too hard!*—out and out into the void, crutches outstretched like shadow wings.

In the backseat someone's breathing abruptly deepened, stretched to a hum. Then Teyib next to him was humming too.

Sam tightened his grip on the wheel and quickly looked down at the speedometer. Without thinking, he'd taken the limousine up to seventy! This stretch of old 199 had been clear for a while now, ahead and behind, and he'd had nothing to judge by. He lifted his foot from the gas and immediately, before he even knew he was going to do it, lowered it again and boosted the car up to seventy-five.

"*Ya automobile, ya ghameel,*" the humming now broke into song, "*Min warrah sahbaak, annah raqbaak . . .*"

239

Eighty. Then he was touching eighty-five, ninety! and holding it there for the briefest moment . . . before easing back. But for that moment he was pushing off the top of the stairs again, leaping out above the staircase, out and out, crutches aloft and flying.

## Out of Here, Where?

*The Uncle improves in stages. Some days he is almost his old self again. Look how he laughs to hear Teyib describe how the monk, so wide looking in his too-tight apron, used to jabber on about recipes. The sleeves of his soutane rolled back to the elbows, flour dusting his black beard. The Uncle laughs so hard, Teyib must stand back with the razor and wait.*

*"Cold cooks," the Uncle says finally, as Teyib continues shaving him. "Usta be dat's whad dey call us back at Sbarbaro's, back in de old days." Switching between Arabic and English, he explains how all apprenticeship begins with recipes, how in the days before glutaraldehydes, which keep muscles from setting, you needed to work quickly to position the body. And you had to do it immediately after the washing. Step by step, like following a recipe. If a woman was big breasted, you first had to suture her close to the nipples and pull the breasts together to hold them in properly.*

*The Uncle sometimes goes on and on like this, but Teyib prefers it to the weeks of silence. Sometimes the Uncle will begin to chuckle at something that has come into his head, and Teyib will lift the razor away so that he can laugh freely.*

*Shofia's kitchen had been well equipped and, when he could work there alone, a pleasure to use. But that was her mutbakh and not his own. Best was mutbakh Teyib, which they permitted him to set up in the attic apartment of the big house; with his own hands he opened the pipes and reconnected them, flowing gas to fire the ancient stove and prepare dishes for the Uncle in his little house across the parking lot.*

*Yesterday, while the Uncle ate what Teyib had carried over to him—a breakfast of quince jelly on freshly baked khubz Arabi, sheep-milk cheese and cracked green olives—he touched a napkin to the corners of his*

mouth and pointed out the window toward the big house. "We shuttin'
down," he said in English.

Yes, Teyib knew. He'd already emptied out the fridge and the
cupboards. He sighed and indicated the breakfast tray. This was the last of
it. "Where to for me now, Uncle?"

"Outta here."

"Where?" Not back. Not where he came from!

"Nah!" The Uncle waved away the very idea. "Just outta here."

"But out of here where?"

The old man pointed to the window, "Out there! See?" Then, smiling,
he called Teyib habibi, as if he were his own blood. "You got to go, habibi.
We awl did it. Awl of us. Me, your Uncle Yousef, Afifie, your Aunt Libby.
Your fadder. Now, you too. G'wan, git. Go home, pack'em up your things!
You been here too long awlriddy!" He swatted the air as if at an annoying
fly. "Allah ma'ak, yallah!"

"My father?"

"Yes, your fadder he give me his blessing for you." Then, reaching
out, the old man took Teyib's head in both hands and kissed him on the
forehead and called him Sammy.

# 19

Teyib joined them in the casket selection room, balancing a tray which he set down on the polished lid of an antique coffin they were using for a serving table. The tray bore five shot glasses, a bowl of ice and a pair of small covered dishes. Waxy pulled a flask of *arrak* from his suit coat pocket. He appeared to be improving, sometimes going an entire day where he was his old self again. Then, abruptly, the here and now would drop away from him, and he would begin talking as if Khaleel were in the next room. Under the suit coat he wore a flowered shirt, open at the neck. Flashy, yes, but it did give color to his face. His hair was slicked back, what there was left of it, thinning waves of gray and white whose ends rose across the nape of his neck in white curls, like a miniature surf. Smiling, he held up the flask. "*W'Allah,* the real thing," he announced, "straight from Zahleh in the Mountain!"

It was Sunday evening. At supper, just before dessert, Libby had called a brief meeting of Tammouz Enterprises where she announced her decision to close down the mortuary for good. Mickey Shaloub's law office had begun drawing up the paperwork. And that was that. No one seemed surprised, least of all Uncle Waxy, who'd summoned the men to gather here afterward—Aboodeh, Gene Moon, Sam, even Teyib—for a toast to his permanent retirement. The casket selection room, added back in the sixties as part of the basement expansion, was long and narrow, and as well lit as a car dealer's showroom; the long sleek row of display caskets added to this impression, as did their model names: the Marquise, the Brougham, the Seville, the Limited DeLuxe. And now, like unsold cars, the caskets needed to inventoried and labeled for return to the manufacturer, a task Libby had assigned to Aboodeh.

During supper, Sam and the others couldn't help double-taking at Aboodeh, who'd come to the table wearing the first leisure suit any of them had ever seen, mint green. Even more surprising was how he'd received Libby's news, in silence, with nothing more than a wry smile.

Waxy signaled Teyib to pour. Sam was no judge of *arrak*, especially straight, without water or ice. It tasted as strong as ever, heavy with anise flavor. And he supposed it was good, joined the others in telling Waxy so, anyway. They finished off their glasses and Gene Moon was first to ask Teyib for a refill.

"This time, put some ice in it, will ya?"

Gene Moon swirled his glass, watching how quickly ice turned *arrak* cloudy. "Suppose I've tasted worse back in West Virginia." He threw back his head and swallowed, Adam's apple bobbing up and down his skinny throat. "Well hell," he began, though coming from him it sounded more like *wail hail*, "my people practically invented this stuff. Moonshine's what *we* called it, though." He set the shot glass down on the coffin lid, tapped his finger for a refill. "And it didn't need that licorice flavor, either."

"This here's no moonshine, Brother," Waxy said, pouring, "and it ain't no Log Cabin, neither. *Anesone*, that's what *he* call it!" Waxy topped his own glass. "I give'im a little taste one time, and he call it *Anesone!*"

"Who?" Sam asked.

Smiling expansively, Waxy turned to Sam, ready to pour him another shot. "An' you *Baba*, he's the one took me over dere to meet'im."

"Meet who?"

Waxy made the gesture for patience, thumb to fingertips. "After your Baba, he bring me and Libby over from the old country, he tole us, don' even unpack you trunks. From New York City, Grand Central Station, we take it the train awl the way to Union Station, Chicago, Illinoize." He sat back, sipped at his *arrak*, taking one of the exaggerated pauses that Arabic storytellers take, before continuing, "November the nine. Nineteen an' t'irty." He fell silent. Maybe he wasn't pausing, maybe he was drifting.

"In Chicago—" Sam prompted.

"Cubs Grille, corner Addison and Clark. A football game goin' on across the street in Wrigley Field. Everybody puttin' down bets. They send us upstairs where they serve the bootleg."

"Wrigley Field," Gene Moon said, "hah!"

"Back in dem days," Waxy remarked, "if you got no bootleg, you got no leg at all, Brother!"

"Shee-ut," Gene Moon turned, muttering out the side of his mouth, "Wrigley Field's *base*ball."

"His eyes was gray, and his eyelashes long like a pretty girl's eyelashes. Forst thing he ask, 'Where you from, originally?' 'From Syria,' we tell 'im. So he wanna know is the wrestler from Chicago calls himself Boogie Saab the Syrian Slammer, he's a relative to you? 'Don' know, don' wanna know,' your Baba he tell him. 'Lookit me, skinny fella like me. I wan' the shit kicked outta me, I coulda stayed in the old country and let a Turk do it!'" Waxy wagged his head, laughing. "Your Baba, he was a *welad ben-douq*, talkin' to the Big Fella like that! Your Baba say, 'Lookit my brother here, he can't speak hardly no English, but he come to America to be *American*. See his hands? They wanna do *American* work!'" Waxy smiled. "'What's his name?' 'His name Abdullah, but in America, he's gonna be Al.'" Here Waxy performed a little double-take. His mouth formed an O and he widened his eyes. "'*Al* you say?' 'Yes sir. Al.' So he look at me like this." Waxy leaned forward, one eye narrowed. "'C'mon, *Al*. I know a fella he do American work, the only 100 percent American work there is—an' that's a National Fact!' Next day he send me in his car to Sbarbaro Brothers Funeral Home—his driver was a colored fella from Davenport, over in Iowa—and the driver he tell Mr. Sbarbaro, 'Put this Syrian fella here to work.' An' that day I start. Monday, November the ten, nineteen an' thirty."

"Wrigley field, you say?" Gene Moon studied his glass with a patient half-smile. "Wrigley Field isn't football, it's baseball."

"Smarty-ass, whaddy *you* know, you wasn't even born yet!"

"He looked good tonight, my dad. Didn't you think?"

"He did, Bud. I'm not sure everything's getting through to him, though."

"It will." Aboodeh was all confidence. While the others were getting up and leaving, he'd asked Sam to stay and have another *arrak*. "To celebrate."

"Celebrate what?"

"I got word, a new shipment's being put together, and it's gonna be heavy ended, just like I asked them for."

"New shipment? What new shipment?"

Still smiling, Aboodeh gestured for him to keep his voice down. "It'll be heavy enough to cover Larry Morton's loss *and* ours."

"Bud, Aunt Libby is shutting us down."

"Yeah. Yeah." Aboodeh's smile grew stiff. "But Tammouz & Sons is in *my* name now."

"The *building*, not the *bus*iness."

"So far, all Libby's done is have the papers drawn up. Mickey Shaloub says it'll take a good long while before they're done and filed. Meantime, you saw my father tonight. Tell me he didn't look like a man who's ready to get back to work. So, never mind Libby. This place is in my name, and we're going to start accepting calls again. Down the road a little, when she sees how working perks him up, keeps him going, she'll *want* us to stay open. And you, you'll thank me, too, after we recover your investment. With interest."

"Look, I invested my Khaleel money and it's gone. I lost money, but that's all I lost. I'm out, Bud, and I'm lucky to be out. You know what? You should get out, too. If Larry Morton and the Mutranehs want to keep this thing going between them, then let 'em go find some other middleman. There's plenty of other mortuaries that handle Jim Wilsons."

"Get out? And pay off Larry Morton with what? As it is, I'm losing my house!"

"Aunt Libby'll help you."

"I'm already in hock to Aunt Libby. But you want to know what's worse than crawling back to her? It's watching 'this thing' take off without me. Look, Sammy, from day one this venture was *my* idea. It came to me, and I knew it for what it was: an idea whose time has come. Sammy, the train's arrived, it's in the station."

Sam tasted the *arrak*, then put his glass down on the coffin lid. "You know what, Bud? Fuck the train."

"But this is *my* train." Aboodeh's voice took on a plaintive tone, entreating his cousin to understand. "Can't you see that?" He looked down into his empty shot glass. "I'll get this business back on its feet, and that'll put my father back on *his* feet. It won't take long."

"It won't?"

"I already contacted the county and had them put us back on the rotation list. And as for the shipment, Beirut's calling as soon as they get it ready to send." He leaned forward and put a hand on Sam's shoulder. "I need you, Cuz. I can't do this alone. Right now all I need, all I'm asking, is that you sit in the office and cover the phones."

"That's it?"

"I'll do everything else. But while I do, I'll need you standing by. Because from now on, it's just a matter of waiting for that phone to ring."

Next morning, Aboodeh was all business as he led Sam into Uncle Waxy's office and sat him down with a pencil and a memo pad. "Right now all I'm really waiting on is the overseas operator."

"What about removal calls?"

"I think it's a little soon for the county rotation to call on an indigent, but if they do, take it."

"Bud, you're not licensed to do a prep on your own."

"That's right, Cuz. Which is another reason I need Dad working again. We need him, and he needs us, because if he doesn't work, he's gonna wither away." Then, with a friendly cuff on the cheek, he left Sam sitting at the desk while he went downtown to meet with Mickey Shaloub; together they were arranging a strategy for getting the business up and running again.

Sam had never before known Tammouz & Sons to be so quiet during the day. No piped-in music, no clack of the adding machine or police-band static from Libby's empty office. The house was so quiet that when the heavy black desk phone did ring, he nearly dropped the *National Geographic* he was paging through.

"Good morning. Tammouz & Sons."

A detailer wanting to demonstrate new snap-release hose-pump attachments. No sooner did Sam hang up than a second call came in, a barely audible female voice that faded in and out of a buzzing background before the connection abruptly broke off. Most likely an overseas operator. Sam went back to his magazine, expecting a call-back. None came.

Next day, he'd thought to bring with him a thermos of coffee and a sandwich which, out of boredom, he ended up eating early. Next to the phone, pressed beneath the desk's glass top, lay typed-out prompts for addressing callers. (*We're sorry for your loss. In this time of need, Tammouz & Sons is ready to assist you . . .*) On the other side of the desk was a stack of assorted holy cards for the families to choose from.

Tired of magazines, Sam picked up the holy cards, squared and shuffled them like a poker deck. Dealt himself five, fanned them out. Three Blessed Charbals and a pair of Our Lady of Lebanons. Full house. But riffling through, he saw that they were nearly all Blessed Charbals or Our Lady of Lebanons. So he cleared a space on the desk and began constructing a house of cards, stacking tier on tier when the phone jangled and sent everything flying.

He picked up the receiver, heard static for a moment, and then clear as a bell an operator's voice—her accent sounded French—asking whether this was Tammouz & Sons Mortuary. Sam waited. She asked again, this time reciting the phone number. Hearing his own breath, he held the receiver away from his mouth.

Again the voice asked, "Is this the mortuary Tammouz & Sons?" Her tone had turned authoritative and insistent, as if aware that someone was there listening, and deliberately not responding.

"Allo?" She began to again recite the number when Sam silently, gently, placed the receiver back in its cradle.

On Friday, he brought a portable radio along to help pass the time. Pouring coffee from the thermos, he lifted his cup in salute to the icons on either side of the desk, Mary in tears and St. Michael triumphant. *"Daime,"* he said, *May we always meet together like this.*

The all-news station reported that in Lebanon masked Christian Phalangists were fighting a pitched battle with Shi'a militiamen. The weaponry on both sides, a UN commentator observed, had recently escalated in power and sophistication. Arms shipments to the Phalange, he said, had been traced to Romania, Bulgaria, West Germany, Belgium and, oddly enough, Iraq and Israel; the Shiites, it was believed, were receiving armaments by way of Syria and Iran; the Sunni factions got much of theirs from Libya and the Gulf states; and the Mountain Druze, having no natural allies, were said to be developing ties to the Soviet Union. A world war in miniature, the commentator opined, and by proxy.

Sam turned down the volume and returned to the task at hand, completing the student loan application forms and transcript requests spread out on the desk before him.

The phone rang as he was addressing an envelope to Ohio State University. He took his time sealing the envelope and applying a postage stamp before he picked up. The static was bad again, but the voice of the overseas operator, a male this time, came through clearly enough. The call was from Beirut, the operator announced, urgently adding that service might go down at any time. Sam heard another male voice, deep in the static, repeatedly, insistently demanding to know whether or not the operator was in contact with Toledo in Ohio, the Tammouz & Sons Mortuary. Sam recognized Phares Mutraneh's clipped, British-sounding accent. "Wrong number," he replied. And, feeling something of a *welad bendouq* himself, he broke the connection.

Of all the applications, Ohio State was the most likely to accept him for the coming fall quarter. Columbus would be a good fit. Away, but not too far away. The first step away.

"Just my luck," Aboodeh said, gritting his teeth as he and Sam struggled to maneuver the body bag up and onto the guttered table. "Nine times outta ten, these bums're skinny little shits." The bag's weight kept sagging to the center, throwing them off balance. "My luck, I get number"—a final heave and roll did the trick—"ten!"

They both took a moment, catching their breath. Then Aboodeh pulled open the long zipper to reveal—as per the accompanying coroner's report—a white male, the face still wrapped in paper toweling. The body was thick built, pot-bellied. No wonder lugging it in had been such an effort. The autopsy scar, a large Y cut into the torso, had been hastily closed with a simple baseball stitch. "Good enough for who it's for," the morgue worker's standard wisecrack about indigent cases. The surgical lights made the man's skin look sick-white, and his chest hair like angry black scribbling. Sam let his breath out.

"Don't go getting woozy on me," Aboodeh said. He tugged the sides of the bag down off the arms. "Until Teyib gets Dad dressed and down here, I'm going to need you. Y'hear me?"

"I hear you," Sam said, pulling on a pair of latex gloves. "I'm fine."

"Good. Then let's at least start the disinfecting before they get here." Aboodeh pointed to the Porta-Boy. Sam pressed the power button, and the sanitizer began its steady clack-and-sigh. The first step was to wash the body with soap and water. Aboodeh scrubbed while Sam directed the hose, lifting an arm or a leg to get at the undersides.

After towel-drying the body, Aboodeh began to spray disinfectant into its cavities. The Dis-Spray's sweet, orange-peel scent always turned oddly offensive, and Sam clicked the exhaust fan up to medium-high. Aboodeh sprayed into the mouth, the nostrils, one ear. He turned the head to get at the other ear, but then thought of something and set down the can of Dis-Spray. "Oh, by the way. A message came through from Beirut yesterday. On my home phone?"

"Oh, yeah?"

"The Mutranehs finally got to the bottom of what happened to that delivery. You'll never guess."

"What's to guess? It never got sent, that's what happened to it."

"Wrong. They sent it, all right. Problem was, we never *found* it."

"What do you mean? You tore that Ziegler box apart."

"One place I missed, though. And it was right under my nose. Our noses." Aboodeh gave a nod down toward the body lying on the guttered table between them.

"You mean it was in the body? *Inside* that old woman? Why would they do that to her?"

"They didn't, I mean the Mutranehs didn't. It was the professionals they hired."

"Professional what?"

"Smugglers. They sewed the packets inside the body cavity because that's how professionals do it over there. Come to find out, using a false compartment, like me and the Mutranehs did with that first delivery? Turns out it's considered very amateur."

"So all that Lebanese Blonde—"

"Up the chimney at Doyle's."

"But how were *we* supposed to know they hid it inside the body?"

"They're professionals. And they assumed *we* were professionals, too."

"So, did you tell Larry Morton? What'd he have to say?"

Aboodeh shook the can of Dis-Spray. "All Larry Morton has to say is we lost his investment, and we have to cover it."

"Or else . . . what?"

"We won't have to find out what. Because we're gonna make this thing work." Giving the can another shake, he nodded for Sam to lift the man's legs and spread them. They were beginning to spray into the rectal area when the prep room's double doors sprang open, startling them both.

"National fact," Waxy announced, his voice, high and wheezy. Leaning a little on Teyib for support, he was wearing a work smock and a heavy rubberized apron. Teyib's apron, floral with petaled scallops along the edges, must have come from Aunt Nejla's kitchen.

"What national fact is that, Uncle?" Sam, having learned not to trust his uncle's good days, studied Waxy's face and the way the old man moved across the room.

"What the two-a-you's working on right there." Waxy raised a forefinger. "Anal sphincter, he's the smartest muscle de human be-ins has got!" He wasn't joking, his voice was serious, teacherly, coming from that part of him that needed to present lessons.

"*Lah-ah!*" Teyib exclaimed; literally meaning *No*, but drawing the word out that way gave it more the sense of *You don't say.*

"*Ma'loum,*" Waxy gave the standard response, *It is taught.*

Sam looked to his cousin, but Aboodeh was pointedly ignoring all this. Finished with the Dis-Spray, he was now gathering and tossing used towels into the laundry bin.

"The anal sphincter, he is the only muscle," Waxy said, "can tell the difference whad's pushin' on him—the solid, the liquid, or just the gas. He knows. Smartest muscle." He shook the forefinger for emphasis. "National fact."

"Well, that's great, Dad." Aboodeh removed a pair of latex gloves from their dispenser on the wall. "Now that's settled, what do you say, you ready to get down to work?"

Waxy reached out eagerly for the gloves. "You betcha!" He pulled one on, wiggled his fingers, then pulled on the other. He looked at his hands and made a dry-spitting sound into each palm—*puh! puh!*—and clapped them together. Yep, he was ready.

Aboodeh positioned himself at the head of the guttered table and began peeling the paper wrapping away to reveal the face. It was jowly, distended-looking, like the rest of the body. The eyelids, beginning to part, showed no iris, and the dark, bristly jaw hung low and to one side, stupidly, a thing unaware of itself.

"Looks to me like next up's a shave," Aboodeh said, adjusting the rubber neck block. He unwrapped a new disposable razor. "Right, Dad?"

Waxy didn't need to be reminded of the protocol. After the washing came the shave. *Ibn Arab* or *Amerkani*, rich or poor, at Tammouz & Sons everyone got the full treatment. None of that "good-enough-for-who-it's-for" business here. Smiling, he said to Sam, *"Habibi, il* Barbasol." Then turning back he pointed out to Teyib a patch of pebbled skin along the dead man's jaw. "When this happen, we call it *ashar bedani*, in English *the goosey bumps."* As Waxy went on to explain the need for careful shaving, his voice, his entire demeanor seemed transformed, charged with an alertness that Sam hadn't seen in him since before the accident. Maybe Aboodeh was right. Maybe getting back to work *was* what the old man needed. "The razor nicks the goosey bumps, they turn brown. You can try'n cover the guy up with the cosmetics, but he won' look good."

"Look good?" Aboodeh muttered as Sam reached past him for the shaving cream. "This bum didn't look good *alive!"*

As the shaving began, Waxy stepped up to his son's elbow and hovered there, breathing out little *ih . . . ih . . .* sounds with each careful draw of the razor. On the other side of the table Sam laid out instruments for the next step, making and probing the neck incision.

Waxy dabbed the newly shaved face with a wad of toweling. Then he looked down at his own hand as if he'd just discovered it there. Straightening, wincing up into the bright lights, he suddenly teetered. It lasted only a second—Teyib quickly put a hand on his back and that was enough to restore his balance. "Lend me a hand, Brother," Waxy said. Grasping the string of the *djrab il khirdee* at Teyib's neck, he tugged him closer. His voice was an urgent whisper, "Stay lucky, Brother!"

Determined, Aboodeh kept on working; he made the incision, found and clamped the carotid artery. Then he began working a popsicle stick into the incision. "Dad?" he spoke without looking up. "Ready in a minute."

Waxy stared down at the table and didn't move.

"Dad?"

He wasn't even blinking.

Finally Aboodeh stepped over to his father, took the wad of toweling out of his hand, and guided him around the table to where the exposed neck vessel lay propped and waiting to be pumped.

And still Waxy continued to stare, only now the object of his intense scrutiny seemed to be the artery, slippery and dark like a stretched earthworm. A pair of vascular clamps and a popsicle stick inserted beneath kept it from sliding back into the incision. Aboodeh drew a length of hose from the pump and gave it to his father. Waxy looked down, seemingly puzzled by this new thing in his hands, coiled tubing with a nozzle that ended in a thick needle made of clear plastic. He stood there, doing nothing with it, so Aboodeh took the nozzle away and replaced it with a scalpel. Positioning himself behind and to one side, he put one hand over his father's and began to guide the scalpel. Their backs blocked Sam's view now, but he heard a wet sound and knew they had opened the artery, releasing its pooled liquid. Aboodeh took the scalpel from his father and with his other hand took up the plastic tubing again, again put the nozzle end into his father's hand. Closed the fingers around it.

Getting the nozzle into the artery could be tricky, Sam knew, even under the best conditions. After a few jabbing tries, Waxy let go and the hose dropped to the floor where it thumped upon the tiles, spurting water at their feet. Quickly, Aboodeh spun the pump's spigot to shut off the flow. Using a clamp to regain a hold on the artery, he nodded toward the nozzle, directing his father to retrieve it. Waxy looked down at his wet shoes, then looked up again. Smiled. But made no move to pick up the hose. Teyib reached down to get it for him.

"Leave him be," Aboodeh said. "Let him do it himself."

"Hey, hey Cousin," Teyib said, "I'm just lending the hand."

"Cousin?" Aboodeh gave a snort. "Tell you what . . . *Cousin*. You helped all you're going to help, got that? Dad's okay now. He doesn't need you anymore. So back off."

"No *br*oblem," Teyib said as if to smooth over a misunderstanding, "no *br*oblem." He bent over and picked up the nozzle.

Aboodeh let go the clamp he was gripping and made a little show of methodically stepping around the table, elbowing Teyib aside and snatching the nozzle away from him. He spoke quietly, his voice seething, "You don't belong here, you understand that?" He came back around the table and once more began trying to manipulate his father's fingers into keeping hold of the hose.

Teyib made no move to leave. He remained where he was, fingering the cord of the *djrab il khirdee* at his neck, as he watched Aboodeh again reach up behind the table for the spigot handle. Adjusting the water pressure caused the pump to buck, startling Waxy. He threw his hands up and uttered a distressed, childlike sound, "Yih!"

"*Likun ya* Cousin, blease!" Teyib pleaded, mixing Arabic and English. Aboodeh, adjusting the water pressure so it wouldn't pop the nozzle out, shut everything off again and looked down at the floor. He stood that way, staring hard.

"Better go," Sam whispered.

"No way, guy!" Teyib stared at Sam, wide-eyed with disbelief. "*Haram il shoum,*" he said in Arabic. "*Mahou ayb?*"

And that was all Aboodeh needed to hear. He growled like a dog and whirled around, upsetting the tray of suture needles. "No!" The word burst out of him suddenly and in full shout, booming off the tiled walls. "You! *You're* the shame! *You* are the big wrong. Understand me? And how come nobody ever fixed that *haram*? Me! *I'm* how come! One phone call to the INS, just one, and you're gone for good—you understand that? Right back where you came from! You understand *go*? Go! This is *my* family, *my* business! Leave my father alone! Now go!"

And then the outburst ended, just like that. The room was silent, only the continuous whir of the exhaust fan, the sanitizer's steady click-clack-click. Sam stood perfectly still, waiting to see if the rage had yelled itself out. Uncle Waxy stood slumped against the edge of the guttered table like a discarded puppet, hands hanging at his sides. Even his face looked slack; he was gone from here, lost in his own head somewhere.

Suddenly Aboodeh started up again. "What? You think I'm kidding?" His face was red and getting redder with the heaving of his breath. "Do you?"

Thinking Aboodeh expected an answer, Teyib opened his mouth as if to reply. Exactly the wrong thing. Before Sam could intervene, Aboodeh had leaped around the table.

"I said *go* and I fucking mean it!" He pointed at the double doors. "*Go!*"

Teyib took a step back, eyes shuttering. He touched the cord at his neck. Suddenly Aboodeh was right in his face, slapping his hand away from the cord.

"That's not yours!" Aboodeh grasped the cord and yanked hard at it, once, twice, jerking Teyib's head down with it, but the braided cord held. "It's mine!" Aboodeh ripped away the apron bib and began wrenching the cord over Teyib's head until the *djrab il khirdee* flew out of Teyib's shirt and spun around Aboodeh's wrist.

Teyib rubbed his neck and began backing warily toward the swinging doors. The front of his throat looked as if it had been touched with the edge of a hot knife. Then he was through the doors and gone.

"You goddamn *better* go!" Aboodeh shouted after him. "I see your face again, I *am* sending you back! Soon as I'm done here I'm calling the INS! Hear me?" He was shouting so loudly now his voice broke. "One call," he croaked, "and it's right back where you came from!"

Wheeling about in the doorway, Aboodeh paused long enough to fix Sam with a look before shouldering past him. And there behind them was Uncle Waxy, down on his hands and knees, reaching under the guttered table for the suture needles that had spilled. Sam started to get down to help when he saw blood on his uncle's fingertips, two spots of it welling flat against the latex, and he was instantly on his feet again, scrambling through the cabinets for the Cavicel.

"C'mon, Dad," Aboodeh was saying. "Easy does it." He lifted his father by the armpits. "Let's finish up, now."

"No," Sam said, "wait." The Cavicel he found was a new jar, and he was fumbling now to peel back the plastic seal.

"No?" Aboodeh laughed dryly. "Well, you can scram too." Then he noticed the Cavicel. "The fuck's *that* for?"

Sam gave the plastic seal a yank and it came away from the jar with a little pop. "Your dad must've pricked his fingers trying to pick up the needles."

Aboodeh took hold of his father's hands, examined one then the other. "This isn't *his* blood," he said. "It's on the outside of the glove. He's fine."

"Fit as a fiddle!" Waxy announced, his voice too bright.

"Put that away," Aboodeh said, "before it gets wet."

It took Sam a second before he realized what his cousin was talking about: right behind him were the triple sinks, half filled with water, and here he stood with an open jar of Cavicel. "Your dad can't take this," Sam said, understanding that what he was about to do he must do quickly. "He's your *father*, Aboodeh." Quickly, then. He reached over the sinks, twisted open the tap full force. Remembering all this afterward, he wouldn't be sure whether Aboodeh had looked up at him with that blank expression before or after the jar of Cavicel slammed into the water. He would only remember taking a deep breath and holding it as he rushed over to grab hold of Uncle Waxy. Had him to the doors, one hand over his uncle's mouth and nose, just as the chemical reaction caught up to them. The smell was sulfur mixed with wintergreen, but far more pungent than he'd ever imagined, a thing he felt more than smelled, a burning-cold ice pick thrust up into his forehead. It knocked him off his feet, through the doors and down onto the ground.

Out in the parking lot, their eyes watering and their breath steaming in ragged gasps, Sam helped Uncle Waxy to his feet. Immediately, the old man bent over the snow and retched, but nothing came up. Cavicel's fumes aren't poisonous, Sam knew that much. His uncle's discomfort was probably as much from the agitation of being suddenly grabbed and sent in a series of plunges through the doors, up the stairs and out into the winter air. After a moment he seemed to recover himself, allowing Sam to assist him across the lot. They were halfway to the bungalow when Aboodeh caught up with them. Waxy smiled over at Sam, wondering why they'd stopped.

"You fucked up for the last time," Aboodeh said. He was panting for air and he needed to wipe his nose.

"I didn't fuck up a thing," Sam said. "At least not this time."

"Huh?" Aboodeh took a step closer, his fists clenched. "What're you telling me? You dropped that shit into the water on purpose?" He cocked his arm.

"I didn't drop it at all." Sam let go Uncle Waxy's elbow and backed up against a parked hearse. "I tossed it in," he said. Expecting Aboodeh to swing, he flinched when he felt Uncle Waxy take hold of his sleeve.

"Lunchtime," his uncle said. "C'mon, Sammy."

They'd gone only a few steps when Aboodeh took his swing, but by the sound of it, he'd struck the fender of the hearse, slamming his fist against it twice in quick succession. Sam winced just to hear it. He turned to see Aboodeh straighten up, his whole body coming alert. Like a dog sighting a squirrel—the image flashed through Sam's mind, and he almost laughed. In an instant, Aboodeh tore across the parking lot, chasing something, just like an angry dog. That something was Teyib, scrambling out of the bushes by the corner of the house,. He bolted across the snow, outrunning Aboodeh, who soon stopped short, panting and shouting after him,

"You'd better run—whatever the fuck your name is! I'm having you sent back where you came from! Back! Hear me?" Aboodeh arched his neck and heaved the words one at a time across the lot: "BACK! WHERE! YOU! CAME! FROM!"

Waxy was still smiling, but he was shaking his head, too, as if mystified. "Sammy, where's he goin' to, you cousin?"

Sam led his uncle toward the side door of the bungalow. Behind them, Aboodeh was taking off in the Lincoln, rear tires spinning slush around the curve of the driveway.

Sam got Waxy settled on the sofa, then went back out and took a look around the bushes where he'd last seen Teyib. The little guy wasn't there, of course, and the snow was so tramped over there was no telling who any of the tracks belonged to. When he called Teyib's name there was no answer. Who could tell where he'd gone? Far, he hoped.

⌦

## MORE BLONDE THAN BLONDE

*Miller time, he thinks, and slowly pulls back the tab on a can of warm beer. It is his first liquid all day. He dares not turn on the tap for fear that whoever it is moving about downstairs will hear and come search him out. The doors are locked, all the windows shuttered. At night he creeps down the steps and checks each one himself. The air in this house cannot move, and remnants of the chemical stink remain in everything. During the day he sits at the top of the attic stairs and listens to the footsteps below. Workmen carrying things out, closing down the house. Sometimes it is the Aunt Libby, retrieving files from her office. Even from up here he can feel the air freshen a little with the opening and closing of doors.*

*Best simply to sleep through the daytime, or try to. As he had done in Beirut, keeping himself out of sight. And the best way, Zeid his teacher had taught him, is like this, right under their noses. He misses the sun. Only at night, when the house grows quiet again, can he light a candle. Flush the toilet. Open a can of beer. Miller time!*

*His food is from cans, too. Sardines, tuna, smoked oysters. He doesn't understand how it is that Americans mock the taste of Spam. Is it not a subtle enough flavor? Spam is best when fried in its own grease, but he dares not light the stove. He must wait until the movers are gone, lest the*

256

smell of cooking lingers in the house. The smell of the attic stove, a cold, dark hulk, even that makes his mouth water.

Out of habit, he touches his neck for the string. The string is gone, of course, the djrab il khirdee with it. Just as well, he thinks. Americans must dare on their own to be lucky.

He has his radio to help pass the night. Hour after hour he listens through the hissing earpiece. The season now is basketball. Weeknights WXYZ will replay entire games, even to the beer commercials and the ads for the auto dealer called Uncle Jack down on the corner of Nine Mile and Mack. Jack. Mack. Arabic too is filled with rhymes, but none as harsh to the ear.

Soon he will need to venture out again for more food to feed himself, more batteries to feed the radio. Outside, the snow has yet to melt—the winter here lasts so long—but this is America, and the sidewalks are quickly cleared.

Carrying a candle to the bathroom, he is reminded how, in his eagerness not to be recognized, he has overused the bleaching peroxide. His hair startles him now every time he looks in the cabinet mirror. More blonde than blonde, it has become almost white; he resembles a khityar, an old man. Indeed. But at least a khityar Amerkani. He uses his weak eye to give his image in the mirror a wink, American style, with a smile and a curt little nod of the head.

Taking the candle to the stove, he checks the pipes behind it, runs his fingers over the connections he'd put in with his own hands. Soon the gas will flow again and he will touch a candle to it. But not until the workmen and the movers downstairs are finished, only then dare he light the gas and cook himself a proper meal.

One morning the house is quiet and he thinks, finally they have finished their work and are gone, but then the radio reminds him that this is the holiday of the Nativity, the Christian Milad when all of America shuts down. Two days later, the workmen are back.

Patience, he reminds himself, sabr. The day of his freedom surely will come. Until then, keeping out of sight is easier to bear knowing it is only for the time it takes for Cousin Aboodeh to cool down. How long? A few weeks, maybe a few months. Sabr, he reminds himself, patience.

Sometimes when he plugs a fingertip into his good ear and listens, he can hear a dull, steady whir, like a fan going. Sometimes he hears faint voices *begin to form and echo out of the whir, sometimes there is singing in his head, the singing of Fairouz or Abd il Bak'r of Cairo, and sometimes even his own voice. That stops him, the sound of his own voice. He must remind himself, then, that this is America. And that here in America there is radio. And here in America there is television, too. And that both are filled with the sounds of other people. Always, one can find a sports program here in America, in the middle of the night even. It is the American way, this, the cheering of great crowds in the middle of the night.*

*Sometimes before sports events an organ plays the same song he used to listen to when the television finished broadcasting late at night. On television it is sung by a choir of voices, and the words of their singing explain everything. The brave find a home in the land of the free, they sing. In the old country he had walked past ticking cars but he was not brave; here he will be brave. He is changing. One must be brave to be free, free to make a home here in America, one must dare to be this much alone.*

*Years from now, after he has changed, perhaps he will return and, unbeknownst to all, cook for Aboodeh the meal of reconciliation—for that was what the old monk had called* mjedderah, *the pottage of lentils and onion that Isaac had made to soothe angry Essau.*

*It pleases him to imagine that day, himself standing to one side while Cousin Aboodeh tastes the* mjedderah. *How his eyes will widen with the pleasure of that first bite.*

*"Who are you, Friend?" Cousin Aboodeh will want to know. "What is your name?"*

*Teyib will have to shake his head in wonderment then at how much America has changed him. And even now, tonight, touching his white-blonde hair, he feels himself surrendering to the change.*

*"My name," he will reply, "is an American name." It is a name that no one can question. A name that cannot be sent back to where it comes from. Because America is where it comes from.*

*At that, Cousin Aboodeh will extend his hand. "Tell me the name, Friend." He will be smiling, his anger undone, like Essau's anger, by the dish of reconciliation.*

*In reconciliation, then, he will return the smile. He will take the hand and introduce himself, "I am Mr. Jim Wilson."*

# 20

Three days, five days, a week, and still no sign of Teyib. When Sam stopped by Aunt Nejla's asking for him, all she knew was that some time in the past week those delicious meals had suddenly stopped appearing on her kitchen counter. Across town, Aunt Shofia said it had been more than a week. He asked around at the Yankee, but Nikki hadn't seen him either. She was busy taking down garlands of Christmas tinsel from the front windows, and his questions seemed to irritate her. In a mood over something, she frowned as she used a razor blade to scrape at remnants of cellophane tape. More bad news from the bank, most likely. But now wasn't the time to ask, not while she was like this.

The last place he expected to find Teyib was in the little apartment in back of the store, and it was the last place he looked. Gene Moon handed him the spare key, explaining that he thought Teyib must have moved out; he hadn't heard anything stirring back there since before Waxy left the hospital. Long before. "Come to mention, I been thinking. Since nobody's usin' the place anyway, I'm gonna ask Libby if I kin have it back." The carryout beer and wine business was picking up, and he wanted to expand the back room for storage space. "Maybe put a walk-in cooler back there. Libby'll go for that, dontcha think?"

"I don't see why not," Sam said. He looked down at Teyib's spare key in his hand. "If it's good for business, Aunt Libby'll go along. She's got a nose for things like that."

"Well," Gene Moon chuckled, "she's got a nose, all right."

Working the double locks didn't feel at all familiar anymore. It felt intrusive, like barging into a stranger's house. Inside, the air itself smelled of somebody else. Of some stranger's life. Sam shook his head. It was hard to believe that he'd ever felt at home here. Everything about this place looked so temporary, so thrown-together—the janitor's sink, the jerry-rigged shower and toilet, the alcove sprinkling plaster down on you every time somebody climbed the stairs. And as for Teyib, no doubt he was long gone by now. From the looks of things, he'd taken with him what few cooking utensils he'd accumulated. Sam followed a faint vinegar smell to a shelf above the sink, to a cracked jar of pickled *lifit* that had glued itself to a dried puddle of beet juice. It looked like blood.

He paused briefly at the alcove beneath the steps. He wanted to summon in himself some sense of what it used to be like here, when here was his own home, this his own bed—but there was nothing to summon anymore. On the shelf above the toilet tank he found a bottle of peroxide. Probably in case Teyib cut himself cooking. Except that the bottle was nearly empty. Was he a blonde again?

He gave the place a final once-over, then closed the door and double-locked it. Gene Moon had the right idea, this *was* a storage space. Never meant to be anything more than a temporary refuge. A place to move away from.

Locust, Erie, Mulberry, Huron, Buckeye. Teyib had learned the streets of Little Syria by walking them. Now, walking these same nighttime streets, Sam was half afraid he'd find that the little guy hadn't run off at all, that any minute he'd catch a glimpse of him passing beneath a streetlamp, just strolling along the way he used to, hands joined behind his back in that posture of foreigners strolling along. Up Superior, across Chestnut, down Ontario, across Ash. A roundabout route that gravitated, eventually, toward Tammouz & Sons. Turning a familiar corner, Sam barely recognized what lay before him, and he had to stop a moment.

The clock and the neon legend, *In Time of Need,* were dark. That was it; he'd never before in his life seen the sign turned off. The entire property looked abandoned. The house and its grounds within the stone half-fence were dark, the wrought-iron driveway gates chained and padlocked.

Once upon a time, *kaan makaan,* all the lights here were kept lit, all the lamps and chandeliers and wall sconces, the coach-lamps flanking the driveway, electric remembrance candles flickering in the visitation parlors. During the three days of a visitation, families practically moved in to Tammouz & Sons, going out only for meals, and at night when the place closed. In the evenings things sometimes got boisterous, and there might be outbursts of laughter followed—as if one naturally opened the door for the other—by tears. "Go ahead," they'd encourage one anoth-er, "let it out." More often, though, being a people who were by nature dramatic in their grief, they needed little prompting. Some would begin calling out before they even reached the visitation parlor's arched entry. "Take me with you!" they wailed in Arabic, the language of their mothers and fathers, "Bury me, too!" Weeping openly, they paid their respects, then dabbed their cheeks and went off to the sitting room for coffee, sometimes lacing the coffee with brandy or *arrak,* while sisters watched their younger siblings, chasing them down the halls. In the restroom, babies were diapered. Everywhere people were talking, embracing, unit-ing and reuniting ("Too bad it takes something like this to bring us all together!"), sobbing and laughing in the very same breath some of them. There was such life in the place back in those days. Now, with practically the whole neighborhood moved away, finally Tammouz & Sons, too, stood empty. Now that the dead were no longer brought here, the place seemed to be full of ghosts. Sam was about to turn away when he heard a rustle of movement on the sidewalk behind him.

"That you, Sammy?" Aboodeh's voice, and then Aboodeh himself, stepping into the light of the streetlamp. He didn't look so good. Coat-less, his hair matted and whorled. He was wearing that mint green leisure suit again, and it looked as if he'd slept in it.

"Bud? Where've you been the past couple days?"

"Detroit," Aboodeh said. "Got back a couple hours ago."

"What is it?" Sam asked. "What's wrong?"

"What's wrong? I'm out, that's what's *wrong.* They decided to cut me out."

"Who? Larry Morton?"

"*And* the Mutranehs." He stared at Sam a moment, eyes flat with menace. "Like you really care." But there was also defeat in his voice, something self-pitying that hollowed out the anger he meant to convey. *See what happened to me? Everything I planned is ruined. And all because of you!*

"But I do really care," Sam said.

Aboodeh sneered, or tried to, curling his upper lip. "My cousin," he said. Then, as if the anger still wouldn't come, he sighed and seemed to sag into himself. "But I suppose all that means shit to you."

"All right," Sam said, "you want to know the truth? All that 'my cousin and me' shit? It *is* a load of shit. *My cousin and me against the world,*" he recited the adage in Arabic, *"my brother and me against my cousin.* You follow the logic of that, Bud, step by step, just like a recipe, and you know where it takes you? Right to *Me against my brother.* It's a recipe for disaster, and it's exactly what's going on right now over there in the old country. That's their whole fucking civil war in a nutshell."

Aboodeh didn't reply, only leaned his head a little to one side, as if suspicious and, at the same time, maybe catching a glimmer. Maybe a door was opening. But no. Deciding to keep that door closed, he made a sniffling sound and turned his attention over toward the house. "Never saw it so dark before," he said.

"Yeah, they must've boarded up the windows."

"New locks, too, all around." Aboodeh sighed. "Libby's gone and shut it down for good this time." He thrust his hands deep into his pockets. "Anyway, it doesn't matter anymore. I'm out." He kept his eyes on the sidewalk. "After the notice was in the *Blade* about the mortuary closing permanently, Larry Morton went behind my back and got the okay from the Mutranehs. Then he took the venture to somebody else."

"Another mortuary?"

"Except that this one's up in Detroit." Aboodeh slowly nodded his head. "Which makes sense—right? Not only is it closer to distribution, but the new place happens to have its own on-site crematory facility. Smart, eh? Good business." Aboodeh looked away, toward the house. "I couldn't hold up my end, Sammy, so they went around me. I'm not the middleman anymore. I'm not even in the loop."

"Well, screw 'em. They can keep their loop."

"But it's my idea they're using, Sammy, *my* idea, and now they won't even let me in the back door unless I buy my way in. Worse, I still owe for that missing delivery that got burned up."

"That wasn't our fault!"

"Doesn't matter."

"What'll you do?"

"Well," Aboodeh flicked a glance toward the house, "the insurance is in my name."

"Don't even joke."

"Who's joking? Eventually Larry Morton and the Mutranehs are gonna cover their losses, *and* make a profit on top. But what's gonna cover *my* losses?"

"Bud, it's not like we're gonna starve. Let's face it, we were like kids playing with fire."

"We? *I'm* the one who got burned."

"Hey, I got burned, too. *My* Khaleel money went up the chimney at Doyle's, too. I've had to apply for scholarships and student loans."

"Student loans?"

"I got accepted." Sam waited, but his cousin didn't ask. So he told him anyway, "Ohio State. Fall quarter, I leave for Columbus."

Aboodeh smiled grimly and gave a little nod.

"Buddy . . . ," Sam began, then stopped. He wanted to put his arms around him, but knew his cousin would resent the gesture. "Things'll work out for you. *Other* things. They will. I really, truly believe that." And in just the saying of the words Sam realized that he *did* believe them. It came to him also that things would work out for Nikki, as well; that someday, sooner than later, probably, she'd find someone else, and make a home of her own; he believed it now as sure as he also believed that this first step he was taking in a few weeks would be the step that would take him all the way away. Mama would live alone, and probably die alone. And in his absence this North End neighborhood, changing now in front of his eyes, would keep on changing. One day he would come back and not even recognize the streets.

Sam meant to stop over at the Yankee that night, or the next. But he didn't. Instead, he gathered and sorted his things for going away, emptied his closet, his chest of drawers. And put off seeing Nikki.

Restless to get moving, he went for drives, sometimes in a lazy weaving route through Little Syria. Moving *out* of here, the *ibn Arab* used to say, was the whole point of moving *into* Little Syria in the first place. Maybe so, but maybe too they'd forgotten what a comfort it had been, newly arrived, to smell wafting through the screen doors of strangers the very same cooking as back home in the old country? *Sish barak* and *awarma, beitinjain* and spiced *heshweh* rice, *laham mishwee* broiling over the outdoor coals. Sundays in Riverside Park, the get-togethers there were like the *j'nayneyeen* picnics in the old country, how the music would suddenly start up, hands clapping to the lute-like *oud,* and how old men in suspenders would twirl hankies in the air to begin a snake-dance while children kept rhythm on little *derbekee* drums and those blackened clacksticks they called the bones. Off in the shade the old women used tongs to keep live coals gingerly balanced atop folded leaves of blonde tobacco. Sam liked to be near them, to lie back in the shade and close his eyes and catch that sometimes chocolatey whiff in the tobacco smoke, listening to the soothing hubbly bubbly of the *nargilehs,* the riffling of cards dealt out for a game of *basrah,* the sound of Arabic itself a consolation, soft and guttural, as familiar as hearing his own name whispered before sleep.

Other times Sam's drives would take him all the way up Monroe and then back across to Cherry and by the Yankee; on New Year's Eve he drove out to Galena Street. Slowing past Nikki's apartment building, he peered up at her shaded windows, then drove on.

Uncle Waxy had given Sam the mortuary's old flower-car to take down to Columbus. Front half a '62 Cadillac DeVille, rear half a pickup truck with tail fins, the flower-car was a throwback to a more lavish time when funeral processions often called for at least one such vehicle to follow the hearse like a portable flower bed.

The V8 engine would be hard on gas mileage, but on the other hand, Waxy reasoned, a Cadillac would provide better protection than the Volkswagen Sam had been looking to buy. Also, since Sam wouldn't be moving into a dorm room but an unfurnished apartment, its truckbed would come in handy for carting down a desk and a bed and the exercycle. Sam had resumed workouts to keep his hip limber, but lately he hadn't felt much like marking distance on the map. When he'd left off cycling, back when Uncle Waxy was in the hospital, the red line of his progress had traced the Mediterranean coast from Lebanon to Turkey, across southern Europe and down the boot of Italy, making the hop at Sicily, before rolling across the Sahara in a straight line to the Nile delta and Alexandria. A good place to leave it, now that he looked at it. Coming out of the desert to water and food, to people. He took the map down off Mama's wall, careful so the Scotch tape wouldn't leave marks, then folded and put it away.

Nikki's shift ended at four, the quiet hour after the bar patrons had all gone home and the breakfast crowd hadn't yet started to trickle in. The sidewalks were empty, and the Yankee's windows lit up the whole corner. Standing there, waiting, Sam half expected a figure just now rounding the corner to be Teyib, but it turned out to be a stranger, a bum who looked up into his face as he passed then immediately looked away again, as if Sam had uttered some rebuke.

Through the Yankee's glass door he saw what he took to be a new waitress, sorting her tip money out on the counter. Her hair was shorter than a boy's, and Sam didn't realize she was Nikki until, reaching up to brush a strand of hair back from her face, she suddenly stopped as if remembering there was nothing to brush back.

He stepped away from the door and watched as she swept her tip money off the counter—quarters, dimes, nickels, Christ, even pennies. Removing her apron, she stepped into the back room to punch her time card. When she returned, coat and purse in hand, she paused to ease the kink out of her neck, a slow stretching roll from one shoulder to the other. Squeezed her eyes shut, opened them wide again. Those big brown eyes that the shorn hair made even bigger. So changed. And in a few minutes, even more of her world would be changed. Not that what he had to tell her would come as a great shock. She had to have seen it coming. He pulled so hard to open the door it banged against the plate glass.

Nikki looked up, startled. Then she smiled. "Hey, Sammy!" she said, and right away he regretted such a lighthearted greeting. It wouldn't make this any easier.

"Nikki, what did you *do?* Wow, I barely even recognized you."

"Pretty short, huh?"

"You look so different."

"I suppose. I don't know. You like? It's kind of a pixie cut, I guess."

"I like it," Sam said.

"Liar."

"No, it's such a *change,* is all. In a good way. Makes your eyes look huge."

"I don't know." Nikki looked at her reflection in the plate glass. "Maybe I'll grow it back." She shrugged. "And the money was good."

"Money?"

She hesitated, as if considering whether to go into it. Then, she gave out a quick sigh and explained that she'd done it for the house, for repair money; her hairdresser had brokered the hair to a wigmaker. "Sheila's been after my hair for years," she said. "Kept telling me you get good money for natural blonde."

"You *sold* your hair?"

"Why not? Money's got to come from somewhere. Besides, not even a week and it looks like it's starting to grow back already. Way I figure, that makes it free money." She started to put on her coat. "And how about you," she said, "where've *you* been all this time?"

"No place. Just busier than usual. Lots of stuff I needed to get done." He helped her with the coat. It looked new, down-filled nylon. "How's Deano?"

"He's fine."

"His allergies?"

"He's fine."

Abruptly, a siren kicked up, loud and close by. An instant later a police squad car appeared, its double gumballs spinning red and blue. They watched it speed by, take the corner and wail on north up Erie.

"Uh-oh," Nikki said, "they're after *some*body."

"That reminds me," Sam held the door for her as she stepped outside. "You haven't seen Teyib around, have you? Since last time I asked?"

"No." She thought a moment and shook her head. "Not at all, come to think of it. Why, something wrong?"

"I think he might be laying low for a while," Sam said.

"What happened?"

"He and my cousin Bud, they sort of got into it."

"In that case, laying low sounds like a good idea." She stopped under a streetlamp and fished the car keys from her purse. Because the Yankee lot was small, employees weren't allowed to use it. Nikki usually found a spot around the corner. "Don't tell me you're out looking for *him* at four in the morning?"

"No. I came here looking for you."

"Oh?" She took a step back.

"I've been applying for student loans. Which I got. And a small, partial scholarship."

"Yeah?" She waited, car key in hand, rubbing her thumb against the brass.

"Well, that, and a loan from my aunt Libby, and I ought to have enough to see me through my first year."

"What are you telling me?" She forced a smile, but he didn't want to see it. He looked instead at the key in her hand, how her fingertips were white from pinching it. She opened her purse and dropped the keys back in.

"My first year goes well, there's other scholarships I can apply for. And part-time work. But right now, I'm figuring to just get down there and, you know, get my feet wet."

"Down there? Down where?"

"Columbus. I got accepted at Ohio State." She stared at him, silent. Then she turned away and started up the street again. He followed. "And also," he said, unable to keep his mouth shut, "I felt I *needed* to get away. On my own."

That stopped her. "On your *own?*" Her hand went up as if to touch her hair, hair that wasn't there anymore.

"I don't know why I put off telling you sooner," Sam said. "I'm sorry. Guess I knew it would disappoint you, me not being there to help fix up your house."

"My house? Hah! Not anymore it isn't."

"The bank?"

She gave a little nod, intending, probably, to show a gesture of sad acceptance. But instead it looked quick and bitter, like the tossing aside of an ugly thought. Her rusty Ford Galaxie was just ahead, parked beneath a streetlamp. She opened her purse, then snapped it shut and turned to face him. "The loan officer said I needed to come up with enough to cover what I owed for last month and this. That's when I had Sheila cut my hair. And it still wasn't enough." She thought of something and laughed. "Isn't there a book about that? Where a woman cuts her hair off to buy Christmas presents?"

Another siren sounded, a firetruck this time, so loud and close they both turned to see. After it passed, the vibrations of its powerful engine thrumming, Sam said, "About Columbus, it's not the other side of the world." But even as he spoke the words, another part of himself saw right through them. It *was* the other side of the world.

Nikki said nothing, simply stood looking right back at him, and for a moment he wondered whether she might be giving him room to back down, to announce confusion, uncertainty, vague doubts he'd been having. More sirens began wailing, but distantly; the fire was far away somewhere.

Finally, she spoke, eyes narrowed, her face quizzical. "Then go," she said, "but don't think I'll still be here."

Now he was silent. He understood. She needed to be the one to do it. That was Nikki. Accept or refuse, it had to be her call. She made love the same way.

She unlocked her car door, but didn't make a move to get in. Instead, she hesitated a moment, then took a step toward him. He hoped it would be a goodbye slap and not a kiss. It was neither.

"I need to get gas," she said.

"What?"

"I'm almost out of gas. Can you lend me something?"

He'd watched her put her tip money in the purse before they left the Yankee. Even so, he took his wallet out. "Sure," he said. He felt oddly relieved. "What d'you need?"

"Ten." She rose on her toes and looked into the wallet. "You got ten?"

He had ten. He had two five's and a twenty. He resisted the urge to just give her the twenty. No. He handed her only what she'd asked for, the two fives. She put them in the pocket of her uniform. Then she got in her car, but after starting the engine she rolled down her window as if to say something. When he bent to listen, she reached out her hand and with her forefinger touched his lips, tracing a slow caress down to his chin. Then she pulled away from the curb and drove off north toward Galena Street.

The sirens began to drop pitch as each wound down, one after the other, down and down to an abrupt, low-throated stop. The northern sky was lit by a throbbing orange glow which Sam at first thought might be coming from all the way off in Point Place. But no, the fire had to be closer than that; much, much closer, he could smell it. Above him, he heard windows opening. People in upper-story apartments were sticking their heads out to see, their faces lighting yellow-orange as they turned north and found the fire. Sam finally saw bright flames bursting out the top of a building only a few blocks away. At least it looked that close, although as he crossed to Erie and began a slow jog north, the fire seemed to recede before him like an optical illusion. Now the flames were coming out the roof of a building a little farther down the block, and then just beyond that, a roof this side of Chestnut Street. But when he crossed Chestnut, he still hadn't reached it. If he kept heading this way he'd pass by the funeral home, only a couple blocks up and one over, and just like that he knew that the fire was there, oh, Jesus Christ! He broke into a full run. Across Mulberry, around the corner of Magnolia, and then stopped short. Just ahead firetrucks blocked the street and a crowd of onlookers was gathering.

It *was* Tammouz & Sons. From down the block, he could see that half its roof was ablaze. Flames had engulfed the west chimney and the corner turret, sending up a column of fire that scattered burning debris down onto the tops of the surrounding elms. Sharp, sulfur-yellow flames were shooting out the attic windows.

He glanced quickly left and right, searching for a familiar face, but he saw only strangers huddled against the cold in overcoats and pajamas. Police officers were busy herding the onlookers back past a hastily set-up ring of wooden barricades. The fire suddenly made a deep rushing sound, like a heavy wind. Several onlookers cried out, their voices thin and puny in all that noise. Sam shouldered his way up to the barricade. Just as he tried stepping between two sawhorses, a policeman grabbed his arm and, without a word, spun him back around again. "Was anybody in there?" Sam asked. "Was anybody hurt?"

Across the gravel parking lot, someone who must have seen him try-ing to get through began calling out his name repeatedly in a faint, high voice, *"Sam-MEE! Sam-MEE!"* Searching, he saw it was Aunt Libby, standing on the side porch of the little bungalow, waving at him. She had on what looked like one of Waxy's bathrobes, and Nejla and Waxy were there with her, safe and sound. Poor Libby, she must have driven over in her nightgown. He waved back, and she pantomimed for him to stay put—arms out, palms pumping down, down, like an exaggerated *salaam.* "Sta-ay there," her mouth formed the words slowly, carefully. "We're oh-*ka-ay.* Sta-ay ba-ack."

The fire moved as if it knew where it wanted to go and was determined to get there. Leaping from the west wall, it used the carport for a bridge to cross over to the near wing of the L-shaped garage. There, it immediately flared out across the shingles. As the firefighters turned their hoses onto the garage roof, Sam remembered all his tools stored there, and his heart sank. What the fire didn't destroy, the water would.

A moment later he forgot the garage and everything in it as the entire west chimney collapsed onto the turret in a slow cascade. Firefighters scattered, their huge trucks backing up. A tower of sparks rose up where the turret had been, and maybe it was a trick of the airwaves or the roar the fire was making, but the collapse itself seemed almost soundless, something Sam felt more than heard, rumbling his knees like an earthquake.

"Look at that!" A woman in the crowd pointed.

The chimney's tearing away had opened a wide gap in the wall—the siding appeared to be actually curling back from the charred framing studs—to reveal the rear viewing parlor, its contents shimmering and wiggling in the heat, as if behind a pane of warped glass. And, for a second or two, all of it looked intact, the sofas, the Turkish carpets, the heavy Victorian curtains not even smudged.

"Can you be*lieve* that?" the woman in the crowd asked. She was wearing a raincoat over her nightgown, so she must live nearby, but Sam didn't recognize her. Used to be, he knew the entire neighborhood, and yet right now he found himself standing shoulder-to-shoulder in what looked like an entire crowd of strangers. The woman pushed past Sam to ask a policeman standing at the barricade how the fire had started. .

The cop—it was the same one who'd yanked Sam back behind the crowd line—shook his head.

"Syrian lightning," someone in the crowd muttered. "This neighborhood . . ."

Neighborhood? Sam scanned the crowd of strangers gathered across the parking lot, their faces undulating in the heated air. What neighborhood? If you *really* considered the neighborhood, you'd see that nobody could call this Little Syria, not anymore.

But he'd no sooner had this thought than he saw old Aunt Afifie poking her head out of the crowd, her deaf-loud voice piercing the noise of the fire. Then the air quivered, and of course it wasn't Aunt Afifie at all. It was some other old woman who'd probably moved in recently.

And yet, gazing over the crowd, Sam thought for a moment that he'd picked out Uncle Yousef standing on the lawn over by the darkened *In Time of Need* sign. But no, that too was someone else, some stranger raking his hair with the fingers of one hand, just like Uncle Yousef.

Sam closed his eyes and opened them again. It wasn't his eyes playing tricks on him, *he* was.

He could conjure up all of them if he wanted, old Zbaideh with her two pairs of glasses; around a corner of the bungalow Boutros and Boulos walking arm-in-arm together. Why not? That woman across the way, her elbows resting on a wooden barricade? Stare hard enough at her, and she could become Aunt Dorah smiling that mysterious, knowing smile of hers that said, *I foresaw this all in the grounds of a Turkish coffee cup.* And those two women up by the far edge of the driveway, they might be the Abdu sisters, uttering Arabic exclamations of awe at such a fire. And there would be his mother, too, heaving herself up onto the curb—*acch!* and *ouf!*—to join the others gathering there. Around her all of Little Syria, or what was left of it, shimmering in the heated air. And why stop with the living, why not Khaleel, his sad smile and curly-thick hair? *And you, too, Baba.*

Sam watched as the firefighters gave up trying to save the funeral home and turned their hoses onto nearby trees and the roofs of the surrounding houses to keep the fire from spreading. Police began to move the sawhorses even farther back, widening the ring of barricades. A team of paramedics draped yellow slickers over Waxy's shoulders, over Libby's and Nejla's, and led the three of them down the porch steps and across the lawn to a spot farther away from the fire.

When what was left of the roof came crashing down, such an enormous cloud of sparks spun upward that an awed, collective shout arose from the upturned faces. You'd think they were watching a Fourth of July fireworks finale. Even Waxy seemed to enjoy it as he turned to look up in glee, clapping Libby on the shoulder and pointing at the sky.

And Sam felt it too, in a way. Despite himself, he couldn't deny feeling a faint inkling of something like—joy. This didn't surprise him. Mourners at wakes used to mention it all the time, albeit with a measure of guilt, that muted thrill upon recognizing the undeniable message underlying all great loss: *After this, everything will be different.*

# EPILOGUE
## . . . a Recounting

The blaze that erupted at Tammouz & Sons Mortuary on that January night in 1976 had to have started off very hot very fast. Most likely a gas explosion, the fire marshal concluded. It gutted the house, one corner burning down into the brick foundation with such intensity that the basement rooms directly beneath became ovens; glass instruments melted, as did the shells of metal caskets in the display room. After a series of delays getting the gas shut off, the fire department had been able to do little more than concentrate on containment, wetting down surrounding trees and roofs. The preparation room, with its chemical supply cupboards, was where the flames had burned hottest, but investigation determined that the fire's downward burn vector indicated that its point of origin most likely had been the attic. They were even more certain upon learning that there was a working kitchen up there. The slowest gas leak is all it takes, the fire marshal explained to Libby. You shut a place up and let the fumes accumulate, and one day when the conditions are right, "Ka-boom!"

Ka-boom. Right. Whatever the expert says. Sam kept glancing over at Aboodeh to see if he was hearing this. Later, when they were alone, Aboodeh took him aside. "Those looks you keep giving me, I know what you're thinking. But you're wrong."

"Oh, so you're not getting the insurance payoff?"

"I *am* getting it. And it's not as much as you think, either."

"But it's enough to get you off the hook with Larry Morton."

"Barely."

"Then how am I wrong?"

"Sammy, it wasn't me. Not that I wasn't considering it. You bet I was. But I swear to God, it wasn't me. I'm saying I *would've*, yeah. But I didn't." Aboodeh shrugged. "Believe me or don't."

Sam did believe him. In his heart he knew the investigators were right: it was gas, it had started in the attic. In the little kitchen up there.

Less certain, according to the investigators, was the question of whether or not the fire had claimed a life. Combing the ashes, they'd found a scattering of human teeth along with charred fragments of what looked to be human bone, so an official inquiry was opened. "Tammouz & Sons was a family business," Aunt Libby said, and she assured the investigators that everyone in the family was accounted for. Aboodeh claimed to remember a jar of teeth his father might have kept in one of the prep room cupboards. "A little jar. Remember, Dad?" But Uncle Waxy, smiling genially, was no help. One of the investigators had a beard. "Michael Rakosi," he'd introduced himself, but Waxy kept calling him *Aboona*, as if addressing an Orthodox priest. "How about you, Sammy?" Aboodeh asked. "You remember that jar, don't you?" The investigators turned to Sam. No, not really. It was possible, though. The whole place was so cluttered. But something he *did* remember, an entire shelf down there of stored cremains containers.

"Stored what?" Rakosi asked.

"Cremains, the remains after a cremation," Aboodeh explained. "Ashes mostly, sometimes small pieces of bone."

"And sometimes," Sam added, "teeth."

At that the investigators looked at one another and put away their notebooks.

Because nobody had seen Teyib for nearly two weeks before the night of the fire, it never occurred to them that the handful of human remains might possibly have been his. Nobody even brought up his name.

When the yellow tape came down and a bulldozer roared in to finish what the fire had started, Sam stood by on the sidewalk. There was a cold, steady breeze that day, and it kept sending gray ash flying with every thrust and scoop of the toothed shovel. Watching the ashes lift and scatter, Sam muttered *"Inshallah t'slim,"* under his breath, a blessing for the dead. Probably not even the right one, but it was all that came to him. Something for the little guy anyway, a kind of funeral.

In September of that same year, 1976, Sam left for school. On the day of his departure, his mother set out for his lunch a freshly made bowl of *rishta* soup, lentils with roasted noodles in a broth of crushed coriander. "Don't you have it backward, Ma?" *Rishta* was traditionally served to celebrate the *end* of a long journey. She clicked her tongue, *tch!*—old country for *no*, and explained that *rishta* was also served on the occasion of a child's first tooth. Then she smiled and quickly dropped her gaze, as if she'd made a joke.

All summer long he'd kept picturing her alone in this place. No bread baking, no simmering lamb shanks. Just herself, standing at a cold stove, her gas bill unpaid, and the fridge, that groaning, overloaded fridge of hers, empty.

But now that this day had arrived, she seemed to be handling it better than he was. And her fridge wasn't empty yet, he could see that as she packed him a *zoueideh* of leftovers for the road. A woman of her generation never traveled without a *zoueideh* lest, God forbid, her family might have to pay money at a restaurant! And the *zoueideh* was always huge, sometimes requiring two shopping bags, because God forbid her family should have to make do without a taste of cinnamon lamb sauce out there in America. And none of them ever left for a road trip without first blessing the car. Most households kept a little bottle of holy water stored away, which they refilled at the church fonts. Mama's special reserve came from Our Lady of Consolation shrine in Carey.

Mama took the stairs sideways, descending them one step at a time, left foot right foot, pause; left foot right foot, pause. Every movement an effort for her. One hand on the banister, the other clutching the little bottle of holy water.

Praying in Arabic, she stepped around the car and sprinkled each tire (wetting the left front twice, Sam noticed, and missing the right front entirely—but he didn't correct her), then the steering wheel, and finished by flinging—up to down, right to left—a wet cross upon the hood.

When Mama was finished, she embraced Sam one last time, then stood waiting on the pavement. He turned the key in the ignition, and she solemnly held up her right hand for the final blessing, thumb and two fingers joined. Her lips moved as she crossed the air before her in two slow sweeps, like a patriarch. When she finished, her hand opened up, fingers fluttering, and her blessing became a wave goodbye.

Columbus was only a couple hours' drive from home, but that short step away would lead to another whole series of steps away—to Nashville for medical school, residency in Chicago, and when his studies proved more expensive than even Libby had anticipated, to the Northern Plains, where he signed on to a federal program for rural areas in need of doctors. During a stint on a reservation in South Dakota, he learned that nearby Rapid City had once courted Al Capone, offering him refuge at a time when Chicago's newly elected mayor had shut him out. How Uncle Waxy would have liked to have heard about that. To everyone's surprise, Waxy survived Tammouz & Sons by several years. When the end did come, the news didn't reach Sam in time for the funeral—he was away on a camping trip with Rita, a graduate student from a nearby ag college—and after he did finally make it home, he found Aunt Nejla so distracted with grief that she seemed to have forgotten that he'd ever left town in the first place. Day and night she sat in the parlor of the little bungalow, softly nodding her head as if in agreement with something; perhaps the foreknowledge that by the time the summer was out she would be rejoined with her husband and her elder son, Khaleel.

Aboodeh sold his parents' little bungalow and used the money for a down payment on a house far from the North End, in Sylvania, a suburb of Toledo. Shortly after that, to no one's surprise, Salma divorced him, and he moved into an apartment up near the Michigan line. On Sam's visits back, Aboodeh would take him for drives through the old neighborhood. One Christmas, his cousin described a new venture he was embarking on, a cemetery lot care program that would provide the "missing link in the perpetual care industry." The concept was simple: while cemeteries only mow the grass, his franchise would see to everything else—making arrangements with gardeners, florists and other maintenance workers to trim around tombstones, repair damage from vandalism, plant flowers and shrubbery, remove graffiti. For a single, up-front fee, the company would maintain a grave for twenty-five years. "Previous to now it was family members who tended the graves," he said, "but today, families are dispersed. And that's the real selling point." He looked excited, as if he believed his own words. Salesmen, they say, are their own best customers.

In the space of a very few years, an entire generation passed away. It seemed as if on Sam's every visit home, Aboodeh had a new loss to report: Aunt Afifie, then Uncle Yousef, both Abdu sisters within weeks of one another, Aunt Zbaideh, old Boutros who was laid out, per his wishes, with a cigar in his hands instead of a rosary.

Libby retired as head of Tammouz Enterprises. Shortly after, Gene Moon closed the carryout and moved the business out to the suburb of Maumee, where, sensing a burgeoning trend, he reopened as a purveyor of fine wines to the carriage trade. The Yankee Cafe was sold off, but otherwise remained pretty much the same. Having coffee there during a visit home, Sam told Aboodeh that Rita, his girlfriend, was almost finished with school and had been offered a position in Minnesota with a large agri-tech firm. Sam laughed, "You can't call them seed companies anymore!" His smile faded. "Anyway, if she goes ahead and takes it . . ."

"You're gonna follow her there."

Sam nodded. In fact, he'd already had an interview at the St. Clare Clinic. "It's a great place, and I think they want me." He explained that the clinic was nicknamed "Little Mayo" because of its proximity to that famous medical center. "And the myth that that's where all its doctors went to school."

"By the way, did you see this?" Aboodeh took a *Time Magazine* out of his jacket pocket and showed Sam a passage he'd highlighted in yellow marker. It was an article about Brigitte Bardot, and the passage was about the war in Lebanon and how much she missed visiting her favorite restaurant there, where the waiters catch your fish after you order.

Sam laughed. "Well, what do you know."

The waitress working the booths came by to top their coffees. After she'd moved on, Sam asked about Nikki.

"Married," Aboodeh said. "And divorced. Not all that long after you left for school."

"Who to?"

"Nobody we'd know," he said. "Some guy from up in Michigan where she used to live." Aboodeh blew on his coffee. "Works at a bank up there. A loan officer. Broke up his marriage for her." He put down his coffee mug and gave Sam one of his level looks. "You had a close call there, Cuz."

"We both did, Bud." Sam shook his head. "What're the odds."

"What're the odds," Aboodeh echoed.

In medical school Sam had been taught to go with the odds. To trust in numbers and percentages. Cancer metastasizing to the liver and brain, untreated, maximum three months from date of diagnosis. Those were the numbers. Which is why he would laugh whenever the numbers were thwarted, or seemed to be, at places like Lourdes and Fatima, at Medjugorje, and even at little Carey, Ohio. Our hopes tell us one thing, but we deny logic at our peril.

Back in the old country the war would go on for another fifteen years as one peace accord after another failed. Out of a population of three million, more than a hundred and fifty thousand people would be killed, most of them noncombatant civilians; another hundred thousand would be permanently handicapped. Nearly one million left homeless or displaced; tens of thousands kidnapped and disappeared. The last two hostages would not be released until 1992.

Those were the numbers.

The year Sam accepted a position at the St. Clare Clinic, he brought Rita home to meet everyone. How strange it felt to climb the staircase of his childhood alongside her, and to see her seated across Mama's enamel-topped kitchen table with its view of pigeons and flat tarred roofs.

That she loved his mother's cooking didn't surprise Mama so much as how this little red-headed stick of a girl managed to polish off two helpings of her *menazleh* stew. "Take care," she warned him in Arabic, in front of Rita, "lest this one grow fat!" In English, she offered to show Rita how to prepare *menazleh* stew.

Reluctantly, Rita admitted that she had never really been very handy in the kitchen. "Love to eat, but never really enjoyed cooking."

Mama had to sit down. Turning to Sam, she had to think the words in Arabic before changing them over to English for Rita's benefit. "Then this one here," she said, indicating her son, "he gonna hafta do it, the cooking."

When it was time to leave, Mama saw them to the door. Standing at the top of the stairs, she embraced Rita, then stage-whispered to Sam, in English, "A good girl!"

Those were the last words he would hear from her lips. Shortly after that visit, Mama suffered a stroke while sitting at her window above the empty store. Libby reached Sam at the clinic, while he was dictating the day's charts. Rita hurriedly packed him a bag, and he drove through the night, arriving to find his mother unconscious and the death watch already begun. As a physician he knew what was being done to ease her going, the drugs, the supposed anesthetic effects of dehydration. And when it was all over, he also knew what was being done to her at Doyle's to prepare for viewing. In keeping with her instructions, Mama had been dressed in the rose-colored outfit she'd picked out for herself in anticipation of when she would no longer be expected to wear widow's black. Baba's photograph was pinned to her breast like a corsage. Kneeling, Sam propped a small framed picture of himself next to her elbow. And there they were again, according to her last wishes, the three of them together.

At the visitation he stood near the casket receiving people and thanking them for their condolences. They turned and looked into the casket, some of them crossing themselves before kneeling to pay a moment's silent respect. Rising, more than a few commented favorably on how good she looked, how peaceful. For this, too, Sam thanked them. Then, before they moved on into the lounge where coffee and sweets had been laid out by the Altar Sodality, most of them would linger as if waiting for something else.

Sam knew what for. At Tammouz & Sons they used to call it "the recounting," and what it amounted to was a relating of the departed's final moments, told in response to that one question, implied if not asked outright, that visitors usually feel compelled to pose: How did it happen?

"He seemed okay after supper," a widow's recounting might begin, "but around eight o'clock he complained of a little heartburn. For dinner that night I cooked him *tobagh roho,* the eggplant casserole. I told him to take some Tums. He was reading the paper. I was in the kitchen, finishing the dishes and before I knew it I heard a noise . . ."

Dishes. The paper. Recountings are laced with the ordinary, the day-to-day, yet these are the things that visitor after visitor asks to hear about. Although some might discourage such constant telling and retelling as burdensome to the widow, at Tammouz & Sons Waxy held that the recounting is in itself a consolation. How else to comprehend an event as startling as a miracle, and that, like a miracle, promises to change everything that comes after it? That someone you touched every day with your body, someone whose clothes are still in the closet you shared, whose hair is still on your pillowcases and in your drains, is forever gone, forever and ever and ever—how can we begin to grasp such a thing? Only human nature, then, that we feel obliged to render it back into the realm of the ordinary, to recount that which our eyes and ears were witness to.

So Sam did his best in relating Mama's final morning, the way her fingers fluttered with the minor strokes that had begun assailing her, the brief moments of seeming alertness and that one, sudden, bright look she gave him, beatific, almost a smile. What else was there to say? In the fullness of her years, with a loved one at her side and in no discernible pain, she experienced what the nuns in school must have meant by a happy death, the kind they used to tell you to pray to St. Joseph for.

And beyond that? He let the visiting Melkite Rite bishop who officiated at Mama's funeral take it beyond that, figuring his guess was probably as good as anybody else's. The man wore a black veiled pillbox hat and what looked and sounded like large golden jingle bells sewn along the hem of his robe. His beard was white, meticulously trimmed. He delivered the funeral homily in High Arabic. Mama would have been impressed, although Sam understood hardly a word of it.

At the mercy meal afterward, he saw new faces among the familiar, the children and grandchildren of cousins. Libby took him around, introducing him to his own relatives. "Nobody makes grape leaves like this anymore!" one cousin announced as he forked another helping onto his plate. (His name was Ryan, or maybe Brian . . . and *maybe* he was a cousin.) The grape leaves were laid out on platters in tight little rolls served hot alongside ice-cold tangy yogurt. Sam couldn't help taking a measure of pride in the compliment since he had helped make them, working far into last night, he and several of the older women. He'd joined in against their protests. Sleepless anyway, he was grateful for something to busy his mind. They must have made an odd picture, the half-dozen of them in their flowered and polka-dotted aprons, there amid the professional stainless-steel equipment of the church kitchen as they wilted the fresh leaves, filled and rolled and boiled them, pot after pot after pot, stacked them in alternating tiers between layers of sliced lemon, drizzled the stacks with olive oil.

~

## THE OTHER SIDE

*"It'll happen before you know it," Sam tells his daughter. "You'll see."*

*"Daddy!" Libby is learning to roll grape leaves, and she's growing more discouraged by the minute, and not without reason. Her last effort resembles a stubby, half-exploded cigar.*

*"Just keep at it," he tells her. He has charts waiting for him at the office but he resists the urge to hurry her. "You'll get the hang of it."*

*"Sure I will—when I'm forty!" She is in fact fourteen. Her hands are still baby-dimpled.*

*"Your hands will learn before you do," he says.*

*"How?"*

*"Remember learning to ride a bike? One minute I was running alongside, keeping you balanced, and after a bit you looked and I wasn't there? You were riding a bike before you knew it."*

*"Daddy, I fell. Remember?"*

*"Only after you looked and saw I wasn't there anymore. Up till then you were riding on your own. Your arms and legs already knew what to do. Same thing with grape leaves. It's all in the hands. C'mon now, try again. Veiny side up, a small spoonful of stuffing. Smaller than that."*

*These grape leaves are for her older sister, just starting her freshman year and already homesick. St. Paul isn't so far away, but to hear Leila on the phone last night, you'd think it was the other side of the world.*

*"How did you learn to make grape leaves, from Sitti?"*

*"My mom was a terrific cook, but no, these are my cousin Teyib's grape leaves. The stuffing recipe, even how we're rolling them, just the way he rolled them."*

*"He? A guy showed you how to make these?"*

*"And why not?" Sam lets his voice project a greater offense than he actually feels. "A guy's showing you right now."*

*Libby rolls her eyes at that, but she does try another grape leaf, and with more success. Then another.*

*"Better."*

*With each try her fingers seem to grow more confident. Teyib's grape leaves? Not for long. Tomorrow, when they are packed in ice and ready for shipping, these will be Libby's grape leaves.*

*His fingers still have on them the faint tang of lemon. Soap never seems to get it out completely, not even the Chloroxylenol they use here at the clinic. Some nights after he's cooked, Rita will turn to him in bed and taste the garlic on his fingers. "You're delicious," she says.*

*Now, Dictaphone mike in hand, he glances briefly at his notes then fixes his gaze on the narrow, moonlit window of his office.*

*". . . While on beclomethasone inhaler 3 puffs b.i.d. indications no*

distress period. HEENT exam comma nose was mildly boggy without purulance or polyps period."

*Back at home, his daughter's grape leaves are finished, cooked and cooled and stored away in the refrigerator, ready for sending to her sister at college. Libby might be asleep by now, and Rita would be in her study off the great room, putting the finishing touches on the presentation she's giving at a conference next week. Sam, too, needs to finish up so they can all have tomorrow together. Some nights dictating charts goes quickly. You talk so fast into the mike that you don't even listen to yourself. You get into a groove.*

"TMS were normal period oral pharynx was clear period. Neck was supple comma lungs comma CTAP comma heart RR and R period."

*In the doctors' lounge they talk sometimes about how it is dictating alone at night in your office, what a temptation it can be to slip in a joke or a too-candid observation. Someday soon this will all be digitized, but for now the tapes of dictation are sent to the clinic's basement typing pool, where, every morning, they are listened to by one of the dozen or so medical transcriptionists—all of them women. One transcriptionist is usually assigned the same handful of doctors so that she gets to know their voices, their pronunciations, and the patterns of their speech. Dropping in a pun or a joke is like putting a message in a bottle and sending it downstream. Will she recognize your joke, or will it get typed automatically into the medical record? It's tempting, trying to get a laugh out of a woman who listens to your voice day after day, a woman you've never seen. This allergist, he has a sense of humor, you want her to say to herself, the allergist with that hint of an accent from somewhere or other. Is it Middle Eastern? He's human, he has feelings about what he does.*

*Outside a wind has kicked up. It swirls shadows in patterns over his white shirt. His hip aches from sitting so long, and he shifts position.*

*On the corkboard above his desk, suspended from a pushpin, is Uncle Waxy's djrab il khirdee. When Sam visited last summer, he'd helped Aboodeh move Aunt Libby into a nursing home. Opening her bedside drawer, she'd lifted the djrab il khirdee by its braided string and asked them if they knew what it was. In a hurry to get out of there, Aboodeh shook his head as if to say Don't remind me. What he didn't get was that she'd asked in earnest. She really didn't remember.*

"It used to be Uncle Waxy's," Sam replied. Then asked if he might have it.

"What for, habibi?"

"To remember him by," he'd said.

He shuts off the Dictaphone.

To remember all of them by. Because that first step away took them all the way away. None of them thought it would. Booking passage, they simply hung their luck like this talisman around their necks and boarded for a new land. There, no matter whether they embraced America or held back, one morning, kaan makaan, they awoke to find themselves at home, but still here, on the other side of the world. And this fact, like a death or a birth, is a marvel they are obliged to remark. It came upon us unawares, they tell one another, this change as terrible and as wonderful as a miracle, and it needs recounting, how we left the old country and became Americans, how it happened before we knew it.

TEXT DESIGN BY PAULA NEWCOMB

TYPESETTING BY DELMASTYPE, ANN ARBOR, MICHIGAN

TEXT FONT: FAIRFIELD LH

Fairfield is a fifty-year-old typeface that has had a recent facelift. Rudolph Ruzicka, artist and book illustrator, designed light and medium weights of Fairfield for Linotype in 1940 and 1949, respectively. For Fairfield's 1991 release as an electronic typeface, designer Alex Kaczun added bold and heavy weights, he also added small capitals and old style figures, swash capitals, and a set of "caption" typefaces (sloped roman style). With its straight, unbracketed serifs and abrupt contrast between thin and thick strokes, Fairfield harks back to the modern typefaces of Bodoni and Didot, but has a distinctly twentieth-century look.

# Who Sleeps with Katz

Also by Todd McEwen

*Fisher's Hornpipe*

*McX*

*Arithmetic*

# Who Sleeps with Katz

Todd McEwen

**Granta Books**
London

Granta Publications, 2/3 Hanover Yard, London N1 8BE

First published in Great Britain by Granta Books 2003

A CIP catalogue record for this book is
available from the British Library.

1 3 5 7 9 10 8 6 4 2

ISBN 1 86207 613 8

Typeset in Perpetua by M Rules
Printed and bound in Great Britain by
Mackays of Chatham PLC

To Lucy Ellmann

*This girl is almost awkward, carrying off*
*The lintel of convention on her shoulders,*
*A Doric river-goddess with a pitcher*
*of ice-cold wild emotions*

—Louis MacNeice, *The Kingdom*

*You've got to think of everything.*

—Louis-Ferdinand Céline


*A guy can't always be thinking.*

—Tom Kromer

# The Old Mental Capital

*Well, I am often taken for a Yale man, by Yale men. That pleases me*
*a little, because I like Yale best of all the colleges.*

—John O'Hara, *BUtterfield 8*

—have you ever heard anything so stupid? said MacK. You know what I mean—the whole problem in this god damned town was never hippies, yippies, yiddies, dippies, nimbies, dinkies, darkies, dorkies, chinkies, hunkies, yuppies, eyeties or The Yankees—the problem has always been *Yalies*. If only they would stay in New Haven, and hadn't been led to believe they have any need or ability to poke their pusses into New York's affairs, or a *duty*, yes a duty to jump into their J. Press pajamas and run the Stock Exchange, some God-given seat awaiting them . . . —You don't have to shout, said Isidor, I know what you're . . . —I mean this is the pernicious thing, said MacK, perhaps really the only pernicious thing in New York—I'm really not kidding—Yale. *Yale* and its *foreign insistence* on maintaining whiteness at the altars of, in the citadels of power—I'm telling you it's the one thing which prevents New York from running *utterly smoothly*, man, the dream of polyglot democracy that it is and must become.

—Polyglot! said Isidor. Pretty big word for a guy who hadda be excused from his foreign language requirement. —Yes, which it *must become*, said MacK, his famous vocal cords hitting the perfect resonating frequency of the carbon diaphragm in the telephone on the marble table—the achievement that must mock the rest of this country for what it is—that *does* mock. It. —Why are you quoting John O'Hara to me at eight o'clock in the morning? said Isidor. —Well, there is a point, said MacK, I was looking at it last night.

1

He's part of this White Culture which I'm just completely at the end of my—I'm flabbergasted and unable to comprehend any longer why and how anyone can continue to defend it, celebrate it, re-invent it—what does this great white culture, this white civilization, which all the idiots want to cherish, to keep pristine from the blacks and the Japanese and the Europeans and the gays and the Jews and the women—of what does it consist? I mean, let's really think—John O'Hara? Pearl Jam? Lawrence Welk? Elementary school book and Bible watercolor depictions of the past? CBS? —Not leaving out *your* great employer, said Isidor.

—The Carpenters, said MacK, Fenimore Cooper, John Grisham? Red Skelton? Hallmark, Microsoft? Mobil? Bill Clinton? Jane Fonda, Walt Disney, American Gladiators? Pat Robertson, Gene Scott? John Willie? Loni Anderson? Jaclyn Smith? The AFL? I'm asking you, man, said MacK, I mean I'm asking all of the religionists and cross-burners and anti-abortionists and professional athletes and cheerleaders and militiamen prancing through the woods in camo, waving Bowie knives and their third grade spelling, I'm *asking* the gymnastic child-abuse coaches—*this* is what you've got? THIS?

—Yeah, yeah, I know, said Isidor. What *I* got is a gut with no coffee in it. Whadda you got? —Oh, well, he called . . . —You mean the doctor called? —Yeah. —Yes and? —Hm. News for you. —So! Gee Whizz, it . . . —Let's meet up about six. —Where? —The Hour? —Okay. All right.

—Aside from my rambling and now, for me, useless analysis of the ills of New York, that call was an absolute *hymn* to male brevity, said MacK. He looked out the window in abstraction. —This music is not blending with the traffic, he said. —*What's* the matter? said the Non-Anglophone.

The jazz wasn't working with his view of the Drive. Rain dark-ened the pavement and tail-lights shone on it in a way which usually pleased him. There were still bright trees in the park. All his life he had been pursuing a soundtrack, yet he balked at the *literal* application of it, those things you stick in your ears that go sss! sss! sss! sss! until you think you must go mad. He just liked looking out of the window and playing the correct record, or to carry the music in his head. What do you think is the meaning of this? Is it composition of a new sort? —You could make a piece, he mused aloud, for pre-recorded Bach, low-angle sunlight and falling leaves. And the stagehands have a script so that the leaves fall the same way each time. —Très arty, she said. —Would you cut that out? said MacK, you're not from France. —You don't know where I'm from. —Yes I do. —What's going on out there? —'Light rain', as we say on the radio. —Untie me? I want to see.

This recalled him to himself and his surroundings. His small pink 'music' room, the only one in his apartment which faced Riverside Drive. The marble café table from Paris and the inguinal hernia it represented. Coffee and bread and butter. The cat in the chair opposite the one she was bound to. The cat adored her. It jumped down and rubbed against her restricted ankles. —Sorry, he said. He loosened the ropes round her ankles, and calves, and thighs, and wrists. He wore his usual black shoes and trousers, white shirt, black waistcoat and long white apron. She hadn't spent the night but had only just come upstairs for breakfast, which he'd fed her. —Can I get you something else? he said. —No, she smiled. Just the check. She stood in her high shoes and looked out the window.

For rain and snow you need brushwork. That or Bach. You need cool jazz if nothing else is to hand. You need Ed Thigpen. *There are moments when you need Ed Thigpen*. But where *was* Ed Thigpen when you needed him? Mr Taste. But today of all days . . . —Do you know what was funny about jazz? said she. The explosion of people named Benny. Blowing into things. Was that not a surprise to everyone? The Bennies? Suddenly thousands of pieces of the shellacs and hundreds of people named Benny exist. No? Formerly an outré name, a name of a man with a gun. Also, later, Oscar.

He found some Bill Evans in which there were brushes.

—What's the *exact* relationship of jazz to traffic? he said. —Of course I do not know, and neither do you, she said, but if you get the right music it will always look right. I love it best for the evening cocktail this month, and all winter long. You always balance the lights with the outside. And the martini. The sushi. And dear cat, she said, tickling it. For breakfast I think it a little nicer in the summer, I like that, the coffee with the window open so you keep discovering the aroma maybe in the breeze?

This music reminded MacK of West 58th Street, the old studios there. How the nightly iterations of the show's orchestra fused with the slim traffic and particular lights of that street. West 58th felt like a *New Yorker* cover in the Seventies, or maybe the *New Yorker* imposed that. They impose so much.

Cars left colors behind them like leaves; the rain shaped them. Music will stop time in the city occasionally. But always there is duty.

He looked at the taxis especially, yellow against the black road and green and red of the park. He put on Lester Young's 'I Didn't Know What Time it Was'. —Bye bye, she said. She kissed him on the neck and tickled the cat, put her coat on over her lurid, unbreakfast attire and went out through the kitchen and down the back stairs chez elle.


The usual folderol extricating himself from the doorman before he heard something utterly stupid. He was sure that he caught something damaging out of the corner of his ear as he fled up the side street towards Broadway.

# Upper Broadway

It's about my first love, he said, looking up at the traffic light—it changed and he stepped off the curb. When he first came to this neighborhood the stop lights were old, with only red and green lamps—no yellow—they trusted you back then. They thought you were an adult who could make up your mind. When he discovered the stop lights, he had immediately wished them older again, of the type which gonged and put out a little flag STOP or GO. Never had been much to say about these few blocks, the incredible merchants who surround a university, selling knock-offs of fashionable shoes, roach traps for twice what anyone pays in the rest of the world or even below 110th Street. It is likely, MacK thought, that a sandwich costs fifty dollars here now.

The bar where he and Isidor learned to drink gone for years, replaced by the hamburger chain where no one learns anything, though they study misery. Here is the hardware store where he did buy his first roach trap, here still the small grocery where a wild-haired man caressed your hand in giving change, baggy eyes shifting. All in all a gentle introduction to town, one roach and one pervert.

Paused a block south. Had thought there wasn't much to do with him and Isidor here, had thought that for a long while, but how? It hadn't been the university neighborhood to MacK for years, not till today. That was where the bar had been, and here was where we learned to smoke, where we took it up seriously for good and all, MacK thought—ruing it, and ruing that he had drawn Isidor into it.

## THE CITY SPEAKS:
## OF COURSE WE SELL TOBACCO SIR.

Their first purchases here at Ben and Nat's—the yellow pouches of 'Teddy', MacK's calabash with a porcelain bowl—ah, later Nat and Phil's after Ben *succumbed* to his self-prescribed ten imitation Habanas i.d., which they all thought ironic and even—funny.

Now that my lung cancer is here, has *finally arrived*, MacK thought, tipping his proverbial hat to those who had predicted proverbially it would—including himself and his loving, paranoid parents, whom he would now precede in death—he set himself the task, on this walk, of deciding, as a poetic and furious concept, which cigarette in the whole world had given it to him.

**30 cigarettes per day × 365 days × 25 years
= 273,750 cigarettes,**

of which how many might you recall? But it is axiomatic among tumor-
ologists that it is not 273,750 cigarettes that you puffed away to
nothing, rain or shine, yours or someone else's—and what does *that*
matter? —you going to go find them? Blame them? They won't even
remember, you, Bud—filter or no, happy or sad—but *just one*, a single
speck of a fleck of smoke from one mean-minded piece of horticulture.

*Really, quite a lot has to do with the old neighborhood.* MacK thought
that it could have been the *first* cigarette he ever really smoked, a
'True' (Blue) in the resonant, tiled bathroom his sophomore year,
where he declaimed Chaucer on advice, and became an
Announcer—but *smoked* in imitation of his Renaissance professor,
who exhaled the pure thought which killed scholasticism oddly and
ironically in this smoke. *Ass Hole (Blue). Ass Hole (Green).* But what bad
luck that would be—it wasn't fun enough for MacK's poetic and
furious concept.

He'd told the doctor he wouldn't want to fight it, and with some
repugnance, an attitude which seemed to be left over from the
national treatment of *conscientious objectors*, the doctor agreed to
send MacK to another who 'sympathized' with patients who, *inexplicably*, believed that when your number is up, it is up. A physician
who would help MacK manage, at least experience, if not enjoy, his
dying, rather than frustrate it, filling his last months with a lot of
morpheated *pep talk*. (You read the papers.)

—*You want a doctor that sympathizes.* —Yeah—scuse *me*.

When he was twenty-five, his hated long-time family doctor told
MacK he would contract it, just as *he* had. Good news! It was his
last appointment with the man—and in fact MacK was his last
patient. Good! —Why do you think I should get this too? said
MacK —*Because you're a bitter little shit just like I am.*

Cold breath of the river up 114th Street; a wink of frost bright on
the stones of the park, which MacK could see beyond the building

on the north corner down there, where he'd lived for a year. It is remarkable how you cannot remember your personal history of every thing and every place in town—you'd go nuts—even though you touch upon these every day. The cold burnt-coffee smell of the West Side in winter. The airshaft apartment he'd thought grand, and the depressing fact that the girl he would spend ten years getting over had moved into the *next building*, that he could actually see her fluorescent desk lamp—which he had loved—far below his kitchen window. The many wind-cooled hopes of Riverside Drive.

But it *was* with her that he'd smoked one of the first. An endless, cried-over salad of the 1970s—you remember them. You know the feeling of the new-democratic gourmet foods sticking in your throat—*quiche lorraine, guacamole, Mateus*—all this crap jamming up your gullet was why everyone constantly burst into tears between 1970 and 1980. In a dark steak and ale emporium—Lincoln Center, to his dismay. —Buy us some cigarettes, she suddenly said, I could do with some raunch—as if she'd awakened to the fact that she was playing a part—the Breakup Scene—they were suddenly to be adult, *to wallow in their own disaster*. Always good news. But how had their tenderness become raunchy, he thought—his tears, though splashed on a lot of turkey and Swiss cheese, were *genuine*.

She looked cute with the 'Kent' and it tortured his sense of loss. 'Kents' from a machine! —which he never smoked again because of that deep, turbulent scene in that dark stupid place—also because 'Kents' smell of the shit-heaps in burning termite nests.

'*The* Broadway?' someone'd written him when first MacK came to town—how seldom you think of Broadway with the name ringing; just a long street with an intense multiple personality disorder. Was Broadway, in midtown even, ever conceived to be glamorous any more? Who has stranger ideas, SAILORS or PEOPLE FROM OHIO? All anyone *thunderstruck* by the word Broadway needs for the disabusement of magic—and they do need this—is a stroll down Broadway in the 100s, thought MacK, as he waded through discount shops, bales of socks, misspellings: Shot of *Whisey* 50¢. But having not walked in the 100s since returning to the neighborhood he was a little surprised that the university had managed to drive wedges of pretense into the place—now there was *espresso for white people*; before there was merely Cuban coffee—for everybody.

At 103rd Street MacK looked again toward the river; halfway down the block on the left was an apartment he and Izzy shared during the Bitterly Cold Winter of 1977, as the newspapers were calling it in November already. Their bankrupt landlord rasped at them through the mouth of the receiver—the Official Receiver—they wouldn't get any heating oil unless they paid their rent—and they said they weren't going to pay any rent unless they got heating oil RIGHT NOW; also the ceiling of MacK's room was like unto a sieve. —That's no reason not to pay, said the Official Receiver. —I can't think of a better one, said MacK. Isidor grabbed the phone and announced he had begun to 'chop up', as he put it, the Mission style oak furniture in the living-room and was burning it in the massive Hugh M Hefner exposed brick hearth of the place—it seemed a Playboy Mansion for cockroaches. —I'm freezing, he said to the Receiver, and that is the sound of your client's dining ensemble warming me up—the oil truck arrived within the hour; the stains of the guy's heaving splattering rush are on the sidewalk still.

MacK had smoked some 'Camels' in that apartment when he and Isidor had the idea of taking Broadway by storm. The theater district, not the 100s. Remembered a number of snow afternoons with the 'Camels' in a holder—which always outraged Iz.


—I'll tell you right now, said MacK to himself, but aloud, in a conscious nod to Isidor, perhaps, today—which cigarette it had better *not* be—any of the damp cigarettes offered me by any god damned drunk *Brit*. Those are the people to get you really smoking, not *play* smoking. Of *course* I'm blaming them! he said to a woman coming out of the smallest laundromat in the world—he remembered it well—they smoke all the time, no sense of STYLE, they call their cigarettes *hairy rags* and to set seal on themselves as the *ashtrays of Europe*, they will actually *talk about death*, thus courting it, while handing them around—not in the *Think on this when ye smoak tobacco*, cut-down-at-eve sense but in grunting through their 'arses' about everything being out of your control so you might as well just 'top' yourself! 'MATE!'—the whole United Kingdom one lost, blurry empire of cut silk.

Fuming now, approaching 96th—the familiar large street tube poured out clouds like a big 'True' (Blue). The big idiot off whom MacK had taken literally a hundred 'Marlboros' in the McAnn's near Herald Square always said the same thing as he, smiling, opened the flap, politely pulled one cigarette an inch up from its fellows, and pointed the pack at MacK like a Luger: *I'm not going to go alone*. Well, said MacK, you haven't. But it would be better if you had. For me.

—But what about every stunk-out bar where I *haven't* smoked? he said. What of that? And what about those who have bored the crap out of me, offering me thousands of cigarettes late into the nights I was loveless—and now your filthy 'pretty smokes' have killed me, what of that? And stopped to get his breath, leaning on the stone ledge at the entrance to the IRT, seeing himself doing it at the same moment—seeing a man who couldn't walk, who couldn't get his breath—*such as you might see*. Implored the god of the IRT—here it was, for worship, succor, or at least for transport off this scene.

## The Gods of Town

*Most dreadfully sorry* but we don't care, do we, what is going on out there in that god damn country. We got our own problems in this our town—we have needs; *'People have NEEDS!'*—we want to LIVE—whereas nobody out *there* can sound a solitary *fart* about being alive—that god damn country is only about death, living death. Consequently we have our own systems of belief. Where is 'Jesus' and that crowd, we would like to know, when you are twenty minutes late for a meeting, it has just begun to hail, *painful* big stones, there are no cabs and no public telephones, there is no scarf, no UMBRELLA maybe! This is *important*. This is your *life*. Well—he is not there. But here are these little telephones, the new guardians of our existence—in shape so like the lares and penates of old—they even cradle themselves, benign and observant, in their own altar in the home. Here is the IRT. Here is the doorman.

How *not* to worship as gods, that is the question, the lady who brings you coffee, the delicatessen with the most reliable head cheese in the world, the sturdy humming motor of the elevator which lands you with a soft kiss on the floor where your meeting is? What of the utility and lovable, dependable stimulus of the Non-Anglophone's goatskin boots? We don't *take for granted* the egg cream, the smell of roasting chestnuts, the umbrella-vendor, fresh shellfish, the No. 1 train, the many Restaurant Martinis of quality, the surpassing fresh cigars—we *worship them here* because THESE ARE THE GODS THAT DELIVER.

Modern life demands flexibility, does it not? Even the *Romans*, a people hardly renowned for their *tolerance*, were happy to take on a new god that seemed useful, wherever they went. They looked into the local religion, gathered its gods to them, and worshipped them with enthusiasm and respect right away! OK they enslaved and murdered the *people*, but they liked all kinds gods!

Of course there are some gods which are simply too exalted for the men and women who crawl like dogs, like *bugs on the street*, to petition directly: the IRT, City Hall, the gas company, the guy who brings seltzer, what the hell is his problem anyway? But in New York, *and only in New York*, you have the freedom to order your pantheon as you will. You like George Bellows better than the man with the THING under his eye at the deli, FINE. And you can mass your gods in order to petition the big boys—there may *be* a way of contacting the gas company through George Bellows and bourbon on the rocks. Set up your altar and do it. We don't bother with CHURCHES.

Like the guy said, in mythic thinking 'distinctions between natural forces and social conventions are not clearly perceived'. Oh, BUDDY! Isn't that your life in New York in a f***ing NUT SHELL? We need more of this fine mythic thinking.

MacK's patient attention to the gods of town had spawned a renascence of painting and sculpture—you see he *suits himself*—which he assigned conveniently to pre-existing public works of art: the monument to the martyrs of the *Maine* at Columbus Circle was for him a kind of ancestor screen, the little gold guys various uncles, aunts, teachers and cartoon characters in decreasing order of favor. He could in Central Park delight in a blindfold *William Powell* [the chief god of Manhattan life] *Riding the Porpoise of Gin*. *Bette Davis* [his female counterpart] *Crowns Johnny Carson with the Wreath of Morpheus*. And the great tableau beloved of us all, near the boat basin, *The Polizei Welcome Mass Transit to Brooklyn with Eros and a Pomeranian while Abe Beame Beckons to Dionysus behind a Cheeseburger Wrapper*.

In classic and agreeable fashion, Central Park is a god and also the *abode* of the god.

—

Hundreds and thousands of TREES connect our island with the heavens.

We got complicated gods: the Chrysler Building, the Metropolitan Opera, the Board of Estimate, the Port Authority (Gee Whizz!). We got simple: eggs scrambled with calf brains by Hungarians on a winter morning, drums, *toupees* (the garment district their HQ). We got subterranean rivers from the old Underworld.

'The altar or the inscription could be carved with the figure of the god or with the symbols of the god's powers.' Take a look at your COCKTAIL NAPKIN!

We got the all-seeing sun and the moon which peeks at you when you're doing something you shouldn't maybe. We got all kinds statues replete with divinity.

We have our Mayors: divine kingship is a form of polytheism.

And—sadly—our gods are countered by demonic forces. The IRT wrestles with quite a few—no names need be named but there is sometimes a powerful demon at work in the token-booth at 50th Street. Wears a dirty blue shirt. The weather, in February, is a demon—or at least a bitch. There is Asbestos. There is the guy who lived upstairs from Isidor with the dogs. The dogs themselves. F***—*all dogs.* AND, as a kind of Miltonian-size *counter* to all the striving, scheming, smoking, buying, selling, thinking, stinking, drinking and LOVING in this our town, there is, across the river, NEW JERSEY. So it's a struggle—what isn't?

We *believe* in the power of objects—why else would we cut up our credit cards, remove the license plates from the car we abandon at 128th Street and the West Side Highway, throw *pennies*—malign, time-wasting demons—into the GARBAGE, if not to quell their powers when we no longer need or want them?

Why do you take a complimentary ballpoint pen from one restaurateur and not the other?

*Some* people place their cheeseburger wrapper in the gutter rather than the litter bin—they believe, obviously, that there in the gutter its magic will be sapped, rather than amassing new, rebellious and rowdy powers in the confined space of the bin with its *partners in chaos*.

If you will take a moment to observe us, with charity, you will see that we are indeed all of us a-worshipping these gods. In this our town. The stern old gods are gone. They got 'mono'—then they died!

In the RCA Building, one of MacK's gods, lived many of his others: microphones, light bulbs, the mischievous god which hovered for him around things made of stone. The great god Radio of course and her nemesis Television. Under Nancy Schwartz's little suits, the gods of silk and night and just-possible orgasm. But of the thousand reasons MacK loved the RCA Building, the proud container of his little struggle to exist, the most salient and wonderful was that Rockefeller Center celebrated, perpetuated the great, meaning gods of the ancient world, Prometheus, Poseidon, Atlas—and others of recent memory, Washington and Lincoln (both deified to the point of unreachability), the steam locomotive, burly-armed linotype operators on the altar of the Associated Press Building . . . even the glory of the American Girl in a skating skirt.

Defy you to identify a glossier chamber of the HEART OF CAPITALISM, and smack dab in the middle of it is an ecstatic swirl of the best of gods. What theism could the capitalists promote other than a wild, rich, doomed, FUN, multifarious one? So *please*—enough of this 'partnership' of 'Christ' and corporation. They *can't* go along with 'Jesus'—there's no PERCENTAGE in it.

Any other line of thinking is

**BALONEY!**

# Upper Broadway

The breathlessness was panic—nothing had changed in his chest in the three days since he'd got the *real* good news for modern man. There hadn't been much pain yet and he didn't wheeze—the whole thing had cropped up as *back pain*—he was still thinking of going back to work *for as long as his lungs didn't make noise*, he'd said to Shelby Stein, *production noise*, that was a good one, and as long as he didn't spatter his beloved microphone with mucus. Yes, the good news—you're going to croak, you've *got* to. More people have got to die, and faster, and many must die by cigarette. Do your bit, MacK said to himself, so.

He was sitting on the steps now—*in people's way*—and leaned against the low granite wall, his head far down enough that there was

14

no escaping the idea he was in distress—though escape it the people of Broadway and 96th would for a few moments longer, he thought. He had trained himself through years of coffee, tobacco and hangover-induced panic (*Change your life*, his hated family doctor said. —Change *this*, MacK replied lamely, though the method is a sound one) to think of DESTINATION, of Isidor. A tear escaped his dream-eye, the lazy one filled with sand after an imagist night—though perhaps that was the cindery wind of the subway—and fell on a perfect circle of ancient black gum at the same moment a hand in a glove came into his field of vision and a man asked if he were all right—if he needed help? *Contact* can break that cycle, even if everything seems compressed and malevolent, terribly near; even if he only thought of the man as his glove and couldn't remember his face in the following days. —No, said MacK, it's just some bad news, thank you. The helping hand of New York—which never doubt—may quickly be withdrawn if it expects you are wasting its time. —You think *you* got bad news! said the hand, in walking away, it seemed to MacK, who still hadn't sought the hand or face of the voice.

Only a few blocks from home, he reflected, but the IRT roared and filled its mouth and lips with old electricity—you could hear the express coming from WAY away—the distances of Manhattan seem doubled in that dark. On cold days the rails sing rather than whine or grate, sing, rush like a river—MacK sat halfway down the steps to the totem-booth and its massive priest, listened to the rushing as if to that of his western river, where, it struck him, he had smoked one of the great cigarettes of his existence, and that he owed it to himself and to humanity that he *decide* on which cigarette he'd *like* to have done him in, perhaps more than selecting the most craven one for *blame*. It was a 'Camel' bought in a lodge shop, thrilling with the odor of inbreeding, on his way up through the mountains. The sort of place which deals only in cigarettes, chewing tobacco, jerky, bait, beer that tastes of trout, and pocket watches on a faded card by the cash register. Remembered all this with the fond painterly clarity which all trips away from Manhattan acquire—it was true that although MacK had grown up only a hundred miles from that river, it had never meant a god damned thing to him until he had gone to New York and got perverted, as his mother said, started smoking—and later got in the habit of returning to the river for *romantic purposes.* —*Jetting around?* Isidor had said, invading yet *another* life?

The first 'Camel' he'd had out of that pack was one of the most ennobling—*the bite of tobacco beside a river* being one of the sublime manly moments. Though how many manly moments like that can you take till you wind up in this predicament, completely *unmanned? The bite of tobacco beside a river*—not in the sense of advertisement, but really—get your yenidje into that pipe and flame it yellow, yellow as the yenidje and the aspens around you at altitude—the smoke rich and white as fresh birch bark—and you begin to wonder, MacK said to himself, but out loud, what this plant is put on earth for, if not our consolation? You can't make shoes out of it.

*The bite of tobacco beside a river*, the stones under the water made silver by the moon seen closer and specially from the Sierra, and, so he thought, Red waiting for him in the tent, all woman (make *seething* noise between teeth), though while MacK had been having these male epiphanies one after another she had taken her credit card up to the hotel and got herself a room—having thought not much of this four-day exit from Manhattan—especially after slipping on something in the camp's washy toilet block—with this guy who after all had a top job, of sorts, even if it bored the crap out of him—she thought the tent unspecial and wanted to be closer to the bar and room service and the little shop selling not bait but designer resort wear. *Here?*

The rest of that pack of 'Camels', MacK reflected, were among the worst he ever smoked, creating an ulcerish BILE which ultimately led him to need to get away from Red and—quite possibly one of these, subsequent to the great first one, was It, *the* one, gave him his bad news, his good news, along the lines of the theory that calf-headed babies are born to rape victims and Republicans after congress with escaped mental patients—*congress*. Smoke a cigarette when you're miserable, *eating yourself up inside* as the saying goes, and that'll kill you. That was the Red story in a nut—transcendent at the beginning and very soon he'd found himself alone with his petty 'realizations' on the bridge; the silver and all that turned to tar.

Panic and all this scum from the past aside, MacK felt happy for a moment, on the steps of the 1, 2 and 3 trains, realizing he had two jolly lists to make, the cigarettes he *wanted* to have killed him, and the ones he would *despise* for doing so.


People walked around him grumbling—a little. You're always sorry to see someone sitting on the subway steps, aren't you, because they're going to ask you for money maybe or—this is the distressing thing—they've *given up*. And you that close yourself. But, MacK thought, should I despise the cigarettes I *didn't* enjoy for killing me, or assign a nobility in doing so to the ones I *did?* What about all those *airport misery cigarettes?* Or the little cigarettes they sell in France—no bigger than a roll-up—which he stood smoking one after another, much as one may discover one has absently eaten a ONE LB bag of candy—looking out at a much rainier version of Montmartre than had been predicted by . . . anyone, especially MacK and Red. Man was she fed up this time. 'Gravités', they called them, the little cigarettes sold by weight and not number—what an idea, like you were stuffing handfuls of shag into your chest. But come on, every cigarette is a misery cigarette. You make fun of 'True' (Blue) for being the ass hole's cigarette? Come, they're *all* ass hole's cigarettes, the lot of them—the holiday exotics, the *papirocii* of Moscow, the 'Gitanes', 'Sher Bidis', 'Turkish State Monopolies', 'Gold Flake' for God's sake—thought they didn't count, eh! What about down on your hands and knees digging in the waste basket for flu cigarettes, the ones you tried to eliminate from your life forever by running them under the tap? The Sobranie 'Cocktails' in little milk-glass cups at weddings—what if it were one of those? *Damn* you'd feel an idiot. The *brands* you found yourself unwrapping—you caught yourself once in a while in a dim acknowledgement that you really did need to smoke *anything*. —*You're some smoker, eh?* said the man in the bar in Cork, who'd only been sitting next you for an hour, through several small cigars, three 'Major Extra Size' and now a pipeful of 'Erinmore' bought up the road—and for *them* to remark on it . . . Of course the same guy approaches you on the way home. —*Any fags?* and you proudly hold out your closing-time purchase, a new pack of 'Carroll's'—and he turns up his nose. —*No 'Majors'?*

—The most delicious cigarettes in the world, said MacK out loud on the steps of the IRT, I say it who shouldn't. —Crazy one, said a guy with a little boy coming down and avoiding MacK.

The irony is that you smoke most when you're unhappy, because of the illusion of happiness. But what if life suddenly worked out? Or you roused yourself and made yourself happy in some way—or it happened by accident—what else are you propitiating these gods for?—and there you are, with this mine of phlegm inside you, waiting for your *happy* self to breezily tread on it and blow you a hundred feet in the air and scatter you all over town. Well *then* you've got something to worry about, so there you are the same old miserable bastard; but isn't that the same reasoning that *keeps everyone smoking: Ah, pal, ah'm f***ed awready*—yes, but are you? When the doctor looks at you as he did me the other day, said MacK, *that's* when you're f***ed, and it hurts, and it would have been a moment to avoid.

—Here, said someone—here. And pressed a five on MacK and hurried down the steps, do you think anyone has time to wait for thanks in this our town? They're all very modest. MacK looked down at his clothes, which were very nice, and felt his chin, which was smooth, and in feeling his chin recalled the recent haircut and the morning's shampoo (he'd started crying when the water came on—*the shampooing* as they say in France—what the Hell do *they* know about '-ing' anyway?)—but he had to take stock of himself in this way—there being no mirror—to be reassured he didn't look awful and that it *was* odd that the lady had given him five bucks—proof he'd been speaking aloud, he guessed. Proof that to sit on the steps of the 1, 2 and 3 and *say* something assures everyone you've *lost your senses* and that you should be given money to go away—but what do they know, you could have been reciting the *Aeneid*—which would only shore up their case—oh you can play music or even SING, like that *ass* on the steps at 14th Street, *Sa-ha-hahm-hm whay-ay-aeayeare o-ho-ho-o-verr the ray-ee-ay-ee-hain-hain-hain-boww*—etc—and everyone's comfortable but SAY something, talk, declaim, and you're suddenly much closer to arrest than you ever have been. Imagine yourself a Demosthenes, why not, strutting up and down the platform, your mouth stuffed with tokens—wouldn't work so well with twenty Metrocards—though 'twould be more hygienic.

Now the thing about talking out loud in public, or talking to yourself, which are not the same thing, although everyone thinks they are, is that you OUGHT TO DO IT. Everyone *does* do it, in the office pod or cubicle, at home, during the shampooing, MacK thought, again recalling the morning's shower, he'd cried in it, but *had also talked a deal of good sense*, planning out today—the walk, hitting the street—a brave act, face town with what you know, hit The Hour with Iz at the end of the day. There's a basic dishonesty in society today about talking 'to yourself'. Who does not say, *aloud*, to himself or herself, when stepping into the shower for the shampooing, 'my brother in law is an incredible weasel', or 'the next time I see Sid Herkenhoff I ought to pop him in the nose'—or 'if only I could get S—W— 's trousers down, what a picnic that would be'? Don't *kid* yourself, people are saying stuff like that 'to themselves' (though that's erroneous), something like that about *YOU* right now! They're saying it to people they *wish were there*, people they wish they had the gumbo to say it to—or people they wish they *were*—all over town—NOW!

—Why should saying something aloud brand you as insane, MacK said, why should *that* be the index of what is mad, of mad behavior —compared to running for office, being a lawyer, working on Pine Street, going on Outward Bound, or to church, buying a new house, 'deciding' your partner is not attractive, moving to the South or the West, neglecting your education, or thinking something on TELEVISION was really pretty interesting? HAH? '*Yes, they're making some marvelous programs these days*—' If anything, said MacK, coming very close to the theories of Isidor at this point, Izzy who truly *cannot* stop himself speaking aloud in public any longer, which is part of the reason he confines himself increasingly to his tower—there've been a few run-ins with the police—it really ought to be ENCOURAGED BY CITY HALL—it's a good way of getting to meet people and promoting HARMONY—relationships wouldn't be based on physical attraction, but in *mutual understanding*. If everyone talked about her crap, his crap aloud, all the time, then you'd move seamlessly from your own preoccupations into someone else's—or, say on the 96th Street downtown platform, into everyone else's—and then back into your own—like jazz—it would be jazz—you'd stop looking at everybody's hair and legs and chin clefts and tits and briefcases and suits and you'd really know what they're about. —It *isn't* mad, he said, it makes perfect sense—it isn't talking to yourself, it's merely a conversation with someone you haven't *quite met*, MacK said, WHAT'S WRONG WITH IT! The big priest in his bullet-proof Plexiglas shrine glanced at MacK wearily, heaved a sigh—reached for the phone.

MacK stood and went back up to the street; none of that crap today. Merely a man who looked fine, with some bad news under his belt, and a mission. No picaresque veerings into small hells—at least not until you get to Isidor—just a guy with a problem and a couple days off. A love of town on a bright day. Why not?

Why not place under arrest all these people talking 'to them-selves', into these *little phones* . . . they really *are* insane.

# That's Laughs Tonight

Spiritual journeys are hugely dull—they sell—but if you're reading one you ain't having one. MacK tried to think of his journey down-town as something other. A *celebration*, he thought, and began to laugh—it was a word they used at work. To the Presentation Department over in TELEVISION, *celebration* meant cutting up all the segments of a hit series into bits and linking them with bullshit espoused by someone who'd never had a hit series, either because the original star had just died of a drug overdose or because some-one on the 15th floor saw a hole in the schedule (usually in the summer) and by drinking extra hard devised some sort of anniver-sary relating to the series, the master copies of which were COSTING THE COMPANY MONEY by sitting on a shelf in Burbank or over in Lyndhurst.

But a *celebration* involves work by editors, thought MacK, and so is much more the mark of respect than the *tribute*, which is the simple re-running of one episode, because some ass hole has defi-nitely died—all a tribute involves is the Traffic Department clearing air time, with sponsors getting bumped, perhaps rounding up some of the original sponsors (a 'special tribute')—and Presentation affix-ing a solemn logo or freeze-frame to the head or tail of the episode:

**IN MEMORY OF SO-AND-SO**
**1947–1999**

with something nauseating like *Still Laughing* or *We Hear You* under-neath, *gods* is television depraved. MacK remembered a Production Standards meeting he'd attended three or four years before, something they had twice a year—the president had said they needed to 'ensure that there was *continuity of recognizability* between all networks'—and a fight broke out between the Presentation Department and the Video Department—strictly a matter of opinions, and morals, and money—over what *was* a respectful amount of time to display such a memorial shot. Presentation said you could cut to it before the production logos but after the network logo, hold it for three seconds, and fade it out in two, thus making it an easily-handled five extra seconds, which could be dealt with as they usually did, by speeding up and chopping the production logos, and by dropping network into the locals' laps three or four seconds late, let *them* take up the slack, tell their idiot anchors to lay off five seconds of drool with the weather girl. Guy from Video—older hand after all, probably thinking of JFK's and even FDR's funerals—rose up out of his chair all Cavendish and ruffled Brooks Brothers offense at this: —Why it's an outrage, which was the first time MacK had heard *why* used as an interjection in years—let alone the word *outrage* in the RCA Building—you've got to *fade up* at least in four, give people enough time to read it a couple of times—*Read* it?! said someone in the back—let it *sink in* for Christ's sake, and fade to grey scale in four or five and *then* to black! Anything else looks like playing pin the tail on the donkey, the guy said, slightly overtriumphantly.

Of course it didn't end there—Programming stepped in and ordered Research to come up with a *numerical value* to be assigned to every network personality, past and present, news, sports and entertainment, based on their peak numbers (to aid decision-making they also requested a value based on each personality's *mean* numbers), which would be used to compute the length of hold on memorial messages in the future. —Damned if I'm going to lose *over two seconds of prime time* on someone who didn't really pull viewers, looking at the big picture, you know, over all, said the guy from Programming—he was a deputy. Then a fresh fight broke out over *tributes* which Video said ought to be more or less the same but Programming and Presentation quickly decided could be forced on to voice-over if time was tight—and when was it not?

So that got dumped on MacK's counterpart, Shelby Stein, Chief Announcer of the TELEVISION network, who had to go write a memo to the announcers about being 'solemn and quick' in such a situation—when no memorial tag would be displayed and the network's grief would have to be demonstrated purely by voice-over with the end credits before hitting the promos for later shows—*Solemn, yes, and God damn quick*, Shelby wrote. *You must move quickly back to a normal promo tone, which may be difficult in the case of upcoming comedy.* Presentation made a half-assed commitment to providing more serious promos if there was to be a memorial v.o., pushing a news special or an upcoming documentary, except that there weren't any any more, and everyone knew they wouldn't do it—Presentation doesn't do jack shit. *Tapes showing your ability to do this to my office by January 23rd—they will as usual be cleared by Programming and if not satisfactory I will assign you a coach.*

[SAMPLE ANNOUNCE]
THIS EPISODE OF *PET TRAUMA WARD* HAS BEEN SHOWN AS A
MEMORIAL TO SO-AND-SO—OUR FRIEND. !TONIGHT ON
*BONACKER*—! SEEDHEAD FINDS A PIECE OF WOOD—[CLIP
:07] —AND BONACKER CAN'T BELIEVE IT! —[CLIP :04]
—THAT'S LAUGHS TONIGHT ON *BONACKER*! —[LAUGH
TRACK TO STING & LOGO—NETWORK I.D. —TO
AFFILIATES.]

Shelby could write a memo that made you think; the veeps thought it was all simple how-to. The *veeps* cleared the *memos*—you believe that? After meetings like this MacK often went down to the lobby and walked under *Sert's great mural, 'Time'*—as it said in the souvenir book and as you heard the tourist guides bleat—looking at the clouds and noble machines. Those were the days maybe, he thought, when airplanes didn't smell like businessmen's crap warm with coffee and artificial creamer—the workers, the vision, everyone *reaching*, for *something*, I don't know . . . But MacK often imagined

23

that *Sert*, Rivera's replacement, might have left a little *space* for Lenin, even though they'd literally kicked Rivera's *huge ass* out onto 49th Street, thrown his brushes, palette and beret after him—*Get lost, pendejo!*—thought the *invisible Lenin* might be near this big nude, perhaps a relative of Prometheus, the big gold guy taking a bath outside—since Lenin had a *beard* he might have wanted to stand near the *locomotive*. At times, say on a dark winter afternoon, the lights in the lobby gave a vibrancy to the mural, a real lift and swirl to all that black and brown old capitalism.

—But you know, said Shelby one day when MacK had taken *him* down to the lobby too, after a meeting about which letter, N, B, or C, was supposed to sound the grandest and most proud—if you were really looking up through these clouds, up through the building, you wouldn't see the sky or the sun, said Shelby. The sky is out *there*, he said, and gestured toward the skating rink—what you'd see is *fifty stories of asses sitting on chairs*. Some people in the lobby took note of this, partly because Shelby's voice was loud and famous, whatever he did with it . . . when he was buying a round at Hurley's he often said joyfully *This is on me!*—he had nothing to spend his money on, Shelby—which sounded so much like *This is NBC* that people looked and one of the duty announcers who was having a highball in the back choked on a rock and ran upstairs, thinking he was hearing a cue. —*And some of them ain't bad looking*, said Shelby, who was one of those who use quaint contractions to state something at once risqué and beneath him—but which in fact he was thinking about all the time.

There are three cool entrances to the RCA Building, and MacK always came in the one designated 50 West 50th Street because he was usually coming from the 50th Street subway, and liked to walk by the Music Hall; Shelby preferred 49 West 49th Street because he was coming from some big-spenders' garage and it was closer to the bank of elevators for the TELEVISION floors. For smoking Shelby liked to stand outside the 30 Rockefeller Plaza door—*There's a canopy and sometimes GOILS*, he said—he thought people might recognize him—though who would have recognized him unless he were speaking?—he simply looked like somebody hanging around smoking. If he and MacK agreed to have a drink at Hurley's, they each took their favorite exit and met at the door of the bar on Sixth Avenue and sneered at each other.


Bored at work, often left profoundly alone on the twentieth floor for hours with nothing to do except wait for the red light to come on, speak his piece, mark his log sheet (☐ FED TO KEY STATIONS ☐ FED TO NETWORK ☐ FED TO LIVE NETWORK ☐ CONTINUITY NO.___ AUTH N SCHWARTZ) —at times it seemed odd to him he should be entombed in this electrically live though acoustically dead casket on the twentieth floor—a little live cancer cell in the grey dead tissue of the RCA Building, using this great apparatus, this swelling organ of vacuum tubes, granite, lamps, diorite, elevators, carpeting, of *power*—just to open the microphone and say things like 'This—is NBC' or 'Stations, promo feed T-5-B will be sent three minutes early today, at 14:24:30'—when he could have been offering a few of his own opinions—at any rate, began a hobby of lists and charts, where most would be happy with acrostics, or JUMBLE—a double-entry day-book of his modest erotic life. Bought a solid accountant's book for this, full of appealing graph patterns and columns— decided to add up the particular talents of each lover and arrive at an over-all, logarithmic rating—talk about raising the next power—which was bound to depress him, since whoever got the highest value would still be unavailable, and still no doubt pissed off as Hell—ye *gods* he'd broken it off miserably with them all— there'd be no going back and declaring *You are everything on this chart!* and reflaming bedtime by dint of statistical analysis.

Of course a lot of the more refined tastes had to belong to the conjecture of nostalgia, since he hadn't known about the uses of string, many of the useful portals of the body, &c, &c, *until he moved to New York and got perverted*, as Isidor used to say. The chart was

| Mlle. | Levres. | Talons. | Ficelles. | Toucher. | Jeu. |
|---|---|---|---|---|---|
| Eliza | As if she had once known how. | I. Miller. | Wouldn't hear of it. | Dreamy. | Laughed in face. |
| Nadia II | Like a SOLAR FLARE! | Hauts! | Worrisome night of her green garden twine. | Velvet, or poss. chowder. | ! 'You be a Hungarian impresario and I'll be girl w/ three-hand piano act' ! |
| Girl from BMT | The little octopus! | C. Jourdan, but kept taking them off: played w/ them when she was in shower. | Refused to be released. Lost sleep. | Somehow, sand got in. | Cowboys— again. Had to buy toy 6-shooter. $ 7.95 |
| Pegeen | A tad gloppy. | Wore flats contr. to instr. | Lost half-hitch somewhere. | Perfect. | Asked me to talk like Lloyd Bridges. Refused. |

becoming more complicated with regard to the *fourth* dimension, as he was extrapolating and deducing the possible erotic aspects of women he had had and others he had not had, from their business and weekend attires and attitudes. Nancy Schwartz, for instance, he was almost positive must own smalls of maroon satin, a projection based upon the qualities of several blouses she wore when visiting Master Control. Maroon was going out of style—it held an unremarkable but assumed place in his erotic pantheon—much as in the delicatessen you *assume* there to be mayonnaise on your sandwich. He was sure, looking at the chart, that Francine Buzza would have enjoyed climbing on top of him, if he had only known such *filthy pleasure* five years before, and whenever he would open this *f***ing* book he achingly, sobbingly wished he had asked to see Bunny Watanabe's shoe closet.

### BUT IT WAS ONLY A HOBBY—*!*

Gods the *office*, thought MacK, who hadn't decided when to go back to work really or if at all. Why not go down and stand on Fulton Street for the rest of the time? Rest of your *life*. *Your life*, after all. What's going back to the office going to do but remind you of the good news? But *Lenin* turned MacK's thoughts of the lobby funereal—he'd never been able to bear the very dark, back part of the lobby—where they sell the tat—he had a horror of the black marble well leading to the lower level—do you hear me? *he hated the lower level* (he hated the lower level of Grant's Tomb, too) hated the way the brass squares set in the black stone curved down there—and was bothered every morning when he walked past the security desk by the thought that there had been a huge, possibly eternal staircase there at one time, walled up quickly in the Fifties when the whole building was trashed for TELEVISION in an absolute panic—they'd needed a scene dock. Hated the idea of *walled up*. When MacK was in a bad mood the black lobby seemed a mausoleum, now perhaps forever. He felt the same way at a cash machine, just off Madison

Square, a special one, as he thought, designed for bankers, surrounded by *too much granite in a soft shape*; it was too creepy to get your money out of a little tomb anyway. So: a CELEBRATION, this walk, MacK thought—at least the five seconds—and grey scale would be nice.

New York is a good place to die. You have your St Vincent's. You have your elegant Madison Avenue mortuaries.

The air seemed to have cleared—or the smog that panic is maybe. Who needs the subway? Gods—the office!

## That Day

He thought: a snow day ten years before, ten *years*, the kind of idea which makes Isidor squirm and profane. There they were leaving Isidor's tower, bundled up, MacK on a visit from one of his god damn network outpostings, joyful in an inadequate overcoat from some stupid part of the country where these things are a matter of form and not of keeping warm. The discreet, the usual sidelong glance from Isidor at what MacK was wearing. Grey snow, not yet slush, snow determined to stay a while and make you cold. And some falling, just enough to speed you the couple of blocks. There were these Irish joints they'd never been, over beyond Third, which needed enumerating. Came out of the tower just to 'walk around'—the porage underfoot was their Enabler as if they needed one.

Out of the tower, past the doorman who was wearing *his* snow day face—a combination of the child and soldier in each of us. —Going to be mighty cold later, Gentlemen. Doormen always try to tell you what to think about the weather. This doorman was known to wear dresses in his time off, so Isidor, *sotto voce*: —Hardly a day for chiffon, Frank.

It is pleasant to have to put the struggle of a snow and noise walk into the conversation. The snow excusing you from the judgement of the city and giving always that sense of holiday. Even on Pine Street it is said they enjoy snow.

It was one of those places that appears ready to serve Guinness at an early hour. Down some steps from the street and through an oddly suburban door, past neon signs. Already some wet patches on the floor. But pool tables . . . —How can you pay attention to your beer, asked Iz, making a face at the sour pasteboard of his pint, if you have to do stuff with a lot of BALLS? Drives me nuts. The bartender, a man of degraded affability, could tell they had come not for the pool but for the drink and they did not care for the drink—these bartenders *should* be nervous at eleven o'clock in the morning—but why are we embarrassed when we do not like our drink, when we do not love the environment in which we drink our drink? Why is it not OK to put down our drink, or ask for another, or simply, Americanly leave? But perhaps to leave is European—what one wants to avoid is an abuse of self, even though in beer with the distinct taste of last night one has been insulted and impugned. To have to put down the glass and leave under the dull smirk of billiard players—! But their footing in the vortex of the day was established.

It was not so many minutes to McSorley's, where Isidor broke with history and had two darks, so as to stay in the *stout spectrum*—MacK fortified himself with two-and-two, gods but they get smaller every year, and for his *petit déjeuner* the liverwurst and onion sandwich *avec la moutarde de old maison at home*, which are too well known to admit description. Isidor never eats before dinner. The snow fell and they wished the fire had been lit, but the history of the stove and the broad backs of other men kept them insulated from the world, truly, at their table. This is why you come out into the world in snow—to be professionally repackaged against it. And to hear nothing—but the infrequent car on 7th Street. With lunch-cool stomachs they emerged in an hour, having discussed that branch of history which dealt with the two of them at that table—the day was now surely styled

**That Day**

in MacK's mind—and faced into the snow and the secretive destination of Wally's, a very old bar in an unmarked courtyard in the
West Village. One never knows, do one, is Wally's going to be open
for business but as they were together and MacK was wearing the
needy talisman of a pathetic coat this was a day of luck, of significance. And if Wally's were open it would be the quiet chapel of the
hours of afternoon, a family of aloof dogs napping by the fire. And
it was not inconceivable, given the flakes which sketched HOLIDAY
outside, that it was not too early for a martini, on a day like today
when MacK was visiting town in a *gauche overcoat*—he'd gotten *looks*
from people he knew on a brief stop at the RCA Building—a Wally's
martini, which were more *décor* than anything. MacK took off the
inappropriate coat and felt himself slipping on an invisible garment
of the past, sitting in Wally's—a comfortable cultural mackinaw
sewed for him by the Wilbur Sisters or Irma Rombauer—felt all the
streets they'd traversed return to the way he and Isidor had always
wanted to see them, how they looked in 1945. Out of pre-addled
bonhomie he'd said the word *Gibson*.

The thing arrived in a wet glass of pure patina, it tasted as if
made wholly of onion pickle juice. MacK had sipped at it and
though initially overwhelmed, felt he should react with optimism
and so pretended he was driving through one of the many *Onion
Capitals* of his youth, father saying *Hold on, there, you've never had
one of these before have you?* So maybe this is what it's supposed to
taste like—though I don't recall, MacK thought, Cary Grant
making any one of the faces I would now like to be making. —This
tastes a little . . . is it supposed to b-hee . . ., he said explosively
and handed the glass to Isidor who took a mouthful and rose up
crying no No NO!, rushed for the bar and collared the soft hippie
with the red beard. —This is *onion juice*, man, said Iz, are you
insane? Guy hick-blinked and then revealed he'd used the last
onion in the jar and had simply upended it into the ice and the gin.
—But this is *madness*, said Isidor, don't you have a strainer? Bring
my friend a martini right away and use an olive. I could have your

license for this. (Isidor, for some wild reason, believed that barbers and bartenders were still all issued with *licenses* by the State of New York—therefore that there was some kind of Masculine Amenity Authority that would haul into JAIL the asses of those who would make with a sloppy drink or cut your hair into peculiar *shelf-like formations*.) The fellow meekly obeyed. *It was quite possibly the only martini mixed at that moment in town by a feller in BIB OVERALLS.* One of the dogs opened a contented eye but that was as far as Isidor's ripples went. And so another, then on to a brief sample of an ale or two and it was time for to meet Sylvie at Sevilla for dinner. That Day.

The streets were quite dark and there were lots of people coming TOWARD the boys many of whom no doubt had Wally's in mind. But a Wally's full of custom which was the only way *they* had ever seen it. And it was not so many blocks to Sevilla, which is located, I tell you now, AT THE CORNER OF BEDFORD AND CHARLES.

And here was Sylvie, muse and nurse, in the window, waiting for MacK and Isidor, looking rather decorative, Christmassy the year round she was, like Celeste Holm, the goddess of nice New York girlfriends. —Can this girl perch on a bar stool and look expectantly festive, said Isidor, or what? Even though she's just come from therapy . . . —*Therapy!?*, MacK recoiled, what kind of therapy! —Search me, said Isidor.

Heaven has a specific address; and there they always address you specifically. They're all from Galicia, these *angeles*, and so they twang at you, solicitous *guitarrons*. Roberto the bartender's *O.Y.U.?* as he slides the Isidoronic martinis toward the boys; Sylvie looks on with her iced Xeres. No fool she. None of this *What have you done to me!?* for her. These were among the best Restaurant Martinis in town because Iz had trained Roberto over months. He had *trained Roberto*. True to the phlegmatic spirit of his native village Roberto took this penetrating customer's instruction without rancor, including it in the ups and downs of life which he suffered in their totality, in every glance at the world through his sad blue eyes—truth to tell a color remarkably similar to Isidor's.

It is not known whether on That Day Sylvie found the boys merely gay company, a bit the worse for wear, or completely nuts and strong in their disbelieving. But she played along as though life was merry and it was. What had been slowly taken through the afternoon was readily absorbed by the planet *mariscada*—its orbiting moons of frozen beer. When not waiting on them with *short-jacketed alacrity*, as MacK had characterized it in his index of waitering, Carlos stood by the table and exchanged ideas about the latest films. —The guy's mad for them, said Izzy, and I like hearing his point of view because it is always, elegantly, 100% wrong. Not because he's from Spain, but because he lives in Queens.

MacK leaned back cautiously at one point—the carpentry of the booths was untrustworthy—and observed

## ISIDOR & SYLVIE: A TABLEAU

Iz perspiring, digging for clams at the bottom of the pot : Sylvie dabbing her mouth and looking at him in a way that was at first monitory but ascended to loving : reflective surfaces of the bottles and glassware and Isidor's spectacles : Sylvie's necklace : soft sweet wools of their clothes : the co-incidence of their flesh tones and the general ease of their being together : a city love made of companionship and romantic feeling for this our town.

How could *this* be? : out into the wet snow for a look-in at the Minetta, to which Sylvie agreed, she always agreed to let the boys have their fun, unlike some women in some chapters we could name, frantically trying to *pull them apart* at eleven o'clock in the cold!

Discussion and then experiment ensued on the subject of the martini as *digestif.* If Sylvie objected she held her peace as sense of a sort was still being made, and anyway she could easily flee the several blocks to home.

The Minetta was bright and Isidor took up the command of the bar, inspecting the bartender's equipment, holding his glass up to the light, MacK felt suddenly he was back under the glaring copper frontier-style *kitchen lamp of childhood*, father showing MacK some simple chemistry experiment. The science MacK never understood, but the *effect*, such as turning a clear fluid violet, was certainly something known to the early religious japesters—mess around with people's drinks and *man* you have their attention. Sylvie still looked at Isidor with something like love, and MacK, still partly in his chemistry lesson, recognized, as he did from time to time, the similarities between Isidor and MacK's own father, the slightly drooping moustaches, the restrained 'aviator' frames which emphasized the sadness of the eyes which MacK had spent his life trying to animate—when you think about it.

But rather than stay and stay and make fools, away from the bright light and across the chilly park to the tower. Sinking into the leather chairs in front of the sharp-smelling fireplace, stroking the cat who watches the humidor being brought out—it had oft thought of taking up smoking; Sylvie excusing herself and going for bed; the lights of downtown for the seeing and jazz brushwork underscoring the blatter of wet snow on the window. The cigar. Quiet descends. Some talk of the past.

The armagnac. The calvados.

But *then*, the rising of a new idea. A clean, reasonable, sane idea! Up and out, like youth itself, to the Knickerbocker, just up the street, really—why not just one or two? —After all, not every day a guy brings a coat like *that* to New York, said Isidor—you'd love to be outside *using it*, wouldn't you?

So they drifted like snow as you do in happy dreams, the short-subjects before the nightly monster movie—up the little street and on to the big street—watched over by the god of late errands, making them deaf to the entreaties of 8th Street and invisible to the malcontents of University Place.

One or two, a whiskey, a beer in the pleasant Knickerbocker —guys playing music in the rear in an open-handed spirit—men appreciating the pretty women who would come out on a night like this—the people of this our town enjoying themselves—and truly, with the minimum of urbane distance—*liking each other*.

## *This Again*, or,
## the Routine of the Empty

In the cold months, Washington Square seems in suspended anima-tion, it glistens and suggests birth later, like some icky pod or *sac* in a biology film. MacK, rambly on his way to the IRT, often avoided University Place as he might again be ensnared in his awful ROUTINE OF THE EMPTY:

At the all-night grocery on 10th he would buy a large can of beer, for taking uptown, which was unnecessary; it was often too cold to pronounce *Oranjeboom*—he felt it a trap. Then across the street to the news-stand to plant himself defiant, bleary and nervous in front of the rack, searching for *Bulletin of the Leg Scientists* (THE LEG STANDS AT THREE MINUTES TO MIDNIGHT!), would mumble and then had laboriously to enunciate because of the suggested humping *Pack of plain 'Camels' please* and fumble fumble with f***ing money, which seemed an inappropriately real element in these repetitious, bull-dozed codas of evenings, of which Isidor and Sylvie were ever unaware—*fumbling* in front of the genial news vendor. Out to the street with all this *silly booty*—a magazine he disdained.

Always recognized he was doing it again. *You're doing this again* he said on many nights, out loud like Iz. He felt his eyes to be as wide open as searchlights, though they were puffy and nearly shut; thought he could take in the wonderful human sounds of this our town through his gigantic radio-telescopic ears. So he would grad-ually get to the IRT at 14th and Seventh, having journeyed blotto through this, one of the sleepiest parts of town there is. St Vincent scatters sand in your eyes around one-thirty. It is frightening to recall, the next morning in your bed of acute pain, the city in such a deranged state, everything so hysterically slow, so stretched and zinging. Indeed it is remarkable that a person in such a blasted and forlorn condition can make himself understood, to the genial news vendor, to the priest of the tokens, make himself presentable enough to his own doorman to be let in the building (Boris has standards after all). It is, in fact, *a tribute to New York*.

On the coldest night of the previous year, when it was foolish to drink at Isidor's tower, equally foolish to go out into the cold, he had *found himself doing it again*; the can of beer stuck to the flesh of his hand even in the grocery. It seemed madness to search the magazines (*Frozen Gams, Lap Land, Leg-Cicle*). Crazy to think of drawing his hand out of his coat to light one of the oddly stiff 'Camels'.

On Fifth Avenue, a man and his dog in front of the Forbes Magazine building—possibly frozen to it. Guy *sitting on the pavement*, it was too much to bear, *the cold floor of New York*. Was there not a room of any sort, anywhere in town where he could be inside, even the IRT? The dog was too cold to sit down, it wasn't going to *lay its nipples* on the cold stoop of the Forbes Magazine building, f*** that, it thought. It stood and panted and gave MacK a look doubtful of its master—the *dog* knew, or at least believed, *hoped* that the guy was being a little theatrical. MacK felt propelled toward the man and the dog, by what in the Oyster Bar or Hurley's would have been martini-fuelled bonhomie, but out here at this temperature and because of this squalid scene, the near frozen beings, the cold-hearted Forbes Magazine building, was a story of survival, an *arctic adventure*. MacK thought he had to *keep the man talking* in order to keep him alive. The man's polyester yarn hat, his beard, his coat seemed to indicate he was going to sit there all night, on *Fifth*, where hardly anyone would come by. Though he was in this state, he started to look a little bored and worried by MacK's going on and on. Now the dog gave MacK the same look: *Okay buddy see you later*. MacK gave the man twenty dollars, the cigarettes, the matches. And the can of beer, though he later thought it might have been medically wrong. Kept the magazine—not that many people into the leg stuff—guy's got a dog.

MacK made the IRT without incident. But here on the uptown platform was the guy singing *Sa-ha-hahm whay-eay-air-air-air o-ho-ho-ver the reay-ee-ay-ay-hain-hain-hain beauwww*—but on the downtown platform he had lo and behold a HECKLER who turned out to be his own FATHER: —Hey why don't you take that shit back to Detroit? —*hain-hain-hain . . . whaaa?* —I SAID, why don't you take that shit back to Detroit? —*Man, I'm FROM Detroit. You know I'm from Detroit, why you tell me to take it back to Detroit?* —Nobody wants 'at around here. [Arrival of uptown No. 3.] —*I see YOUR ass TOMORROW.*

## The Smoking Hero

The apartment buildings of Broadway in the 90s look heroic in a certain light—or perhaps if you are being heroic. There are vistas toward midtown which can be inspiring, or at least they hint of its lure. Sometimes at least in the past Broadway looked as though it might curve down (or up) toward your future—not that it is the only avenue that can suggest things to a young guy or gal. MacK faced south—let the CELEBRATION begin. Guy next to a key shop—one of these guys who just stands there—looking at you as if to say, this IS my employment, motherF***ER, lit up a 'Camel' filter—with its faint aroma of *actual* 'Camels'—funny how one's attention will be caught by the lighting of one particular cigarette—how many were being lit at this very moment—how many loves desires and tempers flaring like matches and lighters all over town? Is New York the only place where you may smoke freely in North America? Thought so. Go ahead! Blow your brains out! —Now that I'm 'not smoking' any more, thought MacK—or amn't I? Funny—they get you in there and tell you a thing like that, and they don't say *I'd cut down if I were you*—*ought to knock it off you know*—it must really be over for me, he thought, and suddenly Broadway looked very sad, as if it led *nowhere*. There was a dark patch, not of panic this time, only of—not loneliness—already missing everyone, already having said goodbye—though he was still standing there, facing downtown. Had it been precipitated by anything other than itself, MacK would have gone for a pack of 'Camels' now, perhaps gone back home and looked out at the Drive, the marble table, the appropriate drink, the cat, a girl. I'm walking into the sunset? he thought—but there was Isidor at the end of the day, so.

But now here's a fellow *asking* for one—and MacK reached automatically as always into the jacket pocket—it still not being cold enough for a MacKENZIE to wear—or buy even—this year's overcoat. There were some. —Thanks, my man. You're a hero, man. You're a smokin' hero. *Me?* thought MacK, walking away from the pleasant transaction—it always is, unless the request for nicotia is a blind and what's really wanted is money or love. Now *I'm* a smoking hero, thought MacK, who'd had his own, he'd worshipped them as fervently as he did the gods of the city:

*Smoking Hero* Mr Playfair himself, the courtly antiquarian bookseller who Izzy'd bought Bibulo & Schenkler from—still around when Izzy started working there in the mid Seventies and MacK had come regularly in and out of the shop. The shop smelled *eloquent*, MacK thought, of latakia and perique. Stained goatee. Mr Playfair used to roll his cigarettes out of pipe tobacco, using some ancient device he picked up in France, a thick metal wallet with mysterious rubber rollers which looked like something that might be harboring *polio*—smoked these with great relish, luxuriously, knowledgeably, in a patent 'ejector' holder—at the memory of which MacK smiled—remembering a summer upstate when, out of sheer boredom and heat oppression, MacK had purchased the self-same holder from a small inbred store at the crossroads—and began rolling Playfairish smokes from his can of 'Forest'. He put these slug-shaped, overly damp cigarettes in the holder and pointedly smoked them on the balcony, to get attention. —Why don't you cut that out? called Isidor from far in the woods, where he was standing with his oboe—don't you know you look exactly like Lillian Hellman?

Alone for a winter month in Vermont—again at the mercy of country-store-as-entertainment, he took up 'Pall Malls', the constant medicament of *S. Hero* Shelby Stein—until he fainted a week later, having snowshoed energetically to the store to buy some more, and back—and in the faintly cinematographic process of fainting he recalled Shelby's manicured but stained fingernails, his large yellow teeth. He never went to the dentist, Shelby, *never*—he was afraid maybe that it would affect his voice—the forced removal of all that vibrating tar—but NBC *made* him go several years later—after craning his neck and scraping around for an hour, with a lamp on his head, the dentist says, *Well, Mr Stein, I'm glad to say you don't have any cavities—OF COURSE WHAT COULD LIVE IN A MOUTH LIKE THAT?* Recalled Shelby's brown, scummy laugh—a good thing he never had to laugh on the air. When he came to, MacK found he'd banged his eye on the corner of the coffee table and went back to 'Camels'.

His distant *S. Hero* cousin, the most glamorous of smokers, who MacK never met till he was thirty—already a barrister in London, though he was several years younger than MacK—he affected at that time a cape, a stick, a limp. He was the first British person of either sex to have designer stubble. Integral to his flourishes of cape, stick, stubble-rub and Romantic Cough was the charming sleight-of-hand he performed with his brass petrol lighter and carton of 'Major Extra Size', *the most delicious cigarettes in the world*, said MacK aloud at 86th and Broadway, *I say it who shouldn't*. He was very well spoken and quickly became an impossibly romantic figure to MacK. The girls thought so too and they lay down by hundreds to help him go over his cases; each wanted to help him up the stairs. (His limp seemed somehow virile—there was never the implication that he was physically weak—the impression he gave was that of man who limped due to exquisite *mental* suffering, on behalf of humanity.) During his month in the London bureau MacK got some of his cousin's cast-offs, though most, when they found MacK could not approach the Queen's Bench, and was American, would only lip him, and British fellation only drives you crazy for a fag while it's going on.

## Upper Broadway

Although on the surface stuck, MacK thought, like those trains possibly sitting below him at the very moment, those trains which arrive in the station briskly, *march in*, to which your mood may correspond, some mornings—they snap open their doors militarily and you think here is hope—the lights are bright and the *precise moments of enticement* this train offers you (maybe it is even a new train!) remind you of the morning's shampooing, deodorant soap—and so on—so you get on, along with the other bushy tails and then the train just *f***ing* sits there—you're willing to give it a minute or two—but there is no announcement, you begin to look at each other—you've read everybody's front page by now—and then the compressor switches off, which means you'll be sitting there a while—and when you realize the doors have been open long enough for the whole car to lose its heat (or in summer its cool), lose its *heart*, really, you see some nonbushy tails have had time to get in now, like rats—they think it's a *regular* train—no no no!—but since they're in, people who just walked down the stairs without purpose, who bought a token without thinking, they have now *made* it an ordinary train and it seems all your good intent is stupid, meaningless bullshit—it seems NEUROTIC. Doesn't it?

He'd decided against the IRT but was standing twenty feet above this god, thinking hard about it—feeling *nostalgic* for all that, if you will, reminded that he might not really be going back to work, which he did usually by walking up to Broadway from Riverside—if he wanted to look at girls he went to 116th and if he wanted to feel a part of the city, to 110th. MacK was never late, but daily gave himself the choice of riding the local to 50th—this on 'humanity' days—and walking over to Sixth; or if he felt architectural and spaced he'd change to the express at 96th—feeling newspapery, overcoaty and busy—and go down to 42nd, walk over to Sixth and up—to look up Sixth toward the Park, especially on a wet morning. He liked discerning the silver and red of the Music Hall marquee, signally when the sun lit that against a dark sky—liked it in the morning or at night, as it mirrored the NBC canopy on 50th where he went into work, and the gun grey sky was close to the color of the metal and this reminds you the city is put together nicely, actually is a living thing, even though architects are always trying to take credit for it—crap-asses. Can you believe they have anything to do with such a place? Up there in their offices, with their manicures and *very neat clothing*; all architects blow imaginary dust off everything all the time—they're sick. They blow.

Standing there stuck like a train, or as if struck by one, tottering, about to die, he thought, though the immediate and imminent end he'd been sure of half an hour before was forgotten—he imagined the usual trip to work, wondered if he'd ever actually be up there again, ever see Shelby, the grey carpeting and the pillars oddly placed in his little wired box? Nancy Schwartz? But now it seemed it hadn't been panic or disease or death but a sweep of nostalgia for his apartment building, which he'd left, what, thirty minutes ago?—and for the warmth, the *possibility* of warmth, of Olive, perhaps only that of contemplating her, which now—

I must call her Olive, because that really is her name and I want all of her to be in this—I can't bear to change it, to see another name here.

# Theo MacKenzie His Building

FIREPROOF CONSTRUCTION THROUGHOUT, said proudly the original prospectus for 407 Riverside Drive—The Wynd—nobody calls it that old sandstone name up there, they call it 407: *You going back to 407?* MacK had seen the prospectus in Olive's apartment—she was on the Residents' Committee and had written a graceful guide for new dwellers in The Wynd—which had gone largely condominium in the Seventies and Eighties—the frankly terrified middle classes massing on their rock poking out of the hydrosphere of racism—not her fault. She'd grown up there. She loved 407. Olive drifted through the building in perfect skirts, thought MacK—how could everyone not have fallen in love with her? To have a spirit like that in your apartment building? Why you didn't even feel that way about the most beautiful guard at the Museum of Modern Art; the Rockettes; the redhead at Rocco, the only (turned out to be from New Paltz, screw it) woman you ever followed down the street even half a BLOCK.

Although MacK made a good living he was still privileged—if that word may be used any more to mean ANYTHING in this our town—and grateful to have got his apartment, its view up the Drive and across the river—or properly, down into the park, as MacK was on a lower floor and could discern New Jersey only through the trees of *winter*. He liked this level and would have felt guilty in one of the more *commanding*—as the ugly phrase has it—upper joints. He had achieved this as a loyal and skilful lover of The Wynd, and many of its occupants, in several ways.

He had known for over twenty years the lovely Mrs Leninsky, Olive's auntie, who'd put in a good word and practically willed the thing to him after she gave up housekeeping by spray cleaner and sensibly went to spend her last years with her brother and his enlarged heart on the ground floor of New Jersey. MacK had known her son Sidney since university and despite many practical jokes upon him in a vain attempt *to get back at Sidney for his personality*—once gluing Sidney's hand to his face (as he slept) with a proprietary adhesive the strength of which was cause for a brutal lecturing of MacK by the emergency room doctor—they remained friends. Sidney even gave me my first job in New York, thought MacK, thinking over his great lusts and little loves for many of the females of The Wynd, not least Mrs Leninsky herself, the kindest, most magnanimous woman in New York—she lived right here, folks—whose spirit of giving and communality never wavered, he supposed, from the night the Nazis kicked down the door of her family home in Vienna. My *crushes*, he thought, on Sidney's sister, on musical girls visiting the Leninskys' over the years, why is desire so extensive in this our town? The surprising tonguing by the cook during preparation for a Thanksgiving dinner years ago, why yes I've always been a member of the family, he thought.

For years he had pictured his triumphs as occurring in the Leninskys' apartment, even in his dreams. Imaginary things, accompanying dazzlingly-dressed Olive in an evening of Bernstein songs on Sidney's Bechstein which MacK can't even *play*.

And now not to survive even most of them. Here I'm to die only recently having got the apartment I wanted? Almost *inheriting* it really—doesn't the word imply immortality? Hell.

Mrs Leninsky was a nice lady. And being a nice lady she spent all her time being nice; she had a job being nice to crippled people and when she wasn't doing that she was out being nice to a lot of other people to whom the Nazis also hadn't been nice and who had great need of people being nice to them even though they were pissed off and crabby, and when Mrs Leninsky wasn't being nice to *them* she was sitting nicely in the Metropolitan and being very nice to the Beaux Arts Trio by understanding what they were doing. Or she was being nice to Sidney *by ignoring his personality*, and being nice to his sister, to the point of practically killing them, or being nice to her niece Olive, MacK's romantic light.

Three years ago, MacK thought ruefully as he passed the notable and oppressive bagel establishments of the low 80s, Mrs Leninsky had managed to sell him her apartment, and at the same time his fitful 'long-term' (*Ha!*) 'relationship' (*double H!*) with Red came to an end—you can only protest your love so long—and your essential innocence—to someone who does not want to hear it. So philosophically and luckily MacK thought, several days after he moved in: HENCEFORTH I CONFINE MY LOVE LIFE TO 407 RIVERSIDE DRIVE.

The cook stopped coming when Mrs Leninsky left—much as I

entreated her, he thought—and it quickly came obvious that this left the Non-Anglophone (real name Olga Ennhopona, from —Romania?). She lived several floors below, with her mother, who wore a headscarf and looked for all the world like the women engaged in that very serious conversation they're having in the rolling fields of tobacco on the 'Balkan Sobranie' label, the carts rumbling away. MacK gave the Non-Anglophone flowers to see what would happen and to return the favor immediately which must be the thing in—Romania?—she shyly sent her mother upstairs with a *sack of dried corn*, which threw things for several months, yet now the Non-Anglophone is often to be found being fed snacks and drinks in my high-backed chair and talking quite witty, he thought. There was too a snooty Pine Street bulless in one of the penthouses, and there was Judy Picklewicz, *Picklewicz of Piscataway*, on the third floor, a tiny blonde who wrote comedy for a living—and this was very appealing was it not? —and whose metallic black legs and very high heels had MacK following her down the tiled hall—but she worked for CBS. For the real purposes of love, Olive.

Only Olive.

Everyone else in the building used a walker and needed HELP ALL THE TIME. *You're such a nice young man.* But he stuck with his decizh, banished even were the many thoughts of Nancy Schwartz at work and the women Shelby Stein literally pushed at him in Hurley's. Mr Polite.

Mrs Leninsky was a very nice lady with no time for doing anything in her house except in what she considered the most convenient MODERN way. She had bought all her furniture in 1965 from Consolidated Modern Art, a tangled emporium on 72nd Street, world headquarters at the time for 'Danish' sofas with alarming fabrics which could not be matched with anything, little blond tables with metallic black legs, which seemed to MacK like tables he ought to follow around, *hassocks*, who really is supposed to sit for an evening of Schubert on a hassock? But they turned out to be useful for certain Non-Anglophonic rites. MacK was satisfied

43

to swallow Mrs Leninsky's furniture whole, had thrown out his own in fact. With few changes Mrs Leninsky's apartment had now some kind of hip, at least as far as MacK had accomplished by 'consolidating' the weirdest Sixties furniture in the pink room with his hernia table and record collection. As Sixties homemaker Mrs Leninsky was a great believer in self-adhesive objects—paper cup dispensers, dish towel holders, shelves even, clocks—*a paper cup dispenser in every room*—I always meant to get the sandblasters in to eliminate the remnant crusts of these, thought MacK, and now too late. What micro-archeology of the Leninskys, he wondered, was left upon the wall?

But he still religiously bought the cups, as a kind of memorial to the generosity of Mrs Leninsky—who'd given him a view—and who'd bequeathed him Olive—he'd hoped. He had to travel some distance to get the little cups but what of it. Man sometimes they were HANDY.


Who knows from fireproof? But The Wynd was solid, replete with things MacK looked for in a building, indicators and providers of stability and oldness: the service elevator, which had to have frosted glass doors on each landing—you *must* be able to see the bright boxes ascend and descend, the friendly uniformed silhouettes—this is city drama and the smooth-running Twenties and Thirties on a *plate*, Busby Berkeley and the lick of expressionism all in one. The inner door has to be opened with a very worn brass handle. The shaft must give off the smell of cared-for old motors, the lovely oils of generations, but never smell of *hot motor*. The service corridors and back stairs, where MacK liked to spend much of his time, on his stoop as it were, smoking and reading the *Daily News*, he required to be painted in grey enamel to two-thirds the height of the walls, then crème. They had to be lit by incandescent bulbs—working in the RCA Building and its cradling warmth, lacking fluorescent fixtures except on the television floors, had convinced MacK for all time—as if anyone needed convincing —that *the extra expense of incandescent light* is the only way forward, the only decent thing, the only light that is inclusive and brings all men and women into civilization itself. As it was perfectly expressed in 1935. Incandescent light IS 'the light of civilization'. Fluorescent light alienates us, ruins our city, our society and our nation. It makes pizza look a fright.

O you ought to have seen MacK before he moved in, prowling the corridors with the Super, though of course he knew the building well already, even some of its recesses, thanks to the cook—MacK approached the Granolithic floor of the lobby with real reverence (so like going to work, though he did not recognize that)—o happy was he that all the light bulbs in the basement were of 25 watts. —How I came to know so many of those people before I moved in, he said to himself, all these weighty West Side Polish and Viennese families. Their altruism and dependability, cohesive like the Granolithic floor of the lobby of The Wynd, the thousand dimly lit polished lobbies of the West Side. And now he rose early, especially on summer mornings, made dark coffee and opened the windows onto the Drive, letting the night's smoky air-conditioning out into the city. He sat in the pink room in any season. Now he thought he might there pass many, or most, of the last pleasant moments that were to be his—before the nurses start showing up. *Nurses.*

Why doesn't Manhattan tip more toward New Jersey, MacK thought, with all these heavy *family buildings* on Riverside and West End? While on the East Side you just have a lot of flight attendants with wicker furniture who *aren't home*—unless Park Avenue makes up for it—but all those hi-rises on Second and Third—the stuff of magazine cartoons—must be light as feathers. Mob concrete like Hostess Twinkies, plywood where there should be sheet rock and metal. But *here* we have the University and Grant's Tomb, which must weigh a ton. MacK was not unfamiliar with certain *lurches of feeling* on the West Side, the slide and dip of hangover, even when safe in his armchair at the marble table, which he felt might be the thing beginning, New York tipping drastically into the Hudson——the *worst* would be all that East Side crap sliding across you as you went under, getting biffed by a lot of bad chef's salads and Lincoln Town Cars and bar stools from those Third Avenue places for people who're afraid of New York.

He would sit at his marble table in the mornings with coffee, he thought, bread and butter, the cat, the Non-Anglophone sweetly still. He would give up the newspapers (he read the *New York Times* in the pink room and the *Daily News* on the 'stoop') and just think about the women in the building. He heard enough 'news' just walking past the News Division on his way to work. You hear a lot of news.

Isidor would almost never visit MacK in The Wynd, even though he liked MacK's ribbon of river, the fleeting slivers of sloop sails in June, could *tolerate* he supposed a martini in the pink room, speculate on what suggestions the high-backed chairs made. Frankly, Isidor had always disapproved theoretically MacK's friendship with Mrs Leninsky, his little courtships in the building, now the infatuation with Olive, whatever went on with the prettily packaged Non-Anglophone, whom he *definitely did not wish to encounter, Sir* . . . Isidor was Downtown Man now and always fervently wished any sightings of himself on the Upper West Side to quickly pass into speculation and folk history. MacK had used his affinities with the Leninskys to BECOME one of them, Isidor felt; this was a shameless inworming, the unnecessary acts of a misguided man, an idiot really squirming and forcing himself into a place Isidor could not imagine *anyone* wanting to be:

### IN A JEWISH FAMILY!

And what's more, *he eats the f\*\*\*ing food!* And this drove Isidor bananas.

*How*, reasoned Isidor, could this proto or sub Wazp (Iz has never been sure how to categorize MacK for his own ultimate purposes), Wazp O' the West, eat matzobrei and mushroom barley soup, challah, rugelach? HAH? And MacK for his part realized this and for his own edification would say to Isidor on occasion, *in public*, that he wanted some flanken, a *good plate of flanken*—and watch Isidor hit the ceiling. How can this guy joke around like this, thought angry Isidor, it's not like he *converts*, it's like he pretends to be a Jew with a Celtic name. The brief stop-over, Sir. MacK had this way of joking around, a synthesis of comedians 1958–1971—he and Isidor did it on purpose to each other from time to time—in some ways it was MacK's real humor—but to top this with the *incredible* claim that he liked flanken, he'd *like some good flanken*, is an insult, thought Izzy, to my intelligence, to my Mama. Oops, thought of her. F***!

On this question: MacK and his ancient, desperate bid to rid himself of the attentions of his cousin Maureen, who relentlessly came at him with a bible and a lot of questions when they were supposed to be having their childhoods! Playing! Finally one day he told her, when she'd mashed him up against the wall of the laundry room of their grandmother's house, she breathing new testament all over him and the bodice of her party dress moving up and down quickly from the hide-and-seek—he finally *said*: Don't tell anyone but I am *secretly Jewish*. It seemed the only response to oppression.

An incident in MacK's disorderly spiritual life which Isidor wouldn't have been surprised to know—though he didn't—Iz too had cousins good only for to escape and revile. MacK always thought it sounded more a sex story than a bid for religious tolerance, A BREAK FOR FREEDOM. It didn't work—she kept after him until he started stealing her underwear, which resulted, in a few weeks, in the *total cessation of their relationship with one another for all time*—and it is a method to be commended. She won't even look at him at *funerals* now. So some things can work out.

—

Sidney, who unnervingly was Olive's cousin, kept *mentioning* MacK to her in this SIDNEY WAY—one of those types of ways which you are never sure helps—off and on MacK had been at family dinners with Mrs Leninsky, Sidney and Olive, during the years he was falling in love, with Olive and the building. A year before Mrs Leninsky left, he and Olive chanced to have a conversation in private—waiting for the elevator—he thought she might take some little interest in him—she suddenly asked *Are you Jewish, MacK?*, not suspiciously but more as if the thought he *might* be had just struck her—he saw it was more important to her than he had hoped. She hadn't considered it previously, he saw, but now that he was possibly more than a guy just around the family, around The Wynd, she needed to think it out.

And his feeble answer, which in Olive's generous spirit and loveliness she has never mentioned to me again, says MacK to himself in the street, and did not hold against me, was a surprised and uncomfortable

**Well SIDNEY says I am*!***

which was supposed to be a complex and rich remark *meaning:* does religion matter?—I am one of the lynch-pin neurotics here in town and something of a comedian and besides I eat a lot of stuff from Murray's Sturgeon Shop so you needn't worry . . . But this made him sound, of course, like a JACK ASS. And how could the Chief Announcer of the NBC Radio Network be so poor at ad lib?


Olive knew nothing of MacK's confinement of his animal spirits to 407 even after he moved in. An affable, curious, game woman. So of course she agreed to see him, friend of Sidney's, what could be wrong with it?

When you are allowed into someone's apartment in the beginning of—? —, politely allowed to look politely around—someone you have not yet kissed—the conversation is IDIOTIC. Even if youse is a natch, even if you will marry and have six children (a tragic youngster, even)—even if you're Comden and Green, Leopold and Loeb, Anthony y Cleopatra, the talk of the first days: —fumble!

But things are happening, you *have* got to the apartment stage—the purpose of which is to allow you to examine the STUFF OF THE POSSIBLE BELOVED. To judge her, him—cruelly? —peremptorily, by it?—if need be. Many a tragic youngster has not been born into the world because her possible mother caught sight of an Al Hirt LP. MacK was quite taken with Olive's stuff—since it was hers, to begin with—and she was part of the Leninskys and 407—his own building!, he had thought with pleasure.

He was anxious to move on to the next stage—which hasn't happened—*It never happened*, he said now on Broadway. Even though they attempted it for several months during which MacK *visibly warmed* whenever the thought of Olive came to him in his electric casket of dials at 30 Rockefeller Plaza. —Our whole relationship, he said, which never occurred and now never can, consisted entirely in the introductory stage! Twenty precinema drinks. *Wine*, too, for too long—before we realized we both prefer *brown liquor*. Unfortunate love—when you make maybe a hot-house of town and try to force a bud.

The closest he had come to her was awkwardly getting up from her sofa to 'help' her (= WATCH and you know it) make coffee during long discussions which to his deep disappointment never revealed or even heralded love—were never personal enough, not at all. The kind of evening you know—how that sort of time feels—you're being *so* polite—it still isn't really apparent what sort of visit either of you thinks this really is . . . Ah, there must be more nice hope each early evening in New York than anywhere on earth. Must be so many guys in the newer jacket helpfully watching women make coffee, women who are desirable and careful, who know how to make conversation, with table lamps lit for a while—until it is time for the Belasco, Alice Tully, the Trans-Lux—hope hot in coffee pots, in tiny snapping bubbles in home-made ice cubes—warmed by pretty lamps and book-lined walls. Hopes which keep the engine of town going. —But the conversation remains that of the movie foyer, said MacK, and what have these people made of things by midnight?

—And the *picture*, he said with a bitterness which was a new and hated thing. He had leaned his shoulder on the wall of Olive's little hallway these times—it led from the front door past the kitchen, into the living-room—her bedroom was beyond—forever—while she made this coffee and they talked of the maddeningly inconsequential. *The doorman made a pass at me last year, funny, me too.* And noticed an enticingly young Olive in this school picture on the wall. Isn't it just great how at age forty you can still witness yourself suffering the torments of the damned—your skin—hair—that shirt!—let's you and I see George Eastman in HELL.

Olive was way in the back—she hadn't begun to turn into what she now was. She looked like a collection of fence palings—looking down at the floor in an embarrassment of adolescence—your shame and disgust and terror at what is happening to you forever preserved. The picture was taken so long ago it had no glamor to it, as everything seems to have now—MacK recognized the asphalt tiles which threw glare at the lens—the flooring of school and supermarket—he could smell sweeping compound. Hadn't he sat himself in the same molded beige plastic chairs which seemed briefly the harbingers of a new world in 1966 until a big dumb guy in Civilization learned to crease and fold them back like an ear? After which your school was filled with chairs without backs?

*OLIVE*, in the back row, where life has not yet started, but two bad girls in the front row ever so slightly flipping the bird, snickering *about* laughing hard, the way girls laugh, as though it's their *last chance* to laugh. So doomed and adult—their earrings and nail polish said it—bad girl, bad teeth—biker chicks at the Lycée Française? —the precocious one the closest to flipping the bird in reality—one arm across her ribbed breasts, grasping her elbow—you could see the giggle—her left hand lying palm-up as if casually on her thigh, the first third and fourth fingers curled just behind the middle finger—oh man she was GOOD—been practicing for years—and this was the picture they distributed to the class! And her friend, in classic *friend* mode, who imitates the bad girl's hair and clothes, so far as she's able in her strictured home, but in whose doughy featureless face you don't find the same *will to evil*, or much of a life coming at all—she's egged on to smoke on the way home but can't do it *at* school the way Princess Flipping Bird could. *You* know, the friend tried to make her clothes provocative, slightly illegal like the Princess's—and now she's married to a nice guy in Connecticut but they have a tragic youngster who occasionally gets write-ups in the local paper. The Princess disappeared from her life in the first car of boys, said MacK to himself still with the bitterness. And there to the left were the large grown up spectacles and pretty interesting lips of *Natalie*—MacK knew her name as she'd signed the picture to Olive—Natalie blurred a little as she was giving her black hair a toss when the shutter fired . . .

Very unfortunately from the first day he visited Olive's apartment MacK became preoccupied with this f***ing picture. It was the energy, the past maybe, not the insolence—of course the intriguing view of early Olive—and now anything seemed able, at the right moment, to make him miserably consider something, *anything* he'd never got around to. This god damned picture had so many potential stories in it—*I call them into my office*—he hires Natalie as his secretary, she was so . . . *loyal*—he runs into Princess Flipping Bird in Hurley's—the friend! —is with her! —suburb—tragic baby—he *sees* it in her *face!* —the whole thing is *ridiculous*, said MacK, they're just girls who went to a school in New York twenty years ago, *twenty*, stupid.

51

And wondered if Olive knew them still. By the time his romance with Olive was half not through, MacK's dream-eye had wandered on to the bad girls and Natalie so many times that he missed the picture in his own apartment and did not know what to do about it. —I should have smuggled it out of her place, said MacK, *out of respect for her*, and had it photostatted and returned it—would have been easy in overcoat weather. Would have put my copy in the same black dime-store frame—kept it by the bed—*I call them into my office*—or the bathroom. Would have been too weird to hang it in the relative place in his own apartment (he had the same short hall containing similar lost bereft and un-figured-out items).

One of the many disappointments of an early death: he wouldn't be able any more to visit this *stupid picture*.

Isidor, surprisingly, had nothing against Olive—liked her in fact—had even invited the two of them to a jazz club he liked and beamed at them across bird-bath martinis—by which I mean of considerable diameter, not 20 ml you merely flick your feathers in. —*Isidor* saw that jazz might be our bond, said MacK, facing downtown and thinking of the streets of the West Village the way you may on a remote corner. *Now* the guy tells me, after I dragged her to Carnegie Hall. *Isidor* discovered she knew all about it, that she could have shown *me* all about it! Where MacK had been feeling like Babbitt with his Beiderbecke cd, she showed him Braxton; MacK stuck in the Holland Tunnel of *nostalgie* and she shows him *Dave* Holland.

So obviously you don't do bondage cocktails with Anthony Braxton and you don't do it with the girl who's introduced him to you and you don't do it with Fletcher Henderson either!, as the Non-Anglophone often pointed out in irritation. (MacK thought she *liked* Fletcher Henderson.) Rooty toot toot.

This meant fortuitously that jazz would lose its theatrical, talismanic role in the dimmer-mellow cocktail hour. He'd indeed been using this all as a sound track for—*pffft!* Much as the ZHLUB of previous generations might buy his secretary some lamé number, fix her a *pitcher* (ugh) *of martinis*—what is *that?*—and stick on *Music for the Love Hours*. Phew!

Isidor beamed at them across the bird-baths and complained about the snacks. —What do you want? said MacK, the heaving sashimi of the Sea of Japan? *These ashtrays are plastic.* —Yeah well, said Isidor, something a little nicer than party mix, with a ten-dollar martini you expect something a little . . . perhaps you and your friend would like some flanken. Waiter? And she laughed. So prettily. But am *I* allowed to laugh at this? thought MacK. —It's funny, he said.


Down Broadway with regained equilibrium, he thought, or at least Librium. Something like that ere long. *So much to look forward to*, as Iz said in speaking of the gradual, nasty, noisy falling apart of his parents. There was a conversation he and MacK had had in the elevator a month before (Isidor will open up personally between the tenth and fifteenth floors of his tower—if the lady with the metal nose doesn't get on)—MacK was admitting he thought the doctor would soon tell him *Yes you're ill, you've had it in fact*, and said to Iz that in a strange way becoming a member of the family of the building had killed him—his immersion in family life had started death ticking. He thought that without taking on the tragic role he had in The Wynd and with the Leninskys he could have gone to and from his 'glittering catafalque' in the RCA Building, the nightly embalming martini, the pretty, immobilized girls forever. —But that was all no good, it's better this way, MacK said. Not really knowing. He didn't believe he wouldn't have died—cerebration must end or you will go mad and moldy—but he felt his aging had been arrested by static routine, as if by the heavy sound-proof walls at work—and that the Leninskys had given it a kick-start. —Yes, you've always been a great friend of the Jewish people, said Isidor.

Who somehow wanted to agree they'd killed him if that proved to be the case.

Now MacK on the street corner thought about Olive in the way dying people think, he supposed: he'd understood nothing, nothing about Olive or New York or jazz or baseball. What *are* these things about? Too late to understand New York except to walk through it several times more. If only he had got away from jazz as the silly soundtrack for looking out the window with, mornings, before going to his entirely absurd job, the very biblical definition of EPHEMERA, helping the winking blinking network hypnotize people to forget their lives were passing by and couldn't come back. Continue with that only so long as it helped him to stare out the window and take his intricate pleasures from town as he could.

But he and Olive had *come close*—that is not failure—to understanding or knowing each other maybe. —If there is to be no more time, there is today, MacK said to himself, during which she may be seen, visited, appreciated. Fixed perhaps in memory. On my way downtown I will just casually POP IN as I pass her office.

# Broadway & 79th

Since he'd stood looking out at the Drive this morning, looking down into the dark cup of coffee, the taste of which he found he paid attention to particularly—its black and astringency made poignant, somehow *pointed* by the doctor's call—the gentle talk of the Non-Anglophone—MacK had pictured the whole day as motion. Had sent his mind's eye as on a camera dolly or crane, all through Manhattan, calling in at various places, seeing people, taking in old haunts—too many actually to accomplish. But wondered, or thought, that this day might be his last day out and about—last *official* day.

MacK ruminated on the main door of 407, which on setting out on his travels he had found open, the doorman hiding in that revolting little room of his—how much the half-open door of

Lenin's tomb glimpsed at two in the morning—as I am sure you are aware—will affect you!—not only creepy that people are doing things in there at night, but the implication that a coming and going from death is possible or even likely—the thought of the *heavy ceremonial door* standing partly open. Something that oughtn't to be open standing casually ajar . . .

Of course *so much to look forward to* as Isidor said—but in picturing the busy day, with Isidor at the end, the soft lights of The Hour, it had all been movement, flight of one kind or another, and here he'd allowed himself to become mournfully sidetracked, by thoughts of Olive, whom he had slightly exuberantly determined to see. *Just popping in* would put light in the middle of the day. Would it be odd simply to walk in to her office, see her look up? But such a thing could happen, he'd been there before—the others looked at him a little knowingly, he thought—she wouldn't have said anything but they saw anyone who came to see her as a potential mate. People in offices are like that—they've no imagination. Whenever MacK had to go to the Presentation Department to see Nancy Schwartz, there was a guy, Ed Zink, who had the office next to hers and *would* wink and up-thumb MacK during his entire transaction with Nancy, which always was very pleasant but for Ed Zink's facial contortions, which as the business went on became more exaggerated and even hideous—women are right, men are predatory and evil. How dare *Ed Zink* make this burlesque semaphore while MacK rested his hand on Nancy's desk, poring over the print-outs, *Projected Continuity Television & Radio Networks 17 February 1600 - 1930 EST Confidential Not To Be Taken From Rockefeller Center—Auth N Schwartz*, looking at her dark hair, resolving to make that entry about the burgundian probability of her underwear in his semi-secret ledger? At least it was still a secret to Ed Zink he hoped.

Meanwhile heading down Broadway, its usual beck. Times Square really is magnetic, he thought—it draws you down, or up, Broadway, but *for what?* There's no point to it any more, it's like dung draws scarabs one supposes, but one does feel drawn *along* Broadway.

# Tombs

Uneasy feelings can accrue in the West 70s. The scary Pillow Bank lives there, and to think therefore about death in a new way, which he already was, thanks a lot. The Pillow Bank, an odd-looking thing built in the Depression, odd that they had the money to build a *monumental bank*. The architect must have been desperate for something to do for quite some time—you can see all his drink-fuelled nightmares of Scottish coffering coming out. The heavy sandstone blocks all have their edges ground down to a softer line. The main door is set back, hiding from the Oriental copper lanterns. If you stand across Broadway the Pillow Bank looks quilted. The absurd soft-looking stone, the lanterns and also the proximity of the Riverside Memorial Chapel on Amsterdam got all MacK's tomb juices going. You can walk by a lot of icky stuff without *having* to notice it—you must—but one stormy day he and Sidney had been walking up Amsterdam, quickly—hoping the sky wouldn't divulge quite its all before they could reach the *Dublin House*—when these two stiffs unloading another stiff let him slip and flop out onto the sidewalk—not ugly, just dead—as if a final comment on the day—and now this IN USE 24 HOURS PER DAY loading dock with its interior rubber curtain and frosted glass and *fluorescent light* and *very ominous clipboards on hooks* is one of MacK's dreaded funerary whirlpools. *Mazel tov* on yer mausolea. Always drawn to, he thought, and repulsed by, marble, stone, granite, particularly black, black with grey, with red, folded—*pillowed* stone, as it folded around the 'sleeping person'. Sweet, dead air. Doors recessed and stairways flattened, the steps wide, to make them easier for—the dead? Indirect lighting—from torchières—which was one of the things that could give him the creeps in the RCA Building, even if he was standing with Shelby Stein and denigrating somebody. In Grant's Tomb the mixture of quiet, eternal stone with sinister *mechanical systems* you only glimpse—ventilators, electrical closets, the feeling that the building is a little more alive than those immured in it, that you are in a slightly grim trap at the moment—the building is on its guard.

Shallow steps, particularly, always going down into a dark well; also any UNEXPLAINED RECESSES or empty, auxiliary rooms—what are they for!

Light playing on the ceiling of a dome, or seen softly in a cupola or cloister—that's what makes you think Lenin is in there. He's at home; he still exists somehow. Pop in.

*Lenin's Tomb* is MacK's name also for a cash machine set in red granite and black diorite, in the wall of an immense temple of the business of the XIX century just off Madison Square, companies that cannot die because their buildings weigh so much, which machine MacK has occasion to consult (the awful weight of the whole building forcing his paltry cash out like squished fruit).

But in his normal travels of the West Side he encounters little tomb-fear; the Pillow Bank is the worst—the soft stones remind him of Isidor's disastrous decision to carpet the sunken living-room in his apartment—there are two shallow steps leading down to it and after they had been neatly done in stone grey wool they looked so like what Mausolus, or rather *Artemisia* would have wanted that MacK could barely walk down them; he sat unsteadily on Isidor's couch with his hands on his knees and after several anguished visits had to request that Isidor have the carpet taken up. No, the Pillow Bank is the worst thing in the weekly round—aside from the back lobby at work. The lobby of the old telephone building on lower Broadway holds some complicated problems for MacK, but you'd only be going there on some sort of historical jaunt, with architects, not likely. *Field trips suck*, Isidor said.

The softness of the Pillow Bank reminds MacK of how they bury people in England. Cozily. Everybody's buried flat in America now, sleeping flat under brass or stone markers pushed down into the grass. So you can gaze at a cemetery and think only of golf. But in (ahhh) *England* they're concerned for your comfort—*after* you've died, that is—your grave is a plump, delicious little bed. For weeks after your burial it will be draped with flowers, while a quilt of thick grass grows. Then you'll sleep tight—warm under your soft blankets of loam. See the fat little headstones, like marshmallows, or toast, leaning back slightly, just like lovely little pillows propped up for reading, *watching telly*, knitting. It's too inviting, the English grave, MacK thought. What's wrong with wanting to be tucked up as if by Mummy forever?

—What's wrong is what's *happening* under there, motherf***ers, said MacK as he stepped off the curb, having come to the end of the block and the city was moving again, with relief. Many possible journeys on the day. But it was suddenly important, MacK thought, to see Olive. He'd give nothing away. Just *pop in* as anyone might have. Her office, the Fairchild Building. Madison again. Madison, Madison, *Madison* figures in everything—lots to do with Isidor, the museum, all the tobacconists. He felt suddenly tilted, like the *Fishermen's Last Supper* by Marsden Hartley in the Whitney. On Madison. And before he actually would come upon the Pillow Bank and had to deal with all of that he turned and *ran!* Straight for Amsterdam and the Park! With cancer!

Never a runner, only a talker and a smoker. F***er. MacK nonetheless was able to gather speed in a convincing way for brief episodes—though perhaps it was necessary to convince only himself today. The day was apple-cold and he might avoid that which he hated most in the world: to perspire. He kept his own bottle of spray cleaner at work to keep MARKS off the console; even though radio studios of the National Broadcasting Company are air-conditioned to 66° Fahrenheit. Up Amsterdam Avenue he ran, past its beer emporia which smell of cold in summer and the comforting fires of 'Marlboro Lites' in winter—turned east to trot nervously past Planetarium Station, the meanest Post Office in New York—and experienced once again the unreasonable depth of his disappointment at this—*Well you in the wrong f***ing line mother-erf***er how you feel now?*—he who so loved the Planetarium and thought you should never name anything bad after it—then things widened and then the trees and turrets of the museum of natural history and smokes in the leaves from a chestnut and hot dog man—the wiener guy checked him with the kind of look you always get when you run but not in running *clothes*—actually a look of pity and disgust—who's gotta run?—guy's gotta *run* over here—though it's often taken for suspicion—the colors of the leaves turning, the smoke which seemed theatrical—the gay *sabretto's* umbrella—his stripy shirt and MacK already felt breathless now and imagined a moment out of *musicals* where he hands MacK a hot dog and MacK would do-si-do around his cart—hold out a buck—he waves it off with a smile—CUZ I'M DYING!—they dance up and down the sidewalk together while large-eyed small animals of the Park environs gather to watch . . .

He slowed in front of the Planetarium, found himself stopping to face it to his surprise but it was the home of many gods, gods of soundproofing and of his early love of *lit controls*, ye gods he thought the Planetarium is where I stored the whole of my childhood here in town without knowing it maybe; here was a god if not *the* god of funerary lighting, and here the surprisingly graceful Projector itself, whirling its dumbbell worlds through its own hysterical night—little gods of recessed Art Deco doorways and double doors and Granolithic floors—he thought in astonishment that the various planetaria of his childhood might have propelled him directly and materially into the RCA Building—but the *sabretteur* was staring at him strangely far from dancing and if there was anything MacK disliked it was: *being regarded with suspicion by outdoor vendors* so off at a trot again toward the red and yellow foliage of the Park, nicely set off he thought by a new black paving of Central Park West just like looking out the window from the pink room at home.

Central Park is everyone's refuge, everyone goes there several times a day, at least in their thoughts—it's why we aren't London tenks gut or Los Angeles—and puffing keenly remembered his old enchantment with it—in the brave bicycle days—the first blinding explosion of autumn he'd ever experienced was here, *right here*—nothing had ever changed color in October, or ever, when he was a boy—but *these* trees were what he had been looking for all his life and to be able to stir himself *into the autumn itself* through his new found and cherished 'Owl' and 'Sobranie' with the chestnut vendors' smoke and the park department's bonfires and all that brightness—what he'd been waiting for since masturbating himself to a pulp in the feeble suburb where I constructed, he said, a little XIX century east coast of the mind, made it out of a worn green Viking edition of Thoreau, Pete Seeger, my tenor recorder, an Osmiroid italic pen, what bushes I could find that did make fall and a horse chestnut I cherished for its brown luster—tried to polish it in the pocket like the old men of the Buckeye State, —*Is that all there is of tradition in your family?* Isidor'd asked, *keeping a piece of garbage in your pocket?*, and when he was finally reunited for that's what it was with the vibrant seasons here, with a particularly vivid pumpkin on Canal Street his first Hallowe'en in this our town he'd thought *I'm alive*, imagine a pumpkin doing *that* for you—but I am a sentimental joe, MacK thought, underneath *this tough radio announcing exterior* I am a big girl's blouse ha ha ha and say it was really time to stop running as everything hurt quite a bit and he had run all the way from Broadway and surely he hadn't run this far since running all the way across the George Washington Bridge early one morning in 1973 to convince some girl that . . . so what, all he got was the father pulling his blanko look.

So waited for the signal here at the West Drive with an affable-looking man who had a golf bag over his shoulder. MacK could not help noticing that each club had a *cover*—had never considered the need for this—imagined it was something his ancestors would eschew, possibly did eschew and were thrown out of Scotland because of it—they do everything so achingly properly, MacK lamented, and chid himself for this too—and then with a start he saw that each tight-fitting leather cover displayed an enameled face—like a little family crowding out of the bag to look friendly out at MacK—and *then* he took a close look at the face on the cover of the—?—driver, he supposed—and realized it was but exactly the face of *Abraham D Beame*, and then in a nanosecond experienced the conviction that the set of golf club covers represented the mayors of this our town and in a flash this was dispelled by the positively *creepy* discovery that they *all* had the likeness of Beame, eleven little Abe Beames! *Abe Beame's face!* So he had to say to the affable-looking man, natch: —Amazing covers. —*Thanks man*. They were still waiting for the light to change—the affable-looking man looked only straight ahead. —They're all Beame, is that right? said MacK. —*I wouldn't know*, the affable-looking man said, still looking ahead. —But where did you, who do you think they, ah . . . MacK trailed off, seeing now the affable-looking man had stolen them only a minute or two before. —*I really don't know*, said the affable-looking man striding off now with the green light, the little mayors joggling for position and smiling goodbye from their bag at MacK who remained still for a moment. And then MacK crossed the West Drive onto a different trail from the affable-looking man and made across the bridle path toward the Sheep Meadow and he saw he was moving like a marionette on a familiar journey—he hadn't intended to visit this old part of life but here were the children of metal, what the Hell is it with this Park, some days there are more statues of kids than kids—perhaps the mayor's idea of safety. The bronze kids glinted through the foliage and now here he was at *SHAKESPEARE IN THE PARK!*

# The Pursuit of Actresses

## WHEN YOU ARE TWENTY-TWO-YEARS OLD
## YOU WILL DO ANYTHING FOR A LIVING

Sidney has a way with waiters: torture. With banter. The busier they are, the more Sidney banters. He drives them mad with increasingly stupid asides until their eyes are so glazed and their jaws so set their teeth begin to crack. What's more, not only is it a chore just getting Sidney's order out from between his idiotic jokes, but Sidney keeps *changing* his order. The waiter can't see that Sidney's orders are throw-away lines. The waiter scribbles on page after page of his pad, he's confused, he's red in the face, he's even starting to write down some of the jokes . . . Then Sidney ambushes the waiter. He's just given his real order, that was his stomach talking, he suddenly *slams* his menu shut and loudly says *And can we have that right away please!* Once when MacK was dining with Sidney and he pulled this, the waiter abruptly wet himself. But that was an extreme case.

MacK is usually embarrassed by Sidney's behavior, but he's happy to be eating with him, on the sort of day in early summer you can enjoy before the very streets swell with perspiration. MacK needs a new job. He wants money, excitement, *l'art*. So Sidney's offered him the first job that has come along at the theater.

Conclusion of enchiladas. MacK bunches up his napkin and burps into its absorbency. Startled from a reverie by this noise, the waiter comes. —Dessert and coffee, says he. —Whole cheese-cake, says Sidney. Yet more charm, thinks the waiter. A shameful scene follows: more banter, frustration, and a lot of cake if not a whole.

To walk off almost a whole cake takes almost a whole after-noon, almost the whole of Third Avenue, north to south. In the

30s, Sidney draws MacK aside. By gesturing he indicates a woman on a bicycle. She wears very short whites. Her hair is cut in a bob; sunglasses of the day. Although MacK notices a particular speckle, a ring-around-the-nightclub look under the eyes, Sidney does not. —That's an *actress*, boy, he says, watch this. Sidney fills his lungs to capacity and pronounces the name *Mlle South Carolina Java*. The bicycle woman turns, peers through her shades at Sidney while remaining in admirable traffic light pose on her machine. A smile impossible to evaluate plays on her lips. —Mamzel, says Sidney, of course you remember me. —Of course, she replies. You put your hand in my bodice. Every night cept Mondies. A taxi driver takes this in and honks urgently. —Huh! says MacK. Sidney starts pulling him up the street. —Her microphone she means, he says, it must of course be placed exactly. MacK follows Sidney round a corner. They stand bent over and panting on the threshold of a luncheon-ette. —I think she likes me, says Sidney. This is the first time the Mamzel notices me to talk to. —There was, says MacK, an element of . . . wryness? —Could go either way, says Sidney, but listen, you ought to hear her sing. In her celebrated role, in her hooped cos-tume she drifts about the stage like a feather from the pillow of our lord.

—What will it be, buddy? says the luncheonetteer. For Sidney has staggered in and sat. —Champagne, says Sidney. —Egg cream for me, says MacK. Guy says to his subluchary:

**Gimme two egg creams out.**

Several nights later. MacK and Sidney in the control room, fondling knobs. Their job. —She's coming on soon, Sidney whispers, wait until you get a load. —Warning electric 29, croons Lampedusa, stage manager and meddling he-bitch. —Just wait, says Sidney. —Stand by electric 29, says Lampedusa. Sidney's eyes widen slowly in thrill. —Electric 29 go, says Lampedusa. On stage, the entrance of Mlle South Carolina Java: whole nations of audience spontaneously applaud. MacK is transfixed by Sidney's transfixment: it's amusing to see a familiar organism come to a complete halt. —29 bloody go, yells Lampedusa. —You mean me? says MacK. Sidney snaps out of it and cuffs him. —Certainly he means you! What are you doing? Go! Go! MacK tweaks the appropriate knob. —Little late I guess, he says. —A little! fumes the Lamp, listen you have a great future, of course it's not in the theater. —Ba-dum-bump, says Sidney. Over the headphones titters of the crew arrive from various dark points. —Don't worry, says Sidney, I'm the shop steward. Only I can fire you. —Good, says MacK, go and get knotted, Lampedusa. —You're fired! says Sidney, that's insubordination.

But on stage something is happening besides the play. In the heat of the summer Park hundreds of bugs are drawn to the gaily lit tableau. Every time Mlle Carolina opens up for breath, tons of 'em fly down her throat. They swarm over her authentic snood. But the Mlle thinks she has the solution: she stops the play.

—Could we have the lights lower please? The Mlle casts heart-breaking looks at the control room. —What's she saying? hisses Lampedusa. He's off book, the swine. —We're on page fifty, says Sidney helpfully. —But what . . . ? —She wants the level down, because of insects, says MacK. —Oh no, says Lampedusa, 33 through 37 are bumps!

Sidney goes crazy. His big chance. In MacK's ear he booms: Master down one and one-half! Ahead one-third, clang of distant telegraph. Outside, things get dimmer. The audience applauds again. Mlle Carolina sweetly bows in the direction of the control room. Inside, Sidney is meltingly in love. MacK and the Lamp are just melting. Throughout history, air-conditioning is too expensive for the likes of them.

After the performance, Sidney bolts headlong from the room and rushes backstage. He hurls himself against the door of the Mlle's dressing-room, scratching with his nails and biting at the paper star. Under this assault the door gives way and we find the Mlle désha-billée. —Mamzel, Mamzel, cries Sidney, it's me, what turned down

the lights for you. He blushes modest. O you can't have forgot.
—Oh. Thanks. And goes back to demaquillating herself. Now
Sidney blushes fulsome to recognize beneath a bulging drape the
winged tips of Signore Bastinetto, leading cad and man. Sidney's
heart breaks dully; he retreats mumbling *Remember me, remember me*.

Several hours later, in the Freesia. Sidney slams down his empty
glass. —Dag nabbum, he says, each and every one ovum.


It is like falling in love with the subject of a painting. You don't, can't
take *Woman Drying Herself* to lunch. You mustn't!


MacK at the fly gallery, throwing levers, helped in the hoisting of
booms by Mouie, vivacious dark and small. MacK's sort really, looking
at history. But he is blind to everything but Mlle Weisswurst, star of the
new play. —What's she got I ain't? whines Mouie. MacK can't hear. He
subconsciously feels Mouie's vivacious dark small presence, her developed little forearms appearing from the rolled slightly up sleeves of a
notorious black sweater. But MacK thinks only of the Mlle.

Lampedusa assumes the role of matchmaker, the cow. —You can't
fool me, he drizzles in the privacy of the control room, the
Mademoiselle! You ache for her. Ah it is ze oldest story in ze world, is
it not? MacK is alarmed lest others perceive his pain. —Why are you
talking like that, he says. —But listen, says Lampedusa, she is, I can
reveal, involved with Signore Mandelbaum. —What! says MacK, that
no-talent! —Ah yes it is sad but true is it not? oozes Lampedusa, he has
an extensive loft and he can seem boyish and sincere, so said the papers.
(Snorts from MacK.)—But I, says the Lamp, subtly will undertake to
apprise the Mademoiselle of your . . . sentiments. —Under the circumstances, says MacK. —Exactly, says Lampedusa. How's that for *la*
buddy-buddy? —And in return? says suddenly suspicious MacK.
—Why in return, says the Lamp confidentially, *stop cocking up my show!*

—

Mouie deserts MacK in her affections, taking up for lack of anything else with Canopa, heaviest stagehand in the world. There are fears for her safety. Sidney and MacK indolently while away rehearsals in the control room. —Our job begins on opening night, says Sidney, just give them work light, anything else is criminal.

They while away intermissions in the Freesia. Sidney grips his rimy glass, he discourses hotly. —She is vivacious dark and small, he says, o those forearms. Her teeth are little candies without the wrappers. —Forearmed is forewarned, says MacK. He makes bubbles in his drink, brooding about Signore Mandelbaum. —Why are they always named Jack? he says. —Who? —Other men.

Sidney is cast down, he suddenly thinks Mouie has a Jack somewhere, a Jack searching for her, although Canopa is a stone anyone would leave unturned.

In the control room as in rooms all the world round, men dream at their jobs. MacK and Sidney's job is to aid the dreams of the pit. MacK dreams of Mlle Weisswurst. Sidney devotes himself to making banter on the headphones with Mouie, crouched up far away in the flies. She seems responsive. Once a night she has to pull a string and make a special effect. —This headphone system is not for frivolity let me remind you? says Lampedusa, warning electric 44, fly gallery 9. MacK's eyes are on Mlle Weisswurst's stunning performance. She is a rare English rose beset by war and brass bands. Tell the truth, the Mlle looks like old photographs of MacK's ma.

Mlle Jo-Ann Weisswurst, Ohio originally, leads a life something between her own and representations of the lives of actresses in jolly old movies. The lineaments of her face seem against her wishes to cast her in inconclusive roles in life as well as on the stage. The Mlle has an expressively wide though dainty mouth, ripe eyelids, a fine forehead. While photographable, her cheekbones are not those of high art. Her eyebrows are of prairie stock. She is petite but not petite enough to play a believably petite person. So she toils in the

English theater's gift to the ages, comedy that is never funny. The Mlle finds no satisfaction in her wobbly paychecks nor in her minuscule apartment which is sometimes hard to find.

Signore Mandelbaum is a lanky rebel. His family of moneyed paleontologists wildly disapprove of his theatrical career even though they send him money. And occasional boxes of bones, meant to entice. Thus the Signore has a welcoming extensive loft and can be, when not shampooed in gin, boyish and sincere. So said the papers.

Lying in the *L* of the loft, the Mlle thinks: any actress secure enough in the hideous insecurity of her profession would never consort with a member of the crew, lackaday! What a dirty bunch of plaid-shirt-wearing drunks. Whew! Perhaps a night with a burly scenic carpenter. But no.

But Mlle Jo-Ann has noticed that MacK's eyebrows are of the hinterland. And so when Lampedusa begins fussing round her dressing-room she takes an unwise interest in his prying, rude, weighted questions. It's not his job but the Lamp is attractively retying the flounces on one of the Mlle's gowns. The Mlle brushes her hair, her black and white heroines smile back at her from the mirror.

—May I say how much I enjoy your performance, says Lampedusa, and your scenes with the Signore, divine! No doubt some of this triumph is due to your relationship with the Signore, which I hope is lovely and interpersonal? —His loft is extensive, says the Mlle. There is a view of Soho and the bridges. He is often boyish and sincere. —But how marvellous! intones Lampedusa like an overgreased trombone, yet, Mademoiselle Jo-Ann, there is another in our happy company on whom your charms they have not been lost. No?

The Mlle searches a drawer for her Japanese fan, for to add the extra coyness. —Why, what do you mean, Lampie? she flutters.

—I mean the worthy MacK, electrician! cries Lampedusa, triumphantly leaving off the flounces although he is in love with them. O Mademoiselle he is smitten, he drools on the knob panel during your scenes. Not the drool of stupidity, Mademoiselle, but the *authentic slobber of love*. He asked me personally to feel you on the matter—I am his ambassador. Since he is a lowly artisan and you a bejewelled glistering thing.

—Yeah, sure, why not? says the Mlle from beneath the panchro sponge. He's got eyebrows from Ohio.

In the middle of the show, Lampedusa starts throwing weird hand-signals at MacK. MacK scrutinizes the rheostats in his purview. —Whassamatta? —You'll find out, says the Lamp, stand by electric 68. —Am I going to be fired? says MacK. —Only I can fire you, says Sidney. —Electric 68 go, says Lampedusa. —Look, what is up? says MacK. —Electric 68 go! says Lampedusa. —You're fired! shouts Sidney, pulling the lever for MacK the distracted.

The need of drama is often strangely met. Lampedusa's errand is it. Is enough for MacK. Over several weeks he begins to dream and drip at his glowing meters, dysfunctional in the knowledge that Mlle Jo-Ann is not insensitive to his finer aspects. It is his distraction from his leaking roof, all the perverts of the BMT, the Bud Abbott demeanor of Sidney, the problematic liquids of the Freesia. Doesn't actually have to approach the object of love—and then—*of course!*

The show closes, for a move to the Belasco, it is said, but some guy named Bernie torpedoes it about 38th Street. Mlle Jo-Ann enters MacK's soul only as a glow, like a distant recalled barbecue. It is easy to think love of those who never arrive.

MacK stares at a blank ream of yellow news, soon to be a smash role for the Mlle, so recently arrived on the stage of this country and MacK's heart. The hour is late. Guy works in the theater for . . . a year? *The theater is a discipline, young man, it is a whole life and you need lots of vague training at state colleges.* And yet he says to himself, *only I can write for her, only I could ever make her really and truly happy.* But this

play smells; it is about two fat men MacK has never met. He telephones to Sidney for advice. —Hello? —Ya think the two guys
could stand litotes in a scene already charged with paronomasia?
—You've awakened me. You're fired.


—Once they told us Indians killed bison only out of need, that
when the things were dead they'd go over and *pat 'em*, on the shoulder, and say *I'm sorry*, says MacK. Isn't that breathtakingly swell? I bet
they never did any such thing. But say they did, what does it suggest
for those who eschew flesh on humanitarian grounds? Might get
'em back on the meat wagon with the I'm Sorry brand of franks. Do
ya think? Are you listening to me?

MacK reflects it is curious that he is drinking cup of café-au-lait
after cup with Sidney. Normally Sidney abjures stimulants, he
cannot be relied upon for dissipation of any kind. He is afraid his
dinky but undeniable *chin cleft* will just melt away. Yet Sidney
grabbed at MacK in 50th Street, dragged him down to Shubert
Alley, into the Petit-Four and started pouring gallons of coffee down
the both of them. MacK's trachea is seared and he doesn't know
what to make of this new Sidney who wolfs coffee and frantically
examines everyone up and down. —See h h here, what's up? MacK's
starting to stutter and bark his words he's had so much Sumatra.
—Nothing nothing nothing, I'm fine fine fine, says Sidney. —Have
I done something to offend you? says MacK, you hardly can look me
in the mug. —No no no, says Sidney. His eyes go round his head like
the rings of Saturn. Suddenly he crushes MacK's biceps. —*She's
here*, growls Sidney, burning with the gemlike. MacK twists in his
chair. All he can see is the ugly double-vent of a big-ass businessman
behind him.

But then it all makes sense. Why Sidney would want to sit in a
little hell like the Petit-Four. Why he would take an afternoon away
from his fresnels, the fresnels that he loves like a woman. Why feign
enjoyment of what to him had always been poison. The Great

Doppo! Even though MacK can scarcely make her out he turns to Sidney and laughs. Might've known!

The Great Doppo appears numinous and nightly in—let us be frank—the great play of our time in the theater across the street. She brings to her role not only her beauty over which men and critics have duelled and gone mad, but insight and a talent that have earned her slavering notices in the papers. Every night the audience is swallowed whole, screaming, into the infinity of History and Meaning by her gigantic . . . green eyes. The Great Doppo chews 'em up and spits 'em out. And they love it.

Sidney is the most spat-out of all, he sees the thing almost every night and on weekends the matinées. Around the Great Doppo is an admiring crowd and her keeper.

Now the strange thing happens, does it not? Sidney begins trying on battle-plans like summer suits. Looking into Sidney's eyes, MacK sees them spin from idea to idea, on the wise of a slot machine. —Do you have a pencil, says Sidney. These management type guys they never write anything down. MacK lends him a No. 2 pencil, ruminating on the former glory of coffee-houses for writing things in, not that the Petit-Four is anything but a drain for waste money. Sidney's being vibrates with the nerve of the hunt, he scrawls with intensity. —Waiter! he calls, take this and a large Venezia i Napoli, double clotted cream, to the Great Doppo. *Avec mes compliments.* Toot the suit!

Departure of penguinlike being. Sidney starts flamadiddling his fingers on the table. He squirms in his chair. Rearranges the sit of his spectacles on his schnozz. Remarshals scarf between jacket and arran, styles his hair with his right hand, un and re buttons his shirt. Advances socks up legs, reties shoe. His pupils are very small. He stares rigidly ahead, his every nerve searches for some molecule of his being or things that orbit it which might be out of place. —What did you write? says MacK. —Oh, merely that we'd met before, says Sidney. I suggested some dimensionalities.

A shadow falls across MacK's brown froth. MacK looks up and

behold! an obviously angry obviously actress, holding a Venezia i Napoli. With deftness and dignity she swirls it into his lap. It's rather hot. —What is the meaning of this, cries Sidney, jumping to his gallant's feet. —This worm sent me this note, says the Great Doppo, I suppose he is your friend. She hands the note *his own note* to Sidney. He reads it laboriously and looks panicked from the Great Doppo to MacK. —There must be some mistake, says Sidney, I've never seen this man before in my life.

—Turds, says the Great Doppo. —Don't talk to him that way, says MacK, he is a member of the General Public. Then, inspiration! as the Great Doppo turns to recommence semicanoodle with her thuggish minder. —By the way, says MacK, that play you're in is drivel. —F*** me, Sidney groans. —O is that so, says the Great Doppo pirouetting. She makes fisties and stores them on her hips. —Yes I'm afraid it's entirely wrong for you. —Perhaps you would care to explain that, say, in my rooms, at eleven o'clock tonight with a bottle of pink champagne. —I guess I have a few opinions. —Well then.

—I was only trying to help you, says MacK in the IRT. —This is my stop, says Sidney, fuming, I'm getting out. Out, please! —What *dimensionalities?* MacK calls after him.

At the door of the rooms of the Great Doppo a knock comes. Hushing her enthusiastically responding hound, the Great Doppo opens up to find atop two legs a quivering pile of flowers, heart-shaped boxes and protrudingly embarrassing bottles of brut. —Ah, do come in, she says. Indicates the way with a waft of Chinese silk, spirals of incense, fractals of parfum and 'Sobranie'. —Charmed, says MacK, trying to avoid the hound, which has a real talent for the underfoot. The Great Doppo excuses herself to ice up. MacK puts himself on the sofa. He and the hound look deeply into each other's eyes and MacK clears his throat a lot.

Tick, tock.

—Well well, says the Great Doppo, arranging her clouds on the far end of the sofa. So you have a conception of the theater. —I . . . —Get over here.

Two bottles of champagne float empty and upended in their bucket. The sampler has been trashed, its various ribbons and pretty papers in disarray all around the room. The flowers droop, mute.

# On the Avenue

—Affairs with actresses? Whose pictures are on buses yet? How different life turned out to be, mercy. It pointedly lacks this sort of thing now, MacK said, emerging from the Park—Manhattan turned out to be strangely quiet in that way, the 1930s can never really happen to you no matter how much you want them—worse still I'd be sleeping under a bridge, not a tuxed smartie macassaring his microphone. O MacK knew the history of his own company's suavity; it was required. Something caught in his throat and he thought *There's a romance to my company . . . there was something exciting and thrilling about NBC that CBS never had. Very cold hearted over there in their cow shed.*

He inhaled the clean but complex airs of the East Side.

But there's never one of a thing in New York. There's the Schmancy East Side, these old towers of granite and brass and iron and velvet, and the glassy ones, the curious squares, defended private streets, no story, even though MacK's larynx is a frequent visitor to the smartest homes. The Quiet East Side, down Second and Third, where hangs Sunday repose. The Crap East Side, spreading nincompoop burgers and teenwear, on a mission from the malevolent gods of Hackensack. The Nibelungen of Nada. What of the Dumb-Ass East Side, a floating world of niteries where some of the 'pages' from NBC demonstrate *yes they can sing*, they make nice—a tiny *nation of yearning struggle* no one ever sees—it plays only to itself and all this sebaceous energy never emerges ever from the pages of *Show Business*—MacK had put in time in these joints years ago when some of his friends were trying to Break In, first you'll have to break out of these sour Michelob mills he thought. How many bacon cheeseburgers could he have eaten watching these crazy kids—they're in their twenties but the head shots made them look fifty, as if they'd just realized nothing was going to happen, like they lived in a TRAILER. Guy who took all the head shots had a camera that did that, a *predicting camera*. If only he had used it for good rather than evil.

—Must get off Fifth, he said, Fifth just doesn't have the humanity of Central Park West, the only real choices are Madison or Fifth and much as it is nice to have the Park on your right as you go downtown, there are a lot of weird people here, people who don't understand anything they see outside their apartments—such as . . . *me*. There really are very old ladies bent almost double by jewelry and there really are pink poodles. —Madison almost always the obvious choice, said MacK as he started across Fifth and got honked at. —Yeah, if you ever make it, snorted a guy who was paid to walk a *dog*. —Wise ass. See this always happens over here right away.

At Madison looked around, always wondering where the *Madison Bar* was—it could only be found on rainy nights when the bus never came—physically it disappeared during the day but no, here it was, its front door a gathered, sleeping face at eleven in the morning . . . a portal to one of the New Yorks that ghosted in and out of Manhattan, the Crap East Side maybe, which like Non New York has no fixed location and can jump out at you anywhere, right when you think you're in the middle of the OK East Side or the Pretty East Side . . .

## The Madison Bar

Last time in the Madison Bar MacK had been stunned, *stunned*, firstly by basketball, which he could never quite believe, that people will watch others sweat in a big stuffy room; men's legs (he recalled the 1962 shorts of Rick Barry and gagged)—secondly by a guy who had brought the Dumb-Ass East Side with him through the door like a fug—it was wrapped around him like an Afghan—talking to two Irish girls through a thick cloud of misunderstanding built of 'Winston Lights' (come *on*) and 'Stoli' martinis—'Stoli' he kept saying, '*Stoli*'—his speech was clear but he must have been blootered as the girls rolled their eyes so—ostentatiously right at each other in the middle of his sentences—you could practically hear their eyeballs plop in their highballs. —*How do you like living in New York?*—he came up with that one, suddenly, several times—*Have you been to any clubs? Have ya been to that new club on 85th?* (Roll, roll: Nah, na yet like)—*Do you know there are more cars in New York than in Ireland?* Guy sounded like reading the left-hand page of a Berlitz. —*Stoli martini Frank, Stoli*—*where do you live?* They didn't answer that one but for some reason they gave him their names and thus having conquered—?—something, triumphed in some small way he got up unsteadily and excused himself—they scampered for the street door while he checked his hair and congratulated himself and smoked and vomited all at the same time in the mens.

Ah poor MacK caught between basketball and this guy whilst trying to put his thoughts of Olive in order; he'd just taken her to the movies. He thought he might write it on a napkin. *She is intelligent, kind, the wearer of experience in life. She looks sweetly tired. Very stylish, looks a humdinger in the rain with her deep red lipstick and delicate skin. Radiates a real beauty of soul.* Here the napkin had run out—and rather than have to ask the bartender whose name might likely be Mort Rushmore for any *favors* he allowed himself to be driven out into the rain by rue and the zoo of the sweaty old Knickerbockers and this guy, the Madison Bore in the Madison Bar, driven out to follow Olive over to the West Side and into her building which after all was his own now, thinking he would never know her and couldn't even get her fine points down on a *napkin*, which one might keep as a souvenir.

—

It isn't only what is *on* Madison as you walk down it. It is the knowledge of *what* you walk through, the miasms of several cultures which can fatigue and enrage. Upper Madison has a homely, family feel to it, what with the Madison Restaurant, snow day cream of chicken and its many saltines. The old people who don't know what to do with themselves all day but go backwards and forwards between two Soup Burgs with a doggie in a little coat. *So much to look forward to*. Hello there. Hello. Walk south and you're in gallery and antique land, or first you're in antique land and then you're in gallery land and there is barely a cup of coffee to be found, *forget* cream of chicken!, *man* how they can treat you from block to block. Then an eddy of glories of semi-civic life, the neighborhood of historical societies, various Leagues, tooth-minders and twisters, tiny private schools and Japanese confectioners who are always empty because everyone is STILL LOOKING FOR THAT CREAM OF CHICKEN, said MacK at a good clip.

Around the 60s you start your descent into Little Tokyo as Iz calls it as it's hard to walk without getting pushed and shoved and having to avoid these people from New Jersey all dressed in *skins*, who have cataracts, who are each carrying something like a kilogram of waste *inside their bodies*, at any rate the big specs so dark they never step aside. WHY AREN'T THESE PEOPLE IN THEIR OFFICES? HAH?

But of course, Sherry-Lehmann, and in the odd pause in all the activity, down around 48th, the Wilbur Sisters themselves. And then of course he felt nauseous about this. Walking down Madison on an autumn afternoon can be pleasing but Madison on the wrong sort of day will drive you mad, you keep getting *glimpses of Fifth*, you think *should I be over there maybe?*, sometimes it looks festive, so *shoot* me. But when you're on Fifth it can seem you're a thousand miles from anything you know . . . the stone wall of the Park presents an unbroken sedulous grey statement of account for blocks and blocks without variation, repeating itself and the corners and cars ad nauseam like the endless background in a cartoon chase; perhaps the

whole of Fifth Avenue is a Möbius strip. MacK had always felt upper
Fifth to be an 'artist's impression' in wash, a matte suspended in
front of the brain's Panaflex. —Of course some people have managed a better grasp of Upper Fifth, he said—they live there, enough
of this *Fifth* jazz—

## Madison & 53rd

A little confused and afraid. —Oh yeah, the Fairchild Building, let's
see, dat's at . . . fiffy toid and Madison, the guy in the hat
said—friendly enough. MacK felt he had somehow forgotten—five
blocks north of the Wilbur Sisters—ought to've clocked *that* when
he visited Olive before—but isn't it true that sometimes you just
don't know where you are in this our town?—it only lasts a few
minutes. Sun on the many panes—you could see how the glen-plaid
steel-cut suits of the early Sixties worked in harmony with the buildings and the haircuts—Madison at work; Madison comes out to
play; crisp piano and very precise brushwork. Jazz like lamps—Ed
Thigpen coming and going through revolving doors of magazine
buildings, his brushes in an attaché case. The Fairchild is one of the
old *gentlemanly* buildings—and there was something related to the
aspect of the RCA Building which offered a kind of communal
warmth—not just expressed in *murals*—but in 1930 Rockefeller
Center was supposed to be a model for the whole city—which
frankly, said MacK, is enough to make you guffaw, given what happened to the whole *country* since then—as MacK and Shelby Stein
frequently *did* guffaw, after breathing in Sert's great mural, *Time*. But
still there was something to cherish in humanism you find here and
there in this our town, stuck like gum on the under sides of
things—an ember—*some*body, at *some* time in history, must have
had a beneficent feeling toward *some*one. Look at the directory in the
lobby of the Fairchild Building: are these not all people, my people,
your people, pulling together? Making and selling things? —*What's*

*wrong with the world of 1957 anyway*, said MacK under his breath, and felt a stab of guilt, betraying the Sixties and their necessary destruction of all that post-war refrigerator horse shit—which of course has been completely *ineffectual*—as we're back to BIG refrigerators and BIG cars, BACK TO BIG IN A BIG WAY—but the security guy frowned.

O pleasing elevators of the Fairchild Building. Actually icky—the cabs remodeled, but the smooth old motors—an excellent, shipshape basement, half-grey walls, 25-watt bulbs to be sure. You know, whatever the *Christian Coalition* may think, there are a lot of plain old offices in New York, offices not made of marble, many offices which lack deep carpeting with secretaries writhing in, thought MacK, even the RCA Building, functional, beautiful, never luxurious—even the Music Hall, which is grand, but its grandeur is for *you,* in 1930. You were wearing a hat. Everything in New York was for you.

In a minute the doors would open on the 18th floor and he'd walk along, as he had several times, down the plain corridor to the door of

## KAM-ART BROS., INC.

where Olive worked every day in the company her father had started. Running it now, really, her father tired and puffing in the city, taking the day off more and more. His hat, suit, overcoat, car—the old routine—but visiting the building something like a former owner or even a ghost. What became important was the still alive hat and journey—he ceased to look into the accounts. MacK loved Olive the more for this, her love for her father and his modest accomplishment, she had picked it up, dealt with the clients in a forthright, honest, lovely way. He liked to see her working along with everyone else, coming out of her father's glassed-in office for MacK's moony visits. Is there anything more attractive to us town boys than competence, assurance? Sign of survival after all—not to veer into that New-York-is-a-jungle, DNA twaddle. But MacK loved her, loved the look of her in her understated and slightly arty suits, her lipstick, her quiet stride.

Kam-Art Bros., Inc., dealt daily with the design of paddy-to-the-touch corrugated boxes for light bulbs, the ones which, once squeezed——. The design for their major client hadn't changed since Olive's father made it in 1964. But! So many things like squeezy boxes have to be worried through the decades, in plain offices like this.

He thought again, as the elevator doors opened and a bell rang, of their movie date, which was both open and closed, and inconclusive; of her inquiry as to his religion. Never thought he would be obliged to answer such a question in New York—but where else? —And now I'm going to die and New York never got around to allowing me to be Jewish—right at the end here when I most need to, he said.

At the office he reached out for the knob—the door with combed-look frosted glass in it, *Kam-Art Bros., Inc.* painted there the day they moved in, in 1959, and never retouched—it did strike him as odd—what was he doing just *showing up*, in the *middle of a business day!?*, he could hear his father—I'm *popping in*, is what I'm doing, said MacK—he'd opened the door and he saw the carpet and the receptionist and there might be a smile when he asked to see Olive.

She was looking at a computerized schema of light-bulb boxes—what else? —the 25-watt, in blue and yellow and white. If only she had known of MacK's fondness for 25-watt bulbs she'd have got him a few from the rep, who always tried to give her bulbs—but are you hearing this, a guy has to *represent light bulbs*. What the——? Even though the package designs were old-fashioned and stark and immutable, Olive had a nostalgia for the days of two-color printing—it reminded her of her childhood—and her moment of reminiscing was confused and then atomized when in a small sequence of flashes through the office—the main door open-ing, confusion of the office lights, sun light and hallway light—she saw in these lights MacK's face, coming in, smiling at the recep-tionist—he's always polite and pleasant, Olive thought in the flashes, MacK's *concise head*—he told her the NBC barber said once *Very concise head Sir*—being directed by the receptionist's pink-nailed hand—now he was looking in her direction. But his eyes weren't his own, were very dark in the slow-moving prism of the outer door whirring on its closer—and Olive was on her feet and going over to him—she didn't run, though she might have, so plain was the news on his face.

The way she looked as she came toward him, the corner of her mouth, her tongue peeping out and preparing her, the *recognizable poignancy of her freckles* shocked him into the realization that she knew, had instantly known why he was there. This hurt MacK because it ruined the pretense he had allowed himself—that he was just saying hello. Merely *popping in* . . . He couldn't say anything. Now I'm a *tragic sick person*, he thought, roaming a building where I don't have an office—could be a matter for SECURITY.

*In the middle of a business day!?*

He was a disquieting sight; he could only mean one thing.


For her part: Olive found MacK stern about things, irascible in his opinions of paintings and movies; not one of those men who turn every organ of New York to their own use—drinking up the Modern like a martini and making the *New York Review of Books* their dripping brunch waffle and staying with a woman just through the current pack of 'Marlboro Lites'—but in keeping to himself, in making time to THINK in his apartment, Olive thought MacK might in fact have New York by a better handle.

She found him nice. She found him confused. She found him ignorant of the simplest intellectually arresting points of jazz and baseball (why *did* he live in New York? —for Isidor). She found him eager and funny and lost in the career of disembodiment he had at NBC and wondered what it meant to him.

Their last conversation had been in her apartment, on the other side of the building from his own—he looking at the picture of the girls from the Lycée—Olive was making coffee in preparation, they thought, for another *inconclusive visit to the Modern*—he'd stopped bothering to keep track of these goddamn visits and he thought standing there looking at the bad girls that there are entirely too many museums in New York—and none of them was going to do the trick with Olive, offer her a glimpse into what might be their romance, show her something eerie and recognizable, tragic or old that stimulates the orgone, eros, the romantic—what is the point of *dragging* these women around museums, Mr New York?

—You know, screw it, said MacK, they *wrecked the lobby you know*. So the Modern was bagged and they sat at Olive's table with wine and her little coffee pot from Naples. She was talking about her poor father's gradual debility and MacK suddenly found the entire great hairy go-round with his doctor spilling out of him, a litany, the way *semen* comes out once it starts—surprised at the thought—pointedly, he noticed himself thinking, because he hated all those people who will top one disease with another:

—*I've got a bum knee.*

—*Yes . . . oh but my BRAIN!*

So here was Olive saying *my father's heart disease*—which he'd every right to have at the age of eighty—and MacK blurting out *I probably have lung cancer,* then trying to trail off, soften it for himself as much as for Olive—*they aren't quite sure*—. His face heated by actually saying these words. Thought he'd know what they would sound like but hadn't really.

She expressed her shock and concern so sweetly. She did not take his hand as he hoped she might. MacK just sat there wondering that he was still outside; outside the family, the building, Jewry,

Olive. And indeed how close was she going to come now to someone who might DIE? Someone who treated her religion as something which could be *assigned* to him, as a cultural whim, or a joke of *Sidney*? Where is my anger? It boiled up that night, MacK thought, I was very angry at this probable cancer right there because before my eyes it was eliminating my chances of love *that evening*.

*Guess I better go*—that's what you say. *Let me know what happens*, she said at the door—he couldn't figure what she meant—he was so full of stupid self-pity, ignoring the complicated reality of their interest in each other. Pondered, in the hall, the biological injustices of the present age which prevented Olive from taking him to her bed for solace—but you're SCREWY, even without these bugs on the loose she'd never f*** him out of 'sympathy'.

But Olive had not been so disinterested in MacK as it pleased him—you know—on some level to suppose. But the EGG TIMER: this expensive plastic clam brooding in the grotto of the bedside drawer, the tyrannical little magistrate of the pockabook—occasionally you allow it a taste of you that few men can have experienced—it gets to know you hideously, thoroughly—a digital incubus you have *paid* for—and when you do think you would quite like to make love you open up the thing and it blinks, in *red*,

NO!

NO!

NO!

The simple disagreement of electronics and desire—she'd figured it would come right in a week or two. Meanwhile, the museums.

After pensively leaving Olive and going down to the ground floor and crossing to his side of the building, he discovered the Non-Anglophone having trouble as always with her door key—he helped her in——her Yale lock (you see what happens?) was installed upside down for some idiotic reason of *supers*. She stood looking at him with her very large eyes. She searched his face, which must have held anguish beyond the usual New York five o'clock shadow of death. Let's face it, whatever's happened to you, by the end of the day you're sick of it. She sat him down and gave him a serving of a goat dish of her people, whoever they exactly were. A large glass of red wine and f\*\*\*ed him against the old refrigerator in her boots which smacked, he imagined, of ENVER HOXHA. And the irony is: with crazy goat-driven sex you don't worry about The Bugs like you just did out there in the hall.

This morning Olive had been thinking about MacK on the subway. Olive remained beautiful on the subway, remote from the subway, even on hot days, even though she used the No. 1 and even though she went through the impossible rigmarole of going to Grand Central and getting the *f\*\*\*ing* F at Rockefeller Center——and even thought in a mode you might associate with *him*, that sometimes she might be beneath the RCA Building, when she was down in that scarily shitty station——and that he was up there in it.

There are plenty of people who are mighty impressed with themselves in this our town, but they still have to go to work——it never struck Olive that she lived in an exciting place even though almost every morning she saw a character from Sesame Street buying a breakfast of hot dogs and cigarettes——no one has time to stop and think that what they're doing would seem impossibly glamorous in that terrible big country out there.

Olive had been a few places and in a few romances which had great unsuitability as her parents thought——Mrs Leninsky's sister and her husband——who of course lived in The Wynd. Ten years ago they'd got one of the penthouses——yes, yes——but like all penthouses it was a mixed blessing——the guy in the other one kept coming out in the foyer in his underpants, raving about forgotten or obscure doughnuts.

But was this part of Olive's reluctance about MacK—that her parents would instantly find out if anything were to 'go on'?—quotation marks like that are the drawback of *buildings*. Where MacK quietly treasured the idea of 'marrying' *into* the family of the building, the building of the family—Olive was wary of making trouble, now that her fate in the firm seemed as sealed as a door in Thebes—as she'd made trouble (for *herself*—her mother and father were confident they'd stop almost anything) with her Italian, her Celt, her Dane, her Fireman, her Orthodox Labor Lawyer already (he chewed with his mouth open)—in her attempts to get *out*.

She talked quietly to MacK now in her father's office, assuring him no one had sensed anything *tragic* or of emergency about his coming—although MacK hadn't heard it, she'd spoken to him and invited him in as normally as if he'd had a suitcase full of light bulbs—what'd *they* know anyway? —*Why did you come to see me?* —I had a call from the . . . —*I know. But why did you come to see ME?* —I was on a walk. I was thinking about the, our building. —*407?* She talked with him in such tones of understanding you could scarcely believe quite such a conversation was happening in an office. Because it was Olive there was a quiet saxophone ballad behind everything, he thought—maybe jazz leaks out of all the glass boxes of Madison Avenue long before the cocktail hour—from when things were largely grey and brown.

If you have a problem in New York, someone will help you. Almost anyone will.

Her quietness and composure and level beauty made him want to weep—but he was exhilarated too, by the city, by the odd feeling of *holiday*, the thought of Isidor at the end of the day. He felt inarticulate—and happy to be with her—and embarrassed about that; still felt he was a visual and sociological problem within the confines of the Fairchild Building.

But now Olive was saying that *she* had had a fright the year before.

Her breast. And now MacK did begin to weep—for the *word breast*—the signals about tissues they were exchanging!—for the pain she might have had, for the worry she suffered—and because her breast he imagined as something ineffably sweet—and he had never seen it.

He choked on all this, seeing she was worried about him but was she also worried about what kind of scene might develop here maybe—was this a moment which demanded rationalism? So be it—rational guy, after all. Degree. Apartment. Place to go in RCA Building. Wanted to say *I'll miss our little chats*—but that was cruel—or *remember me*, *memento mori*—but why saddle OLIVE with that crap, truly *why* break into her life and dump your possible end in her lap and expect her to do something about it? Horse shit!

At the elevator bank, she kissed him, with a meaningful tenderness he'd never have imagined, even his romantic fantasies having only to do with the surfaces of things, the taste of a cigarette at a moment of declaration. First words, never last words. You could say it was because she had been through the 'same thing'—all these doctors, all this coffee and thinking about the end of life—wishing you could call all your life to you at one moment, at your desk—but that had ended and she was going to live—was living—her life become the usual question mark—the downward curve of which toward that **dot** we choose to ignore.

# 50 West 50th Street

> *Four-thirty Sunday afternoon in New York, and the RCA Building*
> *stands up tall and respectfully removes its hat.*
>
> —Introduction to an NBC program, 1940s

With MacK it was always radio—he stood across the street from his favored entrance to the RCA Building—attempting not to think

about the blackest portion of the lobby—gold squares, who cares.
Watched people coming and going under the coffered lamps which
no one but himself ever bothered to look up and love, or be loved by
the old gentler city there. Here comes Nancy Schwartz. —Radio,
he said aloud, in his *known voice*. In the same gawp's way he was now
looking at the metal awning and the red NBC, he'd used to gaze at
the bronze lettering *KGO-810* at the old ABC building in San
Francisco—the scenario, if you will have it, was: a bleak, pitted
adolescent took the train into the city to stand in fog or rain and
stare through heavy plate glass at various hip AM personalities—if
you can accept AM as hip in 1968—three layers of glass which made
something only a few feet away very remote, remote as the network,
teeming away just behind the meter glow and red keys on the engineer's panel—the network, which swept the station up into its arms
for five minutes every hour with a mighty drum roll—and kissed its
tush, Shelby would have said. Discovered something about suavity
from watching the sometimes surprising embodiments of the area's
best-loved voices coming and going from this rather elegant
studio—what snazzy dressers—fell in love with the Electro-Voice
microphone in its suspensory—noticed that someone had taped a
typewritten sign under the Simplex clock at the announcers'
desk—*I CHOOSE NOT TO SMOKE*—and set himself for a career like
that of the duty announcer—a hero the unions have had to give
up—who came into the studio twice an hour, leaned into the microphone and gave a station break rather perfectly making almost all the
radios in northern California throb—the rest of the time he sat
around eating oranges. MacK *peering in* at these guys just making a
living who certainly found most repellent the idea of being worshipped by a *pockmarked monster*—but being a Californian with *by law*
no religious training what so ever, he worshipped what plain gods
were available.

When MacK got in the cab to come to 50 West 50th Street for his
first day of work, it throbbed in the same way as he *over-pronounced*
'NBC at Radio City!' as Isidor was always accusing him of slipping

into work mode. Ignoring MacK's several *years of struggle*, in the wilderness of gabble, doing ads, reading the news to millions who didn't care, not only what the news *was*, but didn't care what it *sounded* like, bastards—and I did achieve it, MacK suddenly thought, but hadn't for years, that his job *was* like the one he had coveted peering into that old radio station in the rain (a little ashamed of this, company man now)—sitting in his studio, the directors in his head-phones— *'Standby announce'*—the red lights tick down—*'And . . . announce!'*—and after all there was not much to say these days.

—Radio is hooey, let's admit it, said MacK looking at the 50th Street entrance, there goes Nancy Schwartz back in, worse than hooey, it's *guano*, but at least there is still such a thing as the NBC Radio Network and my studio and the old elevators and I've been able to preserve the illusion of polish and romance if not exactly *meaning*. Radio began verily as the new tribune of the people in the twentieth century, prac-tically in this very building. And now it only mocks and undermines them. Can you believe that disk jockeys *still exist?*

Radio is adolescence, rejection, revenge. One is always hidden. There are meters. KNOBS.

He still felt something electric in the atmosphere of the older stu-dios on his floor—ye gods five years ago they came up from Engineering with plans for a technical renovation, some digital board with sliding pots and MacK had flipped: —You are *not* going to put *sliding potentiometers* in my studio, he said, this is the *RCA Building*.

He imagined some kind of similarly charged sacred air around altars—and it occurred to him that he felt about all these places the way he did about the TOMBS collecting in his head, which were now becoming more of a preoccupation, because of . . . —So, work will kill you, said MacK, nothing prophetic in that idea.

Last year, standing outside the Rockefeller Plaza entrance with Shelby, who was smoking one of his legion 'Pall Malls': MacK looked up at the sculpted beardy above them, *'Wisdom and Knowledge Shall Be The Stability Of Thy Times'*, and said: —Wait a minute, is this Zeus or Prometheus? —Beats me, said Shelby, I always thought it was Santa. MacK ignored this. But you have to get the pantheon straight. —So *that's* Prometheus, he said, looking out at the gold rink hunk. Shelby hissed his last lungful between his teeth and threw the butt so that it landed just behind the heel of the real door man, a character in a top hat who had been trained to wait for celebrities with an umbrella. Shelby always tried to flip it right there, perhaps hoping for some kind of hot foot. He was under pressures that those in radio could only dream about. He looked out at Prometheus with his slightly yellow eyes. —Yeah well *my* liver ain't so good either, and stalked off under Sert's great mural, *Time*, to the elevators to go upstairs and do promos for *Bonacker*, which was then at number three, and Promotions was pressing so *hard*.


—My years of struggle, smiled MacK, which in fact were not, involving only long shifts on the local station as well. The Seventies and Eighties were not overly difficult at work, but what did make them years of struggle, said MacK, suddenly chilled, was Tumbleson, *she* was the struggle.

Since he was working weird shifts he could often, around four o'clock, walk down to where she worked on Vanderbilt Avenue—filling himself with what he thought of as the *copper feeling* of midtown in an autumn evening, a romantic compound he made for himself of the early street lights, the sun going down on the side of the RCA Building maybe, smoke from the vendors' carts, a pipe of 'Owl'. He would walk her home, to the Upper West Side, where she kept a pewter beer goblet for him in her freezer—a nice gesture to her man—frequently his lips would freeze to it and shred.

He would make grand statements, looking out from her apartment at a large but mundane panorama of the West 70s.

## I LOVE THIS CITY. I LOVE YOU.

What the Hell was he talking about? But Tumbleson was not a romantic girl, she had no little god of New York romance to worship, no James Cagney to MacK's Celeste Holm, and concerned only with the hackneyed epic of Business, she was experiencing the slow disillusionment and sedimentation of time which only working in a midtown office can provide.

Did YOU never make any sartorial mistakes 1970–1980? He bought some shoes near Lincoln Center which seemed *reasonable facsimiles* of tasseled loafers but after he walked in them for several days they became oddly shaped and depressing—they made Tumbleson furious. (Shelby kindly pointed out that tasseled loafers aren't for walking in. —Look at me, he said, I *drive* in—from *Larchmont*. His were tan.)

After a time MacK and Tumbleson began each to believe the other was trapped in *the wrong New York*; and there is nothing you can do about that.

You may think that your face is just you, or how you look. What you put food in and talk out of—but in New York it is a tool, a weapon maybe, said MacK, crossing to the ice rink. You have to hone it, push it through the streets of people, and if you have a sharp, an amazing, a frightening *ferocious face* like *Tumbleson*, you'll get where you're going a lot quicker.

# 44th & Vanderbilt

Which always sounds like something that isn't in Manhattan—ought to be in Brooklyn or on the Monopoly board. *Almighty*, he'd never noticed that the Yale Club was designed by the Pillow Bank guy—must have been—even sneakily tried to make it look like *Columbia*, to *justify* somehow the presence of Yale in New York—as if buggering everything in Pine Street isn't enough. Built this new haven for themselves a few tottering steps from the tracks to New Haven—where is your *courage?*—'We need it right by the train.' F*** you! Remembered the look of these lanterns on copper evenings when he was 'dating' Tumbleson—isn't it fatuous to use the innocent rectangles of the calendar to mean *penetration?*—in the mid Seventies, when no one gave a damn about New York except Isidor and Jackie Onassis. Tumbleson was at a complete loss about all the charms he went on about—never liked Isidor anyway—MacK thought she'd ruined her ability to understand New York at all, working for Yalies, like foreign ground, a consulate.

Today the lobby was even more tomb-like than he remembered it—the tiny sensations you could glean of Vanderbilt Avenue, which after all was *immediately outside*, in bright sunshine, made it and the whole city seem, yes, something to be disparaged and belittled—that *could* be manipulated from in here. Guy in a uniform. —*May* I help you, Sir? —Yes. I wish to book the New Haven Room for the Tie Appreciation Group, thought MacK, as I do every October. But this guy's eyebrow, which ought to be taxidermied and mounted over the marble hearth upon his death, he should *drop dead* as soon as possible, MacK thought—was clearly a thing to avoid stimulating. —Tumbleson, said MacK to the Frank Morgan look-alike.

You expect a Pierpont Morgan look-alike and they have a *Frank* Morgan look-alike.

—Is Miss Tumbleson expecting you, Sir? —She was expecting me for dinner at her small apartment in the mid 70s in the mid Seventies, said MacK. *The guy's eyebrow.* —So no, not in her wildest dreams. The guy phones . . .

MacK used to try to find some warmth or even a welcome in this place—to convince himself that sleeping with Tumbleson made life light and gay, that he was an honorary part of the Yale family—though it was some dysfunctional family—drunk at lunch and staggering around, peering bleary at cabinets of trophies and funerary sweaters . . . *Have you seen the display? Have you seen the display?* this guy Charlie would always say—after his first martini—Tumbleson worked for him—when MacK showed up every other day to share his *truly innocent* NBC vending machine sandwich with her. —*Carter—tryna get rid of martinis, at lunch anyhow—on the attack, isn't he?* Charlie went on and on—*James EARL Carter, a peanut farmer, can you—credit cards too, he hates 'em. Have you seen the display?* But Carter has the right idea, thought MacK, at least prevent CHARLIE from getting his mitts on unlimited credit and the lunch hour martinis. But of course MacK had been a big problem in Tumbleson's life—saw that now. She probably worried for months how to get rid of him. —*You know what they used to tell us in the war?* said Charlie after his third. —What? —*Keep a tight asshole!* —Oh . . . you're it?

Discovered her, composed and presentable behind a large desk in the FUNCTIONS DEPARTMENT, which she responsibly ran now.

—*Look who's here.* She seemed all right. Pretty. —Sorry I'm late. —*Ha.* Looked about the same as before, as *twenty years before*, the kind of thing that drives Izzy . . . —*What have you been doing?* —Well, I've been stuck in the RCA Building for the last twelve years. —*What you always wanted.* —But in the elevator? **Ba-dum-bump!** She smiled; became a little wary. —*What are you doing here?* —I was on a walk and . . . realized the Club looks like my bank. —*!*— —Just thought you might be in. —*Oh I'm in. I've been in.* She paused for a moment in which they both traveled a bit and then grew older. —*Care for a cocktail? I'm the housekeeper, you might say.* Twirled a key on the end of a fine gold chain—just as she used to make provoking gestures out of *Cosmopolitan*, MacK thought.

She led him through blank serving corridors to a bar—the Members' Bar—which wasn't in use. Smelled of chlorine and wool. —*This doesn't open till five—they can get crocked in the dining room at lunch. Still abusing the bottle?* —I'm shocked. Rather it me. —*Martini?*

In an obscure, plentifully stocked bar with Tumbleson!—the stuff of rather desperate phantasy during Redless weekends of the past—now shut sudden away and perhaps cruel from the brightness and inappropriate optimism he'd felt for the last hours, leaving the West Side and wandering happily in midtown which may be thought never to end—always hope and well-being to be found between 59th and 34th—even if but provisionally your own. Her body remembered in her dark suit beneath the darkness that is Yale and its pillowed stone, shuttered against the eyes of Manhattan which would be annoyed to see everyone staggering around in here. In those ties.

—Incredibly, I accede. —*Good for you.* She sounded suddenly tired, like a kick-ass Chandler broad—which she could have been, maybe—if she'd been taller. She had filed down her sweet voice with twenty years of 'Marlboro Lites'. He saw as she lit one and then started up with the glass and metal. MacK leaned on the bar, which was stone and chilly, imagined reclining on it, thought of the cornerstone of the Riverside Memorial Chapel—what an annoying obstacle-course of crypts was Manhattan become.

They raised their glasses to each other silently, almost in the dark.

Isn't it awful to remember what it is like to consciously convince yourself you are in love? Such a huge lie makes every movement painful, every decision agony. For both. MacK was falling in love with the city and supposed he was, or could, with Tumbleson at the same time, or assumed it would happen, *natch*—much as he had *presumed*, when a child, that intercourse occurs when both parties are asleep. Or had *hoped*. He would drift around midtown and rejoice in the tobacconists and shirt stores as evening descended—the copper point of balance between the rapidly deepening sky and the wakening street lamps. Smoke. Prized Autumn, and therefore of course he must be in love with this girl, taking her home most days to the appalling West 70s and that *god awful cop bar*, so that she could shuck her Yale exoskeleton and get her therapeutic helping of violence and sleaze.

Tumbleson turned, with the Yale Club Rubber Martini Olive ($24.95 at Club shop) in her teeth. —*They think this is funny*, she said. *We sell a lot of these.* She squeezed it and it squeaked. —*It's for their dogs.* —That I can well believe. Where do you live now? —*Hartsdale.* —!— —*I'm married, MacK . . . surprised?* —Oddly, I—no. He now learned all about Hartsdale, and about her *doubly tragic youngster*, which had *cysts* and—ironically—could not pronounce its *Ss*—nothing to be done, *but then she suddenly found him out and caressed him*—kneeling, replaced the dog's toy with himself for some moments—got up and turned against the bar—somehow representing the receding aspects of herself and Yale—into which she had never quite disappeared—at least not ideologically, wholly—and they began to move as they used . . . This could be, he thought, one of the last times, *the* last time, and it's with—but what the Hell, she has needs!—that's what she used to say when she'd been with someone else—*people have needs.* MacK felt himself fall back from the city for a moment and observe it—the cycle of fidelity and infidelity, wished or not, worried or not—the Ferris wheel of New York privilege he'd never ridden properly—nor even seen the view. The Yale Club is solidly built, he thought, as her noise came—he started on his—she pushed him back with a small, impatient, yet recognizable hand. Took a mouthful of the cold grey silver, which she had made with real style, he noticed—if only Isidor were here—of course you have to deal with high-octane to get these guys disoriented and down to their ties and sock garters in daylight hours—and put it to him. The old days! He remembered their past funs—which never led to love, no matter how intense—and thought of the beautiful, possible Olive.

Arrived, in Tumbleson's pillowed, stony mouth. Infinite stack of Yale Club napkins.

—Why did you do that? asked MacK, touching her upper arm with . . . *something* strong he was feeling—she didn't know the edge of the world was something he could glimpse readily from the poop of his *Niña*—which seemed the absolute limit of what he might touch—even though she was leaning, relaxed, against the bar, one leg crossed over the other.

—Because we're going to die some day.

Goodbye, all the warmth of Yale.

Had told himself: nothing today—not one—he'd save the capacity for *wonderment* for Isidor and The Hour—but out the big door and around a corner or two to McAnn's, the one where you go way WAY down the stairs and the old bar huddles against the wall in the big dark place—still embarrassed to have usurped the cafeteria of decent office girls of 1950 in the name of the needs of the honestly confused men of midtown. But a glass of beer, a cheeseburger?—a jolly dollop of quotidian smirch after that vivid, chilly twenty minutes in the Roost of the Big Shots—sometimes, Mom, it is just a coolant. Have to remind you that cleanliness and order belong to the land of the imagination. And I am probably the only fellow in the whole joint with lipstick on him, though who can know, he thought, with the first untroubled smile of the day—he caught this himself—it is two o'clock and after all is said and done

**THIS IS A HAPPY TOWN.**

# Why I Hate Food

At the mention of food, thought MacK, it always gradually breaks out a fight. Something has happened to the way people eat; there are too many TRIBES about it. There is the tribe of those who eat only at home, their tiny kitchens stuffed with cookbooks. If they have space they have built kitchen *islands*, under spotlights, grand opera kitchens where the dinner guest drowses drunkly and slowly starves while watching his fat, obsessed host prepare the meal—there is a man on Thompson Street who has an APPLAUSE sign over his island. Its burners in the night. You see it from the imagined safety of your ship. The drums.

Some will only eat in restaurants—they can't, *won't* make you coffee or a drink, even in *anticipation* of the restaurant. But the largest tribe are those who cannot eat the GOOD FOOD WHICH IS FREELY AVAILABLE ON EVERY CORNER IN THIS OUR TOWN. It's right in front of them—but if *sustenance* is mentioned, so is a *taxi*. You could be walking past the GRAND CENTRAL OYSTER BAR even, but no, *NO,* being *proximate* to a place *rules it out*; complicated negotiations must be entered into between every one in the party and you are then forced into a taxi—*the forcemeat stuffing of a taxi*—and hurtled somewhere far uptown, far downtown, and preferably across town from where you realized you were hungry. So hungry. Or *thought* you were hungry! Hasn't your appetite disappeared after one of these *contretemps* asserted of course in the friendliest possible way? HAH?

As we go about town, we encounter a number of altercations, hold-ups, confrontations—it's inevitable—what *look like crimes*—we step around them in the street, on the subway steps, people locked in combat, yes—we observe little tussles out the window of our office or the bus. A has B by the lapels; C uses her stilettos unfairly. But most of these contests aren't crimes—they are people *arguing about where to eat*. It really has come to this. Our town is so disconnected from its sources of supply that where to dine has become a life-and-death struggle—it seems nothing has changed since the Neolithic (excepting perhaps napery). Arguing about where to eat is just as exhausting as chipping your arrow-head and going out to try and kill capybara ancestor; eventually in surprise succeeding and hauling it home, chopping it up and heating it in some unimaginable way.

And supermarkets are all run by JACK ASSES. They take even more time than capybara ancestor.

———

—I truly hate food, MacK said to Isidor recently, I just can't take it any more. F*** food! Of course, *f***food,* he thought immediately—not Bob Guccione spilling Bosco on the rattan, you idiot—but the bachelor picking up little snacks to salt the appetite of his intended—carbohydrates and *rounded* things that might be popped between red lips—things that are slimy—f***food. Isidor became very uneasy when MacK said f***food as it sounded like a put-down of food, which he could not bear, for *food* to be denigrated—F*** FRUIT especially, MacK loudly said in a bad mood one day in Union Square. It's really just sugar and water in a suspiciously plasticky wrapping. Really bad for you. My teeth always ache at the thought of biting apples. *I hate food!*

Isidor's eyes became a wide, morose blue at this. —Keep your voice down, he said under his breath. —It's all the preparation, MacK said, the horrible amount of time—even as a child it drove me MAD to watch people making food, my poor mother, the gas, father raging at his brazier, trying to make it fun, trying to make it—MANLY? Every moment I've spent shopping, cooking, eating and washing dishes I've wished I were smoking, reading, drinking or screwing. Don't you see how important it is to recognize the restaurant, the delicatessen, the pretzel-and-chestnut man as THE ONLY SOURCES OF FOOD? Otherwise you'll end up crying in the street. *Sanctify* the delicatessen, said MacK, the restaurant and their waiters which are closest to your front door, no matter how bad. What better example of the American spirit, of cooperation? Of the primal transaction? I give you something of value, shells or cigarettes, and you feed me. —But why are you fetishizing it? said Izzy, that holy transaction takes place at McDonalds 2,000 times per hour. —Ach, that doesn't count.

—Your argument is a good one, said Isidor, except I happen to know it places you at the mercy of Mary Jo's Deli. I know I know and all the feebleness of upper Broadway, MacK thought, and yes I am made sick with fear standing in Mary Jo's watching flies buzzing in the fittings, how never a single one finds its way even by accident to its blue electric Zing Zing. —Yes I EAT CARDBOARD he said and greeny baloneys because I'm sticking to my theory and it's a good one. Mine is the only theory that helps the ecology of the city and saves me time. Provides jobs. And what is the point of living in a city unless you want to save time? If you want to *waste* time go to Larchmont or Vermont or Montana—where you may pay handsomely to waste your time, waiting in line to buy gasoline or having children—or better, *you can pay people to waste your time FOR you.* Out there. Isn't this the essence of the city? You live in town because you want someone to make your morning coffee for you. Don't you think it's CHEATING to prepare food in your own home? It is only drink that nourishes and ennobles, he said. Admit it! If everyone would *just admit* that then we could send all our wheat overseas to those hungry people—they're not allowed to drink, anyway. We get what we need, they get what they need. —I don't know, said Isidor.

## Bump Bump

Look what happened to the idea of food, MacK said to himself, when, years ago, you were allowed to run your fingers over the prominent contours of the vulva—nothing more—of this girl from Hunter College for three or four hours on a rainy afternoon—in the shower you could still see the dull mark on your wrist the elastic of her underwear incised there. Your poor hand in the exact same position for three hours. You withdrew it from her jeans, bloodgorged numb and purple—if only it had been another extremity—and suggested dinner, which she took as calmly as she had the mauly diddling since three o'clock. —*I'm a vegetarian*, she breathed, doing up the many buttons.

In the old neighborhood, *vegetarian* meant either a muenster cheese sandwich or that Chinese food which had been most boiled in the world—it was losing its molecular integrity. In a state ricocheting between guilt and largesse you took this two-bump beauty (thinking all evening of the pronounced quality of her labia, bump-bump, bump-bump under your fingers) to The Farmyard—*New York's Old-Established Vegetarian Restaurant*, here, in the West 40s. Bump bump, the taxi on potholes outside a garage—rain had come on while you lay on your bed, she staring at the ceiling and you wondering what the hell was happening with your life—nothing. The driver pointed out a modest door and a dingy lighted stair—the taxi went off in a series of puddles and bangs and you took the bored girl's arm out of rocketing chivalry of all sorts. Thunder, suddenly, musically, insistently; lightning across the front of the building, which took on a sinister look thanks to the crenellations of a hamburger joint on the corner. At the same moment this restaurant's venerable sign faltered and—bzzzt—The Farmyard—went out. Bump-Bump went up the stairs, you following, observing with vexation the nautical lacing at the back of her jeans—your recent prison; the scene which greeted you in the dining-room robbed you of air and drew you together—*at last she grabbed you*, in horror movie uncertainty. The shabby peanut-oiled maître d' indicated a SEA beyond of the truly distressed and decrepit; the lame, the halt dining as best they could. Here a man with a growth on his cheek *twice* the size of the growth on the ham and salad tub man at Mary Jo's Deli—hell, twice the size of what he was having for dinner; there a family of hunchbacks in their seventies or eighties *having their food cut up for them* by a waiter with a glass eye. No one a recognizable morphic type, shape, or color, and—you know—that's saying something in this our town. But Bump-Bump rushed to sit down—you lost interest in her body entirely at this point except for beginning to SCOUR HER COUNTENANCE for incipient pallor, growths, twistings—to affirm your moral insertion of her into this menagerie.

The food was classical Vegetarian with a stultifyingly capital *V*—everything vegetal fungal and udderal chopped up and molded at ferocious industrial temperature and pressure to *resemble meat*—only despite these extreme processes the semblance was but slim; each dish with a sickly dairy taste—cold *moussaka* run over by the dog-catcher. Bump-Bump ordered diffidently and seemed determined to notice nothing. When the limping waiter snatched the cover from the platter you stared in fury at your cool parsnipwursts—a shocking reiteration of the late afternoon and its rain—the girl's vulva that of a public monument—and you could barely resist fingering the depression between the two—.

Lump lump, going down. Nothing to be said, apparently, the stuff did require a lot of chewing—it was dawning on you that far from coming to The Farmyard to improve their lot, these wretches, whom you were more likely to have encountered in a fun-house—had in this place, from this food—GOT that way.

No proper ending, thought MacK—New York never lets anything die off completely between two people—but a sequel—several months later in Mary Jo's, Bump-Bump, with bigger eyes and smile, faced him off near the potato chips. *Accosted* him just as he was staggering and feeling ill at the sight of the growth on the ham and salad tub man's face, wondering if he dined at The Farmyard. And she incredulously said, *You're buying baloney!?* Above his ranged fluorescent furrows of browning caking salads, bump bump bump, the ham and salad tub man salivated at her.

# The Little Plate of Childhood

Let us take a trip down Alimentary Lane—before our food moved to New York and became perverted. Here, on a winter evening, is your plate—a jolly Georgian coaching scene—the plate is *brown and white*—and here is just *enough* juice from your little chop pleasantly to obscure the scene ('Catching the Mail')—your little chop is half an inch thick—not insignificant you might say, after all an animal has been sacrificed in your honor—but there is no suggestion of pride or plumpness or luxury in your little chop—there is something insistent about its quality as *fuel*—it is a piece of coal for your engine and since this is a WEEK NIGHT, a SCHOOL NIGHT, it's to be regarded as nothing more—there is a sterility, a NURSE-LIKE quality about mother's kitchen, is there not? Is the little chop itself your nurse? You think about it on the street corner, it is a smell you can conjure anywhere (and have done, even to put yourself to sleep in lonely rooms), your little chop, the broiler, the hood, the kitchen, the hot handles of the pots and pans, the clock, the light, the beans, the rice. Down with potatoes, the role of carbohydrate will this evening ladies and gentlemen be played by White Rice, not sticky together like school rice from a scoop but not of the featheriest and most disparate. Difficult to photograph, a circumspect mound, a tussock of rice with a pat of butter upon it—the butter photographs distinctly and the rice is as always a white shape with disturbing points or shadows. For all New York's claims to cover the waterfront of gastronomy, this is a smell you will never find here, not in the most ordinary corner luncheon-ette or the plainest Sixth Avenue hotel serving the biggest dumbest hicks: the little plate of childhood.

—Ye gods This is all *in* me now, said MacK, these poorly rotogravured and pastel molecules, *inside* and perhaps nourishing something still, some idea of what dinner might be like for someone of RECTITUDE, someone with *character*. I still don't know what half the stuff was that I ate!

—Sure, you *lachrymose schlemazl*, all you eat now or all you tell everyone at the bar you eat is brown rice and vegetables delicately sautéed or oven roasted—how you stay in good trim for a city boy or girl, the balance, god's own roughage slicing all the gin and nicotine out of you. But as Isidor points out, that's all a pathetic throw-back to the little plate of childhood—except for the boring little piece of meat jumping up and down, *begging* to be carried away by the postilions of the mail.

# Destroy All Monsters

In Our Years in Yorkville, there was a battle going on between the epic and the romantic, particularly in MacK's stomach, in his belief in, his loyalty to *two foods* he had decided it was all right to be pre-occupied with—but just *screw* everybody and their restaurant neuroses—*really*, yes. The heavenly GUMBO of Mary-Ann, which he was invited to eat once a month, usually on the 27th, though he could think of no explanation for this—must have been some kind of Catholic reason, a *shrove* thing? 2 + 7 = 9 so OK maybe that adds up to gumbo, hell if he was going to *ask* her, that'd be rude—VS the hot yellow and brown MATZOBREI of Dave and Leo at the D&L Dairy which he could have had every day if he wanted—some weeks he did. Even though it was on the same level as the gumbo, speaking of a little bit of heaven here, it took quite a few matzobreis to balance the monthly gumbo *so in a sense* every-thing was all right. But the more MacK thought about the gumbo and the matzobrei they seemed to be engaged in a contest with each other, one of those end-of-the-world things—the gumbo the world as man has known it with all its and his imperfections and the matzobrei the hot *searing* from the gods that will come on the very last minute . . . that you can still order from the *lunch* menu. Usually two-thirty, three o'clock.

Or more specifically in terms of romance and epic, the gumbo and the matzobrei were playing out a war of the city—the gumbo has *been around*, it *is* romance, the Caribbean, the wonderful polyglot hemisphere; it gathered its flavors subtly many places—it simmers, smolders, seethes, pouts, teases—and you give in, it seduces you, takes you over. The matzobrei is the simplicity and persistent dignity of the proletariat—some days it doesn't taste very good, actu-ally—once MacK even made a face at Dave about it, *what* a f***ing mistake—but one has to eat—so they *say*. One is always basing one's life on the plain things that have gone before, the fish of Scotland, the yogurt of Georgia, cardboard of England; the *matzobrei* is the compressed and slightly tired though still human life of Europe; the matzobrei has been through the grinder, pal, through the f***ing mill—but it picks itself up out of the gutter and is *still being served*. (The particular one Leo'd given MacK seemed to have been through both world wars—but you *expect* it to taste like that, all suffering and sweat—some days in New York that's a rather unpalatable lunch—but everyone has to have it.)

Isidor was a staunch defender of the gumbo—since Mary-Ann would make it for him almost any time he wanted it, natch—so what gave MacK indigestion about the whole idea was that if the gumbo was romantic (and of course Izzy and Mary-Ann had romance, sure, are allowed it) then what food was going to satisfy Isidor's constant defense of the EPIC? (Unless it was the catholicity of what he consumed—anything in any neighborhood at any time—the only food Izzy had ever directly rejected was *funnel cake* at the Ninth Avenue Festival, though he claimed it was the silly *sound* of it, he didn't particularly care that it was *doughnuts* that had been through a *centrifuge*. —It sounds stupid as *bundt cake*, said Izzy—although perhaps the cake is the problem there and not its name. But there are many professional boxers, from places like *Pennsylvania*, who owe their early bulkings-up, that quintessential *luggishness* which pushed them away from life and into the ring, to *funnel cake* and its whole family of frankly unbelievable carbohydrates. You wonder what those from other planets—and they had better get here soon—would make of these things: *Why are they squeezing this glop into hot fat just like waste falls from their asses!* —HOW COULD IZZY EAT GUMBO, KNOWING IT WAS ROMANTIC AND NOT EPIC?, said MacK, who to this day has not been able to figure it out. —Unless he regarded the New World as an *epic romance*, but—pffft! What happens then? The gumbo and the matzobrei *become each other* on a teleological Ninth Avenue and—*voilà*—you have nothing to argue about.

If MacK could have but known it, at just this moment was a new giant come on the horizon to battle the towering MATZOBREI and the antediluvian GUMBO, to knock over some skyscrapers in what might admittedly be a rubber suit, kick some model cars around—fake smoke—little planes swooping on nylon wire. Its name was NAGA. *Huh!*

But he wouldn't be around to witness this ultimate destruction of the city. *Huh!*

## Canned Pears and You

One day last year in Isidor's bookshop MacK discovered the source of all this iniquity. He unearthed, from many overlays and corruptions of the need for food and drink in this our town, the color, texture, temperature, the proteins ('building blocks'—*sheesh!*), the nourishment, the MEANING of his, and Izzy's, youth. Iz stocks tons of ephemera which can make you very uncomfortable about your country and your birthright. In the dark cookery aisle MacK beheld a thing from the antique land we *all* came from, where, woe, mother would get hold of the recipe page in the local paper: *Serving Butter Attractively. Chipped Beef, an Introduction. Cottage Cheese—What Is It?* To wit:

**Down East Clam Dunk:** *Oh, great,* thought MacK, *the* verbe-comme-nom *school of cuisine.* **Blue Cheese Bologna Wedges:** *Bologna—is this spelling supposed to dignify it? 'The FUN staple meat', according to the book. It goes on to describe in surprising detail where it may be wedged.* **Cream of Baked Bean Soup:** *Are you kidding?* **Frank-Topped Zesty Succotash:** *Yiiih!—though it was the most important meat of the period, which encouraged the eating of (canned) vegetables.* **Frank 'n Vegetable Soup:** *And what they did to the letter N! Formerly a kind and useful letter.* **Luau Barbecued Ribs:** *Ah, Hawaii! Shangri-La of the mid-Fifties imagination; now merely the headquarters of minor drug dealers and gas guzzlers.* **Waikiki Kabobs:**

*Spelling just wasn't a problem to our parents. Did you know this? Also try our Waikiki* Nog. **Fiesta Corn Pudding:** *Can you imagine real Mexicans sitting around with bowls of this? They'd hang it from a string and beat the shit out of it.* **Company Cauliflower:** *They arrive, you take their coats, all is early Kennedy jollity, and then their eyes light on . . . !* **Baked Salad of the Sea:** *There was this phrase, 'of the sea', which haunted that time and drifted all around. My uncle once took me to a 'Car Wash of the Sea' in McLean, Texas. And then the idea that BAKING made a thing ready for the table, that it was physically possible to BAKE ANYTHING, as per:* **Baked Cheese Sandwiches, Baked Cheese 'n Ham Sandwiches, Ham 'n Blue Cheese Old Tyme Baked Sandwiches, Baked Swedish Meatballs** *Louis***:** ye *gods*, the ups, the downs, the doomed marriages. **Frank 'n Luau Cauliflower-Topped Baked Hi-Fi Party Rib Coolers of the Sea . . .**

*The bookstore had got very airless indeed; the stuffy aisle—*

MacK could bear it no longer. —Say, he called out to Isidor, as if for air, *Cheesy Ponytail Franks. Place frankfurters in roll. Place sandwiches on rectangles of aluminum foil. Seal carefully and twist ends to give pony-tail look!* Izzy rushed over. There in the dark cookery aisle they cackled and wept together. As he paged through this warped book, Isidor acquired a distant, bilious expression. He teetered. —Don't you hate the word *casserole* and its associated house-filling smell, said MacK suddenly, that of a big earthenware half-glazed dish with a frightening, hollow handle? Doesn't the word *casserole* itself SMELL, of unimaginatively used onions? —Yes, Iz said, how dare they serve dollops of stuff *straight from the cooking vessel*. It strikes at the heart of sensibility. It *deprives waiters of work*.

—*Baked Tuna Ring.* —Oh, said Iz, anything that could be formed into a ring was good. You *reel* from all that post-war sloth. People *will* paint that, said Izzy, as an energetic American time, but really they wanted everything all mixed up with cheese. They wanted it all 'piping hot'. And look: by the time you got to dessert, everything had taken its toll, you'd no energy left to keep cooking: *Refrigerator Cake,*

*No-Bake Confetti Brownies.* —Yes, MacK said, even though preparing the entrées merely involved stirring onion soup mix into . . . *I feel sick.*

No wonder that Isidor and MacK, reared on this kind of thing, are conflicted in their attitudes to food—and everything else for that matter. But while MacK can hardly bear to think about food, was *driven away from it at an early age*, cuisine of the atomic era had determined Isidor on loving food. Trauma ensued—Isidor always asks people about MacK *Did he feed you?* If someone visits MacK, whether uptown or out of town, the first thing Isidor asks them is

**DID HE FEED YOU?**

*The sea is only the medium of a preternatural*
*and wonderful existence; it is*
*only movement and love.*

—Captain Nemo, *Twenty Thousand Leagues*
*Under the Sea*

# The Discovery of Fish and its Waiters

took place on a damp day long ago, Isidor and MacK standing half-relaxed on the prosaic rain-corner of Seventh Avenue and 34th Street. A Monday afternoon, perhaps a public holiday, though you couldn't tell due to the absence of people who *stroll*.

They had just come out of Penn Station,—*that low-ceilinged Hell*, said Isidor, of course you won't remember the old Penn Station. —No, MacK said, I won't, and I'd rather not remember this one either. —I'm telling you, said Isidor, in Hell all the ceilings will be very low, with hot spotlights which singe the acoustical tile surrounding them so it looks like someone has been cooking French toast up there. Architects have got to go.

MacK cast about for something to contrast with the present moment on the dull rain-corner, though contrast is hard won in the West 30s. They had just visited Isidor's parents by train. Isidor's mother, for reasons of her own, believed MacK was a 'Negro' and gave him special, though off-balance, treatment. Isidor's father was fairly sure MacK was not. He took it up with her after the boys had left. —He is more or less like us, what is the matter with you? he said, picking his noonday fight. —Hoo hah! said Mrs Katz, 'more or less'!

There was very little contrast between the Katzes' house and the Erie-Lackawanna Railroad. Sitting on the wicker seats was just as stultifying as sitting on the couch of any parent—no one's choosing *sides* here. There are days, aren't there?, rare ones, when you feel like doing, and can actually do, what normal, relaxed people do. —Radio City, MacK said, thinking of the huge comforting dark to be found there on days such as this; the smugness *Morpheus* feels as you take your wallet out of your coat while passing under the illuminated name LEON LEONIDOFF. —The thing is dwindling but still there, said Isidor, and I respect that. You hear me? I *respec'* that. Let's go.

Yet they remained there on the corner, cold and bleary from the Erie-Lackawanna. MacK was reminiscing over Mrs Katz's food if truth be told. Isidor was put out with him for appreciating it. —What the hell do you mean by thanking her for her flanken? he had said. How dare you thank my murderer? —Oh well, MacK said, I don't know, two boys without their momma. Iz spat on what turned out to be a mouse in the gutter. On MacK's mind was the silver and red marquee at the Music Hall, the warm dark, long purple lights, the smell of a thousand damp coats tidily attended to. MacK looked up and down 34th Street—half way toward Eighth MacK saw a mirroring of the neon his thoughts, a warm old sign in the middle of the block. Already Isidor and MacK were susceptible to commercial overgrowths, barnacles of this kind—*Paddy's Clam House*. As if one, without speaking, they turned in the rain and walked toward it, the orange-white-green neon promising comfort of an old and inexpensive sort. Paused at the door. —Do you eat fish? said MacK. —Well, no, said Iz. And pushed on the door and they were enveloped in the steam and scream of a Fish Restaurant; where they always should have been.

There was a bar. Right as you went in—not original, but there, a little apology for those who came during times of great uproar and had to wait for a table. The charm of small glasses of Piel's for 25¢; part of the spell was looking at the ¢. —One of the last ¢ signs, said Isidor, it must be. They felt like birdwatchers; one could keep a log. MacK looked at his printed napkin, 'Paddy's Clam House', and felt finally a part of the history of his family, all the fish they'd swallowed. —My grandfather and his derby in the clam-houses of San Francisco, MacK said to Iz. He gave me a rare tongue-lashing once, outside Alioto's, he said Chowder, surely you will eat *chowder*, everybody eats CHOWDER?! I said I would have one of the awful hamburgers they grudgingly fry you on a corner of the grill in fish restaurants, but he wouldn't let me be seen with him in Alioto's if I wasn't going to eat fish. He was always going on about eggs, eggs will *kill* you, every egg a *bullet,* yet his favorite thing was to rush into Alioto's in his raincoat and eat six dozens of fried clams. —Hypocrisy is on the rise, said Isidor.

MacK thought of his grandfather going over to a bar while waiting for the cable car to be turned at the foot of Powell Street—he liked the way the sun shone through the little clerestories at him. The bar smelt of brass and hat and glass-smear.

## DRINKS 35¢

It wasn't called a bar at all; oddly, the sign outside said *Laurel Drinks*, and the wiseguy boys of the neighborhood perpetually and freshly wrote SHE DOES? underneath this with chalk and charcoal and dog pooh. Boys like the one the grandfather once was, when he felt the height of the city dizzying, and the freedom which came with dizziness: the freedom to pull the plait of the Chinaman who sold his mother vitriol, the freedom to tie a dog to the California Street cable by its tail, the freedom to hop on and hop off any moving conveyance for any reason. No conductor or Confucian or mother had ever caught him.

The bartender gave the boys big menus. —I don't, uh, said Isidor, what do you—. You should have seen them, side by side, in the mirror behind the bar, perusing their first Fish Restaurant menu, two small worried fellas, perusing it like it'd never been perused. The bartender thought they might be FOREIGNERS who COULDN'T READ.

—I gotta table for you guys, said a waiter, this way. They followed him into the din, into the SEA of white cloths, chairs, coats, people and their fingers, people talking about their ties, their stomachs, businesses—some spoke of cars, f*** *cars*. Being at 34th and Seventh, there was a bit of talk of drapery. —My parents are afraid of fish, said Isidor. —Yeah well that's very tough, said the waiter. —It's the sensuality, MacK offered, as they sat. —No, it isn't, said the waiter. —They're from Poland, said Isidor. —What do you want from me, MacK said, I'm afraid too. My dad used to take me to a *trout farm*—we floated on a lot of slimy water and caught fish who were drugged and hypnotized to OBEY. The whole thing made me very apprehensive. These fish tongued up their own silt all day which was scraped off the bottom of the pond and made into pellets which became their suppers. —*They ate their own defaeces?* said Isidor. How'd they avoid scraping up mud too from the bottom? —It was lined with cement, MacK said, blushing with awareness that he was unworthy of sitting here—what truck had he with fish—save the truck which came and emptied the brainwashed trout into that hideous basin in the semidesert? MacK leaned toward Iz. —I used to throw up at the end, he said, it was the quality of the water we were floating on and this orange pop out of this cooler-which-didn't-cool-it. I'd had no contact with a fish and no expectation of eating one, but *blugggh!* —Pretty funny, said Isidor, looking around, nervous. He felt the conversation was inappropriate for other tables.

It is odd of me, always to have despised the very idea of fish, thought MacK, considering that when young my favorite place was a tidal pool; at night after perusing *The Illustrated Book of the Sea* I often dreamt of a life under the waves, swimming effortlessly with my special friends the giant sun fish and the nautilus . . . That is until things got complicated and *they all turned into dreams of suffocation.* —My mother would boil a king crab all day, MacK said to Iz. The smell filled the house, even the *sofa cushions.* We had to brain her with the pot lid to get her to quit.

—It's extensive, I almost said universal, said Isidor, the child's hatred of fish; it's sex of course—salty, raw, pungent, inflamed, raving, pervading, a mystery to which they are not admitted. They are excluded from fish and from the rites of the parental bedroom and so they hate and fear both. —Thank you, MacK said, after a pause during which they both thought they *had* been a wee bit audible. —Where anyway is all this *salty pervading* sex you've been having? You're skating, you know, awful close to the old fishpussy thing. We are not men like that, men who think that pussy is fish and fish pussy! Men who work for a living! —Would you *stop* talking about this? said a man at the next table. —See, I have problems with, continued Isidor, red, low—I could never get past the affinity cats have for fish and couldn't sort the metaphor. —What metaphor, MacK said, it isn't a—

—Ha ha ha!, what do *you* guys know about *pussy?*, said the waiter, standing there; rocking on the balls of his feet. Big smile, greying hair combed back, short white jacket, beneath it a short white apron, black trousers and shoes. White shirt and black bow tie; towel and pad in hand—MacK could have given his description to any policeman. One's affinity for such get-ups is strong, is it not? —the orderliness of those who play *petanque.*

Smiling, engaged, affably hostile—he had taken in the conversation of these boys at the salient word and was including himself in; had already put Isidor and MacK in his 'little world'—but expressions like this are very irritating—there is only *one* world, after all, and those who would make *special worlds* usually have the purposes of capitalism in mind— *'Welcome to the World of Golf'*—or belittlement. He's in his own world, twirl finger by temple.

### —What'll ya have today—

The menu was large and daily set in tiny Fournier. Bluefish, oysters, snapper, crackers, sauces—these things raced in arcs of ice water around their heads. Isidor was stunned by the menu and its choices, all the words he was unused to conjuring—

### —Okay fellas what can I get yiz—

MacK too clammed up as he stared at the verification of everything he had ever encountered, in a way—the fingers of an old weird-O in his palm, the glistening of girls, the manners of the staff of the IRT. Isidor, subsumed in the menu, saw the city's past, and in the new words found poetry, found his calling: an invisible, partly Gershwin stair was built right beside him which led in several years to the door of his bookshop. You could almost hear the hammers and saws. The waiter's pad was thick; orders now being sweated in the kitchen curved round it to the back; a stripe of royal blue carbon paper; it seemed properly a quality of the waiter's plump hand, spoke richesse just like the menu—

### —. . . fellas!—

—of a sudden they plunged and ordered, MacK a dish of steamed clams, since that was a thing Grandfather had belittled him about, and a finnan haddie, which MacK conceived looked like Grandfather in his derby. And salad—that is, iceberg lettuce and ½ small tomato under thick putty-colored Goo. *Please*. And Isidor *chowder*, New England to be sure—if he was going to eat this it ought to have the Brahmin's luxury, the surroundings of Paddy's notwithstanding. He had long coveted the hexagonal cracker. And bluefish, as it sounded clean, proper, big game. Maybe. No one is too sure of their Hemingway any more.

—*No bluefish*, said the waiter, looking off to the side and turning over a page of his pad—as if there were *never* bluefish—isn't this the kind of thing that drives you nuts—you go into a place where the menu is printed in Fournier *every day* and immediately the guy tells you *no blue fish*. That is New York, pal. —*Then snapper*, said Isidor, snapping his menu shut like he came there always maybe. He hoped by doing this not to have his stock lowered in the kitchen or with the waiter. —You wanna stay with your beers there? said the waiter. Oh there must be drink with fish as surely as there must be astringent après le rasage. —White wine, Isidor fairly shouted; then he looked up at the waiter through his appealing brows—what kinds do you have, he said. —All kinds, fellas, said the waiter, moving quickly away and making a violent sign to the little bartender, yelling *TWO WINES!*

MacK goggled at the place, the black and white waiters moving with many difficulties through the autumn exhalations of the coats and the energetic, ordinary talk in the air like knives for icy pats of butter. Here a whole realm to share with Isidor! —When I was but a babe, in front of the motherf***ing television, MacK said, there were vast restaurants under the sea—the waiters were penguins and lobsters played castanets in the floor show. —Yeah, I know, said Izzy—the orchestra was all trayf. As usual after visiting New Jersey, Isidor was feeling tinges of guilt. —But there's nothing wrong with this! I think we have *got* to have more and more restaurants and waiters and glassware and fish and white wine for everyone, said Isidor looking around excitedly, or everything is going to EXPLODE. Civilization *really will be lost* in slips between pizza box, computer keyboard and drooly lips.

—A Fish Restaurant, clamorous yet efficient, is the obvious model for government! MacK said to Isidor. For how is anything going to get *sorted out*, out there in that god damn country, unless everyone can get together? That's how the country was *founded*, people *got together*, in a room, a Fish Restaurant . . . ! Iz suddenly blotted his mouth and then leaned over toward the tank of lobsters. One of them seemed to approach him, waving its claws with some kind of vague message or greeting. —PREPARE FOR GOVERN-MENT! shouted Isidor.

MacK felt he understood the city for the first time—how it actually works, how it is the engine of civilization and libera-tion—saw the place of delicatessens, waiters and restaurants in a great scheme, and of the FISHES themselves. It really couldn't have been planned better by Moses himself. (Robt.) I give you something of value and you feed me. What could be . . . greater? More his-toric? It generates an energy which runs the city along ineluctable lines. It explains *everything* that our town is a Fish Restaurant, that it raves and pervades, that there is noise and rudeness, rudeness which is salt spray, the pungent flesh of things which get done. Paddy's was so like life . . . everyone was being mistreated. O God they loved it. The source of all rudeness, or bracing American character, may be the flesh of fish, which TANGS, and keeps us in mind of the old city, the old mental capital, keeps us on the old cold streets of sunsets and harsh ideas, keeps us going back and forth across New York Bay on the *Mary Murray* and the *Cornelius G. Kolff*—when taking the Staten Island ferry always wait for a boat with a *nice name*—over the fishes, our sustenance, our salvation. Would that it kept us fighting the Revolutionary War, which everybody out there in that god damn country has ceased to do.

It suddenly struck MacK that waiter panache and aplomb, a *real* waiter's, are needed to survive in town today; to preserve the forms of civilization. —Isn't the waiter's attire the ideal town wear? he said to Isidor.

*The Apron*—none of the city's dribblings, especially in spring, would get on you, the rusty water from awnings, melony sludge from disappearing ice at the fruit stand. Nor do your own spillages, unbal-ances of beer, pose any threat to your true costume, neither the

cigarette-ash coffee and milk covered tables of the Village—pffft!
—the INDUSTRIAL LAUNDRY takes care of your apron overnight
at agonizingly high temperature and pressure.

*The Clean White Shirt*—a religion in itself, gentlemen, your credo
to the world, you maintain; you endure. You can be as ordered, as
eternal a *tabula rasa* as the white tiles, granted on which you may
have lain, of the giant Mens Room of any great hotel. What we put
on *over* the clean white shirt, an apron, a shop-keeper's coat, a suit
sharp-cornered for to prick people turning the corner of Pine
Street, doesn't matter—just for the moment.

*The Towel*—why you don't see everyone carrying a towel in New
York I don't know, he thought, unless that's what they have in those
plump briefcases and bags, lots of nice white towels. If it ain't
money. Never *known* such a place for getting stuff on you, never *seen*
so many people who need a bit of wiping before they get to the
office. If each had his waiter's towel, there would never again come
that moment when you must stutter obvious things to the
groomed, embalmed, refrigerated receptional beauty, having just
blown in off 100° Fahrenheit Street to drip and flake and *breathe* all
over the frighteningly clean formica of her station. (Confidential to
Mr L Bean of Freeport: *'These robust 100% Egyptian cotton Belgian
waiter's fore-arm towels are the best we've seen . . .'* Missing a trick
there.)

What *is* that stuff on the banister of the IRT, south stairs, 14th
Street station (downtown side)? It's there every day. Again
—towel—rectified.

*And the Black Trousers*, thanks to their buddy the apron, don't show
cigar ash, soot, fish blood, that stuff on the IRT banister (south
stairs). Sober companions of the clean white shirt, ready for *anything*
after work, the quiet assertion of non-denominational faith in the
possibility of people if they would *just get serious*; if they would be
Scottish or Portuguese just for a little while?

---

—The waiter is the backbone of civilization, MacK said to Izzy, and ultimately its savior. —I agree, waiters are at the heart of everything, said Isidor. Let's judge everyone we know by how they treat the waiters. Before we finally and officially all *become* waiters in the city of tomorrow, the last way we will have of relating to one another. *Waiters all!* yelled Isidor. Although, he said with menace, some of us would like to think we are waited UPON. —But we all *serve something*, said MacK. There is no real neutrality, aloofness, no escape of one's streetly responsibilities in New York. There is no doing nothing. Always there is duty!

It would be an admirable goal to be the rudest fish waiter in New York; it would make you the kind of King of all this. MacK propounded a theory of waiter attire for himself and over the coming months adopted this costume for himself, black trousers and clean white shirt. Dressed this way, he thought, he could quietly show people where to sit, just anywhere, or even what to do. He would get money and tips. Pick up valuable Pine Street information from people he encountered every day. He could become

## THE CAPTAIN OF THE NEIGHBORHOOD.

—New York is the last place where the graces of waiting table are real, said Isidor. An honorable profession in decline, like those of sign-writer, street-sweeper, tobacconist, whore. Do you think anyone is paid a living wage to bring you a biscuit in *Seattle*, or even a piece of meat? Even though they nourish and sustain all those uptight people of the Northwest? —Pffft!, MacK said. —*It used to be a living*, Izzy said. Waiters raised happily disorganized families in the shadow of the hotel, their collars open on Sundays.

Imagine who comes to call when you offer a job waiting table *these* days. By the Sixties college students had all but replaced waiters from the union hall; then in the Seventies it was high school students, then in the Eighties it was Reagan and so the most unbelievable collection of retard-Os, junior high girls on drugs, pathetic PhDs, out-and-out nutcases—no one would stay more than a month or two, unionize *that* if you will. Where were all the guys with little moustaches? Imagine Reagan destroying everyone's livelihood and sense of well-being just like that! Imagine Reagan *your waiter*. He destroys practically every job that he can't do himself, then falls victim to his own obliteration of the economy and he's serving you your meal:

—*Waiter? Waiter. We also ordered some new potatoes.*

—*Well, you know . . . on new potatoes . . . a lot of people in this country . . . I've spoken with them . . . and . . . well, they think that old potatoes are . . . well . . .*

—*Shut up!*


Paddy's Clam House braced, scarified, excoriated and cajoled them. The fish they ate went down in a trance. It was a little under and over cooked—the food at Paddy's was never very good—tasted of not much except New York and ice water. What mattered were the textures and the texts of that hour. Isidor's meal was deep, MacK's horizontal. They began really to spread their proteins through the city from that day.

The waiter put the check in front of Isidor the way he had put down their plates, as if serving was not so much an intimate trans-action as it was a reminder that they were merely part of the Great Chain of Being. Now no familiarities or banter.

—Do you realize we will never again discuss genitals with that guy? said Isidor, as they moved toward the hanging coats blocking the door like a mob that might turn ugly. —We could hang around, MacK said, see when he gets off.

As usual after visiting New Jersey, Isidor was feeling the horn and wanted intoxicated. In the fine spray of indifference, brine and sarcasm of the Fish Restaurant he imagined bright legs in the Radio City Music Hall; legs like sardines. For the first time Isidor and MacK experienced that temerity for the glistening streets given by flesh of the sea.

# The Far East

A lot of this has to do with what you see walking around in the rain—the connection for instance you make between the dull grey light in the upper floors of Isidor's book shop—the smell of paper and the rain outside—the specific city you choose to live in. Each man, woman, child, dog and cat in New York has to spend all day choosing in which city to live—it's different for each.

Many years ago, thought MacK, there was an apartment. It was WAY over on the East Side, in the lower 80s, almost at the river. The city that Isidor was gradually choosing to live in radiated from his and Mary-Ann's possessions in this place—especially from their books, skeltered across three old bookcases such as any second-hand book dealer might have been happy to have—Mary-Ann had worked for one of the sea-musty antiquarian dealers of Florida. She'd long been interested, as was Izzy, in the histories of strange things and places, as well as food, and her books reflected her journey from the hot confusion of school in Boston to the unremunerative delight in sampling the seafood, salty men and ephemera of Florida, to her next, and current adventure, New York. Mary-Ann was a girl with a lot of outward poise, despite the Worcester accent, but due to the men and the salt and her reading she was a tigress: energy shone bright from her forehead. But Mary-Ann's looks, her books, her dalliances were all shut at the moment.

Her faded cookbooks: mostly from the 1940s, some very salty, from her kitchen in a sea-blue hut she rented in Coco Palms for the season and a half of her 'exuberation', her father called it. Being a policeman. Some quite moldy books on the history of Florida and its coast, some others on the South, with which she had fallen out of love—she couldn't understand it and who from Massachusetts can.

—

115

It was almost as if no one cared about New York between 1965 and 1975—they were just going to plunder it—although JACKIE O began trying to save Grand Central—MacK and Izzy had both gaped at the grotesque headline in the *Daily News*: FORD TO CITY: DROP DEAD. But Izzy had been buying up little bits of its past, for what real purpose he wasn't sure yet, though all this knowledge of the city—*I read what I buy, Sir*—had as much to do with how he would make himself as what he would make of New York. He had begun collecting books on the city when he was still at college. For years he haunted the pleasant, plain bookshops of Fourth Avenue, the Peacock, Sundwall's, Bibulo and Schenkler, for books and pamphlets on the japesters and thugs of all decades of the place; he had a few items on the history of the Interborough Rapid Transit Company; forensic pathology; Lenny Bruce (the thumbedest book in the joint); books on jazz as well as records.

MacK, lying on the floor of the little living-room of the apartment. He turned on a table lamp he'd put on the floor next to his 'bed', a collection of pillows and paper towels—sculpted for him by Mary-Ann. He lay square on a hard-on, trying to shock it with the full weight of his stomach—and began to study the books near the floor in the case. The jazz books seemed to have climbed up to where the Florida books lived—and the cookbooks from all over were settling in with the New York material—the books had been making love in the night, Iz's books commingling with Mary-Ann's more easily than they two, maybe.

MacK wriggled—this was the only time when he felt the red-painted floorboards to be uncomfortable—for while you can lie on your dick in bed, and, remotely, pretend the mattress cradles you as a girl might—in a shakedown you're just a stupid f***er lying on his dick on the cold and lonely floor—the pressure confirms it—*you've no girl*.

But this wasn't a problem at the moment; certainly the only thing to worry about was: cutting off the blood supply owing to the weight of MacK's STOMACH, or snagging it on a nail, some of which now raised themselves up from the boards. MacK reveled, or would later revel, in what was becoming a delight of Isidor's and Mary-Ann's apartment, its almost solid comfort, as solid as something you may find when you are twenty-five, as welcoming as the warm windows you glimpse in apartment buildings on the West Side—to which you silently apply the word *family*—or even in midtown: the idea that from a window across the back garden, Izzy's and Mary-Ann's apartment could be glimpsed as book-lined and lit with table lamps; having a sofa. The warm low lights playing on the louvered door and the window shutters, really the wherewithal of a frugal but comfortable city life of 1945.

MacK looked carefully at the spine of a book published by the Princeton University Press in 1948. In tan cloth, it was modestly embossed with a little gold, a dark grey 'label'. From the painted floor MacK strained to reach out in the chill, and opened the book, breathing deeply of its smell, which it seemed was that of 1948: overcoats, buses, ferries, New Jersey itself maybe—also the perfect mustiness, without dank, of the better not-too-pristine used bookstores. *This is the book*, MacK mumbled, *to be seen here, in this book-comfortable room.*

The floor above (presumably) being similarly bare, the nail-heads (presumably) would raise themselves up in alarm at this time (barely *six*) each morning and two enormous dogs woke up, scratching and whimpering for their evil master, asleep in the upstairs equivalent of Izzy's and Mary-Ann's bedroom—but he might as well have come down the stairs in his unfamiliar European pajamas and asked to join them, for all Izzy could put him out of mind. And he was convinced the evil master enjoyed the dogs immorally, though it is hard to imagine doing this *absolutely first thing*.

But perhaps it was they who instigated the affair?

Even though it was early, there was a holiday cast to the light coming through the half-opened shutters as MacK lay on his hard-on on the hard floor. From previous experience he knew Les Girls across the hall would begin to squeal 'TIME TO GO TO WO-ORK!' before long, even though it was a holiday. *Les Girls*, four of

117

them in a fit of rooming together in the way of an old film: Iz and MacK had never laid eyes on them, though Mary-Ann had—MacK pictured them all cotton peignoir and roller; Izzy pictured them boiling in oil. Between Les Girls, who woke the whole floor with their 'TIME TO GO TO WO-ORK!' giggling every morning about seven (this was the actual beginning of yups, who later ruled the earth), the Dogs of Sodom upstairs, and the brooding menace of the huge pigeons of the window-sill, Isidor lay awake half the night dreading the period between six and eight—he had begun to wake Mary-Ann with his own impression of the pigeons, *hmou hmou hmou*.

Les Girls did begin to squeal 'HAPPEE THANKSGIVEEN!' in cascades of Daytonian nasality.

## Thanksgiving Day

The Dogs of Sodom were going down the stairs and MacK could see light come from under Iz's and Mary-Ann's door and he was elated; *Thanksgiving-day*. The sun sharp across the spine of the Princeton University Press book reminded him of the orange paper band on 'Thanksgiving Day' pipe tobacco, sold only at this time of year in Boston, an old-fashioned shop with the leaves outside in Park Square almost blown away. Old-fashioned irresistible packaging, though after several years' game partaking of this heavily Virginia-based *grand old tradition*, MacK and Iz determined the following year to shred up the label and smoke *it*.

*Thanksgiving*, never very important in his orbits, which MacK recalled most profoundly experiencing at the beach with father. Leaving the poor 12-lb bird to its slow mummification they drove over the hills, MacK rejoicing in the few deciduous trees to be found in their cryogenically preserved portion of California—he was missing the East where it seemed he'd always belonged, where only comes the atomic flash of fall. The weather at the shore was dull, though not properly cold. MacK was also missing the girl who'd practically *thrown him out of the east coast*, and he tramped up and down the beach with his father and their dog, feeling too hot in his eastern jacket, feeling utterly left out of Thanksgiving, the holidays, altogether, even though here were the elements, Dad, Dog, Walk, Jacket, and Natural Forms, even though not radiantly deciduous. The holidays were coming; now they were here—but *he* was not going to get drunk on the spirit of the holidays, not stumbling, libidinous and crude on sunlight combined with the TV, the tumbling freshet of phone calls from elsewhere . . .

Looked out across the waves while the Dad described what-all machines the ancestors were hooked up to these days, looked warily into some of the green dark culverts of the waves and remembered the undersea genre of animated cartoon—lobsters and eels were lining up outside the Oyster Bar about fifty feet out and twenty feet down from where he was standing—all dressed up and being shown to their seats by penguins for their Thanksgiving dinner of—sea turkey?—is that a name for—well—polyps for cranberries.

And missing the proper atmosphere of the holiday in the home of the girl who'd thrown him out of the East Coast—*there* every-one went in for *communal leaf raking and smoldering* before hacking and eating the bird up . . . But MacK happily back in the east now, the girl somewhere unknown, he thought maybe the West Side, or Philadelphia. Happy on his hard-on with Isidor about to get up.

Izzy and Mary-Ann both the bleary type, irksome to MacK, who was from a long line of neurotic work ethic people. Very *pale* people. Saturdays father scraped outside with a *hoe* until the little MacK got up and felt guilty for not gardening. —*Oh, up already?* —Yes, my dad. Mary-Ann had a selection of slatternly bathrobes which only

119

added to her charm, that of the open doughnut shop of New England and not its older values. Well—the girl had a selection of everything.

Her attempt? at Thanksgiving breakfast table talk—*You boys goin' out soon for that turkey?*—brought a groan from Iz, hiding from the spirit of the holidays behind the *Times*, over which he now glared at MacK and started picking his first fight of the day: —How come you never read the paper? MacK knew this was a big topic, a sore point, and was amazed and disturbed they would have to fight this fight so early on a holiday morning (he didn't care for holidays except when he was homesick), in front of Mary-Ann, on whom he was still trying to make a good impression so that he might zip over to the East Side and crash here at any time. —It's bullshit, is why. —*I'm* reading it. That make it bullshit? I read bullshit? —You know it's bullshit. What about all the people we know who work there? You yourself said they were idiots. Anyway you spend all your time reading novels, not newspapers. —How do you know? —Because your house is full of novels. And the *History of Magic and Experimental Science* by Lynn Thorndike. —Yeah well that takes up most of the space, said Isidor—but there are things going on in the world, pal. —No there aren't!

At which Mary-Ann got up for more coffee, caughey or kwoffey—as it might be spelled in her dialect, MacK thought, whose own mother's greatest fear on seeing him off for New York was not that he'd be killed in the alley of legend—but that he would come back pronouncing coffee *kwoffey* and orange *arange* and saying *take cayah* all the time—and reminded the boys the butcher was only open that morning, *which they were throwing away.*

Out the vestibule, where MacK always tried to figure the names of the evil master and of Les Girls, the common perfidy of medical tape and stained calling cards and dymo labels on the mailboxes. —This GROMEK *must* be the owner of a Hell hound, he said. —I know what you mean, said Isidor, but in fact that is not he. There was some turquoise twirly girly script hiding behind the drainflower window on one box: Maddy Brown: but neither was that the popular sleepover capitaine of Les Girls.

When they were in the vestibule, whether coming in or going out, Izzy was never in a mood good enough to tax him with questions like this.

The city muffled with holiday, though so far east it is always quiet. But they were far enough from the river the only sound they might hear from it would be a tug's horn; the usual rumble of traffic on FDR Drive was crying out, entombed below street level here, though no volume of cars set the East Side a-vibrating today, hiding as the celebrants were or would be on the Taconic Parkway, in drifts of grandmothers and food, their occupants inside, pounding against the glass, so lately alive. Families.

—Thanksgiving is cruel and can strike without warning, said MacK. —Plizz give generous, said Isidor.

Here in the Far East, thin snow turning to ice on the street and Izzy started swearing. —F***ing cold, man. I can't believe I have to go out and get this turkey, to *have* turkey, which I don't even want. I hate Thanksgiving. Do you realize that no one realizes it's all about eating shit? How does coprophagia honor the *Pilgrims*? Hah? How does my eating the most horrible food, food from *England*, which I don't want, memorialize their f***ing sacrifice, whatever it was? Why am I supposed to be thankful that *they ate shit?* —Because Indians? said MacK—I don't know.

They walked west to First Avenue and then up to 86th and west again. The Lure of the West. Izzy and MacK had 'grown up' on the West Side and had always professed to hate the East Side. They had clung to the West Side like baby opossums. Izzy had the bravery to go downtown once in a while, but for years the Far East remained unknown. The East Side was known to MacK as a boy from drawings in *Mad* ('the dog-infested jungle of East 59th Street') so he thought he knew it. And he was confirmed in this vision of it after visiting a friend's older sister, recently moved into a building on Third Avenue: the lobby was covered in something like marble, there was a crude version of a door man, a rubber plant; all the women in the elevator wore stretch pants and turquoise nylon turbans and talked through their gum. The sister smoked and chewed gum, bit her nails and poked at her crumbling mascara all at the same time, spoke the Queens English. There were delicatessens and tailor shops which could only be the entrances to the headquarters of international spy networks—so there had been no need to re-examine the East Side for many years—this, after all, is an East Side digression—and so was Izzy's life with Mary-Ann.

The connection between East 86th Street and suburbia is profound, thought MacK, for here at nine in the morning on Thanksgiving Day it is practically dead. It was a morning on which you particularly noted the small confluences of hard corny snow, dog shit and cigarette butts, because there were no souls out with their Yorkville story-faces to look at: the very old Germans were not eating potatoes in the Ideal and the very old Irish people were not eating potatoes in the Blarney Stone and the very old Hungarians were not eating goulash at the Budapest. East 86th Street and Second and Third Avenues would only partially rouse themselves this morning; Yorkville would roll over, look at the clock and calendar of Thanksgiving, smack its chops, and be snoring again by three o'clock.

John the bartender, who Izzy cultivated, was still asleep in Queens. The old lady who ran the very odd German candy store, who had a condition which made her mouth swing in a sort of fleshy reticule—way down *here*—wasn't to be seen standing behind her rows of blue mice, tenks gut.

Izzy won't stay in Yorkville, MacK thought, but he's growing here somehow—we'll all acquire our first grey hairs over here one way or another. He titled their existence at this time 'Our Years in Yorkville'—but you didn't notice *him* making a move over here.

## Something from Schaller and Weber

Which was open, bright and empty. Isidor always felt the need to say something rude or sarcastic whenever he opened the door of a shop—why?—why did Sidney never use the seat of a toilet, except to slam, crouching with his ass low down in the bowl just over the surface of the water, who did he think he was?—Tarzan?—*Why?* —because these are men!

Didn't smell like Thanksgiving, smelt like bauernwurst, which was OK. But an odd feeling to look at trays of delicatessen, MacK thought, something tugged at him, prickled his waspie gonad, lit the fuse in a tiny cranberry-shaped bomb of guilt—he ought to be sitting in a frame house in Westchester, leaves in varied reds framed in the dining-room window. But that would be the Tumblesons, so f*** that.

*Jocularity.* A dangerous commodity to have or open a squat container of (in this case a hung-over Schaller and Weber counterman) around Isidor. *Used carefully it can warm and enrich our lives; used foolishly it can destroy them.* Guy thinks he knows Iz—may or may not—anyway acts like he does, mit the extra impetus of the barren holiday feel in the shop maybe, here they are open for bizniz and there's no pipples. So:

—Whudda *you* want? MacK can feel Iz's hangover bristle like a gorilla suit under his overcoat. —You don't know what I want! —(Smile cracks a little, but) That's why I'm asking! —Oh yeah? Well I came in here to see about a big bird I can stuff—right up my ass! How about that? Iz smiling but that steel challenge always there and MacK knows there may be no dinner in about three seconds; so does the guy. —Ah, there's no need for that, you little ****. (The word that isn't said—but the fight has happened; Izzy instantly furious, his dark blue eyes shooting sparks all over the counter and the pickle trays.) Guy turns around and goes into the back muttering what name? —K-A-T-Z, says Iz, now of course the whole show is up, the guy's won, at least on the German front. Guy broke the rules, reflects MacK, perspiring by a display of Bahlsen biscuits; he made a joke first.

From the back: —I got a lot of Katzes. But Iz relents, inexplicably, except that he nearly always does, if that is some kind of explanation. —Oh yeah? Lotza kotz? Lotzim kotzim? But how many TOIKEYS?, using the guy's *own vowel*. Guy pokes the head around. —East 83rd, says Iz. Guy grins, sort of, and walks toward the counter with it.

MacK looked down at the Bahlsen biscuits and thought of the apartments where people offered them, on thirty-year-old 'modern' plates, such as are stacked by Mrs Leninsky and stacked again in Rosenthal's mother's kitchen, unchanged since 1957—Rosenthal, several months before, trying to make *fudge* in *SoHo*.

The very idea of which.

She'd spent so many years eating nothing, the charming Rosenthal, but pulses and millet, as in rejecting her mother and all her cookery, that MacK thought it must surely be a fudge of dark lentil bubbling on the stove in the tiny apartment where he always tried to make love with her but often could not because of the size—his style was cramped. And Rosenthal was chary about access to the front door at all—she threw him down a key in an unerotic sock if she'd decided to let him in. Too, his earthy gonad had often been flooded by the Upwardly Mobile Brewing Co., Inc., around the corner. Man, she hated that brewery. *Fudge* she'd let him have! Rosenthal was, incongruously, drawing on the girl scout aspect of her upbringing—there was one—it was just too long ago for things to solidify—as MacK often noted. It could not be made to coalesce, not by boiling it for an hour beyond time, not by beating and pounding on it. But it was a domestic liquid so it could be made to freeze. Eventually. So Rosenthal hacked it into chunks which she then rolled into cylinders, wrapped in foil, and froze 'em again. She gave MacK a small one which destroyed the pocket of his beige overcoat on a hot AA train seat which was making a pounding noise. Took the larger one up to her mother in the suburbs who, on seeing the penile foil emerge from the suspect city daughter's bag, launched herself forward and exclaimed (and here is the point, you—) *Ooo! Somezing from Schaller und Weber?* Imagine the expressions on this elegant post-European mama as MacK's suspicions crossed her face: that true fudge would be hard to make below, say, 35th Street; that this was *lentils*.

But now Rosenthal eats meat and cream and lives in Montpelier! There's no escaping geographical declination! Hooray!

Woke to see Isidor at the cash register, deciding whether to take it all out on the woman—but the little gods of Thanksgiving, Cotton Mather and Elmer Fudd—available in candle form—gave Iz a tap on the head—there'd be no fight today. Get drunk on the spirit of the holidays, or—

—It's eleven, said Izzy (loudly, once again in the doorway)—let's get a beer.

It was ten.

They schlepped the turkey between them in its exciting red fishnet, as once they'd hauled a butchered sucking-pig onto the IRT, having made an offering to each god in the station beforehand —token, gum, mints, chocolate, phone . . . as long as their change held out. There was consternation among dog owners, as there followed consternation between Isidor's cats, who knew the thing was hanging in the bathroom all night to drain the last of its blood into the tub. But it was MacK's grasp of reality which had disturbed Isidor, when MacK said, *the best meat comes from kosher butchers*—though for a moment before he smacked him Iz had agreed—drunk? Quit your fooling!

# The Bavarian Inn

The Bavarian Inn, now gone. Kicked off the street, out of Yorkville and precipitating the whole neighborhood's decline into a souvenir and cheap hat shop of TAT; now all of East 86th looks and smells like the familiar pissed-upon cubbyhole in the subway where your man sells umbrellas and cigarettes. The whole joint is fluorescent-lit and yellow and black and red and the radio is on, thanks to the thug who jemmied the Bavarian Inn out of the world.

Under a very high ceiling which you took to be Bavarian (there were beams, though MacK had never examined them as he thought he should—neither he nor Isidor had ended up lying on the floor here so there wasn't that ease in looking); there was some kind of Germany that never existed, except on post cards, beer bottles and in watercolor drawings in *Holiday* magazine twenty years before. The walls were dark green and covered with cuckoo clocks and a papier-mâché alp. There was a big bar looking out onto 86th Street, where you might watch an older, more settled New York walk by, with a modest supper and the late edition in its string bag, as if the window screened out anything after 1960—

Standing one night at this corner of the bar, MacK had proudly announced a very short-lived intention to *marry Tumbleson*—it lasted most of the evening—at which Izzy visibly blanched and said *I feel as though I hardly know you*. MacK was filled with remorse—marriage was a complicated issue, they'd be parted, he'd be krazyglued to West End Avenue, or—it'd probably never stick. But bonhomie: he bought several rounds of drinks for Isidor, Mary-Ann, Pietro Arditti and the bar, for which Izzy rebuked him: —Jeez, get a couple drinks in this guy and he starts *buying* everything. Which was *his* form of remorse.

There were big steam tables between the bar and the dining area—where you ate hasenpfeffer and königsberger klopse handed you by a Yorkville hausfrau in an amazingly tightly laced Bavarian bodice; this invasive plumpness rather like the little hasen—*All up front but rather dull meat*, said Pietro Arditti; and in fact there was a man who played 'The Third Man' and 'Edelweiss' on an electric zither. But no one was going to eat here today—MacK and Iz were surprised to find the place open, the steam tables empty and cold. The bartender looked around feebly, as if he'd forgotten *not* to open. Had he passed the shuttered Ideal and whispered *gott damm* to himself? His upper lip drooped like those of the dead elks which drooped over them all from on high.

But they didn't know this guy, with his lip and polishing cloth—Iz was fresh from his confrontation with the meat head at Schaller and Weber—guy wasn't looking too friendly either, though the welcome here was often like one you get at Grand Central: *Go f*** yourself!*

—What can I get ya? (At least he speaks.)—Two Club Weisse, please. —Ja, kindl weisse is for the old ladies, eh, Ludwig, the guy says, over his shoulder, which is bad, MacK thinks, he's saying something about Isidor to someone else.

This is a guy, Izzy thinks, whose glass smearing and toothpick-lingus will not be interrupted by the finer points of pourage—and he was right—the glasses aren't cold, they aren't wet—guy pours them into the glasses like they were *Schlitz*—is surprised then alarmed by the huge amounts of foam, stares out at the street, pussyflicks his toothpick some more, finally slubs another gulp into each glass and pushes them over to the *fellas*, leaving the rest in the bottles; not a lemon in sight. Said the eyes: holiday, gof***yaself, right? Lights a cigarette.

Isidor's head did something funny, but there was no explosion: was the holiday muffling him too, tamping him down? Was he thinking of Mary-Ann and the apartment and the low lights and the books? (One's thoughts do tend homeward when one's given a wrongful drink.) Izzy was seduced by the holiday, even though he was not going anywhere with football and raking and preturkey sandwiches and 'Prince Albert' pipe tobacco and the local LITTLE BIG game—*Yeah these kids put on a pretty good show, doing really great this year, gimme this over pro ball any day*—Just think, you could be in the suburbs today—but that would mean the Tumblesons, so f\*\*\* that. But this is what is killing our country, what has killed it, the idea that conversation can be had about anything, that you have to have an opinion, that you have in fact to AGREE with everyone any more, MacK thought, try this at the tail gate party—*I think that this school stinks and that everyone who goes to it is an idiot, I ought to know because I went here, I think this is a tremendous waste of time, it's cold, this is my only day off this year, I'd rather be inside my house with a bottle of gin reading* Moby Dick *and getting blown by my wife, I don't know why we force these kids into this, what kind of sick ambition does it instill in them, NO, I don't like sports, or you, you're all a bunch of Nazis, what I want to know is WHY IS EVERYBODY DOING EXACTLY THE SAME THING AROUND HERE?*

## The Dublin House

Was Izzy so hypnotized by the holiday's ancient inaudible cry that he was becoming philosophic? Faced with this lugubrious mug-wiper . . . —They fired John last week, said Iz, from the other place, sons of bitches, he said. (The first bartender of his personal cultivation.) Droopy glasswipe didn't pay any attention to this, aside from coming alive in some tiny way at the obscenity, which was some indication he might be more on *their side* from now on—though you can't tell—but he obviously didn't know who *John* was, though the job of Germanically dispensing bier up and down East 86th Street makes a small fraternity—screw him—Izzy could talk in comfort.

It is the weaning stage of your Manhattanhood, the cultivation of your first bartender, the stranger for these two barfellows, Isidor, belligerent and ready to talk about anything, certain that K-A-T-Z is blazoned on him, constantly bothered by this 'certainty' on the streets of Yorkville, and John, a man smelling of a one-bedroom in

Queens (evincing the attentive yet ultimately unsuccessful grooming of a fifty-seven-year-old single man), with a discernible Germanic sourness—funny that *they* should have bonded, thought MacK, while Iz's and his assiduous *West* Side attempts to become Celtic, or at least Disno-British—Holy Mother o' God what for did they spend all those hours in the Dublin House?—the ordering of pints of Guinness, the herringboning, the flat cap (Izzy looked good in it and MacK did not, another sartorio-historic riddle)—were stonewalled by Jack, the worshipful red-faced stoic who ran the place. The strongest abjuration he ever gave a customer raving in a pool of Powers: *take a rest*. And said to MacK who would suddenly (politely) blurt out of nowhere deep concern over the current physical safety of Walter Mondale: —*Don't you worry, lad, your man's all right*. But in Jack's last analysis they were still boys who smelt of that college approach to drink, the bar a library in more ways than one, not because Iz was Katz and MacK was *too* polite, not talking New York, but because you boys are too young (he never said this)—you're not part of *this* New York—why don't you move on and let West 79th Street sink away from the world, with its Woolworths around the corner and the last IRT station with those f***in' cylindrical token-eating machines—leave us alone boys in our lack of focus.

True—try to find a *cohesive idea* on Broadway between 79th and 74th—the bend, the *bend* f***s everything up!

# The Bavarian Inn

—*Fired!*, said Izzy, you believe that? —What for? —Ah, business is bad—somethin'—I don't know. Although: MacK had not thought much of John when they finally met—another sour lifetime Manhattan bartender—you let enough of these guys in and they people your dreams. But John and Isidor had bonded over the ring—perhaps the whole thing was a set-up?—and Izzy had taken to stopping by over there to watch the fights. —I went to the

bathroom and there was a guy goose-stepping up and down in front
of the mirror, said Iz. —*Zat's nuthink*, said MacK, did you know last
summer I went in there with Alasdair MacNiel of Ugadale, a real
Scot from Scotland, famous BBC announcer with a queer red face
and ears bent by the no doubt one Victorian pair of iron baby for-
ceps in Inverness—a red beard which looked like he *glued* it
on—and this thoroughly inebriated Bavarian clocks us from the
bar and immediately comes over and sits with us—oh he was
Yorkville through and through but you could've put a little loden
jacket on him showing off his big pink drunk ass and one of those
pipes that looks like a toilet—he had a moustache which yearned to
walrusize itself and become the cause of the First World War—sits
with us and starts accusing this *Celt* of being a member of MOSSAD.
—Gee Whizz, said Izzy. —You know, said MacK, you're trying to
tell yourself the guy's just an early afternoon drunk you can *deflect*
with amiable chat, but whatever you venture, the weather, the
slightly more serious assertion that this man is a guest in our city,
*buddy*—and the guy's till-like response is—again and again
—*Nonetheless, you are in the Mossad; nonetheless, you are in the
Mossad*—and then you get a look into the guy's eyes and you see that
flame—the guy is mentally dive-bombing this Jew, he's found a Jew
at lunchtime here in Yorkville! But of course Izzy saw that fire all the
time around here—though the restaurants were good and so was the
Paprika Shop, street life, shop life is not always great for a Jew in
Yorkville . . . MacK saw he didn't need to finish. MacNiel of
Ugadale's pure comment when they'd got four or five blocks down
Third Avenue, away from the guy bumping around like a pinball in
his little box of Naztalgia and hate:

**'Now—I wasna very comfortable wi' *that*.'**

Half the Club Weisse had topped up Izzy's resentment of that—that
den of iniquity—*why I oughta*—here in the solemn quiet of the

Bavarian Inn, through which oddly filtered the breath of the waspy holiday from the suburbs, which discomfited Iz and perhaps thus gave him strength against this discomfiture, he headed for the old wooden phone booth. —*Back in a minute.*

## The Heidelberg

One of the last of these, with a molded seat; light, a fan that comes on as you shut the hinged door—the telephone *dings* as you drop your nickels—pretty comfortable, thought Izzy—the bastards answer, some guy who turfed John out of his job—the bastards are *open*—why?—why today? Just so the right amount of bier can be drunk to accomplish errands Germanically before Yorkville sinks under the waves of Thanksgiving and America.

    —*Heidelberg.* —Hindenburg? says Izzy in his best perverted Peter Lorre. —*What!?* —Hindenburg? —(In great annoyance) *Nein, nein! Heidelberg! HEIDEL-berg!* —Well, says Iz, you're still a big gas-bag! —and hangs up, knowing the torrent of German to come just from the inspiration.

## The Bavarian Inn

Another? No, it isn't feasible, the glasses, the guy . . . —Besides, this is not *drinking* time, said Isidor, this is a *holiday*, do you hear what I'm saying? A holiday—no *drinking*—we have to *enjoy* ourselves. Disgustedly leaves a tip with *such* a *slap* from wallet already that MacK's eyebrow goes up in a *huge* demonstration of emotion and Izzy says—Hey, I have to drink here ya know. Suddenly defending the guy, thought MacK—that they were enjoying disliking so, silently, during the tall not-quite-rights.

# Thanksgiving Day

The walk back to Izzy's was less inspiring than the walk from, for now the turkey had been acquired. There was a necessary component to Izzy and MacK's walkings, alone or together: NEED, the NEEDS each conceived, or that the town, in its infiniteness, forced on you, or *conceived for you:* you NEED that THING; to live in this our town is to agree to obsessive-compulsive disorder, *gimme* it, the whole *place* is one obsessive-compulsive panic attack. Treatment for this has yet to be devised. Some of these were gourmettish needs pressed on Isidor by Mary-Ann but some errands come rattling out of the subconscious—you don't really want to know what has given rise to them. Then too Izzy's and MacK's errands had for years sometimes converged and sometimes not, on the planes of the real, the imagined, the nonsensical:

A few weeks before, a journey to the Paprika Shop was for Iz a Mary-Ann errand, so contained a bit of duress—he didn't like to be sent out for things as at that time his only conception of house-husband—though their union lacked blessing—was sadly monochromatic; but paprika pleased him as did the Paprika Shop and its astonishing *sneezing* proprietor, its many *serious drawers*—its genuine claim to be the oldest going concern in Yorkville; for MacK the same trip had the imaginary *necessity* of acquiring a recording by *Kecskes*, a Hungarian clarinetist, whose name he had been carrying on a slip of paper in his wallet *for four years.* —I'll sell you Kecskes—**hapci!**—if you want him, boy, said the proprietor, who had magyariana as well as twenty-six kinds of paprika, but he's no good—**hapci!**

People have needs.

———

There was a heaviness which you had to admit eventually overrode *holiday*—they'd remember it as an unusually cold one. The crusts of snow haloed with dog pee and various oils, the post Club Weisse landscape—surely Izzy was looking homeward now. Even East 83rd Street, which in Izzy and Mary-Ann's block was of blank, even idiotic aspect (*no one home?*) had acquired holiday warmth: here and there you saw a lamp lighted in a front room and people sitting around, doing—somethin'—I don't know. Tell you one thing—you saw fewer idiots slowly bloating in front of TV than you would have out on a holiday walk and looking in people's front rooms out in the suburbs—not none, but fewer—having come from a couch of pre-turkey cold cuts and little kings, rousing themselves in an effort to create room in their gigantic stomicks before the onslaught of cholesterol and relative-bagging—digest, digest, digest—the lamps, leaves, TV—but that would be the Tumblesons—so f*** that. *Course those city folks have a lot of problems too ya know. OH yeah.*

—Where are the dogs of Hell? said MacK as they entered the porch or vestibule. —Ay, where are they? said Isidor—I think they're *in* Hell. Welcome back.

To enter the Katzenmurphy apartment they . . . opened the door, which put them in the middle of the kitchen ($8' \times 8'$). It was full of smell from Thanksgiving already—Mary-Ann was cooking bitter cranberries and chopping up bread and celery—turkish and hamish smells were cuddling the floorboards and walls.

## How Describe Mary-Ann Murphy

In her element, her shape in the steam? There was a—seamless? —American energy of the past, and of now, running through the Katzenmurphy apartment, situated here on East 83rd Street, on this holiday; running through Mary-Ann's upbringing, which you took to be one of rollicking sisterly hilarity and the charm of Worcester, if New England can be said to exert a kind of 'charm' on New Yorkers—who uneasily feel that it is some kind of prettier, embryonically better version of New York, where Federalism didn't go wrong—like a painting maybe—they can think this if they want so long as they don't visit it—through Mary-Ann's past and Florida and her cookbooks right into Izzy; her cooking running into his mouth, but that was not it altogether.

# What Isidor Had Found
# What it Means to a Man to Find It
# Or—Most of It

Mary-Ann was in herself an amalgam of several ethics important or sub-consciously cherished by Isidor, admired by MacK. She embodied the careless charm you saw in that girl on the bus. In an ancient pin-up calendar—that was it—found behind boxes of nails in the garage. With very little effort you could imagine Mary-Ann's lips rouged redder—and while most girls' hairstyles of the late 1940s were hideous, the way the top looked like a *volcanic plug*, the rest of the hair empoodled around it, yi *yi*, you could imagine finding Mary-Ann while flipping guiltily through the thing—her round figure energizing the housedress of the decade; she's fanning a reluctant barbecue with the hem of it, the whole she-bang—MacK and Izzy thought, suddenly needing to lean against various walls and take her in, cooking, Mary-Ann in the steam—against this combination of innocent household economy, lipstick, the beauty parlor and other such old-fashioned ideas and pretty legs in sheer stockings peeking from under a prim apron, heels higher than necessary to the task and of an arresting color. *None of this* going on—Mary-Ann was very modest and never showed off—if Izzy enjoyed dioramas of any bygone era—Mary-Ann would be the perfect canvas for it, thought MacK, getting strangely thirsty—then it was in the privacy of their room with the paint-thick door wedged shut, only the *hmou hmou* of the pigeons to bother them. Pretend you're f***ing in Paris why dontcha?

Mary-Ann had a job of the sort you get by *neglecting your education and doing what you please*, according to her father, being a policeman. *O sure, just following your nose around the country for a few years like some kind of*—as MacK well knew—Tumbleson had told him he had to eliminate half his employment history from his curriculum vitae—*Can't you hold a job?* He had given up on his head and was just following his vocal cords around. Mary-Ann now worked dutifully with good humor if not soulfully in a TV production house of no merit—one of the many office floors one can find oneself in on Lexington Avenue in the 40s. The glamour America attaches to television is *hilarious*, thought MacK. This company post-produced, which is a technical term meaning *to f*** around with*, some rock music crap you had vaguely heard of but never seen—and amazingly employed ten or twenty people, all of the same age, who didn't look as though they lived in New York at all. Lexington is one of the avenues on which you can feel yourself slipping out of New York—perhaps Lexington and on lower Second and Third is where a lot of these people live—you find yourself walking on a block in which all the stores suddenly look naïve, suburban—the bars are fake bars, the news-stand sells the stuff of supermarket magazine racks—nobody reads this crap in New York—the pastrami has no smell—the rest of the country laps around the edge of Manhattan—just see what things look like at the other end of the Queens Midtown Tunnel—it's like a little wrong-way telescope—foreign; that god damn country.

Izzy worried about her, and about nothing more so than her job, where he thought they mustn't use her intelligence; sure they value her for her tits alone. Parallel with her Catholic modesty and good-heartedness Mary-Ann liked parties—if she got tipsy it was in the way you'd expect her pin-up to get tipsy—her cheeks went pink as champagne and she began to hiccup, giggle, flirt and bounce and flounce. (More than once MacK had felt her foot on his foreleg under the table—no matter.) Iz maintains, no doubt, thought MacK, the most ghastly fantasies of her behavior behind the scenes at rock concerts—it was the phrase 'all areas' flapping on the pass on her breast that froze him to the marrow—'all areas' indeed; it drove him mad, mad do you hear?

But do you see what he'd found? A femininity from outwith the city (he did not believe in its 'cold heart', but) and surpassing any current exemplars, a pretty, honest, voluptuous GAL as your aunt might rasp, slightly out of the concept of the generation; like taking up with a wartime fantasy of your uncle's.

It more than suited Iz. He was fond of reminding, *i.e.* scathing, MacK and Pietro Arditti and Sidney and the others with the fact they hadn't liked Mary-Ann, hadn't liked her at all when he first upped scope and spotted her—with the incredible sNobberY of one's twenties they couldn't see any farther than their own diplomas, didn't see her history, the curves she could throw (in the broad sense), hadn't tasted her GUMBO—which reeked of mature knowledge of the world, erotic adventures among old books and a few salty men of Boca Raton, just an Old Bay State girl giving life a whirl. MacK had no idea where Isidor and Mary-Ann had met but they seemed remarkably easy together—he went to her apartment with Izzy and tasted the GUMBO there—despite the glum fluorescent lobby of the little walk-up in the East 70s and the barely-there spindly furniture, still positing tropical exuberation somehow even in that dark little space—*yeah, might be something to this woman after all*—phew!

## Thanksgiving Day

Izzy dropped the turkey heavily on the floor, tried actually to bounce it on its ass—*Hope you're satisfied!*—he hated carrying things as who does not—Mary-Ann gave out with a grin born in that family, MacK thought, the kidding, absorbing the ever-changing moods of the truculent policeman, perhaps that was it, whereas in *MY* family, he thought, there was no kidding about being in a bad mood, you couldn't burlesque anything—*Why I oughta*—mother hated Abbott and Costello—MacK prevented from wearing his clip-on tie without a clasp—But LOU COSTELLO doesn't wear a tie clasp!—*Go to your room!*

You boys have been to the Bavarian Inn haven't you, said Mary-Ann. —So shoot me, said Isidor. —I ought to—why don'tcha *tell* a girl when there's fun to be had? She chopped at a stalk of celery. —You wouldna liked it, said Izzy, it was very depressing. But get this—we made a crank call, 'cause of John. —Ya did? What did ya say? —Called 'em a gas-bag, said Isidor. —A gas-bag? —'Cause of the Hindenburg. —? —, said Mary Ann. —Yeah, anyway. Want me to cut up onions? And they revolved toward preparing the dinner together and MacK felt the holiday creep over him again, like fog from the river. He offered to help *chop*, why does this word have to do with every aspect of Thanksgiving?—but you can't help a couple prepare a meal, because: that is a *fight*. On Thanksgiving the heavy weaponry comes out—MacK's eyelids had been twitching since he and Iz had arrived back at the Katzenmurphy, in anticipation of an argument over the size of the turkey. Everything in the kitchen was of reduced size—the oven looked, in comparison with the ovens out there in America, across the rivers, like some kind of toy—the turkey looked giant, something you see girls in pencil skirts screaming at on TV late at night, and bloated, like the balloons floating hideous and jovial over the very cold crowd on Fifth Avenue at this very moment—the crowd that always wonders *Is that it?* at a certain point and then rejects these looming icy grimaces in favor of *molecular motion*, a quick walk home, their ovens. The Katzenmurphy sink was really a wash-hand basin. The toilet was small, like the plentiful little toilets of kindergarten, and in order to fit the angle of the tiny bathroom it had been necessary to procure, at some time in the dim past of Yorkville, a miniature toilet that was perfectly *round*, this doesn't fit the normal anatomy and one always had an odd feeling after sitting there and emerged from the bathroom with a queer expression on one's face which Iz could recognize and laugh at.

—Where do you get little spatulas like this? So you have room in here to flip a pancake or omelette? —I got that at Hammacher Schlemmer, MacK, said Mary-Ann.

—No no, you just go f*** yourself in the front room while we do this, just relax, enjoy said Izzy. So MacK sat with several of his favorite books of theirs, one on the civilization that ANTS have, the other describing the ickier procedures of the medical examiner. The brain is encased in a bony box.

Before the queen had seen all her workers die for the season and before the thoracic cavity had been aspirated with the trochar—the page where MacK always got dizzy and gave up—the carcase of the turkey had been stuffed—with natron?—and crow-barred into the oven, having been greased to the purpose; the counter was wiped and Mary-Ann was washing her hands and hanging up her apron—Izzy came in and put on a record.

*Now the terrible waiting begins. Now you hear the Great Clock of Your Aunt begin to tick and tick and tick ever more slowly—the ticking of the Puritanical bombs in a hundred million turkeys—out THERE.*

They drowsed, in a little nap of tea, wine, the *New York Times*, gardening books. Izzy and Mary-Ann argued a little. They spoke in an old-couple way MacK had not heard before but how else can you talk on Thanksgiving, the thing *gives* you white hair. *Did you remember butter for the sprouts? When are you going to roast the potatoes?* WQXR ('*The radio station with cheese between the slices*') sounded particularly dreadful: aside from carrying a Service of Thanksgiving® from St Patrick's and playing a few Ives songs it had no way to deal with the holiday so it was reduced to playing anything that could be dragged out of its 'library' with *hunting horns* in it. So over the course of the day this created a mournful, hollow feeling in the gut—and at the back of the sense memory a desire for *schnitzel*; not poultry and berries.

—Zzz.

## The Commendatore

At four o'clock the door bell rang and Iz jumped up—f*** this! They had all forgotten Pietro Arditti. You may have looked forward to having company when an invitation was made, but when you have shared the vicissitudes of the day then he who comes *MERELY* to eat—even if he is your good friend on any other day—shows up, doesn't know the drill, hasn't heard the day's jokes—he's going to get it in the neck—at least around here, thought MacK, who still had the coroner's handbook on his stomach, and rose from under it with psychological difficulty.

—Ya *friend's* heah, said Mary-Ann, who sounded even more like Edward Kennedy when she was put out.

—Gee Whizz. Iz pressed the button on the corroded speaking device in the kitchen, into which there was no point in speaking—its bizarre appearance suggested its conduit led not to the porch where Pietro Arditti was ringing but down, down beneath the river, down into one of the dwarf-staffed engine rooms of New York. Down the stairs you could hear the inner door bang open, almost feel the cold of the late afternoon, and a lot of puffing and blowing echoed around the mosaic and enamel hall. —Hey why doesn't QXR just play those records of *whales* on Thanksgiving, said Iz, it'd be just the—HOW ARE YOU! he boomed like a foghorn at the spouting Pietro Arditti before him.

This is all going to be a strange contest in bluster, and self-parody oddly aimed at hurting one's opponent, though sometimes not. GREAT!

Pietro Arditti was weighted with little decorative paper bags from the finest stores. —You look like a Christmas tree, said Izzy, grabbing them from Pietro Arditti's sheepskinned mitts—this was Iz being charitable and jolly. —Gee, Christmas, said Pietro Arditti, tomorrow's the day it begins. The thought pierced them all and shut 'em up for as long as it took Mary-Ann to think of a wreath on a Boston door; Pietro Arditti to think of egg nog; MacK to recall the coffeeish smell in the toilets of 747s and the aroma of oranges and 'Royal Yacht' following plum pudding; and Isidor to stumble in horror over the little bags, imagining the imminent descent of grasping madness—*tomorrow*—for this our town is a reasonable place is it not, brotherhood abounds except in the days before Christmas, when a guy could get killed just trying to walk from 50th to 53rd and Fifth on December 21st 1977 at 3.35 pm, thank you very much. —Gee Whizz, he said again and yanked Pietro Arditti's coat off, having to jump up and clutch at the guy's neck to do so, his penultimate act as host for the evening as it turned out. —Come in come in, said Iz, go in—though it didn't count—as you were standing always in the kitchen you knew you had to go into the only room that wasn't bed or bog.

—Whatcha got there, Pietro Arditti? said Mary-Ann looking at the little bags the way everyone in this our town looks at little bags. —Bhh-po-ho!ho! blew faintly yulish this mighty cetacean loosed from his aquarium, nothing less than the World of Business® itself—and these were the unremodeled days of Carter when the tiled lobby of Pietro Arditti's offices looked like it was designed to be full of water, instead of shit. Sorry. Have a drink! GREAT!

Iz and Pietro Arditti puffed and blew at each other remarkably in the Sinclair Lewis style; Pietro Arditti gave Mary-Ann several kisses and squeezes—a few darts passed between her and Iz—though he knew she relished this about as much as the paper cut on her pretty lower lip she got almost every day on Lexington Avenue—the huffing was partly comedy, take-off on the genre of business cats whose subaltern Pietro Arditti was—in those days—but as they got older there was to be more bluster, panic and less parody to it—-regrettably.

MacK blows too though he is out of practice, hiding from Tumbleson as he is he doesn't hear the overweening weenying of business every day. *The man works in a soundproof box.*

They carried the packages into the living-room. There were bags from Sherry-Lehmann, from Dunhill, Bonté, Zabar's and—the *Carnegie Delicatessen!?* Iz poked his puss into all of them but wouldn't use his hands.

### Working with your hands = not good!

Pietro Arditti had brought : a Chateauneuf and a bottle of the Madeira wine of St Edmund Hall, Oxford—*pretty interesting*, said Izzy, as if to convey he acknowledged the pedigree of the stuff although it was something he would have decided against himself, would have abandoned staring at the mead and rainwater shelf in the gloomy belly of Sherry-Lehmann, the dark leviathan of Madison Avenue, one of their inquisitive pomaded suits breathing in your ear—no. —This isn't dessert wine, you know, said Iz at his politest, it's the Brits, man, they sop up this crap with their f***ing tea at four-thirty—somethin', I don't know. But thanks—*in a way*. —I know that, said Pietro Arditti, who didn't. These friends—for so they were—were still a little in the dessert wine stage of life—it's touching : three 'Montecruz' cigars, a Churchill for himself, a Panetela for Izzy, since they went to work entirely in suits, and a Rothschild for MacK, who was tidy and squat and one of the RCA Building's bohemians. —Hmm, said Iz, not bad, what a guy, &c, though again his tone suggested he had discovered pastures beyond the Canaries. He'd been insulted the year before upon discovering the brown delights of 'Partagas' to see Pietro Arditti immediately take 'Partagas' up as his own, and at a grotesquely loud party at his West End Avenue brownstone refer to them as 'Party Guys' while drinking sangria and leaning on his tiny marble mantel, the one thing of interest in the place, cocking his head and winking. *Plenty of jobs in finance!* : Oh and also from the Dunhill family vault a pretty box of Sobranie 'Cocktail' cigarettes for Mary-Ann, who cooed, genuinely—though not her style: she favored tough-girl smokes like the 'Picayunes' she picked up in New Orleans or 'Home Runs' from Baltimore—Mary-Ann knew her way around lots of the uriny news stands of the East, knew how to kill time near every major train and bus depot. Isidor struggled to maintain a front of detachment, but his eyes were widening just as the others' while Pietro Arditti plundered the helpless little bags : eight *petits-fours* (Iz turned up his nose) : Madeira cake (acknowledged its place), and struggled out of the bag : a huge BRIOCHE—at which Izzy rolled his eyes and began to mouth—*Wh—th—f*—and Pietro Arditti triumphed—*For breakfast, you nuts!* Iz smiled (though his eyes weren't)—*You think you're staying for breakfast?* —and in the middle of this Mary-Ann quietly took the chic red-and-white Bonté bag for herself—: two bags of dark roast coffee (Iz grunted; coffee was like tap water to him) and : —*A pastrami sandwich!!??* cried Iz, who grabbed and hefted it accusatorily like you might weigh a baseball you were thinking of throwing deliberately at somebody's head.

—Give me a break, man, said Pietro Arditti, I been going great guns since seven, *I* didn't know what time we were gonna eat—gotta carry all this crap around over here. Over there. —I can't believe this, said Iz, here a beautiful goil's making a big bird for a guy, blowing her brain out, and he brings a big Geek-A-Roni sandwich to ruin his dinner wit'. —With which to ruin, said MacK. —Oh Isidor, ca'am down, said Mary-Ann, the poor guy's been rushin' around. —Gee Whizz, said Iz, I suppose you want a glass of wine with that—a *fine wine*—after your tough day. What the Hell are you talking about? You didn't go to work today. —I was on the phone a lot, said Pietro Arditti. —How long till we eat? Iz asked Mary-Ann—and unceremoniously uncorked a bottle he didn't bother to show the label of.

—

Each took his booty off to a corner of the apartment. Pietro Arditti was left to wrestle the great sandwich alone on the settee—the difficulties of eating it produced lots of creaking noises—the settee was old wicker—they might have been in a little holiday boat of joy. Mary-Ann poured herself a glass of the red wine as Isidor was looking at his cigar in the opposite corner—she selected a green Sobranie 'Cocktail' and puffed at it while rinsing the sprouts. MacK stole between them and opened the miniature refrigerator for a beer—they seemed to have shrunk. Now the *sandwich noise* was over—*Jeez, you OK now?* said Iz in an exaggerated version of Pietro Arditti's own gas station accent—Iz put on some music.

What was Pietro Arditti doing in New York? —he himself sometimes wanted to know. His training had taken him from the Providence Plantations to New York and back up to Harvard and then back again to town. He was a guy who was fast developing the 'idea' that he didn't 'want' to live in New York, for various 'aesthetic' reasons: *i.e.* even with a Harvard© M.B.A.® he didn't think he was going to make enough money to live in town—and just what do you think everyone here lives on?—millions?—he did not mean enough to *live* here—but enough to *cushion* himself with Checker cabs and wine *against* this our town, which rained blows and affronts like cats and dogs down on him wherever he went. He was not a man to go with a flow. MacK and Iz, late night work: scenario for a grand opera, *Don Arditti*, in which the metal Roger Williams atop the Rhode Island State House comes to life, takes a bus to Port-of-Authority, as it is known to every taxi driver, grabs Pietro Arditti out of a meeting at the Hilton and drags him back to New England for good (forceful *operatic laughter: A Ha ha ha ha ha ha ha!*)—along with every other Ivy Leaguer in the World of Business®. But the sandwich had helped Pietro Arditti out of his townish discomfort for today.

—

143

Although the table was small Mary-Ann had come up with a miniaturized homey look for their spread (except for the turkey which
could barely fit)—the potatoes were in a tureen and the cranberry
sauce in a cut glass dish with a spoon representing the *'CITY WALLS
OF ST AUGUSTINE'*—something of her grandmother's—and the
holiday seeped through the windows again in the city light of late
afternoon—they felt snug and festive; the *size* of everything . . .

MacK didn't like the look of the bread basket—an affair of stout
twigs and the feel of workshops—pardon—for the unfortunate. It
looked like the home of the *Lame Squirrel*—the other animals
brought him his Thanksgiving dinner—don't *ask*—winter was
coming—his big big-eye tears—but as this book was still resting in
the natal place—he might picture where—MacK choked up. Later
in the evening he thought of opening a spot in the Village, The *Lamé*
Squirrel—sense had practically deserted him.

Pietro Arditti went for a potato first thing. It was sautéed in
butter and olive oil, a mixture of alcohols known only to Mary-Ann
and one of the tatterdemalion cook books with the little mousta-
chio'd chef again going *buon appetito!* on the cloth of the
spine—Pietro Arditti pronounced them excellent thus: OH MAN!
Mary-Ann smiled, Isidor too, proud of her, vain even. They ate,
each surprised to find themselves together, eating, on the holiday in
the city, when it always seems that everyone travels on Thanksgiving,
the helplessly stuffed families in cars, the freezing late trains, the
planes with their smell of coffee'd businessman shit—but if that is
so, why do you not end up *knocking at the door of an empty house?*

MacK took a gander at the stuffing and for a moment his
bohemian folding chair became the large hard chairs of his own
family's dining-room, it was memory of the *translucent celery*, which
he'd had a horror of, that did it, and the turkey, a thing they had only
twice a year, cooked without a lot of help by his fretting mother,
who had all the cooks of OHIO looking over her shoulder and
making *little noises* with their mouths; you can barely see over the
edge of the table and you hate nuts, cranberries, the *translucent*

*celery*—the dining-room chairs are still too large, even today, MacK thought—he and his sister were not going to get any bigger—and now his little parents were shrinking.

The conversation limped, or was desultory: Pietro Arditti had not yet caught up with the tenor of the day, though as they ate—and this is the warm, Dickensian paragraph—and felt in their bowels the warmth of TRADITIONAL AMERICAN FARE—this improved. Too, if you were eating with Mary-Ann, there was always opportunity to praise her. —OH MAN, said Pietro Arditti again, as she and MacK rose to replenish the tureens, isn't this great, MacK? And here the Latin School raised its head, though it was buried far in the dead New England leaves of his brain: —*These guys are a real couple of Epicureans.* MacK heard the bottom of Isidor's wine glass strike the table and a high, sharp inhalation. —IT SO HAPPENS, said Izzy . . . —It's starting, said MacK under his breath to Mary-Ann in the kitchen. —Oh deah!

—YOU'RE MISUSING THAT TERM LIKE EVERY OTHER JERK OF THE PLANET (one of Isidor's most hated expressions, anything to do with *the planet*—you can see the emotion)—WHAT DO YOU MEAN I'M AN EPICUREAN?

Pietro Arditti's eyes slid back and forth—already!—looking from Isidor to the empty bohemian chairs of MacK and Mary-Ann and back again—if only they had been sitting there!—he *became pink*—with challenge, he'd had Latin and Greek after all, fat lot of good it does you, the uniform of the Latin School on an afternoon bus in downtown Providence—the motto on the escutcheon of which the rough boys translated as KICK MY ASS, might as well be painted on your back!

—You know, said Pietro Arditti, hedonism—pursuit of pleasure. C'mon, what are you—MacK and Mary-Ann brought the amazing potatoes. —Oh what are you boys arguing about? said Mary-Ann, half-consciously becoming the mother of each.

—You think Epicurus went around telling everybody to pig out, don't you, said Isidor, just eat the Geek-A-Ronis all the time, like you? That what you think? Cause I have news for you, pal—the Epicureans lived on water and bread made from one of those near-impossible grains—barley?—bere?—*somethin'*—I don't know—and a pint of wine a day—and you can bet it wasn't like that Chateauneuf you're drinking or the other one YOU brought (there were duelling Chateauneufs) or even that Madeira you so *kindly* purchased and they weren't smoking no maduro maduro either—

—Hey—

—No, YOU hey—Epicureanism *is* a hedonistic philosophy, scumbag, but in hedonism, the pleasure—which *is* the criterion—isn't sensual. Epicurus taught us—*us,* dick head—that the *higher* pleasures are the ones to be sought—peace of mind, *ass hole*, and social justice and civilization and all that shit. You want to find someone like *you*, who thought everyone should eat huge Geek-A-Roni meatball heros all the time, *mnuh mnuh mnuh*, and burp and fart and bonk—you go back to Aristippus, he's the guy for you—the Cyrenaics, they're just like you—they can't think of anything but whatever big fat Geek-A-Roni or broad with her legs spread—*Isidor!* said Mary-Ann—is right in front of 'em, and they *told* everyone that was the only thing that could *ever* be thought about. You believe that?

—Wuh, said Pietro Arditti—

—But even *that* guy, Aristippus, finally had to admit that all this lowbrow getting, all these *Rhode Island pleasures*, chewing up tons of fat *mnuh mnuh mnuh* and getting drunk off your ass every night like a f***ing GEEK, they brought pain. PAIN! Get it, ass hole? You guzzle booze, you get sick—you screw every hole in sight and society breaks down, people go ape shit—so even the Cyrenaics in the end, the *pigs* of the philosophical world, the guys with the fanny packs and the Geek-A-Roni sandwiches and Big Gulp soft drinks and big dicks and big slurpees and BIG TITS—even *they* admitted there might be some higher pleasures to be sought—*Like the pleasures of debate?* said Pietro Arditti—which didn't cause an equal amount of PAIN, said Izzy. So that's what Epicurus built on, the pursuit of *those* pleasures, not stuffing your face like a meatball at my table and

grabbing my girl's ass when you came in the door, *BASTARDO*.
— Isidor, said Mary-Ann.

Pietro Arditti felt slightly abused. —So I suppose you're leading a lofty life here. —Yeah! —On East 83rd Street! —Yeah! —Pursuing high ideals. —Yeah, I *am*—cause I know all about the *pain*. —Ho! —Yeah in fact I *am* an Epicurean, if you want to know, in the real sense, not the shit head sense, because I am a civilized man and I *know* my history and what the pleasures of the intellect are

### 1. Jazz
### 2. Wine
### 3. Paprika

not like YOU who seem to have forgotten everything you ever learned. Don't you think my parents would have preferred a sane, orderly world, filled with good feeling? What do you think the Nazis were except a bunch of Cyrenaics? —Now, hold on a minute, said Pietro Arditti. —*You* hold on—and Iz banged into the kitchen as he was about to *lose his temper*.

Brought out the next bottle of wine—in fairness, they did recognize it was faintly funny to be eating their way through this argument—in this pause they recognized that, even Isidor smiled a little, though the moray eel of his argumentum was not going to be got off Pietro Arditti's leg without being CHOPPED off. —The state must go, said Iz, summing up, raising his glass, the state must go and logic with it. It sounded suddenly like a toast so they all lifted theirs—

### The State Must Go!

—Who would like some more turkey and potatoes? said Mary-Ann, who under stress of the argument pronounced potatoes like *Badedas* which set MacK wondering what Edward Kennedy uses in the shower. Old Spice soap on a rope. —F*** turkey! shouted Izzy, expansive now that he'd conquered Pietro Arditti—cheese! *Send me some Cythnian cheese so that should I choose I may fare sumptuously.* We want cheese! We want cheese!

147

—We don't *have* cheese Isidor, said Mary-Ann, you know that. Or if we do it's that stoopid Cracka Barrel, which you hate.

# A Guy's Mother

MacK and Pietro Arditti were on thirds, Mary-Ann and Isidor decelerating. —What's the matter with you guys, said Izzy, you some kind of Stoics? —Yeah, said MacK, his mouth full of cranberry so he looked like the guy that chews betel nut in *National Geographic*, it's our duty to eat this dinner, our selfless duty to society and it doesn't matter how much we eat because pain is not an evil. (Hoping to defuse . . .) —Yeah, well, said Iz, you're a great stoic like Aristotle—Onassis. Have a cigar.

GREAT!

—But there was pumpkin pie and fruitcake first (how Dickensian *now?*). Pietro Arditti, who had after all watched the storms come and go across Isidor as much as the rest of them, opened the Madeira which they thought a cooler thing to try than port—though Izzy said ominously: —Of course you know I have armagnac for later. So what else is new? Since he finally realized no one had been doing any talking. —Perhaps Mister Argumenti will favor us . . . —That reminds me! said Pietro Arditti, get this. I changed my name. You should call me Mr *Ardent* now. —*WHAT!?* said Isidor in a very loud voice . . . *MISTER!?* —Isidor, said Mary-Ann. —Yeah I changed my name along with my religion. —MacK's turn to choke, on his fruitcake which had soft glacéed pineapple in it which did something subtle, from the past, to the walnuts—since he'd grown up in California and had no religious instruction whatsoever, believed in the gods of the city, and had to keep everyone he knew strictly categorized so as to abjure their beliefs (not to their faces)—he was afraid of being drawn into one monotheism or another. Pietro Arditti had till this moment filled the very important New England Italian Catholic niche which now gaped in

MacK's brain like a robbed grave—iron letters weeping rust down a marble surface—

—What the f*** are you *TALKING* about, said Isidor, and in a similar tone: —What have you *chosen*, said MacK, and: —What religion ARE ya, said Mary-Ann.

—I'm an Episcopalian, said Pietro Arditti, in a tone which said nothing of joy, of blessed relief, of happiness, or justified and courageous pride in finding the right way to a god, but smelt only of 'I got the car washed' or 'Honey, I'm home'—which is about right. Izzy's eyes were not so much bugged out as they had flattened themselves against the insides of his glasses—they looked as though they had been painted on, in there.

—I can't believe this, he said, looking down at his dessert plate like the pieces of cake on it had just performed a sexual act. —You eat dinner with a guy and then you find out you didn't even know who it *WAS!* I'm dumbfounded.

Of course he wasn't—he immediately went on the attack.

—Everyone have to change their name when they become an Episcopalian? —Certainly not, said Mr Ardent. I—just like the way it looks better. —*WHAT YOU MEAN*, said Isidor, is that World of F***ing Business® doesn't like names that end with a e i o u and sometimes y. That it? You're having the big vowel movement—like we need another wasp in this town. Thanks a lot!

MacK thought furiously about the demolition of Pietro Arditti's—Mr Ardent's—niche in his pantheon—this was an offense against his aesthetics as well—the wider Ardittis occupied quite a few important though contradictory slots in MacK's columbarium worldview (he used them for a number of things): pious people of the working-class; the franchisees of a major petroleum company; situation-comedy Italians; people who really know how to find a pizza pie in Providence. He was particularly upset to think that what he had imagined to be a heritage of lively debate, heated argument but at least out in the open, and the rude good nature of the Old World was now to be abandoned by Mr Ardent, whose children would be raised in an atmosphere of air-conditioning and fruit cocktail. (The two achievements of high Episcopalian civilization—air-conditioning cools ardors and prevents clothes from being stained by . . . *perspiration*; fruit cocktail is colorful and *digestible* and fits most neatly into the USDA food pyramid, a great little god which we all worship, admit it. But stay—isn't it really a *triangle?* Come on.) Any racial energy will be lost, thought MacK, becoming an Episcopalian is like taking Emily Post to bed. And isn't this just as Izzy says, part of the homogenizing terror the World of Business® is wreaking on Pietro Arditti? —on all of us? He must've changed his front name too—Pete Ardent?

The idea that everything that can possibly be a business *ought* to be a business—and that if it *is* a business then it is all right—porno, armaments, nuclear power, cigarettes, *'HEALTH FOODS'*—because business and growth are the ultimate necessity—as if it is now deemed necessary by everyone to cheat Earth of all its resources as quickly as possible, so we can *move on*, to—?, thought MacK. —Dessert? said Mary-Ann, who would like more dessert? And, thinking of what leaving her own ostensible church would precipi- tate in her family (though her connection to it was as tenuous as had been her attachment to her school uniform at 3.15), she said, What does ya mother have to say about it, Pietro Arditti? —Oh, well, said Mr Ardent, chillingly casual, I'm an Episcopalian now so I guess mothers aren't very important.

—*P - h - e - w !* whistled Izzy. The guy gives up on his own mother, you believe this? All you have to do is abandon the Mother of God, not your *OWN* mother for Christ's sake.

So MacK was very sad as this seemed the dead bell of exubera- tion, Pietro Arditti the indefatigable *party guy* become *the party man*, a biddable apparatchik of Pine Street. *Izzy* didn't care for they were all rotten, all the Christians and their categories, denominations—as he uncorked the armagnac he said it was wrong for Mr Ardent to neglect his mother, *to say such a thing on Thanks-f\*\*\*ing-giving—all I'll say*. Except that the whole thing is *really—f\*\*\*ing—weird*. But I suppose, said Iz, you've enjoyed that holiday meal much more than ever before, now that you're practically a f***ing Pilgrim and a Daughter of the American Revolution.

Mr Ardent bristled a trifle at this increasing assault. But he was just *so much larger than Isidor* that he knew nothing could happen to him.

—Why don'tcha lay off? suddenly rose up Mary-Ann. Pietro Arditti—I mean, Mista Awdent's just tryna make his way in the world like the rest of us, *Isidor*. He can change his name if he wantsa. I think it sounds *nice*.

—That what you think? said Iz—think I should change my name to Ichabod Crane? Think MacK should get away from that creeping swart Celticness and go totally Anglo-Saxon? Mr Manning, Mr—Kenilworth?—what the f*** does your name *mean*, anyway? What's a *Kenzie?* —No idea, said MacK. —And what about you honey? said Iz, such a beautiful goil with the name of Murphy, which will keep you the scullery maid and brick-layer you so obviously are. —Oh stop it, Izzy—though she *was* bothered by the name of Murphy, which she felt at times in New York a hugely weighted, laughable hat of some kind. —Why don'tcha lay off? And he did—cuz he was five times warmed—by his friends, by the valences of debate in which he had traveled, by grand holiday fayre, by armagnac, and by the knowledge that he was at this very moment contemplating the finer things in life and had contacted high ideals—having run the history of Epicureanism from sensual pleasure right up to peace of mind in one evening—never mind how it was achieved, by kicking Mr Ardent in the bottom. This is a warm, Dickensian paragraph too. And, MacK thought, the holiday still drifted around the room, and even though important things had been stated frankly and even baldly, their group, it had to be admitted, was ever cohesive, held together, as was the little school in Epicurus's garden, by the charm of Isidor's brains and personality.

*So there are these two maggots on the edge of the sidewalk, say around Murray Hill, it's a summer morning and they're wriggling around, and one of them happens to fall into the gutter, into a dead cat. So several weeks go by and one day the maggot who stayed on the sidewalk runs into the other—his old friend. My my, he says, just look at you—I've been struggling to get a living up here but you're so sleek and fat! How'd you do it? And the other maggot says, Brains and personality, brother, brains and personality.*

Isidor had achieved what the Epicureans could only theorize—he withdrew himself each day more and more from external influences (he for one believed the gods have nothing to do with us) the IRT, the IND, Times Square, Schaller and Weber, cops, jocks, and WQXR; and therefore 'lived like a god among men'.

What happened to the Madeira cake?

Mr Ardent was not insensible to the spirit of the holiday—and while he had felt under attack, as he often did by the time dessert was finished at Izzy's and Mary-Ann's, he saw that Izzy had ascended to some higher philosophic plane—that he'd calmed—that he'd *shut up*—so he smiled while taking a paring knife to the end of his Churchill—after all, he'd done the right thing for his career in World of Business®, whatever Izzy thought—and spoke in imitation of Isidor's imitation of *his* voice. —Leave my mother out of this; your mother wears Army boots! —F*** you! So they were happy and here there was a warming scene, Mr Ardent putting on the large sheepskin coat in which he moved through the city, a thick and hardened side of meat; the soft silk scarf he had been affecting lately—the gay blue harbinger of a suit to come. Izzy slapped him on the back in a completely theatrical way, out of his conception of hale fellowship in the World of Business®, but also gave him his hand, once Mr Ardent's were in the frighteningly untanned-looking muttony gloves which matched his coat. Several kisses on the cheek from Mary-Ann, who was happy to see the boys parting so equable—the holiday night air was running up the stairwell and smelled of Christmas coming. —Well steer clear of culture, that's my advice, said Isidor. —You'll be able to do that easily, said MacK, now that you're an Episcopalian—they shook hands. Mr Ardent went down the stairs and stood for a moment adjusting his scarf and gloves in the unpainted vestibule of Isidor's apartment building. With the Churchill at full throttle Mr Ardent looked like an eye-rolling cap- italist fish from the undersea night club. There was a cab on Second.

There is also holiday in washing dishes, the odors of dinner mingling with that of Joy Joy Joy and the percolator put on to help the clean- ing up—a final jot of armagnac—or a bottle of beer as MacK studied the amalgamated dinnerware of Isidor and Mary-Ann while he carried it to the sink. They'd both owned plain white dishes—Isidor's were heavier, stolen from diners maybe—what after all is the purpose of diners?—Mary-Ann's thin, as from an import shop smelling like excelsior and incense—both owned three each of glasses for red and for white, a small number of pots (Mary- Ann knew exactly what she needed to make the GUMBO in the pill-box of her previous kitchen). Both had owned one corkscrew *moderne* apiece, both hated oven mitts and tea towels. So putting their kitchen together had taken no time—a sign?

Isidor began idly picking his after-dinner fight. —What the Hell are you defending that guy for? he said as Mary-Ann brought in the table cloth. —Well, I know it's ridiculous, Isidor, she said, I can see that—but he's down there with all those stuck-up basteds on Pine Street all day an' he gets nervous I guess—he's only tryna make a living ya know. —Think I'm not trying to make a living? —I didn't say that. What is wrong with you? —I think it's an outrage . . . guy changes his *name?* and his *religion?* just so he can join the Yale Club? —Well if he wantsa join the Yale Club whatsa matta with that? —You're starting to sound like a Rockette. —What's wrong with soundin' like a Rockette? My sista's a Rockette! —I know, I know—he'd forgotten. —Yeah, what is wrong with Rockettes at all, piped up MacK, recalling the sista's stems—wondering if intervention was needed and if this was it—they display 'em in old-fashioned *get-ups* to be sure, but they are the legs of today. He suddenly thought he *shouldn't* mix into this. —Remember the time we used the bathroom at the Yale Club? he said, deciding to address the subject under discussion—or its ancillary. —Yes I remember said Izzy, annoyed, there was a time when wearing any kind of tie and a stupid jacket legitimized you up the wazoo in this town . . . no more, man—now they look, they actually look at the cloth and the cut, baby—I have to go to the *Roosevelt* for a midtown squizz. —Although, said MacK, the guy in there is very friendly. —Yeah. The *black* guy is friendly. —Yeah. —No more of that public restroom shit for Mr Ardent, said Isidor—he'll be handed the key to the executive washroom before you know it—YEAH, BABY! —You boys are terrible, said Mary-Ann.

—Know what? said Izzy to MacK, I think this is a very beautiful girl, don't you? —Um, yas, said MacK. —But she's got some krezzy ideas in that head I think. —Stop it, Isidor, right now, she said. —So we're going to go a couple of rounds about it, if you don't mind. —Oh Isidor, not tonight, said Mary-Ann, it's *Thanksgiving*. —Exactly, said Izzy, in his best horror movie accent. —Full of beans aren't ya, comparing one guy to another like that? Think I don't put bread on the table? This poor schmuck and I dragged that Jesuitical turkey of yours all the way from Schaller and Weber, the empire of the franks! —*Via* the Bavarian Inn I think, said Mary-Ann. —So what, we got thirsty dragging it, said Iz from the bedroom, that OK with you? And came out with the gloves. —Those new? said MacK. —You bet they ah, said Mary-Ann. —I love her Everlastingly, said Iz.

# The Champ

There was an overhead light in the living-room, which they all hated—it destroyed the apartment's book warmth, and made the beige walls bleak, like a place in which there were only arguments, cartoon tenement parents yelling at kids—if you saw it from outside. But Iz climbed up on the table and unscrewed the large white globe and replaced it with a reflector flood he kept under the bed,

Mary-Ann wiped her hands on her apron and tutted about having to do this after making dinner, after all. —Come on, said Iz, tomorrow's a holiday too. —Almost wish I *was* going to the office, so, she said. —Come *on*.

GREAT!

—Have a cigar, man, said Iz, sit down, enjoy yourself. Have a beer. He helped her with her gloves on and got his own laced; she with her teeth. They looked at each other and then at MacK for a moment—which was supposed to be some sort of beginning? *Ding*, thought MacK—Izzy turned off the kitchen light—they started circling—MacK lighted up.

—So, think that guy ought to've changed his name, huh? said Iz, plying her with a few inquisitive jabs. —I never said that, Isidor, and you know it, said Mary-Ann. She was lighter on her feet but obviously hadn't been studying long—mostly her guard imitated Izzy's—she was still in her cardigan—she'd taken her shoes off so as to approach his level. The upper part of Iz knew how to box, or at least how to appear to box, thought MacK, reflecting also it was ironic that Iz was now in his white shirt sleeves and dark trousers—whenever MacK wore the same Izzy screamed at him *What are you, a Portuguese waiter? Two espresso!*—and therefore looked like the referee. Iz spent two hours on a heavy bag downtown every Thursday. He wanted to hang one up in the Katzenmurphy, but it would have taken up all the remaining space, being the largest thing in there by far (saving the visits of Pietro—*Mr Ardent*). But while he'd developed quite a chest and shoulders pounding the King of Unresponse, he hadn't looked to his footwork.

—*The champ is looking a little sluggish tonight!* —*Can't agree with ya more, Ed!* —*We had reports from training camp that the champ has been hitting the armagnac as well as the heavy bag!*—*'s been skipping skipping rope!* —*Well it doesn't look like he's been skipping any bouts at the old training table!*—*He's a capacity crowd unto himself tonight, Ed!* —*The champ looks muzzy!*—*the champ looks like he's swallowed an entire toikey wit all da trimmins . . .*

—Would you **shut up?** said Isidor. —Sorry, said MacK. Izzy and Mary-Ann's eyes were bright as they circled under the flood lamp. Izzy started scoring points on Mary-Ann, but he wasn't putting anything behind it—lady after all. Mary-Ann didn't know how to block him and was getting red in the face. Izzy scored on her shoulder, her sternum, and made a little point of goading her solar plexus. —God damn it, she said, and her eye grew beady. —Oh, *god* is it, said Izzy, not something a nice Catholic goil says—course you could *change your name*—hhh! (he scored a right above her breast)—like Pietro Arditti and then God couldn't find you. —Isidor, I'm warnin' ya, said Mary-Ann, stepping back and shouldering off her sweater, dragging the sleeves over the big red gloves with her mouth, now she circled again, in her black leotard—her cheeks very red and her eyes dewy.

—Come on, ya little runt, show us what ye're made of—ya sawed-off little loudmout'. —What? I'm a loudmouth?—and he braised her chin—think I'm going to take that from a cop's daughter? —I'm warnin' ya Isidor, quit makin' personal remarks while weah boxin' or ya gonna get it. Ya little Epicurean ya. —What! I'm not an Epicurean! —C'mon, Eppy! —I told you, I'm not an Epicurean, not in the way *'MR ARDENT'* says I am—the big geek—don't you understand that? He doesn't know the—Mary-Ann almost got him in the bag. —I say you *ah*. —I am not (swings a little wild). —Oh yeah? Where were you and MacK today? I think your day began at Schalla and Weba. I think ya drank some imported beahs at the Bavarian Inn. I think ya came back here and ate a gigantic dinna, that *I* cooked, and drank two bottlesa fancy—*French*—oof—wine (she was starting to hit out crazy now; she didn't connect)—ya smoked a big fat CIGA ya friend brought ya, and ya guzzled about a quata bottla armagnac—also guess what? —What, said Izzy, starting to sweat. —Those cans of plums ya bought at Zabar's? —What about 'em? —Look at the label, Isidor—theyah called *'EPICURE'*. Iz swung a big right at her: —*I'm going to give you!* —and Mary-Ann fell, 'intentionally, without a blow'.

Izzy stared down at her on the floor, eyes wide in disbelief

—You're disqualified, he shouted, that's DISqualification. Mary-Ann lay fetchingly on the floor looking up at Izzy with her pink cheeks and moist eyes, breathing hard. He went for her—here was a brief descent into PANCRATIUM and MacK looked away briefly, not really thinking *Ding!*, before Iz realized the bout was still on—they staggered to their feet and breathed at each other like rhinoceri. —You're disqualified, he said. —I'm disqualified? she said, I'm going to bust ya Epicurean ass—I'm gonna send ya off to a higher plane where ya can canamplate the good. —Oh yeah? —Yeah! said Mary-Ann, and found *such* an uppercut some-where within her girlish interior—an uppercut you couldn't believe—that MacK rose out of his slouch on the couch and the dogs of Sodom upstairs snuffled and growled just it seemed with the hissing air immediately prior to her connection with Isidor's chin—really just hauled off and—as you could imagine people doing in these tenements fifty years before, to the tune of boiled dinners and life in the back yards; children playing in and out of the laundry—dogs—really just f***ing *flattened* the guy. He was slowly lifted in the air along with some of the furnishings, pictures, potted plants and the wicker chairs, there was a low roaring noise such as is supposed to precede earthquakes, and Isidor fell onto the floor as heavy and sack-like a thing as Mr Ardent or the big bag at the gym. Mary-Ann stepped back and calmly began unlacing her gloves with her teeth. —Wanted some cheese huh, she hotly said—dropped the gloves on a chair and went into the kitchen—looked at herself in the shaving mirror over the sink —smoothed her hair—dipped her finger in the stream of cold water—then daintily touched a few drops over each eyelid and came back in. Isidor might have had a big lily sticking out of his chest. Slapped him, without animosity, certainly none of that which had powered her uppercut, what an uppercut, you shoulda—he opened his eyes and *actually said* Where Am I? —Ya on the floor ya crazy Epicurean basted.

# Mary Ann's Mary Janes

Armagnac, the antipuritan poultice of the evening, first to float the gang slightly above and away from the holiday—now to bring Isidor firmly back down into it. His eyes were Xs. —Come on, honey, said Mary-Ann, time for bed. Good-night, MacK—can ya make up ya bed on the floor? You know where everything is. It's more comfortable than the couch I always think. —How does she know that? wondered MacK as he dragged the cushions off the furniture to make the Mondrianic arrangement of pillows and other things on which he would lie. Faint light came through the blind and shone on a print, a dark skyscraper of the Thirties.

MacK roiled in his mosaic bed, reaching occasionally out to hug the puzzle of pillows back together—a crevasse closed on him—he sprang to fill the shape. He replayed the bout in his mind and was warmed by the idea of Mary-Ann in her black leotard, circling, feinting—Iz called her a Rockette, but here is no bad thing, a Rockette in the house would be . . . Well she sure is a curvy GAL and can she cook? Brother. And some fighter.

A number of weeks before, MacK had arranged to meet them at the Plaza Garibaldi. He decided to drop off his overcoat at Izzy's, since it had become suddenly too warm for it—don't you hate this?—or hang it up in the Bavarian Inn and see how it looked—phone Iz from there to ask if in late afternoon a Club Weisse appealed while they waited for Mary-Ann, who never got uptown before 7.30. —I'm stuck doing some stuff, said Isidor, but drop it off—we'll meet you for dinner. Izzy had a desk he prized made from the front door of his last apartment on the West Side—he'd unscrewed it from the hinges and thrown it in the van, last thing. —I need a bigger desk in the new place. —?—said MacK. —Hey, they never gave me any heat here, so what do they need a front door? He did accounts at the desk (he hated doing them in the shop) though it was usually covered in cigar boxes and soaked-off wine labels—much room was taken up by the large desk lamp Izzy used to monitor the decantation of wine into his carafe.

So MacK stopped by with the awful burden of his coat—what is worse than having the wrong coat, having to labor under the thing that is making you hot?—in fact, carrying anything is crap—*it is not urban*—it ought to be country folk and suburban idiots who *carry* things, bundles of sticks, washing, designer ice cream, the bodies of girls they've had to murder because of violating the cousin laws. Theoretically you shouldn't have to carry *anything* with you *ever* in the city, thought MacK, since *everything* is available on every corner . . . But Mary-Ann was home! Late afternoon light in the living-room, only the second, short time of day that actual photons found their way into the place. Izzy had buzzed him in, but when MacK came through the kitchen and through to the living-room he found them—sitting—that is, together—Mary-Ann was on Isidor's lap, which, why not, but. Iz told MacK to put his coat down and they'd meet him in a couple of hours, with more than a breath of solemnity—*somethin'*—*I don't know*, MacK thought. It struck him that Mary-Ann looked quite autumnal, in a plaid skirt and knee socks—well—so what, she's from Massachusetts—and was probably the only woman in that whole 'television' company who wore a *blouse*. —You guys OK? said MacK. —Yah. He *backed* out of the room, away from this—Mary-Ann's mary janes, brand new and barely touching *en pointe* the floor as she sat in Izzy's lap—well interrupting anyone is the pits; ought to be a misdemeanor.

MacK rolled left to right as if sea-sick, wedging himself permanently—as he found—in its usual spot. The curvatures evinced during the bout—the mary janes—these were good things to sleep on—thanks.

———

*Muffled, from the bedroom:*
   —Whoa, say, whuddya call that?
   —Say hello to 'Mr Ardent', honey.


# Baloney: Election Day

NOVEMBER you associate with topcoats and the grim visages of Next Presidents in black and white—*colors* are for the *powerless*—but Primary Day in summer is always bright. Mayhap it's the only day you have any say-so, the only day on which to *celebrate* this damnable process, which ruins both sleep and wage-earning, and causes nothing to improve but only to get worse and worse. This business of keeping the lorises on their toes. The last person you voted for—should he or she even have been DOG CATCHER? *No.*

Isidor always awoke to it with relish—uncharacteristically whipped out of bed leaving Mary-Ann behind—she was from Massachusetts after all and had no confidence in politicians—they kept getting shot, thrown in jail, they *lied,* they wore *helmets.* —You are what is wrong with this country, you know, said Isidor, beginning to shave and loudly hum. 'My Country, 'Tis of Thee.' He did this every primary-bright morning. From under the pillow: —Oh puh-*leeze*, Isidor—f***offwhydontcha?

Such is the breadth of opinion so charmingly allowed in this our town. —Wake *up*, said Isidor, it's time to exercise your franchise. —That what ya callin' it now?

MacK arose with pride from the '14-15' puzzle of his bedding. Sunlight dribbled down into the little back yard and through the small window of the living-room and there was that undeniable clairvoyance you receive, from time to time, that a perfect summer morning awaits you. He had arranged to VOTE with his FRIEND.

During Our Years in Yorkville MacK took every opportunity to sleep on the floor of the Katzenmurphy apartment. He was living at this time on *West* 83rd while Isidor and Mary-Ann lived on *East*

83rd. It was the only point in his existence, he thought now, on his grand north to south *victory tour*, when going *west to east* was my focus. It said much of his affection for the two of them, and not a little about his feudal loneliness.

Back-and-forth has never had the force of up-and-down, he reflected.

The familiar and frustrating hour to wait and watch Isidor drink his little gallon of joe and read the *New York Times*, which on election day he always did with *extra ferocity and flapping*. Mary-Ann primped, plumped and cooed—it was always a nervous morning for her as her patriotism, neither greater nor lesser than yours, was subject to attack.

At ten o'clock the three of them stood at what each privately thought of as the Corner of Decision, 83rd and First, not because it was election day but because at this corner one decided whether to face north and go up to 86th and apply for succor to the crosstown bus and/or the Lexington Avenue subway, or to become part of the vast particulate suspension of humanity and filter, in any way you could, toward midtown. Iz kissed Mary-Ann goodbye. —*Commie slut*, he said. As she crossed the street she waved back at the two voters: —*So long, suckers!*

Isidor made to cross the avenue but MacK swerved. —No! said Iz, no! Not another sandwich, you're going to have to get a special pocket made. But followed him into the deli. —Baloney and swiss on a roll, lettuce and mayo? said MacK. —I know, said the guy.

Isidor could do *nothing* about MacK's being very impressed with the baloney here. Or that MacK had now acquired the habit of buying a baloney and swiss on a roll whenever he passed, whether to or from Iz's—business hours permitting. Sometimes he ate them and sometimes he didn't—given the ban on breakfast at Isidor's they sometimes came in handy—though Iz would come out of his bedroom and shout if he heard the hallmark rustling of deli paper. Some nights this sandwich was one of the elements of MacK's bed on the floor—more than once his pillow. This sandwich was banned from Isidor's refrigerator—to no avail. —How can you just *walk around* with a sandwich, said Isidor, where is your briefcase? —These don't fit in my briefcase, said MacK. His was the rather slim *Briefcase of Ideas*. —Lead on if you please.

—It seems logical, said Isidor, to get a balanced view. He was always talking of this. So they spent an hour in the rather dirty Blarney Castle, while MacK watched Izzy read the *other paper*, for which Iz would never pay. He was sometimes inspired or even swayed by its brand of nutty populism—some elected offices in the land did benefit from his annual perusal of it. He affected to put it down with a dismissive plop after rubbing it in the puddle, crumb and ash of the bar. —Guess I've heard what the hairy apes have to say. —You shouldn't talk that way you know, MacK said, one of these days that wretched paper of yours is going to go out-and-out Republican, instead of *hiding* it all in the 'Living' section—and then you'll have to read this one. —Well that is a day I can stand to wait for, said Isidor, secretly wishing that the city had a newspaper worthy of the name, not just all this *prose*.

—*It is time*, he said, although every political soul in the bar considered *staying* in the bar with its air-conditioning, free newspapers and mess.

Down a side street in the beautiful city morning—there were flowers in pots on black-painted fire escapes of the brick tenements, which seemed patriotic as all get-out, thought MacK. —We go in here, said Isidor. He pushed open a door, above which were flags flying, and bunting. Inside was a linoleum-covered stair. —After you. MacK climbed the stair and found himself in what looked like a room where you might have to hang around for a long time while someone re-lined your brakes or hid and smoked before fixing your teeth. The walls were shiny wood-effect paneling, the lights, glaring on more linoleum yet, were *fluorescent* (but one makes sacrifices for democracy, he thought). There were frightening chairs and standing ashtrays filled with sand, reminiscent of the auto club or the telephone company when it served the people, and frightening magazines devoted to the male desiderata. Aggressive-looking rubber plants postured in pots with little flags stuck in the artificial soil. There was a window, with a ledge, such as you beg at for dispensations in places like this. It was very Non-New York—the two Voting Men might have been in Queens; or Columbus. —Where are the booths? said MacK. Izzy walked over to the window and pressed a button that said PRESS. —Keep your pants on, he said.

—*Who* keeping his pants on? said a voice as the window slid open. What can I do for you gentlemen? —We are here to vote of course, said Isidor. Isn't it election day? —It surely is, said the pleasant receptionist. Who you want to vote for? —Hey, she's not supposed to—, said MacK. —Would you let *me* handle this? said Izzy. We want to vote for Lily and Donna. —You in luck, said the receptionist, they waiting for you solid citizens in Voting Booth Number Seven. Now *she* pressed a buzzer and a door next to her window came ajar. Iz made for this with surety in his *shoes for a guy who walks* and held it for MacK. The receptionist watched MacK cross the floor. —What in the parcel? —It's a *sandwich*, said Isidor, you believe that? —Now I seen *everything*.

MacK followed Isidor down the hall. —I don't think I brought my sample ballot, he said. —Guy brings a sandwich and not his ballot, said Iz. He tapped at the door of Voting Booth Number Seven.

The booth was sunny and looked out on the street. A breeze came through the windows decorated with bunting, which MacK had seen from below. —What's in the package? said Donna, and MacK was immediately charmed by her. She wore a blue dress while Lily was in red and already welcoming Isidor with white gloves. —This booth suit you, said Izzy, or you want another? —I curse machine politics, said MacK. Things are so much more straightforward in California. —Are you from *California?* said Donna.

There was a large sofa. As usual Isidor got down to things quickly on the left wing of it: —Tell me, he said to Lily, as they began working together, your opinion of the Sanitation Bill. —I'm against it, Sir, she said. —The bill!? —No, silly, GARBAGE. —Good. Wow.

MacK had not studied the ballot, being from California and therefore without political training or awareness, so Donna had to draw him out. —My! And how will *you* be voting today? she said, though who or what she addressed—. —I always vote my conscience, said MacK. —Bullshit! panted Iz. —You seem eager enough, said Donna, look, Lily. —Mmm. —Tactics are important, are everything, said Isidor—so Lily took up something else with him.

The flags and bunting in the breeze behind Donna: MacK felt he was falling in love. What an impressionable guy.

The old republic reared its head.

After some martial, stirring minutes Isidor again said it was important to get all points of view. So they exchanged places. —Switch-hit voting, said Isidor, democracy, baseball and hot dogs. —I know you, don't I? said Donna.

Isidor's guidance. MacK's vigor.

The levers were pulled and the boys' intentions for the city and nation were plainly registered. It seemed the Republicans were to do badly today, as we generally hope to be the case in this our town. Lily smoothed her red outfit with her white gloves and reclined on the sofa. After tapping over to the door to receive a tray of cocktails and tea from an unseen hand, Donna draped herself nicely over MacK in an armchair. MacK opened up the baloney and swiss and offered it round. —Good god, said Isidor, but the girls tore off a morsel each and seemed to relish them. Isidor was always concerned with decorum and this was a good thing. He knotted his tie and took out his wallet. —No no, said Donna, poll taxes are always paid on departure. Someone was sneezing up a storm in the next room: —**Hapci! HAPCI!** —There there, said a girl.

Isidor paid at the sliding window. He paid in the *coin of fun*, that commodity we all work so hard for, to jingle in our trousers.

On the street, election day seemed even more beautiful than before. Iz and MacK walked toward Lexington Avenue. They were content to be silent as trotting in front of them was a girl in pretty pink shoes. Voting together as they had was perhaps the fullest expression of their friendship through another medium—though there were the supplementary media, beer and shellfish.

# The Far East

Still there in the morning—perilous near conjunction of the cuttly underside of the thing and a big nailhead—the light came in perhaps as yesterday and MacK got up and collected a few of Izzy's books and a few of Mary-Ann's—the most powerful gods in the house. The day after Thanksgiving is a nightmare to define in city terms. A few people are allowed to sleep in, but most must work, must act like they didn't jiggle their endorphins the day before and cloud the mind with sport—they have a desperate epic journey on their hands—they've got to get to the office before *THE SHOPPING* starts. The dogs—it remained to be seen how much sleeping Iz and Mary-Ann had managed.

According to Isidor, he felt calm. Very calm. Nothing like a K.O. for the effects of armagnac—hadn't he said this for many years? —where does that leave yer Ibuprofen hah? —got to hand it to the girl.

By the time the three of them hit the street the lucky ones had made it to work—there was a bustle to East 86th but this would pale. —Just think what it's like about 50th and Fifth right now, said Izzy in his over-coat. They shuddered. —But where we gonna go today? I'm freezin' already, Isidor, said Mary-Ann, let's take a bus or somethin'. Iz agreed to take a bus to Fifth because of the wind and the Bavarian Inn.

It was only four or five avenue blocks but the 86th Street crosstown carried them from the still-quiet still unexplored Far East right into the blaring zooming semi-suburb Yorkville was becoming. The snow had left the streets mostly but it clung to awnings and roofs and threw enough of the light of a pretty winter day into the bus to lighten the feeling of doom. Izzy and Mary-Ann huddled, Iz in his overcoat-as-battle-tank posture, *thrust into the masses* at the apocalyptic hour of 10.45 am. Behind the driver sat the mother of the worst-behaved kids in New York, they're screaming, they're yelling, jumping up and down on the seats, the mother is very tired, with bags under the eyes from Hell—you could imagine what Thanksgiving had been like for her—no, you couldn't—it was probably all over the walls from cranberries, from stuffing—she had a prematurely sallow face, a face not from New York—but you could tell she thought she was going to die here, maybe today. The piercing screams and craven misbehavior of these children were annoying everyone, who had of course left their houses in the best of holiday spirits—if *that* isn't enough to make you vomit—Christmas begins today—hooray—particularly the driver, who found himself the captain of a bus that couldn't move, in traffic that was becoming monumental—his bus was *failing to live up to its only purpose*, which was to go back and forth and back and forth on 86th Street driving him insane in a few short years. They were totally bogged in front of Gimbel's, where a Saint Nicholas rang a bell, which you could hear above everything, the insidious nasty high and possibly electrically amplified note of the impending holiday, even in the bus with its stuck windows and thumping heater and the engine which might only *idle* ever again. In her desperate sallowness the young mother grabbed her son's head and twisted it around so he was looking at Gimbel's—or traffic—*he* didn't know. —Look, there's Santa, she said (the *Santa* might have formed part of a prayer for release from her agony), Santa! Wave to Santa. God *damn* if this doesn't still work, as MacK observed, and saw that Izzy saw too—*Santa* and kids' mouths drop open, their movements become drugged . . . —*Santa!* said the boy to his sister, and they suddenly began banging as hard as they could on the flabby plexiglas windows of the poor old bus, *screaming* SANTAAA! SANTAAA! HI SANTAAA!, which was an even greater violation of everyone else's civil liberties—and after two minutes of this *f***ing* daemonium during which the bus suffered two changes of the Lexington Avenue stop-light without being allowed to move an inch, the driver turned in his seat and spat at the boy: —*There's no such thing as Santa Claus*, at which the entire bus broke into HEART-WARMING APPLAUSE.

The little boy looks away from the window, stays his hand with which he's been banging like a bitter guy in a prison movie, in mid-swing—looks the driver over carefully, from cap aslant sticky-outy hair to the dirty shirt, silly badge, trouser stripe cadged from a mailman it looks like, to the *track shoes!?* and says—F*** you. At which the entire bus breaks into HEART-WARMING APPLAUSE.

There is nothing that delights us more than when an employee of the MTA gets it and gets it good. Truly: *there is nothing more delightful*.

—God damn kids. Isidor hated getting off the bus on Fifth Avenue, even if he were going to walk down Fifth Avenue—he didn't like the way the bus had to wait, or the way it turned, its loud signal clicking on the dashboard, it drove him crazy—*Goin' crazy!* —consequently he always got off at Madison. So they stood, as many people do, shivering and knocking their hands together in front of the Madison Restaurant, or Soup Burg, thinking they'd only just eaten breakfast but that one of those cups of cream of chicken soup—small pack of saltines . . .

They had to decide as usual which avenue to walk down. —Hey, how come we never walk down *Pak*? said Mary-Ann, folding her shoulders about her in the cold. —*Park!?* said Izzy, *Park* is where you go to *die*. Or get shrunk and *then* die. —Aren't you completely crushed, chimed in MacK, and annihilated by the heaviness of those buildings? Their tomb-like suffocating weight? What they look like under the vapor lamps? (No response.) —Are you kidding? they both shouted, Park Avenue is DEAD MATTER.

# A Gibson Girl

The day was museum-cold, with the reflected quiet light which pulls you into the Whitney or the Metropolitan or the Modern and lets you feel cozy about being there. (Not the *Frick*, which is surrounded by its *own weather* left over from the Scottish Enlightenment and flavored with cold tea and Frigid® brand embalming fluid). No, the museums that make you feel loved! The museums where the pictures love YOU!

Always this coat-room madness; Izzy almost always refused to give up his coat—he thought the attendants rude—he wandered the museums of New York like they were bus stations—not that the Metropolitan resembles anything else—but it is a god and must be placated—you cannot *walk by*. Isidor planned a little progressive dinner of consuming art for them (he believed in eating his enemies)—three courses of his favorite painters—they wouldn't be staying here long, but Mary-Ann always checked her coat because she liked holding the big number in her pocket while she looked at the pictures. —I'll give you a number to hold, said Izzy.

John Sloan painted the very 27 November they had just walked out of—you could almost hear the high note of Santa's bell among the strollers on his crisp day—even HI SANTAAA!, although no one was as badly behaved in 1910—only the *breakthrough* of television has made *that* kid possible. There was the same light reflected from snow secreted on the tops of awnings, and some of the roofs—men and women looked happy enough—happy even—on the street; it looked as though conversations were going on, not just when friend met friend, but that there was a *general conversation*—in which, back then, everyone in town knew they were necessarily engaged—if you were rotting in a back room, diving under the river to build a bridge, hatching an evil plot, sitting in a club behind high windows, you were engaged in the conversation, the exchange which is this our town—even Isidor couldn't avoid it—though when he walked alone he sometimes sought refuge in his own summary pronouncements—*Oh oh, crazy one!*—others heard part of the encyclopediac storm of controversies which consists in I Katz—he talks to himself.

And so do ten or twenty thousand other people in Manhattan—including a guy at the corner under the El in Sloan—his teeth are clearly visible—he's not smiling, he's quietly forming a word—there's no one listening except John Sloan maybe—the word may be SHADDAP—he's talking to himself—*you've got to.* It would be wrong to say Sloan's street looked any friendlier, any more open than it does today (it was Murray Street, near City Hall—oh maybe there were a few more people living around there then—they were only just getting used to the idea that they could fill up Manhattan with masonry—*go ahead, pave and pave and pave me boys, you won't hurt me!*—you *can't* hurt me—just getting the idea that outer space loomed directly above them, uptown) for New York is an open and friendly place. If there were anything different about John Sloan's people it was merely that they had a little more time on their hands—not much—but after the job they'd come out on the street, and the marketing (not the way *you* mean) and the odd drink would be the evening—they'd not to rush back to their apartments to speak on the telephone or watch television or work some more—work was *over*, this was *night*.

—That's the way to live, on Murray Street, said Isidor, who had already collected a ton of not so much Newyorkiana, visual, ephemeral, fictional, intangible, as it was a complicated series of references showing actually and exactly HOW TO LIVE in New York—how other people did it successfully—people of all sorts. Not just Sloan's people who were *extremely tired*, but menus from restaurants long gone, timetables for Fifth Avenue buses in 1928, in 1955—pictures of people in the subway, the skyscraper lithograph in Iz's small living-room uptown, which was blocky, but *examined* the thing, you could see, from the favorite angle of the guy who drew it.

Izzy's collection was his legend to the New York he was building, decision by decision, to live in. MacK liked the hats and Mary-Ann the light reaching out from bar and shop—it made you want to get down to Murray Street right away, *that* Murray Street. Seemingly without having to move their eyes from the canvas across the wall of the museum, the velvet rope, the ticking hydrometer maintaining life in Art's veins like Lenin in his box of jelly, across the guard's stoically uninterested midriff, they went from Murray Street uptown maybe to the fights with George Bellows. Iz stood in front of it a long time, his lips bulging ever so slightly, their need of cigar—smoke circled around the fight, under light much stronger than the bulb at home—Iz contemplated the sweating indoor night of sixty years before for what seemed an hour—the black air above the ring, black as the night building in the lithograph at home—everyone else in the gallery was quieted by the power of Isidor's concentration—he wasn't looking at the painting but was, obviously, *in* it.

### THE CITY SPEAKS:
### OF COURSE WE WILL GIVE YOU ROOM
### FOR YOUR EPIPHANY
### —IF YOU'RE REALLY HAVING ONE

Who knows what correct atmospheres Izzy was storing up; what he could apply to these neighborhoods when he was next there or what mustard-plaster of understanding he could stick to the next prize-fight he attended. —See honey, he suddenly said, taking Mary-Ann's arm, see how that guy is leading? Look at the power in that rotation, how the guy's arm doesn't extend all the way, he's throwing a strong punch there honey, but he's reserving a lot of power in his upper arm still, see? Mary-Ann looked at the fight, through the smoky light of the drawing and through the imaginary cigar smoke with which Izzy had now filled the gallery. —Did ya bring me in heah to show me how to hit? she said. Because I know how to hit ya. Isidor expected his laugh to hurt him—the armagnac—but it did not, thanks to the K.O. of his H.O.—a brilliant discovery—must be the adrenaline, he thought. —Thought you could pick up a few tips, honey, that's all. —Why I oughta . . . —Honey, honey.

Today's museum food was a tiny, cold Thanksgiving in a sandwich, without Badedas, without wine, without armagnac, without the stimulant of debate even, bloated and hung over as everyone in the Metropolitan Museum of Art was. Without the knowledge of the quietly teeming holiday teasing the edges of Manhattan, rolling the city in the light proper to the coming month. Too, 'Mr Ardent' wasn't there. Like all museum food this had a patina to its leading edges, tasted first of oven, then corrugated board, then polyvinyl chloride, smelt of Windex and the warm, coffee-laced shit of slow-thinking businessmen all at the same time. —If you needed *another reason for never leaving your apartment*, said Isidor, so many people come to this great museum that they have to *kill* you so you won't come back. That will be $17.54 apiece. MacK was then all for leaving; Fifth Avenue had ultimately a way of creeping in and *getting* him, even if he were enjoying himself—in other words it suddenly made him feel he was at the very least an entire avenue away from a bar. He usually exited by way of the armory, where his opposition to epic (or what Izzy had long contended was an opposition to it and a perverse will *not* to understand the way the world worked) was temporarily expressed in his love of romance; lots of huge axes to chop heads with and plenty of ornamented helmets to roll them in—this was one part of the museum in which it was harder to find a connection to life outside, on Fifth Avenue—but maybe not. Often there are Japanese tourists in the armory *laughing* at the samurai armor of heavy wicker: why? Izzy said MacK could visit the armory if he wanted to, but that he was going briefly back upstairs (Mary-Ann had gone to Flanders for half an hour). Iz wanted to look at his girls, as he called them—MacK went with him.

Having the same taste in turn-of-the-century girls they both liked spending time in the marriageable company of Charles Dana Gibson's women, whenever they were available—their chestnut hair upswept, their sleeves, collars, hats—their penetratingly intelligent and worldly eyes. —But there is no Gibson Girl today, said Iz. —The guy's a mere illustrator, piped up one of the guards. —Sez you, said Izzy—there's only a few guys allowed to use a pen around here? Rembrandt, Dürer, that's it? Walk down the street, man, take a look.

But there they were in front of a Sargent—a black-haired society bride with the same commanding expression, a pure warm white skin, skin which warmed the pale rose of her dress. —Skin of the rich, said Isidor, you get it from a bottle these days. They'd visited her often enough that MacK hadn't noticed how like Mary-Ann she was (obviously this woman never used the word DON'TCHA—although if it had been invented, why not, this woman could have done *anything*)—and he felt jealous—Izzy had taken a step into one of his old New Yorks—with Mary-Ann, into her and it—he could live in the dark-haired pale-skinned world. Perhaps it sent him out of himself and into Fifth Avenue twilight in 1900—heavy on carpets, floor clocks, carriages passing outside? —What do you think it was like to be in her company? mumbled MacK. Imagine her sweet voice. —Who are you, said Isidor loudly, Edith F***ing Wharton? But these women suggested an honesty in the *conversation of the city*, which was being had more directly then—or so they liked to think. Looking at its boiled front you might think the Metropolitan only a gateway to various heartbreaks of the past, crunched-up stuff from people who gave up, were schmecked, killed—a huge *pain in the ass*—but for Isidor here there were entranceways to the city and his love for it; to Mary-Ann and her love. So was she also part of his collection, part of the clues to New York he was always gathering, filling the shop and their tiny apartment with? Isidor and Mary-Ann fit their little place well—she represented a number of decades, was the women of New York, in the low light of their place in the evenings. —Pretty good-looking broad, huh, said Isidor, as he always did. ——In thinking about the past, said MacK, it's important to decide how noisy it was.

# The Grim Reaper

——How was Flanders, said Iz to Mary-Ann, in the sun on the big steps. ——A little cloudy today, Isidor. The warmth of the afternoon was hard to credit but there was also the spiritual warmth of the chestnut vendors and the warmth of FEAR, fear they might be sucked down Fifth toward 59th and below where the first of twenty-eight days of incredible inhumanity, of reckless and pathetic acquisition, little people being squashed by BIG PEOPLE with more expensive shoes, dirty and tired-looking women weeping silently in front of Gristede's, of Whelan Drug, having lost heart even to hold their hands out—in short, Christmas®—had just begun. ——Times Square, said Isidor, will be just about going about its business today—you can't buy anything there except souvenir belts, fake IDs and condoms that taste like *strawberry shortcake*—you believe that? I saw that in a window. ——You can dump ya god damn kids off to go to the *movies* ya know Isidor, said Mary-Ann. ——Ahh, that's nothin'.

It seemed a reasonable goal.

Assuming you believe in these antiheroes.

The ring had been gnawing at Izzy's subconscious and he took it into his head to visit the bar at Jack Dempsey's. What you want on a semi-holiday: you want something old, beat-up, you want anonymity, you want something stupid, yes you do, to *hide behind*. Dempsey's no longer really smelled of the 1940s but there might have been a slight odor of the city in 1955 or even 1960—something about the tablecloths, the fans, the glasses of ice water?—when Izzy's mother would bring him into town on the bus and walk, painfully disapprovingly, to Herald Square and back to Port-of-Authority, having purchased *one thing*, her rule—a slip, a bird cage, a door mat . . . But in front of the Mutual of New York building Izzy had an attack of defensiveness. —I can't take him to Dempsey's, he said to Mary-Ann as if MacK were not there. Not the Grim Reaper. —Oh Isidor that's so silly, said Mary-Ann, who always leaned forward when in motion, like Miss Clavell, whom she also resembled—but that was only a Catholic connection in MacK's mind maybe? MacK was wounded. —Wait a minute, he said, is Jack Dempsey's so important a spot in your solar system? Surely it is robust? Surely ONE VISIT by me in your *color guard*, cried out the *Reaper* now in the middle of Broadway, the 8 x 10 glossies and clippings and cartoons all nostalgic for the ring and JACK and RUNYON and LARDNER and LIEBLING, surely a MINUTE'S DRINKING THERE, A SEVEN-OUNCE SCHAEFER, WILL NOT CLOSE JACK DEMPSEY'S FOR ALL TIME!?

Isidor had smelled a rat, which if proven to exist had the alarming possibility of robbing him of all he held dear—the past New York, the city of *ago* which he was a-building in his mind—tunneling through New York as if it were a giant cheese—finding his way between only things he admits into *his* New York. *Exempli gratia* technically Isidor wasn't walking, *didn't exist*, once he left, say, the New York Public Library until he arrived at the Wilbur Sisters—because there was nothing he passed going up Fifth to 47th and then over to Madison, which COUNTED . . .

(MacK did this too—his search for the 1940s, the vanished radio world, the smell of hot vacuum tubes, dust on shellac pressings—he discovered a route from the RCA Building to Harvey Radio and then on to several musty theatrical sound houses, and a recording studio on West 47th where a little old guy in a cardigan and brogues was happy to talk to him and show him his collection of microphones, some of which were RCA 77s and GE velocity mikes which he was *still using*—and must, MacK thought, have the *spit* of very famous people in them—the place began as a CBS studio during the war and as it had their good engineering was sold on after—to him, Mr Sweater, as if he was a cat that lived in the joint—guy still makes a living recording *voice only*—Peace Corps promotional programs—Father Nodolny—all the stuff that gets wiped or goes in the trash can in all the radio stations of America, MacK thought.)

. . . But the *rat*—Isidor shifted from one foot to the other and looked MacK up and down, disdainfully, disgustedly, even fear-fully—to Isidor MacK had acquired a hooded cloak, a scythe, his hands sloughing flesh . . . —He killed Lundy's, honey, he *killed Lundy's*, said Isidor, suddenly very resistant. There was some humor buried under that—somewhere. A little. But positively father and husband-like: grim. —Aw, he did not, said Mary-Ann, the place was gonna go anyways—ya said so *yaself* after ya had the chowda. But Izzy had begun to notice whenever he came upon a bar, a restaurant, a *space*—for that's what these were, atmospheres which fit into his schema—if he took *MacK* there, within a few months, or even weeks, the place closed, forever. Iz's theory about it was grow-ing—in his mind the visitation of MacK had closed or was going to close the Bavarian Inn, the Dublin House, the Madison Bar, Keene's Chop House, Sweet's, the Gloucester House, Bruno's Pen and Pencil, McSorley's, Gage & Tollner (the evil *influenza* of MacK reaching across the East River), Lundy's, and who knows, even Lindy's; Ratner's, the Gold Lion, the Old Town Bar, Bill's Gay Nineties, the Lambs Club, the White Horse, the Juniper, the Oak Bar at the Plaza, The Oyster Restaurant and Bar, Yonah Schimmel and now Jack Dempsey's itself. Iz's idea of how and why this was happening was *racial*: he persisted in thinking MacK a bringer of a wave of *westerners* to the city—not that MacK worked on Pine Street—but Izzy felt this huge *influx*, wasps, WASPS who knew nothing and would never know nothing about Manhattan. Visiting the ancient eddies of tap room culture they initially revel in them, but on the second or third visit find them dirty; they begin 'upgrad-ing' each neighborhood so as to force something old and not American, as it's defined in California or Kansas, or in the midwest, OUT. But Iz also thought the problem could be what he thought of

175

as MacK's *pathological affability*, an odd combination of ease and demur, morality and carnival, sourness and generosity, which directly came into contact with the waves of feeling, the fights internal and external, the New York sounds embedded in the plaster and wood of the walls of these altars and temples of his—Iz believed in those chaps who show up with lots of dish mikes, flood lamps, wire recorders and bowls of mercury at haunted houses, and extract the wailing emotional history of the building groaning from the wall. —I'm half French, said MacK. —Oh *yeah*, said Isidor. Very French guy.

At the mention of the Lundy Brothers they'd all twitched, a tinily involuntary turning toward Brooklyn—Isidor saw the whole thing, the vaulted ceilings, exotica of the twenties—the stolid, heavily letterpressed menu of unadorned oysters, pan-roasted fish; the millions of small paper cups of tartare sauce, the ice water which smelled of bread, vice versa—vanilla ice cream in a dish—but most of all that Lundy's was obviously a farm, not a fish farm, a fish *waiter* farm, the nursery of the race of New York fish restaurant waiters—bred 'em up here from sprats and sent them in tank trucks of brackish water to Sweet's, the Oyster, Paddy's, Gage's—also a big demand for them in Hoboken—a steamy sheen to their skins after some years, their eyes begin to stare, and are glaucous, they work their mouths, looking for oxygen?—their constant and usual phrases, *What'll it be?—I'll haveta check—No idea, Bud.*

—We can't take him to Dempsey's, said Iz, it'll go OUT OF BUSINESS. —*Isidor*, even supposing it might, said Mary-Ann, what do you cayah? How's it worth saving—witout da *champ*—da champ *in poison!* Isidor gave her a very long look. For here was the voice of a true champeen.

—You may have a point, said Isidor at long last starting across the street—but don't pull anything funny. Don't order stuff they don't have—get a beer or a martini or a highball—*What else would I order?* said MacK—and leave it at that. *You too,* he said warningly to Mary-Ann—if you want wine, ask for *'a wine'*, not a glass of Bordeaux. You got me? —Yes Sir.

And they went south and west into Dempsey's, where the huge and ancient maître d' looked at them, this is *Jack Dempsey's,* mind you—1977 AD—like they were so much *air* or popcorn smell blown in from the Square—and followed their slightly unassured progress to the bar with the look of a guy who was going to treat them as *tourists,* or *complete* idiots, or *baboons*—this always drove Isidor crazy—being treated badly as a *tourist*—not badly as a *resident.*

## I Never *Wuz* a Grand Duke

The bartender looked like a barber. Didn't say anything either. —It's creepy—surrounded by people who don't know a thing and this guy treats you like some interloper or hick, said Izzy, remembering the protests of the fellow who'd suddenly pulled in front of him in a new BMW on the *sidewalk* on Second Avenue—Iz tapped the guy's tail-light with his by now well-broken-in brogue—the slick fellow leapt out of the car—wild-eyed with the fear of being in NEW YORK CITY—*I'm not some naïf from Ohio—you know—that you can just do things to!* —But you are, said Isidor, pointing to the license plate—you are from Ohio. I think you *are* someone I can do things to. Guy drove away which was too bad, Iz needed a fight that day.

At the bar. Isidor nervous in Dempsey's. A look between MacK and Mary-Ann. —Gimme a slug a whiskey, said MacK. —Let me have a *pousse-café, s'il vous plait,* said Mary-Ann, demurely outlining the obscenely appropriate glass with her curvy hands—to wind Isidor up. —What!? he yelled, turning red, I'm afraid I *must* intercede for my friends, they're INSANE—which was good Iz talk but not a word you slung around in Jack Dempsey's; for what place stated The Old Mental Capital more certainly? Guy still looking at Iz—You people have a problem? —*No,* absolutely, said Izzy, *flushing* with embarrassment. —*Problem here, Don?* —*I dunno . . .*

How often do you see a red Isidor?

—My *friend* and I will have a martini. Very dry, straight up, olive. My *other* friend will have——? A wine please, said Mary-Ann, twinkling, piercing the brow of this guy who looked like a fisherman now. Not a bad-looking gal you thought he thought—oughta show her the wine list, what's she doin' with these toids?

Let's admit it, the wine list was

### You want Red? Want White?

—How do you get salt-and-sun skin like that, said Isidor, as the guy bent, mixing, the short back of his little jacket of the past riding up, the clip-on suspenders—in Times Square? —Maybe it's workin' with oysters that does it, said Mary-Ann. Isidor was beginning to feel he could, or should, cultivate any bartender, all the bartenders of Manhattan, for that is what you have to do, if especially you are too self-respecting to get shrunk. *Some days you just want to hug every bartender in New York.* But he began to get uneasy, looking at *this* guy, imperturbable, immutable—he sent out an Ozymandian challenge to everyone in the place, or specially them maybe—it dawned on Izzy that the guy was unreachable—he wasn't a sour Manhattan bartender, but a sour *New York* bartender, who came in every day from an outer borough, or maybe beyond, some place that wasn't even in *town*—just to do *this*—no sense of commitment to Manhattan, and if that is what you lack how can you pour a good bottle of beer or make a good martini? The beer will be sloppy, with foam on the sides (though not in the way you might get a foamy beer downtown or in a McAnn's—which historical sloppiness would be OK), it won't be in the right glass—the martini will taste of water—it won't necessarily be watery but it will *taste* of water—the guy'll *saunter* over and refill it from the shaker—like this is supposed to be classy—even though the ice has ruined what's left in there . . . Sling your hook, buddy.

—Ach! spat Isidor suddenly, when I'm Mayor there's going to be a law, you have to live in Manhattan in order to tend bar. I am going to license them like DOGS. One eyebrow must have gone up 3mm on Ramses over there—but truthfully—he could have posed for the Sour New York Bartender postcard had someone been pervert enough to issue one—but even in New York there wasn't—but *if there had*, you could sell a lot of 'em. Isidor felt betrayed here in Jack Dempsey's—he had always thought of it as truly suiting his purposes, a way-station for perambulating the West 40s *of* the Forties, and Fifties—granted in a stupid way—but he had already pierced its supposed patina, who cared if they had a Dumont television over the bar—it was a FRONT for a plain Times Square cynicism Isidor didn't like—it was a souvenir shop—they might as well have been selling falafel? *Falafel?*—he could imagine Ramses saying it. If a place isn't going to be real, it ought to be genuine, or at least nice.

Traffic went by in a perfectly ordinary fashion—you'd never have known Thanksgiving was the day before, that the eclipse and apocalypse of good feeling had begun. There was plastic holly and mistletoe over the bar but it had been there many years. Izzy liked the idea the mistletoe might have been hanging here in 1950. Light came into Dempsey's in an interesting way—the large windows on Eighth Avenue were slightly tinted (the Fifties) and the bar area was hung with venetian blinds. The light came in slightly cleansed and perfectly horizontal—Iz raised his glass and looked through the gin and around the corner of the olive; decided that the drink could actually turn light silver, could add to its strength—made light (and surely this was real light? passing through Dempseian filters) glow with the insistent chilliness of TV in the old days—that perhaps the qualities of light on all the TVs in all the old bars came flowing through gin—boxing, *Requiem for a Heavyweight*, Kennedy vs. Nixon, Walter Cronkite . . . Light from the past, which perhaps you could make in the alembic of your drink—you didn't have to go sit in *Dempsey's*.

But they drank these drinks and everything was unremarkable as pie. Ramses received their dough, including a shaved version of the usual Isidorean tip, as Pharaoh would have noticed you pissing in the Nile. He turned away immediately and his starched jacket stated he was positive he'd never see one of them again. MacK's shadow, though hardly skeletally handling a scythe or anything curved except his own slouch . . . perhaps fell across the façade as they left?

Isidor was disgusted to find a crowd gathered around a Santa on the corner of 49th. But then delighted to see *Santa was in chains* and the crowd enjoying it too! This was a real bonus—the day after Thanksgiving and New York was already giving it to Santa. But then depressed again to find it was a protest—the *I.L.G.W.U.*, 'Santa of the Sweat Shops'. As they walked east Iz fondly remembered the Hunchback of Notre Dame on his little turntable of humilia- tion—had to admit Santa looked awfully good in such a pose—it set him up emotionally for weeks. EXEUNT MIDTOWN OMNES, after Santa is led away.

## What Is To Be Done?

The bus up Madison. Packed. Some people had already had enough of the most enraging day of the year. As they got into the upper 60s and antiques began to appear, MacK saw a shop in which he had complained bitterly to a girl that she was buying a *LALIQUE* box. He was unused to spending money at that time and didn't know anyone who bought *LALIQUE*, therefore he was only a trainee New Yorker—he's lucky they let him stay—they haven't made it very easy for him. Has run up quite a bar tab though, so that'll see him through. Her question, 'What's wrong with *LALIQUE*?' served only to emphasize the Grand Canyon of culture which separated them (MacK firmly staying on the north rim). It wasn't *LALIQUE* at all he objected to—not knowing what it is and still not—but the idea that he might, or ought to know what it is, and worse the idea that he might or ought to feel at home in this expensive shop and with the idea of buying something merely for the pleasure of buying it (not even that of owning it) (it was hideous)—and the idea she might take it home and sadly put it somewhere on her sad family's very clean shelves (they were constantly locking each other up in drying-out clinics and even mental hospitals)—the idea that the poor ugly little $400 box wouldn't stand the ghost of a chance of making anyone happy in her climate-controlled clinicky family.

Could have said to Isidor, *I was once in that shop with her*, but it was already past and it wasn't much of a story: *Once we argued there.* Though a story you seldom forget. Whereas some men will wander the streets looking up at a window here and there, or fondly remembering a tryst in the rest room of a petit resto, even feeling nostalgia for a caress gained in a taxi at a particular corner (let us hear it for 34th and Second. Woo!), MacK's romantic map consisted in the pin points of fights and breakings-off. He'd been summarized *a cold-heart* at 42nd and Fifth (frighteningly central and public) and tremblingly, brimmingly 'let go', for *having different concerns,* all the way up Second, in the 80s, on a block that seemed to have been cleared by the police for her purpose—he couldn't recall why there—oh *immature*, to be sure, but couldn't remember what they were doing up there—fighting, surely.

This bus was full of people who had the fear—they'd seen enough—but it didn't smell like Christmas yet, that mixture of boughs in the open air, snow coming, your coat, sprayed by the women who've no idea who you or they are, who spray you, in department stores, vacantly, with perfume; and soup, alcohol, cigarettes. Valium and Prozac may have smells. Everyone seemed very *vertical* so it was just the usual Friday afternoon skanks—with a few people who'd braved the initial shopping. Everyone up and down in black and grey and dark blue—some of the uptown ladies in dark brown but looking a little self-conscious about it. A hat or two and small fussy brassy brooches. Isidor stood on the rear steps, one step down into the well, having got Mary-Ann a seat, and feeling squeezed.

A tall boring-looking guy, a sort of Mr Reasonable, who looks like he lived around 84th and Madison, one of those kind of joints, he starts *staring* down at Isidor in the well. Not exactly moving toward him as though he has to get out . . . The bus stops, someone gets on at the front, it moves on. The guy's glasses and *hat* strongly suggest that waspie pre-eminence: *I'm a real New Yorker, not you, blah blah blah*—a strange look which looks outer-American in New York (or boring, like the bus is suddenly full of bankers or people who went to *YALE*), totally stuffy Manhattanite if you hit him on the head, put him in a sack and dumped him out in New Jersey or Arizona—which would be a good idea—he'd f***ing *FREAK OUT* but would then start running the local Chamber of Commerce—he keeps staring down at Izzy who has to keep looking away, the guy is so silly-looking—that body, that mien.

—*Excuse me*, the guy says very pointedly, almost theatrically, *I don't think it is a very good idea of yours to stand in front of the door where people will have to exit.* Says this to *Isidor Katz*. Mary-Ann flinches in her seat and MacK stops listening to the guy going on next to him about a work thing—amazing how all these conversations sound the same, it could be Shelby Stein and the guy from Programming, on bus, subway, at lunch, in elevators—*In any case I think Bob should look the figures over before we send them out to the coast*—who has not said this? What the Hell is it about? Everyone *already* work for the same company? But ingeniously Iz immediately matches the guy's volume and tone: —That so? It happens that it's not my intention to block the door, *Sir*—*I'm* prepared to move out of the way at any moment. For your information I am standing here because the bus is very crowded, you notice that at all? I got on this bus at Madison and 48th. I do not know where you got on, but it was certainly after that; *ergo*, I do not believe there is room for

*YOU* and your prissy hat [someone laughed] on this bus and if you're so f***ing [the guy blanches—he knows he's in unfamiliar jungle now if he didn't before—he's never even seen a *movie* with that word in it] concerned about civic proprieties then you, *YOU*, Sir, ought to have refrained from getting on this bus, *THAT* would have been the action of a man of *principle*, you could have waited for the next bus and the next and yes the next—but excuse me, you're probably an extremely important person who simply must, *MUST* get uptown—*on the bus!* [General laughter.] *Sir*, I don't propose to interfere with any person's entering or leaving this bus, *or* with their civil liberties [the bus slows as it approaches 79th], unlike yourself, you proprietorial J Press cock-sucking eugenic skunk. [A quite elderly lady who seems to be enjoying what Iz's saying comes over to him in his well—the bus halts and the door opens—Mary-Ann and MacK move up with some others to disembark.] —Now watch me, says Isidor, see what I do, I'm going to *help* these people off the bus—I immediately relinquish my place on the step and I *help them off* as a truly civilized person might do, as he *MUST* do, as he *is doing*, ass hole [he reaches out to the old lady]—May I help you, ma'am? —Oh, thank you, very much, she says, looking around at the others as though she had suddenly found herself on television. —I don't make *summary judgements* about people, they're all my brothers and sisters, let me give you a hand [to a large lady with packages] here, you see? I'm *not* going to stand for your insinuations and I'm *not* going to listen to you run down the people of this city and this nation, says Isidor [climbing down on to the street now, to the guy, whose expression is one of the grimmest imaginable],

## SOCIALISM FOREVER!

shouts Isidor—the doors close and the bus goes on up the avenue, to the strains of the 'Internationale' and not 'Silver Bells' or maybe both if you have the stomach for that kind of imaginary segue—Izzy didn't even need to shake his fist at the bus retreating with the white guy in it—he knew that was a cliché but it was one he loved—and he was pretty good at it too.

Mary-Ann's eyes were bright with admiration for Isidor. The three stood on the sidewalk in contemplation of the resolution of the drama—her cheeks were red in the cold. What a grand girl she was: she'd taken Izzy's performance as gallantry; what's lacking in town. MacK saw she cared deeply for Isidor, and, always grateful for insight, came over a little teary, being hungover. Isidor half-turned to them, but kept an eye on the bus till it was out of sight; then allowed himself only a *You believe that guy?* Mary-Ann took his hand and he walked several blocks with her this wise until coming to himself and becoming annoyed and embarrassed put her hand in her coat for her. —I always knew something like that would happen, he said to MacK, once I moved to the *East Side*. He knew no one in Yorkville—except John, who was *fired*.

# The Day After Thanksgiving Day

MacK associated female warmth with six o'clock, when women dress for the evening, and thought of a rainy day when he watched Rosenthal getting ready for a dinner they had been invited to on the West Side, where—he thought—he would be able to show off this classy dame for the first time in a gracious old apartment with table lamps and sofas (so rather unlike Rosenthal's tea-stained futon and deckchair phone booth in SoHo)—real book-lined city living as he endorsed it—and Rosenthal was brushing her hair, putting on a wool dress; her glasses, the warmth of her skin and eyes, all filled MacK with a feeling of arrival—acceptance—of course these book-owning lamp-burning dickheads didn't *like* Rosenthal at the party—she did keep talking about her spastic colon—but so what? —MacK had never been so warmed than during her dressing, watching her attention to small things. He compared Tumbleson's approach to her garments and herself unfavorably: there were two aspects of it he could not accept. First, Tumbleson was a Debbie. MacK had grown up on a street where everyone was named either Mark or Debbie—even the parents; *Debbie* was a name he early applied to the bright, conversational, yet fundamentally unsympathetic women—built with white bread—of Episcopal America—underneath which there is such a coldness and such a deadness of intellect, and such a willingness to be derailed confused and beguiled, that MacK sometimes thought the only place for them all was Washington DC.

Let us speak plainly. Talking about the Christians and the other Devil-may-care people of our country, completely engulfed by the nation's television imago, who have no culture, who still mentally wear the twinset and pearls of a classical *evil girlfriend*, pleasantly steely and steely pleasant—*one says this through clenched teeth*—people who haven't a thought in the head and don't need to, because if you have a career these days you don't have to think—this is why parties *suck*—the Debbies don't let go. MacK shuddered to think how Tumbleson was acting now she'd found out about Rosenthal—but in contrast to Rosenthal's warmth, evinced in her choice of fabrics, her way of moving and dressing, there were two aspects of cold Tumbleson, one attitude which MacK felt she always used against him, a breezy ease and beauty, especially in the summer. Tumbleson made a point of sleeping past the alarm, even unto 8.45, the point of causing MacK to panic—and then *slipping* out of bed, *slipping* out of her nightgown, *slipping* on a cotton dress, *slipping* into her shoes and *slipping* out the door, having paused at the mirror only to *slip* on her lipstick with a stroke and to shake her hair into its lovely place. *MacK*, who after all had ablutions, to take up half the morning, felt *diseased* compared to this. But there was a more straitened, rigorous Tumbleson, who was raised to embrace, who did embrace, the goal posts and waspie altars, who though she expressed herself happy with MacK was constantly on the lookout at the Yale Club for someone with a legal or Pine Street bulge—a Tumbleson who wore imaginary sweater and pearls under her import shop trousers and her Charlie perfume; a marble girl who professed to be having a good time while she had already determined that the grim future was only the grim family (like hers), a Tumbleson who was, in short, a *miserable f\*\*\*er*, who *would* have been at home among the marketers and marketeers, who seemed to have forgotten most of what she learned (having in fact treated her college like high school, floating across a sea of Schlitz on a raft of 'Marlboro' men)—the people offer as high proof of her coldness Tumbleson's bedtime dramas of chastisement—which MacK had been at first forced to administer, get used to, and to which he was now highly and unfairly addicted—clearly the habit of someone who was having a good time before she stopped smoking and drinking and f\*\*\*ing and would finally at the age of—twenty-eight?—grimly go in search of money, a Debbie of the first water although Debbie was not her name.

The long-suffering tobacconist *Seligman* had had to endure her interrogations at Christmas and on MacK's birthday—*What's the difference between this blend and that one?*—of course he set himself up for this, early—making the fatal mistake of everyone who chooses a business involving many many tiny things and objects and their collision with people who *want* but can't understand them—the madness and doom of stationers and hardware men—but told MacK he couldn't bear to have her in the shop again. —*I felt dizzy, Mr MacKenzie; I couldn't play chess for the rest of the day. I don't like that woman, I'll be honest. Smoke judiciously, Sir.* —I'll be honest too, said MacK, and he had gone out into the snow to again ponder the Rosenthal/Tumbleson jumble.

# Plaza Garibaldi

If you would only allow a sketch of the look of 75th and Second at six o'clock on the evening of the day after Thanksgiving—we don't often get the big vistas in town—so we notice what to others might seem minutiae—the exact color of the bite of sky between one building and the next, the specific quality of dirty ice that makes you slip and fall on your ass on Murray Hill between 36th and 37th and Madison on February 14th 1977 . . . Thank you. The block in which the *Plaza Garibaldi* sat was in one of the neighborhoods wherein dwelt, as MacK thought, many of those who are *unsure* of New York—they may not be staying long—okay!—thanks for coming. There was a peculiar air of REASSURANCE about many of the businesses here, including a comedy club—well, people need to laugh—but they were also being reassured, Isidor said, that they needn't venture into DANGEROUS MIDTOWN for entertainment. The delicatessens have a sterile, foreign quality—the pastrami has no smell—do you get it?—the pastrami has NO SMELL—for people who think they *ought* to like pastrami since they now live in New York—in timid slices out of vacuum 'paks' from the supermarkets of suburb—*Hi, ho, the deli-o, the pastrami has no smell.*

As if to underline the tentative natures of the inhabitants of Second Avenue between 70th and 90th Streets, MacK recalled—in walking across 79th with Mary-Ann and Izzy—the sudden appearance and disappearance here of a girl he'd met on one of his forays out into that god damn country. She had taken a job at ABC—yeah, yeah—and was completely out of her depth—flipping out would be an understatement—could only make herself walk from the apartment she'd rented to the job and back. She began to phone MacK constantly—he didn't know what to do—till one afternoon she invited him over to meet some of her *relatives*, who were to indulge in one of the great nightmares of life in the metropolitan area—*driving a sofa into the city on top of their car*—the poor f***ing bastards. The Hellishness was short-lived—her uncle was quite a parker!—they adjourned for the chef's-salad-and-carafe-of-white-wine in—again—one of these places. A *nautical* motif, with nets, floats, rope, which—technically—is not allowed in New York. The aunt, who'd seemed real, became voluble, then boldly, demonstratively drunk. She disappeared into the ladies and it was full two hours later that the uncle and the proprietor pulled her out into the street by her feet. —*It's just*—*everything's so*—, she said over and *over* again—of course who has not thought this?—and the unhappy ABC-girl—could have told her—disappeared from New York almost as fast as had the kind, interloping station-wagon—the aunt's legs kicking out of the window—toward the George Washington Bridge.

Second Avenue looked just about right for a dinner between friends on this year's very cold vision of the day after Thanksgiving. —Turkey mole? said MacK. —Forgetaboudit, said Iz in his finest put-on Bensonhurst. —Bet you five bucks.

A small amount of rich grey light left in the sky, and four lamps over the façade of the Plaza Garibaldi. Chilly, but—and perhaps this was the holiday again—the three approached the front door with a warmth—of expectation?—certainly Isidor was fresh from his triumph over Mr Reasonable and was gasping for a margarita—his current favorite drink in his current favorite restaurant. So as Pedro the maître d' always said in taking your coat—*Chili today, hot tamale*, which MacK could not believe, that a person from Mexico thought that was funny.

Rosenthal had just arrived.

Once inside there was always a brief flurry of absurdity, plastic plants and gold and green spotlights, which resolved itself—once Pedro had waddled away under the mound of your wool—into something slightly less hideous but which became pleasant when you got loaded.

GREAT!

The always (to be) uncomfortable beady encounter between Isidor and Rosenthal—who could nonetheless get along for an hour or two, although during a two-hour dinner Izzy's head of steam sometimes built so that by dessert Rosenthal almost had to flee. But tonight the little god of Thanksgiving, Spencer Tracy, blessed the four and brought them together maybe.

—How ya doin? —I'm fine, Isidor, how are YOU? (A slight kindergarten note in this—*And what's YOUR name?* —made MacK sweat a little—but things were to be OK. —Hi, Mary-Ann. Kiss.


—Your glasses look very Protestant tonight, said MacK to Rosenthal, almost Episcopalian. MacK loved Rosenthal's holiday look. Her cheeks were red from the walk to the Far East from the Lex, a long ride from SoHo. There was a little tension as the waiter came over—the usual tension before Isidor discovered what everyone was going to drink, *i.e.* that they *were*. He offered Rosenthal a gin and tonic, staccato fashion; Rosenthal was in one of her millet phases—it has to be said, even though you could point to the Rosenthal of TODAY who partakes of meat and bourbon and has no spastic colon. She replied that she did not like the *taste of alcohol*, at which Iz properly erupted—of course she did, she must, who didn't, and even if she did not, *that was not the point* of alcohol whatsoever.

—Don't you live in New York? he asked—this is your *medicine*; it may be bitter but you must have it, and shall be the better for it. The Isidorean pharos was open, the full candlepower of its arcs trained on poor Rosenthal; so early in the evening. MacK was afraid Izzy had already classed her as a bean-eater. —*No*, said Rosenthal, standing up for herself in a way MacK liked, for who dared, though he too found her resistance to drink baffling—I don't need alcohol to constantly readjust, and sour, my view of life. —*Yes you do*, said Isidor—don't you see how absurd that argument is? You're saying, *Life is good—everything is pretty much OK.* —No! said Rosenthal, hurt by this truth. —Yes you are, said Izzy—life's good and there aren't so many problems with the world, not any you can't address—that's what you're saying. With a clear head you can survive life, its vicissitudes, control it, conquer it, live it, love it—right? —Well, said Rosenthal. —That is so *f\*\*\*ed up*, said Isidor, it's almost beyond me to address it; your point of view denies the existence of crime, corruption, greed, jealousy, poverty,

ignorance, religion, impotence, Nixon, the IRT, insurmountable obstacles, I don't *know* . . . ——How the f*** did you even GET here tonight?
said Iz, this city, in case you didn't know, contains all our moral history
as a nation and living in it constitutes a necessary embrace of our
achievements and failures—what did you *walk past*, may I ask? ALL
THE LOVELY PROBLEMS, said Isidor, that evolved with us, that
EVOLUTION, and nothing else, brought up *with* and *for* us, to suck
us down the drain as soon as it becomes necessary. Don't you see this
means, on a human level, as one human being to another, that I CAN
NEVER TRUST YOU? That I can't *bother* with you since you don't
see what is all around you? ——*Whoa!* said Rosenthal—who had once
spent a *flanneled year in Oregon*—gimme a gin and tonic! She has
comic timing, beamed MacK. The lighthouse shut down, or at least
the foghorn; Isidor was satisfied but watchful like a cat.

They didn't trust each other one bit, even and especially after
that—Izzy realized she had merely *knuckled under*, which pissed him
off. But though he was usually on his guard against the tackier
blandishments of that decade, Isidor warmed under the twinkling
lights in the fake trees by the fake fountain in the fake Plaza
Garibaldi.

## Not Love Just Yet

Rosenthal's reasons for hanging out with MacK remain obscure.
She was intrigued by his working above 14th Street—although she
est née in the suburbs (*dynamite high school French*, MacK thought,
though girls shouting *Crassan, Crassan!* in Bonté could impress him)
she had spent so many years downtown that someone who had regular paid employment was *rara avis*. Rosenthal moved into SoHo
when it was merely a place, practically before it had *gouache*. MacK
and his triangle (meaning the present three points, implying nothing) were odd, to her, and the triangle, especially Izzy-at-the-apex,
thought Rosenthal must be mad to live in that little place—if you

lived uptown you were drowning in boredom and all its excrements but at least you had room. But to MacK, spending time with Rosenthal down there was impossibly romantic (though this has now been commercially catechized FOR you, it may be rehearsed): the little shops, the ginkgo trees, street corners and cobbled streets in the rain, bookstores where they didn't care about you, but about books; the unfamiliar and disgusting foods to which she introduced him (millet in many unsuccessful disguises)—pretending one is in Europe (the mark of someone who hasn't yet embraced town, but fun nonetheless) watching the old fellows at *bocce*. Their romance—his—was fraught, as MacK was slow to discover Rosenthal was a *taster*—with six or seven chaps on the go at once, besides the neurotic painter whom she thought of as the *boyfriend* and who constantly said *She's not my girlfriend* to the world. Ah! *these* days no one like Rosenthal can afford to move onto *Spring Street* and do nothing but live. She was particularly interested in Isidor; none of the people of her suburb—nor those at her nice, friendly college—nor the strutting intellects of SoHo had a *smidgin* of self-hatred; Izzy's lush endowment of it kept her willing to eat with him and MacK—by now she could withstand the accusation of Nice.

Rosenthal!, of tribulation, *the never quite*. They had stood and sat, she and he, in various places, in various poses, for some considerable time. On and off. MacK sometimes saying It, or sometimes something like It, and sometimes not. They had *been around*, had the odd Sicilian late night slice and the dawn taxi cuddle. What had come of it, see for yourself. But on a previous freezing holiday they stood in the Park, at the foot of a formal garden. MacK feigned newfound delight but in truth he was f***ing cold and knew the place well—he had regularly been going there, practicing saying It, as if with Rosenthal, several moons, on any noons he could spare.

The garden made her exclaim—he supposed it was the plan, for all the flowers were asleep or dead. The chill was not merely weather cold; the pergolas were planted with the cooler herbs, the mints, and lemon thyme. Twined and bare a tunnel of twigs stretched before them toward an octagonal-lighted building—the toilets, mused MacK, but good old him: however cold and wet he began to brim with arbor ardor. They looked at the bower and at each other. Rosenthal's glasses fogged. Opportunity was not knocking so MacK went out, so to speak, onto the porch where it cowered and boldly dragged it inside. MacK, or maybe it, licked his chops. —Do you realize, said MacK, we're about to go up the garden path together? —About time Sir, she said. Picture him!, the picture of elation. Up they went, but bear in mind, this is not metaphor, there were two people walking in a garden. Up they went, not touching, it would have been too awful to have to release her gabardine-smooth arm too soon; she always demanded release, in order to run around and exclaim over dead birds or rhapsodize about theatrical posters. At the arbor's terminus were benches damp and green ranged around a fountain, which was drained, as MacK, no—as he longed to be. They stared, at the two copper children of the fountain, diaphanously clothed. MacK began to wonder where the water came out, when it did—Rosenthal was looking too. —Nice-looking kids, she said, boy and girl or boyish girl and girlish boy? Or girlish girl and boyish boy? —Goyische boy and Jewish girl, said MacK. Frightened of the nursery, MacK arose reluctantly and to examine slowly slid down the icy empty fountain bowl. —Now I'm here! he called. He faced these copper children. Mother would call them angelic. Staring at flesh, even rendered in hard metal, could give him to morbid ponderings on his physiological future. The thighs—a hint of musculature—around back—MacK felt sick—he remembered with relief he was standing in the large stone basin. —Do you like him? called Rosenthal. —This is *him?* said MacK, no, I hate him. Although she is all right. He had lost track already that these were copper children—embroiled in the erotism of the ? shared moment—looked again at the thigh-green, the line above where the diaphanous napkin-suits gave way. Soon there would be exciting conflict here if they were not related—again forgetting—then imagining them sickeningly to be friends life long as in English novels who would never try it on with each other—faugh!

In the process of thinking this his diaphragm grew warm and heavy with questioning. —*Does the female every truly desire the male?* he asked, addressing still the flanged copper crotches but, of course, meaning Rosenthal. —What! she said, for she truly couldn't hear. —Even, he went on, in incensed boudoirs, even after romantic monochromatic cinema, even after drinking the optimal glop liqueur? Do they? Lust? You can tell me. You *must* tell me! MacK screamed—she eyed him rather distantly but that had been the story. She whispered lowly—*Yes*—he realized it was vagueness, and not audible proof exactly. —Your tone, he said, it reeks of qualification and emasculating doubt. Rosenthal stared at MacK, evangelical—*I have experienced lust*, she said; his knees shook—the implication, so plain, was that she had, but never when he was in the vicinity—he wanted to fling himself at her feet or onto one of the decorative prongs of the fountain, the boy's toe maybe, extended in the sculptress's attempt at innocence—*Yes*, she said.

Once they sat on the steps of a celebrated mausoleum—despite the solemn air he was trying to breathe of the place, *jugglers* leapt about in front of them—Rosenthal was *exulting* in the sunshine—as if she were in *California*—ye gods! MacK stroked her neck in futile daydream—*Let's go to your place!* she said—her meaning clear. In astonishment and joy MacK tripped over his laces and cut his forehead; they did go to his place but to ransack the medicine chest—the sense of *emergency in the park*, the time of bandaging, the smell of tincture merthiolate iced their blood—the day ended in frankfurters. Sadness of yore.

MacK climbed out of the fountain. Rosenthal was particularly beautiful in the cold grey light. Her mouth hung slightly open as she dwelt, leagues away, on other men. MacK wondered if he could really kiss her on that chill bench—of what value are such damp proofs of love? Even coming there so often middays, turning to empty space and saying it, could he now? He rotated toward her in an earnest twist of his torso—his precisely practiced Currier & Ives Suitor's Body Posture (send 25¢ in coin for complete instructions—no stamps). —Listen, said MacK, oft here at noon—*Nph!*—his prepared oration cut short by the fullness of her lips! —Enough? she said—at least he hoped it was a question. Certainly not!— reaching—. But for what, and on what level of the spirit, of honesty? They embraced. —Your coat's dirty, she said. This is where MacK always fell—in the midst of his passion, they noticed his *flaking details*. —*Yes, yes*, he laughed, so desperate, so nonchalant—they are the same thing. Their heads close by—their hands and arms in a sick panic of nonlocation—they again viewed the fountain— transformed for MacK now from sentimental junk into a jubilant Triumph of the Spirit©—out of a pain in the ass, art—the copper children playing out the great drama. —Let's go far away, said MacK. —He stood, and ran in the direction of Fifth Avenue, flailed his arms to signal the pitifully unexistent European express bus. —Come back! she yelled, come here. MacK approached the bench, regarded once again its low damp feel on his legs and end—so many times he'd sat here, adeptly executing the dentitions and fricatives of bliss.

She looked at him in good humor, too good maybe—she often laughed at him at Just the Wrong Moment. She opened her mouth—her stomach growled—leonine—MacK was excited. —I'm hungry, she said. But without the select tone of romantic double entendre, no suggestion that *MacK* might make the meal, except like the wieners of bandage day. —*Come, let's eat*, he said—turning to disgust himself with the sight of the two oxidized brats, still trenchant in their pose of innocence.

## Lucky Garden

Rosenthal was dreaming of men or the meal to come maybe. Canal Street, teeming with vegetables, whiffs, radios; the slit throats of ducks—MacK persisted in questioning her about lust but would she answer? When the question got over steamy she would stop and root through vegetables, caressing round ones and throwing phallic ones around fitfully, treating them like *dirt*. All around, radio blare and a stifling neon buzz as of summer pond insects—the gantlet of squat ladies and their smelling shopping bags—finally the *Lucky Garden*. The Lucky Garden may be lucky but it is also popular—how could it possibly be lucky?—the luck of their usual table was lacking and MacK and Rosenthal were forced to stand for a time—the proximity of the ladies with lines in their faces and the shopping bags barred MacK from pursuing lust. Instead they two chatted friendly about storm drains and the ponytails of dancers. MacK held they were thicker and shorter until *c.* 1957, the tails, not the drains, with a growing trend toward long wispiness which peaked in 1975. Rosenthal held quite the opposite view.

*HUA*, the waiter—the thick *rubber* menu—sea crow in red eye sauce, shining root with black blubber—thank you. In the booth behind, Hua held this colloquy with people not of these parts:

—What is this pork fried rice? —*Ah, pork fi rice is, ah, rice fi with pork. You want?* —Well—is it any good? —*Yah!* —Okay, well, I guess we'll have some of that—whuddya think, Jane? —Mmm. —*One pork fi rice.* —And, uh, what is this won ton soup? Hua leant over the menu and squinted. —*Ah, wa ta soup is, ah, soup with wa ta! You want?* —Well, I, uh, is it good? —*Yah!* —Okay, well, I guess we'll take some of that. —*One wa ta soup.* —Uh, two please. Sir. —*Two wa ta soup!*

*Ye gods*—but the lubricated iridescence of MacK's and Rosenthal's food pushed him again toward the physical, the carnal—the in his view advisable—the briny slime-play on his plate, the voluptuous rises, the cruel dimples he could make in its heavings with his wooden stick— ah!—the way he could bind the turgidity of the sea crow with white strands of his onion—Rosenthal noticed—fueled by her food she was going on between mouthfuls about the Other Team—but since his first steps MacK had felt only revulsion and pity for the National League and couldn't listen. He took the check from under his water glass, where Hua always put it, and as she babbled and ranted about those poor fools who lack a hitter-designate, who can *never have heroes*, he wrote to her on the back:

*Darling. Even though at this moment you are speaking of the Metropolitans, I really think I have fallen in love with you and all this elliptical hanging is driving me nuts. Nuts do you hear. I know I've never written you before but I thought this might be a way of saying that I'm trying to get you into bed. Why are we being so polite?*—as she was *still* talking about Shea he placed it slyly on her saucer—and by the time MacK stopped thinking dreamily about her discovery of the note and how wonderfully the evening would be bound to go, he found she was talking about trees—he jumped in with his petrified opinions about the craven municipality of liquidambars and the overriding importance and beauty of birches—there was no doubt the food had given them a relaxed but stimulated feeling—perhaps it was that chemical—he hoped it was conducive to lust—she finished vilifying the nation's major arboreta. —Sure the Scotch pine is a dangerous Yule tree, said MacK, but what do you do? —Crusade, she said, and then suddenly *Hua was screaming*. —*!Waaah!* He came over and beat his fists on the table. —What! shouted MacK. —Note! he wailed, O so dirty note—from *Missy!* —wild of gesture he threw the *check* down on the table before MacK could figure out . . . Rosenthal whapped Hua in the face with the rubber menu—*What's the big idea?* she yelled—Hua pointed to the billet doux. She read it. —Enough! said MacK, grabbing Rosenthal's wrist and the rubber menu, Hua, please accept my apology. I am the author of that filth, not she. Missy is innocent. —*Huh!*—Yes, a great wrong, said MacK, caressing her wrist since he—aha!—had it. Hua went away to sulk where the teapots are stacked. Rosenthal read the back of the check again with charming eyes out of the animal world and blushed—something he had never seen. She turned it over and began arithmetic. —I'll get it, she said throatily.

Hua presented her with a minty toothpick on the way out but she refused. —No MSG for you next time Missy.

The lamps over the wet street—MacK bathed in the light of dark promise. On the CC she took his hand—took his *pulse* actually. When she had established the diastole she turned to him demurely and said: —What do you think of a fellow who lets a girl pay the tab so easily? —I thought you said you would pay, you said you wanted to pay, *you paid!* MacK could see passengers worrying about him; he looked at them ferociously and they went back to their newspapers *of lies*. —Getting back to lust, he said. —Getting *back*? —To the *subject* anyway, he said. Damn if he was going to give it up no further away than it usually is. —I just cannot believe, said MacK, that you women, so floral, would ever want a sweaty spotty man on top of you, writhing and croaking—it makes me ill for all of you. —I'm not a 'you women', as it happens, she said angrily. —You mean to say you're the only one who has lusted? —Not at all, they're not *all* sweaty and spotty.

So that was it! They weren't?

She pulled him off the train—one is never lucky in the Lucky Garden to drink enough. —But where? he said, they're all the same around here. She took his arm. —So what *do* you think of a fellow who lets her pay it all? —I don't think about it. Who is he?

In this dump, people sized them up from the unconquerable claims of their booths—every bar a little Klondike—revenge often comes to sit in places like this. —Maybe you've lusted, said MacK—he could say the word loud with luxury in the clatter of this dump—maybe you have—for men—*but what about beer?* They drank—all sin and spite and smile. —It's true, said Rosenthal, that when men have wrassled their lust for beer is when many of us lust after *them*. ——Because, said MacK, that is when we are unaffectedly adorable, poetic and kind. ——*No*, it's just man smell, said Rosenthal, beer and cigar and leather. Drives me rather wild. ——Today began, harrumphed MacK, in the loveliest public garden, it began with an earnest dialogue on lust charged with meaning and implication and promise——now we exchange tawdriness even as we breathe the menthol smoke of this Hell hole. ——Yes, said Rosenthal. She took his hand——its wholeness——not the artery.

# Plaza Garibaldi

Race was the circus ground on which Rosenthal and Isidor were never to agree. But out of respect for MacK, or possibly the holiday, they put away the guns of heavy issue.

What Mary-Ann and Rosenthal made of each other was polite, if nothing else——and it may have been nothing else. But when these fellows were together, Mary-Ann and Rosenthal slid abominably——according to everyone——into the roles of guardians, or vestals, or even low, gum-chewing usherettes. Thinking about Our Years in Yorkville, even though he continued to live on the West Side——MacK still gets the taste of Pedro's mother's fresh tortillas and of margaritas in his mouth——still excretes their salt, he thinks. This is the only genuine paean possible, on behalf of these three or four people, to the decade in question, the bright little lights in the trees, the baskets of tortillas and the electrically puréed guacamole, the margaritas in goblets the size of toilets and then the traditional MacK–Iz parting of the ways——Izzy taking the high road of wine to brandy, MacK the low road of beer but arriving in Sot-land afore him. The girls had a good time but felt they had to rein things in, because they wanted to be able to come back to the Plaza Garibaldi and sometimes it was conceivable Izzy and MacK could have too much fun even for Pedro; *arriba*.

There *was* turkey mole and MacK collected $5 from Iz. It struck him this night—the bastard son of Thanksgiving but settling down to the Plaza's own kind of continued nonspecific festival, nondenominational Mexican gaiety—looking at Rosenthal and at Mary-Ann—that what they had here: —What we have here, he said to Isidor and to them, is a couple of Game Girls. —What are you talking about, said Izzy, who was nervous MacK was casting some kind of aspersion on Mary-Ann. —No, said MacK, listen, been thinking all about it—if you don't mind my telling you 'bout this be-YOU-ti-ful goil, he said in a weak imitation of Izzy's stand-up Bensonhurst (he hadn't practiced or thought to use it till now—it was no use at work)—I mean *Game Girls*, in the sense that they're with us; they'd go with us anywhere, wouldn't ya girls? —What do you mean, said Iz, I'm not going anywhere, I'm *not leaving*. Are you talking about going camping again? Because if you are . . . —Camping! beamed Rosenthal—bringing herself down firmly one notch with *everyone* for about twenty minutes (Isidor *camping!*).

MacK had had a vision: World War II and he had to go fight, at least some of the time. —!—said Isidor. —Rosenthal is battling on, you know, said MacK, seeing us through it—it is an old-fashioned chicken farm, out on the Island, the hen houses are dark red. A sunny morning in the winter of war, the ground covered with ice—you drive up in one of those *rounded cars*—she comes out to sell you eggs—they're rationed—she sometimes delivers them in a rounded station-wagon, with *wooden sides* and *dark green fenders*—she's gamely keeping the chickens &c. going because she loves me. Mary-Ann could be doing the same thing, he said, because she looks sincere and wonderful, too—the way they both look when they put their hair up—it would go perfectly with the wood on the sides of the station wagon and the brown eggs in racks, and the sun bright but low in the sky because it's a morning in the war and you're lonely. —Er—what are you talking about? said Isidor. —I think it's sweet, said Mary-Ann, MacK thinks we're beautiful and loyal—that's how he's expressin' it. Here he felt a foot slide up his calf! —That's what you think of me? said Rosenthal, a wartime chicken farmer?

MacK looked from one friend to the other; he said nothing, yet he felt he hadn't told the half of it, the stirring love for and of the Game Girls in their slightly mannish mackinaws—the denims or twills of war, the *trousers of war*—the head scarves but beauty coming through. He gulped, having suddenly had an epiphany: —I apologize, he said, I just realized I've been having an emotional fantasy about *Mrs Harmon*, the lady who used to bring eggs to our house—her Nash Rambler—her hair, I now see with horror, was very like Rosenthal's when in a girlish or old-fashioned design—I even remember the egg lady's *barrette*. —*What*, said Isidor. —It's something Rosenthal favors when we lie around her apartment on Sunday. —When the suburbs, said Isidor, creep into the city and reclaim the hearts of those who are their own? Like some f***ing *monster* movie . . . I hate to interrupt this. —No you don't, said Mary-Ann, you love to interrupt. MacK hated having to explain his affections in this way. —Let's not go into the shrinky side of our bringing eggs, said Rosenthal. A turkey mole was carried past them to another table—MacK collected $5. There was nothing more to be said about chicken or war or, for the moment, the prettiness of the girls, glowing now with the warmth of their chilis and tequila whereas before they had glowed with their inner fires against the cold city. It wasn't mean to them; our town was quite nice to both these girls.


Rosenthal was determined, as always, to get some *personal sweetmeat*. Why go out to eat if people aren't going to talk about themselves? Otherwise you could stay home and read a book. The thought had never occurred to MacK, who usually found himself there for the beer, unless it also involved Izzy, *then* there would be *talk*—that was a reason. Sometimes there was something spicy to go with beer—but MacK was never a respecter of foods, which drove Isidor mad. —How was New Orleans? said Rosenthal. —Oh, we ate *saw* much, said Mary-Ann, Isidor spent almost every day at Galatoire's—I couldn't even get him to take a walk. —We did visit the famous World's Fair, said Iz. —We did not visit it, said Mary-Ann. —Yes we did, said Isidor. Mary-Ann turned her head pointedly toward Rosenthal. —We went up to the *fence*, she said, Isidor was too cheap to go in. —*What!* yelled Isidor and Pedro looked up, though he didn't flinch—he was used to Isidor already, for today. —So we just walked *around* the whole thing, several times, said Mary-Ann, around and around this screwed-up inna city industrial wasteland, just *starin'* *in* at the WORLD'S FAIR. —You have to admit it didn't look too hot, said Izzy. —But to have gone all that way Isidor. —I don't see what you're complaining about, you got your *beignets* and your Picayunes. —Oh, Rosenthal, would you like one? said Mary-Ann, drawing the pack. —Sure! said Rosenthal, which flabbergasted MacK. —I think those lack millet completely you know, he said. Listen, the girl was changing—and for a second here they were again, the two pretty girls on the Home Front.


But was there a better picture to be had of the desires and tendencies of Isidor and Mary-Ann? Walking around the perimeter of the WORLD'S FAIR, which couldn't HURT you—what was he afraid of anyway? Mary-Ann with her New England pluck; the thing certainly couldn't have hurt *her*—and Isidor outside the chicken-wire fence, unable to go in, in some weird way, even for the chance to laugh—*LOUDLY*—at that screwy country. One can only imagine the concrete and plastic bayou, the miniaturized streetcars of desire—because he *didn't* go in—he felt he was being kept out—Iz took all fences personally. There was his fear of America—he was in it enough for his own taste—the WORLD'S FAIR might have been too strong a dose of it. The sight of people having FAKE FUN—he was probably right to avoid it. Instead he took it on himself to single-handedly keep the *French Quarter* in business while everyone else went to the FAIR.

201

Fake fun is something New York is still low on, thought MacK, though 57th Street has for some undiscoverable reason become simply a conveyor belt to the great engine of the perplexity of the people—and someone is trying the same thing with 42nd; let us all watch our backs. The gods willing, this will fail and the pimps can get off their glueboards on Eighth Avenue.

Late under the little lights in Pedro's tree—Izzy and Mary-Ann reliving the arguments and dinners of New Orleans; MacK and Rosenthal cruising on some wave of collaged nostalgia, but this is what it was like when they were in their twenties—they thought they were growing into, or more secure in their coupledoms—you think, *this is adulthood*—but it isn't. Sitting in a restaurant and having a job is not being an adult; adulthood is precisely the *opposite* of those things. Adulthood itself is what lasts, sometimes grinds; not Mary-Ann and Isidor, MacK and Rosenthal; not the Plaza Garibaldi, not the holiday outside. New York lasts. The awful weight of self-awareness goes; at fifty you never think *I have a job and am sitting in a restaurant*—life becomes a whole, details cease to matter or, it seems, even to exist—everything's a blur. New York lasts.

In a moment Rosenthal would want to go to MacK's—and by the time they got to the subway she wouldn't. She'd want MacK to come downtown and then wouldn't, actually in love with her subway rides *solo* more than anything, still treasuring being a city girl on the—whoop de *do*—IND. Some people lead charmed lives.

Heat—in the friends—Pedro's hand. The blast of the night cold in the spirit-hot face. *Sobering* is the word they have got for it . . . in *Hicksville*. —Bavarian *Inn*, said Isidor. —Oh no ya don't, said Mary-Ann, time to go home. —Wait, said MacK, rocking on his heels in a breeze of reassuring chatter issuing from the comedy club. —No no, said Rosenthal, c'mon and walk me to the subway. MacK had a confused vision of subway tiles, Rosenthal's little place; he really always wanted to sleep near Isidor and Mary-Ann—the nails in the floor—but you're supposed to be *keen,* aren't you. —Let's go, boys, said Mary-Ann, fun's over. —I can't believe we're being *dragged away*, said Isidor . . . —I *know*, said MacK, and now Isidor was . . . gone . . . entirely yanked around the corner by Mary-Ann in the snow.

The warmth of Rosenthal, her overcoat, on the way to the Lex, which if MacK squinted had mackinawish tendencies. —The trouble with you and Isidor, she said, is

> **You guys love each other so much
> you don't know what to do with it.
> SO YOU DRINK.**

—Hey MacK, wheah's ya *hat?* called Edward Kennedy from around the corner. He could hear her struggling with Isidor. —Yes, said Rosenthal, where is your hat?

My *hat*, MacK thought, with a pang. He had been so recently bereaved of it, far away in the f\*\*\*ing Hamptons. When he had turned from his hat for the last time, his eyes stung and it was not the wind. It was a sentimental hat—that is, MacK was sentimental about it. It was of fearful green stuff, like oiled pork crackling, lined with a large green and white tartan of—another insult to aesthetics—vinyl. Shaped like the Devil's Postpile, with a neat brim. A snug 7⅜—his *HAT*—now subject to the Law of the Sea. MacK at sunset, 4.37 pm—stood, waiting for his hat to be washed ashore—it bobbed merrily. Would the spite of nature end if we left off torturing her? Somehow the sea around his hat (already no longer his) became the color of rain slanting on the stone street where he had bought it. To it he then turned a face impassive, an Easter Island head—for its own dear sake. His hat was a begging-bowl, turned up to the sun in the waves—the sky a bouquet of trout skin spraying like the 4th of July from the crumpled vase of—his hat. A *bird* had come, flying low and skimming—skiddingly perched upon it there in the waves—actually sat on the brim and there and then in the waves, used it as a pot; while MacK watched. He didn't like that bird, it had the whole Atlantic but it had to use his hat. He tried to accept—forgive—he had loved his hat so, the incident was probably inevitable. It was time for the hat's Appointment with the Duke of Edinburgh maybe—MacK had always known of this Appointment—there was a small card pertaining to it sewn inside the sweat band—the Royal arms. He Stood, Waiting for His Hat to be Washed Ashore. He stood on the beach, suffering vague guilty feelings that he was unread on the subject of eternity. It was deep winter, the beaks of the shore birds chattered—not with gossip nor rebuke, but with cold—the sun could not spark the colors of the grasses stooping by the bay—even the red sign, KEEP OUT THIS MEANS YOU!, was cold and alone.

A *tweed* hat of a similar shape had been denounced by Tumbleson—*It makes you look like a pinhead—like an idiot*—but this one had risen above, and taken MacK with it—he was in normality's realm, and protected from the rain. The sea. *This is America,* he had thought. Twice it had come within far wade-reach—if it had not been deep winter! —if only his love for his hat had conquered his deep affection for his shoes and his overcoat, his fears of virus—although he did quite ruin his shoes, allowing the waves to lave them as he watched his hat. It was at Flying Point, not at Sagaponack as was later reported in the *East Hampton Star.* A hat flying like that, he thought, the refractive day, the mighty Atlantic, his vision suddenly framed and made crystal by despair, could be the subject of a great oil—or even acrylic—on the beach you rarely know your location with respect to the particulars of the bay.

The *sou'wester* had not done—even in its limitless American yellowness—the romance was all—the wearing of it chafed MacK's razor-burn and spirit—the sand flowing in low white winds. So had the *beret* failed, alter scalp as it was for him—had become dark and foul in the week of supposed holiday sea-damp, a sink of pneumonias.

*Could you horse-whip a man for not modeling the dynamics of hats he lets loose on the public?*

Lovers ask—unknowingly—*unfeelingly*—that you sacrifice the very personal thing. Time. Thinking. The drink, the cigarette—perhaps these things are all the same thing: you? They are asking you to give up—that's the way it's always been done—give up some of the molecules, the blocks. In the end, most of us won't do this, now—even a few molecules. So: everyone parts, in our century. So Mary-Ann and Isidor—not that night—some time during the next year it was. They'd gone curiously back and forth about mar-riage—one never knows how to put it—sometimes the teeter-totter does seem right—one exhilarated and up there, the other getting an ass-banging, splattered with mud—Isidor ran back and forth like a child at the beach, daring and fleeing Mary-Ann's foamy bridal tide. The months he wanted to get married she didn't. They were both against it, truthfully, but each had periods when they'd consider it, for reasons of the long, though faint, aroma-like fingers of the suburbs.

*It's bullshit! Let's not do it!*

*It's bullshit! Let's DO it!*

MacK *expected* them to marry but would have been surprised if they *had*. But during one of the months they were both against it, the cat who patrolled the back yards died—and blocks and blocks away—the true ecology of this our town—Yorockefeller University (so called by Isidor because he was usually lighting his a.m. cigar at the corner of 66th and York, where this guy usually sitting at the base of the fancy fence usually said *Yo! Rockefeller!*) broke ground on a new white building for thinking very clean and important thoughts in—no, we don't understand them either, but to be civilized is to pretend that we do—and some very highbrow York Avenue rats and mice began looking around Mary-Ann's and Isidor's street. Looking around in their *bedroom*. Can anything convince you that a *change* may be in order quicker than rodents running across you at night? It must have been when the weather was coming warm, and the river does contribute something to the tenor of life in the Far East—and the Nazi must have stopped clearing up after his Hell dogs—they wouldn't blow him maybe—for there were a lot of cockroaches too—but this is synchronicity gone beyond its normally appalling bounds. During one hot exchange Mary-Ann said *I ain't stayin' around this bug house—mouse house*—and it quickly became a talisman of a kind—in a few weeks it propelled her out of Yorkville, out of town. BUGHAUS! MAUSHAUS! This girl left New York.

## The Wilderness of the Shiksas

Isidor had lost something complex—which is a complicated losing—but natural, and he knew it. Here began several years of going in and out of bars, and, like MacK, wandering. —*That's laughs tonight on Wilderness of the Shiksas.*

Mary-Ann's departure seemed to precipitate the end of Yorkville—as they had known it—but while Izzy was still preparing to leave—for a new life downtown, downtown, everybody's got to go *f***ing* downtown—the Bavarian Inn closed, suddenly and forever, and was quickly remodeled in one of those heartbreaking transformations which are little shows of the rage of non-New Yorkers making an incursion, a midnight raid on Manhattan—like a businessman from New Haven visiting a prostitute on 11th Avenue—the sting of a little insect from outside. The place was boarded up for a few weeks and then there emerged from it a bar seemingly made of the plywood it had been obscured with. It was hard to tell what motif they were aiming for—*I'd say probably the bullshit motif*, said Isidor, as he and MacK stood there sheepish with two glasses of watery Michelob dark—well—one gets curious—*one needs to know the bars.* The place matched what was happening to East 86th Street—it could have been a shop selling souvenirs or crap wool hats or socks—it had a vaguely Irish name—it was a PUB only because it said so—it had as little connection to the Irish people of Yorkville as it did to real bars made out of stone, glass and wood. But East 86th Street was empty of Mary-Ann.

A funny thing—the death of the Bavarian Inn was Isidor's milestone, the northern mossy side of which read BEER and the dry southern side WINE—as if the Bavarian Inn had been the only fount of true beer in New York—though of course it springs from many taps. Izzy moved south, into the heightened connoisseurship of the Village, where *beer*, Sir, is now the libation of *interlopers*.


MacK was walking across East 86th on a bright afternoon—looking for socks—Izzy was still in the neighborhood but not for long. In front of MacK was this frankly unbelievable character—a real *schtarker*—very dark blow-dried hair in a shag—Jackie O dark glasses—tan in a can—okay so he coulda got it at CLUB MED—big fat hands, bracelets, rings—tasselled shoes—couldn't see the trousers for the enormous fur coat, blown and styled by the same hand as the head—guy was walking in the weird way people walk who have formerly been very fat—they waddle still with their toes pointing out—you could see him—for he had *bully* written all over him—lunging around, terrorizing everyone in the schoolyard—but what he looked like isn't important. As he went along he stripped the cellophane off a pack of 'Ass Hole' (Blue)—dropped it and the cover foil on the pavement—lit one from a book of matches—dropped that—opened a pack of Doublemint—threw down the string and top—all the time waddling, with a *soupçon* of saunter—opened the stick of gum, threw the wrapper and the silver paper over his shoulder—walked on, chewing and smoking. MacK felt he was following a truck shedding its load of depressing furniture—but this must be THE GUY who was changing East 86th Street—*he* obviously owned the plywood bar, the shops of dark glasses and batteries—he picked his nose with his cigarette hand and locked himself into the pages of *Mad*, a woman looking for snot with a fuschia pinky nail, cigarette holder in one hand and a Manhattan in the other; there he was, the *Destroyer of Yorkville*. What had *MacK* done compared to *this* guy?

Occasionally MacK thinks of Yorkville and the *'PLAZA GARIBALDI'* if he's on Second or Third in the 60s or 70s—neither he nor Isidor has been there for years now— it's still up there, he thinks—you might find yourself in one of the coffee shops on York Avenue—those places where you seem to find yourself only on the coldest day of the year—but who has anything to do on York Avenue? F*** York Avenue. Noche Bueno.

# In Nature's Realm

OH we all have to spend time away from this our town—it is a curse of living here. Having taken pains to *establish* yourself you are then sent *away* by the gods to see what you might or might not be missing—pastrami?—with luck you recognize it's *nothing* and pluckily come back as soon as you can, though with a deeper understanding of that god damn country. But those who are exiled or even self-exiled briefly are a bit finer and more honorable, it must be said, than those who live their whole boastful lives on Second Avenue and suddenly fall down *dead* from pastrami.

Sometimes—appallingly—one has to leave town because of *romantic feeling*. Not the odd weekend—MacK and that little stick of dynamite from Production tussling over eggs benedict in the middle of the Catskills—but wholesale *exodus*, for months at a time—even telling yourself that THIS IS IT, true love and it doesn't *matter* where she lives—that New York has done everything for you that it will. *Yes, you're a little tired of life in town—getting on a bit—other parts of the country have something to offer—nice to have a garden . . .* Oh, *brother* what shit you can talk!

These things continue to happen and it's just terrible. Even to Isidor—who is not someone you think of as *bursting* to get out of town. One summer night he was wandering around—not so long after he'd moved to the Village—Mary-Ann was still in the air. Isidor thought he might *eventually* arrive at a point where there was jazz and the attendant clear liquors— although he was not in those days in the habit of making for clear liquors invariably on passing out the portal of the office. He walked back and forth on 8th between Sixth and Broadway, becoming disgusted with himself for being interested in various fashions on display and—this was one of the warm evenings which draw students like bugs out of their filthy dormitories—the proximity of KIDS displaying their fondnesses—licking each other between gulps of *gelato* and pot smoke. Iz had long thought of 8th as a boardwalk, summer or winter—it smelled of popcorn, gum, the sweat of mate-search—and is jammed with Guys in Cars sweeping the pedestriennes with binocular eyes and tongues. Even if you're no longer a Guy in a Car you can become susceptible—the atmosphere of musth—and Isidor was, to his discomfiture—though part of the unpleasantness was that same knowledge—that he was perhaps no longer conceivably—or let us say *reasonably*—a player in this drama—or mightn't immediately be conceived as such by the girls passing in their leotards. The beat beat beat of the martini-intricate jazz—its punctual brushwork—took him along like a wave to his usual club. It was still early but here was a trio and here was a bartender. This bartender Isidor had been training-up—he was coming along nicely but sometimes spotted people's spectacles with a too-sweeping ejection of crushed ice and Boissière from the mixing glass. So as to avoid being dotted this way, no regular was sitting at the bar. But there was this oral surgeon.

Their banter will not be recounted; mating sounds so lame when reproduced. 'I'd say it's more a matter of mood', as Khrushchev said—that is, it's a matter of Her receptivity, not Your cleverness. Things just come together, and so, they did—between Isidor and this oral surgeon of Portland, Oregon. Is the predictability of this too brutal?—it's not meant so—just what is the point of elaborating the conversations which rapidly devolve upon one unenunciated foregone conclusion? HAH?

To Isidor, sex is an urban activity—in fact the only *point* to the sexual act—if there can be said to be one at all—over the centuries has been to *build cities*. All that covered wagon stuff, all that self-sacrificing procreation so hideously *implied* in elementary school textbooks is insane garbage. And so is all the sex life of the jungle, the desert. *Tribes*. Sex is no fun in such places. What can be worse than trying to have a nice walk in the woods with someone whose idea of a nice walk in the woods is *anything but?* Is *perverted beyond belief?* Do you even *know* what tree bark feels like against your bottom? Do you know how many ANIMALS might observe you two, even goaded to the attack by your desperate exercises? Think about what a large mushroom would feel like, accidentally squashed by you or the beloved in congress—and how absurd black stockings look under flannel-lined blue jeans. What about all the mentally ill who now live in the woodlands of our country—Millennialists, Nazis, duck hunters who could converge on your frolic, condemn you, photograph you, shoot the animals who had gathered to watch? You don't need cold air or damp *spores* blown onto your organs while you're trying to express the primitive thought. And all that *beach eroticism* is gull shit. You don't want sand in these sacrosanct pockets and folds, you don't need fish swimming around them nor gulls frappity crapping on your head. You don't! And there's nothing exciting about *patches* of sand—*photographic calendars* notwithstanding—what would you say if the beloved had patches of sand and sea-foam and sea-wrack on himself, herself, in the *Algonquin Hotel?* You pull back the sheets and there, by the beloved's attractive underwear, is a *patch of sand* and some *kelp!* You'd VOMIT.

*No*—it's a clean, urban activity—a thing done along precise *lines*, with striking angles to it—if it is to be satisfactory. Yes it costs money to live in town—because of the equipments. Of course you need a cocktail shaker, a strainer, gin—but perhaps most important is the city itself—the dark pane of your window, the lighted city beyond—what is more erotic? *Asking* you. A machine capable of emitting saxophone, piano and brush-on-drum sounds without distortion. Between music and the lighted city will you find pleasing angles of intersection, an architecture (feh!) and an engine. Far from being a *woodland romp*, or even a plushy boudoirish thing of frills, derrières and pillows, sex requires various girders, railings, turnbuckles, skyscrapers, contrasts, *chiaroscuro*—to guy, as it were, desire. Sharp things, snaps, straps and silk coverings—the parachutes for desire expressed, spent commitment.

Jazz—if used wisely it can warm and enrich our lives—if used foolishly it can damage or even destroy them completely.

What could be more natural to an oral surgeon, even if she *were* from Portland? Their night was vivid, kid you not. Strained and loose, strained and slack—if this were a tale of San Francisco you could liken it to a ride on the California Street line, looking down at the gripman's cues painted on the street: DROP ROPE; TAKE ROPE. On this awful day there was, for some inexplicable reason, a word lacking in the vocabularies of both oral surgeon and book dealer and the word was GOODBYE. Which lack of word led Isidor in a few short weeks to have let his apartment—to *Sidney*, gosh sakes—and to find himself knocking on the pine door of opportunity of the Land of Many Uses, the great Northwest itself.

Still more than an employee but rather less than a partner of Mr Playfair's, Isidor negotiated six months' leave from Bibulo & Schenkler. —What are you going all the way out there for? said Mr Playfair—how can you think you are in love with a dentist? But

211

when Izzy looked around, walked around the streets he told himself that this was *exactly* the way desire is to be set and lit and consummated in this our town. Told himself that his vivid night, the curve of the slumbering oral surgeon back-lit by his bit of glittering urban cyclorama (a little slice of Union Square at that time), that nothing and no one he could see on any block promised that vividity and therefore he was going to get him some more of that—while he is not a romantic in the street sense—abjuring and rejecting the word love—observe his actions. Besides it doesn't matter—as you know—that one party doesn't express love if the other does. The word is there on the coffee-table. This oral surgeon was shapely, American—the kind of woman you feel you might get to know if you were allowed to watch made-for-television movies—sun-washed suburban interiors and earnest automobiles—things that ought never to be shown in New York along with television altogether maybe—we aren't prepared for it and most of us can't take it—the filth and the lies—and inasmuch as it tempts us to think that there might be a rapprochement possible with the United States and its people.

Cast a cold eye on Portland, on Seattle—these places where all the scaredy-cats of Boston and San Francisco have gone to drink coffee *without black people*—these so-called 'cities'—can they really pretend they sip cappuccino among the perhaps crumbling but certainly light-toned culture of the Old World? If you want to sit and watch a lot of people in funny-shaped suits drink coffee, why not *go* to Milan? Don't stand on ceremony. Leave now. Yes people there have *time* to drink coffee—if that's your idea of a good time—in the Northwest people are *so afraid of Japan* that they've turned the miracle drug of caffeine against themselves—homeopathically—why Seattle is fast becoming an anagram of *lattés*—it makes them work very hard and to worry worry worry about their Eddie Bauer cars and jackets and boots

which must always be very clean—Mount Rainier and Mount
Hood never get muddy—did you know that?—because all these
white people in fleecewear who weigh nothing prance so lightly
up and down them.

Isidor found an apartment and quickly associated himself with
some book and art dealers in Portland and San Francisco. His card,
wistful already:

**ISIDOR KATZ**

**BOOKS & MANUSCRIPTS**

*ASSOCIATE OF BIBULO & SCHENKLER*

*FOURTH AVENUE • NEW YORK*

He quickly found that life in the Northwest is supposed to resemble,
or has become, a catalogue—one spends a great deal of one's time
having the bedroom closet fitted with intricate shelves—to display
one's spectrum of crew neck sweaters—forest green, teal and crimson especially totemic in the brave Northwest—and acquiring such
sweaters. Socks and shirts—anything that can be made more interesting than it is intrinsically in *different colors* must be stacked and
arranged in the Northwest home—every house a little Federal
Reserve of cashmere and argyle—as if in one of the catalogues or the
stores that are like catalogues. Isidor just put his socks in a *drawer*,
like any other grown-up in New York. This stuff didn't *suit*
Isidor—the whole phony casual tenor of the place couldn't suit anybody who reads a *real newspaper*, he thought—even though it costs
$25 in Portland. So there he sat dutifully for a few weeks in a slate-
grey crew neck and khaki *get-up* that was never really going to let
him *in*—with his $10 cappuccino and his $25 *New York Times*
—feeling distinctly like a kid and idiot.

This didn't please the oral surgeon, who had already begun to
worry that Isidor was not going to *fit in* to the Northwest—what
he did was too old-fashioned and he wasn't interested in re-doing
his apartment in any way to resemble a catalogue or a store that
looked like a catalogue. This oral surgeon was a bore, a sweater

collector and someone who saw nothing wrong in the frighteningly inbred appearance of all the fleecy jogging families of the Northwest. You may say the problem is that orthodontics is a bore because someone has to do it, but the answer is *No*, the only place you need orthodontics is in a superficial empty society—the even, fascistic smile all you need to *get that contract*—we get along all right with our own teeth in New York. Isidor concluded this rather rapidly. Of course, *boys,* being rather dull creatures, we only discover these things after making that big move for love. Making the move is our declaration, which proposes to awe and silence the distant-dwelling beloved for months—to be a statement which will endure—so that no aspect of the emotional life need be discussed once we're ON THE SCENE. What awful, predictable folly. What pathetic animals. Dopes!!

In business Isidor did well, immediately, the book and antique shops of the Northwest containing almost archaeologically the literature previous to 1980—for a time he couldn't believe his eyes—what all these hungry young capitalists drawn from all over—supposedly *OUR ONLY HOPE AS A NATION*—had abandoned in favor of trash. But he very quickly decided it would be best to get all the good books the Hell out of there and safely back to New York, which he commenced to do—the dealers went over like ninepins, blitzed on caffeine—while coming to the realization that the *New York Times* does not New York make, and that Portland was not a city just because they said it was. There was no jazz save cool jazz—and that was pretty tepid—because everything in the Northwest has to go with coffee, the colors of sweaters or music or bus timetables. There are no buses.

How long could you really discuss oral surgery and sweaters? —we have exhausted them here—so Isidor made plans to meet MacK on the rocky coast of Northern California. MacK was floundering about in the wilderness of the shiksas *at the same time*. Down Izzy drove on the coast of Oregon—the most puzzlingly empty landscape he'd ever seen—having left the oral surgeon to her appliances after she'd spoken of his *need to male-bond*. At the same time MacK headed west from New Mexico and north from Hollywood, growing more and more uncomfortable with every hour that continued to *be California*—it's a BEHEMOTH. They arrived about the same time late in the day at a holiday home of the type they both preferred—utterly drab with a sturdy refrigerator with a freezer of great promise. Outside: seals, rocks, redwoods, pines, whales

## ET CETERA.

One of the many towns out there still divided by railroad tracks—like the parting on a balding pate—freight has become an infrequent though alarmingly bulky thing when it does occur in nature—there may be one train a week—but it will take three hours to parade before you. In these here parts.

Waiting those three hours in front of the only blinking light in the whole of this vast ruined economy—in the rain—their engine running. The light reminded MacK of the control panel in his safe warm studio back in New York—thousands of miles away—his tired bored brain flew him across the shiksas and deserts—and circled the RCA Building in a way he would have liked—suddenly swooping in an open window—how often he imagined this.

Iz and MacK sitting there. —It seems the whole f***ing country must pass us by, said Isidor, in the form of this train in the rain. Even the Erie Lackawanna of Iz's childhood and the Pacific Fruit Express of MacK's. This *Hell train* rumbled along between them and LIQUOR. Admittedly: pretty aspects of the trees—folding mists, ocean—mountains which raced away on all sides from this town; the grandeur of its clean but very shut lumber mill, an immense graceful presence on the south hill, pale yellow with expansive lettering of pleasing green. But they stared at the side of the train and could see the word LIQUOR across the tracks—the depressing emporium where it was dispensed in the gaps between the lumbering slow box cars. *The arm lifted* and the cars drove over the grade crossing—an unmistakable sound, cars crossing a railway—its wet boards—in Northwestern rain. You can smell that. —I've an idear, said MacK, whose jocularism was to say it that way in small clapboard towns—we pay homage to the great de Voto with his own special American martini since we're out here in America . . . especially considering the look of this liquor store which will have no gin *you* ever heard of. —Gee Whizz, said Isidor frightened, don't you know that he only admitted of two drinks in the entire world? His rather cloudy though masculine version of the Harvard—beg pardon—martini—and a shot of bourbon? The guy never admitted Scotch even. —*Slug*, he called it a slug of whiskey if you don't mind, said MacK. He was a primitive, but in places like this that may not be a drawback. —He never even drank *wine*, said Iz, shivering. —His biographer described his death, said MacK, as a matter of becoming *electrocardiographically disorganized*. —I'm not surprised, said Izzy, if all you ever did was bump between gin, bourbon, Lewis and Clark *you'd* be disorganized.

Take a look at this joint. There was no attempt at window display. Cases of liquor—ready to go—but who in the shut mill town can afford them? MacK's idea of de Voto devotion involved, as Isidor feared, a domestic gin which might be called *G.'s*; this possibly noble or at least interesting study was taken down more than a notch by the sole availability of Italian vermouth. Isidor began to mope in the wine aisle and he wasn't going to get any happier in *there*—MacK could see from a distance that the labels were an anglo-orthographic rabble. You know the smell of a lousy liquor store do you not—stale smoke, spilled beer, aggressive corks, turkey snacks or corn chips—you can't be sure. A display of dusty corkscrews and stoppers tweaked MacK's memory of the child-oriented utensils at the holiday home. —We need a strainer. Iz flushed and looked around, ever the realist, thank God. —*You* ask 'em; I'm not gonna; forget it.

—Just these, said MacK, placing the *G.'s* and the vermouth on the counter—his eyes flicked briefly at the ICE MACHINE, for St Bernard's recipe calls for 500 LBS. OF ICE—but remembered the generous freezer in the holiday home—though what had they needed that much ice for in 1950? —It's for frozen vegetables obviously, Izzy had said lugubriously, on checking in. —And I need a bar strainer, said MacK. —A what? said the genuinely grizzled man, old before his time, putting their two bottles in a paper bag *without a cardboard separator*, and looking at their twenty as though he could now sell the place and get out of town. —A cocktail strainer for cocktails, said MacK, feeling the floor opening up as you do out there in that god damn country. —I don't got that, said the grizzled man, pushing the bag toward them hard enough that the portions of his long hair unrestrained by his railroad engineer's cap launched themselves toward MacK in a recriminatory way. And HERE was the mistake: —You know where we can get one? said Isidor. As you might in a lot of places but not here. —We *sure don't*, said the grizzled man, shifting the pronoun so as to draw the population of the town all behind him to stare down MacK and Isidor—torches, rakes—KILL THE MONSTERS—the first time he'd looked either of them in the eye—and at that moment MacK realized the grizzled man had *no idea* why they were buying gin and vermouth at the same time. —Thanks a lot, we'll be seeing you, said MacK in an on-air voice. They went past unused rolls of red corrugated paper—sent to Grizzly Liquors by a distillery—*Hit the juice, it's Christmas!*—out the scuffed Plexiglas door into the rain. —Faggits!

—You hear that? said Isidor, settling on the front seat with the holy infants on his lap. —Yeah, said MacK, you want to take it up with him? —Certainly not, said Isidor, although it disturbs me when I think I could get a kicking from someone like that who's so close to my own age. How can someone who's thirty-five have tattoos and a *dirty railroad hat?*—he's so young . . . Iz was close to tears for some reason.

Too weird of course to ask in there about olives—so another

trip, so many *stops*—at last at the tough-looking *Bev's Strip Mall* a tough-looking little super yielded two tough-looking steaks and a squat jar of the toughest-looking olives—they had taken on the dim quality of BAIT; and so home.

This yellow kitchen must have been preserved by archivists. Well-brought-up fellows, they put their groceries where you're supposed to put 'em—considered the look of the bottle of *G.'s* on the counter of red lino. MacK checked the dusty ice in the freezer; Isidor stared at the two bottles summarizing any past number of decades of American sophistication—they struck him as incongruous or anachronistic here in the archaeological kitchen—red lino—pines, rocks, ocean outside—the street lined with sober shingled houses, in each garage perhaps an older but well kept-up car—the whole little town oddly dream-like—the towns Iz and MacK grew up in transplanted to the edge of the sea for one of those reasons dreams have. —Guy called us faggots, said Isidor. —What he said was fag ITS. —Yeah I know, but *aren't* we acting a little . . . urban? said Isidor—looking at the bottles—ashamed to hear himself say such a thing, and MacK astonished. What they both needed was to be *kicked* back to New York. —And that was just the guy to do it maybe, said Isidor. Brave Engineer O'Booze. Isidor seemed suddenly abashed, chastened in the wholesome kitchen and afraid.

MacK made the de Voto martini, which is quite something —strong enough but perverse in the quantity of vermouth—the non-New York taste of *G.'s*—and a suspect fishiness in the ice—but *that* cannot be laid at St Bernard's feet, they should have made NEW ICE on arrival, what were they thinking of? Isidor entered here on his disquisition—why the martini is an urban drink—the Koh-I-Noor of the sexual tool-box—with the geometry of lights outside, stools, dimmers, high heels, so on—such was the extent of the homosexual panic induced by Engineer O'Booze that he had to

## DEFEND THE MARTINI!

—Name the worst place for drinking a martini you ever were, said Iz—I'll go first—a back yard in Alabama. The humidity first *infected,* then *killed* the martini—even though the guy had decent gin, he was one of those who treat it like punch—a pitcher . . . —Yosemite National Park, said MacK—no way to keep anything cold—and the stupid *scenery* overwhelmed the drink and Red's attention—can you believe that, I *made a martini* and she keeps apostrophizing Bridal Veil Falls. —Ah, Red, said Isidor.

Nevertheless they executed several de Votos—eventually raised their voices in a triumph of camaraderie—good to meet in exile—unhappiness was *total* for them both—and these tough-looking drinks went well with the tough-looking steaks broiled in the white gas range of 1950, tasting headily of plentiful methane, Irma Rombauer and Marion Rombauer Becker. —Bernard de Voto must have had a regular *Mississippi* of hangovers, said Isidor upon arising, and it is all the fault of *G.'s.* —Italian vermouth does not help our cause, remarked MacK from the toilet.

These boys had determined to drive south a few miles the next day. —Field trips suck, said Isidor—but he couldn't accept lingering in the holiday home—stack of firewood, stack of board games—the atavistic kitchen threatening him all day. Iz in driving south from Portland and MacK North from Hollywood had been equally annoyed every few miles by small circular signs announcing the Trees of Misery—*'Only 375 miles . . .'*—a grove of hideously deformed *Sequoia sempervirens* belonging to a cruel megalomaniac. The regular appearance of these harping signs had driven them both wild with disgust—finding they were only ten miles from this grove it became their objective.

Isidor behind the wheel of his car—the coast highway took them rapidly away from the town—through big vegetation—here the sea tears at California assiduously and often manages to crack and flood it—it was true that the groves were *'cathedrallike'*, as the brochure had it—but worship seemed a doubtful idea and one felt that outside this cathedral were only grim, enveloping elk—Portland and Los Angeles seemed imaginary.

Sometimes the most comfortable, even cozy road is deadly—in a dark grove, the road submerged and lined with boulders, Isidor strayed—admiring nature, his enemy—the left lane—and immediately had to contemplate the dull insistent face of an oncoming motor home—*Say!* said MacK—swerved to the right and onto a run of boulders, *Where there ought to be a shoulder*, said Iz bouncing—then back into the lane. —I have to tell you that is all drink and your buddy de Voto, said Isidor—my liver is generous but it's not a member of the Justice League of America. MacK slapped Iz like Abbott slaps Costello. —*Quit your fooling now!* —*Waaa!* said Isidor, *I was just tryna . . .*

MacK was truly shaken by this, the closest he'd ever come to death—they both disliked the ignominy of an automotive end—he continued to feel a gag-reflex of revulsion for days to come. But also found himself thinking *Not so bad to get knocked off with him*.

Sad enough perhaps to have *bought* these sickly trees—think of struggling to make this purchase in the Depression—but to have *named* them for whatever feeble associations the original proprietor's mind made of their deformities—to think *that* is what draws people—and it does. The Heidi Tree. The Giant Squid Tree. The El Greco Tree. The Walter Scott Limping Around with his Cane Tree. —The Hitler Tree, said Isidor, walking dispiritedly about, looking at one bent and looming over a lot of little succulents. —Jackson Pollock Tree, said MacK, pointing at one despairing, completely ill. Despite its insertion of the signs into the alimentary canal of Highway 1, the Trees of Misery had actually lost track of what it was supposed to be. However moronic it was to visit these trees, all gloom was banished upon entering the gift shop, a most fabulous example of such a place—it had everything—a *complete* range of cedar ware rubber-stamped 'Trees of Misery'—rubber tomahawks—all kinds of totem poles—plastic donkeys which shat out cigarettes—battalions of shot glasses, coffee mugs and thousands of embarrassing postcards covering not only the Trees of Misery and California's north coast but Seattle and San Francisco and Hollywood and BREASTS—o you can tell yourself you are buying this stuff with a self-aware love of the history of crap but you ARE standing in line buying it, ya jerk—along with the guy saying to his ice-cream smirched kid *Suck up to yer momma if you want her to buy you that, go on, suck up to yer momma!* Ah, gods. Isidor went for a revolting painting of a huge-breasted squaw; MacK key chains, refrigerator magnets and cedar desk implements. —This is *my* idea of squaw-candy, said Isidor.

Toward the holiday home, in brighter weather. Stopped to buy crabs—Izzy was pooped and made to argue taxonomy with the fisherman—who retreated *immediately* behind a sham of mental retardation—Iz's epicureanism was taking a beating in Portland, despite their white walls and posters of roasted peppers—he still flared up occasionally. —*But this man did catch this crab*, MacK intervened.

The introduction of sunlight, two species of seafood here on the edge, after all, imparted a sense of reason, the hope of solving their lives logically. But at table Isidor made further wry comments about his liver, which MacK received in much the same spirit, finding himself in his own miserable woman-chased woman-found Hell—he took it Iz was worried. —You going to drink all of that? —I'm resigned to it. MacK found in Isidor and in himself a new recognition of mortality and was surprised—instead of *resolutely abusing themselves*, they recognized they could feel better without *all* of these liquids; perhaps *some* of these liquids. *Which realization living a complete lie* will bring you to, as MacK well knew. Isidor seemed timid, daily underpinned by fear of death—sobered. Of course you have your frightened moments, but never doubt it or cease to believe it is final. He couldn't have actually said that Isidor felt the same, at that miserable time—not that it came out directly—but we're aging at exactly the same pace, thought MacK. Out to the garage to smoke, preserving the illusion of American health-n-wealth in the holiday home, not to sully please with the bitter odors of the corruptions of cities, as the rules on the back of the kitchen door more or less suggested.

—I used to want to live in the garage, said MacK, but my father wouldn't hear of it. —Male preserve, said Isidor. —More than that, I liked the rafters, the unfinished walls, the high roof where you can hear the rain, said MacK. —What rain, beach boy? —We had some rain, wise guy—where did you get these cigars? —A lucky find in Portland, said Iz—the morality there, the schizophrenia—you wouldn't believe it. HOKAY so everyone jogs during the day in their matching outfits, then they go home and you ought to see 'em eat—cholesterol city followed by these huge childish desserts. In the morning she—I mean *they*—eat this cereal with so many gizmos in it it's like a patisserie. And *I'm* supposed to feel bad for having a CIGAR. Non-fattening. Compact. And they give discomfort to our enemies. —*She*, hah? said MacK, are we going to discuss oral surgeons? Iz's face fell. —Well I've got to give the whole thing up, don't I? It's ridiculous, I can't be part of all this racism . . . it's nationalistic in a weird way, all these *catalogues*, these *designer beers*. —What about business? —I have neatly vacuumed Oregon of its modern firsts, I assure you. Quote—there is nothing left for me here—unquote. —What about her? —Well—here he focused at the ideal reflective distance, MacK thought, and Izzy's eyes and moustache looked rather like his own father's. So this is the warm, Jungian paragraph. —I just have to leave her to this profound emptiness, which she *will fill*—with sweaters. —Wow. —Yeah. I meet her at a club, take her to bed, she's *visiting* New York, I don't know she's practically *hemorrhaging* from sweater withdrawal—I think she's excited about *me*—I go to her brother's birthday *luau*, I'm the only guy wearing a shirt with *buttons*. —!— —So that's the story. And you? What about you, Sir, and the vaunted Southwest?

—Well we have fared much the same out here in this god damn

country, said MacK. I can take you through the whole miserable business in five minutes should you wish it. —Why leave New York? said Isidor, I mean, I more or less had to—I thought—but you? —You glom on to these women, said MacK, they glom on to you—and you convince yourself there is life out there, or out here rather, that you can both live—and it's *so* untrue. —What about NBC? said Isidor. —*Accumulated vacation*, said MacK, it swelled and it throbbed—they said if I didn't take it all right away they'd excise it. A holidectomy. —Nice. —And Red had to go to the desert to make this movie—an expedition to the *vaunted Southwest* with this woman who seems to like me . . . —That's the thing, said Isidor, that *'seems'*.

Now they're going to Have a Cigar and Discuss Women?—so this is the warm, Homeric paragraph?—as they sit and look out the open garage door at the dark sea. —So we get out there, said MacK, there we were in the vast Region of Guns and Christianity—there was the desert, huge and haunting—in fact *really deserted*, deserted in the mind of man. Well you can go out and shoot things but the only place where life occurs in the vaunted Southwest is on television. —Shouldn't bother you, said Iz, media man after all. —What I do in my little room is *futile*, said MacK, but damn if I am not going back there and get all my meals and drinks sent up from Hurley's—see if I don't. But their television is revealing, brother—mainly advertisements for trade schools—a sign that culture has failed completely—the only way you can make a living is by fixing TVs—the thing that ruined your brain in the first place—along with the heat. So we drive across two square states and in Albuquerque she points out this big bookstore. —Really? said Iz. —And a news-stand and she smiles at me coquettishly and giggles *'Last chance!'* So it dawns on me what she's saying—where we're going there's NO NOTHING. No books no music no movies except pornography and *elk-murder*, no selection of gins no single malt no beer except you-know-what no cigars no pipe tobacco. And then we go up and up to this trailer camp in the sky where they're making the movie. —Who's in it? —No idea. I did say I was going to read all of Stendhal one day so I have these *paperbacks* from the *thrift store.* —*Y-e-e-e-c-c-c-h!* said Isidor rising off his bench. —This terrible, empty routine has developed, said MacK, and I say this in *full realization* of the naïveté and dullness of my routine in New York—but somehow there is little drudgery in walking to work from 50th Street. —Well the No. 1 is the people's train, said Isidor, they express themselves there, you get some variety . . . I suppose. —She has to get up at 3.30 every morning and drive down the mountain to the 'location', she comes back late every night, pissed off and half stoned, film people are all the same. We haven't made love since we got there —we suffered from the altitude for a week and she hates me for my constant complaining—there's no this, no that—but damn it; it's *factual complaining*—there really is no this and no that.

—So it's *attitude sickness*, said Isidor. —Once in a while I drive to Albuquerque, which now seems like a cultural OASIS, to get the *Times.* —You!? said Isidor. —Yeah, said MacK. Turns out they only order three copies for the whole state. —What about Santa Fe? —It's banned in Santa Fe. So this is how I'm living. I get up every day and look in the mirror and say *This is how I am living.* I started cutting tiny pictures of pretty women out of mail order catalogues— *Catalogues!* moaned Isidor—yes and the local paper said MacK and this being the vaunted Southwest they are merely gardening or posing in front of new kinds of sinks. I make up stories about them. That's all I do all day. There's this kick-ass bar but you can go in the afternoon and *not* get your ass kicked. After a month the bartender said *What's happenin'?* I said, I bet you I am the only guy in here wearing Clinique® Turnaround Cream. —Gee *Whizz*, said Isidor.

—When I'm overwhelmingly *ultra* miserable I drive over to the next town. It's got a big PINEY LODGE—stone fireplace, antlers, bottles of beer, club sandwiches. It's a desperate scene, man, I put too many *longings* into it. I need it to be New York, just for a moment or two. Clatter. Service. I *can't love Red*, not without bookstores, bars, people in diverse clothing shouting, the sound of breaking glass . . .—So? said Isidor.

—So I asked the waitress out. Out into the woods. —I'm impressed, said Isidor, who nonetheless looked pale. —There's this picturesque rocky *stream*, said MacK, in our town Burger King is a natural feature. We walked along, didn't talk of much, she was from the place—kind of Fifties hairstyle. Then we had one of these thunder showers which come every afternoon. So we ran under the trees—soaked to the skin—and—! There was this penetrating *smell of ozone*.

—I don't . . . said Isidor, shifting in his seat, nauseated by the idea of relations out of doors, picturing MacK and some kind of girl in pigtails, a *tree*, mit *burls*—

—*I'm sorry*, said MacK so anyway the storm ended—we ended—(*Isidor groaned again*)—and we went and sat by the stream. Then at almost the same moment we both got up and started gathering stones from the stream. Large stones like they made the lodge fireplace from. —*Yes?* said Isidor, looking at his watch. —We waded out in the stream and piled them into cairns. We were each making a little shrine. Shrines, what the f*** are you, said Isidor, do you know it's nearly bedtime? —I get your disintegration, you get mine, said MacK. My cairn was of light grey stone, a taller middle section and shorter piles on the sides. Hers was circular, black pebbles. She put two feathers from a blue-jay inside it, and they turned as the water flowed through it. —Yes, *AND?* said Isidor. He was about to explode. —She said, *what's your shrine to?* And I said, this is a shrine to the RCA Building. *Where's that?* she said. It's in New York, I said, 49 West 49th Street, no 50 West 50th Street. I work there. *Oh*, she said, *cool*. What's yours to? I said. She smiled and said *Mine's to love*.

—So you make a *replica of the RCA Building* in the middle of the woods? said Isidor, you think that's healthy?—It simply appeared under my hands, said MacK. It pointed the way home. —So? —I drove her to her place. The car regularly aquaplaned at fifty miles an hour just like it says in all the textbooks. I got back to the house and Red was there fuming, on the phone to her sister—a woman who for some reason is a constant and willing receptacle of Red's mistrust and disappointment and venom about show business and me—in front of her on the table were all my little pictures—the redheads with the new kitchens, blondes riding lawnmowers, brunettes luxuriating on leather sofas in their socks—and she accused me of having affairs with them! —What! said Iz. —*You've been seeing these women while I have to work!* She practically threw me out. *Ai yi yi.*

But after all, one's crazy 'bout one's baby.


Isidor maybe saw his future as irretrievably lonely and tortured—but at least he was *going back to town.* You can't make life happen; nobody can make anything happen. But you can surely be lazy and self-deluded and lonely. The idea that they'd be parting in the morning was already palpable in the smoke, up in the rafters and canoes of the garage. They got off a few loud jokes over coffee in the morning and then it went flat and Isidor made haste to leave. MacK dreadfully sad. He and Isidor always went around thinking they saw enough of each other—or that they could do without it, which really wasn't true.

## SO YOU SEE WHAT TROUBLE YOU CAN GET INTO? IF YOU SET ONE FOOT, ONE *TOE* OUTSIDE NEW YORK?

# Iz On His Own

Toward MacK and The Hour at day's end—walking in his very serious shoes, which he is one of a dwindling band of men in New York to have regularly re-soled, and half of *them* are Yalies—as he'd said to MacK the very day he'd bought them, back in Our Years in Yorkville—*These are shoes for a guy who WALKS*—and walked all of this our town in them. Up and down from his abodes to the Battery, across all of lower Manhattan, way WAY up to the Cloisters. For years and years. Even after he acquired the shop from Mr Playfair, he often left in the afternoon, rain or no, supposedly 'buying'—bull-shit. Out, away from books, the cigarred office. Stopping soon for a cup of joe, of java, mud—the whole old New York thesaurus of coffee—but *no* espresso, *screw Portland*, he said, out loud, too often. Miss Plein would look after the shop. Even though Miss Plein is from Queens and sounds it, THAT doesn't put off his customers because they are the true democrats born of this our town.

When he got Bibulo & Schenkler, half inherited, half purchased, Isidor had had ideas it could become one of the midtown East Side firms—a few very levant titles in a draped window with some Georgian furniture—one of your really discreet side streets—say East 56th? That's a little far north maybe but *you* know. But he quickly decided, after being tortured by some of the *incunabula hounds*, that he didn't give a damn about incunabula, f***ing Gutenberg, or even fine binding. Who gives a damn? *Swaddling clothes, what are we, f***ing Egyptians? I should change my name to Moishe maybe. They'll be asking for papyri next. I sell books, not botched attempts at books!* he shouted in the shop on the day he decided this. He liked smoky old books and that was it. It was funny, but he found he couldn't apply his capable, statistical, finicky brain to the minutiae of very fine books—in the course of several weeks he packed up all the very rarest stuff and sent it up to auction, where it fetched boring, enormous prices. *Screw it*, he thought—East 56th sort of thing would never have suited the history of the shop. It wasn't right to do that to Mr Playfair; why pay gobs of rent, and *be obliged to cultivate an English accent*. So Bibulo & Schenkler, he had decided long ago, would remain a downtown book business in loca-tion and character—the shop would always smell from his modest Montecruz use. Big cinema section, lots of *handled* but interesting firsts—a ton of books on the city.

Poetry he took advice on—*one thing about Isidor Katz*, he thought to himself, *I don't issue opinions on stuff I know nothing about, that's for sure*. His own interests, spicy meats, hangmen, Sing Sing, vanished restaurants and bars, the Fulton markets, Robert Fulton, and Fulton J. Sheen, he amassed with a vigor in buying which often left some of the other dealers open-mouthed. These holies were kept in the shelves around the entrance to his office. Yet—unlike some of our great downtown booksellers—he was willing to sell them. It made him happy to find someone who *liked* the Fulton Fish Market, and—this is unthinkable in the unwritten portion of the constitution of the Antiquarian Booksellers Association (founded 1906)—he liked to talk to people about the books they bought or wanted to buy, can you imagine? But this was the legacy of Mr Playfair, who'd run Bibulo & Schenkler, since *he'd* half bought and half inherited it, in 1940, like an affable professor with liberal office hours.

But forget the shop—you like the sound of it, *you* visit it—Fourth Avenue—you'll see it—he's determined to stay on Fourth Avenue, which has always threatened evanescence, because, Isidor thought now, walking up through Chelsea, particularly *now* I'm determined to stay on Fourth because of how much time MacK and I spent there—why we spent most of our spare cash in college right at the Peacock, and Bibulo & Schenkler—he knew this yet had never thought it much—about his days as a customer in a shop he'd never have dreamt to own. Worried about MacK.

The mud left a dark scum at the back of Isidor's throat; which he liked, whether from java or pipe or cigar or flu or bile rising because something on the street annoyed Hell out of him—always just a little something rising back there was good. *When rises Katz so does the bile*. He'd been walking Manhattan for thirty years, nearly—which shocked him—this was a day for shocks maybe—cleared his larynx of the mud. —*Scum*, he said, out loud, as he passed a news stand.

BLIND PROPRIETOR: F*** you, man.

—Nah, nah, said Izzy—still more than half to himself—the scum put him in mind of a visit to Seligman the tobacconist—walk needs a focus after all—it was time to kick Seligman's ass. And now not just about the whole nasty saga of cigars in the last few years in Manhattan, f***ing-A disgraceful. You start off discovering something of value, from the previous culture, said Isidor, like these shoes for one thing, shoes for a guy who *WALKS*—granted the real property of old Yale farts who can't wait to get 'em off and run barefoot through the deep pile in their club every lunchtime—or cigars—no one gave a f*** about *cigars* in *1978*—except Isidor and Mr Playfair—maybe Jackie Onassis, who knows—they were just for puffy-faced old guys with an irritated drooly lip and an egg-cream eye—then all these *Pine Street* guys come along—they have the salaries—and they buy all the good cigars in New York! —*They even give them to their girlfriends*, said Isidor out loud at the corner of 35th and Seventh. And all the good cigars in New York was a SHIT LOAD of cigars. Sidelong glance from a woman in a very old-fashioned hat. So then you have New York, *New York*, mark you, where everyone really does deserve the best stuff, devoid of cigars! New York, which has always been the most *loyal* to cigars. Screw Chicago—what do they got? They got NOTHING.

## Chez Iz

What is *happening* to *Chelsea*, said Isidor, look at all this arty garbage, man, I tell you—almost as if to MacK, as if MacK was there—it is INtolerable. Where there was recently a perfectly, respectably, *miserable* coffee shop, with a perfect cup of miserable mud—Iz went there sometimes—there was now a yellow-painted GALLERY offering artifacts native to the Gilbert Islands. In the yellow frame of the window a large *tapa* cloth, bark beaten to the merry rhythm of the hydrogen bombs, thought Isidor—but he stopped and contemplated its pattern, as that morning he'd stared at the remarkably similar one graven on Sylvie's back. —Only book dealer currently in Manhattan with a girlfriend with Maori tattoos *after all*, out loud in front of the gallery. Stick that in your Roxburghe and bind it, said Isidor.

But who was going to *recognize* 'the book dealer Isidor Katz' in a man talking to himself in front of a yellow gallery in Chelsea? No danger. Clean white shirt—not a cop in the city'd lay a paw on you, man—say what you want.

After he lost Mary-Ann and drifted, or fled, downtown, *headlong*, and threw in his lot with Mr Playfair, Isidor hadn't known what to do about the *horn*—you get out of practice. Can't go solo—it was an out-of-body experience for Iz anyway—always *saw himself doing it*, so absurd, too pathetic silly and human. Afraid too he'd clock out during it one day. Who isn't? Along with the shop Iz inherited, in a legal-size filing cabinet, a collection of Mr Playfair's leisure time reading from the late 1940s and early 50s—the most absurd magazines ever essayed. But Izzy's casual perusal of them—*What Babes Really Want*—*Cowgirl Roundup*—*Untamed Fury* (girl in a leopard-print tank suit threatening a stuffed ocelot with what was not so much a whip as the handlebar grip from a tricycle with plastic streamers)—*Beautiful But Rough*—*The Big-Opportunity Field Of Custom Upholstery*—*Hitler's Women*—*Bevy Of Brawling Beauts*—*Dish Of Delightful Dreaming*—*Fish Bite Every Day*—never let himself think about *Mr Playfair* leafing through this madness between the Sherwood Anderson first and the *Shepherd's Calendar*—for all Izzy knew the stuff might have come in with some library or other—lot of funny people about. Miss Plein bought a library last year from a *Bronx midget*, who collected everything on miniature railways he could find and also, oddly, a lot of George Eliot—and in practically every book she found a twenty dollar bill.

But once Izzy had secured a pad, he began constructing its ethic. Whereas his place in the Far East had reflected the old booky, homely New York values—the life he and MacK were forever *glimpsing* in windows they passed—and never quite achieved—guy moves to the *Village*, go nuts, right? He found some black lamps which matched his japanned martini shaker. Kind of thing.

This place, in a pre-war tower off Fifth Avenue, had a sunken living-room, bordered by a wrought-iron railing. It seemed to MacK that for a time Izzy sank, along with his living-room. He moved in a pile of the silly magazines—he wouldn't have books at home, for a time, couldn't stand them—even though he was now a partner in the business and life had improved, he was without Mary-Ann, and he'd *decided* to dive—sunk in gloom in his sunken living-room—into a few adventures suggested by this lurid old crap. So there was a succession of jungle babes and vines, cowgirls and lariats, girls with black hair and red shoes who might have been Mary-Ann but clearly weren't.

**Just a nutty little period!**

# Sylvie

One day Isidor came across Sylvie, as you do discover people in town—almost as if they're on a shelf you haven't looked at for a time. She was working at Peacock, where he'd gone to ask about World War II pictorials to fill out a collection of journalism he'd just bought. She turned away from him to the card file and here were these remarkable, combed, *spiced* patterns on her back. Had to ask her out of course, that was obvious, marks on the back. Turned out she was—wait for it—a *second-generation anthropologist blue blood who shared a turret* with her father at the American Museum of Natural History—this father'd 'given' her a going-over by a south seas tattooer for her 21st birthday. So she *had* to be a jungle girl, Gee Whizz, she really was a jungle girl. And she knew all about Isidor's jungle. Sylvie was beyond smart, beyond passionate, and in several weeks she was living in Iz's tower. Things that had been sunken rose up. *As the Katz rises so shall the living-room.* Izzy felt more like himself and reintroduced his books to the place. Oh there was still a jungle aspect—Sylvie liked the bachelor pad lamps and the cocktail shaker particularly—the patterns on her back fit right in with Isidor's design for living.

KATZ PREDICTS! Very few men and women will find themselves settled together in this our town any more—rubbernecking is one of the genetically programmed habits here—if you both assert you're happy together, married even!, you're still looking for the finer thing. But fineness has a limit; fineness is a *finite* quality—and no one can recognize that in New York because you are trained by this our beloved town to salivate after the *infinite*—that is what your guy and gal on the street imagine to be HAVING IT ALL. But something drives you to *act normal* and see what happens. What the hell is it! Act like people and see where it gets you? Wears you down is what it does. You walk the streets and you feel your nest is—not exactly soiled—but perhaps that this wrong person—no judgements, just wrong—is *turning your own apartment against you*. If that is possible.

Martinis get bigger and Bigger and BIGGER—there *is* a bloody limit—disagreements longer, along with the evenings and the heat. You're willing to admit to trust in the beginning maybe, even though you both know this is just an extended bonk, *extruded* even. Plenty people can live with the wrong person but NOBODY can live with the *idea* of the wrong person. The city itself becomes wrong—you cease to be able to see yourself in it—being drained, you lack the vital inch of courage you need to open the damn door and put your foot out.

Don't you see that everyone has that courage here? Except the oldies and the Yalies? They're all BRAVE. That's what it takes to live here—this is why New York whups any other dam' town—it's BRAVE. We continue to live rather than to watch TELEVISION.

But Isidor and Sylvie were of the luckiest—with their intellectual compatibility and mutual style and fondness for games out of very bad mummy or sarong-and-torch movies—as you might imagine —they found each other and did not have to leave town.

Isidor became more like his own customers—this was when he began collecting New York, on paper, in earnest. He also bought furiously for the shop, expanding the Old New York section into an entire aisle on the second floor. *Sunlight and Shadow in Old New York. Brooklyn Waterfront*. Maps, menus, even ephemera, which Mr Playfair had scorned: bus tickets, boxing programs—his apartment and the shop began doing duty *as* New York for Isidor—he lost interest in going out into it. He lost himself contentedly and endlessly in *patterns,* New York's and Sylvie's. On Jungle Night! There was the shop—his tower—and Sylvie, who became—quite simply—his nurse and his muse—*My NUSE*, as Isidor put it—which MacK firstly heard as *NOOSE*—quickly and violently disabused.

—

When Chelsea turns into Times Square you never know—it's always when you're not paying attention. There's the question of the Garment District—an iffy thing to identify these days—and even the older idea of the Fur and Flower District—which somehow floated, ethereally, a little up and over from the Garment District. You're walking along—north—you can already feel or smell Times Square's hot motor—and you get NOTIONS, window acres of machine lace, buttons, edges, elastic—which have never given you any notions other than that you'd better get out of there before someone sews a pink bunny from Hong Kong onto your jacket—nominally Times Square is much more a district for notions than the *notion portion* of the Garment District.

But it's stupid to talk of *districts*—that is for HICKS—every crossstreet is different.

Isidor slowed—the thick leather brakes of his shoes doing this job admirably—as he passed a window rather theatrically displaying theatrical footwear. He recalled his one attempt at Seventies style, a pair of lime green platform-soled oxfords with wing-tip sewing, bought the day after he'd got completely rubbished on mushrooms. Whatever explosive insights to a whole new LIFE STYLE these shoes had been a part of had completely worn off by the time he got them back to his dormitory, though he left them on the shelf next to his beloved *Beowulf* and *Cid*, holding up the *Cid*, for the rest of the year—they cost eighty 1973 dollars. In the present window were some black shoes with ankle straps—Izzy blinked a little, kept moving, and thought about Miss Plein teetering about the shop in such a—but *Sylvie*, jungle night might be edifyingly augmented with—a blast of hot stale DISCO woke him up to the irritating realities of 42nd and Seventh. Across the street he noticed an Orthodox guy—a big one—coming out of a topless bar. Sweating, adjusting his incredibly boring hat—where do they get them so *generically shaped*, mumbled Isidor, you never see these hats in shops—you'd think Ben Gazzara was buried in the last one. But big Orthodox guy? Topless bar? —What'd he think about in there, said Iz. Felt bad for speculating on Miss Plein's sex life and wandered Times Square in disconsolation—over MacK—the end seemed to have been kicked out of his errands, his entrails—thought about going to the tobacconist and *kicking his ass* for killing his friend. Seligman would deny everything: *This is my fault? I've always recommended very moderate smoking*, he'd say that, said Izzy, but it isn't true—all through the Seventies he sat in his f***ing shop with his silent mop-head partner and smoked—they must have got through half a pound of latakia a day—playing chess or pretending to. —Not so arrogant now, are we? said Isidor aloud and got a look from a suburban couple in front of 'Cats'—they're killing the guy, they've killed him, is all, said Iz. The couple obviously came to the theater often enough that they didn't want to *flee* Isidor, but you could tell they wished there wasn't A MAN TALKING TO HIMSELF right in front of 'Cats' so early in the day. They'd thought to buy their tickets early so as to AVOID ISIDOR.

# Naga Mouris

Awful fellow for curry, Isidor—*I'll bhuna you under the table*—always been that way.

When the red dawn of Szechuan first hit New York, Isidor announced to a table of MacK, Mary-Ann and *Sidney* he was going to crunch up, as he put it, an entire Chinese pepper. Black, uncertain eating like a big bug. Bets were placed—he did so—and struggled to show little reaction. —How was it? said Sidney, who had the most money riding on it. —Not so bad, husked Isidor, who picked up his chopsticks and continued his dinner. The conversation resumed and several minutes later MacK reached for the water pitcher—he then saw Izzy had pushed his chair into the *corner* and was drinking directly from the pitcher with both hands. Later, when they were walking across the park, a staggering, crimson Isidor suddenly rushed for an embankment and stuck his head deep into the snow. [Hissing noise.] —That'll be twenty bucks, said Sidney.

Hotter, hotter, hotter—during his year at Oxford he studied little but bitter beer, and started a curry club—bested the Fellows at their own game—Izzy figured his tongue had a lot of Hunan and Mexican training in New York, whereas the Brits had grown up eating *jam*. In the spring he was trying to save his scholarship by characterizing Spinoza's ascending grades of knowledge as the Curry of Opinion, the Bhuna of Reason, and the *Vindaloo of Intuition*—which did little for Spinoza, Balliol, or Isidor. On the last day of term the owner of the 'Mumtaz', where he'd spent all the time he wasn't in the 'Mitre', told him there *was* something hotter than vindaloo, Ceylon, *phal,* and *thal:* NAGA. —*But you will not be finding it with ease, Dr Isidor.* —You shouldn't call me that yet.

Iz came back to New York—his many adventures—the shop—but since 1975 he's been in a kind of cloud—beneath everything Isidor does he's really doing only one thing—like those religionists for whom a conscious chant becomes a relentless, unconscious prayer—he has been thinking about NAGA.

Wandered in and out of Indian groceries and spice shops around 6th Street, or up Lexington, asking for naga. *Asked* these guys, who were just trying to run their businesses—and don't need to have anything to do with obsessed people—though that is always part of business in this our town—in beseeching and pathetic tones, for naga. Instantly they knew they were dealing with a madman. —*You will not find naga*, they all said with charming and nervous smiles, *no no no.* MacK had the feeling Isidor had approached some of these people a *number of times.* Iz would take him into a shop and look around for something that might be naga—without asking. Maybe this is it, Iz said once, picking up a big green thing—the pods in *Invasion of the Body Snatchers.* —*Oh ho ho ho no, that is not naga*, said the shopkeeper, shooing them out onto First Avenue.

One day five years ago there had been a glimmer of hope, Iz thought, in the person of *Sani.* He came out of the back of one of the Indian groceries after Izzy had dispiritedly asked for naga and became tearful upon the answer—came toward him on a cane—a young man on a cane, smoking a *bidi.* He reeked of romantic suffering and turmeric. —*Naga?* said Sani, *it is possible that I could find you naga.* Isidor's compact body flattened and then lengthened—*doyoinnnggg!* —a pointer dog in a duck-hunting cartoon. —*Do you know anything about naga?* Sani asked, coming closer, surrounding Iz with smoke and spice. —*It is not a thing that people . . . cultivate*, said Sani. *It grows only wild, in the hills of Assam. And there, in only one department really, in Sylhet. Call me Friday evening. After we make deliveries I am usually here in the shop, smoking and having coffee with friends. Perhaps I will have news for you.* Like a scene in a Charles Boyer movie, Isidor took the phone number of the shop and went out, up the steps to the street, in the rain.

But come Friday Sani had mysteriously disappeared. Izzy phoned several times only to be told *He's out, he's out.* The third time things got sinister. *There is no Sani here. There has never been a Sani. Leave us alone. Stop bothering us, or things will go badly for you.*

It took Iz weeks to recover. You can't really get everything in New York—it's just something people SAY.

Now wandered into a news-stand. Casually perused *Leg Action, Leg Display, Leg Scene, Leg Quarterly, Leg Geographic, Leg Literary Supplement, Popular Leg, Leg Modeler, Leg & Garden, Inside Leg, Leg Frontier, Leg Theory, Leg & Bass Fisherman, Leg Times-Picayune, Tri-Leg Quarterly, P.M.L.A., Leg Diggity, Leg-A-Rama, Leg Aroma, Leg Neurosis, Leg Mania, Leg Psychosis, Leg Embolism, Leg Aneurysm, Leg Freakout, Leg Nam, Leg Thorazine, Leg Flashback,* and *Knee Joint Action* with his usual *savoir-faire.* Presiding was a man from the subcontinent. With the usual casual indolence Iz asked: —Where are you from? —I am from Bangladesh, Sir, said the man, if it is any of your business (displaying a certain residential period in New York). —*Naga?* Iz asked, not even explaining, he no longer had the heart but carried on the search on a zombie level, the reflex of sadness rather than of hope. Without the hesitation of a second: —*Go to the Madhuban restaurant in Jackson Heights. They will give you naga.*

Out to the street and put up his hand for a cab. Was almost frightened he'd found it—frightened he was going to have to eat it immediately. No time to phone—let anyone *know*; MacK or Sylvie. In the car he wondered aloud if he oughtn't to have taken the BMT. —Is it unseemly, searching for a treasure of the developing world by *private car?* —What is the matter with you man? said the driver, —Naga.


The waiter asked Isidor if he wanted the lunch buffet, steamy and deep-colored in chafing dishes in the window along Roosevelt Avenue. —I want *naga.* The waiter opened his mouth, shut it, and *ran away,* to the kitchen. There was telephony. The owner of the Madhuban, Mr M M Narwal, suddenly hurried in wearing a *spy coat.* He smiled down at Isidor, reached in his pocket, and brought out two soft pods of orange-pink. —I suggest that I can make you a lamb vindaloo with this naga, said Narwal, also perhaps a shad fish curry. Narwal pronounced it *sad.* —Sad! said Isidor. —*Shad.* A man grows these in his own house. I put the tiniest bit on my rice at home

237

last night and my wife said, what is that you have got there, I can smell it over here. This is the naga, I said to her and O gosh is it hot. Narwal pronounced it *hardt*.

Before the naga, a deep red carpet of somosas, pakora, achingly tender pieces of chicken from Narwal's tandoor; a sobbingly wonderful chana bhaji—Isidor BLIND TO IT.

Now the waiters gathered around Isidor's table, the guy from Manhattan who was going to eat naga. He was afraid now—afraid his eyes would puff up, that he would have to apply lotions, tourniquets and scrapers to his soft tissues. That it would be like the *Vindaloo of Intuition* that once forced him out into the streets of Edinburgh, spasmodically waving his arms, where he was nearly run over by a taxi.

But the naga didn't taste like *capsicum* at all—more like perfume—it didn't blister the tongue—it filled Isidor's head with hardt exotic humors. —I'm feeling a little panicky, said Isidor, to no one in particular—I'm hallucinating. Colors plunged that were not in the wallpaper of the Madhuban—a *policeman* on his lunch hour moved toward the chafing dishes with a spoon which, for a moment, became *stupendous in size*.

Now here was Narwal, pulling up a chair. The table was littered with perspired napkins, cups of spice tea, gulab jamun. —Do you know anything about naga? said Narwal, are you all right, Mr—Isidor? My friend has to grow them in Long Island City because of course it is not legal to bring produce into this country. Isidor hunched himself into his jacket. —I didn't know SPICINESS was a thing controlled by governments. —*Oh* yes. Do you know anything about Bangladesh? said Narwal. If only we could become politically stabilized, it could be one of the world's most wonderfully productive countries. We have everything: forests, petroleum, minerals. —And naga, said Isidor, banging his fist on the table, don't forget. —Yes, said Narwal, of course in Bangladesh we still have great problems of the natural world which plague us. Tornadoes, earthquakes, tidal waves, floods . . . —But do these really affect the *naga?* said Isidor—you listen to me—naga could play a big role in redevelopment. *With naga you could rule the world.* —Thank you sir, thank you very much, said Narwal—your bill; I leave you. So he too found Isidor deranged—starry—especially after he'd *got* the stuff.

So often there is no talking to them.

Flagged a gypsy cab, admiring its battle-scarred gun grey body—thought it would do, being blown around in the battle between the monster foods at the end of the world. —Back to Manhattan, said Isidor. —'Back'? said the driver. Cruelly. —Hey guess what, Iz said to the guy, I've been thinking for months that I need medical attention. —So? the guy said. —But what I needed was *Madhuban* attention.

—

Horizontal light and sound of the glimmering river and bridge world—mid-afternoon sun on struts, trains, the water. A real division, thought Isidor, between Manhattan and America—*tenks gut!* —so what Queens has crazy restaurants with naga?—it's still the other place really. Some grandeur (?) along the FDR—homeyness (?) of the small coffee shops of Second. The guy is still hallucinating, is what.

—Here, here, says Iz, off here. Fine. Great. Here's fine—anywhere right around here—*STOP!!!* The driver twitches like a cat and pulls over.

Isidor always felt things were made dark by the Citicorp Center. Ostensibly reflective, it nevertheless seems to draw all life, all light toward it, from blocks around, to suck energy, simply to suck. —Rather like myself, he said—and laughed. Got a look from a curious cop—this was *Lexington Avenue* after all. —Stayin' out of trouble? said the cop, unexpectedly, curiously, *sweetly*. —You bet! said Izzy—taken aback, felt he was recognized in some way—suddenly *existed*, oh dear, instead of being a flying, incisive consciousness, a narrator of the city—they're on to me? Started sassing the cop when he was a block away—more looks. —Trouble with the mouth, that's what it is, said Iz. —I'll stop yer mouth, said a guy in a doorway. —Mouth trouble, said Iz to himself—thinking of MacK and the . . . tumors. —Trouble is, MacK's never used his mouth *enough*, said Isidor at the corner of 58th and Lexington, it's like Sidney always said—his grotesque lack of movement or gesture.

Sidney had once proposed to MacK that he open an *Œconomy of Movement Center*, and he said you had to spell it that way—where those who worried about such things could lose the elaborate gesticulations of the Old World, and become as stiff and still as MacK! *Make a million bucks*, Sidney'd said—*deductible too*. Sidney was the only guy they knew who regularly used the word 'deductible'—to go through life, thought Isidor, with that point of—but here the Citicorp Center. The overhangs, the blue-green corners stealing light—*you steal light from the city?* —Sunlight and shadow in *new* New York, Iz said. Under the overhangs, and in the arcades surrounding the thing—OUT OF WHICH GLASS MAY FLY AT ANY MOMENT—thanks a lot—don't care what they say—there are dark pools, places where the light of commerce doesn't penetrate—where the glutinous hagfish from the executive floors descend to gape and exude their slime—the cyclostomata (*'one of the lowest orders of vertebrates'*—ENCYCLOPAEDIA BRITANNICA) of banking attach, bore into an exotic dancer or two . . . Isidor felt something rising in his blood—fired by the naga—a fight, a fight, the FIGHT he'd always wanted to have with the tobacconist. He'd fight for MacK—why not? Raise a real stink and give up the f***ing stuff *today*, right in front of the guy.

Naga and this brush with one of his possible selves—Isidor suddenly remembered the cop *singling him out*—f***'s sake, you *believe* that? he said. —I'll believe anything, *now*, said a guy also waiting for the light at Madison and 53rd. Up there in the Fairchild Building MacK had been kissed by Olive just an hour or two before.

# The RCA Building

Iz really wished powerfully he could shut up, but there was a tinge of trip surrounding him, and he felt powerless to rein himself in—a little afraid now that his mouth trouble really was getting worse—right there on the street—as he walked. —Is there anything worse than to feel something *inside you* is *getting worse* when you're on the street, said Iz, no wonder everyone's got these f***ing *phones* now, call the mama soon as anything goes wrong. *Mom, I'm having a heart attack on the street. I just wanted to say . . .* Questioned why his steps were westward and remembered he'd got to pick a fight, immediately, with the tobacconist. —Perfect time, after all, go defend the guy, kick that little runt's ass.

Fifth Avenue, seen down the side street, seemed to be an unrolling, inviting carpet, beckoning Izzy toward the tobacconist's— the slightly hallucinating bookseller—he went over. —Gee Whizz this naga is really hanging on, he said. Decided to wander a bit—no hurry after all—the tobacconist's runty ass is always there for kicking until 5.30. Walked down to 51st and turned into Rockefeller Plaza. —Go past MacK's place, he said. The big metal guys on the AP Building still trying to get out that edition—just another dope on the phone, said Izzy, crossing the street and gazing down into the skating rink—Prometheus, his shell, like a phone in his hand—he's on the shellphone, said Isidor, he's talking to the *News* guy about his massive forearm . . . *Atlas is over on Fifth at the moment, whadda you expect, he's going to put the f***ing WORLD down? For YOUR call?* A gay little family of tourists gathered at the edge of the rink, hoping they might find Isidor's talk informative. Across it, leaning placidly his hands on the stone ledge, a security guard, his visor down low over his dark glasses. But obviously looking at me, thought Isidor. —I see ya, ya big palooka. But what were they talking about, Prometheus and the burly reporter from the nearly defunct Associated Press? —About MacK, obviously, said Izzy on the move—*this* was the phone call he was dreading maybe, I was dreading, that's where he works, worked—what'm I *saying?* Guy's not dead and hasn't even told me he's *going* to be dead, definitely, said Isidor. The gay little family slipped away. Isidor gazed into the lobby of the RCA Building from under the awning outside—some *tan* guy standing around smoking—limousines purring in the little street. He thought, sentimentally, of MacK's studio up there—where he'd never been—but thought—the guy's had his hands on some knobs up there—there's some biochemical, some *genetic vestige* of MacK in the microphone, or at least in the screen, said Iz, who knew his stuff—he'd sold a big collection on radio a few years back—and dismissed such a thought.

But whatever news was passing from—let's call him Bud—to Prometheus was definitely *dread, dread news*, thought Iz—and found himself walking over to Sixth, by Hurley's, past all that dreary Irishry where MacK used to meet his . . . *fancy women*, I can say that if I wanna, said Isidor. Hurley's, MacK's martini local—though Isidor appreciated the atmosphere in the little place which had cocked its snook at John D Jr and his play bulldozer—was very hard to take; all those NBC veeps in their suits. Still, something about it, said Izzy. The dread news—found himself wondering if MacK's obit would be in the *Times*—maybe NBC would put it in—last chance to be in the paper, said Isidor wistfully of his friend—he wasn't aware that MacK's name had been in the *New York Times* the day he assumed his job. But it appeared only because of Shelby Stein's promotion to television—the *New York Times* doesn't know or care anything about radio—*running as they do one of the worst radio stations in history themselves*, said Iz heatedly—inserting *actual slices of cheese* between movements of Beethoven. Your Beethoven and cheese station. Pictured the announcer pushing a slice of gouda into the cd deck—those horses' asses in their tartan trousers, their *view of culture*, you don't even see guys at the *Times* dressed like that. Can you imagine asking the Mayor questions in Black Watch pants? He glanced up 47th, its heaving mass of black clothing—oh and there the little wise men in their boat of books—a place he and MacK haunted before Iz was even in the business.

The sweat was back—the naga kept making things a little too vivid—or perhaps it's the DAZZLE OF MIDTOWN, said Iz, its CHARM, to which I've obviously become impervious—and turned west onto 46th. He felt two things, besides the naga's haloes—a slight saliva at the thought of the tobacconist's cigars and large jars of latakia—and a mob rustling in his blood because he was going to have it finally OUT with the guy—the *squirt*, said Isidor, passing the Universal-Brasil Restaurant, Inc., where a little placard beamed in the window, as they might have placed there forty years before, in the movies maybe, though he'd smelled it before his eye met the yellowed card—

## FEIJOADA TODAY

—and because he'd lunched to the hallucinogenic limit at the Madhuban, Izzy felt his various dark systems bubble like the *feijoada completa* in the vats of the U.B. Rest.

As it always referred to itself: 'U.B. REST. CANNOT ASSUME RESPONSIBILITY FOR COATS OR HATS ESP.'—'NOTICE: GRATUITIES ARE THE RESPONSIBILITY OF THE CUST. AND NOT U.B. REST.!!.' What an odd hotbed of responsibility and doom, he thought, for a lot of Brazilians, was the U.B. Rest., Inc., though maybe these guys got kicked out of Brazil for being too Portuguese. It was nothing less than a black, hot mood—and he got the tobacconist's sign in his sights. *Man* he was going to enjoy this, more than naga or feijoada. Saw himself suddenly tall as the Citicorp Center, battling an equally titanic tobacconist—designed by Philip Johnson—who therefore had a hole in his head.

# The Epicure Pipe Shop

West 46th was always a street of our hemisphere—which always amused Isidor: the Brazilian places boiling their feijoada; the moccasin company across the street boiling the feet of Yalies—the tobacconist's had been the first intrusion of anything stylish, so far as anything in 1970 can be said to have been stylish. —But he was a brave arty guy, said Isidor, he had long hair and a SWEATER. Painted the whole place black—displayed the tobacco in white *Japanese bowls* in the window, as if you could pour milk on it and eat it with a spoon. And he'd had some heady blends, 'Owl', Iz's favorite, so stuffed with latakia and yenidje it was like imbibing all the bonfires of youth; reliving every piquant dish or afternoon . . . 'Forest', MacK's—a strange quality of the past, of corks, of wood. Light on leaves, veins of the natural world—with a little *salt*, of adventure, of Stevenson? The incense of several days on which you fell in love. Then there'd been a problem about it ten years ago, suddenly stopped making it, MacK reported to Iz one Saturday—Izzy flew into a rage and *took a cab* there and demanded to know why his friend's favorite tobacco should have been withdrawn—course he should be smoking 'Owl' anyway—but yelling mit scrimming at the poor guy, who still saw himself as doing a *service to all mankind* (though this was to transmute to something quite other)—Izzy had him backed into a corner behind his antique cash register, the motherf***ing *chess set*—when the little guy let out with the incongruity *Most of the people who smoke 'Forest' are no longer with us!* —Gee Whizz said Iz, maybe this is MacK's problem too, though you don't expect to find yourself among the bills of mortality of your favorite tobacconist's. What I mean, you'd be still standing there, hearing about it. Or would you. There was a customer in there on Saturday mornings in the 1970s who had no larynx, but when you're in your twenties you just think—*weird*. And when you're in the West 40s.

## The Epicure Pipe Shop

The tobacconist *Seligman* was never quite happy to see Isidor enter his premises—though he could never quite remember why—at least without his friend, the one with the glasses. The one who used to go on and on and *on* about the yellowing pictures of radio stars in black frames in the Wilbur Sisters, those insane old bitches. *F\*\*\* Madison Avenue*, thought Seligman, why I have ten times the panache they do. Or, did. Wait, I have panache still, *I have panache* he was saying to himself as Isidor came in and up to the counter. Couldn't quite remember why this man—*Good afternoon, Sir*—big smile.

But Isidor found himself capable only of *glowering* for the nonce, glowering at the jars, the pipes *in their little holders*—everything's so *dusted* here, so f\*\*\*ing funereal, he . . . *said*—! —Our customers like a clean shop Sir, smiled Seligman—as to *funereal* I'm sure I don't know what you mean. Issey Miyake and all the Japanese designers use black extensively. How can I help you today? —Yeah, said Izzy, narrowing his eyes and pursing his lips ever so slightly before he could help it in a horrifyingly exact *impersonation of Seligman*—let me have eight ounces of 'Forest'. —!— Seligman remembered Iz now to be sure—and was torn between feigning ignorance of their past, the long past he shared with this customer of his—and saying *I thought I told you*—. —'Forest'! shouted Izzy—make with it! —We don't get much call for that particular blend any more, *Sir*, said Seligman, deciding to stonewall. —How about you make me up a batch special? said Iz—and then smoke it yourself? —I'm afraid I don't—what? said Seligman, who'd been threatened, aside from all the people on the BMT, who he felt hated him, only by one stray unsure robber, who'd got away with $50 and a jar of perique, which Seligman found returned on the doorstep of the shop the next morning—a note:

## TOO STRONG!

Iz was again glowering at the rows of pipes, lurching and looming threateningly over the small glass case of meerschaums and cal- abashes—and sat down suddenly in the black director's chair where Seligman had used to play chess. —Listen, are you all right? said Seligman, can I get you . . .? —He's dead, or almost, said Iz. —With the *glasses!?* said Seligman—the man with the glasses had been his only protection against *this* man, whose name he . . . —He smoked 'Forest', said Izzy. That is, until you took it off the market. He phoned me this morning. —I'm very sorry, said Seligman, in a tone which, even though prissy, Isidor remarked in his distress as the first *genuine thing* Seligman had ever said. —Perhaps there's time for good news yet? —*Nah*, snapped Iz, leaning his head on the glass case which I have done with Windex just this *minute*, thought Seligman—but restrained himself. Customer in trouble.

Of course many have died—not all from my tabacs, thought Seligman—some quit, some left, some had HEART DISEASE FROM BIRTH—for this he steadfastly refused to take any blame—cancer was more than enough fuel for his sleepless nights with that damnable WQXR and the *Oxford Book of Chess*, he thought. —You're not intoxi- cated, are you? he said suddenly—he hated drunks, and this man . . . —Not in the way you mean, said Isidor, suddenly raising his head from the glass surface, where, Seligman noted, there was a MARK. —You ever hear of naga? —I don't believe so, said Seligman—was this to be a calm conversation, suddenly, he thought—is it an African tobacco? —It's not tobacco, said Isidor—*it* smokes *you*, pal. —You're on this? —Forget about it, said Iz. —Coffee? —!

These two were sad. They were sad and would be drawn together today through the various sadnesses of tobacco. (Together they make quite an emotional pair—Seligman and Katz—it sounds almost like a plausible business—the demonstrative, intuitive Katz, the prissy, exacting Seligman. But they never would have agreed on what to sell, not pipes, not *books*, Seligman couldn't even *spell*.)

There are *obvious* sadnesses to tobacco and some which aren't so—sitting there in the shop the whole kaboodle of them ran parallel through Seligman and Iz—they sipped at black bitter coffee—what else would the tobacconist brew on his dirty hotplate behind the case of jars?—coffee black as the placards he'd had made describing his *philosophy*—thanks a lot—THIS IS THE KIND OF PIPE I WILL NOT SELL—*okay*—blah blah blah—black as his turtlenecks of yore, his droopy *moustache* of yore—black and oily as the latakia squinting at them from the jar of 'Owl', as the *feijoada completa* three doors down—it was black.

—People can't smoke as much as they once could, opened Seligman. —Oh? Noticed that have you? —Well I mean, the air is dirtier than it once was . . . Mr? . . . —Iz. —Than it still is? —No, *Iz*—for Isidor. —Isidor. There's also a lot more background radiation. —So? —So everyone gets cancer more easily—that's what's put a dent in our business. —A *dent?*—in your—? —If everything else was clean like it was a hundred years ago you could smoke all the time and nothing would happen—it's my theory.

The long ribbon-cut leaf of sadness running through Seligman and Izzy at the moment was the *nostalgie nicotine*—even though both had grown up in New Jersey they ashamedly longed for the Edwardian era, gas-lit obsequiousness, the beginnings of the idea of *infinite choice*—a blend for every moment—all this masculine bullshit which later went *completely haywire*. A thousand elegant pipe shops, cigar emporia—Gibson girls in basements rolling Egyptian cigarettes, kissing them closed—for long hours.

Isidor burst out: —What I want to know is, what is this f***ing plant doing on earth if it is not for our delectation? It's no good for anything else. The flowers are pale, though they do look good in line drawings—I've sold some plates. Why the f*** is it here?

—They make an insecticide from it, said Seligman, who had absorbed the usual knowledge. —F*** bugs, said Iz—here's what's funny—I've been doing some thinking about it—every single *commodity* that's half way wonderful, by which I mean, FOREIGN TO

HONKIES, who, let's face it, have *nothing*, went through more or less the same thing: a guy SAILS somewhere, he finds NATIVES, they're USING SOMETHING, it's coconut, it's pepper, it's sugar, mace, tea, tobacco—the guy says THIS IS GREAT!!! He BRINGS IT BACK TO HONKYLAND. Jumps off the boat and rushes over to the castle to show it to the KING. King tries it out, thinks GREAT!!! —kings like everything—you imagine that? What a great thing it truly is to be a *King*, people bringing you amazing stuff all the time? —I number several Dukes among my customers, said Seligman. —That's *buying*, said Iz, I'm talking about the amount of *stuff* you get every day, in *vans*, when you're a KING. So anyway the *thing* it becomes a fashion, then a *rage*—everyone's using it—they're trying it out for *everything*—there were people brushing their *teeth* with tobacco at the French court. They start using what-you-may-call-it for medicine, too—but then they go CRAZY, it starts to create an economic hole, besides destroying the poor little place where they grow it—the grey eminences think it's a BAD THING, we have to *regulate*—and then they *tax* it, that is how they show their revulsion—it becomes an *outlaw thing*, a ROGUE COMMODITY—look what happened to sugar—simple enough—when you and I were kids. Look at pepper—you have to go to 6th Street, skulk around, I had to *leave Manhattan* today to get my soft tissues properly insulted. —What? said Seligman. —*Coffee,* said Isidor—*bad* for you now, no, can't have *that*—so in the end we're to be left with what our race—*Broadly speaking*, cut in Seligman—yeah, what our race had in the beginning: beer, and *bere*—and matzobrei—all stuff made from stupid *grains*, stuff around the Iron Age farmyard—it's enough to make you *weep*—we tried everything, said Isidor, throughout history, to get a little zip in our mouths, our lives—but no. I'll tell you this for nothing: we all die. I'd rather die having had a decent cigar and a curry than have had my taste buds smothered by the BIG MATZOBREI since birth. —What do you mean, *matzobrei?* said Seligman. —I've had enough shit sitting on my face, said Isidor, if you know what I mean.

—Possibly, said Seligman, who was squeamish.

—On the other hand, said Iz with hostility, MY FRIEND IS GOING TO DIE FROM SMOKING. So the court physicians in their wigs have the last laugh, think of it—those *frogs* in their *brocades*? How can *they* be right about anything? What are *you* doing, Seligman? Isidor glowered at the racks and jars. Why are you doing this? How do you feel about killing your customers?—it'd bother me.

(Door opened and a guy in a suit came in. Seligman gave him his usual conversation—while he measured the guy's 6 oz. of 'Nostalgie'—an odd concoction of obsequious enquiry and shared smugness, as though he'd run into this guy *later*—as if anyone even thinks much about what they smoke—aside from Seligman and Iz—they're just doing it, aren't they?—the tobacconist doggedly saw his customer to the door.)

—All your customers like that? said Iz, who was hardly ever in the shop with others—how few there were, really. —Most of them, said Seligman—once they get all that snow white hair, I just think, *whew*. Izzy opened his mouth at this. —I'll tell *you* something, though, said Seligman, this whole city has gone to the dogs. —What! said Isidor—*really?* —Don't act so astonished, said the tobacconist. —I'm not, you *ass*. —Oh. Well, let me finish. Do you *know* why the city has gone to the dogs? —No, said Iz impatiently. —It's because of *that man*, who was just in here, said Seligman. —So-o-o, said Izzy, that's him? *That's* the guy who ruined New York. —Not him in particular, Sir, Mr—*Izz*, said Seligman—I mean them. All of them. THEM! —*Who?* —The Yalies, said Seligman—all these *men* who walk around in suits all day and treat me like some kind of person from New Jersey—*Which*, interrupted Iz, *you very deeply are*—Yes, said Seligman, though I am not from New Jersey in that *way*—I mean all these . . . *men* . . . who *take the train*. —You're being incoherent, said Isidor. —I can't be any plainer about it, said the tobacconist—Yalies who live in Connecticut and take the train in here and make too much money and who switched to cigars from their pipes ten years ago. —So that's it, said Izzy. —You think this isn't a tough business? said Seligman. —I think it's always tough being a JIVE-ASS MOTHERF***ER, said Iz. —Listen, you like coming in here to buy my things, said Seligman, let me tell you. —So? —Those cock-sucking Wilbur Sisters almost put me out of business ten years ago. —I won't stand for this, said Isidor, those sweet old . . . —Sweet my eye, said Seligman, they teamed up with that fellow Nachtkapp, from *Vermont*.

(The name of *Vermont* strikes terror and nausea into all the retailers of this our town—its inextinguishable *cachet*, the fact that anything from *Vermont* can be sold in New York for over $3,000, the citizenry's idea that you can get in your car and shoot up the Taconic and acquire wood and wool products uniquely manipulated, books never seen or even whispered in the catalogues of the Public Library or Columbia.)

Iz remembered Nachtkapp, a hulking round-shouldered invader, a guy from *Vermont* who as a woodworker was inventive maybe but who could not shake the hippie dust off himself, the aroma of sandals and soap and candles and BRATTLEBORO out of his clothing and hair and beard. (MacK and Iz examining his wares: *Ponytail alert*, MacK had breathed.) He set up a shop off Fifth Avenue with his Hobbitish pipes and a range of undistinguished wholesale blends, until he cemented a deal with the Wilbur Sisters. —Probably had to *sleep* with them to get those recipes, brooded Seligman, up at his window regarding the passers by on West 46th hungrily. Obviously the whole thing had upset Seligman, who'd made a bid to be the pre-eminent, even the only modern pipe designer in North America—he'd gone out into the woods—*Seligman in the woods!*—how deeply troubling it was too, Pennsylvania somewhere, to find a couple of biddable brother cretins, woodturners out of *Grimm's* who might do what he wanted—the whole project took on Ruskinian overtones—and then this enormous hippie blows into town in his hippie van and somehow got a plushier little shop and all this—boo hoo—attention. There'd been no course but retaliation, Seligman telling his customers that Nachtkapp's pipes were—'not *fine*'—as only Seligman and the legion of purveyors of the exclusive in New York can pronounce the word.

To see Seligman's eye crinkle and sneer when he uses the word *fine*. In fact a customer of his once suffered a very *fine* testicular injury when one of Nachtkapp's Tolkienesque creations suddenly burst and precipitated a firefall of 'Balkan Sobranie' onto his lap. Seligman visited the burnt fellow in the hospital, bringing him tobacco and grapes, and then started telling the story around—*one of my better customers was emasculated by a Nachtkapp pipe.*

—I had to *fight* 'im, *I had to get 'im good*, said Seligman, looking out the window, sounding more Jersey than previously. —How'd you—? —Oh, I don't know, *specials*, that's the main thing, said Seligman. —*Specials!?* —Yeah, sales and things—you know. —Oh *very* ruthless, said Isidor, remembering how he'd been prevented from buying any books upstate for months by a dealer who'd spread the word all around Dutchess County that Izzy had *leprosy*. But Seligman had really been able to cancel out Nachtkapp's *claims to fineness*, just by word of mouth, among the smokers left in New York. *Mouth trouble.* He bruited the word *fine* around so much that it became his own; the Wilbur Sisters had never thought of using it, running a *country store* as they essentially did; Nachtkapp was caught with his tie-dyed pants down using the word *distinguished* which sounds like something the *luggage* trade might use; the Dunhills were off in their upholstered humidor doing god knows what. (MacK had once drawn a chilly parallel, Iz remembered, between the Dunhill humidor, Steinway Hall and the Frank E Campbell Funeral Home. Isidor had insisted it was merely a mahogany problem.)

—Nachtkapp got very nervous at his drill-press perhaps, but within a year a lot of his bowls had burnt through, if you take my meaning, said Seligman. —Where'd he go? said Izzy. —*Vermont*, said Seligman, suddenly hooting with laughter as if it were the funniest answer on earth. —No listen, he said, there's no business in this any more. But I got mad, mad at myself partly, but mad—like I said I got to feeling everyone's hair turn white, and then all the people smoking 'Forest' started to croak, and all these gentlemen

251

who were coming to me got more and more money and they were meaner and meaner. —*Mean* to you? said Iz. —*Yes*, said Seligman—so I thought, you ass *holes*, I'm going to hang in here and see you out. I'm going to keep selling you this stuff and if it kills you so much the better. I'm going to *taper off*, myself, and I'm going to advise moderation in such a way that it will fire them to smoke more and more, and I'm going to rid the streets of Yalies. —Listen, said Isidor, my friend is not a *Yalie*. You've killed your own tovarich. What is all this Yale anyways? —It's just my *name* for them, said Seligman, Yale doesn't produce quite enough people to cause all this *wanton destruction* of the city. But they started it. —Have you ever *seen* New Haven? said Izzy. —God no, said Seligman.

# The Epicure Pipe Shop

Let me tell you something, Mr—? —Katz, said Isidor. —Katz, said Seligman, that reminds me I have to feed . . . —But *Iz.* —Anyway, it's the triumph of the rentiers, *Iz*, said Seligman, all over again. —What! said Isidor—you're a Marxist? —Certainly, Sir. —*A Marxist tobacconist.* —Yes (in the precise tone which had ruined Nachtkapp). —Gee *Whizz* there aren't even any Marxists in the *book* business any more—I can't believe I'm hearing this, the *rentiers.* —I came to New York in 1964, said Seligman—you ought to have seen it. —I went to the Fair, said Izzy. —Ah, the Fair—what a riot of capitalist waste matter—great—but the whole town was just bursting with fun, said Seligman. —Marxist fun? —*All* kinds (severely). But you know who ruined New York besides the thousands of faceless Yalie rentiers, was the *Presidents*—Carter started in on the credit cards, shaming people out of their very necessary lunchtime martinis . . . —You're defending martinis? —*Yes*. No one out *there* understands the pressures on a New York businessman. —You're a martini Marxist. —Yes—of course Ford, drop dead, all that, then you wind up with Reagan, the *one man* in the whole country who was *totally unqualified* to be President, and his calabash—excuse me, *cabal*—of industrialists and spooks up the wazoo—Seligman was beginning to smolder with his theme like a pipeful of 'Nostalgie'—and then Bush who took Eisenhower's *warning* about the Military-Industrial complex and said *Listen, this sounds kinda good, we're going to go with this.* And of course, said Seligman, it benefited no one in New York, most of that corrupt Republican economy is conducted and coffered out in the god damned *West*, Texas, California—*Florida*—he lost heart for a moment—anyway Mr Katz I have perhaps said too much. —You left out Nixon, said Isidor, Nixon didn't do the city any good. —*No!*, said Seligman, won't hear a word against Nixon. Practiced law for a long time in New York—he *contributed*. A marvelous pipe man, Sir—he came in here once out of curiosity. He used to play the piano. —What piano? said Iz . . . well at least you had a hand in doing him in. Alger Hiss used to buy a lot of sickly Cavendish from that guy on Fourth Avenue but that doesn't mean . . .

—*Yes*, who knows, said Seligman. The mutual embarrassment of a protracted political discussion descended. —Look around, said Seligman—it's all class war now. I can't walk down the street without getting yelled at—it wasn't like that in 1964. —Maybe the moustache, said Isidor suddenly—I've never liked it. —Ha, said Seligman, what do you . . . really? Isidor was getting a little steamed now, thinking again how much 'Forest' this idiotically-moustachio'd *Marxist* for God's sake had pushed across the counter into MacK's tissues. —I've always had the same moustache, said Seligman, since I moved into the same apartment—always had the same wife. We got married when we were in design school. I used to sit with her in the kitchen window, looking out. I used to say to her, *I love this city*—before I meant it. It was part of trying to love her. Then I came really to love her, and really to love the city, and then you stop having to look out at the lights and say that. —Very moving, said Iz—your wife a Marxist too? —No, said the tobacconist (the equivalent of the pointed little *yes*, being pronounced *neau*) *neau*, she's a craftsperson. She makes latkes.

—That's handy, said Isidor.

—She'd like me at home now—it seems odd to be looking at retirement when you're in this kind of business—you tend to think of yourself as a little institution of some kind. But for now, Mr Katz, I'm going to keep opening the shop—the word!—my *father* kept a shop—and looking through the obits for my customers. Listen, I want to say that I am very sorry about your friend—but that was 'Forest' trouble and there's nothing I can do about it. Do you think your friend's obituary will be in the *Times?* —Why do you ask me that, said Izzy—how the f*** do I know, you're the *second* guy who's—

The sun came in now at a low angle, just the way it does to show all the shopkeepers of midtown, at least the ones on the north side of the cross streets, that they might go home. It came across the bowls of yenidje and latakia and Virginia and across Seligman's handsome proclamations. WHO TOLD YOU TO SMOKE ALL DAY? —Is there anything I can do for you, Mr Katz? *Autonomically*, it later developed, Izzy asked for 4 oz of 'Owl' and while Seligman fussed with the jar and the scales in the way he'd been doing since 1968, with some slightly loopy, theatrical flourishes he'd convinced himself were Dickensian or *Dunhilllike* Isidor selected a straight-grain billiard from the wall, and picked out a new pipe tool.

—Hey, here's my *American Express*, said Isidor pointedly—guess you don't have a problem with that. —None what so *ever*, said Seligman. He put everything in one of his large grey envelopes (as a Marxist Seligman had always abjured little shopping bags with handles), the shop's trademark—he also used them for mailing latkes to relatives—and dropped in a box of matches—the *staggering largesse* of the guy, thought Isidor, he hasn't given me matches for *ten years*—but it was a sign Seligman had enjoyed talking to Isidor for the first time *ever*. —How'd you know I needed those? said Izzy. Seligman smiled sarcastically. —Sir, it is my business to know these things. Izzy didn't know what to say. Took his big grey envelope which is awkward to carry and won't fit in one's briefcase either and heading toward the door ejaculated an !OKAY!, the friendliness of which startled both of them. The door—its fussy little shopkeeper's bell rang—perhaps for the last time—after all, he'd never have a conversation like that again with *Seligman*. The Unabomber of midtown!

—Smoke judiciously, Mr Katz, said Seligman.


# On the Avenue

Passed the U.B. Rest. now without registering any insinuations of *feijoada*—the avenue ahead was bright and loud and looked appealing—the minutes he'd spent in Seligman's shop seemed like a dark return to some large struggle of the past—like he'd gone and sat in a scene from a very old movie, a painting maybe—or gone to sit in a small family mausoleum, thinking things over, yes. Seligman's *Yes*. A dark scene in a dark shop from a dark movie.

In truth: visiting Seligman—whatever mood the tobacconist was in—always depressed Izzy because he caught an unpleasant breeze of possibility from his own life. Isidor's father kept still a small haberdashery—Isidor could not dissociate his father's shop—its *shopness*—from other shops—which is one reason why he often said something rude, loud, funny, or provocative as soon as he entered a shop of any kind—MAKE A NOISE. It hadn't worked so well at Lord and Taylor last Christmas—rather hard to be entering there through all the umbrella'd throng from Fifth—they didn't know Isidor of course—they didn't take his point—just thought he was a nut who'd got stuck in the vestibule like all the others—he *staggered*—toward the Clinique—threw him out and now he can't even walk on the same side of the *street* as Lord and Taylor. Isidor feared he might wake up one day and find himself the proprietor of the haberdashery, struggling with steam and enamel, the Old World—nothing so airy and light as his book shop, with its upright, individually priced *palpable thoughts*, which can bear him away to anything at any moment—a guy who is wanting to adjust his scarf, turn up the collar of his overcoat as it were, in the chill of a little life he had escaped.

Turned right on Fifth and found himself in a small whirl of associations with MacK—Isidor could feel the RCA Building pulling at his back—MacK's electric office in there somewhere, radiating—felt a pull to the left, to the McAnn's toward Vanderbilt, where you go way downstairs—Vanderbilt!, Gee Whizz—at that moment MacK and Tumbleson were—but after all. Went to head more or less downtown now, get the news, *f\*\*\*!* he exclaimed aloud. Nearly at 42nd now, busy and benign today in a Vincent Youmans kind of way—Izzy stopped to take a look in the window of Nat Sherman, in a kind of knee-jerk of smoking desire, or familiarity—but conscious that Seligman didn't even admit Nat into the *pantheon nicotea*—brightly colored cigarettes, some pretty ugly pipes, accessories that would ream-n-kleen Alfred Dunhill in his grave—*what a f\*\*\*ing tragedy*, Isidor said, aloud, shaking his head, then rushing across 42nd.

The Seligman problems hung over Izzy and the only place he could escape the breath of haberdashery or keeping a shop where claustrophobia is sold in small amounts was to hurry up the steps to the library. *Need books.* Entered as he always did exactly under the name TILDEN, the only one he liked, and scurried across the huge marble lobby before it could be filled with roaring torrents of deep green water—his frequent nightmare.

## Books and Manuscripts

It is Isidor noticing the various stains of the Berg Collection. Mr Playfair had never dealt in mss, being *physically afraid of them*—one reason why Bibulo & Schenkler wasn't an all-rounder of antiquarianship. Mr Playfair thought books much healthier, as they were white things in general, including lots of nice antiseptic ink—he used to fill his bedroom with paperbacks when he had influenza—the idea that in handling a ms you might touch some tobacco ash of Hammett or the vomity spittle of Fitzgerald, however dried, gave him palpitations.

—This is a good thing to do after lunch in New York, said Isidor, aloud—the guard in the middle of the Berg Room immediately caught his eye—Iz held it and continued—perpetuate someone else's neurosis. And smiled—this somehow seemed an acceptable comment to the guard—as if addressed to him—and he let go Isidor's eyeballs with an Official Warning.

The stains recalled the whole trial of literary effort in a particularly awful way—what the words didn't say the residues of coffee, wine and tobacco told—on blue air-mail tissues, the corners pinholed. There was lots of violet ink, violent scrawl and stink: Kerouac's rainbow pads from the corner markets of the road, Auden's economic ledger sheets . . . —Really it's all business here, said Isidor, that's what *I* think. *Sending the third draft of—don't know if you can use—Dear Mr Moss—can't be in America for a year or two.* News print and yellow news print banged and harangued on: Delmore Schwartz apparently had a problem with his ribbon. Red invaded black and built his sorrow. —This was the Golden Age of Typewriting, said Isidor, and of I Will Gladly Pay You Tomorrow—the guard again—wasn't it? A question in the guy's eyes and again an almost imperceptible acknowledgment that he was not going to caution or exclude Isidor, who went out into the big hall now, muttering. —You notice how all those guys wrote their letters on one side? They knew their shit would be pinned up in here like butterflies.

Quickly down the hall to one of the better places to howl while you piss in midtown; but it's no place to make a phone call. Iz decided to let Miss Plein prove herself this afternoon. —What emergencies, after all, crop up in my profession? A chapped morocco binding cries out for 'Fortificuir?' Man at the door with a delivery of silverfish?

# On the Avenue

Isidor headed in his natural direction, down Fifth, moving south-ward—pausing at the corners only as sensibly as anyone else—diminishing rapidly and becoming an ant along with the rest of them by the time he shouldered by Empire—which looked rather upright, stiff and presentable today, not *drooping* like it sometimes does. You couldn't have seen much of what Izzy was thinking now, but as he walked under the canopy—when is this f***ing thing going to get fixed, *finally fixed?*—and wondered as usual why the EMPIRE STATE BUILDING has *discount drug stores* in its clay feet—he noticed a certain aluminum gleam to Empire's sides which seemed like modern light-weight coffins. Now he had to go down and see MacK—he didn't like feeling that head-ing downtown had anything to do with death—but perhaps it was just looking at the poets' letters—thought suddenly with a pain that MacK was in the habit of wearing lots of *dead people's clothes*—from Mrs Leninsky's family—his own uncle even—and he fretted that MacK had caught something from a garment like that. —But, said Isidor at the corner of 29th, as he hurried toward the all-important corner, you don't just throw away a *Pendleton shirt*.

# The Hour

Dim street lights and shaded lamps in apartments in the Village. Steadiness filtered from the modest lighting of old; lamps which have comforted MacK for many years. Soft lighting of the stair in Grant's Tomb, the cloakroom of the Music Hall, the gently coffered, mortuary ceiling of the *old* lobby of the Museum of Modern Art—architects have got to go—like the underbelly of the RCA Building's canopy which mothers MacK from rain and snow when he arrives at work.

There was a soothing city once, MacK thought—a courtly city—lobbies and foyers, though Granolithic, used to welcome you before they became sterile and official and ignored—the vast lobby of The Wynd had since the 1950s acquired all the warmth of the Staten Island Ferry Terminal—he often expected the Last Boat gong to sound when crossing it at night.

Incredibly, a truly comfortable and unknowingly welcoming bar has survived in this our town—or it has been nudged back into comfortability, down here around . . . such-and-such a street. No further triangulation—this can't be shared with you.

Somehow this soft thing managed to survive, like a pretty kitten with a red ribbon fallen onto the tracks of the IRT. You don't want to know *how*. You just worry how long it will be before it is splattered all over the News. You just stand there worrying.

So I have not yet done for The Hour, thought the *Grim Reaper*. Its doorway is set slyly into a stocky building of the 1920s, which, upperly, attempts grace, and flanked by two round lamps glowing like portholes. I have not cursed and closed this place, thought the Grim Reaper, because Isidor and I tend to drink at Isidor's when here in Isidor's neighborhood; I have saved this place for the odd occasion when Isidor feels a need to flee his tower; when he has been thrown out by his *Nuse*; hounded out by the cat.

The exchange, thought MacK the Reaper, the Big Talk, to happen in this soft place, in just a little while. Almost like talking about it at one of the aforementioned tombs, or in the Pillow Bank. But The Hour was not open yet—who IS it that decides when the public needs a drink? HAH?—and anyway MacK was early and anyway it would have been—not sacrilege, but at least disrespectful in the ordinary way—to enter without Isidor. So MacK took a spin around several surrounding blocks, wishing to empty his skull so that the time in The Hour would be

## THE MOST MEANINGFUL MARTINI
## IN THE WORLD.

Memorable—at least to Isidor, who it seemed would be staying alive in order to remember things.

Up the street, a flicker of the Seventies—a brick and tile façade behind which had lived a pair of art students, best friends of his college girl, the one who left him confused for many years about the meaning of himself. Prevented from becoming this or that socially useful item, MacK thought, I became *the most well-known useless person in America*. Discovering his true vocation had been denied him by his carousel of distractions and ladies, none of whom except the beautiful possible Olive would have had it in her to accept any kind of self-discovery once the bales of NBC cash were a permanent part of the landscape of his apartment. But this is no way to clear the head.

Some years ago MacK would blunder through the Village, unaware of its treasures, after the *Mary Murray* bundled him safely back on to Manhattan. He would seek the horizontal copper lights of the midtown evening, and Tumbleson, play at that futile error.

Walked past the worst deli in the world, so bad that this is the exact spot where his argument about having food prepared for you falls down dead. Isidor always refused to acquire a sandwich here before stepping on a subway for the Yankees. —You have to be very careful about mayonnaise, he would say. —A whole sandwich could go off in half an hour? said MacK, knowing it was no use. But Isidor's *countermeasure* was to buy a sandwich *near* the Yankees, in one of those places that sell corn popped in Indianapolis—more than once he left the sunny stands after one of these subs and a paper pail of beer to puke and puke in the stadium's bowel. —Do you really think the Yankees themselves clean all the food preparation surfaces in the neighborhood? said MacK. —Well yes I do, said Isidor. —There's something more at work here than mayonnaise.

MacK lurched at the thought of food, imagining that soon all he would be able to swallow would be some kind of foamy pink fodder.

He was surprised that so much had happened to him in the Village. Time piles and piles things up. He was annoyed at anything that had not to do with Isidor.

Here was the dry cleaner who had offered to clean and hand-press a shirt for MacK, in a leaving-town agony once before an affiliates meeting. Two hours later the man proudly showed his handiwork. The shirt was in a glory. There wasn't a wrinkle on it nor anywhere *near* it. Noble on its hanger, sporting a little ascot of tissue paper which puffed up its throat like a proud bird's. What is more, it seemed no wrinkle *could* be put in the shirt. MacK wore it indelibly for three days through the entire meeting and then on to fishing in the Sand Counties with Red, who was bug bit and testy. In a fairy tale moment, a fish MacK caught gaped and swallowed at him, in his hands, as if pregnant with MESSAGE and then whipped MacK in the chest with its tail and died. From that moment the charm the dry cleaner had put on the shirt evanesced—the shirt became stained, wrinkled, odorous; it displayed suddenly everything that had happened to it in five days of conventioneering, wading and being unfaithful with a bait shop girl while Red slept petulant.

Now of course you could always walk up 8th for a guilty, quick—NO A PERFECTLY INNOCENT AND CITIZENLY, INNOCENT PARTY STARE in a certain shop-window of interest. So he did so. The meek passing by were *unaware of the torrents of filth raging in the famous yet modestly dressed man,* he thought. Guy has a right to look in a shop-window. Could be anybody. Could be for any of a hundred reasons after all, although always disgusted at the idea of being taken for a she-male, yuck-O. Afraid always of a repeat of the Pine Street bulless who happened by here several summers ago, saw MacK gazing at the sexy little things and made a peevish, dramatic *show* of staring at him and then at the shoes, at him and then at the shoes, whirling with her elbows raised in fury and outrage, somebody call the cops, a man is looking at a shoe in a window. But of course as the shrink blessedly said, *that's about HER fears, isn't it?* O clever shrink. Some nice ones here, red calf with dainty ankle straps, about six inches—but as he admired, with all the practiced nonchalance he could summon, MacK felt a small funeral within. It was the funeral of TINSEL. Found himself profoundly shocked at how NEEDLESS it would be to have to lever someone like the beautiful possible Olive into these; if one were in a position to *ask* this, one would obviously have love, *really love*, and what would be the need? MacK breathed out to see if it was the season of locomotive steam yet. Not quite. Breathed in to see if it were the season of crackling. No. And there in the distance was Isidor.

This moment was always one out of books, a romantic moment to MacK; he couldn't say if it were epic to Iz. The feeling that things will be all right with the world for the next few hours. The Republicans can go hang; you're safe, or if they do press a Button at least you will die in good company. Don't want to die in Macy's or even the RCA Building, thought MacK.

MacK looked back at the window—finding it always unbearable, the last thirty yards to be closed between Isidor and himself—a black pair with extreme louis heels—one or the other usually had a witticism or an observation at the ready.

MacK was once standing in front of a cinema, attending an unusually slow approach of Isidor from Sixth—a hot day—and became aware of something like a puppy tugging or clawing at the tail of his jacket. Discovered a neatly dressed but laughably tiny woman of sixty. —Who is that coming? she said. Who are you waiting for? —Ah, nobody, I mean—what? said MacK. —Is he famous? said the little lady, is he *appearing* here? —Well, yes, appearing, said MacK, but not for, you know. Not for money. It's just someone. *Arriving* really.

—Oh, said the lady, but you looked so expectant, as though you were to greet him . . . *officially*. —Ho ho, said Isidor, rolling up, who's this? —Your biggest fan, said MacK, relinquishing all to the control of the God of Sidewalk Encounters. —I'm very pleased to meet you, to have this moment with you, said Isidor to the tiny, almost *invisible* lady. —I'm a great admirer of yours, said the lady. —Oh? Have you been to my shop? said Isidor. —Shop? said the lady, I don't understand you.

It tailed off into confusion and even bitterness, Iz getting ratty with the lady. The two MEAN MEN fled into the cinema and watched a brutal movie from the 1950s, where the crew-cutted hero *abraded* his way through a lot of dishonesty which smelt of 'Kent' cigarette smoke, and women wearing dress-shields, with his head. He wallowed and thrashed through the heartbreaking seediness mother tried to steer you from in train-stations.

Isidor was closing the last few yards, clocking MacK's position in front of the window. MacK hadn't known what to expect from himself at this moment and panicked, as if Isidor might be snatched from him now. Izzy was attempting to look ironic. So MacK could see there was to be a determination to keep things on the old keel. Which was a relief and infuriating. MacK was suddenly afraid of the evening, having today not thought much about what it would be like. He found himself thinking within a new column for his ledger: women who had given him cigarettes but not themselves.

—I recommend red, said Isidor, pulling up in front of the window. I view this as a positive amenity of my neighborhood. —I'm sure I don't know what you're talking about, said MacK. —How ya doin'? —Do you remember the woman *Vicola?* blurted out MacK. —Sure, said Isidor, What-is-his-name's sister-in-law. You cad. —I spent a very hot summer with that woman, said MacK, *sans* AC or even a refrigerator. We went out to this bar on Broadway every night which had this enormous *fan*. We smoked all their free cigarettes (Isidor's eyes widened at this bold mention of the dirty little engines) night after night, said MacK. She got me going, that was one of my periods. And all that smoking *amounts* to sex, really—there's something streamlining, skeleton-fluorescing about it but we would go home for a grope out of *school*. —Why tell me? said Isidor looking nonplussed. —She was completely mad, said MacK, and rather well-endowed. —Takes one to know one, said Isidor, I mean, ah, the mad . . . what are you saying, it's all *her* fault? And immediately Isidor looked stricken; this was to jump the gun. —No no, said MacK, turning away at last from the pricey *talons*—you just think Why Not? What else is all this about? He felt bad about Isidor and the gun.

So *this* is the guy with the random anecdote, thought Isidor. The footing has yet to be found here. —We could go in and buy a pair each, said Isidor. —She'll think *we* wear them, said MacK—forgetting his stance of ignorance on the subject—that's out. Do you subscribe to the idea that they are a missing snatch or wi-wi? —At *$120 a pair?* said Isidor I think not, Sir. No. —Then what? —I think, Sir, said Isidor, staring off perhaps by chance in the direction of New Jersey, at fourteen one is clammy. I think one is pocked. One is unworthy of meeting the gaze of girls, but still one has simply the need of admiring them, and one finds one can look down, at their choice of adornments there, which one thereafter associates with their charming personalities and little affectations. Their own ideas of beauty or provocation to be found there. And one looks down and down forever. Think about it: the height of your sexual powers is the lowest point of your existence. —Oh.

They then walked in unexpected silence to the closed door of The Hour. Shadows moved upon the blinds. Promise but as yet no cigar. —They open at six? said Iz. So, this is defusing something, he thought. Possibly for the better. They looked at each other, MacK angry at himself for being a little mired still in a useless part of the past. —We could always get a pre-martini beer, said Isidor in his

Joisey accent. We could do whatever the f*** we wanna. We don't
gotta wait around for these jerkoffs. —Okay, said MacK, in some
irritation, feeling in fact a distinct *Lack o' Wanna*, having desired The
Hour to be open now, he and Iz to be the first customers, friendly-
welcomed, everything in readiness. So they would have to circle the
neighborhood as well as the subject.

But the subject won't *wear* a street corner, or a 'forced march', in
Isidor's phrase, even though it is an angry thing, and you do see
people arguing about it on corners; their mission is to defeat it, at
least for the night, give it a lethal injection. That's legal in this state.
That is the method preferred by most of the condemned.

But not so easy—where the hell are they going to go? Isn't *everyone* you see in the streets around this time of the evening looking for
a place to say something important? Isidor said: —Since the unfortunate death of Bradley's, indeed of Bradley himself, one feels little
beck in this quarter. MacK felt a breeze as he turned to look at the
near avenue. —We could walk to the Juniper, he said.

Mutual, stony, sickening awareness. Turned and walked together
toward the problematic place. —I wouldn't worry, it's entirely possible, said Isidor, that we will be too early for all the asses that infest
the Juniper. People like that, even though they're going to spend the
whole night there, are so confident of their infestation, like insects
and their globalization, that they don't observe the rituals of
opening. Indeed, these asses are impervious to pleasure and don't
have any idea of the importance of being the first foot in an expectant and ordered bar. —It can almost be the little death, said MacK.
—Huh, said Isidor. They crossed the avenue and pushed through the
acclaimed, soiled door of the Juniper—shabby, considering who-all
the *Juniper* said had pushed in before you.

—But oh the asses are here, said MacK. Waiting to fan out to all
the *other* bars, perhaps even into The Hour. —Gee *Whizz*, said
Isidor. Like they had shouldered their way into a smoked beehive, or
a cool cave which they were revolted to find lined with bats.

We don't do ourselves any favors, we men, by smoking, by sneering while we drink, nor by scratching ourselves and chewing gum while giving our opinion on an article in the paper to the bartender. It would be well to remember that the bartender reads the paper every day with more attention than you do, which is why he says only

—yuh—

while you kick up the dregs of stupidity; why he stares down at the filling glass. He can't believe YOU'RE here again.

We don't do ourselves any favors by burping and farting and spitting next to each other in the GENTS, in fact they ought to take that sign down. And as for trying to start the *same* tit-bit of conversation with the ureter adjacent—. The Juniper, in all its glory. Don't mean to pick on, of course. Two pints.

*Beer*, on a cool night which anticipated the velvet of gin—Iz and MacK both dead and confined to this *roadside hut on the way to paradise*—if like so many you imagine it as the Taconic Parkway. So the thing closed in, darted at them maybe. Isidor said: —These drinks don't count ya know, simply do not count.

Don't need to tell you they left the Juniper two bubbled furies—floated through the door of The Hour soon after, indeed the first to arrive and in better spirits instanter.

# Martini I

The Hour is a place you almost can't believe in—you sit at the bar with your eyelids flickering, you think someone is about to fling something at you or strike you; someone outside the window is going to shoot you. Isn't this place as softly lit as the cupola of Lenin's Tomb, isn't it about to be invaded by loud people, their music, their ideology? But no.

So they are at last here, considering the spectrum of bar-light, a comforting halo of old-movie and places you have inherited, perhaps where your parents used to go when they were in love. MacK and Isidor said nothing for a few minutes. Things go back and forth between two men while gin settles in. Things *fly* back and forth. The conversation to come lights up in each like a distant town.

—Can't you give us some nuts or something, said Isidor, here we're paying twelve bucks apiece for these drinks you know GOOD HEAVENS. Isidor thought The Hour approached perfection, if not the sublime, but found the staff over familiar—and weirdly reluctant with the snacks. And in the weeks since the *thing* is in some certainty bruited upon MacK—knowing, really—this is the first moment the idea

### HEAVEN

comes to him and he thinks he really has to pick which one it is to be, for as the poet laureate said you will go to the paradise which you *believe* awaits. You can pick it YES YOU CAN.

—I'm going to have blond wood furniture and grey carpeting, said Isidor, intuiting all from MacK's absent expression, and showing that he could speak very naturally on the subject. It's going to be on the upper East Side. Heaven has an exact address. —That's not far, said MacK; he had never considered a *convenient* next life. —Commuting is for asses, said Iz. There's this indirect lighting. —I'll bet, said MacK, thinking that the only source of light in the heaven of Isidor would be from the fire of Hell; that he would have *planned* it that way. —It's a large round salon, straight out of Fred Astaire's bigger hangovers. There are comfortable sofas and next to each sofa is a tall stool, and that's where the waitress sits so you can admire her legs. When she's not bringing you your drink. —Oh? said MacK, feeling Isidor had stolen into his head one night with a flashlight and mask. —Or, said Iz, there are stools they used to have in shoe stores and you sit on the top part and the waitress sits across from you with her feet up on the slanted part and you admire her legs and shoes. You can even tie and untie her ankles. It doesn't matter. The food is all shellfish and Spanish sausages, but it doesn't kill you and there are steamed vegetables for when the saints come around to make sure you're eating healthy and enjoying yourself. MacK considered the scenario and apart from wondering at the idea that Isidor's heaven had authoritarian saints, and if it were quite a good idea to be so specific, he experimented by putting G de B, from American history class in 1967, in it. Boing! Like a charm it worked. —This seems a little decadent, said MacK. —They're not strippers or anything, said Isidor, they're wearing *suits*. —Well it seems okay for a while said MacK but you'd tire of it (thinking he wouldn't.)—No I wouldn't, said Isidor. —Yes you would, said MacK. —No I wouldn't. —Yes you would. —No I wouldn't. —You would too. —No I would not. —HEY! Mr Katz! This from a man who looked totally out of place, ye gods he looked like a *student* or worse. What was he doing in The Hour? Ordering *beer!?* Bah! Iz turned aghast on his stool, you'd think it'd been the voice of his mother. —HEY Mr Katz. How are you? Isidor took in a lot of oxygen in a hurry, a shame. —*I'm fine thank you very much for asking me BUT WE DON'T NEED ANY POEMS TODAY!* And followed this up with a frighteningly piercing gaze MacK didn't think he had ever seen before. Shrivelling of young fellow. —Oh. Oh okay. Okay sorry. He retreated into a semicircular portion of the bar lit with blue lights. It was the children's area.

—You mean this instep thing—you see I do not mince words—to remain your pre-eminent concern for *eternity?* said MacK. —Yes. —Overriding our deep and mutual ministrations to this very drink here—to the bars and restaurants of old—to the mystical smokes? —That's the way it is, said Isidor. He didn't seem very sure. This pissed off MacK and he decided that since this was supposed to be *the* evening in which things, nay, every thing, was had out, he would try for higher ground.

—I go for the intangible, said MacK, it seems safer. I think there must be a heaven only of smokes. —I had a fog one in mind for a while, said Isidor. —Same thing in a way, said MacK, conciliatory, but he went on: one will just be suspended, a taste bud as it were, in the volumes of memory in smoked and smoky things; the world is about to go up in smoke anyway . . . what could be more natural? —This is a little depressing, said Iz. —Not just smoke, said MacK, but extraordinary smoke, smoke that is smoked. Opening a tin of latakia on the first day of October. Every day would be the first day of October. That is a heavenly moment—the oak paneled library where we used to—*You can't smoke there any more*, interjected Isidor, *I checked*—Anyway, said MacK, I could float in that for eternity, or let us say a long time, in the Wordsworth and Chaucer and Keats that latakia smoke contains. —Keats, said Isidor, I don't know . . . —Better than hanging around with a lot of *fetishists*, said MacK. When I am thirsty the trout-brown angels bring me lacquer bowls of lapsang souchong. There is a hint of cigar leaf some days as in the old Sobranie No. 10. —The yellow tin, said Isidor. Puked once after but it was classy. —And when I am hungry, said MacK, they bring me the salmons of Argyll smoked over peat of the Hebrides, and a glass of Laphroaig. And anyway you are *always* puking, so . . . —Hey, I got smoked salmon in *my* heaven, said Iz, *plus* you get girls. Goils mit legs!

Laphroaig, latakia, lapsang . . . all the beautiful possible Ls! thought MacK. Suddenly. One might snuggle, even settle down with Olive before a fire of birch logs, their impossibly white smoke, in some mountain cabin forever away from All This (*this perpetual, annoying belief in escape of those not born in New York*):

When sunlight manages in, it is dappled, our red house, standing in cool churchly dark, alone—we're out days. The wooden furniture cools. The beautiful possible Olive makes flanken and I just sit on my ass. The darkness of the forest here, this elbow in the redwood road, can't be penetrated with my reading lamp. Things over-arch our path home. The dark muscles courage from the fog and the smoke of our fires. The brightest thing is *Schlitz* beaming from the tavern window. Folks are nice to us there. We don't stay late. Weekends we tell stories and watch each other bathe. She feels safe when I build a fire . . . it's cool enough to do so every day. She dries her pretty hair by the hearth, sometimes wafting the smoke my way. Smoke fires me when I take her in my arms. I'm a bear. She thumps. And maleishly not contented with love, I have to spook her. —*O no, I've left the ax outside : on the woodpile : in the dark.*

Smoke and girls, they thought now, gin doing what gin telepathically, clairvoyantically does to two people, could be invited into the idea of a third heaven, the heaven of the restaurants. —This telepathy is really . . . said MacK. —Whew, said Isidor, it's . . .

## Martini II

But here and now in the red aorta of The Hour, their friendship seemed weighted down in the prow by what they were not discussing. Not so much as on the deck of *Titanic,* trying to keep your toes from being sliced by violin strings and your ass out of tubas, but things were canted and MacK and Isidor knew that. Isidor looked out beyond the red lit area toward the blue, where the poet sat all indigo in his surplus jacket with cigarette. —How can anyone drink their beer over there, said Isidor, look what color the foam is. I find that rather lurid. —He's a poet, isn't he? said MacK.

The martinis in The Hour were not of the Caracalla size favored by the bulls of Pine Street, but they weren't of the old Restaurant size either. —What about this, said Isidor, do you realize they have 'smalls'? The boys were insulted to notice a small elegant glass displayed behind the bar, DEMI MARTINI. —If I tip my head like this, said Izzy, things feel better and that glass makes sense. I think I might slow down.

This sitting here should not be ruined by any plunges, MacK thought, I'm not here for an orgy but for quiet love of things. And just enough neck oil. —*Deux demis*, said Isidor to the pup in the white jacket, who was a craftsman without a haircut, as it turned out.

MacK felt a sting of guilt, but it was not a time to suffer this and so he spoke. —I have something to reveal, he said. Isidor started, his eyes widened and he looked ahead at himself in the mirror. —You mean . . .? —No, it's not that, ah gods not yet, said MacK, who'd forgotten for a *second* why they were here. It's that I already had a martini today. Isidor turned to stare at him as if World War II had begun again. —Really, he said. I never heard of anyone doing that ever before. —Well, it *was* in midtown, said MacK, and it *was* the lunch hour and it *was* . . . the Yale Club. —I see. So you're flying, is that it? said Iz. What a place to spend your . . . he didn't finish. —Don't worry, said MacK, it's been . . . sucked out of me. —Good, said Iz.

—Can we get back to heaven for a moment? said MacK. —Where do you think it is that you are? said Iz. —I think really, don't you want to make sure the food is good? said MacK—the delight of leggy company and the comfort of smoke aside, don't we really think it will be a sort of restaurant? Heaven might be a *regular table* and you sit there day upon day. —It's not about gluttony, said Isidor quickly. —Not at all, said MacK, it's about a comfortable seat and a table in front of you for eternity. —See, you always have to have this *table*, said Isidor, you know that? You're always squirming and sweaty when there's nothing to *hide your lap*. —I guess so, said MacK, ignoring this aggression, after all, one will have to eat, drink, smoke and write postcards. For a long time. He thought of his studio in the RCA Building, the comfortable chair, the neat piles of Things to Say, the clock and the controls slanted toward him, *To Network, To Key Stations, Master Control, Standby, Announce, Flag Announce, Telephones 1 2 3 4 5 6 7 8 9, Network News, Presentation Only*, the Neumann microphones in their suspensory which floated so easily into any position. Maybe he could take it with him as a drinks holder? —It's not that, said Isidor, it's that sometimes in your life you have to stand up, use your legs, proclaim your midriff to the world, be seen in total. —Really? said MacK, it hardly seems requisite now. Isidor blushed. —Yeah.

Silence.

271

—You may well be right, resumed Isidor, the white cloths would seem true to judeochristian iconography; the vessels. —We can construct heaven, said MacK boldly. After all, everyone else has. This guy was talking to me on the bus—he started complaining about Scientology, EST, the Forum, B'Hai, the Mormons . . . —Complaining? —Yeah, he said he didn't like 'made-up' religions. And I said *Oh! You think THOSE are the 'made-up' ones?* —What'd he say? —He got off, said MacK. —You silenced him. —He got off, that's all I know, said MacK. —Where? —Church Street. —*HE GOT OFF AT CHURCH STREET!?* shrieked Isidor, who sometimes believed MacK never thought anything out. —Oh.

—So let's *make* with the heavens, said Iz. —I nominate the waiters, the long bar, paneling and chowder from the Tadich Grill in San Francisco, said MacK. —Yes to paneling, said Isidor, but I do not want to spend eternity with those guys. I want the waiters from Gage & Tollner. —Well of course we don't want waiters with *wings*, that is for sure, said MacK. Don't you find it revolting, in religious painting, when you see an angel's back, *where the wings come out?* —Don't get me started, said Isidor. An angel may be a waiter but that doesn't make a waiter an . . . They looked at each other and then simultaneously said: *Paddy's Clam House.* —And why not, said Iz, they're already there, maybe. A Fish Restaurant the model for heaven. —You'd better let me pick the wine, he said nervously. —So? —Sherry-Lehmann's catalogue of 1963, he sighed. —And the cigars? —What are you *talking* about! Isidor barked. THEY'LL HAVE CIGARS!

Then Isidor pictured Seligman wandering marbled halls, wringing his hands and checking on all his killed little businessmen.

—You pick the sunlight, said Isidor. —From Paris. —Done.


This was very embarrassing because here was the thing now almost out in the open. Practically *on the bar*, with the nuts and the stack of napkins. The bar, whereon the man in all the jokes comes in and

plumps a strange machine, or an octopus, or a set of ladies' under-
garments, or a little duck on a fruitcake tin.

So, MacK : —Look it's curtains, really. The guy said. He knows
I don't want to do anything about it, he's pissed off—so that must be
why he was—*brusque*.

(A choke-making word.)

—What he said was that he had to give up and stop counting the
*nodules*. I hate that word. And that was that, as far as *he* was concerned, even though *I* need to've had many, many more women and
less to smoke, possibly that would have been good, said MacK, in a
disorganized way. Was he beginning to feel electrocardiographically
disorganized? —Here I'm going to die without having had enough
sex, said MacK. What everyone dreads.

Isidor glared at his martini. He asked that its best silveriness
emerge now and bless MacK and himself with the most important
quality of the martinis they'd had in Jack Dempsey's, years and years
ago: namely to exist in the past, at least for one moment. Please.
That old-television silveriness that always stopped time. Before. But
of course if you're saying there is a Before, then it never did stop it,
Isidor thought. Very ruefully.

MacK and Isidor had both raised themselves and turned straight-on
to the mirror behind the bar. For the next while they addressed each
other's reflections in the mirror, for face each other they could not.

—Aren't you angry at the smokeables? said Iz, after all, they've
done you in. —My pipe never hurt me, said MacK, it was
cigarettes. One, to be exact. Isidor's eyes bulged out. —One!?
he said, his indignation rising on a number of fronts, *which* one?
—I'm not sure. —Those 'Gauloises' didn't do you a pack of good,
said Isidor. —*Au contraire*, said MacK, they do you just about a
pack of good. —If I were you I'd be completely pissed off, said
Izzy, I'd punch out every smoker and doctor in town. They
collude. I'd want to kill and kill and kill. —*No time*, said MacK.
Which silenced Isidor. —There's literally *no point* in being angry,
I find, because I've lived here. Known you. There have been

many rounds of pleasing drinks. We VOTED together. And I've had a really good microphone at work for the past fifteen years. —What! said Isidor. —You know, the Neumann. —I can't believe I'm hearing this. And MacK felt an awareness of how many times he'd denied things to Isidor, days when they weren't in sync. But these were not many.

—But, see, I'm not going to let you get away with this, said Iz, and he immediately felt like crap again, because he had to; MacK *would* get away. —Hey, man, these little drinks have *reduced the scope of the discussion*, said Izzy.

## Martini III

Brought by the bright boy. —Thank you, bright boy, said Isidor, who meant only to cherish, but felt rude. Let's get to the bottom of this. —Why? said MacK. —So we can *move on*, of course, said Iz. We don't want to talk about this *all night*. Do you want to talk about it all night? MacK felt something askew. He had imagined that after he and Isidor sat down in The Hour that there would quickly come nothing more to be said. He realized he had imagined nothing, no life beyond *his ass* on *this seat*. How stupid. No more talk and therefore no more Isidor, no more Isidor, no more world. As if *Isidor* was going to die. And of course this was all a bit hasty; his carcinomas were obviously not in the business of doing him any favors, but why ought they to kill him in a comfortable bar with his favorite drink and man? No, no, they are far too obtuse for that. So: —No, said MacK, I don't want to talk about it all night.

—*Good*, said Isidor, I just wanted to know how you *feel*, I mean, these things are sent to comfort us, and we embrace them, we embrace them with enthusiasm because they are godsends. And it turns out that months or even years ago these *things*, these compounds *rounded* on you, and now you're—. Think of all that travelling we did on the IRT, *going* to Seligman, *going* to the Wilburs.

I mean, what I want to know is, WHAT IS THIS PLANT FOR? Does *everything* we like have to *kill* us? Loving something, and knowing that love, causes your death? Inevitably? Because time passes and you feel things. Maybe that's the way we all die, thrusting ourselves into the perfect drink, the girl with the highest heels, the best job, the best book. Think about it, said Isidor, you eventually find the best book to read and it *kills you*. You have to *insure that time will pass* by chasing the gods that offer the most. Otherwise you can't be sure that time is going by, and while death will come, he will come merely to throw a blanket over your head and hit you with a frying pan—*Dunnng!* MacK reflected on this. —You never liked the Wilbur girls, he said. —That's not exactly true, said Isidor. I disliked all the pictures. Their famous dead customers. I'm not going to smoke a pipe from some dump just because *Herbert Hoover* did. What does Herbert Hoover know about smoking? —What does he know about *anything?* said MacK. —Metallurgy, said Isidor, since you ask me.

—No—what I have to say to you, said Isidor suddenly, is this. He rose. *O no*, thought MacK. Isidor held up the nobler-sized drink and squinted through it, first at MacK, then with some blurring at the rest of the world. Saw his silver wish come true.

—I always believed, said Isidor, that when our mutual, clownish attempts at quote normal unquote life, I mean our attempts *to mate* had failed, and failed ultimately, that when all the women we have courted and chased all over town totally and finally rejected us *forever*, that we would end up together, I mean sharing a place. That we'd live that long. Of course I have Sylvie now, and the shop. And a cat. But without being superstitious, or disloyal to Sylvie, and to the cat, to my future with them, I still always believed that I would end up on my way to the Battery with you, or McSorley's, or Seligman's. Or I thought we'd finally leave the city *successfully*—don't stop me please I know this is *pure* fantasy—and live on an island in Maine or maybe even become retired FLORIDA GUYS, stranger things have happened. Just two old *guys* who pretend to think. Who carry on

275

with culture. I read the *New York Times* and you drive me crazy with television, and all the stuff you personally *remember* from television. These two cynical old skunks who religiously observe the cocktail hour and you could hear them cackling for hours if you walk by their house on a warm evening. We end up talking like Abbott & Costello. In the local store we're very polite but often giggle. Occasionally some very pretty women come to visit us. Women who like us but can't stand us for more than a WEEK a YEAR.

—There's always lots of bottles, said MacK, but we keep the place up. —That's right, said Isidor, still looking through his drink with one eye. We grow a lot of coriander, capsicum, and hops. —Fag its, said MacK.

Here Isidor caught himself.

—What I want to say is that this STINKS. I reject the idea that LIFE could come to an end just as a simple sum, so many cigarettes, martinis, taxi rides, books, laughs. Nights. I mean to say: if we really are ORGANISMS, then we ought to DIE IN THE FOREST. Biodegrade. We ought to quietly become leaves and granite. Just slough away in soggy blue shreds from the tide pool.

—I thought, said Isidor slowly, the city would save us.

MacK turned away.

The inward movements of friendship.

The world had tipped toward them for an hour.

—So what I'm *saying* is, said Isidor—he reached out toward MacK with his drink—is that this is your cure. *I'm telling you*, you get this down you, you walk out of here no problem. Think about the *Lenni Lenape*, man, I know, I know, Lenny Who? said Iz, heading MacK off at the pass. You know what they used to do when they got poison ivy? —No. —They used to *eat* it. No kidding—they break out in a rash, they don't go for *calamine lotion*, they f***ing CHOMP DOWN on the stuff, they swallow fistfuls of it and Boom. So I say: more to the more. Me and this martini sez you're going nowhere. You're CURED.

Izzy stopped looking at MacK through his martini and took That Sip of it.

MacK turned back to the bar and looked at the olive in its triangular silver cloud. —I'm *cured*, he said. Cured. I'm cured. And off he went to the gents.

—Gee Whizz, said Isidor in a whisper. I get *naga* and the guy *dies*.


—Do you know that in all our fair heavens, said MacK, who looked a little wet on his return, and spoke a little bravely, we included nothing from Sevilla? The boys realized they had included nothing from Sevilla, which does have many heavenly Restaurant and Manhattan qualities.

*The waitering is done in short jackets.*

*There is ice water which tastes like New York.*

*The clams are dirt cheap.*

*There is Tabasco for the steaks.*

*There is Roberto, student of Isidor, beloved of the gods.*

*It is located at the corner of Bedford and Charles.*

You sort out your heaven, but of course it is not here. And they were not men to drink all night any longer, they are reasonably sober, sober reasonable men. One is ill. That Day had come down to This. —What you wanna do? said Isidor, wanna eat? MacK contemplated the pink foam of the future. —Perhaps. —Want to go to Sevilla? —Sure. Or, maybe . . . They both felt the heavy weight of the medical. Felt it here. And here. —It's not so hard, said Iz, just when we finish up here we could walk, you know, right over to Seventh, and then down to Bedford, and boom. MacK flared after staring at a map he was trying to form in his mind with the grid of bottles behind the bar. —Why *Bedford*, he said, you just walk over to Charles and then *down* to Bedford, avoiding Sheridan Square like a good fellow. —Bedford and Charles don't intersect, said Isidor in his most challenging matter-of-fact. —It's located at Bedford and Charles, said MacK. —What are you talking about? said Isidor, there is no such corner. —Look on the matchbook, said MacK, it *says* Bedford *at* Charles. —That's *IMPOSSIBLE, YOU*

*ASS HOLE*, said Isidor loudly and he couldn't believe he said that and neither could the bartender, young Matt, who though lacking intrinsic presence was still the bartender and as such his startled glance at Isidor carried some small authority. Isidor waved at him—Sorry—and burped. *Waaap*. MacK looked at the illuminated bottles. —I didn't come here to be insulted, he said. —I don't think you can be too sure about that, said Isidor apologetically.

Inside: Isidor was angry and bereft. MacK was desolate but it was too at Bedford and Charles.

—It's not 'located' there said Iz. Softly: I'm telling you. After this pause, of anguish, Isidor said: Look at us. We're having our *last fight*.

Got their coats, which had only just shed the cool air of their earlier walk through the neighborhood, and took them through the red and blue areas of cocktail out into the cold. MacK thought: if we go to Sevilla, there will be all that, and this will not be it. But then after Sevilla it will be it, and perhaps that will not be so good as it is freezing and who knows if I will be full of bonhomie as usual after Sevilla or maybe tonight it will just be *the aftermath of beef* and that would be intolerable, that *that* would be it.

—It was a 'Marlboro', said MacK, from that stupid idiot in McAnn's. Or one of the god damn Brits and their god damn 'Silk Cuts', I've almost decided. Isidor looked at him. —Of course it couldn't be one that you *enjoyed*, he said, that would never do, would it?

—No, said MacK. Listen, I don't think Sevilla tonight, he said, looking uptown. —Not hungry? said Isidor quickly, I understand. —It's not that, said MacK, I'm not sure that it *exists* any longer. —Sure it does, said Isidor, looking down. —I'll just go, said MacK. —We could go tomorrow, said Isidor, feeling around in his coat for—? He pulled out a mashed instance of the grey envelope by which

## SELIGMAN

is known in midtown and the various suburbs, and handed it to MacK. —Oh, said MacK looking rather delighted. Inside was a pipe of his favorite billiard shape and a four-ounce pouch of 'Owl'. —The cure, said the shaman Isidor. Neither MacK nor Isidor were *thinking* what this *meant*; it was their old exchange. Because of this, now far from tears, MacK filled the pipe and stood on the curb looking like an overly friendly lamp post. They regarded each other. MacK breathed in, a setting-off-uptown intake. The air in his nose was cold. —Have you ever, he asked Isidor, had a certain, exact hair? A special one that you coddle, a TOY HAIR? That you let grow maybe, while exterminating all the others, on your eyebrow, or ear, or maybe even in your nose? In the morning you can't wait to get out of bed to see how it's doing? And test its springiness?

Isidor looked up and down the street. —Gedaddahere, you crazy nut, he said. He took a few steps away. MacK's smile began to wane and so did his color. Suddenly this was intolerable, they were being pulled apart by two hateful little gods, right there on the street, yanked apart with twice the decisiveness of Mary-Ann and Rosenthal—but half the strength. Isidor turned and walked toward the south. He didn't look back. *These are shoes for a guy who walks.*

MacK stood looking after him. He lighted his pipe—'Owl' never burns very well until it has been breathing New York itself for a few days. He lighted the pipe and, like Early Man bearing fire, carried the flavorful embers of the Old World, of *Isidor*, uptown.

STRANGERS IN BLOOD:
RELOCATING RACE IN THE RENAISSANCE

JEAN E. FEERICK

# Strangers in Blood:

## Relocating Race in the Renaissance

UNIVERSITY OF TORONTO PRESS
Toronto Buffalo London

© University of Toronto Press Incorporated 2010
Toronto  Buffalo  London
www.utppublishing.com
Printed in Canada

ISBN 978-1-4426-4140-2

Printed on acid-free, 100% post-consumer recycled paper
with vegetable-based inks.

**Library and Archives Canada Cataloguing in Publication**

Feerick, Jean E., 1968–
Strangers in blood : relocating race in the Renaissance / Jean E. Feerick.

Includes bibliographical references and index.
ISBN 978-1-4426-4140-2

1. English literature – Early modern, 1500–1700 – History and criticism.
2. Race in literature.   3. Social classes in literature.   4. Blood in
literature.   5. Human skin color in literature.   I. Title.

PR408.R34F44 2010      820.9'355      C2010-902794-9

University of Toronto Press acknowledges the financial assistance to its
publishing program of the Canada Council for the Arts and the Ontario
Arts Council.

**Canada Council** **Conseil des Arts**   **ONTARIO ARTS COUNCIL**
**for the Arts** **du Canada**   **CONSEIL DES ARTS DE L'ONTARIO**

University of Toronto Press acknowledges the financial support of the
Government of Canada through the Canada Book Fund for its publishing
activities.

*For my children, Liam, Sean, and Brynn*

# Contents

# Illustrations

# Acknowledgments

This book has benefitted from the support and feedback of family, friends, and colleagues over many years. It began at the University of Pennsylvania under the excellent guidance of Rebecca Bushnell, Peter Stallybrass, and Phyllis Rackin, without whose mentorship the project never would have reached fruition. I owe them a great debt of thanks for posing questions that would productively resonate across many years. At Penn, I was also fortunate to come under the influence of brilliant mentors – including Margreta de Grazia, Maureen Quilligan, Robert Turner, Sean Keilen, and David Wallace – and an amazing group of graduate students, including Jim Kearney, Jane Degenhardt, Jonna Mackin, Tyler Smith, Erik Simpson, Erika Lin, Jennifer Higginbotham, and Cyrus Mulready. These friendships sustained me then, as they do now.

At Brown University, I was fortunate to have colleagues more generous than I could ever have anticipated, most especially in James Egan and Coppélia Kahn, who read and responded to every word of each draft of this book, but also, at a crucial early stage in reshaping the book's argument, in Leonard Tennenhouse, whose encouragement aided me in significant ways. I am grateful as well to Brown colleagues Bill Keach, Melinda Rabb, Ravit Reichman, Beth Bryan, Stephen Foley, Kevin McLaughlin, Rolland Murray, Philip Gould, Tamar Katz, Virginia Krause, Tara Nummedal, and Esther Whitfield. For Brown's brilliant graduate students – especially Corey McEleney and Jason Zysk, Jacque Wernimont, Laurel Rayburn, and Julia Shaw – I am appreciative and awed. And for institutional backing from Brown in the form of a Faculty Development Fund and the means to accept the William S. Vaughn Visiting Fellowship at Vanderbilt University, I am most grateful.

I owe profound thanks, as well, to my colleagues at Vanderbilt University and the Robert Penn Warren Center for the Humanities for their support of this project in 2005–6, when I was the William S. Vaughn Visiting Fellow, particularly Mona Frederick, Leah Marcus, Holly Tucker, Lynn Enterline, Katherine Crawford, Kathryn Schwarz, Carlos Járuegui, Jonathan Lamb, and Sean Goudie. A more collegial, inspiring, and spirited group could not have been conceivable.

I would like to thank as well the following colleagues in the field of Renaissance studies for their support and inspiration: Amanda Bailey, David Baker, Emily Bartels, Lara Bovilsky, Patricia Cahill, Dympna Callaghan, Sheila Cavanaugh, Mary Floyd-Wilson, Kim Hall, Jean Howard, Karen Kupperman, Kathleen Lynch, Carla Mazzio, Steve Mentz, Hiram Morgan, Barbara Mowat, Vin Nardizzi, Michael Neill, Lena Orlin, Gail Kern Paster, Kristen Poole, Katherine Rowe, Matthew Senior, Gitanjali Shahani, Laurie Shannon, Elizabeth Spiller, Garrett Sullivan, Marjorie Swann, and Roxann Wheeler. My year as a fellow at the McNeil Center for Early American Studies at the University of Pennsylvania was richer for getting to know Dan Richter, Roderick McDonald, Martha Rojas, Hester Blum, and Birte Phleger. And to the many scholars and writers not specifically identified in this list from whom I have learned and by whom I have been inspired, I am honoured to give something in return.

For pushing my interests in the direction of Medieval/Renaissance studies, I would like to thank my incredible mentors at Georgetown University, Joan Holmer and Penn Szittya, whose examples of scholarship and ethics still sustain me. For consolidating this orientation in the direction of early modern Ireland, travel writing, and utopia, I would like to thank John Carey at the University of Oxford. And for ensuring I didn't stray much beyond the circuit of Renaissance scholarship, I thank especially my dear friends at the Folger Shakespeare Library, especially Mary Tonkinson, who imparted to me her profound love for the craft of writing.

For recognizing the merits of this project and for supporting it through publication, I would like to thank my editors at the University of Toronto Press, Suzanne Rancourt and Barbara Porter, as well as the three anonymous readers for the press who pushed me in the best of ways. Heartfelt thanks is due as well to Toronto's typesetter – CAPS and lowercase – for their heroic labours at a crucial time in the book's publication. To Alison Kooistra for last-minute, yet meticulous assistance with the index, I am deeply grateful. Parts of chapters 3 and 4 appeared in *Early American Studies* and *Renaissance Drama,* and I thank the publishers of these journals – the University of Pennsylvania Press and Northwestern University

Press – for their permission to reprint them here. I thank as well the John Carter Brown Library and the Huntington Library for permission to reproduce images from their collections.

Portions of this book have been presented at various forums, and I am particularly grateful for the thoughtful responses of audiences at the Early Modern Center Colloquium at the University of California, Santa Barbara; the Renaissance Colloquium at Yale University; the Shakespearean Studies Seminar at the Harvard Humanities Center; the Group for Early Modern Cultural Studies at Vanderbilt University; and the Inhabiting the Body, Inhabiting the World Conference at the University of North Carolina, Chapel Hill. I would also like to thank the members of the SAA seminar I co-led, 'Shakespeare at the Limits of the Human,' for their dazzling insights. And for opportunities to benefit from the archival holdings of the Folger Shakespeare Library in Washington, DC, and the John Carter Brown Library at Brown University, I thank these institutions and their staffs.

Ultimately, it has been my family and friends who have sustained me through the intense labour involved in writing this book. For friendship and solace, I thank in particular Margaret Houk, Stacey Vitiello, Ann Goings, Kavita Sahrawat, and Raquel Buranosky. And for the unwavering assistance of my children's caregivers, Fatima Zahrane and Cora Padilla, I express my deepest thanks and appreciation; without them, this project would not have been possible. To my siblings and in-laws, for reminding me that there is life beyond the academy, I am grateful for the broader view. My parents, Emalie and John, are the most generous people I have ever known, sharing time and resources without bound. For nurturing the literary, aesthetic, and analytical abilities required of this book, I can never express enough thanks to them. They stepped in amid many a crisis, giving extravagantly of their time, labour, and love.

And, to my husband, Bill, for keeping me anchored with affection and love amid my trials and tribulations, and for reminding me that there is still room for play, I owe much.

I dedicate this book to my three inquisitive children: Liam, Sean, and Brynn. They have effortlessly buoyed my spirits and kept me grounded amid the abstractions of my work; I am grateful for having their company across life's journey.

STRANGERS IN BLOOD:
RELOCATING RACE IN THE RENAISSANCE

# Introduction: Bloodwork

## Racial Dislocations

In the last two decades, critical studies of race, as brought to bear on the English literatures and cultures of the sixteenth and seventeenth centuries, have proliferated amid considerable debate about what it means to posit a modern taxonomy of difference in a period that many would characterize not just as 'early modern' but as 'pre-modern.' Such criticism has questioned if *race* signified as a category for this period, seeking further to name the distinctions of identity it described. If one of the landmark collections of essays on the topic expressed this tentativeness explicitly in its title by marking the term *race* with scare quotes, subsequent engagements have continued to focus on the ways 'racial' identity for the period might approximate modern paradigms.[1] Whereas *race* used to be considered an invention of Enlightenment epistemologies, critics of the early modern period are increasingly discovering traces of its modes and logic in the earlier period of the sixteenth and, especially, seventeenth centuries.[2] That there was 'something like race' in the earlier periods seems to be a consensus. Xenophobia, religious intolerance, and ethnic rivalries often feature in these critical narratives as approximating the racial distinctions that will become normative for modernity. In such accounts *race* is a category that hails outsiders, strangers, and foreigners, peoples, that is, marked by differences of culture, colour, and condition. As such, *ethnos* is the category that studies frequently rely on to illuminate the content of early modern race.

Guided by Michel Foucault's notion of a genealogical history as a method of illuminating past discursive formations, I attempt in this study a different kind of project, one that departs from dominant approaches to race in resisting the temptation to limit the early modern category of race to the concept of ethnos. Crucially, Foucault's theorization of historical analysis seeks to disperse the notion of origin, committing itself instead to the 'dissipation' of linear models of causation and emphasizing the 'discontinuities' that register within and between historical periods.[3] In the previously unpublished lectures that Foucault gave at the College de France in 1974–5, he attempted to use these strategies to think himself into the form of an earlier category of 'race.' Notably, he rejected the idea that race for the earlier period was, in Ann Laura Stoler's words, 'based on the confrontation of alien races' and argued that it was produced instead through a 'bifurcation within Europe's social fabric.'[4] He thereby wrenched the term away from dominant contemporary meanings by narrating how racial thinking erupted from tensions internal to European polities. He identified its connections to the breakdown of long-standing social hierarchies, suggesting how it was used as a powerful political weapon, one that stoked the period's revolutionary sensibilities. That he was challenging guarded beliefs about a general similarity of racial form over time was registered in the negative response his lectures sparked for its immediate audience. And yet, his instinct was, in my view, a good one, insofar as he sought to pry beneath the seemingly stable signifier of *race* in order to identify the different objects it describes and the varying mechanisms through which it operates across time. Pursuing a related project, I seek to identify and explicate moments of discontinuity between early modern racial ideologies and modern ones.[5]·Although critics have increasingly cast suspicion on strict periodizing boundaries for overstating rupture as a model of historical change – as against theories of discursive sedimentation, layering, and rearrangement – most critics nevertheless grant that early modern racial ideologies are not coextensive with modern racial ideologies, that they bear distinctive and even arrestingly different features.[6]

Indeed, turning to the literary texts identified by modern critics to be most implicated in the 'race thinking' of early modern England – plays that have been read to define and instate barriers between 'insiders' and 'outsiders' on the basis of cultural and phenotypical difference – it is compelling to consider how much these texts confound the tendency in modern racial ideologies to emphasize taxonomies of colour. If critics have identified plays like *Othello, Titus Andronicus*, or *Lust's Dominion: or, The Lascivious Queen*, for instance, with instating oppositions rooted in skin colour, what is remarkable about these plays – and many others that might be positioned alongside them – is how insistently they locate the difference of colour in relation to a still more powerful, because more dominant, cultural divide attaching to social station, to the difference of blood. In these plays, differences of colour emerge, as it were, in dialectical relation to social rank, allowing social tensions originating with the difference of rank to be resolved, mitigated, or exploited with reference to this emerging difference of colour. As such, they expose, with uncanny similarities of representational strategy, the social dynamics that enable colour to accrue value as a cultural marker of difference, revealing how its emergence is predicated on and entangled with the decline of a deeply established system of difference that places a metaphysical value on bloodline independent of colour, complexion, or culture. As such, these plays depict the processes that enable disparities of social power to be actively rechannelled into emerging modes of difference. They dramatize the collision of competing systems of difference and suggest the need for thicker accounts of race for this period – studies, that is, that will question not only the singular attachment of this category to taxonomies of colour but its axiomatic connections to ethnos as well.[7]

To pursue these patterns a bit further, we might consider why it is that Moors – to take just one group at the centre of discussions of early modern race – who are represented in drama of the late-sixteenth and early-seventeenth centuries are often figured as royalty or nobility, or, in the case of the less typical lowborn Moor – such as Aaron of *Titus Andronicus* – are marked as social aspirants, defined, that is, by the drive to bend the rules governing a strict social hierarchy. In *The Merchant of Venice* it is a *prince* of Morocco who assumes a place among Portia's many highborn suitors, while *Othello*'s Moor of Venice not only boasts exceptional military stature but indicates his descent from a noble line at the play's start. So, too, the blood-feud portrayed in *Lust's Dominion: or, The Lascivious Queen* features Eleazar, Prince of Fesse and Barbary, who has been captured in war prior to the events of the play and assimilated into the Spanish court. Like Othello, he scorns the attempts of some members of the Spanish nobility to associate his dark skin with depravity, powerfully countering:

Although my flesh be tawny, in my veines,
Runs blood as red, and royal as the best
And Proud'st in Spain.[8]

For a brief space of time, he lives to embody this claim, seizing the Spanish throne from his Spanish dispossessors and recoding the significance of his embodied identity by referring to his 'countenance Majestical' (3.6.2059). If throughout the play he is figured as precipitating the mangling of the Spanish royal body, it is both his dark skin and his princely identity that afford him this power. The combination, I suggest, allows the play to make use of his tawny skin to 'out' the theme of festering bloodline that riddles its representation of the Spanish court.[9]

In short, what links all of these plays is the way they embed the difference of skin colour within entrenched social hierarchies. Again and again, the difference of skin colour emerges in the context of a contestation of social hierarchies expressing a hereditary order. Does it matter that we have de-emphasized the rank of these figures in order to argue that their skin colour is the more constitutive site of their identity? Surely the plays qualify such readings by directing our attention to the intersections of these axes of social identity – colour and blood – and by dramatizing their intricate relation. The persistent proximity of these markers of difference, I suggest, is a symptom of an important cultural transition, one that records the fracturing of one racial system and the rise of another. Literary critics to date have been exceptionally attentive to the uneven emergence of colour as an axis of racial identity in the early modern period, but they have not adequately theorized the ruptures to a system of race-as-blood that preceded, accompanied, and enabled this cultural development. The decline of this earlier racial system is the cultural transformation that this book seeks to explicate. It is a race system that will appear foreign to many, involving few references to skin colour or phenotypical difference, since these qualities do not yet anchor the category *race* in early modern England. Rather, in English literature of the late sixteenth and early seventeenth centuries, *race* is most frequently used and understood as a mode of social differentiation that naturalizes a rigid social hierarchy within a polity.

Some will no doubt dispute my identification of a blood-based social hierarchy with a racial system, preferring the designation 'class system.' Yet careful consideration of early modern terms and categories indicates that *race* was the category that named the difference of social location for this period. What gets lost in translation when the difference of early modern terms and categories are softly elided in preference for modern ones? Following Raymond Williams, I would argue a good deal. Williams long ago urged careful attention to shifts in language as a crucial gauge of the movement of social formations, insisting that the changing meanings and relations among words attest to the ongoing adjustment and reconfiguration of social categories.[10] Attending to language across time involves recognizing its constitutive force, acknowledging its status not as 'a "mirror" to a separate reality' but rather as an active agent that produces and shapes 'realities,' one that actively creates and controls social forms.[11] If, then, language is the medium through which a culture distils its internal logic, we should heed the period's dominant definitions for the term, which tell us more than a little about what early moderns thought they were describing when they spoke of race. In contrast to Marxist critics, whose challenge has been to identify class formation before *class* as a word or category existed,[12] critics of race face the challenge of semantic excess. Indeed, far from leaving no trace in the earlier period, the word *race* appears with such frequency in early modern texts that it invites us to presume a continuity of semantic meaning between early modernity and modernity. Its long shelf life has discouraged careful consideration of the ways a singular semantic unit – *race* – can describe quite distinct social formations across the historical divides that anchor its meanings. Consulting the *Oxford English Dictionary* urges a more sustained explication of such semantic rumblings, since it provides compelling evidence that *race* in sixteenth- and seventeenth-century England describes a social system radically distinct from that invoked by its more modern cognate. In fact, the lexical trace it records suggests that *race* then and now refers to different social bodies and propounds different symbolics of corporeality.

Unlike nineteenth-century notions of race, which would draw in part on that day's available medical terminology, using the language of genetics, species, and other emergent classificatory divisions,[13] the earlier period produced the term's meaning in relation to a quite differently configured social system. Denoting not the broad groupings that would come to dominate its meanings in the late eighteenth and early nineteenth centuries, the earlier period used the term *race* to express a system of blood. It referred to 'offspring or posterity,' to 'breeding and generation,' and identified a contracted group as represented by 'a house, family, kindred.'[14] Raymond Williams seems to overlook this word in his classic compilation *Keywords*, but in his analysis of how the concept of *class* develops (unevenly), we find traces of the category I am describing in the terms '*estate, degree, and order*,' which were 'widely used to describe social position from medieval times.'[15] Surveying a range of early modern materials to identify and weigh the conditions that enabled but also blocked the emergence of the modern notion of race, Ivan Hannaford captures this word in its early modern incarnations.

Notably, his findings estrange our expectations in naming 'an exclusive quality,' identifying a privileged group within a social body, at first kings and bishops but subsequently a wider group of nobility and gentles. As an identifying tag, *race* was far from universal in its application; that is, everyone did not enjoy the privileges that it expressed. As Hannaford observes, 'to belong to a race was to belong to a noble family with a valorous ancestry and a profession of public service and virtue.' As such, 'not all members of a civil society are members of races.'[16] On the contrary, *race* was a term that denoted a social elite, most often used to identify those of 'worthy' blood. Sir Philip Sidney, for instance, could boast his membership in a 'noble race.' And we know that many scrambled to establish their own connections to ancient 'races' by purchasing or fabricating coats of arm.[17] To be of a 'base race' was an oxymoron; baseness precluded membership in a race. This is not to say that it could *never* be used to denote baseness – after all, Caliban is described as being of a 'vile race' – although this might express in oblique form his claim to a patronym.[18] It *is* to say that such references are not common in early modern England. *The Winter's Tale*, for instance, contrasts members of a 'nobler race' with those of a 'baser kind' (*WT* 4.4.95, 94), reserving the ascription race for its elite incarnations. If we have come to think of Othello as a member of the black race, we should consider what it means that he defines himself altogether differently as a man 'of royal siege' (*Oth* 1.2.22), a phrase that insists on lineal identification and values rank as the dominant social classification. To be marked by inclusion 'in a race,' as Othello claims for himself, was to announce one's participation in an elite group.

Indeed, by way of contrast to modern usage, Shakespeare, Spenser, and their contemporaries generally employed *race* with reference to a person's birth and lineage, suggesting its close affinities with properties of blood and a heritable order. Strikingly, this locution reveals how the early modern category of race could describe differences *internal* to a polity, even enable and support identifications across national and political lines for people of similar social location, indicating that the boundaries it instates abide by a quite different logic from that of its modern cognate. Critics of race have often acknowledged such differences, perceiving these ideologies of race to be analogous to modern class formations. But they have also tended to bracket them, concerned as they are to elucidate the origins of racial dynamics more proximate to modern ideologies. To do so, I suggest, is to overlook a crucial discursive phase in the making of modern race. For what early modern writers named and understood as race – a category proximate to that of rank – had deep, if oblique, connections to the later ideology. The clearing of this earlier ideology was, I suggest, an enabling condition of modern racial ideologies. Insofar as we translate the *race* of which I speak into *class* and/or collapse it into a study of ethnicity,[19] we miss the opportunity to explicate a crucial moment of cultural transition, one that saw a massive realignment of cultural categories, such that today we have difficulty imagining the possibility that the social boundaries instated by *race* might distinguish one English person from another.[20]

Race was, I have suggested, a way of 'speaking the body' quite distinct from modern paradigms first and foremost because it defined the body primarily through the qualities of its *blood*. That is, it propounded distinctions of rank above all else. Sir Thomas Smith would express these connections in mapping out the distinctions between different social ranks; the gentry and nobility, he urged, were made 'noble' by 'blood and race.'[21] The two terms signified as one for him, as they did more widely within early modern culture. To be 'of a race' was also to be 'of the blood.' William Harrison, himself a man of modest origins, would echo this formulation in his *Description of England* where he defines gentlemen as 'those whom their race and blood, or at the least their virtues, do make noble and known.'[22] To be 'of the blood' meant enjoying a metaphysical separation from one's social inferiors, although Harrison's qualification to this coupling – 'or at least their virtues' – expresses an ideological system undergoing transition.[23] Sir Thomas Elyot would try to express these associations in moral terms in *The Book Named the Governor*, his educational tract for gentlemen. Here he would urge, 'Where virtue is in a gentleman it is commonly mixed with more sufferance, more affability, and mildness, than for the more part it is in a person rural or of a very base lineage; and when it happeneth otherwise, it is to be accounted loathsome and monstrous.'[24] As Gail Kern Paster has argued, Renaissance homologies associated base men with base metal/mettle, suggesting a cultural logic that conceived of lowborn persons as 'made of unworthy and insubstantial materials.'[25] Elsewhere Elyot would devise the etymology for race or nobility, urging that 'for the goodness that proceeded of such generation the state of them was called in Greek Eugenia, which signifieth good kind or lineage, but in a more brief manner it was after called nobility, and the persons noble, which signifieth excellent.'[26] Conversely, Henry Howard, Earl of Northampton, would attack those responsible for conferring arms in increasing numbers on those he considered his social inferiors, characterizing this pattern as a sort of 'infection' unleashed upon the 'noble scions of true noble houses.'

He described the 'base blood' that such heralds were complicit in 'clearing' as 'a kind of leprosie.'[27] In the logic of this culture, divisions of rank expressed divisions of deed and potential as transmitted through the quasi-immaterial repository of blood and as reified in landed holdings.

If scholars have observed the connections of race to blood and lineage in the past, I suggest that they have not fully inhabited the implications of this clustering. In fact, the conceptual overlay of these terms for the earlier period, while acknowledged, is usually regarded as subordinate to the 'more important' task of analysing the status of concepts and practices that only later get positioned in syntactic relation to the word *race*. As such, critics of race have been inclined to explicate the contours of an emergent social formation at the cost of analysing its relationship to a dominant one. Literature of the period, by contrast, repeatedly emphasizes the connections between emergent and dominant ideologies of race. We must take time to consider these relationships and ask how these differences impact the stories of race that we have thus far told. How might it affect the readings we produce if we follow this period's ascriptions and understand blood rather than skin colour to be the somatic referent anchoring this system of race? At the very least, it gives me reason to believe that our stories have been incomplete, proposing new directions, even a new set of archives, for 'race studies' in the Renaissance.

How might inhabiting the sanguinary nature of race alter readings of the period's literature? I might begin in a suggestive way by urging that textual moments frequently read as expressing a modern racial logic often equate villainy with an attack on noble lineage, linking it to a disregard for the symbolics of blood. Such moments record how an emergent racial idiom – particularly one valuing skin colour – is used to unsettle a dominant system of race that locks power together with bloodline. Iago's villainous identification of Othello's colour as bestial and barbarous, for instance, can and should be read within the context of Iago's attack on the privileges of blood and rank. In and through this language he strikes out at the seeming inviolability of Othello's descent from 'men of royal siege,' recoiling from his abject lowness in relation to Othello's higher social rank. When he complains 'Tis the curse of service' to Roderigo, giving voice to the discontent that festers within him, he indicates his rejection of a system of 'old gradation,' of hierarchy that locks men like himself into positions of social subordination (*Oth* 1.1.34–6).[28] He also implies his readiness to use any weapon at his disposal to release its grip on him, including misogyny, patriarchalism, and xenophobia, as we witness in his verbal assault on Brabantio. We can see how forcefully he strikes out against this principle of social hierarchy – one that confers benefits readily to those of race and blood – in the case of Cassio, who is not implicated in the same way Othello is in a modern racial paradigm. In analogizing Cassio's decorous gestures to clyster-pipes, Iago assaults his gentility in ways analogous to his debasement of Othello; that is, he takes the marker of rank and blood in Cassio – his courtly behaviour – and sullies it through association with the fecal abundance of the lower body – sign and symbol of the commoner, of base blood. His interactions with Cassio, if viewed through the lens of modern categories, seem to express the disdain of one 'white' man for another. And yet I propose they be seen instead as an integral part of Iago's assault on an early modern system of race that understood social hierarchies to embody 'natural' principles. Through his abuse of both men, Iago labours to bring high blood low, both materially and symbolically. To that extent, Shakespeare retrieves the etymological association of 'villain' with servile status.[29]

In the case of Othello, Iago's challenge is to deploy a language that will nullify his stature and breeding. That is, he seeks to situate him at a remove from the community of blood that has dominantly defined him, just as he seizes on Cassio's vulnerability to alcohol to isolate him from this community. It is instructive to notice that Iago and Roderigo sample a few discursive strategies before discovering the efficacy of a language of colouration many would read as expressing a modern racial logic. When they descend on Brabantio's household, they first taunt Desdemona's father with the image of Othello as thief, conjuring the spectre of a low-born man rapaciously feeding on Brabantio's patronym (*Oth* 1.1.79–86). It is also significant that the play's elite characters – excepting Brabantio – never echo Iago's linkage of blackness with monstrosity, and that even Brabantio expresses initial resistance to such slanders when he perceives Iago's most inflammatory language as the utterance of a man who has lost his wits (*Oth* 1.1.92).[30] For the play's senators, Othello's nobility is a self-evident fact, as it is for Othello, who presumes that Brabantio's anger in response to the elopement will be neutralized not only by his service to the state but also by his high birth, though, he admits, ''Tis yet to know' (*Oth* 1.2.19). Insofar as Iago succeeds in convincing Othello that Venetians equate dark skin with villainy and barbarity, we might observe how Othello's internalization of these views is accompanied by a sudden change to the qualities of his blood. He feels and allows his blood to rise to passion and distemperance, even to an epileptic fit, undergoing the degenerative slide of blood's debasement. In presuming that Othello's blackness has always-already excluded him from a Venetian system of power, critics overlook these locutions, positing instead a metahistory of racial dominance.[31] The source for Shakespeare's play – Cinthio's *Hecatommithi* – foregrounds another way to understand what race means in this play. In closing the tale by describing the ensign's next set of victims, the one detail Cinthio insists on is that this episode, like the one we have just read about, revolves around 'a person of good birth' – that is, someone of noble race, not, as we might expect, someone of African ancestry. This source text may help us see what our own positioning historically has occluded: that race in this period refers to a social system built in, around, and through the symbolics of blood.

Revaluing race as blood might also evoke a rereading of *Titus Andronicus*, where the language of darkness that comes to define Aaron is part of a larger dynamic that expresses an attack on and a disdain for the metaphysics of blood. Those who read the play's articulation of difference primarily alongside an axis of skin colour overlook the extent to which the bodies of the play's characters are shot through with differences of blood. Like the upstart Iago, Aaron believes he can usurp, co-opt, or claim the privileges of blood and lineage, a violation that consumes much more stage time than references to him as a dark Moor.[32] That the absence of a noble lineage, rather than white skin, may be the dominant obstacle for him is suggested in his words to his son: 'Villain, thou mightst have been an emperor' (*Titus* 5.1.30), playing, as I have argued is the case with Iago, with associations of 'villainy' and servile status. In fact, it is his attempt to breach these distinctions – to contaminate the noble blood of the Queen, his mistress, with his common blood – that triggers degrading references to his dark skin colour from the Andronici.[33] The fact that his blackness comes to denote his depravity only once he has flagrantly disregarded a hereditary order suggests the continuing sway of this earlier race system.

*The Tempest*, too, might submit to a different sort of reading if we foreground race-as-blood, one that might have the added effect of suggesting adjustments to how we understand the racial dynamics that underpin colonial relations. In the case of Caliban, though recourse to a racial discourse rooted in skin colour is confounded by the play's indifference to his colour, the play is clear to identify his ur-villainy – his attempted rape of Miranda – as expressing a desire for the privileges of a pedigree. As Jonathan Goldberg has argued, Caliban's error is failing 'to recognize the unbreachable difference between kinds';[34] he covets and yet disrespects noble blood, much as do his henchmen Stefano and Trinculo.

These three characters are linked in the logic of the play not by a modern racial discourse of blackness but by their disdain for and will to violate the social hierarchies instated by bloodlines. That is, it is a central part of Prospero's project to position all of them – and especially that native who most threatens his claim to rule on the island – as beyond the community of race and blood that he seeks to refortify by clustering them at a remove from the island's nobility. Yet his aim is hardly a secure achievement at the play's end, since we come to see Caliban, Stefano, and Trinculo's incursions on the privileges of rank – specifically, their scheme to overthrow Prospero and seize the island for themselves – as an iteration of the drive toward imposture and usurpation that defines the elite community on the island. Antonio and Alonso have already violated Prospero's bloodline in illegally seizing his right and title, and Sebastian attempts to repeat their actions against Ferdinand. Attending to race as a system of blood forces us to reconsider the cultural work that these narratives are performing, to read them not for the oppositions typical of modern racial ideologies but for the ways they express the unravelling of an earlier racial idiom.

**Racial Scions**

If critics of race have tended to identify skin colour as the period's dominant marker of difference, I propose that its role in either blocking or enabling access to social power should be seen as in relation, and even as subordinate, to the symbolics of blood that express this period's cosmology. Foucault early identified this period's rootedness in a language of blood as marking a fundamental break from the 'more directly biologist (racist) system of modern heredity.' He describes the earlier period as one where 'the blood relation long remained an important element in the mechanisms of power, its manifestations, and its rituals. For a society in which the systems of alliance, the political form of the sovereign, the differentiation into orders and castes, and the value of descent lines were predominant ... blood constituted one of the fundamental values.'[35] In Foucault's account, this symbology of blood 'gradually gave way to a new order of power: under modernity, the workings of blood and death were replaced by a concern with sexuality and racial proliferation.'[36] If Foucault offers this overview of historical change in the context of his larger exposition on modern sexuality, in this book I hope to provide a necessarily partial account of the literary processes that enabled the undoing of this older system of race in the late sixteenth and seventeenth centuries. In the chapters that follow I read the literature of the period as betraying evidence that this sanguineous system was itself being subject to dispersal. If my reading of race here is firmly bound to blood, therefore, it does not presume that blood's meanings were static or unitary.

In fact, my account draws on a range of narratives of blood that animated English culture of the sixteenth and seventeenth centuries. In its ideal form, blood could be conceived of as a repository of sacred principles and properties, the locus of a family's virtue and social standing. A family was animated across time by the self-same properties of blood and temperament, constituting a single organic body capable, in theory, of infinite reproduction. Such lines often had recourse to the botanical image of the tree for self-representation and can create the appearance of the social body as a group of stately trees. But imaged together, each seemingly separate tree was but a branch of a unitary tree, sharing one origin and one sap-blood across time. The apparently separate and competing bloodlines of powerful families in sixteenth- and seventeenth-century England ultimately coalesced into one and the same consanguineous line, whose origin was expressed and embodied in the figure of the sovereign. One of the first maps printed to honour King James's ascension to the English throne makes these connections explicit. The map depicts the landscapes of England and Scotland flanking a genealogical tree that takes its root in William the Conqueror and flourishes, atop layers of branches with royal scions, ultimately in the buds of King James and Queen Anne.[37] An ornate border surrounds both images of land and royal tree and is constituted by the names and coats of arms of the lands' noble families. As this image demonstrates, the royal tree and its noble scions offered itself as a representation of 'the' social body of sixteenth- and seventeenth-century England. If such an iconography would seem to exclude the vast majority of the inhabitants of England – the group who together could claim no name or blood – it did. In the representation of this body as a plant body – a tree – such commoners occupied the 'no place' of being lesser vegetative growths, even weeds, threatening to grow beyond bounds and overtake the elite arboreal body while also requiring its protective shade to survive.[38] If there is a crucial border that race-as-blood insists on, then, it is that between the elite body – unified across time and space – and the mass body – dispersed and disordered like the image of a 'Beast with many heads,' which one gentleman observed of a group of commoners rioting to oppose land enclosure.[39]

Indeed, land was at the centre of this symbolics of blood, as we can observe in and through the period's naming practices whereby the nobility were named for the land that anchored their identity. A quick glance at Shakespeare's histories or tragedies can confirm this point, as when Antony addresses Cleopatra as 'I am dying, Egypt, dying' (*AC* 4.15.41), or when Hamlet Senior is referred to as 'buried Denmark' (*Ham* 1.1.46) and his ancient rival as 'ambitious Norway' (*Ham* 1.1.60), or as Bolingbroke's name evolves from Hereford to Lancaster in his rise through the ranks.[40] The Ditchley portrait of Queen Elizabeth perhaps most explicitly speaks the logic of race and blood as rooted in land by superimposing the embodied image of the Queen atop the entire landscape of England – if Cleopatra *is* Egypt, so Elizabeth *is* England. Even as the period enabled new means of advancement through the wealth and riches won in trade and the professions, as social historian Keith Wrightson has argued, 'the establishment and maintenance of gentility depended upon the acquisition and retention of landed wealth.'[41] Race, blood, and land were the coordinates of the social body I have been describing.

But if these terms signified in relation to each other, their connections were hardly static in this period. Social historians have debated the speed and extent of such change, and the recent tendency has been to understand the early modern world as one where social hierarchies were 'unstable and contested,' perhaps more so than previously suggested. Influenced by sociological models of power's operations, historians have moved away from accounts of the social body that see it as comfortably dichotomized along a gentle/non-gentle divide or as locked into place. They contend instead that the powers of a landed elite were subject to constant negotiation, not only in relation to the monarch but also to local notables. Michael Braddick and John Walter, for instance, emphasize the range of forces that worked to delimit gentle identity: 'Lineage and wealth – in the desirable form of "broad acres" – were necessary prerequisites for their social pre-eminence ... But this in itself was not enough ... they had to meet a definition of gentility they did not themselves control and which was changing in the light of larger cultural trends.'[42] Addressing the same question of how to account for the degree of continuity and change that attended the period's social hierarchies, Wrightson theorizes that 'the key to the distinctive social experience of early modern England may lie in the developing ambiguity of its social relations,' what he elsewhere describes as the age's 'social realignment.'[43] Other historians have underscored these changes by tracking subtle modulations to 'everyday rules of behaviour,' to changing ideas about demeanor and conduct.[44] My own interest is in how writers registered and shaped changes to a hierarchical social body in their representations of the body's internal physical properties. If race propounded a symbolics of blood in this period, we might expect that a challenge to its rules, which tightly governed the distribution of cultural power, might be conducted in and through languages of blood.

Such a challenge is audible, I suggest, in the widespread notion of degeneration that rose to prominence in the late sixteenth and early seventeenth centuries. I read this discourse as conveying the fraying of the period's dominant system of racial identity. In emphasizing the unstable and variable properties of bloodlines, the language of degeneracy pointed to the fault lines that hovered beneath the ideal language of blood as securing an intergenerational continuity of identity. If families had the potential to 'come into' and 'out of' property, such movement could be understood within a larger discursive system describing blood's malleability, evidenced in the breaches of nature between parent and offspring. Degeneration, defined in the *OED* as the act of generating 'something of an inferior or lower type' (v. 6), was a phenomenon that plagued those of blood. In *The Governor*, a text offering advice on rearing the children of nobility, Sir Thomas Elyot portrays the material properties of blood underpinning nobility as requiring fortification by a range of material practices. Everything from a sanguine wet nurse to a gentle tutor to exercise and study of precise texts are offered to elite families as supports for raising children of noble temperament. But the potential for breaks in the transmission of noble blood also haunts this text, as it does the accounts of noble lineage that make up the period's chronicle histories. Here, too, the possibility for a decline in blood is ever present. In Hall's *Chronicles*, John Talbot, 'erle of Shrewesbury,' is praised for 'not degenerating from his noble parent' in displaying true valiance. And in Speed's *History of Great Britaine,* 'Young Commodus' is described as producing a 'degenerating Son.'[45] Shakespeare's *Henry V* seems to invoke this conceptual framework as well in understanding the young Hal's early years of moral errancy as consisting of 'wildness' and 'addiction' to 'companies unlettered, rude, and shallow' (*H5* 1.1.27, 55–6). In imagining Henry's body as eventually transformed into a 'paradise' that can 'envelop and contain celestial spirits' (*H5* 1.1.31–2), Canterbury speaks to the restitution of Henry's nobility of blood. The spectre of decline that Hal suggests in dramatic form was part of a cultural commonplace that could describe potential failings in even the pure bloodline of the then living monarch, Queen Elizabeth. Required on numerous occasions to defend her decision not to marry, the Queen would frame her defence through this language of degeneration, urging that children of noble families often degenerated and that therefore marriage could be no guarantee of a suitable heir. This language of falling away from one's kind or from one's 'gen' – what one author described as the 'erasure' of 'ancient-marks of gentle-blood' – was invoked in the context of England to explain blood's anomalies, its unpredictable movement.

In pointing to failures of blood, degeneration expressed the period's system of blood as in effect part of an open bodily system. If on the one hand blood was described through a metaphysical language that saw it as carrying the immaterial essence of a family and race, it was also defined in and through its material form and was a fluid of earthly qualities. As one of four types of humours thought to constitute the body's internal constitution – along with bile, phlegm, and choler – blood-as-humour was inherently unstable. It was part of a metaphorics of liquidity: humours flowed, boiled, churned, and stirred within the contours of a porous vessel. Hence in pondering Hal's various transformations, Shakespeare's bishops explain his blood's debasement by reference to his physical activities, his participation in 'riots, banquets, sports' (*H5* 1.1.57), as much as his moral compromises. They also invoke the logic of plant life to explain his sudden regeneration. Perhaps, they reason, just as 'wholesome berries thrive and ripen best / Neighboured by fruit of baser quality' (*H5* 1.1.62–3), so the young Hal has all the time been properly cultivating himself, bud and fruit of the royal tree as they perceive him to be. If noble blood transmitted immaterial principles of virtue, it was also perceived to be vulnerable and required discipline to perfect, maintain, and rescue it from potential slippage.

## Migrations

Thus far I have suggested that the Renaissance was characterized by a racial system that yoked land together with blood and gentility. I want to emphasize, as well, that this symbolic system was subject to rupture and dispersal, yielding a set of conceptual quandaries in the period of the late sixteenth and seventeenth centuries. We have seen that a governing image for this social body was that of a multi-limbed tree sprouting from a land mass, one expressing a deep attachment to English soil. Like other 'natural' growths, this trope suggested that the social body was in part constituted by its rootedness in England, that it possessed attributes uniquely derived from that soil. It was a commonplace, after all, within the period's language and logic of botany that plants tended to absorb their qualities from precise physical conditions – from the soils, climates, and topographies that nurture them. These ideas were translated to social and political bodies as well. Jean Bodin, for one, had popularized the notion that climate determined political formation, understanding it to underpin the diverse political arrangements structuring different nations. When Sir James Perrot took it upon himself to update the chronicle of Ireland, he, too, would pay respect to these theories, arguing that 'the soyle and scituation of the contrie' helps determine 'mens dispositions' and the political forms that they prefer.[46] Such ideas generated a good deal of worry when James assumed the English throne and urged the union of England and Scotland into Britain. Eager to placate such worries, the Earl of Northumberland praised King James's admission of Scottish noblemen to the Privy Council in commending 'the many scions of true noble houses planted at the council board, upon our saviors own presumption that thistles cannot bring forth figs.'[47] Since the thistle was symbol of Scotland, the Earl seemed to be insisting on the unique contribution, indeed irreplaceable role, that the Scottish nobility would provide the newly created British body. But his words also intimate that a soil as proximate as Scotland could produce a kind of nobility quite unique from that yielded by its sister soil of England. More distant geographies, by implication, would produce still different 'kinds.' Colonization – in Ireland, Virginia, and the West Indies – collided with these theories of identity rooted in land and soil, catalysing profound revaluations of the period's dominant account of blood. Efforts to reproduce the social body of England in new soils, that is, had the effect of unsettling the system of race then dominantly constituting England's social structure.

Juan Huarte's *The Examination of Men's Wits*, a text that enjoyed considerable popularity in its English translation between 1592 and 1616, places these quandaries at the centre of its representation, grappling explicitly with the relation between migration and lineal identity. In one section of the text, Huarte attempts to explain why Francis of Valois, King of France, insisted that only a Jewish physician could cure him of a long-lasting illness. Having already identified the skill of imagination necessary for medicine as unique to people inhabiting Egypt, Huarte attempts to explain why Jews might possess these qualities. Arguing that 'the varieties of men, aswell in the compositions of the body, as of the wit and conditions of the soule, spring from their inhabiting countries of different temperature, from drinking diuers waters, and from not vsing all of them one kind of food,' Huarte suggests that the four hundred years that the Jews were forced to live in exile in Egypt had shifted their collective dispositions. Paying close attention to their access to particular foods and waters and their subjection to particular climatic conditions, he argues that their previously 'strong bodies' – and by this he means bodies with sufficient heat to digest harsh foods like onions and leeks – were transformed into 'subtile and delicat' bodies. These conditions took such a 'rooted condition' in their bodies that they were transmitted to their offspring, who were found to be 'sharp and great of wit in matters appertaining to this world,' and therefore very able physicians. By altering their environment, the Jews had in effect diverted their collective genealogy, transforming the traits that they transmitted to their offspring. For Huarte, generation was anything but a static or monologic process, bloodlines anything but fixed. Blood could and would absorb changes from new cultures and environments.[48]

If those of race and blood living within European civil centres were increasingly faced with the spectre of racial decline, of behaving in ways that might mar their ancient names and titles, Huarte's account suggested that migration, too, could have profound effects on a bloodline. In studying a case where lineal attributes seemed to have improved under the force of transmigration, he opened up the possibility for viewing such changes as potentially liberatory; in fact, his account of how environment could change a family's nature intimated that birth might not be the absolute determinant of social identity many assumed it was. A similar view was articulated by some of the earliest settlers in Florida. In the extensive compilation of voyages published as the *Principal Navigations, Voyages, Traffiques, and Discoveries of the English Nation* (1589), Richard Hakluyt included an account by René Laudonnière of the early settlement of Florida by French Huguenots. He recalled an address made by John Ribault to men newly arrived to the plantation, which urged them to settle there permanently. As Hannaford reports, he reminded them that in France 'they were unknown to the king … and [to] the great estates of the land,' urging further that 'they were descended of poor stock' and had little chance for social advancement. He offered the fledgling plantation as a space that might overturn this rigid social system, one where virtue could be 'regarded' as highly as birth, so that more men could 'be found worthy to deserve the title, and by good right to be named noble and valiant.' Florida, he intimated, might be the place where these lowborn men could 're-race' themselves, ascending the social hierarchy armed only with discipline and hard work. He also made it clear that no such option would ever be available to them at home in France.[49]

His appeal to these men reminds us that colonial transplantation was a powerful engine of social change, one that was redrawing pre-existing boundaries of racial identity, even as it was inventing new ones.

If we have seen that degeneration was sometimes invoked to explain anomalies at home, I suggest that once movement to the colonies assumed a critical mass, the social changes that this discourse described were pressed with greater urgency. Here bodily systems of blood began to unravel in profoundly unpredictable ways. In revealing that the 'fixed' lines of race that were a central feature of that social body were fallible, subject to dispersal under the pressure of migration, colonization had the effect of destabilizing the English social body. Critics of early modern Ireland have long ago heeded the significance of this discourse in the context of the Tudor conquest of Ireland, where English settlers living in Ireland since the Norman invasions of the twelfth and thirteenth centuries were charged with having degenerated from their noble anteced- ents. But I revisit this language and this context among others to argue that what the newly planting English feared, obsessed over, and, in some cases, embraced in using this language were not merely cultural altera- tions but racial alterations – that is, alterations that had an impact on a system of race-as-blood. Through this language, they worked through the implications of inhabiting another soil, sorting through how their acts of 'planting' – a term that they preferred to colonizing – would affect not only themselves but their descendants. In reflecting on how gentle blood might become distempered under the influence of the hot climate of the Indies or how exposure to the bodily fluids of Irish women might confound genealogical ties, their reflections run up against and expose the limits of concepts that had long defined the English collective. When they question whether those transplanted to distant lands will maintain consanguinity with family members in England once their bodies had absorbed the imprint of different climates, diets, and cultures, they also, in effect, interrogate the strength and viability of bloodlines. And when they question whether displaced gentlemen will be able to sustain their gentility at a remove from the court and civil centres, they also imply that gentility might be less an inherited essence than a function of place and context. Collectively, I read these moments as catalysing the decline of a long-standing system of race.

The literary texts that I take as my objects of analysis in the chapters that follow often speak of changes to the transplanted English body by attending to and modulating shifts to the body's physical properties in ways that literary criticism of the period has overlooked. My readings will uncover a range of textual moments where modulations to blood are perceived in and through accounts of its homologous fluids – breast milk, sweat, and spirits among them. In the unusual attention that authors of colonial matters paid to dietary shifts, climatic difference, and cultural practice, I argue we are hearing these writers actively modify, revise, and adjust the period's dominant account of blood. My book demonstrates how this charged fascination with blood's fluctuating principles under the pressures of migration and resettlement were anything but innocuous. By focusing on blood's alterability and indeterminacy, writers were actively interrogating its status as a transcendent signifier, the cornerstone of the social hierarchy structuring England from within. They contributed to the remaking of a substance that was intimately connected both to their place within a social hierarchy (i.e., as elite, middling, or base men) and to their sense of themselves as English. In effect, their representations ruptured the attachment of blood and social power and established the conditions for modern notions of race. If criticism on early modern literature has been attentive to how difference comes to attach itself to skin colour in this period, it has not yet explained the break with older conceptions of race-as-blood, which enabled this process.

Although the authors I analyse are, as I said, linked in their status as English, they also came from varied social stations and are far from uniform in how they perceive England's investment in colonization as well as in the stances they take to old and emergent embodied systems. I consider Spenser's representation of transplantation to Ireland in two chapters. The first positions Book 2 of *The Faerie Queene* within the context of the struggle in Ireland between the low-level New English administrators and the Old English elite who blocked their ascendancy. Focusing on the political implications of the book's emphasis on distemperance and degeneracy, I argue that we can locate a carefully modulated attempt on Spenser's part to diminish the cultural power conferred to those of race and blood, as was the case for his rivals in Ireland, who justified their power on the basis of ancient bloodlines. In his anatomy, the active achievement of temperance replaces birthright as the marker of gentility, since inherited bloodlines, as the book shows in countless vignettes, frequently decline. Men of high blood seem 'naturally' to gravitate to positions of social pre-eminence, desires that are compounded in the loosely regulated contexts of the colonies. If Old English lords and Irish chieftains claimed Irish land by virtue of their birth, Spenser challenges their possession by exposing their blood as degenerate. By fixating on notions of temperance – the ideal balance of the body's blood and humours – Spenser performs a sleight of hand, shoring up the claims to land that he and an entire middling planter class were making. This chapter lays the terms for the book as a whole by showing how a seemingly insignificant embodied discourse – that of temperance – would become a powerful tool for reinventing the social body.

In another chapter that moves beyond Spenser's epic to his political tract on Ireland and engages a wider circle of New English writing on Ireland, I observe a preoccupation of these writers with the material practices of nurture for colonists in Ireland. In the constant troping on the figure of the Irish wet nurse in this literature, I detect a widespread cultural unease about the potential of foreign breast milk, conceived in this bodily system as homologous with blood, to rewrite English paternity. As such, her breast milk threatens to deluge tender English heirs with alternate bloodlines, confounding familial and national identification at large and raising the spectre of racial decline in colonial milieus.

The next section of my book moves to the more distant context of the New World and the genre of tragicomedy. Because tragicomedies generally depict aristocratic families threatened by separation and distance, they are a particularly fruitful place for observing how representations of displacement speak to and are implicated in modifying an English social body. In the first chapter of this sequence, I read *Cymbeline* alongside tracts promoting the colonization of Virginia and suggest that both sets of texts disclaim the association of degeneration with the colonies. Suggesting that British bloodlines are most at risk being subject to luxury at home, the play and tracts defend the idea that the harsh western landscape of 'Nova Britannia' will restore such blood to its ancient noble properties. Colonization therefore emerges as the ultimate safeguard of British blood – reconfigured along a horizontal plane – while the court's emphasis on rank and the differences inherent to elite blood signals, in effect, the contamination of an ancient British bloodline.

The fifth chapter, which focuses on two 'island' plays – *The Tempest* and *The Sea Voyage* – responds to the potential confounding of English gentility in distant soils with reference to the dynamics of gender. Where *The Tempest* identifies the obstacles to reproducing the elite blood of Europeans in venues far from home only to evade them, John Fletcher and Philip Massinger's later play, written when Virginia's settlement was established if also besieged, seeks to resolve such obstacles. Notably, the play carves out a privileged role for aristocratic women in this regard, suggesting that under precisely delimited conditions the colonies can be a viable site for the reproduction of gentle blood rather than the occasion for its necessary decline.

The final chapter considers settlement in the Indies following the introduction of slavery in English plantations. Here I read Richard Ligon's *True and Exact History of the Island of Barbados* (1657) to suggest that even in the context of chattel slavery an emergent racialism is impeded by the continuing sway of an earlier racial system rooted in blood, which placed a strong emphasis on gradations of rank. That Ligon's epistemology is not yet poised to accommodate the oppositions of an emergent racialism (white against black) is evident in how he conceives both of genre and physiology. Calling his text a 'history,' rather than a 'natural history,' implying a continuity between natural and human forms, Ligon describes Barbados as a site 'naturally' governed by hierarchy, as manifested in the differently embodied animal spirits he perceives each of the island's inhabitants to possess – vegetable no less than human. The presence of high spirits and elite forms in the Barbadian landscape indicates that the plantation will have little difficulty supporting English gentility. His text, then, implicitly refutes the charge that a tropical colony, like other distant plantations, will produce a degenerative slide for English settling there. But insofar as his enthusiasm for 'high' spirits bespeaks his royalist identification, it expresses a defensive bid to cling to blood as the defining principle of the English polity in the face of its erosion.

Once Englishmen began to settle beyond the shores of England in significant numbers, blood's meanings altered. For those not entitled to colonial lands by virtue of old systems of blood, colonization invited the occasion for inventing new languages, different systems of blood to justify their newly landed status. For many, the concern was to demonstrate proximity to those who remained in England in part by stressing how moderate and temperate their blood remained though subject to foreign conditions. By fixating on changes to blood through their obsession with degeneration and temperance, the literature of this period actively modified, revised, and adjusted the period's dominant account of blood. It is these moments – those that describe and sort through English transformation abroad – that I see as evidence of the period's racial system of blood coming undone. To the extent that I make this claim, I concur with George Fredrickson, who argues in his short history of racism that 'the rejection of hierarchy as the governing principle of social and political organization ... had to occur before racism could come to full flower.'[50] Translating the implications of this idea into my own terms, I would argue that the social body imagined as a community of blood had to be reconstituted and reimagined as part of this process. Colonization forced this redefinition upon the English, who in crossing to the colonies began the long process of writing a new social body.

# 1 Blemished Bloodlines and *The Faerie Queene*, Book 2

## 'Growing strangers'[1]

In the crucial last years of the Nine Years War in Ireland, the Queen sent Essex to Ireland, charging him with the task of putting the axe 'to the root of that tree which hath been the treasonable stock from which so many poisoned plants and grafts have been derived.'[2] The 'root' to which she referred was, of course, the arch-traitor, Hugh O'Neill, whom the Queen herself had propped up a decade earlier in an attempt to counter his kinsman and then powerful Irish chief, Turlough Luineach O'Neill.[3] To her chagrin, the sapling Hugh had taken all too well to his native soil of Ulster, raising himself to unexpected heights as arch-rebel and leader of a rebellion that swept the entire country. If she had nurtured this fledgling branch of the O'Neill clan in the hopes that it would fortify her royal authority, her prediction failed horribly, for the tree had grown awry, spreading the poison of treason rather than the fruit of the royal will. In the Queen's estimation, Hugh had grown too mighty, and he needed to be violently cut back. Hence, Essex was commanded to 'raze' a family she deemed threatening and volatile, one that had grown without bound.

But O'Neill was hardly the first to pose a threat to the monarch on such terms, and the organic metaphors that the Queen here uses to represent his unpredictable rise to power were frequently used to describe men of English descent, where they were, I will argue, a sign and symptom of a much larger crisis of identity precipitated by the Elizabethan conquest of Ireland. Ever since the first round of English conquerors had arrived in Ireland in the twelfth century, Irish soil had served as an alternative base of power for high-ranking English families, who received extensive powers and privileges in their capacity as proxies for the monarch. As a result, families like the Butlers and Fitzgeralds, the Lacies and Burkes, established themselves as powerful dynasties there, ruling with near-sovereign power over an Irish population of would-be subjects, and serving as a constant cause for concern for the English monarch. In his own account of this early period, the attorney-general of Ireland under James I, Sir John Davies, would observe of Henry II: 'it is manifest that he gave those Irish lords the title and style of kings.'[4] Just beyond the reach of English oversight, Ireland seemed naturally to foster the growth of over-mighty subjects, both English and Irish. What had changed in the late sixteenth century, after a series of rebellions beginning in the reign of Henry VIII with the revolt of the Earl of Kildare and extending to the rebellion of the 14th Earl of Desmond in the late 1570s, was that these tensions fed into a much wider social conflict. In rebelling, the Old English threw down the gauntlet, pushing back on the monarch's attempts to limit their many long-standing privileges, particularly their freedom to billet men on their tenants, a practice known as coyne and livery.[5] They cast these measures as encroachments on their birthright, as attempts to repudiate their heroic ancestries, claiming that their long and illustrious genealogies were thereby being razed.

In arguing as much, they placed the issue of bloodline at the centre of their dispute with the English, defending themselves by reminding the Queen of their ancient service and noble derivation. As Sir Nicholas White, a member of the Irish Parliament, charged in 1581, the men sent to Ireland to implement reform aimed at nothing less than the 'rooting out of ancient nobility,' an affront he likened to 'artisans that persuade owners of ancient houses to pull them down for altering of fashion wherein they seek more their own setting a work than to do the owners' profit.' He reminded her how the 'seed of English blood' – those of Old English derivation – had laboured without pay since 'their first planting,' urging that they be reformed rather than 'supplanted' by a group unable to 'govern themselves.'[6] Not surprisingly, it was on precisely these terms that the men sent by Queen Elizabeth to administer the land – those we refer to today as the New English – fought back. Faced with this argument by descent, New English writers like Spenser, Bryskett, and Moryson found themselves revaluing and questioning the significance of blood, stock, and lineage as principles of power and rule. Almost all of these men – like the New English at large – were of middling rank, the 'second sons, impoverished soldiers, and indigent poets' who saw in Ireland 'the otherwise impossible prospect of ascent to the ranks of the landed gentry.'[7] In attacking the Old English, they sought to bolster their prospects for social mobility in Ireland, but their arguments had the more radical effect of striking at the root of England's own social hierarchy. Indeed, displacement to Ireland, with its suddenly loosened system of land tenure, enabled these New English settlers to launch a critique of English systems of identity that was nothing less than an assault on a long-standing racial system predicated on blood. In attacking lineal identity as the de facto basis of social power, they were hacking away at one form of race and inadvertently making way for another.

As such, their writing is crucial for theorists of early modern race since it crystallizes the connections between race and lineage in this period that critics have routinely acknowledged but not yet adequately theorized.[8] More specifically, their writing enables a view of the ways that earlier idioms of race jostled up against emergent ones, revealing the uneven movement between competing systems of difference that compellingly defines the early modern period. Bloodlines, their writing reminds us, served to anchor a dominant early modern ideology of kind, whose attempt at 'clearing' by the likes of New English writers like Spenser was radical and liberatory – in the way that Marx observed of the decline of feudalism – until it yielded to an equally oppressive, yet different logic of 'kind.' In this chapter I focus on the effort that went into dismantling this earlier system of race by those who felt its edge sharply and stood most to gain by its repudiation – the New English community, among them the poet Spenser. As such, my argument extends the work of critics who have suggested that Spenser's poetry and prose express a guarded critique of ideologies of the English 'centre,' a critique many associate with the years he spent living 'on the margins' in Ireland.[9]

Indeed, 'clearing' is a fit metaphor to describe the process initiated by the New English, since it extends the tropological vocabulary that they favoured in representing the political field of Ireland. Like the Queen, who used the stunning image of a tree growing unpredictably to describe the Irish rebel, they, too, leaned heavily on botanical metaphors. Such images were commonplace in the context of Ireland, where homologies culled from plant life underpinned the very effort of colonization.[10] In part, these associations derived from Roman antecedents, as conveyed in and through the Latin word *colonia*, which denoted a group whose activities were defined first and foremost by the working of the soil, thereby emphasizing a strong attachment between person and soil. Settlers drawn to Ireland echoed these associations in referring to themselves as 'planters' and to their movement abroad as one of 'transplantation.'

They were also urged by propaganda seeking to encourage migration to Ireland to view themselves as the 'good seed' that would transform the 'waste' of Ireland into a garden, a *hortus conclusus.* In the words of Sir John Davies, 'the husbandman must first break the land before it be made capable of good seed.' To leave it to the Irish, or Old English, as New English writers would increasingly imply, was to let it 'grow wild again.'[11] O'Neill's monstrous growth confirmed the charge that one New English writer levelled against both the Irish and Old English living in Ireland: they had become dangerous 'weeds' needing to be supplanted or at least 'kept downe.'[12] '[T]he new planted English' offered themselves as the stewards who would restore orderly growth, both properly enclosed and bearing fruit, to this barren land.[13]

In their hands, the use of the plant metaphor was a powerful weapon that could serve to undermine Old English assertions of power. Specifically, it enabled them to expose the huge fault line that ran beneath traditional notions of race, which identified blood as the bearer of differences of 'kin' or 'kind.' Entering the English language in the early sixteenth century, the early modern word *race* described identities configured in relation to lineage or genealogy. Although the word seems to have been absorbed into English as a translation of the Italian *razza*, the Spanish *raza*, and the Portuguese *raça*,[14] it was layered on top of pre-existing English words and concepts, most notably that of *stock*, a word that the *OED* entry repeatedly uses to define the earliest meanings of *race*. In such instances, *stock* appears as the material referent for that which unites or connects a 'family,' 'kindred,' or 'tribe.'[15] As such, the concept of race from its first usages drew heavily on plant terminology, since the word *stock*, stretching deep into the medieval period, had long described parts of plant bodies, as in a 'tree-trunk' or 'stump,' a 'stem of a (living) tree' or 'plant,' as well as 'a stem in which a graft is inserted.'[16] As early as the fourteenth century, this plant language was already being used by the likes of Chaucer and others in what the *OED* describes as a 'figurative' sense to denote bonds among men, as in 'the source of a line of descent; the progenitor of a family or race,' but also a 'family, kindred,' an 'ancestral type from which various races, species, etc. have diverged,' and a 'pedigree, genealogy.'[17] John Florio's Italian-English dictionary would compress these elaborate etymological developments in defining *race* as 'a kind, a broode, a blood, a stocke, a pedigree,' compellingly supplementing the vegetative substance of 'stock' with the human material of 'blood.'[18] Looking to his definition of the Italian word for *stock*, which is *stirpe*, we see the same associations. The definition reads 'a progenie, a generation, a stock or kindred, a race, issue, or nobleness of birth, an offspring, a house, a bloud, a kinde, a pedigree. Also the root, stem, or stalke of a tree, plant or herbe, a yong branch or set.'[19] If critics have observed that Spanish authors were beginning to use the word *race* in the late sixteenth and early seventeenth centuries to denote the introduction of an undesirable element to the bloodline – one they tended to associate with Moors or Jews[20] – English writers like Florio[21] and Spenser tended instead to associate the word with high birth and noble derivation, as in Florio's phrase 'nobleness of birth' or Spenser's praise of Sidney's 'noble race.'[22] Blood was the transmitter of the privileged marks of race or stock, conjoining the generations of a family across time just as the trunk of a tree anchored an intricate web of branches.

The force of each of these interlocking concepts – *race, stock, blood* – was to track continuity across the ruptures of time, imagining a body linked inter-generationally through a palpable substance that lived on despite the passing of any individual body. But even the oldest stories of these racial lines conceded that the trans-generational continuities could, on occasion, suffer rupture. Wilfulness or sin was one way this might happen, where an offspring might deliberately choose to defy a nature transmitted to him in his stock or blood. But another powerful rupture had been associated with migration or long-term transplantation. In the account of the postdiluvian world, for instance, the migration of Noah's three sons – Ham, Shem, and Japheth – into three distinct geographical spheres provides an originary account for the diversity of the world's people.[23] In moving out beyond their ancestral lands to distant lands, each of Noah's sons was perceived to suffer the blunting or 'rasing' of shared genealogical marks, a process that some would describe in a botanical register as a kind of deracination, an uprooting. Such narratives powerfully defined moving away from one's familial roots as an act that might very well sever those roots, one that might break the genealogical ties of race altogether so as to spawn separate shoots, races with distinct attributes. Although monogenesis argued that all peoples derived from a single progenitor, it also quite clearly suggested how readily those of 'familiar' identity could become estranged.

If, therefore, the equation of races with vegetative growths originated as an expression of cross-generational stability and the fixity of racial stock – as in the image of a towering tree extending indefinitely – in the context of large-scale migration, such aims were undermined. For in the same way that plants depended on soil, climate, and cultivation to ensure proper growth, a people taking root in new soils absorbed the risk of alteration. The observation was a commonplace for early modern writers. In his essay on Raymond Seybond, Montaigne would observe, for instance, that 'Men are not only influenced by the place ... but like plants, they will assume new characteristics when they migrate.'[24] So, too, political theorist Jean Bodin, in contemplating the origin and nature of national differences, would argue that 'we see men as well as plants degenerate little by little when the soil has been changed.' People were observed to differ from their botanical counterparts only in how long it might take for such changes to take effect. Bodin argued that whereas transplanted plants 'quickly lose their identity and adapt themselves to the nature of the soil,' 'men do not change the innate characteristics of their own nature easily, but after a long period of time.'[25] The plant metaphor, therefore, emphasized the indeterminacy and vulnerability of racial stock to a range of agents, viewing the seed as only the beginning of a complex process of generation.[26] This potential for racial mutability was registered in the organic terms that early modern writers used to describe the fate of people so displaced: they 'grew' awry; they 'decayed';[27] they 'altered'; they 'degenerated.' In his account of linguistic difference, Richard Verstegan encapsulated this point with force: 'meer strangers' were not at first strange; rather, they became that way because they 'dayly grew unto more and more alienation.'[28]

Such phrases – particularly this notion of 'growing' strange – direct our attention to a crucial difference between this early category of race and those that came to supersede it: they identify early modern racial identity as alterable and conditional, and as deeply connected to social practices – mores, customs, and culture – no less than the physical practices we call 'nature.'[29] The porous divide between these concepts emerges with striking force in Sir Francis Bacon's natural history, *Sylva Sylvarum*, amid a discussion of how to apply pressure to and even collapse the features of distinct plants. Observing that transplantation is one way to alter plant form, Bacon notes, 'The rule is certain, that plants for want of culture degenerate to be baser in the same kind; and sometimes so far as to change into another kind.' Withholding culture – that is, acts of cultivation – results in a physical lapse for plants that can be so substantial as to alter their fundamental nature. Elsewhere Bacon indicates how considerable the change might be when he notes: 'It is strange which is reported, that basil too much exposed to the sun doth turn into wild thyme,' describing this process as a 'very great change.'[30] The reasoning that allowed Bacon to imagine one plant turning 'kind' – that is, leaping the divide between one plant and another – was consistently transferred under the power of homological thinking to people, as is readily visible in the archive of New English writing on Ireland.[31] In each context – human and botanical – acts of culture are regarded as having the power to shape nature, as being easily absorbed into nature's eminently pliable fibre. Hence, in the absence of certain cultural practices, nature would be expected to decline. Early modern racial ideologies thereby articulate with compelling force what modern racial ideologies seek to bury: the ever-present prospect of racial reversibility.[32] If race denoted the noble markings that descended through a bloodline – the qualities that King James would note 'run on a blood'[33] – early modern writers observed with increasing frequency that racial identity needed to be supported, that it required a range of prophylactics in order to maintain the mark of distinction it conferred. Post-structuralism and post-colonial criticism have recently equipped us with the tools to deconstruct the oppositions that underpin modern racial thought, but early modern constructions of race already practised a version of such thinking, insofar as they openly conceded the precariousness of racial lines.[34]

## 'Wrestinge ... Auncestrye'[35]

Nowhere was the lability of racial stock and bloodline emphasized more than in the context of New English migration to Ireland, where planters had good reason to stress how much the Old English community had lapsed. Here, the New English developed the charge of degeneracy on the part of their Old English rivals into a powerful indictment, speaking of their 'wonderfully degenerate' Old English counterparts not (yet) in the anxious tones of those who fear for their own survival – as critics have been inclined to argue – but rather with the enthusiastic vigour of men anticipating their own social ascendancy.[36] Their criticisms were hardly new. Following the Anglo-Norman invasion of the twelfth century, it had become a commonplace to observe that these high-born settlers had grown away from a line of noble progenitors.[37] In embracing the Irish language and Irish customs and in combining with the Irish through fosterage and intermarriage, it seemed these early conquerors had allowed the outward marks of their noble lineage – namely, a set of behaviours coded as civil and courtly in England – to slide. Degeneration was the name for such a decline. And it was an indictment of their bloodline, suggesting that they had failed to live up to the behaviour established by their forefathers and expected of men of high rank. That the term described a violation of rank can be deduced from the fact that the charge was also used as an indictment of gentlemen living in England who violated decorum in some crucial way. Hence the chronicler Thomas Walsingham records how John of Gaunt ridiculed members of the House of Commons following a contentious Parliament in 1376 with the charge that their petition should not be regarded since they were degenerate knights ('degeneres ... milites') who were pretending to be lords or princes of the land ('reges sivi principes').[38] Here the word served to denigrate a group perceived to threaten a naturally ordained social hierarchy, to discipline those perceived to have stepped out of rank. Such usages were echoed in early modern chronicle history as well, where they appear in comments seeking to account for a genealogical rupture in the historical record, as when John Speed describes Commodus by reference to his 'soone degenerating Son.'[39] If in such cases the rupture of degeneration was understood as resulting from a flagrant abuse of privilege, it was analogous to the rupture that was imagined to accompany long-term resettlement in Ireland. In this context, too, degeneracy identified a debasement of and decline to an aristocratic bloodline. Of course, in this earlier moment, *only* men of high pedigree – brothers, sons, and uncles of the monarch – were sent to Ireland, where they were to serve as proxies for the monarch remaining in England.

Patterns of conquest and settlement were different in the late Elizabethan period when efforts were stepped up to subdue Ireland. In this moment, the majority of settlers were not high-ranking aristocrats but rather mid-level administrators, men who had never known and yet, we might speculate, had always envied the privileges of their social superiors. This group had a strong interest in curbing the will of their social betters in the form of the Old English, since it was they who blocked their claims to large tracts of land. As such, the New English had a vested interest in reviving the ancient charge of degeneracy against them. As Richard McCabe has suggested, 'accusations of cultural "degeneracy" were potent weapons in [the New English] struggle to supplant their Old English rivals.'[40] In his political tract on Ireland and his book of the governor that appears in his epic, Spenser was at the helm of such efforts. In both contexts he sought to fissure the viability of blood, stock, and lineage as the mainstay of Old English power in Ireland. He did so by staging the spectacle of Old English blood declined, by demonstrating the extent to which bloodline was an unreliable gauge of a person's merit, one that did not necessarily ensure the transference of virtuous attributes in the teleological fashion conjured by words like 'line,' 'lineage,' and even 'race,' with its alternate early modern sense of progress from one point to another.[41]

To assert as much is to revise a customary view of Spenser as a poet who was unqualified in sanctioning an aristocratic ethos, a view that takes his connections to the staunchly Protestant Sidney circle as evidence for his unwavering support of the political system empowering these patrons.[42] Yet it has been nearly a decade since Debora Shuger sounded a challenge to this view when she made the daring claim that Spenser's political tract on Ireland was an indictment of an aristocratic culture of violence, professing signs of affiliation with something resembling what she tentatively describes as a kind of 'bourgeois social order.'[43] Shuger's reading of *A View of the Present State of Ireland* portrays Spenser as someone labouring to articulate and to defend an ideological position valuing the 'new' men who sought land and rapid upward mobility in colonial contexts, as the New English clearly did in Ireland. Although Shuger casts doubt on the extent to which her reading might hold in the context of Spenser's epic[44] – since the antagonistic attitude toward aristocratic culture she discovers in the *View* seems to counter the epic's professed intent to 'fashion a gentleman'[45] – I suggest that she may, in fact, move too quickly to concede to traditional readings of the poem, which tend to locate it on either side of a polarized political field. Either Spenser is of the Queen's court – a staunch defender of an absolutist ideology and the 'arse-kissing poet' that Marx mockingly imagined him as[46] – or he is the mouthpiece of his aristocratic patrons, whether Sidney, Dudley, or Essex.

Weighing the context of Ireland forces us to qualify both positions, to see them as oversimplifying a more complex political and poetical field. For Ireland created possibilities that were not readily available at home, producing conditions that enabled a wider set of political positions and interests. It did so by allowing 'mere' civil servants like Spenser to aspire to land formerly bound to noble families – the Butlers, Fitzgeralds, and Clanrikards of Old English derivation among them. At home, there had been no large-scale redistribution of lands since the early Reformation when the monastic lands were dissolved, an event that historians have long acknowledged as having had the effect of pressuring an aristocratic ideology that attached land by 'natural' right to bloodline.[47] As such, the conditions enabling social mobility were limited. But in Ireland, where Desmond's escheated lands were being distributed among English of a wide range of social positions – to gentlemen like Sir Christopher Hatton and the just-knighted Sir Walter Raleigh,[48] and to mere captains like the

Norris brothers – these desires were stoked. Here, low-ranking officials like Spenser – whom we must recall 'served' his way through Cambridge as a 'sizar'[49] – came into repeated conflict with men of rank and privilege, like his Old English neighbour Lord Roche, whose lands Spenser was actively pursuing for himself.[50] If in attacking these men he tried to erode the foundation upon which their privileges rested, a further effect was to split open a system of race-as-blood and make way for a less exclusive system of identity based on the merit of earned virtue. In this view, gentility was properly a practice, rather than a birthright, something to be worked at rather than derived through one's blood. In valorizing temperance as the quality that defines the one knight in *The Faerie Queene* who is conferred the title 'Sir' in bold letters on the book's title page,[51] Spenser draws attention to the importance of what one 'achieves' with one's blood rather than the 'kind' of blood one might inherit. He who is truly temperate, the book suggests, *makes* himself so.[52]

Hence, for Spenser, as for some of his New English cohorts, colonial displacement catalysed what Willy Maley describes as a process whose aim was to '[refigure] metropolitan identities,' a process that I see as pressuring a system of race with close affinities to rank.[53] To argue as much is to position Spenser's representations of the Irish within a complex 'racial' dynamic. Armed with a seemingly more naked exposition of his ruthless position on conquest in the *View*, critics have demonstrated his role in portraying the Irish as a barbarous people, a group eager to disclaim the benefits of English civility. Moreover, some have observed how this tendency to figure the Irish as uniformly depraved, with its drive to represent a complexly stratified society as a single homogeneous and subordinate group, is strikingly similar to modern racial ideologies. And yet there is a compelling difference in the racial dynamic of this earlier moment that I seek to draw out: namely, its embeddedness in still dominant ideologies that identified differences of social station – noble as against common or base – through the language of 'kind.' It is this steep social hierarchy that bedevils and blocks the emergent opposition – English against Irish – that critics have tended to perceive and emphasize.[54] A hierarchy of blood blocks the polarization of English against Irish by fostering identifications between Old English and Irish lords, who are linked through a feudal ethos, and by fracturing English unity by pitting Old English lords against the New English men, who tended to be their social subordinates. As such, and as critics have recently begun to observe, the diatribe against the Irish is absorbed into a larger target – that of the over-mighty subject.[55] It is this figure's ill-government that is credited with sanctioning, if not producing, Irish depravity. Some of the Irish tracts – especially Spenser's *View* – articulate this with precision: the Irish are recoverable as English subjects – even described as being now 'somewhat more Civill' – but not while they live under the purview of Old English lords and Irish chieftains.[56] It is these men, claiming the prerogatives of their ancient bloodlines, whom Spenser makes 'villain,' exposing the extent to which they have grown base in blood through wilful neglect. If English monarchs had long assumed that the Old English were able governors – of the Irish but also of themselves – Spenser's goal is to call their bluff, to show that their declined blood makes them unfit to be the rightful heirs of Ireland. He does this by demonstrating in countless vignettes how bloodlines, like the stock of plants to which they were linked, transform and decay over time if not given proper attention. To the extent that he shows how much blood's properties alter through various acts of mingling and mismanaging, he confounds their value as a measure of a person's merit and as an indicator of a person's true allegiances.

**Bloody Lines**

Traditionally, it has been the fifth book of *The Faerie Queene,* with its portrayal of Artegal's quest for justice on behalf of the damsel Irena, that has been the locus of criticism concerned with the poem's relation to the conquest of Ireland. More recently, however, critics have interrogated the logic supporting such a view, which implicitly imagines Ireland as a finite object of representation neatly bound to a single book of the epic, rather than as an active ideological field that might lay claim to the entire poem. One critic has compellingly intervened on these terms to propose that 'Spenser's project is nothing less than the making of Irish colonial society,'[57] suggesting that Ireland stands, as it were, at the poem's very centre. The force of such an assertion is not, it bears clarification, to offer Ireland as 'the' key that unlocks the intricacies of Spenserian allegory, but rather to propose that the social and political dynamics of Irish society, which were the very conditions of the poem's composition, cannot help but pervade the entire poem. We can intuit this from the abundance of Irish place names and objects that abound in all the books, one critic recently even identifying a brotherhood of knights in Ireland who denoted their fellowship through the emblem of the red cross, revealing the layering of Irish meanings within tropes long presumed to have an exclusively 'English' referent.[58] But, more at large, we can see the hand of Ireland in the poem's broad thematic concerns with the nature of rule, law, and conquest; with civility, savagery, and the soft divide that holds them apart; as well as with the implications of distance, exile, and estrangement from a courtly centre. My own concern is to suggest how Spenser's charged relationship to the conflict in Ireland imprints itself on the epic's second book, which takes a hard look at the polemical issues of race catalysed by this context.

Of course, scholars have already culled Irish intimations from a book that otherwise might seem removed from political concerns given its extremely 'private' focus on bodily management. Hence, Stephen Greenblatt early on read the book's final canto, with its representation of the seductions of the Bower of Bliss, as recording the gendering of discovery, and David Read has understood Spenser's emphasis on temperance as informed by a broader English colonial ethos eager to portray English conquest as removed from the ruthlessness of Spanish conquistadores.[59] If these readings have the value of insisting on the book's imbrication in colonial dynamics, they suffer from moving too readily to freeze that field into a set of oppositions, failing to observe the intricate exchange and modulations of identity – both English and Irish – captured in and through the epic's representation. That is, both readings tacitly work from the assumption of a unified English identity, one that gets shored up in and through the production of an 'other,' whether Irish or Spanish. But my own interest is in what the book's representation of temperance does to *English* identities, specifically, how it encodes and seeks to resolve a fracture internal to English society, one that gets overlooked when we too readily homogenize a diverse group of English interests under a single nominal rubric – that of colonizer. The reality was infinitely more complex. Those who set out to subdue foreign lands were as divided by rank, station, and interest from each other as were those they left behind, and the colonies often served as de facto crucibles where these pre-existing rivalries were sorted out.[60] It is with this point in mind that the anthropologist Ann Laura Stoler, in an effort to bring Foucault's writing to bear on the topics of race and colonization, argued for the need for a more supple language of difference, demonstrating how frequently colonists made use of their displacement to reconfigure the metropole.[61] In the case of Spenser, the notion that bloodline should serve as the arbiter of social power was a long-standing assumption of English political life that tensions in Ireland led him to challenge.

Of course, that blood is central to the book is explicitly signalled in the book's subtitle – 'Of Temperaunce' – a phrase that announces the book's dedication to a virtue representing not only physical 'moderation' but the more specific act of 'mingling or combining in due proportion' various physical substances – passions, humours, spirits – carried by the blood and shaping the body's complexion.[62] Concerned with the limits of 'life in the body,' as against the temptations of the soul that the Red Cross Knight must face, the second book of Spenser's epic defines bodily life primarily as a function of regulating one's blood. Hence, bloody imagery pervades the book, with variants of the word *blood* appearing no fewer than sixty-two times, and its conceptual counterpart – the word *race* – appearing eleven times, more than in either Book 1 or 3.[63] If Guyon stands for order, balance, and rule of blood, the book seems to delight in dramatizing blood that is out of place, directing us to figures who are encrusted in blood, spurting blood, and embalmed in the 'mucky filth' associated with the body. Time and again we see blood wandering off course, not only inflamed to violent passion within the contours of the body but erupting beyond its bounds and absorbed into a surrounding landscape.[64] Its eruptions create havoc both for individuals – who are challenged and tormented by its rapid shifts – and for larger collectivities, particularly those conjoined by ties of blood.

Indeed, kinship bonds – or their failure – are a principal concern for Guyon, who is unique among Spenser's knights in being a protector of orphans. Where many of the epic's other books depict knights defending damsels in distress, or, in the case of Britomart, in hot pursuit of a male beloved, Guyon is instead a guardian of the young, the one knight whom we see devoted to the chivalric role of 'Defending ... Orphans right' (3.2.14.6). Hence, in the 'Letter of the Authors' we learn that he is called forth from court by 'a Palmer bearing an Infant with bloody hands, whose Parents he complained to haue bene slayn by an Enchaunteresse called Acrasia' (717). Although this account is overturned by the events that open Book 2, which find Guyon discovering Ruddymane and his not-yet deceased mother in the 'real-time' of his adventure rather than before its inception, both episodes point to the priority of the babe and his protection as a crucial part of Guyon's mission. But what, we should ask, does the babe have to do with temperance, and what larger cultural dynamics are figured in this central episode, which serves as the pivot for the entire book, the origin for Guyon's vow of revenge toward which the book crescendos?

The son of Amavia and Mortdant, the babe Ruddymane is first discovered by Guyon and his Palmer puddling his hands in the 'streaming blood' of his mother's lethal wounds. Her blood oozes onto the child, marking his hands and spreading outward to defile the 'bubling foun-taine' that she lies beside (2.1.40.2). Blood also dominantly defines the child's father, Mortdant, who has a range of sanguineous markings inso-far as his armour is 'besprinkled' with blood, and even in death he dis-plays fully blooded features in having 'ruddy lips' and 'rosy red' 'cheekes' (2.1.41.3–5). Although his blood-coated armour evokes images of knights in heroic combat – even serving to redouble the force of heraldic insig-nia which often contained markings called gules to denote drops of red blood[65] – we learn that this knight has died not in battle but through his own acts of distemperance, having prostrated himself before Acrasia, the enchantress whose powerful curse overpowers his wife's attempts to cure him with purgatives. Departing from home and from his expectant wife in search of heroic adventures, he soon abandons this quest, seduced as he is by the witch's charms. Though his wife eventually learns of the treachery and sets out to rescue him, doing so proves her demise and, possibly, something worse for their son. For the babe comes to have his parent's crime indelibly marked on him, destining him to a life devoted to 'mind[ing] reuengement' (2.2.10.8).

If blood is a charged signifier in this tableau – one that denotes the failure of an otherwise thriving bloodline – it has the power to absorb those beyond its racial circuit, ensnaring even Guyon in its representa-tional grip. The mere act of witnessing this family's carnage produces a passion within the rescuing knight that threatens to 'frieze' his 'fresh blood' (2.1.42.3), nearly killing him with extreme pangs of pity. His reac-tion crystallizes, by reiterating, what the scene stages: disjunction, eras-ure, death without heroic memorialization. This threat echoes through the episode. We see it in the caesura – the dead poetic space – that brings Amavia's lament to a halt as she dies, and in the seemingly trivial material effect that her cries produce for Guyon. Indeed, upon hearing her shrieks, he and the Palmer respond by staying 'their forward steps' (2.1.35.9), thereby setting aside both the 'hard assayes' (2.1.35.2) that have thus far engaged them and the steed and spear that are the means and emblems of such heroic achievement. When Guyon returns for his martial supports, he finds they are gone. We later learn that they have been stolen by Braggadocchio, but for now we know only that they pre-cipitate Guyon's turn to pedestrian life, the plodding and patient course of movement on foot. As such, the genealogical 'race' that has lapsed for Mortdant – his death in the bloom of youth – impedes the chivalric 'race' of adventure (2.1.32.7) that Guyon until now has actively and forcefully pursued, suggesting that Mortdant's actions possess the potential for spreading contamination. Mortdant's errancy thereby ensnares himself no less than his entire family and those who seek to rescue him.

If this episode has tended to be interpreted in conjunction with the Christian narrative of original sin, emphasizing the taint that adheres to all mortal flesh,[66] I suggest that it reads, as well, in secular terms as an emblem of genealogical rupture, denoting the blemishing of a noble bloodline.[67] This emphasis on lineal identity is captured not only in the clustered bodies of a father, mother, and son, but also in their placement beside a fountain from which flows water saturated with blood. These disseminating waters, like the many rivers that feature in Spenser's poetry, can be seen to emblematize the wandering paths and unanticipated mergings of bloodlines, signalling the flows of generation. In 'Colin Clouts Come Home Again,' for instance, Spenser developed the genealogical symbolism of rivers in his account of Mulla and Bregog, the two Irish rivers who conjoin against the will of the 'father,' Old Mole, who prefers to see his 'daughter' matched with the river Allo, Spenser's name for the Blackwater. He extends this familial metaphor in the 'Cantos of Mutabilitie' in describing the union of Fanchin, Spenser's spelling of the river Funsheon, with the stream Molanna (7.6.40–53).[68] The disloyal maid, Molanna, is punished for aiding Faunus in his plan to spy on the bathing Diana in that her flowing waters are impeded – 'whelm'd with stone' (7.6.53.4) – on their path toward union with Fanchin. Rivers abide by genealogical patterns as well in Book 4, where we get an account of the origin of the three Irish rivers – the Shure, the Newre, and the Barrow. Here the three rivers are imaged as the offspring – the 'faire sons' (4.11.42.8) – of the nymph Rheusa, whose delivery of these children is imaged as a pouring forth (4.11.42.8) that serves to generate the river lines. In each case, the flows of rivers denote genealogical flows, whose origins and mixtures are sometimes chaste but also sometimes expressive of illicit desire.

In the context of the Mortdant episode, the waters of the fountain double as an image of Amavia, whose blood flows into the river as she dies. The mother, like the river, is a life-source. Moreover, just as Amavia's wounded heart gushes 'a stream of goreblood thick' (2.1.39.7), so this 'bubling fountaine' flows with 'purple gore' (2.1.40.2, 4). But the airiness of the fountain's pure waters also clearly contrasts with Amavia's thicker blood, setting off through opposition the parents whose bodies are strewn beside it: against their excess of desire, the fountain's waters originate as a protection for a chaste nymph, and against their inability to protect bodily thresholds, first when Mortdant submits to Acrasia and then when Amavia subjects both herself and her baby to 'danger and great dreed' (2.1.52.9) in disguising herself as a palmer to search for her spouse, the stream guards its waters in not allowing the boy's blood-stained hands to be cleansed in her waves (2.2.3). As the Palmer explains to Guyon, the fountain thereby manifests its 'chaste and pure' (2.2.9.7) virtues, having emerged to protect a nymph from the stain of Faunus's lust.[69] But in refusing to 'drink' the blood on the child's hands, it also serves the function of reproducing this virtue for the child, becoming a kind of prophylactic for him. Its insoluble waters guard him by preventing the 'erasure' of the blood-mark that holds his identity, ensuring that he does not fail in the same way his father has. Amavia has already related the nature of that failure when she tells Guyon the origin of her despair; she recalls, 'me he knew not' (2.1.54.5). If Mortdant's memory of his origin has been washed away through contact with Acrasia's waters of excess – symbolized by the charmed cup (2.1.55.3) from which he sips in her bower – his son's identity will be preserved in a more chaste form, symbolically transmitted to him by the Nymph's stony flesh, fixed as rocks – the 'two heads' (2.2.9.1) at the stream's origin. His bloody hands are ensured by such contact to live on, serving as a 'sacred Symbole' and an 'endlesse moniment' of 'his mothers innocence' (2.2.10.7, 9, 5) in contradistinction to the forgetfulness of his father. The chaste river initiates, then, a reform to a declined genealogy, to a failure of race.

If righting this failure depends on protecting the memory of one's origin, Guyon extends this memorializing project in transforming the river's action into verbal form in calling the child 'Ruddymane,' naming him for the mark derived from his parents. This, he tells Medina when he entrusts her with the child (2.3.2), will remind the boy 'T'auenge his Parents death on them, that had it wrought' (2.3.2.9). This act of naming clarifies the nature of Guyon's role as defender of orphans. It suggests that protecting the child requires not only care for the individual but salvaging his lineal relations, the bonds produced by blood. Indeed, as the episode reveals in charting the rapidity of Mortdant's lapse – which has occurred in less than a year – Faeryland is a place where kinship bonds readily vanish, 'like vapours,' in the way that Spenser's *Ruines of Time* observes of greatness at large.[70] In that poem, the spirit of the ancient Roman city of Verlame laments the erasure of greatness, while the speaker grapples with the loss of a Leicester, Sidney, or Walsingham. Though cities and houses rise and fall, the poem suggests, their heroism can persist through the labours of poets, who memorialize their names in their immortal lines. Similarly, without Guyon's crucial intervention, Ruddymane will suffer namelessness and oblivion, the same fate that Spenser's *View* associates with the 'adventurers' who first sought the heroic conquest of Ireland.[71] These Old English planters – 'the Audleyes, the Talbotes the Tutchites, the Chamberlaines, the Mandevils, and the Salvages' – though of 'antient dignities' in England, had left no 'memorie' or 'signe' of their former greatness once they moved to Ireland.[72] To Irenius's chagrin, the memory of their great stock had been vanquished over time, their names utterly forgotten by their own children's children. Indeed, only the Irish could reveal that the 'Macmaghons' were 'auncientlie Englishe, to witt, discended from the fitz Vrsulas ... a noble familie in England.' And no one would know that Lord Bremingham's race was now the 'Maccorish' clan, or that 'the great Mortymer ... forgettinge how great he was once in England, or English at all is now become the most barborous of them all, and is called *Macnemarra*.'[73] Like Mortdant – whose name shares the same root as that 'most barborous' offender Mortimer – each of these adventurers had left his family in pursuit of honour, moved by 'high corage' (2.1.50.5). But like Mortdant, each of them had only managed to give the gift of erasure to their offspring, severing the 'budding braunch ... from the natiue tree' (2.2.2.6) and destining them to being 'scattered' and 'withered' (2.2.2.5, 7) – even orphaned. Insofar as Guyon gives the orphaned Ruddymane a name that attaches him to his origin – even if one marred by his father's failure – Guyon remedies this failure, positioning the errant child on a new 'race,' one that directs him toward the 'dew vengeance' of righting 'guiltie blood' (2.1.61.7, 8).

Compellingly, this episode concludes with the Palmer bearing the child in his arms, while Guyon 'his sad fathers armes ... did lightly reare' (2.2.11.3–4). The punning play on the word *reare*, with its doubled sense of carry but also nurture, alerts us to the detail's significance in the larger dynamic of 'rearing' that surrounds Guyon.[74] Curiously, at the same moment that he gathers up the dead father's arms, he also discovers his own steed and spear to be missing, a detail whose explanation the narrator defers for a later time (2.2.11.9). Rather than entertaining us with this distraction, we are invited to focus on the transference of martial symbols, along with the exchange of the child from one man to another, which this episode records. Through this sequence of exchanges, Guyon comes to possess the primary symbols of Mortdant's patronymic: his armour and his heir. Iconographically, then, he absorbs the father's identity, becoming a surrogate father for the orphaned child. The prospect of a similar kind of exchange arises in Spenser's *View*, when the topic of 'wardes' comes up. In this context, Irenius observes how much harm results from the bonds that connect knights to lords in Ireland, which allows the children of the former to be raised 'in the warde of those Lordes,' with the effect that they are 'brought vpp lewdlie and Irishe lyke.' This matter could be rectified, he argues, were 'those ward-shipps ... in the princes disposition,' since the Queen 'would take better order for the bringing vpp of those wards in good Nourture, and not suf-fer them to come into so badd handes.'[75] Ruddymane is saved from such a fate by Guyon's intervention. Although his hands register the stain of his father's declined blood – and evoke Irenius's image of 'badd handes' – they have been reclaimed, turned against those responsible for first infecting 'with secret filth' his father's blood (2.2.4.7). Insofar as the epi-sode positions Ruddymane as the ward of the tempered Medina – 'that virgin pure' (2.3.2.1) who resembles Irenius's Queen – it seeks to heal the corruptions of kin-ties that governed Irish politics. Eudoxus might well serve as a voiceover for Guyon, then, when he observes, 'I hould yt noe wysdome to leaue vnto them to much commaund over theire kyn-red, but rather ... to gather them vnder the Commaund of Lawe by some better meane.'[76]

If, then, this episode seems to value lineage as a principle of order – even lamenting its disruption in the form of a Mortdant or his Old English counterparts – it also points up the limitations accompanying this system of identity, subtly insisting on its reform. Noble bloodlines, it reveals, falter, bending to the powerful undertow of degeneracy. If not constantly maintained and guarded in the way that Ruddymane's red hands will remind him, they do and will decay. The ability of bloodlines to transmit virtue intergenerationally, therefore, is revealed by this epi-sode to be profoundly conditional. Moreover, if Guyon appears to be a protector of sabotaged bloodlines, insofar as he rescues Ruddymane from oblivion, it is also crucial to consider how his actions actually serve to reconstitute the nature of family bonds. Like the Irish and Old Eng-lish wards imagined by Irenius, Ruddymane is grafted onto a new race, in this case that emblematized by Guyon himself. Indeed, in the episode where he submerges the child's hands in the waters, which many critics read as an emblem of baptism, the child is symbolically reborn, or, we might say, re-raced, made a son of Guyon. The knight does, quite clearly, place him on a new course, line, or race – the telos that will constitute his future. If these actions are framed as efforts that connect the child to his natural parents – his begetters – they also remake the child in the image of Guyon. For like his protector, Ruddymane is directed toward venge-ance, toward righting a wrong, Guyon's principal concern throughout the book.[77] His father, by contrast, was bent on fame, departing 'to seeke aduentures wilde ... his puissaunt force to proue' (2.1.50.6–7). Ruddymane's quest is therefore of a fundamentally different nature than that of his father. If his father was about self-aggrandizement, and the pride that seeks the attention of heroic heights, his son will be, like Guyon, more 'pedestrian' in pursuing 'dew vengeance' (2.1.61.7). Not only is the child bound to Guyon through the vow they make as they bury his parents (2.1.61), but the child is symbolically brought low when his blood is mixed with earth (2.1.61.3), a detail that seems to mark a break from his aspiring father.

### Ireland's 'Unnatural' Family

The family romance that comes to define Guyon's quest was also writ large in New English representations of the predicament of Ireland. These tracts sought to discredit the Old English by portraying them as the 'unnatural' offspring of a parent whom they had neglected and forgotten. Such a charge is obliquely registered in the tract by Spenser's friend and contemporary, Lodowick Bryskett, whose *Discourse of Civill Life* reads as a prose counterpart to Spenser's epic in praising virtues like magnificence and temperance and in featuring vignettes that seem to have stepped right out of Spenser's poem of faery. In it we hear of men turned into beasts, of the mistaking of a person behind a bush for a deer, of the fallacy of hoarding money as 'muck and pelf,' and of Lycurgus's temperate powers to withstand the charms of a 'witch or inchantress.'[78] Indeed, Spenser himself appears as a character in the tract, as one of the men who convene outside of Dublin to discuss ethical life. Here he is described as completing a poem on the topic of moral life, and he directs his interlocutors to this text for his own treatment of the topic of 'civil happiness.'[79] It is in the context of discussing the merits of a notion of honour predicated on duels and violence – a feudal ethos defended by both Irish chieftains and Old English lords – that Bryskett explores the possibility that 'family' might turn upon itself. He notes how men sanctioning such views 'are not ashamed to say ... that a man for cause of honour may arme himself against his country ... yea euen against his father, and with cursed hands violate his person ... so long as the one ceaseth not to be a father, and the country forgetteth not her citizens.'[80] Here, citizens assume the posture of children to their country's parent, and the imagined rupture of blood ties emerges as an act of 'forgetting,' one produced through the violent acts of 'cursed hands.'[81] If the preferred metaphor here identifies the conflict as occurring between a father and child, Fynes Moryson, who would succeed Spenser as secretary to a lord deputy of Ireland, would modify the gendering of the family dynamic in his own accounts of the situation in Ireland. He, too, would depend on familial metaphors to describe the estrangement of the Old English from the English monarch, but he would conceive of 'the State (as a mother) with open Armes [who receives] her disobedient Children to mercy.'[82] In imagining the Queen as tending toward maternal dotage, Moryson figured the political predicament of Ireland in terms similar to Spenser. In his view the Queen, like Amavia, was a woman who risked everything in loving too well someone who had strayed beyond rescue. Though she might apply purgatives, 'wise handling and faire gouernaunce' (2.1.54.6) in an attempt to effect his 'deliuerance' (2.1.54.9), such solutions would prove only transient. As Sir John Davies observes of the House of Desmond, the family he blamed for first degenerating: 'yet could not the king's grace regenerate obedience in that degenerate House, but it grew rather more wild and barbarous than before.'[83] Like Mortdant, whose reform at the hands of Amavia bends to Acrasia's deeper claim, the Old English cannot help but backslide.

Where these writers depict the situation in Ireland through a set of binary figurations – a parent as against a child – Spenser's poetic representation of a similar dynamic differs in triangulating the political dynamic, thereby creating a more mobile symbolic field, one allowing for the difference that he associates with New English ascendancy. In his vignette, notably, it is the father, rather than the child, who stands for forgetfulness and the degenerative slide that it encodes. He is the one whose wilful actions produce the unnecessary spilling of blood. Ruddymane, by contrast, is associated with a future in which order might be restored; he picks up where his father has left off, symbolically stepping into his shoes by walking off – under Guyon's surrogacy – with his bloody armour.[84] If the armour revests him with the heroic quest abandoned by his father, his bloodied hands remind him specifically of his mother. As the Palmer notes, 'they his mothers innocence may tell' (2.2.10.5), deviating from the symbolism of the patronym in establishing a *maternal* origin for the orphan. To that extent, the episode stresses the unbreakable bonds between the 'new children' of Ireland – New English Ruddymanes – and mother England. Unlike their Old English counterparts, these new men will never forget the mother who bore them.

If the trope of the orphan crucially informs Guyon's mission, it also figured prominently in an unpublished tract by a New English planter written in the early 1590s, in the context of a stinging critique of the Queen's policies in Ireland. Casting its lament as the 'crye of the father-lesse orphanes,' the text appeals to the Queen to abandon her Old English children, warning that they no longer could be said to share 'ore nature' since they were 'no more Englishe.' Pushing up against the limits of the familial trope central to his argument, the author insists, 'They nowe retaine nothinge of that they were but the bare name… And why? Because the blood of theire Irishe mothers, hath wasted away the natu-rall love they bare to theire mother England.' One mother, as it were, has displaced another in their affections, resulting in the charge of unnatu-ralness and betrayal. In cajoling the Queen for being reluctant to break with them, the author intimates that the same charge will attach to her, should she fail to defend her children newly orphaned in Ireland. Flirt-ing with the accusation of illegitimacy, he urges, 'The bloode of youre most renowned and magnanimous father remaining in you, would have boyled out longe ere this a revenge.'[85] Not acting on her part, the author suggests, is tantamount to proclaiming herself a bastard, confirming her own degeneracy from a princely bloodline.

By emphasizing that Old English blood had been marred in Ireland – both by Irish mothers and their other begetter 'the earth of Irland' – the author of this tract gives voice to a larger cultural shift that was coming to define this late sixteenth-century moment. He suggests that race – as determined by blood and descent – may not be an airtight determinant of identity, and that place of birth should supersede it as a testament to one's true 'nature.' He reaches this striking conclusion when he describes the Old English as 'naturall plants of theire owne soyle,' iden-tifying their native Ireland as 'their naturall mother' and implying that they have become alien to England. He contrasts their status with that of New English planters, who know Ireland only as a 'stepdame,' a rela-tion that renders their adopted land in terms fully subordinate to their land of birth – England. A similar shift can be observed gathering force across the archive of commentary on Ireland throughout the second half of the sixteenth century. It is most audible, I suggest, in the language used to describe the Old English community. As early as 1541, in the wake of the Kildare rebellion, an English act declaring Henry VIII king of Ireland recognized no distinction between English subjects living in England and those living in Ireland, referring to the king's 'English sub-jects in Ireland' as against his 'Irish enemies,' who were to be conquered and made English subjects themselves.[86] Defining identity exclusively in relation to the sovereign, the act identifies loyal settlers living abroad as English subjects in no uncertain terms.

So, too, in the period leading up to the Desmond rebellion, it was customary among English deputies in Ireland to refer to the Old English by reference to their English lineages. Hence Lord Deputy Sussex – who controlled the English effort in Ireland from 1556 to 1564 – described the Butlers, the Old English family he most cultivated as his allies in Ireland, as 'for the most part of English bloud or name.'[87] Similarly, in a memoir of his service in Ireland, Sir Henry Sidney repeatedly refers to the Old English community through phrases like 'gentlemen of English race' and men of 'English lineage,' connecting them to English circles of power by reference to their bloodlines. Indeed, at times it seems he is at pains to make these connections, despite the ravages of time so lamented by Irenius. While in Galway, for instance, he records confronting a 'Mack William Eughter of English race, and by surname Borough, there called Burke, but in Latin anciently and modernly written De Burgo.' Evoking the Latin version of the name, it seems, serves to authorize or demystify the Gaelic rendering, just as the memoir insists throughout that the Old English had willingly submitted to Sidney and that they were 'desirous to live in loyalty, and under the laws and subjection of the crown of England.'[88]

Increasingly, however, those critical of a 'soft' approach to these Old English lords sought to identify and emphasize a difference. They did so by speaking not of the enduring bonds of blood and lineage, but rather of the changes wrought to blood by soil and nurture, thereby suggesting the impermanency of bloodline, the rapidity with which a race's markings could be 'rased.'[89] Those critical of Sidney, for instance, charged that he was 'guided in the government by councilors of *Irish birth*' – a phrase that described the Old English community – and Lord Grey famously dismissed the Earl of Ormond, cousin to the Queen, as leader of the Munster army on the grounds that only an 'Englishe governor' could be entrusted with that role.[90] Moryson, serving in the late 1590s, took this emphasis to a new extreme, repeatedly associating the threat of the Old English with the fact of their being 'borne and bredd in Ireland,' more radically redefining the community by naming them 'English Irish' to emphasize that they were a 'mingled race.' Indeed, he occasionally seems to drop the label 'English' altogether, using the term 'Irish lords' in an indiscriminate manner to describe men of Irish and Old English descent alike.[91] Davies would reinstate this fissure, observing it as a feature of the past, when he noted how tensions routinely erupted between 'the English of birth and the English of blood and race.'[92] Although he was narrating events long past, his history articulated with precision the syntax of the late Elizabethan and early Jacobean moment. For it was this moment that was producing a cataclysmic shift away from the language of race, bloodline, and lineage to that of birthplace as the defining anchor of identity.

### 'Failure[s] of the seed'[93]

Indeed, that bloodlines are fallible and errant seems to be a dominant theme of canto 10, which features Arthur's and Guyon's genealogical journey through their 'countreys auncestry' (2.9.60.7) in the form of the histories provided by '*Briton moniments*' (2.9.59.6) and '*Antiquitee* of *Faery* lond' (2.9.60.2). We have already seen that the epic's second book opens by identifying Guyon's quest as centrally concerned with righting violations to race and generation in that his quest revolves around a blighted family and the powerful undertow of degeneration. The tenth canto returns to this theme with a difference. Where the earlier episode isolates the transgression of blood to a single moment and a single generational crux – marking the passage from Mortdant to Ruddymane – the later one pans out, providing a vision of two distinct genealogies moving across time. But the episodes are linked in that both centrally feature an injunction to remember: in the one case, it is written in blood on an orphan's body; in the other, it is preserved in ink for a foster son. Like Ruddymane's hands, Arthur's chronicle is both a testament to his origins and a reminder of how bloodlines fail, how they deviate from the fixed lines presumed to govern them.

Indeed, as Harry Berger Jr long ago identified, what begins as a lofty account of the 'famous auncestryes / Of my most dreaded Soueraigne' (2.10.1.7–8) quickly devolves into an account of genealogical rupture. After four stanzas of praise to the Queen, we get sixty-four stanzas of 'sweat and blood which marked British history.'[94] If nobility of race is the principle presumably reified in this episode – insofar as the poet begins by celebrating the Queen's 'linage' for stretching 'forth to heuens hight' (2.10.2.3, 5) – blood-ties are also the episode's nemesis. Looking back into the archive of his ancestry, Arthur discovers the various forms of depravity that have ensnared his bloodline. The vile passions of pride and disdain have led brothers to kill one another, sons to prey on their parents, and mothers to victimize their sons. If the ideal of bloodline

suggests a continuity of race and purpose across time, this episode exposes that idea as wistful fantasy. For Arthur's royal ancestry is no less rid-
dled by distemperance than is Ruddymane's lineage. In fact, one of his
most ancient ancestors – Locrine, eldest son to Brute – seems to reca-
pitulate the very failures embodied by Mortdant. The 'soueraine Lord'
(2.10.14.1) of a Britain divided at his father's death, Locrine is admired
for instating a 'quiet gouernment' (2.10.14.8) over Britain and for his
heroic defense of the land against the Huns who disturb the land's peace
with a 'flood' of 'violence' (2.10.15.5, 6). But a form of forgetfulness
(2.10.17.3) soon upsets his noble posture. Proud and complacent after
his victory – perhaps too assured of his greatness – Locrine falls under
the grip of 'vnwonted ease' and 'voluptuous disease' (2.10.17.2, 5) in the
form of his desire for a woman. Like the fallen knight of Guyon's opening
adventure, this king allows himself to love 'leudly' (2.10.17.6), breaking
the bond of marriage. Emasculation is the result. Not only is he 'van-
quisht' in battle by his wife (2.10.18.5) and placed 'in bands' (2.10.18.7),
but his incontinence spreads out to the innocent, ensnaring the 'sad
virgin' Sabrina, his illegitimate daughter (2.10.19.6). Echoing the scene
of the chaste Amavia's death, when her blood blends with the waters of
the nymph's fountain, the chaste Sabrina is 'poure[d]' (2.10.19.7) by
the revenging Guendolene into the Severn River, her innocence paying the price for her father's concupiscence. The bloody lines of this
'moniment,' like Ruddymane's bloody hands, memorialize the crime
and remind those who come after of blood's rapid transformations. If, as
Berger argues, the history breaks from its chronicle sources in withholding a sense of 'moral causality,'[95] in dispensing with a telos it also strikes
a blow to the early modern ideology of race-as-blood. For if the earlier
episode with Mortdant illuminated the degenerative slide that was the
'fatale destynie' of Irish soil, this episode exposes such decline as a threat
haunting the very centre – England's own royal bloodline.[96]

Indeed, Locrine's is but the first in a series of such failures, where
royal heirs refuse to embody the merits of their bloodlines. The virtues
of Brutus's line suffers decline for a range of reasons. Either an heir
proves by nature, like Madan, to be 'vnworthie of his race' (2.10.21.1),
or he seeks too doggedly to enjoy the exclusive privileges of sovereignty,
to horde the power and privilege conferred by blood. So Cundah, grandson to King Leyr, envies his brother's share of sovereignty, leading him
to kill him so that 'he none equall knew' (2.10.33.9). And Porrex and
Ferrex kill first their father and then each other, so driven as they are by
'greedy thirst of royall crowne' (2.10.35.1). Even Bladud, who is singled

out for his civility in being the deliverer of arts from Athens, succumbs to pride, seeking, like Icarus, 'to excell / The reach of men' (2.10.26.8–9). Indeed, if there is one recurring failure that governs this sequence it is that those of noble blood – who have inherited political power as a function of birth – seem to gravitate 'naturally' to tyranny, to unbounded political appetite.

Indeed, after seven hundred years, we learn there is scarcely a 'moniment' (2.10.36.8) of Brutus's royal bloodline remaining, so consumed with self-butchery has it been. In the charged botanical imagery that served as the iconography of early modern race, we hear how 'The noble braunch from th'antique stocke was torne' (2.10.36.4), as the genealogical line comes to a screeching halt. In fact, it seems precisely the point that an end is inevitable, surprising only that the bloodline has managed to extend itself across so many centuries amid all the internecine warfare.[97] In the next sequence of stanzas, and, specifically, with the rise of a new ruler, this state of affairs is rectified but only because bloodline, as a principle of rule, has been dethroned. Peace and stability, that is, are reinstated by a figure who is defined by the absence of a noble bloodline. Indeed, that this figure has no familial connections to speak of is crucially underlined by the poem's withholding of a name for him. Naming, as we have seen in the case of Ruddymane, is of defining importance for Spenser and his contemporaries, insofar as it establishes lineal connections. The Old English, in particular, were scorned for rejecting 'their very English names (though they were noble and of great antiquity),' an act that was perceived to deprive them of race, to remove the '*marks or differences* ... of that noble nation from which they were descended.'[98] And so the fact that it is an unnamed man of law who assumes the throne – on the basis of his merits, his 'matchlesse might, / And wondrous wit' (2.10.37.1–2) – signals not just the introduction of a 'new dynasty,'[99] but an attempt to modify the entire dynastic system. This man – whom only our textual notes identify as 'Donwallo' – is singled out for not having a noble pedigree, and for earning his path to rule on the basis of his deeds. Deviating from the various chronicle sources to which he had access, Spenser chooses to narrate his rise to power as a function of an election, describing how he is chosen by princes who convene at his request (2.10.37.6–7).[100] Although the laws of succession resume following his death, yielding the Briton line, it is implied that principles guiding 'dew successe' (2.10.45.7) have been reformed. Notably, rulers of this line are defined by their deeds and virtues, and when such actions lapse, as happens for Archigald (2.10.44.4–5), deposition is invoked as a political corrective, one that serves in this case to reform the king's behaviour. Moreover, in the absence of a viable heir – as in the period when Lud's sons are in their minority – election, rather than blood-based feuding, is the default political mechanism (2.10.47.2). The new ethos of this line is signalled as well by its adherence to statutory law, by the desire to limit the powers of the land's over-mighty subjects, those of a previous era who rule 'By strength' and 'without pollicy' (2.10.39.8). So we see Donwallo overthrow the petty kings of Albany and Cambry – the land's marcher lords. And we see that Guitheline and his wife Dame Mertia (2.10.42) rule justly in accordance with a set of 'wholesome Statutes' (2.10.42.6). The new era inaugurated by Donwallo comes to stand for a new state, where the singular power of elite blood and the aspirations to untempered power that it signifies are brought to curb.

If this journey into the bowels of Britain's past evokes for its Arthurian 'foster Childe' (2.10.69.5) feelings of 'secret plesaure' (2.10.68.8) and 'wonder' (2.10.68.9) in providing a survey of the 'natiue land' (2.10.69.2) he has not seen since birth, it also serves the more didactic function of exposing the contemporary problems besieging England's foster children living abroad in Ireland. For as the *View* repeatedly argues, stepping foot into Ireland is like stepping back in the pages of history, occupying a land bearing an uncanny similarity to 'England … in the raigne of Henrie the second.' The social relations that govern each land – Norman England and Elizabethan Ireland – are, Irenius insists, 'worthie of sharpe correction' and would offend any Englishmen were they 'now vsed in England.'[101] The implication is that they are intolerable for Englishmen living in Ireland as well. For Ireland, like Britain in a bygone age, is a land gripped by the 'tyranny of great lordes,' by men whose noble bloodlines have enabled them to raise themselves to 'immoderate greatnesse.'[102] Indeed, across the vast range of tracts on Ireland by New English settlers, as Debora Shuger has demonstrated, the Old English are impugned for enjoying excessive power in Ireland on the basis of their ancestry. Davies's account of the process by which these lords '[grewe] out of frame'[103] reads as an echo of the abuses that characterized the line of Brutus: 'those large scopes of land and great liberties, with the absolute power to make war and peace, did raise the English lords to that height of pride and ambition as that they could not endure one another, but grew to a mortal war and dissension among themselves.' He concludes, 'great estates and royalties … begat pride, and pride begat contention among themselves,' identifying their internecine warfare as 'the chief [impediment] of the final conquest of Ireland.'[104] Diagnosing the same social ill, Moryson argues that the 'yoke of the great lords' was enabled by claims based on descent, since these lords defended their actions by arguing 'that their Progenitors did not only giue them lands to till' but also 'challenged right of Inheritance in their Tenants persons, as if by old Couenants they were borne slaues to till their grounde.'[105] Richard Beacon, too, understood the dangers of high blood in Ireland, noting how the Old English lords 'grew unto such greatnesse as they acknowledged no superiour,' holding 'for lawes their owne willes and desires.'[106] Living in Ireland was like living in ancient Britain, which was, in turn, like living in that 'happy land of Faery' (proem to Book 2, 1.7).

Indeed, it seems at every turn that Guyon encounters coupled figures who embody the abusive feudal relations that these writers identify as the source of Ireland's intractability. Atin's devotion to Pyrochles, for instance, is characterized by a steep hierarchy that resembles the relationships between lords in Ireland and their tenants and horseboys. His devotion to his master is blind, with his master's will wielding the force of law for him, in the way that Spenser observed was standard practice among a lord's vassals.[107] Moryson indicated how corrupt these bonds could be in observing that 'the Country people living vnder the lordes absolute power as slaues ... obey their lordes in right and wrong.'[108] Announcing his subjection to Pyrochles, Atin describes his relationship to his master in almost these precise terms: 'His am I *Atin*, his in wrong and right' (2.4.42.5). He later risks his life by jumping in a lake 'his Lord to ayd' (2.6.46.1), demonstrating the extreme devotion produced by 'dread of daunger' (2.6.46.2) or fear. Similarly, Sir Huddibras, whose name is identical to that of one of the kings of Brutus's line (2.10.25.4), seems to enjoy freedoms associated both with those ancient ancestors and the Old English. Described as 'great of name' rather than 'good of deedes' (2.2.17.3), in contradistinction to the line of rulers authored by Donwallo, Sir Huddibras engages in 'cruell combat ioynd in middle space' (2.2.20.3). If on the one hand this suggests his rejection of the middle path of temperance, it also connects him to the space running through 'the very lapp of all the land,' Irenius's description of the middle space of the county palatines. Originating as a privilege that granted lords great powers to subdue border territories or pales, the privilege had since devolved into an 'abuse' to 'robb the rest of the Countries about yt.'[109] The anatomy of bloodlines that centrally informs Guyon's quest for temperance, therefore, exposes the 'heroic code of the armigerous aristocracy' – wonderfully parodied in the blood-encircled flames rendered on Pyrochles' shield – to be a cover for the 'hot, wilful and stubborn' behaviour that Sir Henry Sidney associated with the rebel Earl of Desmond.[110]

## Earthly Spirits

Moryson casts such ideologies as outrageously obsolete when he describes the new names taken by these Old English lords. Mocking them, he notes that 'some[,] as if they were knights of Amadis of Gaule, and had the valor of those errant knights, were called the knight of the valley, the white knight, and the like.'[111] His words – specifically, his scorn for the professed principles guiding 'errant knights' – lead us to a concluding question: if Spenser shared Moryson's disdain for a warrior aristocracy wedding political power to bloodline, why does he devise the figure of a knight errant to oppose this ethos? For a critic like Debora Shuger, the presence of 'crusading knights' in the epic poem is enough to indicate its distance from the 'bourgeois' vision of the *View*. For her, this fact evidences the poem's complicity in a chivalric ideology.[112] My own sense is that we need to parse the figure of the knight more precisely, allowing that the repetition of a term or social category – such as knighthood – across discrete texts and moments creates only an illusion of stasis, since different texts and moments press change incrementally by assigning new meanings to a familiar word or social category. Curiously, in the case of Guyon, Spenser seems to go out of his way to connect his knight to traditional knightly figures and the genre of medieval romance. Hence, his hero's name echoes the name of famous romance heroes, as in 'Guy of Warwick' or 'Guy of Burgundy,'[113] and he seems to step out of the pages of a romance, in being associated with figures like Sir Huon and King Oberon (2.1.6.8–9). Moreover, as I indicated above, he alone has the title 'Sir' proclaimed on the title page that introduces his quest, singling it out for our attention. But if these romance tags seem to suggest the poem's sanctioning of a feudal ethos that Guyon embodies, there are also suggestions that the text may be pressing subtle modulations and adjustments to this ideology. For one thing, Guyon denotes a quite precise kind of knightly identity. We know, for instance, that if he is of 'noble state' (2.1.6.5), he has only recently been knighted, an event that seems to be associated with a previous trip to the land of faery, when he presumably earned the honour in the field fighting on behalf of 'king *Oberon*' (2.1.6.9). His, then, is a recent ennobling, born of deed and merit, rather than one inherited through an illustrious lineage.

Moreover, the poet seems to go out of his way to name a difference between Guyon and the poem's other knights in defining him as of 'Elf-in kynd' (2.10.71.2), as compared with the princely Saxon origins of the Red Cross Knight and the royal British origins of Arthur. Exactly how we should read Guyon's label is ambiguous, since the designation 'Elfin' means a range of things in the poem – sometimes suggesting nobility, sometimes creatureliness, and still other times a figure's origins.[114] Looking to the 'rolls of Elfin Emperours' (Argument 2.10, l. 3), we get a more specific account of what the term might imply, where we learn that the race originated from earthly creatures – being 'deryu'd' from beasts (2.10.70.6) and animated by fire stolen from heaven – and that the line was raised to fame by virtue of their 'mightie deedes' and 'braue ensample' (2.10.74.4, 8). This earthly quality is reiterated when Guyon refuses Mammon's offer of a match with his daughter, Philotime, on the grounds that he is an 'earthly wight' of 'fraile flesh' and an 'Vnworthy match' for one of such 'high estate' (2.7.50.3, 4, 2). Earlier in the canto, Guyon had represented himself to Mammon as one of 'high heroicke spright,' who values 'Faire shields, gay steedes, bright armes' as the 'riches fit for an aduent'rous knight' (2.7.10.6, 8, 9). But his words here seem to express a form of hubris. As the canto proceeds, for instance, we observe how this 'heroicke' spirit ensnares him and results in his near death, since it has prompted him to follow Mammon deep into the tunnels of the earth. Moreover, we might intuit considerable irony in his attempt to associate himself with a set of knightly accoutrements that he spends much of the book either deprived of or seeking to reclaim. His horse and spear are stolen by Braggodocchio as early as the book's second canto, never to be returned in this book, and his shield is seized by Pyrochles during his 'deadly fit' (2.7.66.9), while Arthur borrows his sword (2.8.40.1–4) to defend him. When he awakens, Guyon immediately notices his missing weapons – asking 'what wicked hand hath robbed mee / Of my good sword and shield?' (2.8.54.1–2). And yet it is notable that from here on out, he needs and uses none of these traditional knightly weapons, depending on his own feet, the Palmer's staff, and the 'subtile net' (2.12.81.4) to capture Acrasia.

In fact, the disappearance of his steed, and the plodding course of walking on foot that it necessitates for Guyon, seems to be particularly important. Not only does it occur at the crucial moment of his discovery of Ruddymane, officially marking the start of his quest, but it lasts for the entire length of the book. If it marks symbolically his control of his passions – traditionally figured as a steed – it also serves to lower him physically, insisting that he remain grounded in the earth and implicitly curbing his aspirations for height. In contrast to the high adventure pursued by Mortdant, which results in his undoing, Guyon's course will be defined by a labouring ethos, one of 'derdoing' (2.7.10.1), with the emphasis on 'doing.' There is some reason to believe, then, that in these 'quirks' and 'evasions,' Spenser is providing the image of a 'new' kind of knight, a new ideal of what might count for a 'good' race. As against the high and 'hot' blood of a Desmond or a Huddibras, Guyon embodies steady qualities of blood, grounded by contact with the earth and the pedestrian labours that Guyon most emblematizes.

Spenser's friend, Bryskett, in his own account of civil life, holds out a similar ideal. In responding to criticisms that in leaving his public post he had surrendered the opportunity to 'have risen to better place,' Bryskett responds, 'It is a perilous thing for men of weake braines to stand in high places, their heads will so soone be giddie, and all climbing is subject to falling. Let men of great spirits, of high birth, and of excellent virtues, possesse in Gods name those dignities and preferments, which the favour of the Prince and their sufficiency may purchase vnto them.'[115] Guyon, we might recall, says something similar when he reproves the match with Philotime. Her court reminds him of the merits of lowliness in depicting the viciously competitive ethos that informs her courtier's bids 'to raise themselues to high degree' (2.7.47.1). In the land of faery, by contrast, only one 'kind' of man seems to be able to stay the course, only one 'kind' of man able to complete the 'race.' Earthly, plodding, and patient, Guyon embodies a new principle of blood, one that replaces the distemperance of high blood – with its boundless dash to degeneracy – with the temperance of blood 'made good' through countless acts of self-restraint. Rejecting the pattern of monstrous growth that characterized Old English lords in Ireland, Guyon stays low. In that respect, he resembled his author. For though Spenser toyed with his derivation from the noble stock of the Spencers, he would wear his blood with a difference. Where that family would 'boast of Armes and Auncestrie,' petitioning for a coat of arms in the mid-1590s, Spenser would urge, by contrast, 'I meanest boast my self to be.'[116]

# 2 Uncouth Milk and the Irish Wet Nurse

## The Politics of Breasts

In the account of ancient Briton resistance to Rome's occupation that appears in Holinshed's *Chronicles*, William Harrison highlights the revolt of Boadicea, the famed British queen of the Iceni tribe who led an army predominantly composed of women against the invaders. Though nearly successful in driving the Romans from Britain, Boadicea and her followers receive scant recognition for what are arguably a heroic display of nationalist sentiment and an ideal embodiment of ancient British vigour. Instead, Harrison chooses to emphasize the savage effects of Boadicea's leadership, describing in gruesome details the physical mutilations performed by her warriors on the bodies of their female enemies. Remembered not only for killing captives, they are also recorded as 'spar[ing] neither age nor sex: women of great nobilitie and worthie fame, they tooke and hanged vp naked, and cutting off their paps, sowed them to their mouthes, that they might seeme as if they sucked and fed on them.'[1] This gruesome image of women suckling at their own breasts resonates in uncanny ways with a similar account of mutilations performed on the bodies of English soldiers during an invasion of Wales. Familiar to Shakespeareans as a source text for Shakespeare's Henriad, the complementary episode describes how Welsh women mutilated the 'dead bodies of the Englishmen, being aboue a thousand lieng vpon the ground imbrued in their owne bloud' by '[cutting] off their priuities, and [putting] one part thereof into the mouthes of euerie dead man, in such sort that the cullions hoong downe to their chins.' In addition, the account describes how 'they did cut off their noses and thrust them into their tailes as they laie on the ground mangled and defaced.'[2] Both incidents are remarkable for staging political resistance to English invaders and Roman colonizers in graphically sexual terms. And yet, the latter account has been given much more scrutiny than the former, which has come to critical attention in Jodi Mikalachki's study of the engenderment of British native origins. Perhaps this is because castration, as a trope of resistance, neatly abides by the model of conquest that critics of colonialist discourse have put forth, which tends to figure invasion as an act of phallic penetration enacted upon a space coded as both feminine and passive.[3] Castration simply reverses an act understood to be penetrative.

But how, we should ask, does this aggressive mutilation of female breasts figure into the dynamics of conquest and plantation that are represented in this episode? What is it about the lactating breast that so concerned these ancient Britons, and why would this event capture the attention of early modern English chroniclers such that they would record it in detail? Moreover, why is it that this episode, when held beside the Welsh incident, seems to figure the breast in terms so proximate to those used to describe the genitalia of dead Englishmen? Why, that is, do these episodes figure lactating breasts and inseminating penises as homologies for one another?

I begin by proposing that this image of mutilated breasts captures in vividly materialist terms the crisis of race and lineage that I have been tracing as a consequence of colonization. That the punitive violence involves an assertion of boundaries is clear. And that maternity is implicated in the categories of difference under threat also seems evident. The violent gesture not only infantilizes the conquering group by figuring them as nurslings, but it also debilitates them by symbolically denying them the powers of maternity insofar as it insists on autologous nurture. If the mutilated women were in fact Romans, as the army's defensive posture suggests, the image seems to argue that 'mother' Rome should direct its 'lifeblood' back to its source, urging a return home of Romans and a circumscription of the Roman empire. If, on the other hand, the enemies represented are British women who have joined force with the Romans, the image works to reprove their alliance with the Romans, rejecting their political openness by violently constricting their somatic boundaries. In both cases, mother's milk is closely guarded, the mother's body forcefully enclosed. And yet, it seems perhaps still more crucial that although we are not made privy to the geographical origin of the victims, we are provided details about these women's social standing. Indeed, far from being indiscriminate attacks, these assaults are directed specifically and, it seems, exclusively against noble women, the 'women of great nobilitie and worthie fame' whom Harrison describes. In figuring the violent securing of elite women's bodily thresholds, then, the episode reveals that concerns about the inviolability of race and bloodline lie at the heart of early modern debates about conquest and colonization and underpin the detailed attention to maternal nurture that this context occasioned. For the focus on such nurture that informs Harrison's account of ancient British history during the period of the Roman occupation was also apparent in contemporary debates about England's plantation in Ireland, a context that frequently evoked contrast and comparison with ancient Britain.[4] By writing the history of their own transformation from barbarians to civil subjects, the English were also working through their colonial agendas. As such, the episode narrated by Harrison could function as a stunning reminder that the mundane choices of colonizers – on matters as seemingly trivial as how to rear their children – could have profound implications for the success of colonial activities. In effect, Harrison's account exposed a failure of boundaries, by intimating that illicit crossover between Roman and British mothers and infants had occurred. It was an error that settlers in Ireland were determined not to repeat.

In the last chapter I showed how Spenser turned an established discourse of temperance against an Old English elite, using it to dislodge the privileges of blood that positioned them as the social betters of the lower-ranking New English who were eager to advance themselves in Ireland. Against the Old English presumption that nobility was transmitted in inalterable form through a bloodline – an ideology that protected their unquestioned right to the privileges and property of their ancestors – Spenser and his peers defined blood's qualities as conditional, as predicated as much on decorum as on ancestry. If this strategy had the benefit, for the New English, of suggesting that elite bloodlines could rise and fall, as they argued had happened to Ireland's elite Anglo-Norman planters, it also destined those in the ascendant position to a regimen of constant self-regulation and self-scrutiny, a kind of ideological fallout that this chapter seeks to illuminate in the very specific context of their charged interest in rearing patterns among English settlers. Implicit in their discussions, I suggest, is an awareness that achieving the desired state of a temperate complexion would be nothing less than an ongoing production, requiring countless acts of self-discipline even from the time of birth. He who sought to 'make' himself temperate had, in effect, to be constantly on guard for potential violations to the body's porous boundaries.[5] Indeed, defending these bodily thresholds in an attempt to secure their ascendancy is precisely what was at stake in the prohibitive stance toward maternal surrogacy that the New English consistently took. For, as critics have often noted in passing, as a class, the New English were more than a little concerned with details of maternal nurture in Ireland, both among the Irish and the planter population.[6] Spenser's own antipathy to Irish wet nurses is explicitly recorded in his political tract on Ireland. But that the same sentiments are imprinted, as well, on the epic, in the precisely delimited patterns of nurture that govern his knights' upbringing, has not yet been charted. Moreover, what has not yet been clearly articulated is how this obsession with women's bodies encodes a concern about the bodily thresholds of the colonizers themselves. We need to ask what was at stake in the flow of mother's milk, such that it features so prominently in tracts otherwise concerned with the politics of conquest. Why, after all, did these tracts treat mother's milk as such a politically fraught subject?

A provisional answer emerges from yet another passage in Holinshed. We have already seen how Harrison's account of ancient England rejects as excessively brutal Boadicea's insistence on maternal boundaries, a fact that, following Mikalachki, we might associate with his general discomfort with female rule and the martial powers of a woman warrior. And yet elsewhere, in his translation of the history of ancient Scotland – originally written in Latin by Hector Boetius – Harrison seems to align himself with the insular perspective that Boadicea's violent acts instate. This section of the history records how the hardy women of ancient Scotland took 'intollerable paines to bring vp and nourish [their] owne children' by nursing them 'with the milke of their brests ... least they should degenerat and grow out of kind' by drinking 'strange milke.'[7] Echoing concerns implicit in Boadicea's violence, Harrison's translation of ancient Scottish practice clearly acknowledges the power of the lactating breast to determine the boundaries of 'kind.' In choosing to breastfeed their own children, these ancient Scottish mothers have embodied the ideal enforced by Boadicea's perverse mutilations. Like the famed woman-warrior, these Scottish mothers regard their bodies as nothing less than political boundaries, construing their decision about nurture to be tantamount to preserving the qualities of their people at large. Indeed, it is their sacrifice of time, effort, and convenience that is credited with preserving the Scot's famed hardiness. Hence, the two narratives, though radically different in tone and detail, speak to a common end: both acknowledge the centrality of the mother to uphold or confound a people's identity through her willingness or refusal to feed her child her own milk. Both powerfully suggest that 'strange milke' – what John Bellenden describes in Scottish terms as 'uncouth mylk' – may very well undo a people's distinctive marks.

## The Milk of Forgetfulness

The same observation had long informed debates in early modern England about the risks and merits of wet-nursing, a custom that, though dominant practice among aristocrats of the time, was increasingly frowned upon by physicans, humanists, and puritans.[8] Although wet-nursing had the benefit of increasing the fertility of aristocratic women, enabling the production of a greater number of heirs during a time of high infant mortality, critics expressed concern about the powerful influence wet nurses exerted over elite children. Indeed, the very status of the heir was called into question as a result of the bond the child might develop with these women both physically and emotionally. In many respects, the connection between nurse and infant was seen to threaten the prior bond between parent and offspring. The concern was that nurse's milk might somehow dilute or even reverse the ties of generation, inducing a puzzling form of forgetfulness in the heir. Classical texts, which played a considerable role in stoking opposition to the widespread practice in sixteenth- and seventeenth-century England, emphasized these powers in striking terms. In a frequently repeated anecdote that originated with Plato, Socrates' student Alcibiades, an Athenian by birth, had suffered a radical alteration to his disposition as a result of being nursed by a Lacedaemonian woman. '[Naturally] ... milde and timorous,' after consuming the milk of a woman of a 'verie stout, and valiant Nation,' Alcibiades had grown noticeably more 'hardy' himself. Jacques Guillemeau, a leading author on midwifery who disseminated this story, substantiated this account by observing a similar pattern among animals. They, too, expressed physical changes as a result of being exposed to non-maternal milk. Hence, he noted how 'If a young Lambe sucke a Goate, it is found by experience, that the wooll of it will be harder, then of either sheepe, and he will proue more fierce, and wild, then is naturall for his kind.'[9] These widely circulating anecdotes spoke to a cultural worry regarding the profoundly determining effect the nurse could have on her charges, and they were invoked as a warning for aristocrats to use due diligence in selecting a woman for the task. Guidelines for such selection processes dated back to the first and second century AD, when

Soranus of Ephesus had codified rules for evaluating wet nurses.[10] Such details as the nurse's age, health, complexion, hair colour, body size, and milk viscosity and colour factored into the selection process, governed in all instances by the goal of choosing someone who approximated the mother's disposition.[11]

These ideas were readily absorbed into humanist thought, making their imprint on major humanist texts of the sixteenth century, particularly those concerned with the upbringing of the nobility. Sir Thomas Elyot's *The Book Named the Governor* is a case in point insofar as it draws on standard classical guidelines in the recommendations it provides for raising aristocratic children. Significantly, he underlines the importance of selecting a proper wet nurse immediately following the delivery of a child. At this point, the parents should take care, he urges, to select 'a nurse ... of no servile condition or vice notable. For, as some ancient writers do suppose, often time the child sucketh the vice of his nurse with the milk of her pap.' He cites her age, health, and humoral complexion as among the most important criteria on which to base a selection, urging, in keeping with classical prescription, that her complexion be 'of the right and pure sanguine.'[12] We can observe these same commonplaces in Lodowick Bryskett's *Discourse of Civill Life*, a translation of Cinthio's *Tre dialoghi della vita civile* written by an English planter living abroad in Dublin, which begins its discussion of civil happiness by attending to the form of infant rearing. Compellingly, guidelines devised for those of 'so high an estate as the son of a mightie monarke' are offered here as 'a patterne to be followed by priuate gentlemen,' suggesting the extent to which Ireland was catalysing a profound revaluation of an extant social hierarchy. The advice Elyot had offered the sons of the land's peers becomes in Bryskett's hands a model to be followed even by the gentry, especially those men who styled themselves a rising class of 'governors' in Ireland. Following Elyot, Bryskett recommends close scrutiny of a wet nurse, advising that the mother's milk is to be preferred to that of 'any strange woman,' but allowing that a nurse 'of good complexion, and of a louing nature, and honest conditions' may also support 'a disposition to a vertuous and commendable life' in the infant charge.[13] In all cases, he warns, parents should take care not to choose a nurse of 'base or of vile condition,' nor one 'of strange nation, lest she should giue it strange or vnseemely manners, vnfit or disagreeable to the customes and conditions of the house or citie wherein it is borne, and wherein it is to liue.' He substantiates this view by noting that 'the minds of children ... are like to the yong tender slips of trees, which a man may bend and straighten as he list.' Because the child is so impressionable during his early years, the quality of the milk that would serve as his 'first fit food' should be carefully scrutinized.[14]

If Bryksett's comparison of the infant to a sapling imagined milk as akin to the 'culture' that might gently direct the sapling to deviate from a 'natural' course, Erasmus pulled a different implication from a similar metaphorical register, emphasizing in stark terms that the nurse could fundamentally alter the child's nature.[15] Observing the lessons of plant life, he argued that just as 'wheat sown in alien soil degenerates into wild oats or winter wheat,' in effect becoming a kind of bastard or base version of its original self, so the infant nursed out to another woman would be liable to degenerate, to cease to resemble his parents altogether. His speaker, Eutrapelus, explains this transformation by viewing the milk as akin to the soil affecting a plant, noting how it will behave like the 'moisture of the soil [which] changes the quality of what it nourishes.'[16] In his widely influential treatise *Popular Errors*, Laurent Joubert would extend the trope of the nurse as a kind of non-natural soil in observing that just as a 'beautiful tree, green and laden with fruit in one region, when transplanted into another, will weaken and shrink because of the humor of the place,' so, too, the child suffers through the 'borrowed and degenerate food of foreign milk.'[17] Where these writers tend to align mother's milk with nature and with nativity, they view the wet nurse's milk as imparting an acquired, and therefore non-natural, disposition. In registering the force of what they took to be a profound threat to the child's natural identity, they raided the arsenal of words that this period leaned on to describe a break in the continuity of nature between parent and heir to represent the dangers presented by surrogate mothers. In their eyes, the child would suffer decline, degeneracy, and transformation at an alarming rate. Their metaphors expressed in clear terms that the wet nurse signified a threat to the seamless notion of generation, which was a central fantasy of early modern culture.[18] She was a reminder that even the elite body was a potentially open body.[19]

Yet another strand of the debates about wet-nursing probed the implications of wet-nursing still deeper. Where writers like Erasmus urged concern on the grounds that the wet nurse's milk could alter the child's inherited nature insofar as it was a kind of 'non-natural' – one of six factors that Galenic medicine identified as having the power to shape the body's complexion – others discovered a still more dire prognostication of her influence aided by Galenic science. For humoral theories significantly exaggerated the potential influence of breast milk insofar as they defined the white substance as nothing other than a woman's concocted blood, in the same way that semen was the whitened form that concocted blood would assume in a man's body.[20] Indeed, the proximity of milk to blood in early modern conceptions of physiology figured high on the list of reasons to abstain from using a wet nurse. In the words of Guillemeau, 'milk is nothing else but bloud whitened, being now brought to perfection and maturity.'[21] The implications of this theory were profound. It suggested that the nourishment meted out to the infant could also pose a palpable threat to the purity of a family's bloodline, by mingling the nurse's bodily dispositions – her complexion – with those transmitted genealogically to the child. Indeed, for Guillemeau, the power of the milk to determine character should be viewed not as subordinate to but rather *on par* with the parents' contributions. The wet nurse becomes for him a third parent insofar as 'the Milke (wherewith the child is nourish'd two yeares together) hath as much power to make the children like the Nurses, both in bodie, and mind; as the seed of the Parents hath to make the children like them.'[22]

In *Popular Errors*, Laurent Joubert would go even further in claiming that the nurse's contribution exceeded that of the parents, declaring that her 'spirits, carried into her milk, have great power and influence in imprinting certain behaviors and complexions in those who first drink them, even more than those coming from the blood and spirits of the father and the mother by way of their sperm.' The Athenian philosopher Favorinus, the mouthpiece for Joubert, likens the selection of a nurse to the process, prior to marriage, of looking 'very deeply into the man's and the woman's circumstances, their ancestry, their blood, and their conduct, so as to have the best lineage possible.'[23] In taking on a wet nurse, then, one was effectively taking on another bed partner, warranting the same strict considerations that were involved in selecting a spouse. In fact, as A.R. Braunmuller so effectively points out in tracing these connections in the context of *Macbeth*, undoing and remaking lineal connections was precisely what wet-nursing could achieve. As he notes, the practice had the effect of making the 'child non-natural and from a genealogical or dynastic point of view invalid, a failed heir.'[24] Valerie Fildes substantiates this reading of the practice when she points out that the nurse 'did not just provide nourishment for the baby; she was believed to transmit to the child, along with her ideas, beliefs, intelligence, intellect, diet, and speech, all her other physical, mental and emotional qualities. Effectively, she was seen to be reproducing herself; the child was the nurse; an extero-gestate foetus.'[25] M. Steeven Guazzo's

*Civile Conversation* traced in precise detail the processes here encapsulated, indicating how a noble and legitimate offspring could become debased and tainted: 'as a child, by reason of the milk, taketh after the complexion of the Nurse, so the disposition of the mind, followeth the complexion of the body; and therof also it commeth, that the daughters of honest women, prove altogether unlike them, both in body and mind ... whereof it commeth, that the children fashioning themselves to the humores of the Nurses, swarve from the love and duetye whiche they owe to their mothers, and have not in them the blood whiche mooveth them to obay or respecte them any thing.'[26] By allowing the subsitution of the nurse's blood, in the form of her breast milk, for their own, the parents would, in effect, be transforming their legitimate offspring into bastards. That is, in disregarding the sustaining powers of mother's milk, they would be depriving their children of 'the blood' which naturally yields 'kindly' behaviour – in the form of a desire 'to obay or respecte them' – from those who are kin.[27]

## The Patriarchal Teat

Familiarizing ourselves with these early modern conceptualizations of physiology leads us a long way in understanding why questions of female nurture appear with such frequency in debates about Ireland's conquest. As the potential carrier of milk-blood powerful enough to alter a genealogical line – indeed, as a mediating figure who could step between an heir and his paternal origin – Irish women were perceived by New English writers to be Ireland's best concealed weapon, capable of dispensing metaphorical death to Englishmen through the transformative power of their breasts.[28] Again and again, New English tracts on Ireland trace back to Irish women the deviations it discovers among not just Irish sons and husbands but also those English men and boys who have fallen short of English expectations.[29] All of them, it could be claimed, had sucked at the teat of an Irish woman at one time or another, instating and/or reversing the benign marks that an English bloodline had once wrought on them. If the wet-nursing tracts had warned against placing infants with nurses of 'base conditions' or in the hands of 'strange women,' Ireland yoked the two threats together in the notorious figure of her barbarous women.

Indeed, the disorders of Irish women more generally tended to be writ large in texts by New English settlers, crystallizing their antipathy for all things Irish. Against the New English insistence on a well-bounded, temperate body, Irish women were described consistently in their accounts as defying boundaries, as being the site of dangerous contaminations and mixtures. In discussing Irish methods of preparing food, for instance, Fynes Moryson, secretary to Lord Mountjoy prior to Ireland's defeat in 1603, cannot help but betray discomfort at the sheer openness and availability of Irish women's bodies. Ever keen to emphasize Irish barbarity, Moryson discusses Irish milkmaids, highlighting their excessive physicality and earthiness and noting how the customary manner of preparing grain allows that her 'more unseemly parts' become mingled together with the corn. Elsewhere he signals the Irish woman's indifference to the rising thresholds of civility,[30] in describing how she would coax the milk from an unyielding cow by washing her hands in 'cowes dung' and sodomitically putting her 'hands into the cow's taile.'[31] In Moryson's assessment, the Irish woman is barbarous because she exceeds normative bounds and defies 'natural' laws, proving a site of troubling exchange between human and animal, nutriment and excrement.

For Moryson, Irish women seemed to confound as well the 'natural' distinctions governing gender differences, as expressed in their custom of urinating from a standing position and their excessive consumption of alcohol. Moreover, insofar as Irish women were perceived to experience 'little or no payne in Chyldebearing' and had 'such strang ability of body presently after [deliuerance],' they were blamed for flouting what English Protestants understood as the divinely ordained consequence of woman's sinfulness. Her ease in this disregard was symptomatic of a wider set of failures. Attributed to a custom of breaking a (pelvic) bone during childhood, such facility in childbearing easily translated for English colonists as vaginal openness, an indecorum confirmed still further by their perceived verbal openness. Moryson explicitly collapses the upper and lower bodily thresholds of Irish women when he observes how it is customary to 'gossop and drincke with wemen' immediately following delivery.[32] Indeed, in recalling the case of 'a Soldyers wife deliuered in the Campe,' her speed of recovery is translated into her ability to continue marching 'six myles on Foote with the Armye' within a matter of hours, violating codes of decorum prevalent in England not least by mixing domestic affairs with martial activities.[33] The repugnance that these accounts convey are reiterated by Barnabe Rich, famed author of countless military tracts on Ireland, who stands against the breaches of Irish women by figuring himself as fully continent: 'I will not speake of those affaires belonging to Child-bearing women, that are no lesse uncivill then uncleanly.'[34] Clearly, for New English writers, Irish women embodied a profound form of boundary violation. In Moryson's words, they 'doe openly the most secret necessities of the body.'[35] In opposition to the notion of a closed, elite body that social aspirants like Spenser increasingly figured themselves in relation to, the Irish woman denoted the open body – one routinely associated with the ungoverned posture of the lower ranks.[36]

If, as these accounts suggest, the mere act of viewing an Irish woman's body provoked a kind of titillating voyeurism that threatened the undoing of English civility by requiring writers to speak of indecorous physical events, contact with her bodily fluids posed a still greater danger. In the anger, energy, and angst that these men expressed in repudiating the practice of sending English children out to Irish wet nurses, the New English worried about nothing less than the invasion, destruction, and sabotaging of their English bloodlines. They worried and alerted their communities to the potential 'Irishing' of English boys, which was an all-too-common transformative trajectory for settlers in Ireland. Indeed, this insistence on bodily borders was what defined their difference from the Old English settlers, who had, in their view, lapsed from formerly elite identities and ancestral houses precisely because they had diluted their bloodlines with the baseness of 'yrishe staynes.'[37] Professing the difference of their own civility required that they refuse, at all costs, the same permissive exchange of bodily fluids.

Indeed, again and again in New English texts on Ireland, planters are warned not only against intermarrying but also against fostering their children to Irish women. In his *View of the Present State of Ireland*, Irenius, who serves as the mouthpiece for New English settlers in Ireland, goes so far as to describe Irish mothers and wet nurses as the twin adversaries of the colonizing enterprise in Ireland. At all costs, he urges, the English should avoid fostering their children to Irish wet nurses, arguing that to do so is to undo one's lineal identity as expressed in linguistic, political, and physiological terms. Not only, he urges, will the young suckling imitate the nurse's tongue, since his first speech derives from her, but, and I want to emphasize what scholars have consistently overlooked in this passage, 'they moreover drawe into them selues togeather with theire sucke, even the nature and disposition of theire nurses, for the mind followeth much the temperature of the bodye: and also the wordes are the Image of the mynde, so as they proceding from the mynde, the mynde must bee needes effected with the wordes: So that the speach beinge Irish, the harte must needes bee Irishe.'[38] In this complex epistemology – which will be recognized for its continuities with the midwifery and courtesy texts earlier analysed – body temperature determines mental structure determines language determines national allegiance. The cycle, as identified by Spenser, is set in motion by virtue of the nurse's body temperature, that is, her complexion.[39] The threat here is not, then, as critics have tended to imply, limited *merely* to a cultural plane. That is, the passage does not figure degeneracy as exclusively a cultural dynamic.[40] Rather, what the passage reveals with painstaking precision is that physical difference – here the nurse's complexionate qualities – is entangled with and around cultural difference, as in the child's language and national orientation. Her baseness and strangeness – which together define her as Irish – figure a pollution of the balanced 'English' temperament prized by the New English, threatening him with the condition of indistinction that he was so determined in Ireland to rise above.

Indeed, so prevalent was the threat posed by the Irish wet nurse that she figured as a regular trope in New English political writings at large for that which was contagious, transmissible, and unbounded. In establishing his central claim that coyne and livery, the practice of billeting troops on the populace and requiring provision for horses, was the land's crucial failing, Richard Beacon, friend and co-planter of Spenser, would turn to the metaphor to express his condemnation, describing the practice as 'the very nurse and teate, that gave sucke and nutriment to all disobedience, rebellions, enormities, vices, and iniquities of that realme over fowle and filthie, here to be expressed.'[41] This policy, which enabled Old English overlords to drain their freeholders of property and possession – reducing them in the view of many New English to the condition of slaves[42] – positioned them in the New English imaginary as on par with the child fostered to a nurse, who, though seeming to provide nourishment for the child, was actually performing a violent kind of draining. Through the seemingly beneficent act of giving milk, she took language, lineage, and allegiance from her English charge,[43] reducing him to a cipher of his former self. By dispensing milk that was also blood, she threatened to reverse the child's patronym, adulterating the offspring before he even knew the need to defend himself.

It was her power to 'play' the father in this respect that so reviled New English writers. They observed with scorn how Irish men seemed so comfortable with and even encouraged female control of the central rituals of patriarchy. Irish men, in their view, emasculated themselves by granting women this power to 'author' them. Moryson, for instance, spills no small amount of ink in condemning the power of Irish women to determine patronym in naming the 'true Father of each of her Children' while lying on her deathbed.[44] As he elsewhere expands, 'maryed wemen giue Fathers to their Children when they are at the point of death ... And these bastard Children euer after follow these fathers, and [think] themselues to descend of them.'[45] Irish women's powers in this regard subvert – indeed, stand as the antithesis to – English patriarchal culture. If in England a father would 'author' his child at the moment of birth, conferring the benefits of the patronym in accord with the 'natural' processes of reproduction, in Ireland, women – in many cases not even wives – would 'author' children on their deathbeds, allowing the mediated force of their words to determine consanguinity.

The ability of Irish women to confound the logic of blood that dominated English cultural systems extended still further. For what was most stunning to English writers about the Irish practice of fosterage was its sheer disdain for the bonds of 'nature' – for 'real' kin-ties – and its privileging instead of various 'artificial' productions of blood-ties. In explaining the intricate rules governing fosterage, Moryson notes how 'They seldom nurse their own children, especially the wives of lords and gentlemen (as well mere Irish as English-Irish). For women of good wealth seek with great ambition to nurse them, not for any profit, rather spending much upon them while they live, and giving them when they die sometimes more than to their own children. But they do it only to have the protection and love of the parents whose children they nurse.' He observes further: 'old custom is so turned into a second nature with them as they esteem the children they nurse more than their own, holding it a reproach to nurse their own children.' Perversely, in his eyes, 'foster-brothers – I mean the children of the nurse and strangers that have sucked her milk – love one another better than natural brothers.'[46] The language here is precise: 'strangers' become brothers under the suspect rules governing Irish fosterage, with the result that fraternity is rendered but a fiction. And yet, as was so often the case in Ireland, the difference being defined proved unstable, yielding something like a hall of mirrors: for, as Sir John Davies would observe of the power of these fraternal connections, 'they were tied together, vinculo sanguini.' Although not born 'in blood,' the strong bonds that resulted from this rearing practice indicated the extent to which one could be *made* 'in blood.' In fact, in the eyes of the Irish, as Davies would record, blood-ties produced by birth were little if not transient and inconstant, scorned as an ineffective method of forging bonds between people. Foster relations, by contrast, 'do participate of their means more frankly and do adhere unto them in all fortunes with more affection and constancy' than those related by birth.[47] That Irish women controlled the processes whereby an inherited bloodline was transformed into something different – where a child was quite literally re-raced – struck at the deepest and most entrenched roots of patriarchal English culture, to the horror of the New English.

And yet, in another regard, the tendency in Ireland to 'make' blood may also have stoked the envy of New English settlers. For one effect of a loosened system of blood alliance was a much greater potential for social mobility than was customary in England. This fact was not lost on the New English. On the contrary, they observed with frequency how most everyone in Ireland claimed the privileges of blood that were reserved in England for only a precious few, the first born of gentle birth. Davies, for one, would observe that 'there are not to be found in any kingdom of Europe, so many gentlemen of one blood, family, and surname, as there are of the O'Neills in Ulster, of the Burkes in Connaught, of the Geraldines and Butlers in Munster and Leinster.'[48] Moryson would observe with still more scorn how even the 'basest of them wilbe reputed gentlemen and sword men.'[49] So, too, we can hear in the *View*, in Eudoxus's words, a kind of mixed admiration for Irish villains like Feagh McHugh, who, 'beinge but late growen out of the dounghill,' has successfully 'lifted him self vpp to this dangerous greatenes,' so that he 'begynneth now to overcrowe, so high Mountaines.'[50] Seeing a version of their own bid for social ascendancy in these recently 'gentled' Irish men, the New English took it upon themselves to expose the 'commoner' lurking behind such Irish 'gentlemen.' When asked by Eudoxus how the English can in right and conscience reverse O'Neill's claim to his 'Signiorye,' for instance, Irenius responds by revealing the man of base blood who hides behind the image of a powerful Irish chieftain, a would-be descendant of the 'five royal bloods.'[51] O'Neill, he claims, never 'had any auncyente signiorie in that Countrie'; rather, he 'made him self Lorde of those fewe people' through 'vsurpation and incrochment.'[52] Similarly, in Irenius's hands Feagh McHugh is exposed for being the descendant of a 'man of meanest regard' in former times, whose claim to 'that countrye or the signorie' is 'most vaine and arrogant.'[53] As such, Irish chieftains, in Spenser's account, are exposed for being a group of commoners who have, for too long, wrongly enjoyed the privileges of elite men. Indeed, as a group 'on the make' themselves, the New English were pressed to name the difference that distinguished them from these Irish 'boys.' If, as chapter 1 argued, one way that they justified their own social mobility was to cast the Old English as possessing dangerously 'high' blood, another strategy required that the Irish, particularly those enjoying power and land, be cast as naturally low, as little save a 'rude multi-tude.'[54] As such, Irenius's solution to the stalled conquest in Ireland is to make the base blood of these Irish men socially visible, by transferring 'all the landes ... unto English men' and forcing 'those Irishe to bee ten-nantes' 'under everie of those Englishe men.'[55] Such were the rewards to be offered those who could embody a virtuous middling course and properly temperate qualities of blood.

## Tilting with Mammets

If this power to 'make' or 'break' the man was seen as originating with Irish nurses, it is hardly a surprise to find that Spenser constructs nar-ratives of nurture in his epic that shield his knights, embodiments of English gentility, from the influence of maternal figures. Indeed, he all but erases the maternal contributions that might have shaped these fig-ures during their infant years, in effect modelling a course of action that would require banishing the female's lineal contributions as the key to preserving English gentility. In this text, the 'fashioning' of gentlemen occurs by men. This pattern is established at the outset when our author informs us that he has made it his task 'to fashion a gentleman or noble person in vertuous and gentle discipline,' but it is reiterated through the array of male tutors and foster parents who assume the role of fashion-ing – of rearing – his knights.[56] The material contributions of mothers and, perhaps more explicitly, wet nurses – the wet nurse being a figure of unnatural surrogacy explicitly associated in the *View* as in many New English texts with Irishness – are in this text marginalized, systematically replaced with what are presumably the more potent contributions of the male intellect. For, in addition to informing us about his knights' progress in accomplishing the assigned quest, Spenser takes pains to trace their histories back to this juncture, to the moment of their pas-sage from the maternal to the symbolic realm.

None of what we learn about these knights' earliest experiences of nurture is easily equatable with standard early modern practice among the aristocrats for whom Spenser writes, whereby the newborn child would likely be sent out to a wet nurse for the first years of life to prevent breastfeeding's amenorrheic effect from sabotaging the cultural impetus to produce an heir. After that initial experience of nurture, frequently lasting between one and three years, the child would have returned to home until the age of seven, when he would attend grammar school or begin service as a page.[57] In the interim period, he would have been at home among his parents. Spenser alters this pattern in outlining the histories of his knights, first by compressing the time permitted for maternal nurture and later by all but eliminating their contact with a wet nurse. In effect, he enhances what Lawrence Stone identifies as the 'export of children'[58] by expanding the phase of interaction with male instructors. In his narratives of nurture, children are conveyed very early, indeed often as infants, to their tutors, skirting the exigencies of breast, pap, and wet nurse. We learn, for instance, that Arthur was 'soone as life did [him] admitt / ... From mothers pap ... taken vnfitt' (1.9.3.5–6) to be delivered by Merlin to his future tutor Timon. Moreover, his relation to Merlin is described as that of a 'noursling,' presumably suggesting that the food of Merlin's 'almightie art' (2.8.20.3, 2) nourishes him more fully than that received at his mother's breast, which has left him 'vnfitt.' While the mother's function is here acknowledged, if in a position of subordination to that of the male tutor, the material contributions of the wet nurse are here and elsewhere rendered invisible in what are otherwise very closely constructed narratives. Artegall, for instance, is 'from the cradle of his infancie' (5.1.5.2) 'noursled' (5.1.6.8) by Astraea, but this demigoddess is figured as feeding him the 'discipline of iustice' (5.1.6.9) rather than any bodily nourishment, filling the role of a tutor or foster parent before that of a wet nurse. Moreover, she is soon replaced by the male substitute, Talus. Red Cross, too, is mysteriously swept away while in 'swadling band[s]' (1.10.65.7) to be raised by a Ploughman in the Georgic way of life, a description that serves to assure us of his timely removal from the matrix. While we are not privy to the histories of the two other male knights, during Guyon's centrally placed near-death experience the role of nursing is, predictably, assumed by his male tutor, the Palmer. In finding the moribund Guyon lying on the ground, he 'courd[s him] tenderly, / As chicken newly hatcht' (2.8.9.8–9), acting the part of nurse-cum-midwife to his infantilized charge. In fact, of the knights whose past is discussed, only the one female, Britomart, is linked explicitly with a female nurse, namely, Glauce, who appears in the text only to have her authority subordinated to the superior care and knowledge of Merlin. It is he who directs Britomart away from the nurse's wrongheaded solutions to her illness and toward her imperial destiny. And where most of the male knights are described in a state of 'matrix interruptus,' she alone of them is explicitly imaged by the text in a prolonged simile as a suckling nursling, alternately grasping at and rejecting the nurse's breast being offered her (5.6.14.8). In almost all other cases, the originary act of social creation at the breast of the nurse is repressed and replaced by the predominantly male narrative of tutor-student interaction.

None of these details seems to me to be incidental. In fact, references to 'nursing' in this text command considerable attention, appearing in an abundance of metaphors. In the proem to Book 6, for instance, the narrator prays for knowledge of 'the sacred noursery / Of vertue' (3.1–2) and in the House of Pride, Idleness is described as the 'nourse of sin' (1.4.18.6), implicitly defining the nurse as the 'ur-begetter,' either of vice or virtue. Moreover, images of nurturing breasts and suckling infants recur throughout the text. In the House of Holiness, Charissa's bare breasts invite her babes to 'sucke their fill' (1.10.30.8) and thereby signify her unwavering charity. But where the mother's breast is alternately invoked as a source of positive and negative influences, wet nurses make their appearance in the text only to be connected with betrayals and deceits, seemingly transmitting corruption through both their dugs and their flawed dispositions. The foster brothers Phedon and Philemon, for instance, are linked in their treacherous bond of love through the 'tender dug of commune nourse' (2.4.18.3), the origin of a relationship that ends in murder and attempted suicide. Similarly, Radigund's foster child Clarinda betrays her foster mother in herself loving Artegal rather than serving as the conduit for Radigund's love, an act of betrayal that is likened to that of a niggardly nurse

> which fayning to receiue
> In her owne mouth the food, ment for her chyld,
> Withholdes it to her selfe, and doeth deceiue
> The infant, so for want of nourture spoyld. (5.5.53.1–4)

Clarinda's treachery, the extended simile implies, originates with and reproduces the flawed temperament of a deceitful nurse. In each case, it is the nurse's commonness that blights the proper relations that should govern elite identities. In England, such baseness was used to define the labouring poor, but in Ireland, in the hands of an ascendant New English class, the careful discriminations of an English social hierarchy were suspended, with the effect that 'baseness' – the epithet describing those occupying the lowest-most rung of the social order in England – was extended to the population at large.

As such, I read the perversion of maternity most powerfully embodied in the poem by the figure of Error as itself evoking more than just an anxiety of female nurture and more than a concern with domestic patterns of fostering. This episode (1.1.13–27), with its figuration of a radical violation of somatic boundaries between mother and offspring, evokes, more precisely, a concern with the reversal of proper affective bonds that was the identifying hallmark of Irish nurture. Though presumably a mother to her charges, Error's description evokes the malignant patterns of nurture associated above with nurses. A physical analogue to the vice imagined as transmitted to Clarinda by a vile wet nurse, Error's 'dugs' (1.1.15.6) feed poison to her offspring, who in turn deposit their own contaminated bodies in the 'sinke' (1.1.22.5) of her body, producing a grotesque cycle of death and destruction.[59] The episode resonates with the horrific exchange of fluids that Irenius recalls as having passed between an Irish foster mother and her foster son at the scene of the man's execution. He recollects that 'at the execution of a notable tratour at Limbricke called Murrogh Obrien, I sawe an old woman which was his Foster mother tooke vpp his heade whilst he was quartered and sucked vpp all the blood running there out, sayinge that the earth was not worthie to drincke yt, and therewith also steeped her face and brest, and tare her haire, cryinge and shriking out most tirriblie.'[60] The cannibalistic image is offered as proof of Irish derivation from the Scythians, but the scene also emphasizes the barbarity and unnaturalness of Irish maternity, figuring an absolute reversal of nurture. Where the foster mother would normally be expected to give suck to the child, she here 'suck[s]' up her foster child's precious lifeblood. In the compressed cultural logic that governs the account, the blood that the woman once presumably meted out to the boy as milk is now returned to her own body as blood. By graphically reversing the normal processes of nurture, the recollection forces the reader to acknowledge what might otherwise go unheeded: that seemingly innocuous maternal gestures – like that of suckling – have a profound impact on the nature of bloodlines. These two people, though 'strange' at birth, have since become radically interpenetrated. The boundaries between foster mother and child have all but vanished, just as they have for Error and her gorging progeny, who are bound together by a matrix of contaminated bodily fluids.

Although a 'natural' mother to her offspring rather than a surrogate mother whose absence from the *Faerie Queene* I have been tracing, Error, like the aborted images of nurture traced above, seems entangled in the same set of discourses that conjoined, for Spenser and his New English community, 'unnatural' maternity with Irishness. The details of her description, that is, betray an Irish residue if not quite an Irish referent. In fact, the cannibalistic orgy depicting the circulation of infectious maternal fluids between Error and her offspring not only echoes the horrible account of Murrogh O'Brien's execution but also evokes a similarly 'horrible spectacle' during the 1590s famine in Ireland that circulated in New English accounts of the devastation. In a passage not at a far remove from Spenser's own report of the 'Anotomies of death' that emerged from the Irish terrain in the aftermath of Sir Arthur Grey's violent rampage through the country, Moryson reports how his friend witnessed the horror of 'three children ... all eating and gnawing with their teeth at the entrails of their dead mother.'[61] But where this image of an Irish mother would seem to allow for the transference of life to the offspring at the moment of the mother's own death, Spenser's analogous image disavows any suggestion of nurture. Rather, Error's maternal fluids disseminate death rather than life to her charges, evoking the social death that New English settlers presumed would be the price of contact with Irish wet nurses. The emphasis on stasis that the image propounds – in figuring the imminent demise of the clustered bodies – returns us as well to the image of containment earlier observed in Holinshed's account of Boadicea's mutilated victims. Both accounts, I would suggest, invoke an image of foreign maternity rendered gruesomely impotent to mediate a crisis of identity. Both, that is, seek to resolve that crisis by neutralizing the mother's inscripting powers, redirecting her forces 'homeward' through grotesque images of cannibalism. In doing so, these accounts seek to halt her considerable powers to determine a social field insofar as they produce a symbolic representation of her absolute containment.

**Acrasia's Irish Bower**

The same goal could be said to constitute Guyon's quest in Book 2, which begins and ends at the breast of a woman. In the last chapter, we saw that Guyon's quest entails protecting the orphaned infant, Ruddymane, who is named for the blood that his hand absorbs while making contact with his mother's wounded breast. Insofar as her blood leaves a determining mark on his hand – one that I argued should be read as the mark of Mother England, threatened by the lethargy of forgetfulness that has seized Mortdant – it also resonates with that dangerously permanent mark that Spenser associated with maternal surrogacy, the mark of 'first [framing] and [fashioning]' that the child will 'hardlie ever after forgoe.'[62] England's originary mark, the episode suggests, must be guarded, defended against the potentially more powerful imprints of a 'strange' nurse. Barnabe Rich would capture the contemporary resonance of these subject-positions in casting the Queen's relationship to her Irish subjects as that of a 'louing Nurse, nay rather a kinde mother, that did still carke and care for them, with such compassionate love and kindness.'[63] Asserting the prior claim of Mother England as against the unnatural claim of the (Irish) nurse was a project shared by countless New English planters, Rich and Spenser among them.

Indeed, if Guyon's quest opens with the image of a besieged mother, it also concludes with the assault of a figure who, I will argue, shadows the Irish nurse as constructed in the New English imaginary. This figure is, of course, Acrasia – the book's emblem of incontinence. Structurally, her placement at the book's close indicates that she is Guyon's ultimate challenge. Conceived more broadly, she stands, as well, as the chief obstacle to the colonial enterprise. Indeed, Spenser goes out of his way in the book's Proem to suggest to his reader that there may be a connection, even if elusive, between Guyon's land of faery and the 'newly discovered regions' of Virginia, Peru, and the Amazon. But that the poet's adopted home of Ireland is an absent presence that figures into faeryland's representations is also implied in the image of the 'wandring Island' (2.1.51.5) that names Acrasia's abode.

That this geography – this island – registers less the threat of topography than a set of somatic dangers associated with Acrasia is registered in the details of Guyon's journey to her land. In traversing to the island, he meets and must pass through landmarks that read as a microcosm of the female body. Not only must he navigate the dangers of the '*Gulfe of Greedinesse*' (2.12.3.4) or 'grisely mouth' (2.12.6.1) that 'deepe engorgeth all this worldes pray' (2.12.3.5), but he must overgo a mountainous 'craggie clift' that threatens to sink them in 'helples wawes' (2.12.4.2, 9).[64] As the abundance of incontinent metaphors in this canto makes clear – from watery islands, to abundantly creeping ivy, to gates that fail to enclose – the female principle that Acrasia embodies is an engulfing boundlessness. 'Unmanning' the man through her seductive comforts, Acrasia, like the Irish women who feature in every New English text on Ireland, is made to epitomize the threat of distemperance. She is water and fire, enticing men to her lawlessness with the twin weapons of her 'fierie beames' (2.12.78.7) and 'liquid ioyes' (2.12.60.9).[65] In the logic of the text, she is the cause of that backward slide known in New English parlance as 'degeneration.'

But to point out Acrasia's threatening sexuality is only to retrace familiar critical territory.[66] Venturing beyond this observation, I suggest that Spenser includes in his 'anatomy' of feminine excess not just the powers of seduction but those of maternity as well. Indeed, the fountain that lies at the centre of Acrasia's paradise associates her powers specifically with her life-giving function, denoting her ability both to engender and support life. As the fountain's flowing waters suggest, it is her life-sustaining fluids that exert a controlling sway over boy and man alike, united in the posture of self-immersion in her various 'liquid ioyes' (2.12.60.9).[67] This iconography of feminine-maternal power is further elabourated by the description of 'Two naked Damzelles' (2.12.63.6) in the fountain's waters who entice the otherwise guarded Guyon with their 'lilly paps' (2.12.66.6). But it is the 'snowy brest' of Acrasia herself that ultimately focusses Spenser's desire and anxiety (2.12.78.1). Bared and dripping with drops 'more cleare then Nectar,' like 'Orient perles' (2.12.78.4, 5) in a post-coital reverie, Acrasia's breasts are imaged as the focal point of her powers. Issuing sweat instead of milk and arousing hunger instead of satiety, however, their perverse strength involves the disruption of the 'natural' maternal function and a reversal of the nurturing process. Rather than rearing infants into men, her breasts are seen instead to induce regression. Under their 'spell' the man becomes child; stripped of his accoutrements of honour, he submits, infant-like, his 'sleepie head ... [to] her lap' (2.12.76.9). In being remade in the posture of a boy, Verdant therefore comes to embody the threat to lineage that this witch ultimately embodies. For if sexual contact with her has the power to delay the knight and his quest, the episode intimates that a still greater threat is yet to come. In figuring Verdant as suckling at her breast, the episode suggests it is less his own sexual congress with her that will undo him than his *heir's* prostration at her breast. It is this act, proleptically figured in the foetal posture that the man assumes, that will destroy not just a man but an entire race and bloodline. For it is at the lips of the child that her fluids will transmit the complexion of a stranger, transforming a gentle bloodline into the errant lines of Irish consanguinity.

If the dripping Acrasia is ensnared and, provisionally, 'contained' by the outrageously inappropriate tool of the Palmer's 'subtile net' (2.12.81.4),[68] managing the problematic of breast milk on a material level was a more difficult matter altogether. In fact, Spenser was to find that keeping his real-life co-planters from the 'error' of fostering with Irish women would prove a task beyond his control. The project of shielding Englishness from mixture with all things Irish was in fact far from realized in that shadowy counter-image to his ideal faery land known as Ireland. Despite the extensive rhetoric of contamination and pollution that framed his discussion of Irish women, Spenser proved unable to prevent the very customs he feared from being duplicated by his New

English peers, even among his very kin. We know, for instance, that Richard Boyle, the famous Earl of Cork who acquired a fortune as a planter in Ireland and who was a kinsman to Spenser's wife Elizabeth, used Irish country wet nurses for most of his children, until they reached the age of three or four. According to Nicholas Canny, there is strong evidence to suggest that other planter families, too, sent their children to Gaelic Irish homes for wet-nursing: he notes at least three other instances in depositions from Leitrim alone.

Indeed, the textual record explaining these decisions suggests that the polarities that Spenser and others symbolically instated readily disintegrated in the field. Not only did the English, like their Old English counterparts, inadvertently become like the Irish, in some instances they actively *sought* to be like them. At least, that is one way of interpreting Richard Boyle's explanation for why he chose to send his children to Irish wet nurses. Grafting a newly emergent discourse of Irish alterity onto an already existing discourse naturalizing differences of rank, Boyle justified his decision by noting that 'the care of a country nurse, who by early inuring him by slow degrees to a coarse but cleanly diet, and to the usual passions of the air' helped his children to develop 'so vigorous a complexion.' It seems he welcomed the advantages to be had from mixing with a hardy native nurse. Rather than producing children 'made of butter or of sugar,' Boyle went the route of hybridity, understanding this choice to produce not the contamination but rather the fortification of his bloodline.[69] That is, he willingly assimilated the hardiness of the Irish body, much like Alcibiades was thought to have assimilated the desirable qualities of his Lacedaemonian nurse. Her derivation from a 'verie stout, and valiant Nation,' according to Guillemeau, produced a hardy noursling despite the fact that Athenians were 'naturally ... milde and timerous.'[70] Similarly, Boyle clearly believed that the 'weaker' blood of his elite children would benefit from the infusion of the blood of an Irish nurse, perceiving the effect of a fortified genealogy in her complexion where Spenser saw only the debasing spectre of distemperance.

Uncomfortable with the power such surrogate mothers wielded in the contest of nations, Spenser chides the Old English for having rejected their 'real' mother – England. In what is perhaps a wilful slip of the tongue, he accuses them of violating the bond that links mother and child at her breast, likening their investment with things Irish to the act of biting 'of her dugge from which they sucked lyfe.'[71] What he here represses, in analogizing England to a nursing mother, however, is the reality of maternal surrogacy. It was not, after all, English breasts that were consistently offered to the children of English settlers. Moreover, Spenser's insistence to the contrary, the foreign breast was not refused but welcomed, creating bonds with Irish nurses that did indeed challenge ties to Mother England. For, as Joubert reminds us, engenderment was perceived by many to be the lesser part of maternity: 'the affection of the child, its love and intimacy, go entirely to the one nursing it, and because of this, it has no feeling or desire whatsoever for the mother.' It is precisely this ability of the breast to reconfigure the bonds of lineage that Spenser wanted his New English peers in Ireland to heed. He warned them, in no uncertain terms, that tilting with mammets was the English gentleman's most dangerous quest, and that rearing was the better part of conquest.[72]

# 3 *Cymbeline* and Virginia's British Climate

## Tragicomic Displacements

Spenser's associations with Ireland – his lifelong devotion to a career abroad in the colony – invariably shaped his poetic representations and may have motivated the recoding of race that I have argued lies at the heart of his interest in bodily comportment, lineal integrity, and temperate blood. But such recodings were hardly limited to those living abroad, and this next chapter of the book will consider how a set of writers who never settled beyond England or ventured far from her shores contributed to the massive cultural transitions occasioned by transplantation. I turn to drama of the early seventeenth century – particularly the genre of tragicomedy – to explicate how its representations could be a powerful catalyst for challenging long-standing conceptions of race.

Critics concerned with mercantile and colonial exchanges both in the East Indies and a broad circum-Atlantic context have already observed the formative role that tragicomedy played in reshaping English culture in ways that were conducive to the rise of capitalism.[1] By depicting the movement of English resources – both people and bullion – to distant peripheries as less a loss than an investment, tragicomedy, they propose, helped to redraw economic structures, and its attendant affective structures, so as to accommodate burgeoning mercantile and colonial efforts. If work in this vein has tended to anchor its claims in the corpus of John Fletcher and Philip Massinger – whose plays are set with increasing frequency in distant lands – it also builds on critical work that informed readings of *The Tempest* for some time, dating back to the 1980s. Indeed, of Shakespeare's tragicomic romances it is *The Tempest* that is most often identified as shaping colonial dynamics and an emerging racial formation. In Prospero's dominating stance toward the native of the play's island, scholars have observed an imperial posture, a glimpse of European colonial strategies at large, as deployed through a powerful set of binary oppositions. The play's displacement to an ambiguously identified island – whether construed as lying in the waters of the Atlantic or the Mediterranean – arguably serves to substantiate these readings, as does the use of North Africa as an enframing context for its action. Racial dynamics, it seems, begin with the attempt of English dramatists to imagine what it might be like to live beyond Europe. The outward-looking orientation of the play, its investment in spatial displacement, seems to announce its imbrication in a racial formation.

And yet, in assuming that racial dynamics awaits a confrontation with the 'other' – one associated with a foreign locale – critics have tended to overlook ways that other Shakespearean romances are implicated in redrawing the contours of early modern race. I propose that another of Shakespeare's late tragicomic romances – *Cymbeline* – is equally concerned with the reconfiguration of race in this period, although it accomplishes this end through an estranging glimpse at those living within Britain, particularly those imagined to possess the strongest claim to race and blood within the British polity – the royalty.[2]

The play takes as its explicit focus an episode from British history when Rome's imperial powers had been extended to British soil and yet found to be insecure, thereby focusing on a key moment of empire building in the classical world. Rewriting these historical events so that they occur during rather than after Cymbeline's reign, the play engages the struggle that ensues between the British court and an encroaching Roman force. While quick to wage verbal valiance against their enemies, the court figures – including Cymbeline, his second queen, and his son-in-law Cloten – are exposed as an inflated and corrupt group, shadowing the failures of their Roman aggressors, particularly the decadent 'Italian' Iachimo. As a result, the kingdom's future is found to lie in the hands of the next generation of Britons, not only with the king's daughter Imogen but also his two princes, who have been missing since birth. Kidnapped roughly twenty years before the start of the play's action, the princes have been living in the harsh and rustic environment of Wales. It is here – in this far western land – that Imogen unknowingly reunites with them while attempting to evade her father's objection to her marriage to Posthumus, a man whom the king considers of ignoble origins despite the fact that he has been raised at court as a ward.

Significantly, it is only when an adapted notion of Britishness – one that values both noble and ignoble contributions – emerges under the pressures of this untamed western land that this new generation finds the strength to resist the invasion and to cast off the servility that has come to define Britain in the form of a rigid social hierarchy. Through its temporal displacement to an ancient world and its spatial displacement to Wales, the play attempts to loosen such exclusive notions of race. It does so by interrogating the value of blood as the principal determinant of identity within early modern England, identifying geography and cultural practice as equally crucial constituents of identity, forces that the play reveals have the power to affect blood, either by weakening or strengthening it. Where blood had traditionally anchored notions of race – as expressed by the king's view that only a noble match will suffice for Imogen – the play seeks to fashion social identity in more inclusive terms. It makes use of the ancient Briton – renowned for his freedom and his disavowal of hierarchies – to press this crucial cultural revision.

If, then, the play does not seem to be explicitly concerned with a contemporary colonial context in the way that a play like *The Tempest* seems to be, its focus on the Roman Empire and the motives and limits of expansionism suggests the extent to which it is engaging with such issues. To date, critics have tended to narrow its topical relevance to debates about the union spurred by King James's quest to forge a British state. But when we consider that emulation of Roman imperial models informed both the conquest of Ireland and the New World, it should spur us to entertain broader readings. I attempt one such reading by emphasizing how the play's use of geographically based notions of identity, which emphasized the degenerative and regenerative powers of environment, connects it with a set of texts more explicitly concerned with England's colonial activities. In the very years that saw the production of this play, a group of sermons and tracts commissioned by the Virginia Company from 1609 to 1614 actively sought to encourage settlement in another wild, western land, deploying a set of discursive strategies that mirror those evident in the play. Virginia was the focus of this stream of propaganda, and overcoming worries about this land's harmful effects was its aim. Just as Shakespeare's play frames Wales as a restorative space, so this body of writing, in seeking to overcome Virginia's reputation as a dire place fit for beggars, argued that it, too, would have an ameliorative effect on those settling there, intimating further that it might enable men of modest station to restore bloodlines ravaged by time. In emphasizing the constitutive force of climate and geography, and in documenting the wayward paths of genealogical lines, both sets of texts can be seen to straddle a deep cultural transition, one that was revaluing blood as the principal determinant of collective identity.

## Transmigrations

In the concluding moments of *Cymbeline,* when the King is to be reunited with his two lost sons, who have unknowingly been held captive in Wales since infancy, the question of 'identity' is suddenly problematized.[3] Cymbeline's faltering questions as he examines the two men – 'How? my issue?' (*Cym* 5.6.332) – and his expressions of uncertainty – 'If these be they' (5.6.356) – raise the spectre of imposture and suffuse the moment with doubt. How, indeed, *is* Cymbeline to know his sons from any other young men? Their foster father Belarius, eager to reveal and make amends for the role he played in their disappearance, first gestures toward their earliest royal garment, a 'curious mantle, wrought by th' hand / Of his queen mother' (5.5.362–3), which he produces for inspection. But Cymbeline is unconvinced by the 'alienable' object. He looks instead for bodily 'evidence,' for the 'mark of wonder,' the 'sanguine star' that he recalls as having graced Guiderius's neck. The 'natural stamp' (5.6.366) discovered, Cymbeline receives both men as his heirs. The body's physical properties, Cymbeline's demand seems to suggest, are the sole arbiters of genealogy, the only stable identifier of one's family and race.

Although this scene valorizes the body as the locus of one's 'true' identity – as a site marked indelibly by the inscriptions of race and lineage – the play elsewhere calls that very assumption into doubt. Indeed, far from being stable containers of bloodlines, the play repeatedly emphasizes how alterable its characters' bodies are, highlighting how much they absorb changes to physical environment as registered in shifts to climate and diet. The Italian Iachimo confesses as much when the effects of a northern climate '[enfeeble]' (5.2.4) his southern body when he arrives with Roman troops to Milford Haven to subdue a rebellious British population. His body feels and registers the material effect of his movement. So, too, when Posthumus is banished from Britain on account of his clandestine marriage to the King's daughter, his wife Imogen and servant Pisanio suspect that his travels south to Italy have 'infected' him, and his rival Cloten wills it so with his curse 'The south-fog rot him!' (2.3.126). Each of these moments suggests how much the play's protagonists suffer alteration in migrating to new lands, which profoundly implicate both their genealogical identities and those qualities that they associate with their place of birth, as Britons, Romans, or Italians. Crossing boundaries in this play is a dangerous venture, resulting in shifts to identity on a physical and, by extension, psychological level.

Indeed, just as the play intimates that individuals are destined to failure in seeking to preserve an inherited identity under the pressures of new soils and climates, so it tracks how qualities of blood decline over time. The play registers this emphasis on decline in its puzzling decision to incorporate two seemingly discrete historical moments for Rome in a single representational field: so we see ancient Rome staged alongside what seems like a contemporary Italy. In doing so, the play holds constantly before our eyes the reminder that Rome's Italian heirs have ceased to resemble their ancient forefathers, suggesting that a radical break of racial 'stock' has occurred. The play's Italian anachronisms seem to suggest that Lucius's forthright Roman courage has degenerated into Iachimo's effeminate circumspection.[4] We will witness, in fact, how the gentle Iachimo is mastered in battle by a mere British 'carl,' by Posthumus, a figure identified in the play as but a man of modest origins (5.2.4). Indeed, so opposed are the qualities of these two men – Lucius and Iachimo – that they seem to suggest a commonplace about the rise and fall of empires. Narrating how the demise of Rome emerged from within itself, Jean Bodin observed that it was the Romans' 'neglected discipline' that had so weakened them that though 'they formerly excelled all peoples in their reputation for justice and in military glory ... they [now] are outdone in both respects by almost everyone.'[5] Certainly, Iachimo's prostration at the play's end undermines any claim to martial glory. Apparently corrupted by what Bodin calls a 'perverse training,' Iachimo's good stock, what Bodin refers to as the 'natural goodness' of the 'character of the Romans,' cannot immunize him from racial 'corruption.' Indeed, he seems to confirm Hamlet's fatalistic view of an inevitable degenerative slide in which 'virtue cannot so inoculate our old stock but we shall relish of it' (*Ham* 3.1.118–19). Even the noble stock of heroic Romans, Iachimo reminds us, suffers alteration and decline.

In fact, the prospect of racial decline haunts *Cymbeline* in general, complicating its genealogy of Britain and rendering uncertain the nation's embodiment in the future. Recording not only the 'degenerations' of races and nations across time and space, it entertains as well the possibility that races can be revived and restored to a former glory, through a specific set of physical regimens. In the economy of transmigrating peoples and products so central to the play's plot, identity proves anything but constant, racial and national genealogies anything but immune to repeated reinscription. As such, the play extends the engagement with degeneracy that figured so prominently in Spenser's poetry, as seen in the preceding chapters. And yet, where the poet associated gentle behaviour with the forms of courtly decorum prevalent in England, associating a 'slip' of blood with the intemperate freedoms available at a distance from that civil centre, Shakespeare's play records a still more radical account of the alterability of bloodline. For it suggests that even the court – that font of English civility – registers blood's decline. In doing so, it loosens the juggernaut of traditional notions of race and lineage, reimagining the polity in less exclusive terms. For in the same way that Spenser's kinsman Richard Boyle discovered a stronger form of blood in its mixture with the 'earthy' qualities of a wet nurse, so this play retrieves an ancient British polity that defined all Britons as brothers and perceived rank to be the mark not of virtue but of softness. If Shakespeare's romances have traditionally been understood as a generic system poised to protect an aristocratic ideology, I argue that this play dramatizes the ruptures to that ideology and resolves them only by making profound modifications to it. For if the royal family is reunited at the play's end, it is only because it has been radically reconstituted. In symbolically absorbing Britons from Wales, Scotland, and England, the play concludes with a quite different image of the social body. It is a more inclusive body, where consanguinity derives as much from the inscriptions of place as the inscriptions of patronym.

## British Antiquities

To the extent that the play reflects upon racial alteration – upon the slippages that plague both small and large collectivities – it makes evident its own historicity, its status as a cultural object produced in and through the ideologies of early modern England. At the time Shakespeare's play was being performed on the stages of both the Globe and Blackfriars theatres between 1610 and 1611, England was flooded with printed texts investigating the physical and cultural origins of national difference. Not confined to the educated circles of William Camden's new historiography, which subjected historical evidence to cultural and linguistic scrutiny as part of an effort to demythologize the British past, these discourses were widespread in less elite circles. Ideas analysing the causes of national difference, and its essence, emanated from the political theorizing of popular continental writers such as Jean Bodin and Giovanni Botero, authors whose writings were newly translated into English in the late sixteenth and early seventeenth centuries.[6] They in turn were responding to the flurry of newly translated classical texts, including those that dealt with Roman expansion into northern territories, as found in Caesar's *Commentaries* and Tacitus's *Agricola* and *Germania*.[7] As Joyce Chaplin has argued, these classical writings were well disseminated among a broadly literate audience, given their centrality to the grammar school curriculum. It is not surprising, therefore, to find permutations of their arguments appearing in the popular drama, where a diverse theatre-going audience could in turn engage with them.

That the appeal of these antiquarian investigations was a popular and controversial topic can be demonstrated by reference to a series of plays about antiquity that were performed in roughly the same period as *Cymbeline*. John Fletcher's *Bonduca*, the anonymous *Caradoc or a Valiant Welshman*, and William Rowley's *A Shoemaker, A Gentleman* are just some of the plays that competed with *Cymbeline* to entertain London audiences by catering to an interest in the nation's ancient origins.[8] Christopher Wortham has convincingly argued that this shift to ancient topics in Shakespeare's repertoire may be seen as a function of the transition to a Jacobean court. He connects this shift to a larger movement away from plays focused on a recent English past, which had characterized the last decade of Elizabeth's rule, to those concerned with a British or Roman past, such as occurs in *King Lear, Macbeth*, and *Cymbeline*. Wortham reads this movement as in part a response to the exigencies of patronage, emphasizing both King James's announcement of his patronage of Shakespeare's company upon assuming the English throne and the dramatic increase of play-going at his court from the days of Queen Elizabeth's rule.[9] In part, such plays responded to King James's desire to merge Scotland and England into a unified Britain, evidenced by his early emphasis on this consolidation as a fulfilment of an ancient Arthurian prophecy and his tendency to style himself a modern 'Augustus.' To this extent, such plays surveyed the past in an ongoing effort to articulate what it meant to be 'British.' But such retrospective narratives must also be seen as connecting with interests beyond those of a monarch and as responding to more deep-seated questions about national identity. I would suggest that we read them, as critics have begun to read antiquarianism at large,[10] as implicated in an emergent spirit of empire, and as responding to changes to traditional conceptions of identity that were occasioned by westward movement. In looking to ancient models of conquest, these early modern writers sought out models to shape their engagements with contemporary colonial contexts.

What English readers discovered in these texts was a rather estranging vision of themselves as a barbaric, if courageous, ancient people. These images simultaneously aroused their disgust and pride and demanded an assessment of how far they had come (or had slid) from their ancient heritage under the pressures of Roman conquest and, in its wake, the incursions of Saxons, Danes, and Normans. Central to the classical record on the Roman conquest of Britain were ethnographic accounts of the northerners whom the Romans aimed to subdue, accounts that were in turn indebted to the Greek philosophies of Hippocrates, Aristotle, and Plato, among many others.[11] The accounts of Tacitus and Caesar, for instance, record a widespread conviction on the part of Mediterranean peoples that northern climates tended to produce physical imbalances. In his *Agricola,* for instance, Tacitus records the 'massive limbs' and 'ferocity' of the Britons the Romans encountered, which he suggests led them to resist bondage and to desire liberty.[12] Such claims were grounded in natural philosophy and physiological theory, which worked together to categorize people according to their native environment, seeing the body as a porous vessel that was shaped in relation to physical forces such as climate, diet, and topography.[13] In addition to the 'natural' forces determining identity at birth, which were seen as rooted in the seed of the parents, the theory of the body as a humoral vessel also granted a prominent role to various 'non-natural' forces that continued to remake the body after birth.[14]

Such theories tended to divide the world into three climatic regions – the torrid, temperate, and tropical zones – which were in turn connected to dominant physical dispositions among the people inhabiting each zone (see fig. 1). 'Those who live in a hot climate are chilled, but those who live in a cold climate have a hot nature,' Aristotle's Problem XIV concludes. 'Both classes are big, those in cold climates because of the natural heat existing in them, those in hot climates owing to the heat of the place; for growth is due to hot climates and heat.'[15] In his *Politics,* Aristotle connects these physical traits to a people's disposition or temperament, arguing that 'The peoples of cold countries generally, and particularly those of Europe, are full of spirit, but deficient in skill and intelligence; and this is why they continue to remain comparatively free, but attain no political development and show no capacity for governing others.'[16] Clearly connected to Tacitus's conception of the northerner as prone to liberty, such theories would persist well beyond the period of the Roman Empire, exerting profound influence in particular in the early modern period. They would unleash widespread discussion of the

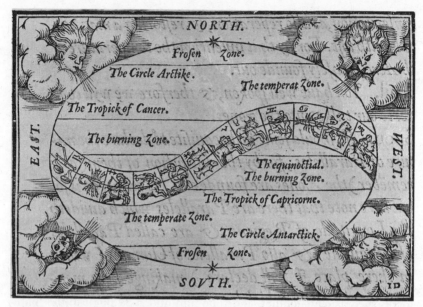

Figure 1. Woodcut depicting climate zones and the zodiac from William Cunningham, *Cosmographical Glasse* (London, 1559), fol. 64. Reproduced by permission of the Huntington Library, San Marino, California.

relative roles of climate and cultural institutions in shaping national character, figuring prominently in the political writings of Bodin and Botero and in the historical projects of Camden and Raphael Holinshed, among countless others. Bodin's widely influential *Method for the Easy Comprehension of History*, for instance, would echo Aristotle's theories in a contemporary context: 'The Mediterranean peoples [i.e., southerners] ... as far as concerns the form of the body, are cold, dry, hard, bald, weak, swarthy, small in body, crisp of hair, black-eyed, and clear-voiced. The Baltic peoples [i.e., northerners], on the other hand, are warm, wet, hairy, robust, white, large-bodied, soft-fleshed, with scanty beards, bluish grey eyes, and deep voices. Those who live between the two [i.e., in the temperate region] show moderation in all respects.'[17] Claiming for his native France the temperate ideal, Bodin participated in a widespread enterprise of national revisionism. Botero would echo these characterizations in his *Reason of State*, maintaining that 'Those who inhabit the extremes of north and south, in excessive cold or heat, have in them more of the beast than other peoples; both are ... ill-balanced in temperament, the one being beset by cold and the other suffocated by heat, the one stupefied by an excess of phlegm, the other rendered almost bestial by excessive melancholy.'[18] Although Botero would follow Hippocrates rather than Aristotle in arguing that northern climates yielded cold rather than hot bodies, he characterized northern peoples similarly as 'tall, broad, full-blooded and vigorous' and therefore 'simple and straightforward' in opposition to the southerner's 'thin and dry' physique, which made him 'sly and artful.' Significantly, both white skin and black skin expressed marginal physical conditions, deviations from the temperate ideal. In summarizing the two dispositions, he concludes, 'they are as the lion and the fox.'[19]

Such revisitations of classical climatology would echo at large through a transnational debate, as authors reiterated and interrogated ancient 'mappings' of the world. These debates would work their way as well into popular texts, underpinning the largest-selling book of the period – the almanac – and permeating the period's drama. *Cymbeline,* too, engages them, reworking these classical theories to England's honour, in valuing the physical benefits yielded by her climate – valour, honesty, and liberty – and minimizing its deficits. The play also obliquely points to one contemporary context where revisionist accounts of climate were deployed – the settlement of Virginia. For although these classically derived theories of nations seem to lock nations together with climates into a static formation, they actually concede that movement to another climate or espousal of new cultural patterns could substantially alter one's native disposition.[20] Bodin, for instance, emphasized a notion of decline in asserting that 'men as well as plants degenerate little by little when the soil has been changed.'[21] Such ideas of alterability could resound with particular force in the context of colonialism, when large segments of a nation entertained the prospect of migrating to a foreign place. What changes to identity would migration entail for such a people?[22] Shakespeare's play takes up these questions, dramatizing the way that such 'geohumoral' theories could come into direct conflict with genealogical theories of race.

### 'DePicting' Lineage

Such contradictory notions of race permeate the play. *Cymbeline* embodies one view insofar as it embraces lineage as a powerful narrative of identity, reading the father as superseding land or climate in authoring identity. Through the titular character, the play engages the age-old meaning of 'race' as 'lineage.'[23] The princely marks that Belarius discovers on his foster sons reinforce this sort of emphasis, since the marks clearly testify to the presence of royal blood that has been unmarred by the long captivity and distant migration of these princes.

But these marks also encode a very different set of potentialities. In alluding as they do to an ancient British practice, they also seem to undermine the stability of lineage, suggesting that far from being fixed at birth by the father's stamp, the body is continually re-created, produced repeatedly through interactions with a surrounding world and its objects.[24] In having Cymbeline gesture to their 'flesh' for proof of identity – to Guiderius's sanguine star – Shakespeare obliquely references the ancient Britons' practice of staining their bodies with woad. Both Camden and historian John Speed describe this practice as a genealogical sign-system, a way of 'externalizing' the internal qualities of one's blood. The marks were attempts to imprint patrimony on the flesh,[25] as Speed explains, leaving 'an vndoubted marke in the Children representing of what Parents they were borne.'[26] Camden, too, elaborates on this practice, linking the ancient word for being 'painted and coloured' – *Brith* – with the national ascription 'Brit' (see figs. 2 and 3). He goes so far as to associate the princely name 'Arviragus' – a name that Shakespeare will use for one of Cymbeline's sons – with 'Aure,' a 'faire yellow or golden colour' often used to paint 'gallant' men.[27] These ancient British customs he links with those of the Picts, suggesting their consanguinity with the ancient Britons by observing this shared practice of 'artificiall pricking.' Camden interprets the Picts as engaging in a sort of genealogical semiotics, noting how 'their Nobilitie and Gentry thus spotted, may carrie these starres about them, in their painted pownced limmes, as badges to bee knowen by.'[28] For both Speed and Camden such bodily practices signify less as an indication of ancient barbarism than as an expression of ancient civility, one that served a function analogous to the elaborate codification of clothes in early modern England. Guided by their observations, Shakespeare takes this process of acculturating the body one step further by transmuting artificial pricks into birthmarks. He does so by assigning his royal heir a natural star-mark on his flesh, thereby designating both his status and his paternity. In doing so, Shakespeare expresses a longing to naturalize culture, to imprint kin ties on the fleshy fabric of the body.

But the artificial sign-system to which Guiderius's birthmark alludes offers an implicit challenge to such identifying marks by revealing them to be the products of 'artifice' more than 'nature.' That is, it suggests a fault line in discourses of status, race, and genealogy by highlighting

Figure 2. Title page, John Speed, *Theatre of the Empire of Great Britaine* (London, 1611). Reproduced by Permission of the Huntington Library, San Marino, California.

Figure 3. Detail of 'A Britaine' demonstrating the connections of the word 'Brith' to the state of being 'painted' or 'pownced.' From the title page, John Speed, *Theatre of the Empire of Great Britaine* (London, 1611). Reproduced by Permission of the Huntington Library, San Marino, California.

the extent to which the body cannot, in and of itself, speak its identity. The external marks are called upon to perform a task not sufficiently answered by the child's blood. They compensate for the body's failures, its inability to receive the full force of its paternal imprint.[29] In adapting this practice for the royal heirs by transmuting the Britons' artificial stains into natural marks, *Cymbeline* would seem to repress the body's alienability – its status as subject to various imprinting processes, which may or may not supplement that of the father. In doing so, it not only domesticates the spectre of a barbarous British past but also moves toward stabilizing a body that otherwise appears capable of profound mobility.

The play's other royal offspring, Imogen, also has a natural mark that attests to her identity insofar as she bears a 'cinque'-spotted mole below her breast that is likened to a cowslip. Like Guiderius's star, Imogen's mole embodies her royalty at the same time as it identifies her place within a patriarchal system. It, too, seems rooted in ancient British practice, disavowing its antecedent even while shamelessly alluding to it. According to Speed, ancient Britons identified married women through marks like 'Moones and Starres &c' that graced their 'pappes,' distinguishing them from virgins, who displayed 'the shapes of all the fairest kinds of flowers & hearbes' across their bodies.[30] In being imprinted by a mark at once resembling a flower and, perhaps, a five-pointed star, Imogen's flesh attests to her complex status in a marriage at once unconsummated and paternally unrecognized; it figures her as both wife and virgin. Transferring contemporary distinctions of dress to the flesh itself, Shakespeare's marks seek to render genealogical ties material and visible.

The more radical possibility that even patrimony may be alienable is explored elsewhere in the play, at a safe distance from the royal family. We learn, for instance, that Cloten has 'derogated' from his mother, resisting the stamp of her shrewdness in his characteristic doltishness. As Lord 2 suggests, Cloten's 'issues' need not concern themselves with falling off, since he himself has already achieved the ignominious status of being a 'derogate,' of having degenerated.[31] Such failures of familial resemblance and, antithetically, the ability to 'make' kin-ties where none 'naturally' exist permeate *Cymbeline*, emphasizing the extent to which the play entertains the possibility that racial identity is materially produced in time and space rather than metaphysically embodied in the blood. Indeed, the play opens with something of a celebration of the regeneration of Posthumus's stock through his incorporation into Cymbeline's royal family, a regrafting praised by the play's first gentleman even as the jealous Cloten villainously decries such hybridizing. The gentleman describes how Cymbeline 'Breeds [Posthumus] and makes him of his bedchamber,' and how Posthumus has received his teachings 'As we do air, fast as 'twas ministered' (*Cym* 1.1.45). The process, moreover, is imagined as exceptionally successful, yielding 'a harvest' in the 'spring' (1.1.46). The governing metaphors of crop production used to describe Posthumus's ascendancy will be echoed later in the play when Belarius describes his two royal charges as demonstrating

> valour
> That wildly grows in them, but yields a crop
> As if it had been sow'd. (4.2.180–2)

Though marked by the valiance that Belarius assumes connects them to the king, Guiderius and Arviragus have come to embody that virtue with a difference – 'wildly.' While on the one hand they retain signs of royal 'cultivation,' Belarius's young charges have also absorbed aspects of the wild environment they are made to inhabit. Both stocks – royal and common – demonstrate transformative potential, the one toward wildness and the other toward civility, when forced, in effect, to trade places. Neither is static.

## Inscripting Geographies

These transformations – the possibility they suggest for the remaking and unmaking of racial identity – form an interesting pattern in the play, pointing beyond the father to a host of agents invested with the power to 'generate' people and nations. Not only nurture but also, and perhaps more strikingly from a modern perspective, 'foreign' geographies and climates impress themselves on characters, unsettling any notion of self-determination, autonomy, or stability. In *Cymbeline*, indeed, place seems intimately connected with the production and reproduction of people. Wales, for instance, is imagined as a borderland, defined repeatedly as the seat, if not the cause, of many of the play's physical alterations, while Italy is depicted as the breeder and exporter of southern deceptions and of the wiliness of a people parched by the sun.[32] Both geographies produce alterations in the play's characters. In Wales, confusions of identity occur, both willed and unexpected: the disguised Imogen's loyalties shift, as do her national allegiances, evolving from British to Norman to Roman. She also experiences herself as undergoing a process of physical alienation, first as a result of her hunger and subsequently from a diet unfamiliar in its full rawness. Hardness is the mother of hardiness, she claims, as she feels herself empowered in ways previously not possible. Iachimo, too, feels himself altered by the 'Welsh' elements, his strength seemingly evaporating in a northern climate whose 'air ... Revengingly enfeebles' (5.2.3–4) him, pressing the 'heaviness' (5.2.1) of an 'honest' disposition upon an 'Italian brain' accustomed to acting 'Most vilely' (5.6.196, 198). The complexions, or temperaments, of characters seem alterable, worn lightly by the body like garments assumed and discarded. If the play interrogates the extent to which clothes accurately designate identity, it also leads us to suspect Cymbeline's tendency to locate racial identity – one's relation to kin, tribe, and nation – on the fabric of the flesh itself. The body's properties, that is, seem every bit as malleable as the identities that clothes confer in the play.

Can we assume, then, that Belarius's two young charges, having spent twenty or so years occupying the 'foreign' space of 'Wales,' subject to its 'foreign' climate and a purportedly 'barbarous' diet, are in fact the 'same' princes they once had been? Do they, that is, contain the stamp of identity transmitted, in Renaissance theories of generation, through the father, the genitor, making them his extension through time?[33] In the economy of fluid physical identity that the play borrows in part from its historical sources, which together grant culture and place the power to remake 'nature,' such an equation is far from self-evident. The princes are arguably self-estranged from their courtly alter egos, physically alien from their former identities in ways that compound the changes wrought by time. Not only do they resist the dictates of common law in murdering the offending Cloten, but, as Belarius reminds us, their blood has been 'chafed' and something very near savagery inscribed upon them by virtue of their exposure to endless physical hardship, to wintery winds and beating sun. Are they British royalty or have they become as alien as those (Welsh) who reside beyond the boundary of the Severn in a land that the play only names by negation as 'not Britain'? Or, as Janet Adelman suggests, has the transformative trajectory moved in the opposite direction, from courtly barbarity to savage civility? Though they are touted by Belarius as the noble products of their father's blood – 'O worthiness of nature, breed of greatness!' (4.2.25) – are they not perhaps 'purer vials of their father's blood,' representing something of a 'split-off and hence protected portion of his masculinity?'[34] In such a reading, their relation to a rustic landscape and their exposure to hardship has managed to regenerate them, to protect them from the potential harm of a paternal stigma.

The play, I suggest, does indeed seek to register a profound physical transformation in these two princes, a break in the transmission of qualities from father to son. Land and climate are raised above the father as generators of races, connecting them to a wider community, to a people linked through their habitation of a specific geography and their espousal of a shared lifestyle. To the extent that it does, the play replicates a tendency in the English and Scottish histories – among its primary sources – to investigate the rise and decline of races, their tendency to change over time and space. The radical contingency of racial stock recurs as a theme in these histories insofar as they grant environment and behaviour, alongside genealogy, a shaping power over disposition. Placing contact with another people's physical milieu on par with intermarriage as events that attenuate racial identity, these texts emphasize the profoundly transformative power of climate and diet.

Critics have frequently demonstrated Shakespeare's debt to Holinshed's *Chronicles* in *Cymbeline*, pointing out Shakespeare's use of the English and Scottish accounts of Cymbeline's rule contained in this multi-authored volume, as well as a range of other passages that draw upon the vast archives of the chronicles.[35] Moving beyond the observation that Shakespeare drew from specific passages for his detail and historical data, I want to suggest a larger affinity between the two sets of texts in their shared interest in the making and unmaking of racial lines. Holinshed revisits again and again the causes and effects of shifts to racial stock, attributing such changes to diet, habitat, and climate – details that resonate with the princes' experience in *Cymbeline*. In Holinshed, identity is externalized rather than seen as primarily a fixed and inherited property of blood. Culture, that is, can rewrite the imprints of race in startlingly direct ways.

Featured prominently in Holinshed's *Chronicles*, William Harrison's 'Description of Britaine' repeatedly connects a people's topography to their physical constitution. The inhabitants of the Orchards, for instance, he describes as 'of goodlie stature, tall, verie comelie, healthfull, of long life, great strength, whitish colour' and attributes these qualities to their 'old sparing diets' and their 'ignorance of excesse.'[36] This praise of a northern climate and a sparse diet – characterizations clearly indebted to the Roman histories that described ancient Britain – is evident as well in the description of the Britons. But here Harrison's praise is partly defensive, directed against continental authors like Bodin who saw the British as a physically strong but weak witted people by virtue of their cold climate. Refuting their claims, Harrison argues that the long days so characteristic of Britain's northern geography enable the sun to produce 'braines' at once 'hot and warmed' and therefore capable of intellectual prowess to match the unquestioned physical force of the Briton on the battlefield.[37] He thereby appropriates Bodin's revisionary strategy, defining Britain as a temperate rather than a marginal geography. In scorning the consumption patterns of contemporary 'north Britons,' whose growing dependence on southern European products he blames for '[ingrossing]' their bodies, Harrison implicitly casts continental Europe as decadent, as a locus of degeneracy.[38]

Hector Boetius seconds this reading when he attempts to account for the differences between the ancient Briton and the modern-day Scot in his 'Description of Scotland.' Qualifying his praise of the Scots' courage and hardiness, he claims that these strengths are predicated on their ability to 'liue temperatelie, and follow their predecessors in moderation of diet.'[39] Alterations in diet, Boetius argues, can break and, in fact, have broken the genealogical continuity of the lowland Scots. By contrast, the Scottish Highlanders are, for Boetius, a model of fortitude rather than barbarity. He praises them as having 'lesse to doo with forreine merchants' than the Lowlanders, and he argues that they are 'lesse delicate, and not so much corrupted with strange bloud and aliance.' He here places consumption on par with intermarriage as a primary cause of racial alteration, urging that dietary abstinence, like sexual abstinence, has produced bodies that are 'more hard of constitution ... to beare off the cold blasts, to watch better, and absteine long,' and making them 'bold, nimble, and thereto more skilfull in the warres.'[40] If purity means disavowing mixture with 'strange bloud,' it also means resisting strange food.

Boetius depicts the Lowlanders, by contrast, as 'falling by little and little from the frugalitie and customs of their forefathers,' leading 'their vertue and force ... to decaie' as well. He blames, above all else, their 'vnnaturall rauening and greedie desire of forreine things' for this degenerative slide. Where their forefathers ate 'such stuff as grew most readilie on the ground,' they now enjoy the 'immoderate vse of wine' and 'gad ouer all the world for sweet and pleasant spices, and drugs,' bringing home 'poison and destruction vnto their countriemen.' He pointedly concludes: 'they were temperate, we effeminate.' A formerly northern body has by virtue of these changes become a stranger in its native environment, proving unable to weather the 'colder regions' because its 'inward parts doo burne and parch as it were with continuall fier, the onelie cause whereof we may ascribe vnto those hot spices and drugs which are brought vnto vs from the hot countries.'[41] Boetius bemoans the loss of 'our ancient sobernesse and manhood' in the majority of Scottish men, detecting only a trace still remaining in some. He thus charts a genealogical break stemming from bad diet and bad daily practice: the Scots through proximity to their English ancestors came to 'learne also their maners,' and so to lose their distinctive racial attributes.[42]

Like Boetius, Camden celebrates the strengths of a robust, because mixed, marginal people like the highland Scots, whom he identifies as the descendants of the ancient Picts. Although often associated with an emergent form of history that ridiculed Geoffrey of Monmouth's ancient 'myth' of British descent from the Trojans,[43] Camden's account is in fact surprisingly sedimented. Camden betrays, for instance, a deep ambivalence about those unenslaved ancient Britons who wandered north and west, far from the reach of the Roman civilizing forces, evading not only 'bondage' to an imperial power but also the softening effects that it brought in its wake. Celebrating their flight from the Romans as a fight against 'servitudes, which is of all miseries the extreamest,' he records their northern migration and the physical strengths such movement produced. They arrived, he explains, to 'these Northerne parts, frozen with the bitter cold of the aire ... Where being armed not so much with weapons, as with a sharpe aire and climate of their owne, they grew vp together with the native inhabitants whom there they found, unto a mightie and populous nation.'[44] Climate here seems to mix with breeding in uniting these two stocks of people and securing their survival.

Those who fled to the mountains of the west benefited similarly. Celebrating these westward Britons as those who 'continued the longest free from the yoke both of Romans and also of English dominion,' Camden attributes their resistance to the strengths they derived from their environment: he describes them as a 'puissant and courageous nation, by reason they keepe wholly in a mountanous country, and take heart even of the soile.'[45] Their simplicity of diet, consisting of 'white meates, as buter, cheese &c,' produced bodies of 'cleere complexion, goodly feature, & lineaments of body, inferiour to no nation in Britain.' Citing John of Salisbury's *Polycraticon*, Camden recounts how these Britons succeeded in making 'inrodes,' in 'assaulting,' 'winning,' and 'overthrowing' nearby English settlements because their English counterparts had been 'so deintily brought up, and loues to be house-birds and to liue lazie, in the shade, beeing borne onely to devour the fruits of the earth and to fill the belly.'[46] Following Tacitus, Camden betrays a distrust of the luxuries that civility breeds, and the physical vulnerabilities that such luxuries produce.[47] He glances back nostalgically at ancient simplicity and fortitude.

Civility at the hands of the Romans was a vexed enterprise promising material comforts at the same time as its 'effeminate' softness subverted a hardy race.

These debates received new and urgent currency in the first decade of the seventeenth century, with King James's ascension to the throne and his pressing demands for unifying England and Scotland into Great Britain and his call to naturalize Scottish citizens under English law.[48] Debates on the topic raised many questions. How much would union produce a conformity of manners? What differences of stock existed between the Saxon and British races? What constituted those differences? What qualities inhered in each race, and to what extent did custom produce those physical qualities? What effect would political, physical, and cultural proximity have on each group? Circling around distinctions between Scot and Englishman, these debates overwhelmingly emphasized the significance of environment.

Sir Francis Bacon, who was at the centre of these debates in his position as Attorney General and who came to be an advocate of the union, himself celebrated, in what seems to be a nod toward his Scottish neighbours, the benefits of a hard upbringing, going so far as to define it as central to imperial growth.[49] While much of his manuscript entitled 'True Greatness of the Kingdom of Britain' has been lost to us, enough survives to convey Bacon's praise of the hardy strength of the Briton, his admiration of the strengths produced in people who occupy the margins of civil life. The Swiss mountaineers, for instance, he praises for having defeated various rounds of invaders. Although characterized by 'stirring and turbulent' spirits, much as many English perceived their Scottish neighbours to be, he argues that such men of strength are essential to empire. Seeming to refute those who resisted union on the grounds that it would dissipate English wealth, he argues further that national wealth makes a nation vulnerable when it is severed from military virtue which he associates with poverty. Because wealth must be 'joined with martial prowess and valour' to be useful, it is 'better when some part of the state is poor, than when all parts of it are rich.'

Writing to promote what he saw as a desirable national agenda of expansion, he urged Britain to model itself on 'most of the great kingdoms of the world,' which 'have sprung out of hardness and scarceness of means, as the strongest herbe out of the barrenest soils.'[50] Iron, he elsewhere asserts quoting Solon, will outperform gold every time in the contest of nations.[51] Though the Spanish 'should of late years take unto themselves that spirit as to dream of a Monarchy in the West ... only because they have ravished from some wild and unarmed people mines and store of gold,' it is 'this island of Brittany' that would do best to fill that role, armed as it is with the 'best iron in the world, that is the best soldiers of the world.'[52] Where other writers were observing the barbarity of the Briton's ancient strengths, leaders like Bacon were quick to connect those strengths to an emergent British colonial enterprise.

In casting the Scots as arguably Britain's leading class of soldiers – describing them as 'a people ingenious, in labour industrious, in courage valiant, in body hard, active, and comely' – Bacon not only echoed the accounts of classical ethnographies but also implicitly diagnosed English degeneracy. Although 'of one piece and continent' with the Scots, the English have been undone by their wealth, their 'reckonings and audits, meum and tuum.'[53] In this respect, Bacon's arguments intersect with the accounts of racial slippage registered in the *Chronicles* and represented at large in a widespread national debate. In his notorious anti-theatrical tract *The Schoole of Abuse*, for instance, Stephen Gosson was quick to echo the *Chronicles'* doomsday sentiment in associating the theatre, like other 'foreign imports,' with civility's effeminizing excesses which he blamed for eroding English manhood. Drawing on Holinshed's portrait of a hardier past, Gosson laments that the Englishman's age-old ability to 'suffer watching and labour, hunger and thirst' and to feed 'upon rootes and barkes of trees,' has been replaced by his insolency, his tendency to 'gape after meate' and 'long for the cuppe.' Worst of all was the substitution of 'banqueting, playing, piping, and dauncing' – all activities associated with the court – for the military exercises central to the nation's welfare.[54] Gosson's call for a return to native origins is framed by the observation that the English have in fact outdone the enormities of their incontinent European neighbours: 'Oh what a wonderfull chaunge is this? Our wrestling at armes, is turned to wallowyng in Ladies laps, our courage, to cowardice, our running to ryot, our Bowes into bolles, and our Dartes to Dishes. We haue robed Greece of Gluttonie, Italy of wantonnesse, Spaine of pride, Fraunce of deceite, and Dutchland of quaffing. Compare London to Rome, and England to Italy, you shall finde the Theaters of the one, the abuses of the other, to be ripe among us.'[55]

**Conquest of Degeneracy**

Responding to this challenge with uncanny specificity, while ironically choosing to instruct through the very medium Gosson so rails against, Shakespeare's play both compares London to Rome and England to Italy, and in many respects confirms Gosson's diagnosis. Through its unflattering depiction of the British court figures, for instance, the play maps distinctively southern vices onto a British disposition, pointing up the extent to which wealth and the contact with southern people and products that it enables has caused degeneration. Cloten, Cymbeline, and the Queen are linked in their depiction as having dissipated the nation's characteristic ancient strengths. Although together they speak for Britain's inviolability, voicing the play's powerful articulation of Britain as 'a world / By itself' (3.1.12–13), in fact their ties to that nostalgic space have been corroded by the various non-native practices each of them has embraced.

Cloten, for example, demonstrates the effeminacy so denigrated in the histories, a condition Tacitus and the British chroniclers following classical authors describe as being 'mollified yet by long peace.'[56] In summarizing Tacitus's famous account, Camden observes that the Roman method of subduing the fortitude of northern peoples like the Gauls and Germans was by diverting them with leisure activities, including instruction in 'liberall sciences.' By encouraging the Gauls to give 'themselves over to ease and idlenesse,' Camden explains, 'cowardise crept in, and shipwracke was made both of manhood and liberty together.' It is, more specifically, their adoption of southern postures – first the wearing of the Roman gown, then their instruction in the Roman tongue, and finally their enjoyment of 'sumptuous galleries ... & exquisite banquetings'[57] – that signals their decline. Though Cloten seems to possess the martial physique of the ancient Briton – humorously referenced by Imogen's misplaced lament over 'his foot Mercurial, his Martial thigh, / The brawns of Hercules' (4.2.312–13) when she mistakenly believes him to be her deceased husband – his native strength has become so encumbered by soft civil markers, the 'unpaid-for silk' (3.3.24) which Belarius mocks, as to be impotent. His preoccupation with the leisure activities of bowling, music, and wooing signals his decline from an ancient standard. And while he celebrates those native strengths in defiance of the Roman encroachment – 'We have yet many among us can grip as hard as Cassibelan' (3.1.39–40) – he also divorces himself from their collective ranks when he urges 'I do not say I am one' (3.1.40). Other Britons, he suggests, will ably disburse an impinging Roman force. He, by contrast, proves unable to answer even the personal threats he poses to Arviragus – 'Die the death!' (4.2.98) – and feels his words soundly answered by the 'rustic mountaineer' (4.2.102). His defeat here dispels the force of his rhetoric and excludes him from association with the elite band of warriors imagined in his own and his mother's rhetoric before Lucius.

As Belarius recalls of Cloten in a former day, he is 'nothing but muta-

tion' (4.2.134), the classic failing of the northerner, as outlined by Caesar, Tacitus, and subsquently Camden, Bodin, and a long line of early
modern ethnographers. Poised between the extremes of his body's heat
and dampness – its excess of blood and humours – the northerner suffers an 'unconstant and variable mind ... [loving] evermore change
and alteration.'[58] As Bodin explains, 'The inner warmth [of northern-
ers] drives them to action ... but moisture brings softness,' a duality that
he describes as producing a 'curious inconsistency of nature' that leads
them to seek alternately war and the indulgence of sleep and feasting.[59]
Inactivity, in other words, forces the strengths of the northern temperament to give way to 'infirmity,'[60] allowing the body's heat to yield to
its softer physical component. As such, the northerner's complexion
makes him particularly vulnerable to a degenerative slide. Cloten seems
to embody just such a decline in his shifting loyalties to Imogen – love
quickly mutating to jealous, even murderous, rage – and in his untempered responses to losing at bowls, dice, and women, the very activities
Gosson identified with English decline. As the punning Lord notes,
Cloten's status is nothing if not 'rank,' festering in too much idle time,
too many inflated words, and too few martial deeds. He reinforces Imogen's later observation that 'Plenty and peace breeds cowards' (3.6.21).
Rather than demarcating a privileged genealogical inheritance, Cloten's
possessions – the land that he has inherited and the fine clothes he
flaunts – have undermined his ancient British genealogy.

Shakespeare repudiates Cloten's genealogical connection to ancient
Britons further through the name he assigns him. Actively revising his
sources, Shakespeare rejects the way these histories narrate how Brute's
line comes to an end. In the *Chronicles* the lineal break with Brute is
identified as occurring in the wake of a fatal civil war waged between two
brothers, which leads to the ascension of a king named Cloten. Not line-
ally connected as were the warring princely brothers to the mythic Brute,
the arrival of Cloten to the throne marks the bitter end of the prized Tro-
jan genealogy.[61] In rewriting this tragic sequence of events, Shakespeare
valorizes the unity of his British princes, rather than characterizing them
by dissension and warfare. He also takes the more dramatic step of violently terminating the progression of Cloten's non-Trojan line by having
Guiderius sever Cloten's 'head.' With Cloten's future undone, that of the
royal brothers proceeds unencumbered, presumably extending indefinitely through time. Shakespeare thereby rejects the genealogical graft
that Cloten embodies, imagining instead the continuity of Brute's (and
Britons') strengths in the future.

In fact, Cloten, it seems, holds a lineal connection only to the play's marred figure of womanhood, the Queen, his mother. He alone of the play's young Britons is defined by a matrilineal genealogy, the others, including both the princes and Posthumus, being linked with the heroism of male ancestors like Cassibelan and Leonatus. None of these admirable men has had sustained contact with his mother, Posthumus being literally 'ripp'd' (5.4.45) from his mother's womb and the princes removed from an unnamed mother prior to weaning. The Queen's womanly strengths aside, it seems she is unable to 'author' Cloten as would a father, producing instead a 'derogate,' a son notable for having fallen off from a noble line. As Guiderius puts it, Cloten fails to be 'worthy [of his] birth' (4.2.96). His characteristic senselessness mirrors his mother only insofar as she dotes blindly on an inferior and unworthy heir. Otherwise, her shrewdness does not extend to a son who is characterized instead as a fool. As the Lords note, she is a 'crafty devil' (2.1.49) and is 'hourly coining plots' (2.1.56). Far from demonstrating the native Briton's 'plain dealing,' the Queen has imported the scheming of the Italian machiavel, what Harrison describes as the southerner's 'subtile practises, doublenesse, and hollow behauiour.'[62] She notoriously engages in machinations to secure the throne for her son and assumes a 'tyrannical' force in her control of her husband. Her alignment with these southern vices is materially rendered through her association with poisons, defined in *Cymbeline*, as in other contemporary plays, as a product of 'drug-damned Italy' (3.4.15). But in contrast to southerners like Iachimo, who prove successful in implementing the connivings of their 'beastly mind[s]' (1.6.154), the Queen only shadows their sophistication. Whereas the southerner's subjection to the sun's heat produces an excess of black bile, providing the conditions for 'highest learning' and 'foxlike cunning,'[63] the Queen is largely ineffective in her plots, duping only Cymbeline.

Where his Queen is associated with Italianate vices, Cymbeline's past expresses affinities with imperial Rome that have altered the plain-dealing nature characteristic of his native people. Nurtured in the Roman court under Caesar, it seems Cymbeline was too much in the 'sun,' learning the Italianate mode of distrust in searching out duplicity to his own detriment. Belarius reminds us, for instance, of Cymbeline's fatal choice in believing the 'false oaths' of two villains before the plain acts of a friend and soldier, one whose 'perfect honour' (3.3.66, 67) was visibly demonstrated not just by feats on the battlefield but a body 'marked / With Roman swords' (3.3.56–7). Cultivating suspicion for a British soldier of 'perfect honour,' Cymbeline is forced to surrender his succession and to accept a wider class of Britons as his kinsmen. Deprived of his sons, he is forced to depend upon the 'valiant race' (5.5.177) of Britons whose sword-marks designate their connection to Britishness every bit as much as do the birthmarks that grace the royal family.

Where the play's primary figures of courtly identity demonstrate various breaks with native British identity, the princes and Imogen undergo a process of re-learning their British ancestry and of resuturing fragmented genealogical connections. Their princely blood, it seems, proves insufficient in securing their connection to their British forefathers. Indeed, we witness the 'renaturing' of princes into native British subjects through immersion in a British environment. If the princes are regenerated in Wales partly as a tribute to the Welsh genealogy of the Tudors, they are also reformed like the ancient Britons, who fled to the Welsh mountains to escape Roman servitude.[64] Following his historical sources, which describe the Britons as 'driuen either into Wales [or] Cornewall' during various and repeated rounds of conquest not only by the Romans but also by the Saxons and Normans, Shakespeare removes his royal princes from the corrupting imports at court and returns them to a native landscape. In addition to being transported to a native climate, being 'hot summer's tanlings and / The shrinking slaves of winter' (4.4.29–30), they are regenerated by characteristically British cultural practices, returning to a simplicity of diet and activity that counters the excesses at court. Together with Belarius, the young princes hunt hares, goats, and venison and live humbly in a 'pinching cave' (3.3.38), donning the simple attire of 'clouted brogues' (4.2.215) in keeping with descriptions of ancient Britons.[65] Engaged in labour despite their royal blood, the princes undergo the 'drying' and remasculating 'sweat of industry' (3.6.31).

Their exposure to British topography, moreover, imprints their bodies with northern features, whitening and strengthening their bodies beyond compare. Though subject to the climate's extremes of heat and cold, Posthumus reminds us that their complexions are, if anything, perfected by the exposure, describing them as 'fairer / Than those for preservation cased' (5.5.21–2), and thereby echoing Harrison's description of the Briton as 'of a good complexion, tall of stature, strong in bodie, white of colour, and thereto of great boldnesse and courage in the warres.'[66] That they demonstrate the northerner's characteristic eruption into wrathful violence, which Bodin distinguishes from the southerner's more 'cunning' pursuit of violence and torture,[67] is evidenced by Guiderius's response to Cloten's accusations of treason. Refusing to qualify or conceal his act, he responds to Belarius's anxious questioning by directly asserting that he has 'cut off one Cloten's head, / Son to the Queen' (4.2.119–20). Such forthrightness demonstrates his ties to ancient Britons, recalled as living 'in a lawlesse kind of libertie, as bearing themselves bould both upon their owne valour.'[68]

Imogen's royal birthmarks are also transformed by the inscriptions of a British land and lifestyle. Retrieving an ancient practice believed to enhance the Briton's military success, she brands herself with what she thinks is Posthumus's blood, calling upon it to

Give colour to my pale cheek …
That we the horrider may seem to those
Which chance to find us! (4.2.332–4)

Like her brothers, she is made to forego the comforts of court life, sleeping on the ground and experiencing the restorative, if harsh, effects of 'famine' (3.6.19). She also assumes the female complement to their labour, by demonstrating her skill as a 'housewife' (4.2.45) in preparing their savage fare. Imogen and her brothers unlearn their royal privilege, labouring to survive like modest Britons. Their immersion in native practices suggests the provisional nature of British consanguinity and suggests that geography and work may have as much power as blood in 'authoring' a people. Like the royal Boadicea, who was said to have behaved 'not as a Ladie descended of so noble progenitors … but as one of the common people,'[69] Cymbeline's royal offspring follow the path of 'tributary rivers' in travelling away from the 'imperious seas' (4.2.36, 35) of courtly life and privilege.[70] Collectively, the royal family distance themselves from wealth, Imogen willingly surrendering her inheritance to her brothers and Cymbeline choosing despite the British victory to pay tribute to the Romans. In making these choices, they assert the virtues of simplicity, rejecting luxury and enacting Posthumus's motto of 'less without and more within' (5.1.33).

In fact, the play resolves the ambivalence it raises regarding the question of human 'dust.' Whether 'clay and clay differs in dignity' (4.2.4) though made of 'one dust' (4.2.248) or whether 'noble fury' can issue from 'so poor a thing' as Posthumus (5.6.8) is roundly answered by Posthumus's triumph. British topography regenerates Posthumus, transforming his 'baseness' and 'rootlessness' into the new identity of 'a Britain born' (5.6.84). The play thus grants 'Great nature, like … ancestry' a role in moulding the 'stuff' of human bodies (5.4.142–3). Early in the play, we watch as Posthumus falls prey to southern 'infection.' He sullies his valorous British lineage when he is forced through banishment to wander far from home through the corrupting south. While demonstrating many of the virtues of his Briton lineage – a line traced first and foremost to those ancestors who fought to preserve British soil against Julius Caesar – Posthumus fails like vegetation that is 'not born where't grows' (3.4.55). In fact, his travels through France and his banishment to Italy tutor him in the ways of a southerner, teaching him both the cunning to deceive Imogen and the vindictiveness to murder her (3.4.31–2). He becomes the consummately jealous Italian, re-enacting Cloten's 'mutation.' Suffering the northerner's soft impressionability, Posthumus proves susceptible to 'strange infection' (3.2.3) through contact with 'drug-damned Italy' (3.4.15). Iachimo himself connects Posthumus's corruption to the excesses of feasting and viands, which denote not just Italian wealth but also Italian degeneracy (5.6.155–6). Cloten's curse, 'The south-fog rot him!' (2.3.126), appears to have been fulfilled when Imogen concludes that he 'Has forgot Britain' (1.6.114). Indeed, Posthumus's border crossings do unearth him, unravelling his ties to his heroic British ancestors and refiguring him as an orphan.

By immersing himself in the raw 'stuff' of his country, though, Posthumus arrests his degenerative slide. He dispenses with civil accoutrements – with 'fresh cups, soft beds, / Sweet words' (5.5.71–2) – and adorns himself instead in the meanest of rags. Shaming the 'gilded arms' (5.6.4) of his Italian counterparts, he testifies by his rags to his connection to ancient Britons who fought with 'neither head peece nor coate of fence' and were the hardier for so doing.[71] '[B]eggary and poor looks' (5.6.10) are thereby embraced by the play not as the antithesis of 'noble races' – signs of those locked outside its circuit of privilege – but as the very condition of such genealogies. Urging Jupiter to peep through his 'marble mansion,' Sicilius insists that the deity acknowledge the centrality of his 'valiant race' (5.5.181, 177) to British identity. In so doing, he suggests a return to the ancient British practice of raising in common all British children, since 'true British Nobilitie is moe [sic] in vertue then in Auncestors.'[72]

## The Britain Beyond

Although these histories of ancient Britain seem to express a radical inward turn on the part of their authors, in fact, these interrogations

of deep-seated assumptions about genealogy's determining drive were
catalysed by England's struggles to forge an identity in a global arena.
The emphasis on antiquity, though, has served as something of a critical
blinder, impeding our ability to perceive the contemporary uses to which
an ancient past was being applied.[73] In returning to images of Roman
imperialism and to originary accounts of ancient British strengths,
Shakespeare and his contemporaries were not merely nostalgic. Rather,
they sought the justifications and strategies that would position England
as a contender on colonial fronts, both with regard to 'British borderers'
and in relation to more distant vistas. *Cymbeline*'s westward movement
thus demands critical attention. Although *Cymbeline* powerfully retraces
the ancient Britons' flight from imperial Roman forces, the play's wester-
ing impulse persists to the closing words of the play with the image of the
'Roman eagle / From south to west on wing soaring aloft' (5.6.470–1).
Although the image can be seen to suggest the translation westward of
the ancient Roman Empire to include the distant land of ancient Britain,
it also gestures beyond its Roman context. It is described as vanishing
in the 'beams o'th' sun' (5.6.472), suggesting a deferral of closure, an
evasion of narrow referents. The eagle points England to imperial des-
tinies yet to be pursued, urging her to assume the role of 'new Rome'
in following the eagle's flight to the west. It was an image that appealed
as well to those urging colonization of Virginia. In his *Nova Britannia*,
Robert Johnson would warn the English not to imitate the mistakes of
the Romans in clipping the 'wings' of empire so that 'shee might take
her flight no more.'[74]

In *Cymbeline* western movement brings regeneration, where stasis in
the English 'centre' leads to degeneracy. Moreover, the play seems to
suggest that such transformations be seen as extending beyond the play's
elite characters to a larger collectivity. Indeed, it is striking that Imogen,
who serves as something of a symbol for the nation in calling herself
'Britain' (1.6.114), experiences herself as profoundly altered (3.6.15–
22) in her movement westward to a land beyond Britain. Her venture
toward Milford Haven, and toward a land that Pisanio describes as 'not
in Britain' (3.4.135), signals a return to the site of Tudor ascendancy. It
was to Milford Haven that Henry Tudor came to take the English throne
as the British/Welsh ruler of the kingdom, an originary myth that both
the Tudors and Stuarts celebrated. Imogen twice visits Milford Haven –
once imaginatively to 'see' Posthumus depart for Italy and then in actual-
ity to meet her returning husband. But in the early seventeenth century,
the port harboured ships for another western land – the as yet uncharted

land 'Nova Britannia,' which many envisioned as an unspoiled Britain.[75] In referring to 'Virginia' as a new 'Britannia,' English colonists performed a conceptual move similar to that of Shakespeare's play: they cast back in time for models to elucidate the present and to shape the future, framing the New World in the terms of the Old World. Imogen's reference to her mother's experience of her own birth (3.4.2–3) as she awaits Posthumus's 'delivery' in this unfamiliar landscape and her tendency to see her travels west as a desirable movement beyond the containment of a 'nest' (3.4.139)[76] obliquely point toward the new colonial context.[77] The language of reproductivity thus parallels the language of an empire being born.

Shakespeare wrote his last romances after a twenty-year hiatus in efforts to colonize Virginia, following the failures in Roanoke in the early 1580s. That he had connections to a rather broad circle of investors who helped to revive the Virginia enterprise between 1607 and 1611 has been brought to bear on studies of *The Tempest*, given the play's oblique relation to the shipwreck of the *Sea Adventure* on Bermuda in 1609. Such connections, which include the fact that two of Shakespeare's primary patrons, the Earls of Pembroke and Southampton, were elected as members of the 1609 Virginia Council, have perhaps been overlooked in critical readings of *Cymbeline*, a play roughly contemporaneous with *The Tempest*.[78]

While I do not wish to claim that this play and the Virginia enterprise are directly related in a causal sequence – the notion of context simply being transmuted to text – I do wish to draw attention to the overlapping discursive grid that defined both textual moments. In fact, it is remarkable to find how closely *Cymbeline*'s themes resonate with those articulated in the Virginia propaganda, a mix of pamphlets and sermons urging plantation, which circulated in the years of the play's likely composition. Both texts circle around competing accounts of generation, weighing the merits of genealogy and geography in determining identity. Reading the two sets of texts together not only helps to elucidate them individually as engagements with nation and empire at a defining moment for England, but it also reveals how colonization actively contributed to the remaking of racial identity in this period.

In the years between 1607 and 1611, the settling of Virginia was an enterprise that few Englishmen were eager or willing to pursue. Quite to the contrary, the early efforts at colonizing Jamestown enjoyed considerable notoriety, provoking dramatic ridicule as an enterprise for Scots and ragamuffins. It was also attacked for its financial and human losses.[79] The

Virginia Company took up the charge and struggled to rewrite defeat in terms of a heroic challenge, commissioning speeches in a variety of venues that would celebrate the colony. It was the role of the Virginia Company to offset the negative associations, to reframe the enterprise so as to attract interest and commitment from men otherwise inclined to heap scorn on the effort. 'Why should any frowne or envie at it, or if they do; why should wee (neglecting so faire an opportunitie) faint or feare to enlarge our selves,' questioned Robert Johnson.[80] Similarly, in a sermon preached in 1610 before Lord De La Warre famously embarked for Virginia to serve as Lord Governor, the residue of popular resistance speaks at large in the words of author William Crashaw. To those who maintain that 'the Countrie is ill reported of by them that haue been there,' Crashaw posturingly responds, 'it is not true, in all, nor in the greater or better part.'[81]

In a subsequent tract, Crashaw replies less circumspectly to reports of the horrible conditions at Jamestown – the shortages of supplies, the need for continual labour, and the resulting disease and starvation – suggesting in his own heightened pitch that such accounts were escalating. In a dedication that he appended to Alexander Whitaker's *Good Newes from Virginia*, he starkly reproduces the accusations regarding Jamestown: 'When they come there, are they not starued, and do they not die like dogges?'[82] Eager now to blame these failures on the factious behaviour of the colonists, Crashaw also abandons the pretence of denying Virginia's pitfalls. With Johnson, who published a continuation of *Nova Britannia* in 1612 as *The New Life of Virginea*, he was acknowledging that 'there is no common speech nor publike name of anything this day, (except it be the name of God) which is more vildly depraued, traduced and derided by such vnhallowed lips, then the name of Virginea.'[83] Clearly, these writers had no small task in reframing the individual sacrifices writ large in this effort as deserving embrace.[84]

Just as Shakespeare's play calls for the reproduction of a degenerate people by appealing to the power of geography and native custom, so, too, the great body of tracts urging transplantation to Virginia point to racial slippage as a primary incentive for planting abroad. In fact, it seems that the authors of these sermons and tracts may have culled the same historical sources so central to Shakespeare – those of Holinshed and Camden – in searching out their framing arguments. Assessing the Englishman's 'nature' and his resemblance to the 'nature' of the nation's forefathers was one line of attack that the Virginia Company's propaganda machine actively pursued. Collectively, these tracts pressure

Englishmen to imitate their 'forefathers' strengths,'[85] implicitly charging those who were lukewarm about the westward enterprise with bastardy and/or degeneracy. Looking to Tacitus's argument that found in Rome's greatness the kernel of its decline, the Company promoted tracts and sermons that warned Englishmen against living too comfortably off the 'fat and feeding ground of their natiue countrey' and of living licentiously in a state grown 'ripe and rotten.'[86] Charging them with having all but 'extinguisht' the 'ancient valour of English blood,' with 'so much forget[ting] themselues,' the Company urged Englishmen to retrieve the 'corporal hardnesse' of their forebears and to 'shake off that dull and lazie humour … into which our nation is now degenerate.'[87] Envisioning those forebears much as *Cymbeline* envisions its ideal British leaders, Crashaw emphasizes that they were constituted through their relation to land and hardship: 'they exposed themselves to frost and colde, snow and heate, raine and tempests, hunger and thirst, and cared not what hardnesse, what extremitie, what pinching miseries they enured, so they might atchieve the ends they aimed at.'[88] Such 'corporal hardnesse,' he suggests, has been lost on their English offspring who scorn the Virginia enterprise and thereby demonstrate their degeneracy, their inability to 'indure winter and summer, winde and weather, sunne and showers, frost and snow, hunger and thirst, in campe or garrison, by land or sea.'[89]

Drawing much of their material from the ethnographic history of Bodin's writing, these tracts posit an inherent warring of 'fluids' at the core of Englishness, attributing the decline to a collective physiological disposition as expressed through inconstancy and indecisiveness.[90] Defining Englishmen as naturally plagued by the 'muddy and earthly spirits,'[91] the impressionable damp humours characteristic of people inhabiting northern regions, these tracts suggest that too much inactivity – the 'want of exercise of armes and actiuitie, want of trades and labour'[92] – has produced a physical decline from the masculine heat of their forebears. They argue that the idleness produced by 'peace and plentie' has resulted in 'self-forgetting.' But the contaminating effects of interaction with foreign peoples and of exposure to foreign places is also blamed for this degeneration. Those like Shakespeare's Posthumus who 'wander from coast to coast, from England to Spaine, to Italy, to Rome ∴. pulling a world of temptations upon their bad dispositions' are precisely those whom these texts identify as standing to gain most 'by these new discoueries, in so great a world,'[93] by a land whose conditions were proximate to those of their heroic ancestors. Framing the New World as a 'Nova Britannia,' as England's uncorrupted alter ego, these tracts argue for a regeneration of native stock through the 'pinching miseries' of a 'harder course of life.'[94] Through the discipline of their new life, they promise, Virginia will be the means by which they will become 'new men,' and, collectively, a 'new mould.'[95] Although framed in the language of 'newness,' these tracts seek to reclaim ancient strengths, to make anew an ancient mould.

Although the Company's propaganda traced these strengths to Saxon, rather than British, forebears, seeking to distance themselves from what they describe as the barbarity of the more ancient Britons, they implicitly appropriate the strengths of people of the 'British margins' for their project, adding the Welsh and Scottish to the ranks of those celebrated as 'Saxons.' Noting the multitude that gathered to ward off the Spanish in the year of the Armada, for instance, Johnson's *New Life of Virginea* recalls a hybrid gathering of some 'thirtie hundred thousand of English, Welsh, and Cornish men,' while also describing Scotland as a 'warlike, wise, and stout nation.'[96] The authors of these tracts seem to follow Bacon in tracing the source of the degeneracy outlined above to *English* softness, to the idleness and luxury that were produced by *English* wealth. But even as they celebrate the 'noble Saxons bloud,'[97] they also begin to move beyond blood-based identifications in striving to anchor identity in geography rather than lineage. Constructed as a new (ancient) Britannia, Virginia is imagined as a space that will replace blood as the authoring agent of a people, extending the benefits of nobility to all. One author anticipates a radical flattening of hierarchies abroad, such that 'thou shalt bee more eminent and famous in a yeare, then at home halfe of thy ranke shall bee all their daies.'[98] Casting its net to catch the lowly British Posthumus as well as the aristocrat, the Virginia Company, like Shakespeare's play, expanded the meaning of *race*. If previously it had usually referred to noble lineage, it increasingly came to mean the nation. Whether that nation was England or Britain remained a contested question.

But if the Company explicitly sought to frame Virginia in the language of 'regeneration,' fears of degeneration lingered in the margins of these texts. Though hard work and a removal from the luxuries of culture certainly boded well for refining natures grown 'soggy' with rest and idleness, migration to Virginia also presented serious questions regarding climate. If British geography and climate had helped to produce them as a people, what would become of colonists when translated to Virginia? What if the land itself could remake Englishmen, transforming them not in accord with their ancient fathers' native strengths, but in the

modes and manners of other Old World and New World peoples? 'Early
in the history of colonization, some had speculated that American nativity would produce radically different individuals – Indians, say, rather
than Europeans,' Joyce Chaplin has argued. 'English migrants faced the
possibility that, in America, they would become a different people and
would be parents of different people.'[99] Worse still in the minds of many
English, they might be renatured in the form of a southern European, as
an Italian, or a Spaniard.

Indeed, in Crashaw's defensive denial of excessive heat in Virginia, we
see anxieties rooted in *European* difference. To those concerned with the
experience of travel itself, he asserts: 'we come not neere the *Sunne*, nor
vnder the Aequinoctiall *line*, to distemper our bodies.' And he argues
that, once arrived, voyagers will find 'it is not so hot as *Spaine*,' but rather
of a temper with which they will be 'well content.'[100] Similarly, Edward
Hayes would seek to assuage fears that northeastern America might too
closely resemble southern Europe to be suitable for English settlement.
Having identified Virginia's location as 'betweene 40. and 44. Degrees
of latitude, vnder the Paralels of Italy and France,' he insists 'yet are
not they so hot,' since the sun's heat is 'qualified in his course ouer the
Ocean.'[101]

As these references to Spain, France, and Italy suggest, Europeans
did not at this time assign themselves a homogeneous transcontinen-
tal identity, certainly not one linking them through a shared phenotype
of 'whiteness.' Rather, early modern European writers identified themselves with a diverse set of 'complexions of body and conditions of mind,'
produced by their exposure to varying climates and cultures.[102] These
varying humoral complexions were in turn visible through the subtle
distinctions of skin colour they observed among each other. According to Bodin, 'under the tropics [people] are unusually black; under
the pole, for the opposite reason, they are tawny in colour … down to
the sixtieth parallel, they become ruddy; then to the forty-fifth they are
white; … to the thirtieth they become yellow, and when the yellow bile is
mingled with the black, they grow greenish, until they become swarthy
and deeply black under the tropics.'[103] To move between and among
Europe's diverse climates invited physiological changes, altering one's
complexion – both external and internal.

In fact, the dangers of moving south to hot climates were thought
to present unique threats to northerners like Englishmen since such
climates were at a great remove from England's own cool nature.[104]
Bodin and others had argued, following classical accounts, that north-

ern peoples moving southward suffered notorious deficiencies. Because produced by a generally damp climate, northerners, they argued, would 'dissolve in perspiration when they make their way to the south or wage wars in the warm regions,' much like cattle, which 'lose their fat, fail to give milk and suffer a general decline.'[105] The same observation resonated in Richard Eden's 1555 translation of Peter Martyr's *Decades* in its account of Hispaniola. In this context, Martyr had recorded the force of tropical heat on natural objects ranging from wheat to cattle. He observed a pattern of transformation among these species, noting how wheat transplanted to this tropical climate 'groweth into holowe reedes, with fewe eares.' Similarly, 'Neat or cattall, becoome of bygger stature and exceadynge fat, but theyr flesshe is more vnsauery, and theyr bones ... verye waterysshe.'[106]

Although presumably recording the effect of such heat on Spanish 'races' of wheat and cattle, the observation would resonate with even greater force to English ears. Indeed, accounts of such transformations litter the early colonial record, as Joyce Chaplin has documented, originating with and further informing European discourses of man, world, and nature. Himself a reader of these early encounters, an author like Montaigne would digest their collective wisdom in saying that 'the forme of our being depends of the aire, of the climate, and of the soile, wherein we are borne, and not onely the hew, the stature, the complexion and the countenance, but also the soules faculties ... In such manner that as fruits and beasts doe spring up diverse and different; So men are borne, either more or lesse warlike, martiall, just, temperate and docile ... good or bad, according as the inclination of the place beareth, where they are seated; and being removed from one soile to another (as plants are) they take a new complexion.'[107] Fears of such transformations are audible as well in the literature promoting settlement in southerly Virginia. Guarding against the worry that Virginia's climate would quite 'undo' them as Englishmen, the tracts again and again claim that Virginia is 'very agreeable to our natures,'[108] that 'The aire of the Countrey ... is very temperate and agreeth well with our bodies.'[109] These authors repeatedly insist that Virginia's climate approximates that of England, Crashaw even imaginatively linking the two land masses through the image of a bridge: 'onely this passage into Virginiea, being into the West Southwest, or thereabouts, is in that true temper so faire, so safe, so secure, so easie, as though God himselfe had built a bridge for men to passe from England to Virginiea.'[110] Conceding that Virginia is indeed lower in latitude than England, these authors nevertheless try to minimize the implications of these differences, analogizing Virginia's climate to the 'south of England,' and thereby casting the as yet unfamiliar terrain in familiar terms. To shore up their claims, they would point to the brief experience of English planters abroad, insisting that they 'doe not complaine of any alteration, caused by distemper of the Climate.'[111] But intimations to the contrary would eventually arrive home. In fact, notions of mutability, degeneration, and racial decline would centrally inform the colonial experience for decades, even centuries to come, attesting to the power of ancient theories of embodiment and eluding the efforts of stage and page to strategically deploy them.[112]

That is not to say that these media lacked a shaping influence on such theories of identity. Quite the contrary. Accounts surrounding settlement in Virginia, like contemporary plays on the London stage, participated in a shift in conceptions of racial identity for the early modern period. Part of the cultural work that together they performed was to replace 'lynes' with 'lands' as the authoring agent of a people, expanding earlier definitions of *race* defined as lineage to include emergent notions of *race* defined through reference to the shared habitation of a bounded geographical space – to nation. Conceptions of identity as passing from one generation to the next were slowly transmuted into spatially based identities. But even as they embraced a notion of 'English bodies' produced by an English geography, such ideas would in turn generate anxieties regarding the instability of land-based identity. For these emergent notions of national identity were expressed in and through discourses of the early modern body, a body felt to be porous, permeable, and prone to change. Just as this body could not defend itself against the ravages of time, neither could it evade the transformations brought about by spatial dislocation. Both sets of experience would be recorded under the term 'degeneration.' Like the bloodlines of noble British and Saxon fathers, which were believed to be subject to dilution through a range of physical agents, national bodies, because the 'products' of precise geographies and climes, could themselves be rewritten by foreign conditions. Denying the alterity at the heart of the English and British races would be the project of subsequent racialisms. But in *Cymbeline* and the Virginia tracts, *race* remains a question and a problem. Is *race* defined by 'noble Saxons blood,' or can blood itself be transformed for better (by the rigours of a Welsh or Virginia climate and lifestyle) or worse (by the heat and luxury of the south)?

# 4 Passion and Degeneracy in Tragicomic Island Plays

## 'Sea-changes' of Blood

In the account of his voyage to Barbados in 1631, Sir Henry Colt provides a detailed survey of the status of English planters abroad. In summarizing the quality of life available to them in the recently planted island – the foods the island can provide, the sustaining power of the soil, the qualities of the climate – Colt also observes how the island has affected the collective complexions, that is the tempers, of Englishmen. The already hot tempers of the island's young English planters, he notes at the start of his account, have grown dangerously fiery. Searching for explanations of this near-universal pattern, Colt turns first to humoralism and to the effects of consumption on the humours to account for the change. The distempered excesses of these men, he believes, derives in part from their overconsumption of hot drinks[1] – the rosemary water, angelica water, aniseed water, and aquavitae that he will recommend his son include among his own staples should he set out on a future voyage. Not moderating their 'younge & hott bloods' by drinking 'cold water,' these young planters have instead allowed themselves to become 'enflamed', to passion and quarrelsomeness, spending their days in riot and idleness and allowing the duties of running a plantation to fall by the wayside.[2] Making his observations just a few years after the plantation of Barbados by Englishmen, Colt was describing part of a phenomenon that would eventually congeal in the phrase 'Barbados distemper.'[3]

Although Colt writes with a distinctly paternalistic concern, urging English planters to correct this mishap, he also seems to suggest they are destined to fail. Indeed, after detailing his various criticisms of their behaviour, he comes forward with his own confession. He, too, it seems, underwent the same alienating transformation. Though he had always lived by habits 'wise & temperate,' while on the island he fell under the grip of these distempering behaviours, observing how his customary two dramms of 'hott water' rose to a frightening thirty dramms in a matter of days.[4] In numbering himself among those who have declined, Colt seems to suggest that few English planters – young or old, gentle or base – can escape untouched by these lands' profound transformations. As if abandoning all hope, he gestures toward a metaphysical explanation of this heatedness to supplement the natural explanation he had earlier provided, noting: 'Who is he [that] cann liue long in quiett in these parts? For all men are heer made subiect to ye power of this Infernall Spiritt. And fight they must, although it be wth ther owne frends.'[5]

In observing the island's centripetal tug toward discord, heat, and disquiet, Colt contributed to a growing cultural obsession among the English of the early seventeenth century about how transplantation could effect reversals on 'civil' planters. In observing transformations that affected the blood – changes that made the already hot blood of young Englishmen even hotter – Colt was addressing a problem that elsewhere was described through the language of degeneration. Just a few years before Colt's journey to Barbados, for instance, Samuel Purchas espressed concern about the possibility that those migrating to Virginia might suffer alteration, urging that adventures to the Americas not make 'Savages and wild degenerate men of Christians, but Christians of those Savage, wild, degenerate men.'[6] In this early period of English plantation, geographies as variable as Virginia, Bermuda, Ireland, and the West Indies were framed through this language of degeneration, which expressed a complex engagement with the challenge of maintaining an elite identity outside England.[7]

By the time the English began establishing settlements in the West Indies in the late 1620s and early 1630s, the question of how transplantation would affect the physical and social identity of Englishmen was already being explored on the Jacobean stage, dating from the period of Shakespeare's romances. Emerging as a dominant genre of the stage during the early period of Virginia's colonization, such romances placed a premium on plots dramatizing social and physical displacement. They staged families divided, heirs seized, patriarchs displaced, obsessively circling around challenges to elite blood posed by, among other things, geographical obstacles. Both *The Tempest* and John Fletcher and Philip Massinger's *The Sea Voyage*, written a decade later, speak to this growing interest in the effects of transplantation on English bodies and English culture.[8] If *The Tempest* obliquely engages the question of whether and how foreign lands might reinscribe the physical and social identity of transplanted Europeans, *The Sea Voyage* makes this problem its central concern. Both plays are set on islands distant from Europe, and both plays likewise avoid precisely identifying the geography of their setting. Scholars have locked in debate over the location of the isle in Shakespeare's play. Some have tended to read the play as broadly allusive to events surrounding the early colonization of Virginia, producing readings that emphasize an Atlantic context and the play's implication in an emergent imperial discourse.[9] Others note that the origin of the Italian fleet's journey in Tunis insists on the island's Mediterranean context and, more specifically, a location somewhere in the Sicilian archipelago.[10] Still others suggest that the island is all of these locations and more, identifying Ireland as yet another site allusively engaged by the play.[11] In a similar way, Fletcher and Massinger avoid specifiying the precise location of the islands featured in their later play. We know little save that the colonists have fled from a plantation in 'the happy islands' (*Sea* 5.2.88) before arriving to the 'unknown world' (5.4.31) of the twin islands they now inhabit.[12] Working from these rather general references, a critic like Gordon McMullan posits that the islands are located near the coast of Guiana.[13] But an exact location is never named. As with Shakespeare's play, what we have is an 'island play,' one that rejects specificity of place and even conjures multiple locations.[14]

This obfuscation of geography is, for my purposes, of the essence. I suggest that to varying degrees these plays represent and seek to resolve the problematic of surviving not in any one specific place but rather in a place far from 'home.' The geographies they describe are linked in being alien to the native lands of the plays' respective protagonists. As Jerry Brotton has argued, we know for certain only that the islands represented are 'distant, terrifying and bewildering places.'[15] Together the plays constitute a sustained meditation on how alien soils affect elite Europeans, exploring the effects transplantation might have on elite blood. Through the French, Italian, and Portuguese figures depicted in these plays, the English playwrights project onto an earlier round of European colonizers challenges that the English were newly facing at the start of the seventeenth century in moving to plant abroad.

Yet despite their similarities, *The Tempest* and *The Sea Voyage* represent two rather divergent figurative resolutions of the problems posed by plantation. *The Tempest*, produced in the context of Virginia's earliest settlement, evokes, even as it sidesteps, the question of how living and reproducing beyond English borders might affect identity. The play gives us reason to believe that inhabiting a different climate, soil, and air could well be a veritable Pandora's box for identity. It is hardly inconsequential that Prospero's magic is founded on his control of the natural elements, granting him the power to produce or withhold the alterity of the island's geography. And it is the qualities of the isle's climate that first lock the newcomers in dispute (*Temp* 2.1.35–60).[16] If the optimism of Adrian and Gonzalo leads them to emphasize the landscape as temperate, lush, and capable of sustaining life, Antonio and Sebastian deflate this account with their own narrative of the isle as a barren and infecting landscape. For them the air is 'rotten' (2.1.48) and fenny and the land itself burned to a 'tawny' (2.1.55) colour. That this discussion implicitly mediates the problem of reproducing far from home, in a place alternately described as 'inaccessible' and even 'Uninhabitable' (2.1.38), is expressed in the sudden turn of this conversation to the topic of marriage, heirs, and both Claribel and Dido. As figures who embody the disruption of patriarchy, these famous queens serve to mark the crisis of lineage occasioned through prolonged contact with lands beyond 'our Europe' (2.1.124). In the image that brings this classical digression to a close, the play's humorists conjure an alternate system of property transmission – one where distant isles can be transported, like any old apple, back 'home in [one's] pocket' (2.1.89–90). In the image of island 'kernels' generating 'more islands' (2.1.91–2) after being sown in the sea, we witness the play's wistful rewriting of migration and transplantation. In this reverie islands travel home, securing lineage and even empire, and thereby absorb the costs of reproduction from a nobility wary of displacement.

If I am right to infer that geographical alterity is this play's Pandora's box, it is a box closely guarded. Indeed, in this play the elements are obedient, they submit to Prospero's power. Although Prospero raises a natural storm and, by implication, the 'sea-change' (1.2.404) of a social calamity in the mariners' revolt against rank and royalty, he also makes it his task to quell both. He actively governs these storms, righting the wrongs he had allowed at home in his attempt to newly embody the role of duke. European social systems and their concomitant identities are produced on the island precisely as they should have been at home, and alterity – of clime and identity – is held at bay. The question of how to reproduce home abroad is not a problem this play seeks to resolve.

When *The Tempest* first appeared in print in the 1623 Folio – itself a collaborative production of Shakespeare's fellow King's Men, notably Condell and Heminge, but also, perhaps, Fletcher – two playwrights for the

King's Men took it upon themselves to rewrite the play. In doing so, they fundamentally altered it, fixating on the geographical alterity that the earlier play had recoiled from in framing Europe as 'home,' as the locus of desire for the play's Italian characters as well as their ultimate destination. Fletcher and Massinger's play has a different trajectory. Using material clearly indebted to Shakespeare's play, they ask and attempt to imagine how Europeans might transport 'home' to unfamiliar lands, both barren and idyllic, as embodied by the representation of the two different soils and climates of the play's sister islands. At a time when the Virginia Council began sending women and children in significant numbers to Virginia, Fletcher and Massinger were using tragicomedy to explore how women's presence in the colonies might implicate the colonial project. If *The Tempest* ultimately reads Italy as home – as the space where the play's romantic resolutions will bear their fruit – *The Sea Voyage* labours to make the *colony* a viable site of romance. Just as Shakespeare's imaginative engagement with colonial matters seems a response to the interest of his patrons Southampton and Pembroke in the Virginia Council, so Fletcher had a spur in his close ties to Henry Hastings, fifth Earl of Huntingdon, who invested in the Virginia project in the early 1620s. A patron to a host of poets and dramatists – Donne, Drayton, Marston, and Massinger among them – Huntingdon had joined the Virginia Council in 1620 and was connected still further to western enterprises in that his brother accompanied Sir Walter Raleigh in his second attempt on Guiana in 1617.[17] Taking up the conceptual problems posed by the colonialist project and the questions that forging a sustainable settlement newly raised, Fletcher and Massinger fix our attention on what it means not merely to sojourn for a time in a distant place, as Shakespeare had done in having Prospero 'reside' on a distant island, but what it might mean to take root in an alien soil. As such, the 'sea-changes' artificially circumscribed in Shakespeare's earlier play become the very condition of this later play. That is, *The Sea Voyage* insists that the extreme threat to identity posed by degeneracy assumes centre stage.

If we take a few steps back and ask precisely what was described through this language of degeneracy, we would be well served by recalling the colonial context of Ireland. Here *degeneration* described a set of changes that were perceived to be closely connected to qualities of blood, although this association has often been overlooked. Through this word New English planters like Spenser, Sir John Davies, and Fynes Moryson puzzled over the Circean transformations that they observed among an earlier round of English colonists in Ireland, those they called the Old English. To New English eyes, reproducing abroad had forced these Old English colonists into a long and gradual process of decline. Fynes Moryson, secretary to Lord Mountjoy in the early 1600s, emphasized the extent to which the decline was related to processes of generation and, by implication, to blood when he observed that 'as horses, cows, and sheep transported out of England into Ireland do each race and breeding decline worse and worse, till in few years they nothing differ from the races and breeds of the Irish horses and cattle, so the posterities of the English planted in Ireland do each descent grow more and more Irish, in nature, manners and customs.'[18] In noticing a decline to 'races and breeds,' Moryson was articulating a shift at the level of blood, that is, one that was capable of producing a break between parent and offspring. By choosing to live and, more importantly, *reproduce* beyond the pale of England's borders, it would seem, English planters implicitly invited genealogical disruption, a fear that I explore in Chapter 2 in considering the extreme measures that some New English settlers took to avoid what they considered a debasing mixture with Irish women.

Degeneration – whether explicitly engaged as in Moryson's words or implicitly described as in Sir Henry Colt's – described more than just a transformation at the level of culture, more than just a shift in habits of dress, speech, and manner, as I have suggested in earlier chapters on Ireland. If we persist in reading degeneration as a cultural phenomenon, we remain wedded to nineteenth-century notions of the body and to a nineteenth-century discourse of 'going native.' Moryson's words tell us something different; they resist these characterizations, just as they derive from an early modern model of embodiment that openly expressed the articulation of nature to culture. That is, changes to culture were perceived to produce and express material shifts to nature. The phenomenon that Moryson describes, and that countless proximate authors described as well, should not therefore be understood to limit itself to 'manners' and 'customs.' Rather, for the early modern period, such cultural indicators have a dynamic relationship to 'nature,' to conceptions of the body, such that they express and in some cases help to produce physical states. Moryson makes these connections overt in placing these two terms beside the proximate term 'nature.' In this instance, moreover, he seems to define nature as the causal agent, a change in nature here producing a shift at the level of culture. In the homology he uses whereby English people are to Irish manners and customs as English horses are to Irish breeds, he defines the change these planters have undergone as one originating in changes to nature, to the physical body.

More specifically, I suggest he was drawing on a widespread belief that the physical body was shaped by a surrounding world and that it would absorb changes from altered environments.[19]

Such ideas derived from early modern tendencies to understand the body through the lens of humoralism. Never sealed off from its surroundings, the humoral body was seen as continuous with the world, as positing a radically porous set of boundaries dividing it from that world. Gail Kern Paster has reminded us of these specific qualities in describing the humoral body as 'being open and fungible in its internal workings' as well as 'porous and thus able to be influenced by the immediate environment.' John Sutton builds on these observations in suggesting of this body that 'urgent steps could be taken to close off its vents and windows, barring the orifices by which external dangers could intrude. But this seasonal body was always vulnerable to climatic effects, and permeated by the environment right through to its cognitive capacities.'[20] In coining the term 'geohumoralism,' moreover, Mary Floyd-Wilson has demonstrated that in this early modern period different geographies were perceived to produce widespread physical correspondences among populations, such that people inhabiting cold climates were believed to demonstrate an excess of phlegm or blood, while those in hot climates were thought to have a preponderance of choler or black bile. She goes on to demonstrate how these associations amount to an early, if estranging, kind of ethnic discourse, since the dominance of any given humour bespeaks a whole range of intellectual and emotional traits in a population.[21]

To the extent that humoralism posited a porous boundary between body and environment, as these critics contend, I suggest it elicits different readings of degeneration from those that emerge at the end of the nineteenth century where the body is understood as a genetic entity. We may laugh when Colt describes how his drinking habits abroad catch him off guard, finding his worries quaint and pedestrian. But I will argue that to do so is to miss the ontological charge of such concerns. For in worrying changes to his humoral disposition through this language of temperance and distemperance, Colt attempted to describe and to modulate physical shifts structuring social identity. That he is particularly attuned to changes of blood – a fluid that was both a humour and the basis for an entire social system – warrants particular attention. In describing blood heated to an extreme – whether by climate, diet, passion, or appetite – writers like Colt sorted through the profound adjustments to identity that colonization occasioned. By grappling with perceived changes to blood's temperature, they contemplated the remaking of a substance that was intimately connected both to their place within a social hierarchy (i.e., as elite, middling, or base men) and their sense of themselves as English.

## Temperate Races

That divisions of rank were intimately connected to the qualities of one's blood functioned as something of a commonplace for the early modern period. To be elite, to be of a race, as I have argued in the introduction, was a function of blood, and being 'of the blood' translated into enjoying both a physical and a metaphysical separation from one's social inferiors. Noble blood was widely thought to embody a tempered ideal, as compared with the intemperate condition of base blood, which was closely associated with 'villainous' behaviour.[22] Sir Thomas Elyot would articulate what it might mean to have noble blood through the lens of humoralism. In *The Governor*, a text produced in and through the medical knowledge that more explicitly informs Elyot's more popular *Castel of Helth*, the basis for nobility emerges as a kind of physiology: 'a gentle wit is ... sone fatigued ... like as a little fire is soon quenched with a great heap of small sticks.'[23] If on a cultural plane noble blood was equated with great courage, Elyot translated what were once thought to be solely spiritual virtues into humoral physiology, reading nobility as the embodiment of subtle heat. His educational regime, moreover, was offered up to readers as a guide to achieving and sustaining this temperate condition, thus suggesting by implication that the 'subtlety' of elite blood had to be actively supported.

As Englishmen ventured to plant abroad in the early part of the seventeenth century, this language of temperance, I have suggested, took on new force, becoming a defining trope of colonialist literature.[24] We have seen that Spenser, in writing his own guide for gentlemen while serving as a planter in Ireland, placed temperance second only to holiness as an indispensable virtue, and that he made use of temperance to question the equation between social status and inherited bloodline. Because temperance was, by definition, a virtue that required discipline and self-restraint, it could be used to contest the privileges awarded to some by virtue of birth and ancestry, regardless of whether their behaviour continued to express such nobility of origin. If Spenser placed the wedge of temperance between race and blood, this embodied discourse continued to resonate well beyond the context of Ireland and Spenser's

writing, mediating at large the cultural shifts occasioned by colonization that catalysed the decline of this system of race. By holding out
the promise of landholdings to those not likely to inherit them at home
– that is, to younger sons of the gentry and men of non-gentle blood –
colonization undermined the sign system upon which accounts of blood
were built. Such associations were reified by biblical exegesis, and were
a structuring principle of early modern England. The story of Cain, for
instance, functioned as an originary account of servitude, suggesting that
those dispossessed of lands and estates had earned their status through
deeds 'unnoble' and '[dishonourable].'[25] By contrast, virtuous sons like
Shem and Japheth were awarded a 'free estate' and a 'famous stocke' to
carry them through time, their virtue imagined as descending uninterrupted through generations of offspring produced by the quasi-immaterial repository of their blood. The metaphysical qualities of blood came
therefore to be reified in the physical world. Those of the blood were
often also of the land, lords who possessed great estates. By distributing
land less restrictively, colonization impeded these associations, placing a
wedge between land and noble blood. That is, land could no longer be
trusted as a stable sign of elite blood.

Colonization problematized blood in other ways as well. In fact, if the
blood of elite Englishmen was reified in land, it was not reified in just
*any* piece of land. Rather, it gathered its particular attributes from the
unique topography and climate of England, a geography granted considerable force by the period in constituting identity. As Floyd-Wilson
has argued, England's climate – its cold and relatively damp qualities –
were thought to produce a shared disposition among all her people, with
smaller variations of dispositions suggestive of differences of rank, gender, and individual quirks. England's climate was the source of physiolo-
gies thought to express themselves through acts forthright and martial,
if not politic and circumspect like their counterparts in more southerly
climes.[26] Hence, to contemplate transplantation to a hot climate such as
characterized Barbados was to contemplate a wholesale reorientation of
identity. In the language of temperance and distemperance so prominent in texts of a colonialist nature, writers of the period express their
imbrication in the moment's reorganization of blood's meanings. I read
the repetition of these terms as indicative of this crisis, as an attempt
to secure the elite English blood of planters from its degeneration into
alien blood – blood, that is, that could no longer demonstrate its distinction from base blood or, perhaps, from the choleric tinge of Spanish
blood. Through the language of temperance, not only did they justify

newly won landed possessions, but they sought to identify themselves as properly English, as anything but alien. This language, however, required nothing less than constant vigilance, because blood could be profoundly altered, as Colt's account suggests, in no less than a 'few dayes.'[27]

## Reproducing Abroad

If the self-identity of blood could be profoundly altered in so short a time as days, it is no wonder that colonists worried with particular force about the extent of alteration that might occur generationally to trans-planted groups. Indeed, Moryson's words sound the alarm that planta-tions posed to blood across the generations, effectively urging English planters, following Spenser, to scrutinize carefully the conditions of their children's upbringing. Colt, too, seems to contemplate the risks of reproducing abroad, if only obliquely – for it is the *young* English plant-ers about whom he expresses particular concern, just as it his youthful son who constitutes his immediate audience. How to guide this young generation in securing tempered blood – which he understands as the defining condition of their elite English identities – seems to motivate his writing. He advises, 'you are all younge men, & of good desert, if you would but bridle ye excesse of drinkinge, together wth ye quarrel-some conditions of your fiery spiritts.'[28] By prefacing his account with a letter to his son outlining a detailed physical regiment should he con-sider moving abroad, Colt guards against the debasements to blood that he observed in and through the distempering excesses of the island's young English planters. In order to ensure that his son's 'stomack' is 'kept warme' – a hot physiology believed to be both a native condition of all Englishmen[29] and one necessary for proper digestion – he advises his son not only to wear a 'wollen stomacher' and to consume foods spiced with hot pepper but suggests as well that he visit 'Mr Wicks in black fry-ers beyond ye playhouse' who will furnish him with 'his best hott waters at 7s ye gallon.' Such waters, he makes clear, were 'our principall proui-sion & dyett,' and he urges his son to use them to aid digestion, 'befoor meals & sometimes after.'[30] But the same waters appear in his narrative as, potentially, 'oyle' in the flame of the planters' 'hott bloods.' Paradoxi-cally, the substance capable of supporting an English temperament was precisely that which might also bring it to 'flame.' Constant vigilance was one's only weapon. Only through careful attention to diet and purgation could these mishaps be avoided. It is suggestive that Colt recognizes only one person on the island as embodying this delicate temperate state –

the island's young governor at the time, Henry Hawley. For Colt, the young governor's ability to temper his own passions was right and fit, the proper expression of his power to adjudicate the quarrels among the island's planters.[31]

If Colt is intent that his son guard against the potential debasement of the family's blood abroad, he is also hopeful that such blood may, God willing, even be ennobled abroad. Imagining himself lord over this fertile land, he remarks, 'would it weer my owne & thus seated in any part of Europe. I will not say whatt I could be in short time, if ye princes of Europe by force or couetousnesse would not take it from me.'[32] Though not 'seated in any part of Europe' and therefore an implicit threat to English blood, Barbados also held the promise of rapid upwardly mobility. Not only does Colt imagine himself as on a par with Europe's monarchs, but he also imagines his son dining, like he had, on a 'pye' so rare that 'ther fathers & predecessors yt liued & dyed in England weer neuer fed dayly wth ... Yett weer they farr better men'[33] than them both. If, then, he prays that his son does not degenerate abroad, he also imagines the many ways that his bloodline might be ennobled by virtue of settling abroad.

Motivated by what appears to be a similar set of concerns – particularly the problem of establishing a stable plantation at such a remove from England – the Virginia Council experimented with structural changes to its own patterns of settlement in the early 1620s. In its *Declaration of the State of the Colony and Affaires in Virginia*, the Council outlined broad shifts in policy to govern the plantation, high among them the decision to send a larger contingent of women to accompany the numbers of men flocking to the colony. Although some women had arrived earlier to the Virginia colony, in general women were the exception to a dominantly male planter class in the early years of settlement.[34] But this pattern was to shift in the years before and up through the 1620s. In enumerating the names and investments of those involved in the plantation effort, for instance, the *Declaration* identifies 90 women among a 1619 shipment of 650 people to the colony, suggesting a new emphasis on expanding the female population in Virginia. The Council announced further that it planned to send an additional hundred 'yong Maides' to 'make wiues' for another shipment of eight hundred planters to be sent on behalf of the Council.[35]

Although this second shipment of women never occurred as expected in 1620, the commitment of the Council to sending women is visible in how they restructured the Company following a royal proclamation of 8

March 1621, which declared that the use of lotteries or public funds to support the Company would no longer be permissible. In response, the Council looked to investors to undertake ventures in return for a share of any profits, and one of the first of four 'magazines' that they settled on was to provide one hundred women as wives for the colonists.[36] What is remarkable about the documents that record in detail the gathering of funds, women, and articles to be sent to the colony is the new emphasis placed on the character of these women. In the opening paragraph of the document that contains these details, the Council summarizes its motives, in part, by emphasizing that they decided to send women not only to appease the 'dejected' state of the planters, but also to allow the planters to construe their endeavours abroad not as a 'short sojour-ninge' but as a 'place of habitation.' Women, they concluded, would be the key to 'tye and roote the Planters myndes to Virginia.'[37] They did not accept just any women. Candidates came with written recommendations from respectable members of parishes, trades, or the gentry. Of the fifty-seven women who were selected, the documents record the social rank of thirty-seven. 'No fewer than eight had links to the gentry,' including the daughter of Sir Gervase Markham.[38] Many more were associated with families involved in trade, suggesting a desire to stabilize the colony not only by encouraging the male planters to reproduce there but by mak-ing women of the best rank and character available to them as potential spouses.

The fact that women were coming to play a more central role in the colony in the 1620s is suggested as well by the presence of their names among those whom the Council identifies as having contributed to the plantation venture. The list that comprises the bulk of this *Declaration* records, for instance, Mary Robinson's donation of two hundred pounds toward the founding of a Church in Virginia, as well as a fifty-pound contribution made by Mary, Countesse of Shrewsbury, and a twenty-five-pound investment of Mistris Kath. West, now Lady Conway. Urging that 'the Colony beginneth now to have the face and fashion of an orderly State, and such as is likely to grow and prosper,' and affirming that efforts are now under way 'to perpetuate the Plantation,' the Council suggests that women will be the key to accomplishing such goals.[39]

If women's reproductive role was deemed indispensable to the colony's longevity, however, that was not to say that the necessity of reproducing abroad did not occasion some uneasiness. In fact, worries are implicitly sounded in the very pages of the *Declaration*, immediately after women's contributions to the effort are outlined by the Council. By insisting that the people of this plantation are 'diuided in soyle oneley' from 'this their natiue Countrey' and will 'continue always as one and the same people with vs,' the Council was already insisting on the hope of reproducing a community of Englishmen abroad. Reading between the lines, we detect a Council anticipating potential differences and disruptions between an imagined 'us' and them. For, as Spenser and others had argued just twenty years earlier, being divided by 'soyle oneley' had often resulted in the engendering of an alien people, the very antithesis of 'us.' The Virginia Council in this document and elsewhere makes clear its determination to guard against a reading that reproduction abroad might disrupt English consanguinity.[40] But these matters would take centre-stage at the Blackfriar's theatre, in a play produced collaboratively by Fletcher and Massinger that speaks to plantations comprising men, women, and children. In this context the problems and potential solutions of such settlements would be openly staged.

That this play responds to the conditions of this moment, when the survival of plantations was necessitating that planters embrace the prospect of reproducing abroad, cannot be overemphasized. *The Tempest*, by contrast, raises questions of reproduction abroad but deflects any sustained attention to the problem of degeneration they unleash. In fact, in localizing such threats to reproduction in the figure of Caliban – who, we are told, earned his enslavement through his attempted rape of Miranda (*Temp* 1.2.350–1) – Shakespeare's play engages contamination of elite blood in its most literal form – by rape – a threat conceivable in a range of contexts, both near and far. And significantly, this threat is one that Prospero contains. The play prefers instead to narrate reproduction as an event tied to home. Miranda, for instance, is nearly three years old when she travels to this island with her father, and the start of yet another generation is deferred at the play's close to a point following Miranda and Ferdinand's return home. In fact, though Prospero has celebrated their union in the play's masque, consummation has been guarded against in overdetermined ways; Prospero warns Ferdinand no less than three times to restrain his desire, asserting

> Look thou be true. Do not give dalliance
> Too much the rein. The strongest oaths are straw
> To th' fire i'th' blood. Be more abstemious. (4.1.51–3)

In the masque's sudden disruption, these prohibitions are formally embodied, together serving to defer the closure of romance – the reproduction of noble lineage – to the arrival home. The play warns elsewhere of the danger of producing heirs in distant geographies in the context of a discussion of Claribel, Alonso's newly displaced daughter and, insofar as Ferdinand is believed to be dead by the newly arriving Neapolitans, his displaced heir as well. If there is a chance that she will produce an heir in Algeria – a possibility that 'new-born chins' will become 'rough and razorable' (2.1.245–6) – the play raises the possibility only to warn against it. Heirs born 'Ten leagues beyond man's life' (2.1.243), Antonio maintains, lose their connection to home by the sheer magnitude of space. In this play, reproducing abroad is a vexed and dangerous activity, and a problem that remains deferred and unresolved at the play's close.

By contrast, Fletcher and Massinger, in 'rewriting' Shakespeare's play, take a hard look at the risks and rewards of reproducing abroad. Like Colt, their play acknowledges at every turn the vulnerability of blood abroad – the perception that noble blood might suffer debasement and that blood-ties might be disjointed – if blood is not carefully tempered. Those who are distempered – and it is significant that the play's gallants are those who fit this description – are associated with genealogical erasure, with failures of reproduction. By contrast, those capable of continence and self-restraint – traits that the play assigns to the captain of a group of French pirates – accrue to themselves the language of gentle blood. In looking to temperance as a safeguard against degeneration, the play produces a new narrative of blood. Rooted not in title, land, or wealth, blood is measured by temperance, which serves as its own sign of nobility, its own estate.

## Tempering Passion

Both Shakespeare's play and that by Fletcher and Massinger follow Colt's narrative in foregrounding questions of appetite and distemperance, all structuring their narratives in uncannily similar ways around banquets and 'hott' drinks and the excesses of passion surrounding them. In Shakespeare's play, however, differences of blood are carefully monitored, and Prospero's control of the climate, the external 'tempest,' is a figure for his control over the appetites of all the aristocrats on the island. He explicitly makes these connections when he asks Ariel, following the successful production of the storm and shipwreck, 'Who was so firm, so constant, that this coil / Would not infect his reason?' (1.2.208–9). Here he suggests that producing such 'infection,' a passionate imbalance, was a central part of his intent in calling forth the storm. If Prospero uses his art to provoke a crisis of passion among the newly arriving Italian nobility – by toying with Sebastian's envy of the throne, Alonso's near-madness, and the group's collective hunger as they grasp at an illusory banquet – it is a temporary and controlled form of revenge that serves to remind the men of their nobility of blood and to reify its difference from base blood. By stoking the 'fumes' of their base passions (5.1.67), he exacts revenge but also stages a purgation of the 'foul and muddy' (5.1.82) qualities of the blood that they, in plotting his usurpation, had already allowed to invade 'the reasonable shores' (5.1.81) of their 'properly' noble minds. The intent would seem to be to spur them to moderate their blood, to purge it of the passions that signal its decline. Insofar as Alonso expresses his wish for 'pardon' (5.1.121), while Antonio appears to remain hardened and unpurged, the play naturalizes his status as ruler. In moderating his passion, Alonso reclaims his powers as king, rule of self here imagined as the precondition to rule of others.

Indeed, we have good reason to follow the play's cues in reading Prospero's failing at home as a version of the passionate shipwreck that Alonso has submitted to while on the island. In recalling these originary events, he tells Miranda that 'The government I cast upon my brother' (1.2.75), while he himself became 'rapt in secret studies' (1.2.77). To the extent that his language signals someone in the grip of immoderate passions – the act of 'casting' rule away suggesting impetuosity and the state of being 'rapt' suggesting impassioned prostration – it describes a ruler who has violated the principle of noble blood and the temperate rule it ideally embodied. That Prospero has spent his years in exile attempting to correct the imbalances of such eruptions we learn from Miranda, who tells Ferdinand repeatedly that

My father's of a better nature, sir,
Than he appears by speech. This is unwonted
Which now came from him. (1.2.500–2)

Later she will note how uncommon passionate behaviour has been for him when she observes, 'Never till this day / Saw I him touched with anger so distempered' (4.1.144–5). But her words also suggest that maintaining a temperate condition – the act of stilling his 'beating mind' (4.1.163) – is an ongoing struggle for him. Through countless acts of self-government, Prospero displays his blood in its properly elite form and establishes his claim to rule. As such, he comes to embody the freedom from passionate infection that he evokes among the islands' newcomers.

In allowing themselves to become subjected to such 'madness' (5.1.118), these newcomers are made to embody their status as 'subjects,' as necessarily 'thrown under' the care of a ruler like Prospero.[41]

In fact, Prospero demonstrates this principle of rule in carefully moderating the passions of the younger members of the nobility, including both Miranda and Ferdinand. From his daughter, he exacts temperate behaviour when he receives her pity for the shipwreck victims with the rejoinder,

> Be collected,
> No more amazement. Tell your piteous heart
> There's no harm done. (1.2.13–15)

Similarly, he seeks to temper the grief Ferdinand feels in contemplating his father's likely death by instructing Ariel to orchestrate a 'sweet air' that would '[Allay]' the 'fury' and 'passion' that has erupted in the young prince (1.2.396–7). If he tempers these his subjects, he also seeks to undercut the authority of his rival, Sycorax, by describing her as ever in the grip of a 'most unmitigable rage' (1.2.278). By emphasizing her subjection to passion, he defines her as unfit for rule.

If Prospero emphasizes his power to temper the passions of the nobility, he leaves the ship's servants – Stephano and Trinculo – to self-destruct by strategically placing 'celestial liquor' (2.2.109) into their hands. By consuming what Colt calls 'hott drinks,' they become enslaved to passion and quarrelsomeness, parodying their quest for upward mobility as emblematized by their desire to lord it over Caliban. Stephano's relationship to Caliban mocks the relationship of king to subject, not least in that Stephano moves to temper Caliban's supposed 'fit' and 'ague' (2.2.72, 87) as I have argued Prospero does for the noblemen. Stephano assumes this stance of paternal care when he concludes, 'I will give him some relief' (2.2.64), while taking steps to do so by dispensing wine. Clearly, the wine does for these men what Colt worried it would do to elite planters – drive them to passionate excess and distemperance. For Prospero, this is exactly as it should be for Stephano and his cohorts, their ill-governed passions being the sign he seeks to evoke of their base blood. He polices the divide separating gentle from base more overtly through his insistence that the courtiers' garments – the body's most visible document of rank – are refreshed and sustained under Ariel's diligent care, a point repeated in the opening act, first, when Ariel indicates she has followed Prospero's orders precisely, and once again when Gonzalo wonders at their clothes' newly starched freshness (1.2.218–19; 2.1.62–5). Bolstering differences of blood rather than meditating on their undoing is Prospero's central concern.

Fletcher and Massinger's *Sea Voyage* is, then, less an iteration of *The Tempest*, as Restoration critics lamented, than a catalysation of the tensions rippling beneath the earlier play's surface.[42] It systematically undoes all the safeguards to identity to which Prospero had carefully attended. In the first scene, the one that establishes clear connections to its Shakespearean antecedent, a ship full of French pirates and planters tries to fend off the attacks of a tempest, culminating in the captain's demands that the vessel be purged of all baggage. An early indicator of the play's interest in somatic matters, the scene develops correspondences between the surrounding storm and the men's rising passions. The ship itself assumes the quality of distemperance when the men observe of the glutted vessel that 'She reels like a Drunkard' (*Sea Voyage* 1.1.13), signalling the play's interest in gentle bodies grown distempered. In fact, the image of the impassioned body as ship on a stormy sea had become such a commonplace that in the year prior to the play's performance the English translation of *A Table of Human Passions* would be framed in precisely such terms: 'For as that tempest is more dangerous that suffers not a ship to repaire to her haven ... So most difficult are the minds stormes, that let a man to containe himselfe; nor suffer him to quiet and settle his disturbed reason.'[43] Under the force of the captain's orders, the ship's gallants are made to toss overboard all signs of their wealth and rising status; doublets, swords, crowns, double ruffs, as well as meats and cakes all drop to the bottomless depths. If Prospero was eager to retain these outward signs of rank, this play is just as eager to dispense with them, forcing a confrontation with unaccommodated man, with little but, in Tibalt's words, 'thy skin whole' (1.3.34). By doing so, this play puts gentle blood to the test, moving to define temperance as against land and wealth as the real essence of gentle blood.

When the play opens degeneration, rather than temperance, is writ large. And heated tempers are to blame. We learn, for instance, that the events that immediately precede the play's actions involved the seizure of a Portuguese plantation by a set of French planters. Based both on André Thévet's account of a Portuguese crew shipwrecked off the coast of Brazil and on Jean Ribault's French settlement in Florida in 1562, these events resulted not in peace and plenty for the French planters but faction and discord, the same passions of heat that Colt had observed in Barbados a few years after this play's performance.[44] Leading to the demise of this colony, those same passions threaten to erupt when members of that earlier colony – led by the Frenchman Albert – set out to reconcile with the other French faction but instead find themselves on a desert island with no resources. Here unconstrained appetites threaten to produce self-destruction for the group. Not only are they at each other's throats verbally, but the one female planter, Aminta, finds herself literally 'put to the knife' before she is rescued. If Shakespeare's *Tempest* imagines a similar scene of crisis in Sebastian and Antonio's temptation to kill the sleeping Alonso, *The Sea Voyage* has no magical medium of patriarchal law and order, such as Ariel embodies, to effect stability. The distempered Frenchmen are left to their own devices, or to those of the ship's captain, whose modulation of his own desires prefigures his ability to temper theirs.

In fact, *The Sea Voyage* poses the possibility of undoing noble blood and of genealogical failure in the context of plantation as the tragic possibility that the tragicomedy has to resolve. As the play opens and the French planters seek shelter during the storm on the deserted island, we hear a Portuguese man and his nephew, Sebastian and Nicusa, members of the original Portuguese colony shipwrecked years earlier on this island, reflecting on how they have found themselves removed from history. They long for a 'little memory of what we were' (1.2.32), and reminisce about 'our kindreds,' 'our families,' and 'our fortunes' (1.2.35–6). The island has removed them from history, from genealogy, from the monuments of blood. The Frenchmen who arrive echo the question earlier put by Stephano and Trinculo to Caliban (*Temp* 2.2.23–6, 55–7, 62–3), wondering if the Portuguese 'islanders' are monsters or men. The French compare the islanders to shadows, sea-calves, and horses, and mock the possibility that they might once have been 'a couple of courtiers' (*Sea Voyage* 1.3.102). If possessors of gentle blood, as they assure the Frenchmen, that status cannot be read from external signs of rank, since they lack the grooming, the wardrobe, and the well-fed bodies that would have made their status obvious at home. Later in the play, another group of Frenchmen will come into contact with these men and will repeat these questions, wondering if their 'noble breedings' are legitimate or just something they 'pretend to' (4.1.30). Gentleness, the play here suggests, must inhere in the blood, the body's tempered complexion must serve in and of itself as a 'noble monument' (3.1.130).

That the French are in no way immune from a similar social failing is immediately brought to their attention by the Portuguese, who warn them to guard their appetites lest they suffer a similar fate. A group ravenous for gold and food, only the French leader Albert shows any signs of one who can rise above appetite. Where his French shipmates dream of surfeiting on medical by-products amid their hunger, Albert undergoes a purgation, his wounds are stitched, and his body is thus newly brought to curb. It is noteworthy that Aminta describes Albert's body as an altar of 'staid temperance' (2.1.23). And yet we learn that this tempered posture is a new one for him. In recounting the events prior to the play, we hear that he had been led by a raging 'heat' to seize as booty the woman, Aminta, who subsequently will help heal him. In travelling with him, she has transformed him from a youth in the 'heat of blood,' to a man of self-control who is capable of prescribing 'Laws to itself' (2.1.28–9).

In fact, the power of Aminta's cold kisses to 'allay [Albert's] fever' (4.3.234) explicitly suggests that the presence of a noblewoman in the colonies actually could prevent degeneration. The unruly members of the French crew early seek to identify Aminta's presence on the ship as the real source of their troubles, blaming her for obstructing their pursuit of 'happy places and most fertile islands' (3.3.83) in turning 'the captain's mind' (3.3.85) to reconciling with her brother, Raymond. They also characterize her as a leaky vessel, turning her into a metonym for the ship and charging her with incontinence for reacting passionately to the storm's force: 'Peace, woman! / We ha' storms enough already – no more howling' (1.1.49–50). But her effect on Albert certainly neutralizes these charges. In fact, Albert attributes to her a process of physical regeneration. Though suffering physical hardship like the others stranded on this stark and barren island, he perceives his love for Aminta as a restorative:

I feel
New vigour in me, and a spirit that dares
More than a man. (2.1.74–6)

Feeding on her love – 'when I kiss these rubies, methinks / I'm at a banquet, a refreshing banquet' (2.1.38–9) – he gathers the strength to swim across the channel separating the two islands. He also steels himself against his hunger on her behalf. Though offered food upon his arrival to the fertile island (2.2.245–6), he honours his vow to Aminta that he will not 'eat nor sleep' (2.1.86) till he returns. In the play's logic, gentle blood is a moral condition that is tightly bound to physical principles. Given the temptations to heat, passion, and distemper that the play associates with travel to hot lands, such blood is hardly something that can be presumed. Rather, it requires constant vigilance, countless efforts at restraint.

That Aminta's power involves not just 'tempering' but 'ennobling' Albert's blood is demonstrated by the way that his control of his body, and more specifically his ability to temper the heat associated with passion and desire, accrues the 'metaphysical' force of a properly aristocratic ethos. Albert, that is, comes to embody the principle of noble hospitality. After discovering the abundance of the nearby island inhabited by women, for instance, Albert returns to his starving Frenchmen and distributes his newly found riches like a patron figured in a country-house poem.[45] Tending first to his lady – 'some meat and sovereign drink to ease you' (3.3.163) – he turns immediately to satisfying the needs of the others: 'Ye shall have meat, all of you' (3.3.167). Even after he learns of the treacherous nature of their appetite, specifically their flirtation with cannibalism, he continues to distribute food. Because this act of distributing food is repeated in this scene, we have to assume this gesture that marks him as the noble patron is central. We observe him and Aminta feeding them – 'There, wretches, there' – and see his bountifulness extend still further – 'There's more bread' – and further still when he tells them, 'There is drink too' (3.3.175, 177, 179). If Tibalt seeks to deny these men food on the principle that they are distemperate and deserve enforced restraint – 'touch nothing but what's flung t'ye as if you / Were dogs' (3.3.173–4) – Albert reverses this pattern. In tending to their appetites, as he has tended to his own, he displays his nobility. It is clear that his blood has been restored to its non-degenerate form. His temperance marks him as a man worthy of his plantation, worthy, that is, of the plantation that the play's end celebrates as '[home]' (5.4.112).

The degeneracy of the other men, by contrast, is connected repeatedly to their respective violations of a landed, aristocratic ethos. Franville for one has joined the crew only after having sold his 'lordship,' leaving, in Tibalt's words, 'no wood upon't to buoy it up' (1.1.134–5). Lamure, by contrast, is intent on purchasing land in the plantations with money 'bred' usuriously, a history of living off of others that directly counters the landed ethos here being valued. Surely it is important that Fletcher's country patron, the Earl of Huntingdon, explicitly embodied these ideal principles and that Fletcher's royal patron, James I, was attempting to enforce such ideals as a corrective to absentee landlordism and rural unrest.[46] The two gallants evoke their failures at home, as abroad, when they reminisce about their distemperate habits of banqueting, where they have 'lewdly at midnight / Flung away' their 'healths' (3.1.30–1).

Such behaviour violates the decorum of an elite society, striking at its core values. They are parasites, men whose threat to Aminta's flesh – 'We'll eat your ladyship' (3.1.128) – translates into a threat to nobility at large. If Albert's command that they 'be better tempered' (1.3.62) goes unheeded by them, it is an oversight that seals their own demise. For the play will move to define such profligacy as the antithesis of generation itself.

In fact, only those who subscribe to the laws of temperance seem up to the task of reproduction at all. That seems to be why Fletcher and Massinger place an island nearby, which in addition to being fertile is inhabited by a colony of women, who, though bound by a vow of abstinence, find themselves in the grip of 'youthful heats' (2.2.24). Just as their male counterparts long for 'princely banquet[s]' and 'dainty dishes' (3.1.49, 38), so this island's younger women dream of sexual satisfaction. As the two parties are brought together, the gallants pray for herbal aids to meet the requirements of copulation that they sense may be upon them. As such, their voracious appetites signal the failure of their reproductive ability, their impotency. By contrast, the other Frenchmen, those who have espoused continency in one form or another, 'rise' to the challenge, Tibalt even refusing the power of anti-aphrodisiacs to hold him back. In fact, in their view, mating with the women will promote continency, acting as a restorative purgative. In choosing the oldest woman as his own potential mate, Tibalt justifies his choice by saying

> the weather's hot, and men that have
> Experience fear fevers. A temperate
> Diet is the only physic. (3.1.321–3)

Women, he urges, are the 'diet' to end all fevers, the 'physic' to cure all distempers. As such, the playwrights grant gentlewomen a central role in producing an uncorrupted version of elite blood within foreign climes and soils. If the play literally depicts Portuguese and French gentlewomen anchoring a planter class of men prone to physical and moral errancy, this representation functions analogously for English gentlewomen. Given their presence in the colonies, the reproduction of English blood, customs, and manners in lands far from England will prevail.

By affording women such an expansive role in plantations, Fletcher and Massinger do nothing less than rewrite the major colonialist theories inherited from an earlier generation. They not only revise Shakespeare's *Tempest* to qualify the role of a strong patriarch in preserving the bonds of blood abroad, but they reverse the gendering of degeneracy that had been so central to Spenser's Bower of Bliss.[47] Fletcher and Massinger give us two models of degeneracy. On the one hand, the play offers the Franvilles and the Lamures, wilfully bent at home and wilfully bent abroad. The degeneracy that they embody precludes place and locality. On the other hand, the figure of Albert serves as something of a shorthand for the widespread cultural assumption, most famously embodied by a writer like Spenser, that transplantation would produce degeneracy. Indeed, it seems Albert is the victim of a genealogical taint originating in the family's decision to transplant itself abroad. Although we know little of Albert's past, we do know that the initial act of plantation was carried out by his father, and that his father is therefore to blame for the original treachery of the colonists, which consisted of the dispossession of a preceding Portuguese settlement. We also know that Albert and his cousin Raymond (brother to Aminta) were ensnared by this patriarchal pattern and fall into the trap of repeating it by sparring one with the other. In dramatizing Albert's ability to break the cycle of deeds produced by blood 'enflamed,' enacted as a pattern of ejecting first one planter then another, Fletcher and Massinger imagine degeneracy as reversible. If their play suggests that the colonies will produce alterity, it refuses to define alterity as an intransigent condition. A compelling intervention in colonial theories, the play's resolution of the problem of colonial degeneracy seems also to have been short lived on the stage.

I have already suggested some of the ways that Shakespeare's own play, written and first performed a decade earlier, guarded against the hard look at blood's alterity that Fletcher and Massinger willingly invite. On the other side of the temporal spectrum, a similar pattern emerges. In the post-Restoration period, when this play was revised by Thomas D'Urfey as *A Commonwealth of Women*, many of the defining features of the Fletcher and Massinger collaboration outlined above were excised.[48] Indeed, this play can imagine no 'Albert,' no figure of degeneracy who must labour to effect temperance, as indicated by the wholesale removal of any character of this name. Our reviser instead is compelled to split him apart, to make two characters of the original Albert. Hence we get a good Marine, who embodies all of Albert's finest qualities and is the object of Aminta's love, and we get a malign LaMure, a character who absorbs the treacherous details of Albert's past, passionately seizing Aminta as a prisoner. D'Urfey's Marine never experiences the pangs of unruly passion that gripped Fletcher and Massinger's Albert to the point that he contemplated raping Aminta. Nor is D'Urfey's Marine visibly staged as undergoing purgation by his mistress, the scene where his injury requires bloodletting and resuturing at the hands of Aminta having been excised from this later play. In fact, if D'Urfey is not interested in imagining how Albert's passion might be reformed, neither is he interested in a sustained engagement with the threat plantations pose to social and physical identity. His play therefore seems to be less about transplantation than it is about celebrating 'home,' defined now not as a European polity (as in Naples or Milan) but a domestic unit. His heroine Aminta, though a Portuguese woman who is described as having been born in a colony, is raised 'home' in England where she meets her love, Marine (20). That she loves this Englishman, as against the 'French-firework' LaMure (17) who has captured her, indicates the proper orientation of her desire. In this play, the problem is not how to secure English blood against the threat of foreign places but how to secure the English patriarch at home. The failure here is disavowing patriarchy through self-exile. Fletcher and Massinger's wayward gentlemen-gallants, violators of a landed ethos, become in this play husbands who spurn their role within the English household. Here they swear to abandon England because they hate their wives and the way these wives lord it over them. They therefore vow 'never to converse with,' 'kiss,' or 'remember' (27) them, wilfully rejecting their children, as well, in urging that they too should 'stay at home' (27). For them, home translates into a place for keeping 'lent, and [chewing] the Cud' (27), a depraved posture that the play sets out to reform. Indeed, by the time these men have experienced enthralment to the women's 'commonwealth' abroad – a female community that we first observe singing songs of liberty, rather than hunting as in the earlier play – these husbands conclude: 'few know the goodness of Wives, till they want 'em. Ah would I were at home.' Henceforth, they promise to live more soberly and to 'sing Psalms' (100–1).

Transplantation, then, is imagined not as a heroic feat of self-rule that noble women enable but rather as cowardly resistance to rule of self, wife, and *domos* – that is, to life at home in England. Clearly invested with post-Restoration politics and the move to disavow republican sentiments as unmanly and unpaternalistic, D'Urfey's play shifts Fletcher and Massinger's focus on mending injuries of blood abroad. Shakespeare had placed the heroic agency for this sort of project in the hands of a noble patriarch, one who had no less than magical resources at his disposal. He uses this magic to control the passions of those around him, naturalizing a social hierarchy by writing it on blood – on its physical properties, whether hot or moderate, impassioned or temperate. In controlling the passions of all who reside on the island, Prospero interpellates them as subjects who require his discipline to still their fits and passions. D'Urfey's English hero, by contrast, in seeking marriage to Aminta, pursues his destiny as patriarch, tending to his own mini-state in guiding his wifely subject. Fletcher and Massinger imagine identity as structured along a different set of axes. For them, Englishness travels not exclusively through crown, land, or *domos*. It exists instead as a quality of the blood, inhering in the tempered blood that these playwrights equated with an aristocratic class: its men and women, and their capacity to govern self and community. [49]

# 5 High Spirits, Nature's Ranks, and Ligon's Indies

## The Kingly Pine

In an entry in his *Diary* dated 19 August 1668, John Evelyn records his first experience of seeing and tasting the Barbadian fruit 'called the king-pine,' a fruit whose exceptional powers he had read about in Richard Ligon's *True & Exact History of the Island of Barbados*, which first appeared in print in 1657.[1] Evelyn's recollection of the event places the royal fruit among a host of other regal emblems: a banqueting house, a richly ornate coach, and an arriving figure of state. Moreover, at the centre of the representation, the axis around which all these signs converge, Evelyn recalls the presence of the monarch, who offers him a sample of the royal fruit from his own plate. The diarist eagerly complies and proceeds to taste the rich confection. And yet, moments later, he concedes that he found the experience to be somewhat of a disappointment. Though he grants that the fruit has merits – in resembling the flavor of a melon or a quince – the fact is that he has been led to expect more, anticipating the 'ravishing varieties of deliciousness described in Capt. Ligon's history.' That is, he was hoping to sample the *king* of fruits – what Ligon describes as 'far beyond the best fruit that grows in England, as the best Abricot is beyond the worst Slow or Crab' – rather than a fruit approaching England's quite ordinary melons or quinces.[2] By referring to the 'rare fruit' of Barbados as one item in a sequence of superlatives, Evelyn confers a stature equivalent to each of these cultural emblems on this princely artefact of nature. His eye moves from the regal figures at court to nature's emblems of royalty as though they were part of a single continuum.

Evelyn's description of the event is compelling for expressing in precise material form the way a narrative such as Ligon's account of Barbados could actively shape the desires of a reading public back home in England. Evelyn has, it seems, been titillated by the profuse praise Ligon heaps on the fruit. If Ligon's purpose in writing is to 'stir the hunger of prospective settlers' for the colonial project under way in Barbados, as Keith Sandiford suggests it was, this account testifies to Ligon's success.[3] Evelyn does betray an appetite whetted by the exceptional products available in Barbados. Moreover, that he attributes the pineapple's mediocrity to the fact of its 'impairment' in transport suggests that despite his disappointment, he yet believes the fruit once possessed the royal properties attested to by Ligon. But I would like to press this episode beyond a claim about how the text may stoke English desires for colonial possessions. I am interested in the cultural logic that Evelyn, like Ligon, expresses in the associations he makes. Insofar as Evelyn's account locates the pinnacle of Barbados's natural landscape – the 'king-pine' – at the English court, where its status as a natural emblem of royalty functions homologously to confirm Charles II's authority, it does more than express a textually induced desire. It encapsulates in small an epistemology central to Evelyn, Ligon, and Stuart ideology of seventeenth-century England, which openly acknowledges the extent to which the social system is entangled with and around the sphere of nature.[4] Not yet devoted to supporting the pretense that these two realms are distinct, which Bruno Latour will describe as the province of modernity, the cultural logic captured in this little episode allows that the realm of the 'non-human,' of the natural world, is profoundly constitutive of the social polity, of the relations that govern the world of humans.[5] 'Pristine' nature – in Barbados or at court – is revealed in this moment to be always already infused with cultural categories and, in turn, to possess the power to uphold or to undermine socio-political relations.

Ligon, like Evelyn, was a gentleman with ties to the court, taking up the royalist cause during the Civil War in serving as a royal official in Devon before seeking in Barbados refuge from the violence in June of 1647.[6] He would remain on the island for more than two years, agreeing to assist Colonel Modiford, who had accompanied him on the journey, in his bid to take over William Hilliard's plantation (22).[7] In 1650 he returned to England only to be thrown into debtor's prison, having offered himself as 'standing surety' for the debts of his long-time friend Sir Henry Killigrew.[8] It was here that he would write about his journey – dating his dedicatory letter 12 July 1653 – although it would wait another four years before appearing in print in 1657. The account begins with the shape of the journey itself, describing their passage from England along the coast of Spain and past the 'Maderas'; embedding an extended description of their sojourn on the Portuguese island of Sao Tiago – Englished by Ligon as 'St Iago' – in Cape Verde; and recounting their eventual arrival to Barbados. Here the form of the narrative shifts, moving from a personal account of daily events into a broad history of the social, political, and natural forms of life on the island from the time of its earliest settlement by the English. Compellingly, had the original plan for the journey been fulfilled, Ligon might never have written this account, since we learn his intent was actually 'to plant' in 'Antigoa.' Such plans shifted when the group fell ill and when the ship from Plymouth, carrying 'men victuals, and all utensils fitted for a Plantation,' miscarried at sea (21–2). Due to these mishaps, Ligon's time in Barbados was extended indefinitely, providing him with the chance to observe all manner of life on the island, details that would later cohere as a 'history.'

Although the account describes an island far distant from the turmoil of England – one positioned in 'the Southern and Western parts of the World' (Dedicatory Letter) – it is a powerful record of and response to the world he left behind, expressing not just a socio-political orientation but a complete epistemology, one perhaps sharpened by the challenges put to it by republican ideology.[9] As with Evelyn, this epistemology achieves powerful expression in and through Ligon's account of nature, specifically the way he perceives the island's natural forms as fully entangled with social principles. As we will see, he discovers principles of rank and order everywhere in the island's rustic landscape, identifying natural forms like the king-pine fruit and the regal palmetto tree in a landscape of presumably queenly attributes. But the conflation of natural and social categories that recurs in the text expresses, I propose, more than just an interest in and excitement about the land's natural wonders, more than just a sense of its strange majesty. I read them as registering a more complex and layered response to the larger enterprise of transplantation, specifically, English efforts to settle the isle. That is to say, in identifying as elite the natural forms that grace the Barbadian landscape, Ligon reveals the island's ability to support English gentility, the very social system being decimated by the wars under way in England. As such, although his account of Barbadian nature seems far removed from the hand of culture, in fact it is intimately connected to its processes and systems, devoted, at heart, to a larger cultural effort to preserve 'aristocratic and royalist structures, styles and attitudes' in the face of their erosion.[10] That he views nature – the natural world of Barbados – as the origin, source, and transmitter of these sociopolitical structures reveals a lot about this moment. It indicates that even at this mid-seventeenth-century point – at the peak of the social transition this book has been tracing – the links between culture and nature – and the naturalizing of a rigid social hierarchy derived from such linkages – continued to anchor English perceptions of the world, gaining forceful expression in royalist writings of the period.

Such assumptions had powerful implications for colonization, since they seemed to require a symbiosis between natural forms and cultural forms. Civility or social distinction, such views maintained, derived from principles present and visible in nature. But in travelling to strange lands, an English elite was forced to confront a powerful contradiction lingering beneath the surface of these assumptions. In England, this contradiction remained concealed – civility was encoded in countless ways in a surrounding natural environment, with the effect that its relation to environment went unquestioned. But in venturing out to distant lands, this dilemma reared its prickly head, raising the question of whether wild, savage, and barbarous lands might sabotage elite cultural forms, whether they might completely erode civility and social distinction. Would movement far from England evoke necessary decline? We have seen how such a view shapes Spenser's account of an Old English aristocracy in Ireland, insofar as he perceives this group as having allowed their distance from court and their proximity to a 'savage' environment to allow their nobility of blood to become marred, defined by excess and even tyranny. Only by tightly controlling that environment – remaking it in civil form – could such a slide be arrested, an argument Spenser develops in his political tract on Ireland.[11] The categorical overlap between nature and culture that continued to be the centrepiece of English culture insisted on a reciprocal relation between these terms, with nature holding the power to support or undo what we today would call cultural forms, and vice versa. To date, critics have tended to emphasize the power early moderns conferred on culture over nature, insofar as our accounts of colonization have tended to be about the 'domination' and 'mastery' of nature. But the idea that nature might act upon and, indeed, serve as a condition of culture – which I read as an ever-present assumption of Ligon's *History* – has not yet been fully appreciated.

The twinning of these categories has profound implications, broadly speaking, for how we construe early modern culture, as critics have observed in the context of discussing the period's production of knowledge.[12] But I suggest that this conceptual overlay needs to inform our accounts of the period's ideologies of difference as well. Critics of race have already identified Ligon's text as crucial material for their analyses, mining the *History* for what it reveals about England's early involvement in the slave trade.[13] His text is widely accepted by historians as straddling a crucial transition, having been written 'in the middle of the "sugar revolution,"' when Barbados shifted from a mixed labour economy – depending largely on indentured servants from England, Scotland, and Ireland – to one primarily dependent on the labour of African slaves.[14] This shift in the dominant mode of production was accompanied, as Susan Amussen has argued, by a 'profound shift in social relations,' requiring the English 'to create new institutional and legal structures, reorganize work, and change their relations with each other.' It 'drew upon and reshaped English ideas of identity,' instating a system of social relations 'where the wealthiest exercised power untempered by reciprocity' and where 'no attempt was made to mask the use of naked force in social control.'[15] In other words, it required a reorganization of a social form 'characterized by vertical alignments of patronage and clientage, paternalism and deference,'[16] a shift, that is, in social relations deeply connected to a system of race and blood. Although Ligon's text is often read as powerfully complicit in these developments, as evidenced by his support of planter culture and a relative indifference to the predicament of the African slaves labouring in those plantations, I see evidence in the text of resistance to these transitions, ideological obstacles that stood in the path of such change. Such a reading is not motivated by a concern to distance Ligon from association with slavery; rather, it aims to show the continuing sway of residual ideologies of difference in this crucial context of England's first slave-holding plantation, and to emphasize the cultural reorganization involved in the naturalizing of slavery.

It is Ligon's account of nature that I see as crucial to observing the continued grip of such ideologies. Although this emphasis is often over-looked in readings concerned with his representation of social relations on the island, in fact Ligon underscores it in his title for the tract. The extended title explicitly announces its focus on natural forms, noting that it will be '*Illustrated with a Mapp of the Island, as also the Principall Trees and Plants there, set forth in their due Proportions and Shapes, drawne out by their severall and respective Scales ...*' It is this representation of nature that can shed light on the changing social relations of the moment, since Ligon's tendency to see natural and cultural forms as embedded one with the other constitutes a significant break between early modern race and the modern category that will supersede it. As Ezra Tawil has argued, modern racial ideologies depend on defining the realms of nature and culture in opposition to one another, construing racial features as inalterable ascriptions of nature.[17] Culture cannot undo the imprint that nature confers in a modern epistemology; biology is a sphere quite separate from culture. The logic of difference that informs Ligon's epistemology, by contrast, conceives of the relation between these terms quite differently. Not positing an opposition, Ligon understands these terms homologically, as versions of each other. If modernity conceives of nature as beyond the purview of culture, in Ligon's moment there is no ontological state of being 'outside' of culture. Rather, the realms that we define as distinct and even in tension, he defines as concordant, as abiding by the same governing principles.[18]

We can see this overlap most forcefully through the ordering scheme that bridges the realms of human, plant, and animal in Ligon's text. Compellingly, the human is not set in opposition to 'the natural,' whether 'animal' or 'plant,' a notion that enables the grip of modern race. Rather, these realms – if we can refer to them in the plural – function as nested versions of each other, each organized internally around a set of gradated differences. Crucially, each is marked with inscriptions of degree, revealing the presence of high and low forms, exalted and depressed forms, and distinct and indistinct forms. And yet, if these relations of hierarchy locate each life form within a precise rank and degree, they also resist defining any one of its members – even the lowest – as 'essentially' or 'naturally' different from the others, as will be the case under the racial ideologies of a later moment. When Ligon speaks of the different human groups in Barbados – planter, servant, and slave – or when he speaks of kinds of vegetation on the island – from the royal palmetto to the weedy 'withs' – he implicitly positions each form within a precise hierarchy, identifying the highest ranking form in each group, but also the lesser and more middling forms that compose them. What this repetition reveals is that if there is a crucial difference of race or 'kind' that Ligon's premodern epistemology expresses, instates, and operates on the basis of, it is a difference of degree.[19] For him, such difference bears an ontological charge, so that the difference of 'rank' that he perceives in the royal palmetto as against the lesser palmettos amounts to nothing less than 'an addition to the nature' (75). If the two kinds of trees share a name – in being both palmettos – they do not share a nature, held apart, as they are, by the ontological difference of rank. Looking into the mirror of human culture that was nature, Ligon perceives a world ripe with difference organized along a vertical continuum.

It is this principle of degree, I suggest, that collides with the oppositional thinking that modern race fosters and depends upon, and that constitutes instead an early modern taxonomy of difference.

To construe relations among living creatures in this way is, I have argued, fundamentally in tension with the logic of modern race and with modern epistemologies more at large. To the extent that we seek to identify the 'origins' of modernity in texts of this earlier era, we will overlook just how insistently Ligon and his contemporaries express premodern ways of knowing and inhabiting the world. In this chapter I attempt to retrieve this very different cosmology, by highlighting its presence in Ligon's text across a range of discursive fields, from natural philosophy, to humoral theory, to generic practice. What I seek to uncover in assessing Ligon's assumptions about each of these fields of knowledge is his tendency to conjoin categories that will subsequently be ruptured: natural forms with social hierarchies; the embodied form of slaves with that of masters; and pleasurable fictions with 'scientific' truths. His assumptions in each of these domains records the continuing sway at this mid-seventeenth-century moment of premodern epistemologies, which signal their difference from modernity by confounding the oppositions that have since come to inform conceptions of knowledge, race, and genre.

**Critical Dichotomies**

By emphasizing the centrality of 'crossings' from nature to culture and back again, which Ligon's text insists on, is to position a reading of Ligon's and other early plantation narratives within recent criticism observing the radical interpenetration of embodiment and environment.[20] This work has indicated the extent to which the early moderns conceived of themselves as quite shot through with the world they inhabited, bearing the imprint of the material world's elemental properties and qualities. In one of the striking metaphors deployed by critics of this school, the human body figures in its properties and attributes as a 'spongy' being, imbibing the diverse and changing properties of a surrounding world.[21] In urging the interpenetration of physical body and natural world, these studies have pressed earlier accounts of the early modern period that located the emergence of an autonomous subject and, by implication, a disembodied consciousness in Renaissance tragedy.[22] Insofar as the new critical school has drawn attention to the profound impressionability and receptivity of a pre-Cartesian subject, by characterizing that subject as perhaps not much more than a 'physico-cognitive space' gathering accretions of various natural properties that it absorbs in travelling through worlds small and wide, it has disassembled the earlier narrative.

But if this criticism has reminded us of the elemental forces that surround and shape human culture, it has also not fully abandoned the 'Great Divide' that modernity instates between nature and culture, in that it continues to conceive of the 'elements' and 'humours' as 'natural' agents separable from, if circulating among, a cultural apparatus.[23] Such criticism has done well to theorize the ways that the realm of the social and cultural is interpenetrated by 'nature.' But I would argue we need to take this insight still a step further by dispensing with the dichotomy altogether, by collapsing the divide of nature and culture that implicitly continues to inform this scholarship.[24] I attempt to move us in this direction by emphasizing how natural and cultural forms work in tandem, demonstrating how a range of political meanings saturate nature's 'purest,' most elemental configurations. Guided as we are by modern categories of thought, it is easy to construe physical elements like hot, wet, cold, or dry; or bodily substances like animal spirits and humours; or natural bodies like fruits and vegetables, which so interest Ligon, to be at a far remove from the hand of 'culture.' But, in fact, even in these contexts we are steeped in its principles, always already 'inside' early modern culture. Such concepts are fully saturated with political meanings, not at all pre-discursive or pre-cultural in the way that a modern division of nature from culture will seek to instate them.[25] Rather the two terms blend into a single concept for the early moderns, embodying a word that Latour relishes: a 'cosmopolitics.'[26] Insofar as the word captures the twinning of terms and categories that will only later undergo rupture, it expresses the early modern social formation, which was fully authorized by nature. As such, our reading practice needs to acknowledge that nature's body, like the human body and the body politic, were metaphors for each other, each realm standing in mimetic relation to the others.

In this chapter I will suggest some of the ways that details of a world we, as moderns, would designate as 'natural' – specifically, Ligon's description of Barbadian nature – can act 'cosmopolitically' to provide a sort of scaffolding for social identity under the pressures of transplantation. It makes perfect sense that Ligon would look to Barbadian nature to gauge the island's suitability for English settlers. For, in the absence of a distinction between the realms of the 'natural' and the 'cultural,' the possibility that unfamiliar 'natural' configurations – like England's newly acquired colony in the West Indies – can reconfigure culture becomes a charged concern. We have seen such concerns become apparent in previous chapters, and we have observed the range of strategies that Ligon's contemporaries invoked to guard against the degenerative slide that some assumed would begin with transplantation. What distinguishes Ligon is his tendency to approach this problem from the other angle, construing the transportability of human culture through the lens of the natural world.[27] There he finds confirmation that there is little reason to worry about the problem of degeneration in the context of Barbados, since the social forms valued by English culture are already writ large in her verdant landscape.

## A Short History of Genre

If my last chapter observed how tragicomedy attempted to project and resolve obstacles to transplanting English communities abroad by envisioning the tempering force of the upper ranks, and especially gentlewomen, the first sustained account of English settlement in the West Indies took a different generic form: that of a history of nature. The title of Ligon's text announces itself more broadly as a 'true and exact history,' positioning itself within what seems to be the wider frame of a general 'history' and directing us to what may seem to be a narrative about the island's civil affairs from the time of English settlement, twenty years prior to Ligon's arrival to the island.[28] But it quickly becomes apparent that what Ligon means by 'history' is a history that will include and even emphasize Barbados's *natural* properties – the island's topography, climate, plants, and animals – alongside and in relation to its civil history – the island's social, political, and economic structures. We may wonder at his choice of title – especially the omission of the qualifier 'Natural' to modify 'History' – in a work that announces an interest in the '*Principall Trees and Plants*' of the island on the title page. But this omission, I suggest, is the generic residue of ways of thinking that hold the early modern apart from the modern. It expresses, that is, a distinctively early modern way of organizing the world as well as knowledge of that world. Ligon was hardly alone in making this choice, as it was a dominant practice in the late sixteenth and early seventeenth centuries.

Indeed, the term of choice for those writing natural histories in the sixteenth and much of the seventeenth centuries was simply 'history,' a tendency we can observe as early as 1541 in Conrad Gessner's influential *Historia plantarum et vires* or his later *History of Animals* (1555). The English translation of José de Acosta's account of New Spain extends this pattern in yoking terms and conceptual categories that *we* might perceive as distinct in being titled *A Naturall and Moral History of the West Indies.* Implicit in the title is the idea that nature's works no less than the works of man can impart knowledge of a 'moral' nature, a conviction that is further conveyed by Acosta's clustering of sociological and ethnographic information together with botanical, geographical, and climatological data.[29] Philemon Holland's popular English translation of Pliny, which appeared in editions of 1601, 1634, and 1635 – indicating renewed interest in the genre just prior to Ligon's journey to Barbados – insisted on the same set of conjunctions in calling itself *The historie of the world: commonly called, the naturall historie of C. Plinius Secundus.* The double title is instructive: it implies an identity between a 'historie of the world' and a 'naturall historie,' suggesting that nature encompasses the world, in all its political, moral, social, cultural, and naturalistic forms.

This tendency to effortlessly mix 'the subject matters of "nature" and "man"' was shared by countless other writers of this period, including Camden, Harriot, and Bacon. It also underpinned a range of disciplines including chorography, historiography, and cosmography, as Barbara Shapiro has demonstrated in research investigating the origins of probability and certainty.[30] Shapiro suggests that writers of the seventeenth century were not inclined to draw a sharp line between 'scientific and humanistic studies,' and that the practitioners of both history and natural history shared not only a common culture but also a common approach to the problem of knowledge and the appropriate means of gaining that knowledge.'[31] These insights have been confirmed by more recent work on *historia*, in which this mode of enquiry has been characterized as 'a key epistemic tool of early modern intellectual practices,' one that 'straddled the distinction between human and natural subjects, embracing accounts of objects in the natural world as well as the record of human action.' Not just a genre but a cognitive category, *historia* 'seriously challenges our assumptions about nature and culture as separate fields of inquiry,' denoting a significant break with the two-cultures world that supersedes it.[32] These studies convincingly demonstrate that the project of writing 'history' had not yet been divided along the axis of human and natural, as it will eventually come to be.

In fact, according to Brian Ogilvie, a historian of early modern botany, this cultural shift would not be fully consolidated until the middle of the eighteenth century, when 'natural history' would become the genre of choice for that which does *not* encompass histories of man.[33] We see this shift well in progress – but still incomplete – at the start of the eighteenth century in a text heavily indebted to Ligon's history, an account of the many islands of the West Indies by Sir Hans Sloane. The title he selects is revealing, in that he calls it *A Voyage to the Islands of Madeira, Barbados, Nieves, St. Christophers and Jamaica, with the Natural History of the herbs and trees, Four-footed beasts, Fishes, Birds, Insects, Reptiles &c Of the last of those Islands.* As with Ligon, the account begins with a journey and then expands into a more comprehensive account. But the differences are crucial too, as this text expresses a different conceptual apparatus from that evident in Ligon; notably, Sloane calls his account a 'Natural History,' as against Ligon's 'History.' Although we might be inclined to read this as a minor difference – expressing what may be mere personal preferences with regard to word choice – we should consider changes to textual content as well. For along with the narrowed title, Sloane's account expresses a more narrow definition of what counts for 'nature.' Notably, man – and the civil, cultural, political, and economic structures that surround him – is mostly missing from this text. The emphasis on 'social organization and local culture' so central to Ligon's capacious history is mostly absent here, reflecting a deep cultural shift.[34] Describing the generic changes visible in the eighteenth century as a kind of epistemic shift, Ogilvie argues that they be read as reflecting a fundamental reorganization of knowledge. It is a division, I would add, that crucially enables modern racial ideologies.

In the case of Ligon's account of Barbados, a range of textual details helps to clarify that his project of history writing will be achieved through close attention to the precise forms of natural objects alongside civil events. The extended title, for one thing, illustrates what it means by 'history' with reference to a landscape and its vegetation. Indeed, the title gives priority to the vegetative landmarks of Barbados – its '*Principall Trees and Plants*' – as against the artefacts of human culture, since the machine that produced sugar from cane – the Ingenio – appears in smaller typeface and at the bottom of the impacted title. But it is the dedicatory apparatus, specifically, a poem on the text written by Ligon's cousin, George Walshe, that identifies this text as participating in a quite precise genre of history writing. In this poem, Ligon is hailed as a modern-day Pliny, one whose descriptive taxonomies neither miss

Nor Heaven, Earth, Sea, nor ought that in them is.
Not a new Star can scape your Observation,
Nor the least Insect passe your Contemplation.

Walshe identifies classical models for this kind of work in the writings of Pythagoras and Ovid, whom Ligon resembles insofar as he attends to a diversity of embodied forms, from rational to vegetable. Indeed, at one point in the text, Ligon indicates that he is quite self-consciously structuring his narrative in accord with a natural philosopher's migration from one embodied form to another, structuring a transition from a section on the island's people and animals as a movement from the 'reasonable and sensitive Creatures of this island to say somewhat of the Vegetables, as of Trees' (66). Histories routinely made such connections, effortlessly moving between the spheres of culture and nature, in much the way Evelyn does in construing the 'king-pine' in parallel with Charles II. In titling his own tract a 'history' of Barbados, then, Ligon indicates his imbrication in an epistemology that yoked civil and natural, scientific and historical, poetic and factual.

As Walshe's introductory poem indicates, he may also have been quite self-consciously modelling his project on Holland's recent translations of Pliny, even attempting to update the classical catalogue with reference to England's newly acquired colonial possessions. In this effort, Ligon was hardly alone. The Spanish had been revising Pliny with reference to their colonial possessions for decades by the time Ligon came to write.[35] Nicolás Monardes's *Ioyfull newes out of the newe founde worlde* was 'Englished' in 1577 and appeared in subsequent editions in 1580 and 1596, alongside Acosta's *Naturall and Moral History of the East and West Indies*, which was translated into English in 1604. English authors had yet to stake their claim to this active market in histories of nature, although it may not have been due to a lack of interest. Paula Findlen has observed that scientists like Thomas Harriot and John White, who were involved in the earlier settlement of Virginia, had hoped to compile their observations of this land into a natural history but found their desires thwarted by political turmoil. The result was that no such 'history' ever materialized. Harriot's *briefe and true report of the new found land of Virginia ...* and White's accompanying drawings offered only a taste of what a more systematic history might have provided.[36] Years later, Francis Bacon would attempt to spur these limping efforts forward, urging the English to join with historians of other nations in compiling natural histories. The 1627 posthumous publication of *Sylva Sylvarum, or, A natural history, in ten centuries* was an attempt to begin such efforts and became a publishing hit, running through multiple editions all the way up to and beyond the period of the Restoration.[37] Elsewhere, particularly in his *Novum Organon*, Bacon encouraged others to extend his own incomplete effort 'in the research and compilation of natural history,' urging that 'we must turn all our attention to seeking and noting the resemblances and analogies of things, both in wholes and in parts.' [38]

Ligon seems to have viewed his work as an attempt to further such endeavours, often casting himself as a Baconian scientist. He explicitly refers to Bacon at one point in his *History* when he puzzles over the absence of springs despite the plenitude of Barbadian caves with moist air. He confesses: 'I had it in my thoughts, to make an Essay, what Sir Francis Bacons experiment solitarie, touching the making of Artificial Springs would do' (98). This tendency to rather self-consciously assume the mantle of a natural philosopher recurs in a number of places in the *History*, as when he speculates as to why, in travelling at sea, they have perfect visibility through the water only when the sea is rough, not calm. This puzzling observation reminds him of 'a point of Philosophy I had heard discours'd of, among the Learned; That in the Air, Rough hard bodies, meeting with one another, by violent stroaks, Rarified the Air, so as to make fire' (7). He commends similar efforts in a slave named Macow, whom he describes as conducting a basic 'experiment' (49) in connecting varying lengths of timber in order to replicate the musical sounds of Ligon's theorbo. The wonder that the incident evokes for Ligon – his surprise that one 'without teaching [could] do so much' – leads him to conclude that 'these people are capable of learning Arts' (49). He himself was well supported in such enterprises by a circle of friends and patrons who promoted his own scientific enquiries. He had been involved in an effort to drain the fens of East Anglia at the urging of Sir William Killigrew, a project that disastrously backfired when inhabitants revolted against the enclosure, ruining him financially and priming him for his overseas trip to Barbados.[39] Moreover, we learn from his dedicatory apparatus that the Lord Bishop of Salisbury, Brian Duppa, urged him to publish on the topic of Barbados and was likely the financial support behind the enterprise, since Ligon completed the history while in debtor's prison. This was the same Duppa, tutor to Charles I, who was patronized by Archbishop William Laud, indicating Ligon's connections to a group of divines whose religio-political insights gained expression in part through histories of nature.[40]

Far from being an exclusive treatment of the 'natural world,' as writing about objects of the natural world would increasingly be framed, in Ligon's moment the genre of *historia* enjoyed very flexible parameters. It allowed him access to a range of genres – scientific no less than poetic – in pursuit of his truth claims. Critics have sensed this openness of form in the range of classifications they have tended to assign the text. Some have associated it with 'travel literature,'[41] while others have argued for its affinities with the 'domestic manual' or with the more political focus of a 'plantation manual.'[42] Still others identify the text with the sentimental literature that developed around the story of Inkle and Yarico, since the originary account of this Indian woman – Yarico – who would save and then be betrayed by an Englishman, first appeared in Ligon's text.[43] But the text is also organized, as I have suggested, by the governing categories of natural philosophy, in explicating rational, sensitive, and vegetative bodies. As these competing narrative strands suggest, the 'True and Exact' claims of the title had not yet congealed into a later form of scientific representation, which would promote the use of a transparent kind of language to avoid what it would perceive to be the distortions of 'romancical' discourse.[44] Ligon's 'history,' by contrast, includes not only the genres enumerated above but elements of pastoral, Petrarchan lyric, and epic romance, which work in tandem with the text's content to advance its meaning. I will turn now to explicating how these generic overlays work in tandem with the conceptual overlays between culture and nature to argue for the text's embeddedness in a pre-modern system of identity, where the difference of race – what early moderns also referred to as a difference 'of kind' – was a difference of degree.

## Romance, Errancy, and Degeneracy

If Ligon's emphasis on the bounty and natural beauty of Barbados might lead us to believe that he welcomed the prospect of planting in the Indies, in fact, the text explicitly confounds this narrative. His emphasis – in form and content – is on the rupture of the Civil War, which he blames for transforming him, a royalist, into a 'stranger' at home. Eager to be transported to 'any other part of the World, how far distant soever, rather than abide [in England]' (1), Ligon accepted a friend's bid to join him in planting a new colony in 1647. He thereby substituted storms at sea for the social storm at home, and a previously settled Ligon ends up being transformed into a wanderer and vagabond on the 'Raging Seas.' If tropes of romance come to describe his own predicament, so they serve to frame his narrative. Attempting to 'place' the text in the opening letter to Duppa, Ligon refers to his text as a 'wild Grotesso' and a 'loose extravagant Drolorie,' invoking the quintessential figures of romance – mixture, hybridity, and vagrancy – to suggest his and England's ontological status of being 'out of place.'[45] Returning form and order to their shapeless condition is the unstated goal that this opening identifies. If his aimless errand initially gains expression in a narrative that wanders into a forest of pleasurable digressions, both he and the narrative will discover a principle of order in the book of nature, which provides a blueprint for stability, both social and narratological.

Just as the text's formal features define Ligon's unplanned trip as a kind of errancy, this concern informs Ligon's view of the creatures he observes at sea, who seem to stray beyond the contexts that normally define them. As he sets sail for what he believes will be a plantation in Antigua after a brief stop in Barbados (21), he observes versions of his own hardships in the life forms he sees. Emblems of displacement – of animals wandering at a remove from their native element – crowd his account. Predators force dolphins from their 'watry Element,' and a change of locale transforms the shark – 'Tyrants' of the seas – to impotence (5). In Ligon's optic, all living forms express attachment to a milieu, and are rendered vulnerable when this bond is disrupted, human no less than animal and vegetable. As such, transplantation is the problem that has been thrust upon Ligon and that the narrative will seek to overcome. If it is a problem produced by fraught political relations, however, he discovers his response to it in the natural forms that surround him. At sea, for instance, Ligon becomes captivated by a species of fish, the 'Carvil,' and a kind of bird that comfortably occupies more than one realm, defying any singular or exclusive attachment to place. He marvels at the bird's ability to thrive equally on land and water, such that he wonders if the 'sea may not be counted their natural home' (4), and he touts the fish's ability to transform itself into a sailing vessel, as he 'Raises up his Main mast, spreads his sails ... and begins his voyage' (6). Transforming the purposeless wandering of his early journey into a wilful and effortless ability to move between places, as he observes these animals have effected, is the goal he increasingly moves toward.

Indeed, this quality of portability assumes greater significance much later in his narrative, when he provides an account of his stay in Barbados. In the catalogue of life forms that structure his observations of the island, Ligon singles out the sugar cane plant for being the island's one non-native vegetable, describing it as having been 'brought thither as a stranger, from beyond the Line' (85). As a transplanted species, the sugar cane models in vegetable form what Ligon seeks to reproduce for English culture. Though he is quick to concede that the plant lacks the royal properties visible in the king-pine or royal palmetto, he praises it for making up in ingenuity what it lacks in rank. He esteems it for being a steward, guardian, and husband, one whose 'special preheminence' is the ability 'to preserve all the rest from corruption' (85). In language that construes the sugar cane plant as an overseer of an active estate, he describes it as 'a strong and lusty Plant, and so vigorous, as where it grew, to forbid all Weeds to grow very neer it,' thereby maintaining 'its own health and gallantry' (87). The plant, then, instates in nature the distinctions of rank that Ligon seeks to secure for English settlers, both those already living abroad in Barbados and those contemplating such movements in the future. If transplantation – and the spectre of errancy that it evokes – is the problem to be overcome for Ligon, the 'gallant' sugar cane shows him the way by keeping a steady course of growth amid the assaults of enemies, and by extending this principle of constancy to other plants through its role as a preservative.

But even as animal and vegetable bodies hold principles of order that can guide English settlers, these life forms are also impeded in ways that will resonate for the project of translating English culture abroad: all face the problem of how to sustain their natural difference, their distinction, from other forms within their group. While the sugar cane, for one, has the potential to serve as an orderly husband, it is also vulnerable to the levelling energies of another growth – the withs – a weed Ligon discusses at length. Defying classification – being neither a tree nor a plant – withs also stand against relations of rank, as conveyed in the vegetable world through properties of height. Withs bring the high low, and undo the fruitful potential of other plants. For Ligon, they signify the principle of indistinct growth, decimating cane, garden, and orchard alike, by their ability to 'creep into every place, and as they go pull down all' (97). Though a creeping plant, he regrets that they do not stay in their place, preferring instead to 'mount to the tops of the Trees, which are for the most part, eighty or 100 foot high' (97). The same threat carries over to the world of human activities, of human culture, which can, at any moment, fall into oblivion. For Ligon, as for his contemporaries, movement beyond England triggers fears of losing one's status, that is, of losing the distinctions that defined one's rank, degree, and place within an English social body. To represent the potential for this cultural outcome – the decline of degeneracy – Ligon develops the theme of wandering that opened his narrative into a full-fledged romance. This is the genre that most forcefully defines his account of their brief stay on the Cape Verde islands, which is figured as a space of moral errancy, one that literally delays their arrival to Barbados and that symbolically confounds crucial principles of order underpinning Ligon's sense of the world as a carefully calibrated hierarchy of life forms.⁴⁶ It is on this island that Ligon constructs a perfect vignette of what it means to stray from social distinction in the figure of the Portuguese master who is the governor of the island of St Iago.⁴⁷

We can see this narrative of self-forgetting take shape when Ligon describes his first sighting of the Portuguese island of St Iago. The island's natural forms identify its social failings. Viewing it from afar, the island appears as a kind of unbroken continuum to the English shipmen, one where rock, hill, and barren soil blend together. We soon learn that the island has the potential for fecundity, since they have arrived during the blighting season of tornadoes, but that its fruitful potential is not cultivated by its Portuguese overseers. The problem attributed to nature is, in fact, a political problem, one positioned as the failing of the island's ruler. A man whom Ligon analogizes to the 'Knight of the Sun' (10), the Governor is an 'errant' knight for undermining his own rule in regarding so lightly principles of social hierarchy. By applying such hyperbolic language to the governor – a reference to the protagonist of a sixteenth-century Spanish romance translated as *Mirror of Princes and Knights, in which Are Told the Immortal Deeds of the Knight of the Sun and of His Brother Roxicler, Sons of the Great Emperor Trabacio*⁴⁸ – Ligon uses a genre associated with Spain and Portugal – chivalric romance – to parody the failure of heroism on the island, the failure of the very principles of rank and blood that underpin the ideology of heroic chivalry. Notably, the governor appears sheepish, refusing to impress his authority over those whom he rules in choosing to live hermit-like in a modest home buried within a hill overlooking a parched landscape. This failure has already been forecast in the earlier description of the island's nondescript landscape, as the political arrangement is a version of the land's natural forms in Ligon's optic; neither has been cared for in a way that might foster civility and distinction. This failure of political rule is expressed in the Governor's domestic arrangements as well, for he has sired 'a *Mollotto*' (9), presumably with one of his 'negroes,' violating the very basic distinction between master and servant in the process. Ligon humorously underscores the social inversions this man embodies in recounting the Governor's arrival to host the English for dinner. The event reads again as an absolute parody of heroic chivalry, as the Governor violently races in atop an aggressive barb, whose 'swiftness of motion' (11) nearly kills him, leaving him in a great trance. In describing the Padre as 'subject to the will of his horse' (10), Ligon translates the episode still further as emblematic of the world turned upside down: the vignette portrays horse ruling man, passion guiding reason, and the high being brought low.[49] From his ill-constructed house, to his unadorned walls, to his habit of serving instead of being served, this governor fails in not holding himself apart, not honouring the distinction that his social role as governor should entail.

In recounting his indecorous treatment of his beautiful black mistress, Ligon completes the vignette. Critics often pause over the passage where Ligon describes this woman as 'A *Negro* of the greatest beauty and majesty together' (12), construing the episode as displaying Ligon's voyeuristic desire for the African woman, a species of the pornographic desire he will express when describing the scantily clad bodies of African slave women in Barbados.[50] His emphasis on her graceful carriage and majestic demeanour do indeed seem to suggest Ligon's admiration of, if not desire for, the woman. But I would argue that his desire grasps at the social distinction he believes she confers. Notably, he is the servant to her 'royal' will, positioning himself as a client of this regal patroness. As such, he offers her 'Trifles ... worn by the great Queens of *Europe*,' which he admits are 'not worthy her acceptance.' And he describes her reward of a beautiful smile as requiring a 'far greater present' than the 'rich silver, silk, and gold Ribbon' he has offered her (12–13). As such, he indicates that his service has been reciprocated through the distribution of a royal reward, one that promises still more favours in the future. This tendency to associate her with courtly codes is visible in every detail of this two-page account of the mistress. In fact, he goes so far as to describe her as a woman of 'far greater Majesty and gracefulness' than he has observed of Queen Anne at court, even when seated in a 'Chair of State,' accompanied by a 'Baron of *England*,' and dancing a measure at the end of a 'Masque in the Banquetting house.' This outrageous comparison complexly embeds Ligon's social desires. Not only does it serve to emphasize his social proximity to the court, but it may hint at thwarted ambitions at home, intimating that the rewards to be found on the islands will far exceed those distributed at home. He emphasizes the extent of such benefits in his description of this mistress's body. Though forced to hold court in the debased context of the Governor's mean lodgings, the Cape Verdean mistress yet conveys her social pre-eminence in the exquisite garments she wears. Recalling with meticulous detail events of years earlier, Ligon describes her garments as if she were standing before him still, recalling her 'green Taffaty' head roll; a 'vayle'; a 'Peticoat of Orange Tawny and Sky colour'; a mantle of 'purple silk' adorned with a 'rich Jewel'; as well as 'Silk' buskins, shoes of 'white Leather,' and jewels to adorn her ears, arms, and neck (12).

Indeed, the language of courtly compliment that he here leans so heavily on suggests a quite different reading of the mistress than has been offered by critics to date, one that gains significance when positioned within the larger narrative arc linking St Iago to Barbados. In the context of the embedded narrative of Portuguese (mis-)rule that I have thus far traced, clearly her majesty and courtliness serve to set off the failings of the Portuguese Governor. Here she quite clearly embodies the principles of decorousness that he neglects, not least insofar as he denies her a devoted train of followers due 'such a state and beauty,' an omission that allows Ligon ready access to her (13). Where she is a model of the order he associates with courtly life, the Governor emblematizes the disorder of lapsed gentility. He has allowed himself to become indistinct, 'discomposed' in word and gesture, as we have already learned from his barbed entry (10).

But there is a larger narrative arc to be traced in and through his representation of this regal African woman, one that is prefigured in the text's introductory poem. In this context Walshe describes how Ligon has drawn a

Landscape in rich Tapestry
....

Attireing all in such a lovely Dresse,
Rich, Genuine, and full of Courtlinesse:
That as Great Brittain sometimes I have seen,
So you've Barbadoes drawn just like a Queen.

Like the courtly mistress Ligon introduces us to in the opening pages of his text – richly attired, courtly in manner, and queenly in essence – Walshe fashions Barbados, as had been customary for Britain, in the figure of a Queen. He offers, that is, an allegorical representation of both lands, linking them by figuring each through a powerful emblem of royal order – the figure of the queen's body.[51] If we interpret the mistress in a similarly allegorical way, she comes to signify beyond her status as an individual whom Ligon has happened to encounter on his journey, taking on greater significance as an emblem of the island's 'naturally' royal properties. Ligon seems to press this sort of reading in what appears to be his reckless decision to compare the mistress to Queen Anne, and in the still more hyperbolic reading of her body in terms of '*Neptunes Court*' (13). In making such comparisons, Ligon encourages us to read this woman typologically, as a symbol of all that these islands might be, were they afforded the care of a stewardly 'husband' rather than the neglect of a jealous 'Padre.'[52]

Indeed, this trope of the regal feminine figure recurs in his narrative, characterizing his visits to *both* islands, as registered not only in the people he encounters but the natural forms he records. Immediately following the episode with the mistress, its main themes are underscored when he encounters at a nearby fountain beautiful black twins, whom he greets with a charged amorous discourse. He falters for words to describe their beauty, noting 'To express all the perfections of Nature, and Parts, these Virgins were owners of, would ask a more skilful pen, or pencil than mine' (15). As with the majestic mistress, these '*Negro* Virgins' (15) seem to signify beyond their individual identities by virtue of the hyperbolic language he uses to describe them. It hardly seems incidental, for instance, that they are adorned with elements of the island's resources, their hair plaited with 'rare flowers that grow there,' their arms with 'pearls, and blew bugle' (16). Ligon tells us they are 'Wanton, as the soyl that bred them, sweet as the fruits they fed on' (16), making their emblematic significance explicit. As such, they are walking embodiments of the luscious landscape, figures of the soil's fertility. But what is equally crucial to observe of these virgins is their status as being unmanned in this 'valley of pleasure' (15). Serving as a kind of analogue to Sir Walter Raleigh's famous description of Guiana as a country that 'hath yet her Maydenhead,' these virgins function within the narrative to stoke the desires of English gentlemen at home.[53] Like the mistress improperly 'husbanded' by the Portuguese Governor, these twins beckon with the promise of satisfying desire, rewards that they are eager to bestow, insofar as they 'counsel and perswade our loves ... and so commit rapes upon our affections' (17). In a compelling inversion of Raleigh's image of an enforcing male conqueror, Ligon imagines himself as a taken husband, one who has been forced into manning these feminine 'Paragons' (17).

The extent to which the episode values natural gentility as a social principle of far greater importance than skin colour emerges when we compare it to another account of rape mentioned in passing in this same Cape Verdean vignette. Ligon records how one afternoon during their stay aboard the ship off the coast of the island, a group of 'passengers' sought to go ashore to have their linen washed. They brought 'divers women' from the ship to perform the necessary labour, women whom

Ligon describes with disdain as having been 'taken from *Bridewel, Turnball* street, and such like places of education.' While attempting to complete their work, he reports how 'the *Portugals*, and *Negroes* too, found them handsome and fit for their turns, and were a little Rude.' He implies they were raped, although Ligon confesses 'I cannot say Ravish'd' as the women's labouring status precludes them in his view from being able to 'suffer such violence' (13). Perhaps still more shockingly, when the English gentlemen depart from the ship the next day to explore the reported beauty of the place, completely unaffected by the 'complaints' of rape and pillage on the part of the 'passengers,' a Portuguese captain assumes they are eager to revenge their women and requests that they return their arms to the ship. Ligon and the other men, including Colonel Modiford, are quick to dispel this illusion, indicating in no uncertain terms their absolute indifference to the predicament of the common English women. Viewing the women – though presumably white and English – as removed in kind from themselves, they treat them as lacking any claim to self-propriety, whether sexual or material. The difference of their treatment at the hands of their higher-ranking countrymen as compared with Ligon's expressions of decorum in relation to the virgin negroes is striking. If dark of skin, even marked by a 'badge' as 'free *Negroes*' (16), the virgins yet bear claim to a form of social distinction emphatically valued by Ligon. It is their lavish garments that attest to this value – clothed as they are in the silks and gems that signify their social distance from the Englishwomen, whose commonness is given material expression in the plain linen with which they are associated.[54] If the predicament of the English women evokes not the least expression of concern from Ligon, even in the very public form of this published record of it, his account of the virgins evokes a kind of erotic rhapsody from him, one that he feels explained to justify alternately as an expression of his artistic leaning, his extended travels at sea, and the island's minimal entertainments. He concludes the vignette with an apology for this passion, for this 'spirit of love, a passion not to be govern'd,' what he refers to in the language of romance as his 'wild extravagancy' (17).

But the high spirits – expressed by high passion – that these young women, and their majestic counterpart in the Mistress, evoke is precisely what Ligon seeks to evidence in his record of these islands. He urges, in effect, that these lands can and will support English social distinction, insofar as they 'naturally' evoke the pastimes of love, painting, architecture, and banqueting that he associates with a courtly readership and that he has evoked in his interactions with the island's beauties.[55] His apology for his outburst, then, registers as contrived, rather than sincere. In fact, we will hear the same voice much later in the text, when he describes the trees that populate the Barbadian landscape. Here we can more readily perceive how his description functions as a literary *topos*, since Ligon waxes lyrical in this later episode over his love not for a woman but for the royal palmetto tree (see fig. 4). He tells us that 'I believe there is not a more Royal or Magnificent tree growing on the earth, for beauty and largeness, not to be paralell'd … as if you had ever seen her, you could not but have fallen in love with her' (75). He sings her praises across four pages. And it is notable that he commends her for the same qualities he admired in the Cape Verdean women, observing that the tree perfectly embodies the 'soyle that bred her' and is so 'chast' as to be a superior model for Vetruvius's column than the courtesans after whom the architect had modelled his more '[lascivious]' columns (78). As in the earlier episode with the virgins, the reverie concludes with an apology for '[tir'ing] you' and he agrees to 'give over' (79). A modern epistemology tells us to separate these episodes as quite different events, with the effect that critics copiously analyse the earlier episode depicting the mistress and virgins and yet quietly pass over the latter discussing the palmetto tree. But if we take seriously what the dictates of *historia* as a genre tell us, then these narratives really serve as versions of each other, the one recording in the world of people what the other records in the world of plants.

Indeed, both vignettes connect in central ways with the larger aims of his narrative. I suggest that they figure in the register of amorous discourse what the history evidences elsewhere in the discursive mode of natural philosophy: that the islands 'under the line' (107), given proper stewardship, do not confound but rather preserve distinctions of rank crucial to English conceptions of identity. Nowhere else, Ligon tells us – and by this we must understand 'not even in England' – is majesty so beautifully set off as in these tropical islands. Not even Queen Anne can rival the regality of this island's mistress. The Portuguese Governor is, of course, blind to these majestic forms, and stands against principles of stewardship. But Ligon – and the English gentlemen whose optic he embodies – are positioned by the text as the islands' proper stewards, those who can and will actualize this potential. In moving from a tone of farcical romance while in the Padre's abode to a Petrarchan discourse and a pastoral rhapsody in discussing the island's regal women, he indicates the range of outcomes that the island holds. He celebrates the fact that the island need not be a site of indistinction, such as the Padre has

Figure 4.   Engraving of the 'Yonge Palmetto Royall' from Richard Ligon, *A True & Exact History of the Island of Barbados* (London, 1657), page 76. Courtesy of the John Carter Brown Library at Brown University.

made it, since emblems of rank and regality are everywhere visible to the well-trained eye. Far from being a racialist fantasy, then, his account of the mistress and her youthful counterparts serves to allegorize the observation that rank inheres – or *can* inhere – in these islands. And Cape Verde holds the lessons that he urges a proper ruling class to heed in Barbados.

## The Order of Nature

It should hardly come as a surprise, then, to find that when Ligon approaches the English settlement of Barbados, the natural landscape is a perfect expression of all that was lacking in the Portuguese settlement. From its first sighting, the land embodies the principle of rank, and the notions of obedience, reciprocity, and mutuality that such a system ideally instates. Not incidentally, the first thing his eye perceives are the 'high large and lofty trees, with their spreading branches and flourishing tops' (20), which he describes as protecting and in turn being replenished by the earth beneath them. A classic symbol of the monarch's protective function in relation to his subjects, the botanical dyad indicates how 'bounty and goodness in the one' is returned with 'gratefulness in the other' (10). Ligon pauses in this moment to conclude that 'truly these Vegetatives may teach both the sensible and reasonable creatures, what it is that makes up wealth, beauty, and all harmony in that Leviathan, a well govern'd Common-wealth,' gesturing at the 'woeful experience of these times we live in' (21). His history of Barbados, then, invites us to consider this landscape as a place that will restore the principles of rank and regality that have begun to wither in England. The natural features of Barbados suggest the possibility of a different outcome. Here, the land's emblem of royalty – the royal palmetto – is described as 'crown'd with' a great head and bearing great 'weight' (76), evoking the struggles of England's own former monarch, but as also benefiting from a kind of natural stewardship in the land. In Barbados the soil honours royalty, providing the regal tree with a sustaining network of roots to prevent it from being 'blown down' (78), unlike its English counterpart.

Moreover, it is here in Barbados that a narrative on the brink of 'forgetting itself,' in emulating the Portuguese-like acts of dilation and wandering, is called back to its English origin.[56] Indeed, in the inscriptions of rank that Ligon perceives everywhere in this natural landscape, he discovers a principle of order that will hold his narrative, and, by implication, the English he seeks to translate abroad, in place. It is the principle of hierarchy, so lavishly on display amid Barbados's natural forms, that enables Ligon to find his footing. Taking his cue from natural philosophy, he organizes his account by clustering material into segments categorized according to the reasonable, sensitive, and vegetable life forms, beginning 'at the top,' with man, and moving downward, concluding with a discussion of the island's plant life. Within each cluster, he varies this method, sometimes beginning with the lowest form and proceeding, incrementally, up a scale of value to the most noble form, and other times beginning with what he considers the greatest form and proceeding down a scale of value. In all cases, precise rankings – as conveyed through terms like 'greater' and 'lesser,' 'noble' and 'base' – govern his groupings. When he speaks of trees, for instance, he begins with the most depraved kind among them, proceeding from the poisonous species, to those that bear 'contemptible fruits' (69), on up to those producing edible fruit, until he eventually works his way up the ranks to the royal palmetto, which he describes as the most magnificent tree on earth. When his topic is animals, by contrast, he begins with the 'largest' (58) beasts, proceeds to 'lesser Animals' (61), and concludes with 'moving little Animals' (63) – what he elsewhere describes through the term 'multitudes' (63) – such as ants and crabs. Across the island's various life forms, Ligon discovers order in the hierarchies of rank that 'naturally' organize relations between one creature, one plant and the next.

So, too, Ligon's method of 'classifying' the people who inhabit the island reflects this tendency to position groups within a gradated hierarchy, expressing an assessment of human difference quite distinct from modern racial ideologies. Most notably, he demarcates three 'kinds' of people on the island – master, servant, and slave – rather than conceiving of the groups as locked into an opposition. Although we might expect Ligon to place considerable stress on the difference of skin colour, since he writes at a time when chattel slavery was just beginning to take hold in this English colony, in fact I propose that he leans on a more labile language of physical difference, suggesting that racial ideologies rooted in skin colour would become consolidated *after* slavery had been implemented as an economic institution, rather than at its inception.[57] Since Ligon lived in Barbados for nearly three years during the crucial decade in which the colony shifted to large-scale sugar production and the dependence on slavery that accompanied it, his text is a key source for assessing these debates. And yet, what he does *not* say is sometimes as revealing as what he does. Significantly, he never once refers to English settlers by reference to their skin colour, although critics will often presume that he construes the English settlers and servants collectively as 'whites.' Although he is, of course, aware of differences of colour, typically referring to African slaves as 'negroes' and even admiringly describing the Indians' 'excellent ... colour' of 'bright bay' (54), when he comes to the Christian settlers – who were of English, but also Scottish and Irish, origin – he does not collectivize them as 'whites.' Instead, he clusters settlers and servants according to religion, place of origin, and, importantly, rank or social location. Hence, the adjective he most frequently uses in association with the servants is 'Christian.'

Indeed, rather than aligning the servants with their masters on the basis of white skin, Ligon tends instead to position them in relation to the African and Indian slaves among whom they lived and worked. The logic of rank, that is, serves to conjoin groups that modern racial ideologies seek to define as ontologically distinct, as occupying either side of an opposition. We see these associations bubble to the surface in Ligon's indeterminate and imprecise handling of the distinctions governing the categories of servant and slave. For him, the two terms are often used interchangeably. On more than one occasion, for instance, he collapses the distinction by referring to slaves as 'servants,' cautioning that they are 'Very good servants, if they be not spoyled by the *English*' (44).[58] Conversely, what he emphasizes about servants – both their abuse at the hands of cruel masters and their tendency toward insurrection – resonates with the details of slave life on the island. Indeed, in one particularly powerful anecdote, he describes how a planter who needed a servant offered to trade his own hog for a servant woman belonging to his neighbour. He went on to propose that the two – both woman and sow – be measured on a scale, with 'the price ... set [at] a groat a pound for the hogs flesh, and six-pence for the Womans flesh.' Ligon records the event for the humour it produces when the man discovers how much the fat servant outweighs his sow, leading him to retract his offer. But Ligon lingers on the episode to inform his reader that such transactions are 'an ordinary thing there,' where it is commonplace to 'sell ... servants to one another for the time they have to serve; and in exchange, receive any commodities that are in the Island' (59). He thereby identifies trade in flesh – servant and slave, human and animal – as the norm of planter culture, and points to the considerable overlap between servant and slave that structured relations in the colony. If there is a problem for Ligon, it is that neither group – slave or servant – is extended the protection that a paternalistic ethos – such as was the ideal in England – took for granted in delineating the reciprocal nature of the bond between master and servant.[59] As servants, he sees both groups on the island – Christian servants and negro slaves – as entitled to a greater degree of protection at the hands of their masters.

Indeed, Ligon confounds our expectations about the island's logic of difference when, using the same narrative principle of an ascending or descending hierarchy that he used to organize his discussion of plant and animal life, he locates the human groups on a hierarchical continuum. Strikingly, he orders his discussion by beginning not with the slaves, as we might expect, but with an account of servants, only then proceeding to discuss conditions for the slaves, and finally concluding with a discussion of the master. That he seems to equate life 'at the bottom' of the human hierarchy with the island's indentured servants, rather than with its slave population, provides some indication of the indeterminacy of the category of slave at this transitional moment, and his tendency to regard both groups under a broader category of servant. It may also be an indirect way for Ligon to underscore his outrage upon finding that 'Christian servants' are typically regarded as the settlers' most expendable possessions, their flesh hardly regarded as worth the cost required to sustain it.[60] In fact, he notes the degradation of their condition by observing that 'The slaves and their posterity, being subject to their Masters for ever, are kept and preserv'd with greater care than the servants, who are theirs but for five years ... So that for the time, the servants have the worser lives, for they are put to very hard labour, ill lodging, and their dyet very sleight' (43).[61]

If Ligon comes down on this tendency to define servants and slaves as expendable flesh – as the planter's living possessions – it was because he perceived planters in Barbados to be actively violating natural principles of difference that ordered the world. Rank, after all, was a principle of English social relations precisely because it was perceived to naturally inhere in the flesh of those it described. If, then, Ligon does not yet construe the island's inhabitants in oppositional relations structured by the difference of skin colour, this is not to say that he had no language for translating the social categories of master and servant, royal and base into physiological terms. Indeed, I suggest that he had a more nuanced system of difference, one supporting a greater range of gradations, as compared with the rigid language of black and white that would soon become hegemonic in planter and English culture alike. It is also, significantly, a physiological term with close connections to discourses of blood. What his text leans on repeatedly and consistently to name differences of this nature – to name an early modern difference of kind

– is the language of spirits, a central physiological concept for the seventeenth century that was associated with animating in varying degrees and with diverse material effects the flesh of plants, animals, and people.

A shorthand for the 'animal spirits' that Francis Bacon would identify as the principle of life connecting all embodied forms, these physical agents were perceived to be the site of exchange between the material body and the immaterial soul. Offering a detailed description of their animated processes in his *Novum Organon*, for instance, Bacon explains: 'For every tangible body on earth contains an invisible and intangible spirit; the body envelops and clothes it.'[62] In conceiving of the body's elements in these terms, Bacon was building on a long tradition that left its imprint on humanist thinkers, who had associated these airy substances with crucial physical processes in the body.[63] Sir Thomas Elyot, for instance, would describe spirits as 'a substance subtyll, styrynge the powers of the body to perfourme theyr operations,' and Marsilio Ficino would observe that 'between the body of the world that is tractable, fallen in fact from part of it, and its soul, whose nature is too distant from its body, spirit is everywhere present ... For such spirit is necessarily sought as a kind of middle, in which the divine soul is present in a thicker body and bestows life on what is inside.'[64]

If spirits left a visible imprint on the works and philosophies of sixteenth-century humanist thought, their function became more pointed with the rise of natural philosophy in the seventeenth century. In his posthumous natural history *Sylva Sylvarum*, Bacon would use these physical agents to define the classificatory principles of his natural philosophy, crediting them with instating degrees of separation between inanimate and animate bodies, so that the latter were understood to possess spirits 'more or less, kindled and inflamed' than the former.[65] For Bacon, variations in the quality of spirits were the basis of crucial physiognomic differences, with some bodies possessing higher spirits, meaning spirits more refined by heat, and others yielding depressed or sluggish spirits in the absence of such heat. Scrutinizing the qualities of spirits in all bodies was a central tenet of the new natural histories he urged his followers to take up. To understand the transformation of a body, he explained, 'one must ask of every body how much spirit there is in it, and how much tangible essence; and of the spirit itself ask whether it is abundant and swelling, or weak and sparse; thinner or denser; tending to air or fire; sharp or sluggish; feeble or robust; advancing or retreating; broken or continuous; at home or at odds with the surrounding environment, etc.'[66] As his language attests, spirits were perceived to be a mobile and lively substance, rarely stable or static. Indeed, their dependence on the blood as a vehicle of distribution throughout the body meant that they were particularly vulnerable to its fluctuations, absorbing its changes in response to diet, but also climate, through their sustained contact. Insofar as they were equated in this period with blood, viewed as blood's purest, most airy force, they assume a key place in the reorganization of blood's meanings that I trace in this book.

In fact, in these seemingly trivial bodily substances I read a major modification to identifications rooted in blood, particularly insofar as these physiological agents emphasize the fallibility of blood. If, as Bacon suggests, different bodies are naturally disposed to possess low or high spirits, his account of these substances also emphasizes that such differences are contingent, that they can be altered by physical pressures whether artificially induced by the hand of a natural philosopher or naturally induced by a changed environment. They are not invariable in the way I have argued an earlier emphasis on lineal attributes in the sixteenth century suggested they were. As such, they are the symptom of the epistemological rearrangement I have traced beginning with Spenser, consolidating his view that by practising temperance one can indeed *make* non-lineal blood gentle. The rising cultural valuation of spirits emphasized that all blood, even high blood, needed to be *made* as such and could not simply be presumed. Spirits were by definition too mobile and mutable to support notions of blood as imparting a fixed difference. As Descartes would observe in *L'Homme*, 'whatever can cause any change in blood can also cause change in the spirits.'[67] If, then, spirits infused bodies with difference, such qualities were alterable.

A reader of Bacon himself, as I have already suggested, Ligon was very much a part of this moment, insofar as he leans heavily on the concept of spirits to explain the differences between the island's various groups – human no less than vegetable. Indeed, in using this concept as a constant touchstone in describing the island's inhabitants, Ligon may have been adhering closely to Bacon's suggestion that such information be an essential feature of all reformed natural histories. Heeding Bacon's call for greater attention to the varying physical manifestations of spirits, Ligon observes their animating presence in all life forms on the island. All living beings – from the weedy withs that threaten to pull down the sugar cane, to the rebellious servants and slaves who erupt in revolt, to the island's labour-wearied first planters – are seen by him as animated by 'spirits' that confer distinctive qualities on each body. Notably, man's spirits are not in principle different from those of animals and plants.

All flesh is infused with these spirits, allowing for various kinds of sympathetic crossovers between the species. Like them, plants and animals experience the vicissitudes of having variously high and low, turbulent and calm, exhausted and persevering spirits. The tenor of spirits in one body as against the next, that is, served as a barometer of difference to organize a group or species from within.

If this language of relative height suggests how spirits could be used to delimit 'natural' relations of rank, such differences are also understood as conditional, responding to acts of studied intervention. Indeed, in many cases their powers are predicated on various forms of cultivation. Hence, Ligon recommends constant attention and vigilance on the part of settlers to keep the spirits of the many bodies they were 'overseeing' properly ordered. In the case of a plant like ginger, Ligon instructs future settlers in stilling its restless spirit, recommending that the skin be scraped off 'to kill the spirit,' so as to prevent it from perpetually growing (79). Similarly, he describes the island's potatoes, used to make 'Mobbie,' as having such potent spirits that they need to be soaked in water until 'the water has drawn and suckt out all the spirit' (31). 'Good ordering,' a recurring phrase in the text, is all that is needed.[68] Indeed, Ligon's active interests in cookery, architecture, and husbandry during his stay on the island are linked through this desire to moderate the 'temper' or 'spirit' of all living forms – whether man, plant, or element – in the interests of maintaining a clear social hierarchy. Not only is he obsessed with finding the 'true temper' (42) of Barbadian bricks so that they will not crack, but he carefully considers how homesteads might be redesigned to prevent settlers from having their spirits sapped by excessive heat. St Iago had no such principles of order, leaving the visiting English gentlemen 'scald[ed] without' by the sun and 'scalded within' by the exertion required to climb to the Padre's inaccessible house. As a result, as Ligon memorably describes, he and the other English gentlemen were 'in fitter condition to be fricased for the Padres dinner, than to eat any dinner our selves' (10). The depletion of their high spirits, in Ligon's account, transformed each of them into 'a dish of flesh' (11) fit for the table. What this event and Ligon's discussion of spirits reveal at large, is that if spirits express differences of rank that 'naturally' inhere across a spectrum of bodies, those differences are not understood to be eternal, unchangeable, and unmovable. Rather, they require the support of the will and careful acts of ordering on the part of the settlers, for their own good and for the good of those labouring on their behalf.

Even elite bodies can be radically renatured if care of these spirits is withheld.

Indeed, he is clear that ignoring these physical agents will explosively redound upon the settlers. He tells us that such was the failing of the first round of planters, who endured too patiently a range of assaults on their embodied spirits. Living in windowless houses for fear of heavy rains, labouring too excessively, and feeding too slightly had the effect of 'depress[ing] their spirits ... to a declining and yielding condition' (41), a process of 'decay' that Ligon insists would grip even the 'best spirit of the world.' Arguing that they were not originally a 'mean' or 'lowly' group of settlers, their physical tribulations produced them as such. He identifies a similar predicament in the current settlers when he speculates that their 'distempers' are responsible for the 'killing ... disease' (21) that hit the island soon after his ship had arrived. He reasons that it is 'the ill dyet they keep' and their tendency to drink 'strong waters, [that] bring diseases upon themselves' (21), echoing Sir Henry Colt's warning to his son about the dangers of excessive consumption, discussed in chapter 4. By dragging their naturally high spirits down through such disregard, these planters have facilitated their own decline. Similarly, in demanding too much of their servants – both Christian and negro slaves – they repudiate natural differences of spirit. He repeatedly and openly speaks out against the standard treatment of indentured servants, pointing out that they are subjugated too forcefully. Observing their daily regimen closely, he recommends that they be given more meat, and objects to their having only one garment of clothing, since labouring in the sun so opens their pores that they are subject to a chill at night. Together such physical strains, he explains, 'exhaust the spirits of bodies unaccustomed to it' (45) and exacts a considerable cost of the settlers. For, like the cassava root, whose spirit carries an explosive force before it is drained, those servants 'whose spirits [are] not able to endure such slavery' (45) – those who have *higher* spirits than the settlers acknowledge – rebound in revolt, as has occurred just prior to his departure for England. Describing this 'combination amongst them' as a kind of human fire spreading from one spirit to another, Ligon heroizes their instinct for revenge, admiring the bond among men whose 'spirits [were] no way inferiour' one from the other (45–6). By subjugating them to a social level beneath that naturally instated by their spirits, the planters have invited this disaster upon themselves. He intimates that a hierarchy governed by incremental differences is to be preferred to one predicated on steep oppositions. His view of the world – in its natural and social forms – as properly defined by gradations stands against the model of absolute subjugation preferred by many planters.

Even among the negro slaves, whom Ligon describes as afraid to revolt since their 'spirits are subjugated to so low a condition' (46), Ligon models a kind of behaviour that seeks to elicit the natural differences that inhere in the group. Susan Amussen has argued that Ligon, upon his arrival in Barbados, tends to homogenize the slaves, not regarding them as individuals, in the way he identified the Padre's black mistress as exceptionally majestic.[69] Yet, I read his narrative about Barbadian slaves as extending, rather than inverting, the kind of optic he displayed while in Cape Verde. We might notice, for instance, that his survey of this group is marked by brief anecdotes of individual slaves who demonstrate exceptional abilities: so we learn that one Macow has conducted curious experiments with music; how another slave named Sambo seeks the privileged knowledge he associates with Christianity; how a young negro girl swam so cunningly in capturing a duck that Ligon insists she be rewarded; and how a free Indian woman named Yarico was ensnared by the treachery of an Englishman, though she was 'as free born as he' (55). In each vignette, Ligon emphasizes the slave's unique abilities, pointing to the exceptions that disprove the rule, as in the case of the slave who died in a fire or another who put out a fire with his bare feet, both of whom he identifies as 'excellent servant[s].' He does not propose that *all* of the slaves are loyal in this way, conceding that in fact many of them express the stereotypical attribute of cruelty, and seeming to view the male slaves in particular as more inclined to express acts worthy of praise than their female counterparts, who go for the most part unnamed in his account.[70] But neither does he accept the rigid subjugation of all of them that has come to inform planter practice. Rather, he contends, there is 'no rule so general but hath his acception: for I believe, and I have strong motives to cause me to be of that perswasion, that there are as honest, faithful, and conscionable people amongst them, as amongst those of *Europe*, or any other part of the world' (53). And he repeatedly scolds planters for withholding the option of baptism from the slaves. As against the tendency to reduce all slaves to a single kind or class, Ligon identifies fine distinctions. In effect, then, each anecdote allows him to model the posture that he urges the planters to espouse at large: a kind of stewardship that recognizes and cultivates the difference of spirit among the members of any group, rather than collapsing those differences through too violent a subjugation. So, on Sambo's behalf he pleads to his master to allow him to be baptized, stressing his resemblance to English worshippers in observing he is 'as ingenious, as honest, and as good a natur'd poor soul, as ever wore black, or eat green' (50); and on Macow's behalf he regrets that his own illness prevented him from tutoring him in the tones of music; and with the young girl, his intervention on her behalf wins her the reward.

The principle of stewardship that he embodies in these instances serves to model an ethic that he seeks to elicit in the planters at large. Hence, he calls upon the planters to be more lenient, urging them to 'cure and refresh the poor Negroes' and 'our Christian Servants,' whose 'spirits are exhausted, by their hard labour, and sweating in the Sun' (93). Given his silence in the face of the violated Englishwomen aboard his ship, his calls for changes seem to register the extremity of planter practice and the threat it seemed to pose to the 'order of things' as viewed by an elite newcomer like Ligon. He proposes a range of modifications to their general treatment, reminding the planters to take care to sustain their servants' embodied spirits by allowing them a 'dram or two of this Spirits' at the day's end (93). He is pleased that Walrond, a planter who consistently stands out in his account as among the island's best, takes his advice and sends for Irish rugs to clothe his servants and slaves at night (44), and has decided to give both groups more flesh in their diet. It is not incidental that Ligon connects Walrond's admirable behaviour to his high social rank in England, indicating that he 'had been bred with much freedom, liberty, and plenty, in *England*' as he could not 'set his mind so earnestly upon his profit' as to ignore his own 'lawful pleasures' or the charity and stewardship expected of a man of his station (35). The implication is that 'mean' settlers are the ones less inclined to understand the reciprocal nature of service, who thereby run the risk of '[spoyling]' these 'very good servants' (44) through their 'extream ill usage' (45).

Indeed, he intimates that the settlers risk spoyling *themselves* – demeaning their own spirits – in being committed to a social system predicated on such violent oppositions. By minding their profit at the expense of their pleasure, such planters allow themselves to be 'riveted to the earth' and bound by 'earthly delights' (107), a posture that associates them with the lowness of servility rather than the height of gentility. In closing his text by outlining what gentle pleasures may best be enjoyed in a hot land like Barbados – particularly music and banquets – he provides what is, in effect, a recipe for maintaining high spirits in a land whose climate, labour, and social practices seek to reduce this natural principle of social difference to naught but sweat.

## Spirits of the Future

Ligon was not alone in perceiving the connections between the concept of spirits and a social hierarchy. At the time of his departure, when tensions between royalists and republicans flared up, a pamphlet written by republican Nicholas Foster framed its indictment of the privileges sought out by royalists with reference to their spirits and tempers. Describing the encroachments of these planters as like those of 'devouring Caterpillars,'[71] he condemns them for having 'turbulent spirits' (38) and for actions derived from 'heate of bloud' (44). Proposing that their actions in Barbados are attempts to reclaim 'great inheritances' (35) lost in England and to 'insnare us in the greatest slavery' (13), Foster reproves the attempts on the part of elite Englishmen to compensate for these losses by making Barbados 'a receptacle for men of their owne spirits' (81). If Ligon construed the principle of spirits as the key to translating social distinction abroad, for Foster spirits denote little more than distemperance, turbulence, and the hot excesses of a ruling class. In his eyes, high spirits should not be fostered and preserved in the way that Ligon would have them, but should be rooted out. For him, they express a pernicious source of social unrest on the part of men who style themselves 'Lords of the Land' (80). As he charges, such men threaten to 'sheath their Swords in the hearts of all those that will not drink a health to the Figure of II and another to the confusion of the Independent dogs' (35–6). It is no small irony that he singled out Walrond, the man of high estate whom Ligon so admired, as the worst malefactor on the island (35–8). Though both Ligon and Foster were familiar with this prevalent discourse of spirits, their diametrically opposed sense of its relations to the 'real' – to social relations – expresses the strains of a culture in the throes of massive restructuring. For Ligon, spirits were the key to preserving distinctions that ensured benevolence and stewardship; for Foster, they stood as the sign of an oppressive social system that condoned the slavish and servile treatment of one Englishman by another.

Future generations would continue to regard Barbados as a colony characterized by coursing spirits, though with quite different implications. Nearly one hundred years after Ligon had visited Barbados and observed its potential to support the spirits underpinning English rank, the natural historian Griffith Hughes would extract a different view using a similar language. Where Ligon considered high spirits a crucial link between gentlemen in England and those in Barbados – as precisely that which would preserve the connection between the elite members of both lands – Hughes understood the 'high flow' of 'Animal Spirits' which characterized those living in Barbados as producing a central dif-ference between all Englishmen and all Barbadians. No longer presuming an equation between spirits and rank, he saw the 'volatile and lively Disposition' associated with Barbadian settlers as expressing instead a difference of nation. For him, the quality wrote in small the difference between 'Phlegmatic Londoners' and Barbadians of all ranks, who had been altered in nature over time by their hot climate.[72] Collectively, they were a different people from the English, the qualities of their blood no longer typifying their relation to an elite group but rather their relation to a geography, whether England or Barbados. Although similar in tone to what Spenser had observed in the sixteenth century of the Old English living in Ireland, in fact there is a crucial difference of emphasis. For what Spenser perceived – and indeed sought to emphasize – was the extent to which the Old English elite had declined in blood. He argued that they were no longer civil or courtly like their peers in England and should be divested of their titles to reflect this change. But what Hughes perceived nearly two centuries later – in the fiery qualities of the Barbadian temperament – was an alteration that had separated one collectivity from another. Although both writers speak of these changes through discourses of blood, the continuities between them are largely superficial. For the terms that defined blood's meanings had radically shifted between the two moments, moving away from gentility and rank – or the differences *internal* to England – and toward nation and people – defining Englishmen in contradistinction to those from other lands.

If Hughes's words suggest the rise of nationalist identifications to surpass a system of race and blood that had breathed its last sighs possibly decades before he wrote, such changes were part of a still larger adjustment to ideologies of race. For in his account of Barbados we hear other reconfigurations of social terms and categories at play. For the way he discusses 'animal spirits' – in language emphasizing their material and physiological properties – captures a cultural opposition between the realms of culture and nature as compared with Ligon's moment. The redrawing of boundaries around these terms is visible in a range of ways. Firstly, we see it generically. Hughes's later account of the colony would describe itself not as a *history* of Barbados, as was the case with Ligon, but instead as a *natural* history of the island. This seemingly insignificant generic shift, like the shift in his usage of 'spirits,' registers a fundamental realignment of the categories that held sway for Ligon, Evelyn, and any number of seventeenth-century men of letters who were also natural philosophers. For Hughes's text defines as ontologically separate concepts that Ligon's text doggedly conjoins. The new genre in which he writes demands, for instance, that the 'literary' be kept separate from the 'scientific.' Hughes complies with the requirements of this new discipline in that he repudiates the 'poetical dress' encumbering natural philosophy in ages gone by. Unlike Ligon, he perceives language that is anything but functionalist or transparent as a misrepresentation, as transmitting the false knowledge contained by 'fables' and 'fancies.'

The new genre in which he writes also predisposes him to conceive of nature as a realm quite distinct from culture – from the realm of the human. We see this in his concern to distinguish data that belongs in a history of nature from that which belongs to a history of man. He makes such distinctions in arguing that human histories necessarily mix pain with pleasure, falseness with truth, since man is prone to moral failings. Nature, by contrast, transmits truth unencumbered with falsity, as the fixed imprint of God's hand.[73] Notably, this view no longer allows that nature encodes social principles and forms, being a realm unto itself. As such, there is no evidence in Hughes's *Natural History* of the homologies that allowed Ligon to see plants ordered by hierarchies resembling social relations or Evelyn to see the same royal essence in the king-pine as in Charles II. Hughes, by contrast, commends Bacon for what he perceives as his preference for the world of nature above and against the world of court. He does so because by the time he came to write his natural history, the two realms so tightly conjoined by royalists of the mid-seventeenth century had come to be perceived as distinct, even opposed to one another.[74] Nature had one set of laws, culture another, and the gap between them would rapidly become insurmountable. It is this later moment – not the moment of Ligon's rank-infused, sociopolitical landscape – that expresses the epistemological conditions for modern race.

# Coda: Beyond the Renaissance

Ligon was a royalist writing at a time of massive social upheaval. During the decade after his trip to Barbados, the system of labour used on the island would transform rapidly, moving from a mixed labour force of indentured servants and slaves to one dominantly driven by slave labour. His text powerfully captures the ideological unevenness of this moment, demonstrating perhaps most forcefully of the texts treated in this book the complex relations that existed between blood and colour as competing and overlapping systems of difference throughout the sixteenth and seventeenth centuries in England.

I have argued that Ligon's emphasis on the difference that inhered in blood, rank, and spirits obstructed his ability to view all Africans as slavish, subordinate, or naturally inferior by virtue of their skin colour, although it is clear that he is quite comfortable with a social hierarchy and the view it propounds that 'nature' predisposes everyone to a given place within its folds. Many Africans do seem to belong in Ligon's view at the bottom of these plantation societies, but it is not at all clear that he believes skin colour justifies these determinations, as evidenced by the unqualified praise that he has for many people of African descent, whether the mistress and virgins in St Iago whom he extols, the various loyal servant-slaves in Barbados whom he defends, or even the well-groomed African soldiers whom he admires in Cape Verde. In many cases, he seems intent on emphasizing African order in contradistinction to European decadence, as expressed in the Portuguese Governor, the riotous revolutionaries at home in England, or the 'mean' planters in Barbados who are bound so 'slavishly' to profits as to be servile masters. Indeed, so ingrained is his conception of hierarchy that it serves to prevent him from viewing many people from England as 'of a kind' with him, impeding the notion that they might constitute a collectivity, whether linked by white skin, Christianity, or English derivation. So we see that his ties to gentility occlude his ability to identify with the English labourers aboard his own ship or with the Christian servants who toil on the island. Although he criticizes their abuse, he also seems more broadly to condone the uses to which they are put. When he recalls how the ship's gentlemen, himself included, were carried to shore on the backs of such labourers, it reminds us that divisions between ranks were a constant feature of social interactions in Ligon's moment, rendered every bit as visible in the details of everyday life as the difference of skin colour.

In concluding his text with reference to a depraved Irishman, a man he describes as a pirate of extreme cruelty and one whose villainy requires that Ligon's ship disembark for England under the cover of night, we see the obstacles that continued to stand in the path of the forging of a 'white race.' In fact, Irish villains – whether pirates, adventurers, or sailors – appear with increasing frequency as a 'concluding' motif in mid-seventeenth-century texts, making brief cameo appearances in which their treacherous dispositions are revealed before they vanish from the representational field. As such, they function as yet another symptom of the cultural change this book has tracked, serving to express and absorb responsibility for these changes through their association with a drive to flatten the social hierarchy. Like the villainous Moors whose relations to a system of blood I tracked in the introduction – the Aarons and Eleazars of an earlier moment – these Irish figures are defined by their utter rejection of a metaphysics of blood, even a refusal of the more expansive notion of spirits, which we have seen became normative across the seventeenth century. This is intimated in Ligon's text insofar as the Irish pirate – Plunquet – strikes randomly and mercilessly at any and all ships; though he is 'bold,' Ligon is eager to disavow his status as 'valiant' (119), separating him out from the ranks of heroically gallant pirates and conquerors – the Drakes of another day – whom Ligon recalls during his visit to St Iago (10).

In explicating these associations, we can hardly overlook the fact that the largest single ethnic group of servants in Barbados consisted of people of Irish descent. It is significant as well that a Master and Servant Code of Barbados, dating to the year 1661, warned of the unpredictable behaviour of these Irish servants, viewing their behaviour as deriving from their 'turbulent and dangerous spirits.'[1] If uninclined yet to identify this Irish population with their English superiors by emphasizing their 'white' skin, this Code reveals the availability of another embodied language to describe the difference of their dispositions – one, notably, closely allied to a system of race and blood. Insofar as they describe this group as possessing disordered spirits, the planters position them against the 'ordering' ethos that sanctioned upward mobility for good English 'husbands'; they embodied instead the threat of rebellion and insubordination, the kind of uprising that Ligon recalls as spreading across the island just before his departure for England (45–6).[2] In revolting, in Ligon's view, these servants aimed at nothing less than taking the entire system down, seeking to raze the distinctions so crucial to him. Their goal was not to make themselves freemen; rather they aimed to be 'Masters of the Island' (46). Like the weedy withs whose destructive tendencies Ligon so deplores when he surveys the island's varied vegetation, these servants were threatening to ascend to new heights by '[pulling] down all'; just like the withs that assaulted gallant cane and regal pine alike, these servants '[made] nothing of' the difference that separated them from their gentle superiors (96–7). As such, they stood for a social system organized by steep oppositions – one with only a top and a bottom and nothing in between. For a royalist like Ligon, such a vision was nothing less than a nightmare, its agents nothing better than servile.

A similar figure of Irish villainy is visible as well in Aphra Behn's *Oroonoko* (1688), where it is the 'wild Irishman,' Banister, who singles himself out for being indifferent to the regal disposition of the heroic Oroonoko; like Aaron of *Titus Andronicus*, Banister is fit 'to execute any villainy.'[3] It is this Irishman who mutilates the African's majestic body, in the same way that Dekker's Eleazar of *Lust's Dominion* assaults the body of the Spanish King. Both character types are defined against a social system of blood, rank, and spirits as an anchoring principle of social relations. But where Eleazar arguably signals the potential for a social release from a system portrayed as corrupt and archaic, Banister denotes the barbarism that will result from its utter elimination.

If Ligon and Behn used these Irish figures – lowborn bandits – to signal the danger of anarchy that lingered behind the repudiation of a monarchical order, republicans saw things from a different perspective. In fact, when republican Henry Neville came to write his own account of an English plantation off the coast of Madagascar in 1668, he imagined a polity that did not value rank as the determining principle of social relations.[4] In the imaginary account of the settlement of this island by an English group during the reign of Queen Elizabeth, we witness the social ambitions of a class of servitors – if not Irish servants, then English servants – brought to fruition in the figure of George Pines. Travelling with his merchant master in a journey destined for the East Indies, the passengers aboard the ship – including the merchant's wife, son, daughter, servants, slave, and apprentice – are separated by a violent storm. Only Pines – the apprentice – and the four young women – the daughter, two maidservants, and one negro slave – survive and arrive safely on the island. After finding the necessities for their survival fully answered by the resources of the island, Pines begins to feel his desire for the women rise, and selects one of the servant women, presumably an appropriate match for a man of his own modest origins, as his mate. But a vision of social parity soon rises within him, and he begins to move beyond the dictates of an English social hierarchy. Having made 'consorts' (198) of the two servant women, he subsequently finds that the master's daughter 'was content ... to do as we did,' and he includes her within his promiscuous orbit. Not long after, sensing the negro girl's '[longing]' for him, he allows her to partake as well, but only in the deep of night since he prefers not to see her dark skin colour while copulating with her (198).

In this would-be (sexual) utopia, sharing women in common comes to stand for the benefits of a republican ethos, specifically the more equal distribution of property – both land and resources. As such, it stands against the principles of rank so central to relations at home in England. Though at first reluctant to choose his master's daughter as his sexual partner, Pines is quick to abandon this code of difference and eventually embraces her as not just his bed-partner but his 'beloved wife' (200). It hardly seems incidental that when he moves to take this step, it is accompanied by the act of demarcating the negro girl's crucial difference from the others. His shift in perspective is enabled by and connected to the articulation of this alternate system of difference, with its emphasis on skin colour as the crucial marker of difference. Philippa's dark skin, therefore, is revealed in the logic of the text as enabling Pines to construct a homogeneous community consisting of himself, his mistress, and the two maidservants, despite the considerable social difference that would separate them at home. That Pines is 'right' in insisting on this new valuation of difference is confirmed by the text insofar as the geneaological line that comes to be the locus of insurrection begins with Philippa's offspring. Though 'white' and as 'comely' as the other offspring (198), hers yet seem marred in character, her dark skin transmitting a kind of behavioural curse that predisposes them to tyranny and lustfulness. By contrast, there are no Plunquets or Banisters to incriminate the two maidservants with depravity; their offspring with Pines are as obedient and handsome as those he sires with his master's daughter.

If the community lives in relative peace after an offending member of Philippa's line pays the price for the line's treachery with his life, the 'evil' of the earlier social system gets reintroduced on the island when a Dutch ship arrives nearly one hundred years later. Arriving at an island by now highly populated, those aboard the ship immediately express disapproval of what they perceive to be the island's unnatural social conditions. Notably, they are surprised to see the man they call the island's 'prince' – William Pine, grandson to George Pine – inhabit such a modest 'palace,' surprised to find 'prince and peasant here faring alike' (192). Indeed, the absence of social distinction is a principle they seem compelled to correct, since before leaving they build a much grander palace for the 'Prince' and encourage him to dine in a 'royal manner,' with delicacies like 'brandy' rather than the water that was customary for them. An allegory, perhaps, for the Restoration, the reintroduction of rigid distinctions of rank on the island – such that the prince comes to have a train of servants – seems to be the demise of the island's commonwealth. The textual response – in plot as well as ideology – is to reaffirm the more crucial axis of difference associated with skin colour. For just as the old system of rank begins to rear its head, another insurrection at the hands of yet another descendant of Philippa occurs, evoking a unified response from the others. It serves as a reminder that some differences are more crucial than others, insisting, as it were, on a realignment of race away from blood and rank and toward colour and ethnicity.

In the oscillation between representations of base Irishmen and slavish blacks that defines texts of the Restoration period, we see English culture grasping at some new literary solutions to the cataclysmic cultural adjustments that reverberated across the seventeenth century. In the shifting relations between terms like *blood, rank, spirits, temper, complexion,* and *servitude* animated across a range of genres, the culture was performing a crucial reorganization of its most basic social structures. Principles of metaphysics gradually gave way to materialism, just as vertical social structures relaxed to accommodate horizontal modes of identification. English literature of this period – the epic and drama but also the chronicles and natural histories – was intimately involved in these developments, actively participating in the remaking of race that defines the early modern period.

# Notes

## Introduction: Bloodwork

1 In her essay '"The Getting of a Lawful Race": Racial Discourse in Early
  Modern England and the Unrepresentable Black Woman,' in *Women, 'Race,'
  and Writing in the Early Modern Period*, ed. Margo Hendricks and Patricia
  Parker (New York: Routledge, 1994), 35–54, Lynda E. Boose was one of the
  first literary critics to propose that racial distinctions in the early modern
  period might differ from the modern category in their affinity with 'cul-
  tural and religious categories rather than biologically empirical ones' (36).
  Other major studies of race for the period include Kim F. Hall, *Things of
  Darkness: Economies of Race and Gender in Early Modern England* (Ithaca, NY:
  Cornell UP, 1995); John Gillies, *Shakespeare and the Geography of Difference*
  (Cambridge: Cambridge UP, 1994); Ania Loomba, *Gender, Race, Renais-
  sance Drama* (Manchester: Manchester UP, 1989) and *Shakespeare, Race, and
  Colonialism* (Oxford: Oxford UP, 2002); Joyce Green MacDonald, ed., *Race,
  Ethnicity, and Power in the Renaissance* (Madison, NJ: Fairleigh Dickinson UP,
  1997); Catherine M.S. Alexander and Stanley Wells, eds., *Shakespeare and
  Race* (Cambridge: Cambridge UP, 2000); Mary Floyd-Wilson, *English Ethnicity
  and Race in Early Modern Drama* (Cambridge: Cambridge UP, 2003); Virginia
  Mason Vaughan, *Performing Blackness on English Stages, 1500–1800* (Cambridge: Cambridge UP, 2005); Sujata Iyengar, *Shades of Difference: Mythologies
  of Skin Color in Early Modern England* (Philadelphia: U of Pennsylvania P,
  2005); and Lara Bovilsky, *Barbarous Play: Race on the English Renaissance Stage*
  (Minneapolis: U of Minnesota P, 2008).

  In his *Racism: A Short History* (Princeton, NJ: Princeton UP, 2002), George
  M. Fredrickson points to discrimination against Jews in Medieval Christen-
  dom and early modern Spain as a type of 'nascent racism' (12), although it
  goes without saying that 'racism' is not equivalent to the category of race.

2 Others locate it in more distant ages. See, for instance, Geraldine Heng, *Empire of Magic: Medieval Romance and the Politics of Cultural Fantasy* (New York: Columbia UP, 2003); and Benjamin Isaac, *The Invention of Racism in Classical Antiquity* (Princeton, NJ: Princeton UP, 2004). The collection edited by Ania Loomba and Jonathan Burton, *Race in Early Modern England: A Documentary Companion* (Houndmills, UK, and New York: Palgrave Macmillan, 2007), in particular, challenges these strict narratives of periodization (2).

3 Michel Foucault, 'Nietzsche, Genealogy, History,' in *Language, Counter-Memory, Practice: Selected Essays and Interviews*, ed. Donald F. Bouchard (Ithaca, NY: Cornell UP, 1977), 139–64, esp. 140, 142, and 162. Foucault urges that as historians 'we must dismiss those tendencies that encourage the consoling play of recognitions' and be suspicious of a 'pretended continuity' (153 and 154).

4 For an excellent contextualization and analysis of these lectures, see Ann Laura Stoler, *Race and the Education of Desire: Foucault's History of Sexuality and the Colonial Order of Things* (Durham, NC: Duke UP, 1995), esp. chapters 2 and 3. For her paraphrase of Foucault's thinking as quoted above, see 60.

5 In general, historians have been more inclined than literary critics to emphasize the absence of continuity between modern forms of race and early modern ones. Ivan Hannaford, in *Race: The History of an Idea in the West* (Baltimore and London: Johns Hopkins UP, 1996), has made a convincing case for the relatively late provenance of racialist thinking, emphasizing how classical political theory imagined the state as precisely that which could '[release] one from nature' (12). He suggests that it is only when nature comes to replace the political as the site of the 'real' – with the implication that peoples and societies are bonded not by politics and law but by nature – are racial divisions conceivable (58). As such, he argues that racial thinking 'is fundamentally an Enlightenment notion' (6). More recently, historians have considered how religion implicates histories of race. In *The Forging of Races: Race and Scripture in the Protestant Atlantic World, 1600–2000* (Cambridge: Cambridge UP, 2006), Colin Kidd argues that 'Race was not a central organizing concept of intellectual life or political culture during the early modern era,' urging that it be seen as occupying the same 'ideological space' as theology, insofar as it was deeply entangled with 'the theological problems associated with the origins and distribution of mankind' (54, 67, and 55). Kidd argues that the Christian emphasis on monogenesis, dominant throughout the seventeenth and early eighteenth centuries, tended to block modern racial divisions in emphasizing a view of 'race as an accidental, epiphenomenal mask concealing the unitary Adamic origins of a single,

extended human family' (26). Not until the rise of polygenesist theories in the eighteenth and nineteenth centuries, he argues, would the idea of discrete races take hold.

David M. Goldenberg, in *The Curse of Ham: Race and Slavery in Early Judaism, Christianity, and Islam* (Princeton, NJ: Princeton UP, 2003), pursues a related project in investigating the scriptural origins of a bias against black Africans in Jewish society of the biblical and post-biblical periods. His meticulous research suggests how a monogenesist emphasis can in theory accommodate an ethnocentric bias given the concept of a cursed lineage, such as comes to attach to Canaan in Genesis 9:18–25. And yet, he shows that the association of the curse against Canaan – subsequently interpreted as a curse against Ham – only belatedly (relative to his study) comes to be associated with black Africans. He refutes the idea that this development might be traceable to the biblical or post-biblical periods, seeing it instead as taking hold during the seventh century, in part as a function of biblical (mis-)translation but also in response to the Muslim conquest of Africa. Goldenberg is reluctant to describe even this later development as 'racist,' as opposed to 'ethnocentric.' Believing that a racialist ideology requires evidence that a 'society's internal structures are discriminatory and its ideology justifies such discrimination' (198), he seems to associate these developments with 'attitudes that evolved from the sixteenth to the eighteenth century,' emphasizing their intimate connections to the colonization of the New World (199). But a close investigation of this claim is beyond the focus of his book, and he relies primarily on the work of literary critic Kim Hall to substantiate this view.

6  Bovilsky's study makes this point with particular force in stating: 'We should not assume that Renaissance understandings of race mirror ours. But the differences between them need not prove interpretively daunting or render the past meaningless for us' (20). Although Bovilsky's aim is to insist on the ways that early modern racial forms resemble and make use of modern techniques of racialization – the use of physical, cultural, geographic, and linguistic features, as well as the inconsistent and contradictory logic that underpins these selections – she yet accepts and elucidates differences of emphasis, describing the earlier period as one where 'racial identifications are especially fluid' (32). So, too, Iyengar has recently made the case for the 'strangeness of early modern racialized discourse' (1).

Though I place an emphasis on the difference of racial form between early modernity and modernity in my account of race, this is not to say I view this difference as 'irrelevant' to subsequent racial ideologies, a critique that Bovilsky has directed at critics who have argued for reading the period as expressing a pre-Enlightenment episteme; see *Barbarous Play*, 24–5. To capture difference, in my view, elucidates the specificity and contingency of modern notions of race perhaps more powerfully than does an emphasis on similitude and continuity.

7 Bovilsky admirably does the former, as does Mary Floyd-Wilson in *English Ethnicity and Race*, but neither interrogates its relation to 'ethnicity.' Floyd-Wilson's title implies that race and ethnicity are roughly synonymous terms, although this relationship is not theorized in the book. By contrast, Colin Kidd, in *British Identities before Nationalism: Ethnicity and Nationhood in the Atlantic World, 1600–1800* (Cambridge: Cambridge UP, 1999), speaks of 'ethnicity' in relation to 'nationhood' rather than 'race,' seeming to hold the terms apart for the early modern period and associating 'racialism' with developments in the eighteenth century and beyond. In his more recent book, he moves to link the categories of race and ethnicity when he argues that for early modern writers 'race and ethnicity involved questions of pedigree: did an ethnic group descend from the line of Ham or Shem or Japhet?' (*Forging of Races*, 58). In pointing to lineage as the axis of these identifications, one he connects to theological debates, Kidd emphasizes an association I seek to draw out still further.

8 *Lust's Dominion: or, The Lascivious Queen*, ed. J. Le Gay Brereton (Louvain: Librairie Universitaire, 1931), 1.2.231–3. All subsequent quotations are to this edition and will appear parenthetically in the text.

9 For a reading of tragedy at large as concerned with the breakdown of ideologies of blood, see Franco Moretti, '"A Huge Eclipse": Tragic Form and the Deconsecration of Tragedy,' in *The Power of Forms in the English Renaissance*, ed. Stephen J. Greenblatt (Norman, OK: Pilgrim, 1982), 7–40.

10 Raymond Williams, *Keywords: A Vocabulary of Culture and Society* (New York: Oxford UP, 1976).

11 For a trenchant overview of how developments in critical theory have impacted the project of writing history, see the introduction to Penelope J. Corfield, ed., *Language, History and Class* (Oxford: Basil Blackwell, 1991), esp. 27–8.

12 This problematic is explored with nuance in a series of articles by Keith Wrightson; see 'Estates, Degrees, and Sorts: Changing Perceptions of Society in Tudor and Stuart England,' in Corfield, *Language, History, and Class*, 32–44; 'The social order of early modern England: three approaches,' in *The World We Have Gained: Histories of Population and Social Structure: Essays Presented to Peter Laslett on His Seventieth Birthday*, ed. Lloyd Bonfield, Richard M. Smith, and Keith Wrightson (Oxford: Basil Blackwell, 1986), 177–202; and 'Class,' in *The British Atlantic World, 1500–1800*, ed. David Armitage and

Michael J. Braddick (Houndmills, UK, and New York: Palgrave Macmillan, 2002), 133–53.

13 See *The Oxford English Dictionary*, sb. *race*, I.2d.

14 See *OED*, sb. I.1a; sb. I.1b and I.1c; and sb. I.2a.

15 Raymond Williams, *Keywords*, 51–9, esp. 52. See also Wrightson, 'Estates, Degrees, and Sorts,' for a discussion of how the three medieval 'estates' get reconfigured in the early modern period. He suggests that in late· sixteenth-century England 'writers did not rehearse the traditional tripartite distinction in their accounts of society. Instead they depicted a consolidated hierarchy of "degrees"' (34).

16 Hannaford, *Race*, 175. Michael Banton extends these views in arguing that earlier usages of *race* indicate its use as an ideological tool to emphasize 'supposed innate differences between persons distant in social rank,' and only later gets used to stress 'differences between people of distinct nations'; see 'The Idiom of Race,' in *Theories of Race and Racism: A Reader*, ed. Les Back and John Solomos (New York and London: Routledge, 2000), 51–63, esp. 51.

17 See, for instance, Lawrence Stone, *The Crisis of the Aristocracy, 1558–1641* (Oxford: Oxford UP, 1967); see also Frank Whigham, *Ambition and Privilege: The Social Tropes of Elizabethan Courtesy Theory* (Berkeley: U of California P, 1984).

18 See *The Norton Shakespeare*, ed. Stephen Greenblatt et al. (New York: Norton, 1997), 1.2.361. Future citations of Shakespeare's plays refer to this edition and will be cited parenthetically in the text.

19 Many critics of race have noted that *race* is related to *class*, enumerating *class* or *degree* as one in a sequence of categories that help to delimit racial codes. This point is made by Loomba and Burton in the introduction to their *Race in Early Modern England*, where they devote a few pages to 'Religion, class, and color' (12–16). Here the editors make the crucial point that '"race" as it was most widely used in this period [was] … a synonym for class. At this time, class was seen as an attribute rooted in the blood, or inherited, rather than a changeable socioeconomic positioning' (14). Although Loomba and Burton are comfortable in translating *race* as *class*, their emphasis on how early modern usages of *race* connect it to inheritance and blood suggests a difference between these terms that should not be collapsed. Where *class* is a term that names a social identity, early modern *race* names a 'natural' or 'pre-cultural' identification, one believed to be transmitted generationally through the blood. It suggests a fundamentally different conception of the relationship between society and nature than exists for modern class formations, one wherein social divisions are ordained by nature.

Bovilsky, too, sees *class* as intersecting with *race* across various social formations, proposing that 'Racist theories encompass specific beliefs about nationality, language, psychology, intellect, religion, morality, vocation, class, gender, and sexuality, to name some significant and interrelated categories' (*Barbarous Play*, 10). Here class is positioned as one among many categories that inflect racial theories. But she comes close to making the point I press here when she suggests in the context of reading *The Changeling* that 'questions of status, rank, and their stability ... are closely linked to questions of race' (140). I would suggest that in early modern England, race is more than just 'linked' to status; it is the ideology that naturalizes such social distinctions.

For a compelling discussion of the connections between racism and 'class signification,' specifically racism's links to 'the aristocratic representation of the hereditary nobility as a superior "race,"' see Etienne Balibar, 'Class Racism,' in Etienne Balibar and Immanuel Wallerstein, eds., *Race, Nation, Class: Ambiguous Identities*, trans. Chris Turner (London and New York: Verso, 1991), 204–16, esp. 207.

20 For the association of social rank with the different lineages of Noah's offspring, see, for instance, Sir John Ferne, *Blazon of Gentrie* (London, 1586), 2–8; and see Dame Juliana Berners, *The Boke of Saint Albans ... Printed at St Albans ... in 1486*, ed. William Blades (London, 1881), fols. Ai[r] and Aii, both quoted in Mervyn James, 'English Politics and the Concept of Honour 1485–1642,' *Past & Present* Supplement 3 (1978): 1–92, esp. 64 and 3. Ruth Mazo Karras has demonstrated that such ideas were prevalent in medieval Scandinavian literature as well, where race was a property that described an elite person in opposition to a member of the underclass. In the thirteenth century, for instance, Saxo Grammaticus speaks of an enslaved king whose regal identity is discovered and described by a princess in the following terms: 'The shimmering glow of your eyes pronounces you the progeny of kings, not slaves. Your form reveals your race ... the handsomeness which graces you is a manifest token of your nobility. ... your visage testifies your true family, for in your gleaming countenance may be observed the magnificence of your ancestors ... your face reflects your innate rank.' Here race is equated with nobility of ancestry and high rank, and it names the 'natural,' physical difference of what we today would identify exclusively as a social identity. Karras goes on to show how such differences were developed still further in relation to colour-coding, with dark skin associated with labourers, 'ruddy skin' with the freeborn, and white skin with the nobility, without any correspondence to ethnic distinctions; see her *Slavery and Society in Medieval Scandinavia* (New Haven, CT: Yale UP, 1988), 56–7, as quoted

in Goldenberg, *Curse of Ham*, 118–19. Goldenberg notes that this tendency to emphasize a tripartite division of society in relation to complexion can be found in Old Norse literature and several other medieval texts from the ninth up to the fourteenth century. He refers to a similar practice in ancient India and Iran whereby different social classes were distinguished one from the other through association with different skin colours: white symbolized 'the priestly caste, red the warrior caste, and black the agriculturalists' (307 n.35).

21  As quoted in Leonard Tennenhouse, *Power on Display: The Politics of Shakespeare's Genres* (New York and London: Methuen, 1986), 36. The same definition of gentility – as those 'whom their blood and race doth make noble and known' – appears in John Cowell, *The Interpreter of Words and Terms ... First Publish'd by ... Dr. Cowel ... and Continu'd by Tho. Manley ...* (London, 1701), as quoted in James, 'English Politics,' 22. The original text was first published in 1607.

22  William Harrison, *The Description of England*, ed. Georges Edelen (Ithaca, NY: Cornell UP, 1968), 113.

23  For a discussion of how virtuous behaviour comes to be emphasized alongside bloodline as a defining principle of gentility across the sixteenth century, see James, 'English Politics,' 58–68. He associates this tendency with the rise of humanism and the introduction of the grammar school education.

24  Sir Thomas Elyot, *The Book Named the Governor* (1531), ed. S.E. Lehmberg (London: J.M. Dent, 1962), 14.

25  Gail Kern Paster, *Humoring the Body: Emotions and the Shakespearean Stage* (Chicago: U of Chicago P, 2005), 226.

26  As quoted in Whigham, *Ambition and Privilege*, 84.

27  Linda Levy Peck, 'The Mentality of a Jacobean Grandee,' in *The Mental World of the Jacobean Court*, ed. Linda Levy Peck (Cambridge: Cambridge UP, 1991), 148–68, esp. 163.

28  For an excellent reading of the social dynamics of service in this play, see Michael Neill, '"His Master's Ass": Slavery, Service, and Subordination in *Othello*,' in *Shakespeare and the Mediterranean*, ed. Tom Clayton, Susan Brock, and Vincente Forès (Newark: U of Delaware P, 2004), 215–29. See also his chapter 'Servant Obedience and Master Sins: Shakespeare and the Bonds of Service,' in *Putting History to the Question: Power, Politics, and Society in English Renaissance Drama* (New York: Columbia UP, 2000), 13–48. For an excellent study of the role of early modern drama in catalysing changes to servant/master relations, see Elizabeth J. Rivlin, 'Service, Imitation, and Social Identity in Renaissance Drama and Prose Fiction' (PhD diss., U of Wisconsin-Madison, 2004).

29  For medieval uses of *vilain* or *villein* in relation to social status, see Paul
    Freedman, *Images of the Medieval Peasant* (Stanford, CA: Stanford UP, 1999),
    10. Othello's invocation of the epithet 'honest' in relation to Iago may work
    similarly to denote his lower status; the *Oxford English Dictionary* suggests that
    it was often used as a 'vague epithet of appreciation or praise, esp. as used
    in a patronizing way to an inferior' (a.; 1c).

30  This is the important point that Emily C. Bartels makes in '*Othello* and
    Africa: Postcolonialism Reconsidered,' *William and Mary Quarterly* 1 (1997):
    45–64. In her essay 'Making More of the Moor: Aaron, Othello, and Renais-
    sance Refashionings of Race,' *Shakespeare Quarterly* 41, no. 4 (1990): 433–54,
    she comes still closer to the point I seek to make here when she argues that
    'Iago's terms of difference are politically incorrect and directly unspeakable
    at court' (450). She claims that Iago's challenge is to undercut the politi-
    cal status that Othello enjoys at court, which makes him an 'authorizing
    insider' and has the effect of keeping 'Iago in the margins of power' (451).
    The first of these essays is rewritten for her book *Speaking of the Moor: From
    Alcazar to* Othello (Philadelphia: U of Pennsylvania P, 2008).

31  For an excellent approach to the play that admirably resists such tenden-
    cies, see Bartels's introduction in *Speaking of the Moor*. Here she argues that
    the Moor is defined in early modern representations not by his presumed
    exoticism and outsider status but rather by his proximity to European cul-
    tures and polities.

32  Loomba's chapter on *Titus Andronicus* captures this insight at its close in
    arguing that 'for [Aaron], as much as for the white Romans, race is indeed
    lineage' (*Shakespeare, Race, and Colonialism*, 90), but this insight is not further
    developed. In my estimation, the centrality of lineage to early modern race
    demands greater attention.

33  I discuss these dynamics of the play at further length in my essay, 'Botanical
    Shakespeares: The Racial Logic of Plant Life in *Titus Andronicus*,' Special
    issue: 'Shakespeare and Science,' ed. Carla Mazzio, *South Central Review* 26,
    no. 1 (March 2009): 82–102.

34  Jonathan Goldberg, 'The Print of Goodness,' in *The Culture of Capital: Prop-
    erty, Cities, and Knowledge in Early Modern England*, ed. Henry S. Turner (New
    York and London: Routledge, 2002), 231–54, esp. 233.

35  Michel Foucault, *The History of Sexuality: An Introduction*, trans. Robert Hur-
    ley (London: Penguin, 1978), 147.

36  Foucault, *History of Sexuality*, 147. See also Uli Linke, *Blood and Nation: The
    European Aesthetics of Race* (Philadelphia: U of Pennsylvania P, 1999), esp.
    36–7.

37  See Peck, 'Mentality of a Jacobean Grandee,' Plate 23, which depicts John
    Speed's Military Map of 1603–4.

38 For the tendency visible in informal utterances throughout this period to compress intricate gradations of degree into a polarized opposition of gentle or 'better sort' as against common or 'meaner sort,' see Wrightson, 'Estates, Degrees, and Sorts,' 44–9.

39 As quoted in Keith Wrightson, *English Society, 1580–1660* (New Brunswick, NJ: Rutgers UP, 1982), 149–50.

40 For the compelling suggestion that this emphasis on landed identity so characteristic of the tragedies figures an archaic social order, see Jean Howard, 'Shakespeare, Geography, and the Work of Genre on the Early Modern Stage,' *Modern Language Quarterly* 64, no. 3 (2003): 299–322, esp. 314.

41 Wrightson, *English Society*, 27. See also Harold Perkin, *The Origins of Modern English Society*, 2d ed. (London and New York: Routledge, 2002), who argues that 'One's place in [the Old] society was wholly determined by the amount and kind of one's own property ... in post-feudal England status followed property' (38).

42 See 'Introduction. Grids of power: order, hierarchy and subordination in early modern society,' in *Negotiating Power in Early Modern Society*, ed. Michael J. Braddick and John Walter (Cambridge: Cambridge UP, 2001), 1–42, esp. 1 and 15.

43 Wrightson, 'The social order of early modern England,' 200–1, and 'Estates, Degrees, and Sorts,' 48–9. James makes a similar point when he observes: 'There could be no whole-hearted rejection of blood and lineage in a society for which this was still a central concept. But uncertainty about the status of heredity in relation to other aspects of honour increased, with a proneness to present honour, virtue and nobility as detachable from their anchorage in pedigree and descent' ('English Politics,' 59).

44 Anna Bryson, *From Courtesy to Civility: Changing Codes of Conduct in Early Modern England* (Oxford: Clarendon P, 1998), 73; see also Michael J. Braddick, 'Civility and Authority' in Armitage and Braddick, eds., 93–112, esp. 95.

45 The quotes from Hall and Speed are cited in the *OED* under the verb form of *degenerate*, definitions 2 and 6.

46 Sir James Perrot, *The Chronicle of Ireland, 1584–1608*, ed. Herbert Wood (Dublin: Stationery Office, 1933), 15. See also Jean Bodin, *Method for the Easy Comprehension of History*, ed. Beatrice Reynolds (New York: Columbia UP, 1945).

47 Peck, 'Mentality of a Jacobean Grandee,' 163.

48 See Juan Huarte, *The Examination of Men's Wits*, trans. Richard Carew (1594), ed. Carmen Rogers (Gainesville, FL: Scholars' Facsimiles & Reprints, 1959), 185–9.

49 As quoted in Hannaford, *Race*, 172–3.

50 Fredrickson, *Racism*, 47.

## 1. Blemished Bloodlines and *The Faerie Queene*, Book 2

1  This quote is taken from Fynes Moryson, *Shakespeare's Europe: A Survey of the Condition of Europe at the End of the 16th Century. Being unpublished chapters of Fynes Moryson's* Itinerary *(1617)*, ed. Charles Hughes, 2nd ed. (New York: Benjamin Blom, 1967), 208.

2  As quoted in Cyril Bentham Falls, *Elizabeth's Irish Wars* (New York: Barnes and Noble, 1970), 239.

3  According to Fynes Moryson, who served in Ireland as secretary to Lord Mountjoy, Irish 'lordes thus raysed never fayled to prove more pernitious Rebells, then they against whome they were supported by us. One instance shall serve for proofe of the Earle of Tyrone raysed by our State from the lowest degree, against Tirlogh Linnaghe, whome the Queen too long supported ... till he had all his opposites power in his hand, which he used farr worse then the other, or any of the Oneales before him'; see *Shakespeare's Europe*, 242. See also Hiram Morgan, *Tyrone's Rebellion: The Outbreak of the Nine Years' War in Tudor Ireland* (London: Royal Historical Society, 1993).

4  Sir John Davies, *A Discovery of the True Causes Why Ireland Was Never Entirely Subdued ...*, ed. James P. Myers Jr (Washington, DC: Catholic U of America P, 1988), 77.

5  For an overview of the struggles between English lord deputies and the Old English lords, see Ciaran Brady, *The Chief Governors: The Rise and Fall of Reform Government in Tudor Ireland, 1536–1588* (Cambridge: Cambridge UP, 1994).

6  For Sir Nicholas White's complaint to the Queen and an account of the rising tensions between the New English and Old English at large, see Nicholas Canny, 'Edmund Spenser and the Development of an Anglo-Irish Identity,' *Yearbook of English Studies* 13 (1983): 1–19, esp. 14.

7  For this description of the New English, see Richard A. McCabe, *Spenser's Monstrous Regiment: Elizabethan Ireland and the Poetics of Difference* (Oxford: Oxford UP, 2002), 128.

8  A recent attempt to explain the connections between *race* and *class* appears in the introduction to *Race in Early Modern England: A Documentary Companion*, ed. Ania Loomba and Jonathan Burton (Houndmills, UK, and New York: Palgrave, 2007), esp. 12–16. And yet, the translation of early modern terms such as *race, rank*, and *stock* into the modern term *class* seems problematic, not least for occluding the transgenerational and blood-based dynamics of birth, lineage, and genealogy so central to the period. The modern concept of *class*, for instance, does not rely on a notion of inherited disposition in the way that lineage and rank do. As a result, I retain the term *race* to describe the early modern notion of genealogical identity.

9 In the introduction to his edition of Spenser's *View of the Present State of Ireland* (London: E. Partridge, at the Scholartis Press, 1934), W.L. Renwick observes that by the time the complete *Faerie Queene* appeared in print on 20 January 1596, the same year he maintains that the *View* was in circulation, Spenser had had no fewer than sixteen years of 'regular experience in Irish affairs' (224). See also Andrew Hadfield's discussion of Ireland as the 'home' that Spenser nostalgically produces in 'Colin Clouts Come Home Again,' in *Edmund Spenser's Irish Experience: Wilde Fruit and Salvage Soyl* (Oxford: Clarendon Press, 1997), chap. 1, esp. 13–16. And see Julia Reinhard Lupton, 'Home-Making in Ireland: Virgil's Eclogue I and Book VI of *The Faerie Queene*,' *Spenser Studies* 8 (1990): 119–45.

10 Debora K. Shuger observes the force of these homologies in noting that 'the Irish tracts presuppose a direct relation between cultivating crops and people'; see her 'Irishmen, Aristocrats, and Other White Barbarians,' *Renaissance Quarterly* 50, no. 2 (1997): 494–525, esp. 508. Eamon Grennan, too, observes the pervasive use of 'the agricultural metaphor' in Spenser's *View*, noting that the tract imagines 'the Irish as being in a state of wild nature that needs cultivation to perfect it,' which he rightly suggests has rather 'sinister' implications; see 'Language and Politics: A Note on Some Metaphors in Spenser's *A View of the Present State of Ireland*,' *Spenser Studies* 3 (1982): 99–110, esp. 101 and 105.

11 Davies, *True Causes*, 70–1.

12 See the anonymous tract *Supplication of the Blood of the English* ..., edited by Willy Maley and Andrew Hadfield and published in *Analecta Hibernica* 36 (1995): 3–78, esp. 38. The full excerpt reads: 'Weedes they are O Queene, the naturall plants of theire owne soyle; the earth of Irland is their naturall mother, a stepdame to us: you can never soe cherishe us, what care soe ever you take about our plaintinge, unlesse you seeke to supplant them, or at the least to keepe them downe from theire full groweth, but that they will overshadowe us, but yt they will keepe the warmethe of the sonne from us.' For a discussion of this tract's 'radical uncertainly [*sic*] about ultimate claims,' see David J. Baker, '"Men to Monsters": Civility, Barbarism, and "Race" in Early Modern Ireland,' in *Writing Race Across the Atlantic World: Medieval to Modern*, ed. Phillip Beidler and Gary Taylor (New York and Houndmills, UK: Palgrave Macmillan, 2005), 153–69, esp. 158.

13 Moryson, *Shakespeare's Europe*, 209.

14 For these connections, see Christopher Ivic, 'Spenser and the Bounds of Race,' *Genre: Forms of Discourse and Culture* 32, no. 3 (1999): 142–73, esp. 143–4.

15 *Oxford English Dictionary*, race, sb., 26 and 6.

16 *OED, stock*, sb., 1a, 2a, 2b, and 4.

17 *OED, stock*, sb., 3, 3a, 3c, 3d, 3e.

18 The close association between the 'stock' of plants and human blood is captured in William Lawson's horticultural tract *A New Orchard and Garden* (London, 1618), where he observes that 'sap is like bloud in mans body, in which is the life' (24).

19 See John Florio, *A worlde of wordes, or Most copious and exact dictionarie in Italian and English* (London, 1598), 313 and 398.

20 In an unpublished essay entitled 'Unfixing race,' Kathryn Burns translates the following definition öf *race* from the 1611 publication of Sebastián de Covarrubias Horozco's *Tesoro de la lengua castellana y española,* ed. Martín de Riquer (Barcelona: S.A. Horta, 1989): 'The caste of purebred horses, which are marked with brands to distinguish them. Race in cloth [means] the coarse thread that is distinct from the other threads in the weave ... Race in lineage is understood to be bad, as to have some Moorish or Jewish race.' The Spanish reads: 'La casta de cavallos castizos, a los quales señalan con hierro para que sean conocidos. Raza en el paño, la hilaza que diferencia de los demás hilos de la trama ... Raza, en los linages se toma en mala parte, como tener alguna raza de more or judío' (896–7).

21 Born in London, Florio was of Anglo-Italian derivation but often referred to himself as an Englishman.

22 Edmund Spenser, dedication to Countess of Pembroke, *The Ruines of Time,* in *Yale Edition of the Shorter Poems of Edmund Spenser,* ed. William A. Oram (New Haven, CT: Yale UP, 1989), 232–61, esp. 230.

23 See Colin Kidd, *The Forging of Races: Race and Scripture in the Protestant Atlantic World, 1600–2000* (Cambridge: Cambridge UP, 2006), esp. chap. 3. See also Benjamin Braude, 'The Sons of Noah and the Construction of Ethnic and Geographical Identities in the Medieval and Early Modern Periods,' *William and Mary Quarterly* 54, no. 1 (1997): 103–42.

24 Michel de Montaigne, 'An Apology for Raymond Sebond,' trans. John Florio, in *Essays* (1603), ed. George Saintsbury, 3 vols. (New York: AMS Press, 1967), 2:297–8. In Donald M. Frame's translation found in the *Complete Essays of Montaigne* (Stanford, CA: Stanford UP, 1958), the translation reads: 'so that just as fruits are born different, and animals, men too are born more or less bellicose, just, temperate, and docile ... according to the influence of the place where they are situated – and take on a new disposition if you change their place, like trees' (433).

25 Jean Bodin, *Method for the Easy Comprehension of History,* trans. Beatrice Reynolds (New York: Columbia UP, 1945), 87 and 144.

26 For a fascinating discussion of plant generation, and how a writer like Sir

Thomas Browne celebrated the 'immutable quality' of plants, as against man who is 'lost in Degeneration,' see Marjorie Swann, '"Procreate Like Trees": Generation and Society in Thomas Browne's *Religio Medici*,' in *Engaging with Nature: Essays on the Natural World in Medieval and Early Modern Europe*, ed. Barbara A. Hanawalt and Lisa J. Kiser (Notre Dame, IL: Notre Dame UP, 2008), 137–54, esp. 145–6.

27  For a description of the Old English as having allowed themselves to submit to 'daily decay,' see 'Tract by Sir Thomas Smith on the Colonisation of Ards in County of Down' in the *Appendix* to George Hill, *An Historical Account of the MacDonnells of Antrim* (Belfast: Archer & Sons, 1873), 405–15, esp. 406.

28  As quoted in McCabe, *Spenser's Monstrous Regiment*, 182.

29  Robert Bartlett emphasizes the cultural aspect of biological terms when he notes 'while the language of race [in Medieval sources] – gens, natio, "blood," "stock," etc. – is biological, its medieval reality was almost entirely cultural'; see *The Making of Europe* (Princeton, NJ: Princeton UP, 1993), 197. Scholars have locked heads in disputing whether biology or culture determines the meanings of *race* at different moments, and whether this difference matters, but they also overlook the extent to which these two concepts and their relationship change over time. Part of my point here is to suggest that early modern culture did not oppose nature to culture in the way that modernity does but emphasized instead a dynamic exchange between them. But see Bruno Latour, *We Have Never Been Modern*, trans. Catherine Porter (Cambridge, MA: Harvard UP, 1993), for a deconstruction of this opposition even for modernity.

30  See *Sylva Sylvarum: Or, A Natural History. In Ten Centuries*, in *The works of Francis Bacon*, ed. Basil Montagu, 16 vols. (London: William Pickering, 1825–34), 4:246–7.

31  The same metaphors underpin discussions of raising, rearing, and educating children; see Rebecca Bushnell, *A Culture of Teaching: Early Modern Humanism in Theory and Practice* (Ithaca, NY: Cornell UP, 1996). In his own discussion of raising gentle children, the New English planter Lodowick Bryskett observes: 'if the seeds of vertue be not holpen with continuall culture, and care taken to pul up the vices which spring therewith ... they will over-grow and choke them' (*Discourse of Civill Life: Containing the Ethike part of Morall Philosophie. Fit for the instructing of a Gentleman in the course of a virtuous life* [London, 1606], 119). Bryskett's text is a translation of Giovanni Battista Cinthio Giraldi's *Tre dialoghi della vita civile*, which is the second, non-narrative part of his *De gli Hecatommithi* (Vinegia, 1566). Bryskett frames the dialogues with his own fictional account of a visit by nine friends to his home outside Dublin.

32  As such, the discourse of degeneration that so centrally informs New Eng-

lish representations of Ireland bears affinities to the language of 'turning Turk' that governed English exchanges with Muslim peoples insofar as both emphasize the potential for rapid transformation. For an introduction to what is now a vast body of criticism, see Daniel Vitkus, *Turning Turk: English Theater and the Multicultural Mediterranean, 1570–1630* (New York and Houndmills, UK: Palgrave Macmillan, 2003). See also Jane Hwang Degenhardt, *Islamic Conversion and Christian Resistance on the Early Modern Stage* (Edinburgh: Edinburgh UP, 2010). Consider the ideological overlap visible in Moryson's account of the situation in Ireland: 'For an English Troope of horse sent out of England commonly in a yeares space, was *turned* half into Irish' (*Shakespeare's Europe*, 242–3 [emphasis added]).

33  As excerpted by Loomba and Burton, *Race in Early Modern Europe*, 152–3.

34  In his essay 'Forms of Discrimination in Spenser's *A View of the Present State of Ireland*,' Willy Maley substantiates this view when he urges that 'postcolonial criticism can arguably both inform, and be informed by, early modern texts and contexts' (74), concluding that 'Spenser's strategy is one of displacement and deferral rather than an unexamined essentialising animosity' (89); see *Nation, State and Empire in English Renaissance Literature: Shakespeare to Milton* (New York and Houndmills, UK: Palgrave Macmillan, 2003). See also McCabe's discussion of the postcolonial concept of hybridity in the context of *Spenser* on page 140 of Spenser's *Monstrous Regiment*.

35  This quote is from Spenser, *View*, ed. Renwick, 58.

36  This phrase is from Moryson, *Shakespeare's Europe*, 215.

37  James Muldoon discusses these earlier observations of English degeneracy in his *Identity on the Medieval Irish Frontier: Degenerate Englishmen, Wild Irishmen, Middle Nations* (Gainesville, FL: UP of Florida, 2003). He does not, however, explore how this discourse relates to conceptions of rank and bloodline, discussing it exclusively in relation to national identity.

38  See Henry Thomas Riley, ed., *Chronicon a monacho sancti albani, Vol. I: A.D. 1272–1381* (London, 1863), 74–5, as quoted and translated in Emily Steiner, 'Commonalty and Literary Form in the 1370s and 80s,' in *New Medieval Literatures*, ed. David Lawton, Rita Copeland, and Wendy Scase, Vol. 6 (Oxford: Oxford UP, 2005), 199–222, esp. 207.

39  See *OED*, degenerate, v., 6.

40  McCabe, *Spenser's Monstrous Regiment*, 35.

41  The *OED* registers this sense of the word in defining it as 'the course, line, or path taken by a person or moving body' (sb., 5a).

42  Richard Helgerson, for instance, compares Spenser's epic with that of Tasso and concludes that the absolutist ideological tug of *Jerusalem Delivered* is quite distinct from the valorization of aristocratic privilege, in the form of an expansive romance ethos, that pervades Spenser's epic; see 'Tasso

on Spenser: The Politics of Chivalric Romance,' *Critical Essays on Edmund Spenser*, ed. Mihoko Suzuki (New York: G.K. Hall, 1996), 221–36. Elsewhere he describes the poem as invested in a 'Gothic ideology of renascent aristocratic power'; see *Forms of Nationhood: The Elizabethan Writing of England* (Chicago: U of Chicago P, 1992), 59.

This view has been challenged by Ivic, who points to Richard McCoy's discussion of Spenser's 'surprising skepticism' with regard to Elizabethan chivalry as an influence on his own thinking ('Spenser and the Bounds of Race,' 165–7, esp. n. 35); see also McCoy's *Rites of Knighthood: The Literature and Politics of Elizabethan England* (Berkeley, CA: U of California P, 1989). McCoy provides quite convincing evidence that Spenser was ambivalent toward the ideology of chivalry, which he attributes in part to his 'long residence in Ireland,' which 'literally set him apart from many of his contemporaries' (128). He sees this pattern in his shorter poems, where opportunities to praise his patrons are curiously qualified, as when he attacks 'mightie Peeres' in *The Tears of the Muses* as men who 'boast of Armes and Auncestrie' (quoted on 132) or when, in *Astrophel*, he 'subtly criticizes' the excesses of Sidney's chivalric pursuits in observing '(too hardie alas)' (as quoted on 151). He traces this pattern even in the epic poem, despite its status as 'one of the most successful symbolic acts of Elizabethan chivalry' (136). The poem's indebtedness to chivalric models, both political and aesthetic, does not translate for McCoy into its sanctioning of such ideologies. Rather, through analyses of Books 4 and 6, he traces the poem's critique of such political forms. I seek to extend that sort of reading to Book 2.

43 Shuger, 'Irishmen,' 510.
44 In note 105 to her essay, for instance, Shuger confesses: 'Only the unfinished final book of Spenser's epic romance seems remotely related to *A View*. Book VII has no crusading knights but instead on an Irish hill top unfurls the ancient pageant of the seasons, in which the annual cycle of georgic labors becomes, quite movingly, the privileged symbol of human participation in cosmic order' ('Irishmen,' 520).
45 This phrase famously appears in the 'Letter of the Authors expounding his *whole intention in the course of this worke ...*' which first appeared at the end of the 1590 edition of the poem; see *The Faerie Queene*, ed. A.C. Hamilton, text ed. Hiroshi Yamashita and Toshiyuki Suzuki (Edinburgh and London: Longman, 2001), 714. All future quotations are to this edition and will appear parenthetically in the text with reference to book, canto, stanza, and line number.
46 See *The Ethnological Notebooks of Karl Marx*, ed. Lawrence Krader (Assen: Van Gorcum, 1972), 305 and 362. See also the discussion of this phrase by Anthony W. Riley under the entry 'Marx & Spenser' in the *Spenser Encyclope-*

*dia*, gen. ed. A.C. Hamilton, ed. Donald Cheney and W.F. Blissett (Toronto: U of Toronto P, 1990).

47 See the classic argument by Lawrence Stone, *The Crisis of the Aristocracy, 1558–1641* (Oxford: Clarendon P, 1965).

48 Raleigh was knighted on 6 January 1585, the same year in which he received a sizeable estate in Munster, specifically in the counties of Waterford and Cork.

49 See Alexander C. Judson, *The Life of Edmund Spenser* (Baltimore: Johns Hopkins UP, 1945), 30–1.

50 For a detailed account of the letters pertaining to the disputed Kilcolman estate – which Lord Roche claimed as his own inheritance – see Ray Heffner, 'Spenser's Acquisition of Kilcolman,' *Modern Language Notes* 8 (1931): 493–8. Heffner concludes that Spenser challenged Roche's possession of some twenty-two ploughlands (roughly equal to four thousand acres), at times using force to do so. For another brief account of this conflict, see Raymond Jenkins, 'Spenser: The Uncertain Years 1584–1589,' *PMLA* 53 (1938): 350–62, esp. 359–60.

51 See Spenser, *Faerie Queene*, ed. Hamilton, textual note to 'Sir' on 157.

52 For a discussion of Spenser's commendatory poem to Battista Nanna's *Nennio, or A Treatise of Nobility: Wherein is Discoursed What True Nobilitie Is, with Such Qualities as Are required in a Perfect Gentleman* (1595) along similar lines, see Ivic, 'Spenser and the Bounds of Race,' 166–7.

53 Maley, *Nation, State, and Empire*, 75.

54 I include myself in this number, as my earliest interest in Book 2 concerned its figuration of the Irish as a humorally distempered population; see my article 'Spenser, Race, and Ire-land,' *English Literary Renaissance* 32, no. 1 (2002): 85–117.

55 For a strong statement of this view, see Maley, 'Forms of Discrimination in Spenser's *A View of the Present State of Ireland* (1596; 1633): From Dialogue to Silence,' in *Nation, State, and Empire*, 63–91.

56 See Spenser, *View*, ed. Renwick, 195.

57 Willy Maley, *Salvaging Spenser: Colonialism, Culture and Identity* (London: Macmillan, 1997; New York: St Martin's Press, 1997), 98. Maley goes on to argue that 'Ireland dominates the poem in the way that the poet would have wished his sovereign to dominate Ireland'; he concludes that 'this dramatically alters the sense of a reading of the poem, making it more politically critical of English imperialist efforts than has hitherto been appreciated' (98). See also McCabe, *Spenser's Monstrous Regiment*, which uncovers engagement in the politics of Ireland in books usually severed from this context, particularly in the books devoted to holiness, temperance, and courtesy.

58 See McCabe, *Spenser's Monstrous Regiment*, chap. 1. He points to Sir John Davies's account of a 'fraternity of men at arms called the Brotherhood of St. George,' consisting entirely of Catholic Old English palesmen (see Davies, *True Causes*, 101).

59 Stephen Greenblatt, 'To Fashion a Gentleman: Spenser and the Destruction of the Bower of Bliss,' in *Renaissance Self-Fashioning: From More to Shakespeare* (Chicago: U of Chicago P, 1980). See also David Read, *Temperate Conquests: Spenser and the Spanish New World* (Detroit, MI: Wayne State UP, 2000).

60 For a compelling discussion of these tensions, see Nicholas Canny, 'The Permissive Frontier: The Problems of Social Control in English Settlements in Ireland and Virginia 1550–1650,' in *The Westward Enterprise: English Activities in Ireland, the Atlantic, and America 1480–1650*, ed. K.R. Andrews, N.P. Canny, and P.E.H. Hair (Detroit, MI: Wayne State UP, 1979), 17–44.

61 Ann Laura Stoler, '"In Cold Blood": Hierarchies of Credibility and the Politics of Colonial Narratives,' *Representations* 37 (1992): 151–89. In analysing the archive of colonial materials about East Sumatra in the late nineteenth century, and noting the surprising discrepancies among colonists as to the cause for rising violence in the Dutch colony, Stoler concludes: 'The "historic turn" in anthropology has been marked by a new contextualizing impulse, one challenging the naturalized ideologies underwriting colonial representations of authority ... [W]e often invoke these texts ironically, assured of the imperial, racist, and sexist logics in which their authors operated. We are able to read them as collective representations because we expect a comfortable fit between a dominant discourse and colonial agents.' And yet, she finds the textual field much more complex, identifying 'a more problematic correspondence between colonial rhetoric and its agents on the ground. Colonial lexicons were unevenly appropriated, sometimes constraining what agents of empire thought, elsewhere delimiting the political idioms in which they talked' (183).

62 According to the *OED*, early meanings of *temperance* include 'the body's state of being balanced, tempered, proportionately mingled' (sb., 3b).

63 For these results, I have consulted the *Comprehensive Concordance to the Faerie Queene 1590*, ed. Hiroshi Yamashita, Masatsugu Matsuo, Toshiyuki Suzuki, and Haruo Sato (Tokyo: Kenyusha, 1990). My count included the words *blood, bloodguiltinesse, bloodguiltnesse, bloody,* and *bloodie.* Interestingly, Book 2 is the only one of the poem's first three books to feature any variant of the word *bloodguiltinesse,* suggesting its unique concern with blood grown awry. However, Book 1 has more hits for variants of the word *blood* than does *FQ* 2 – at eighty – but this number drops to forty-seven for Book 3.

64 See the compelling discussion of Verdant's relation to his environment in

the introduction to *Environment and Embodiment in Early Modern England,* ed.
Mary Floyd-Wilson and Garrett A. Sullivan Jr (Houndmills, UK, and New
York: Palgrave Macmillan, 2007), 1–3.

65  For a fascinating discussion of the description of *Hamlet*'s Pyrrhus as embodying the details of heraldic insignia, see Margreta de Grazia, Hamlet *without
Hamlet* (Cambridge: Cambridge UP, 2007), 94. De Grazia refers to John
Guillim's *A Display of Heraldrie* (London, 1611) for details on these intricate
markings.

66  For a good overview of such readings, see the entry for 'Amavia, Mortdant,
Ruddymane' by Carol Kaske in *The Spenser Encyclopedia.* See also A.D.S.
Fowler, 'The Image of Mortality: *The Faerie Queene,* II.i–ii,' *Huntington Library
Quarterly* 24, no. 2 (1961): 91–110.

67  This locution belongs to Sir William Herbert who boasts 'I have little cause
to think myself blemished by my blood being the heir male of that Earl that
hath this day living nine earls and barons descended out of his body'; see
the introduction to his account of Ireland titled *Croftus, Sive, De Hibernia
Liber,* ed. Arthur Keaveny and John A. Madden (Dublin: Irish Manuscripts
Commission, 1992), ix.

68  See 'Colin Clouts Come Home Againe,' in *Yale Edition,* 530–2, ll. 104–55.
See also the entries 'Bregog, Mulla' and 'Fanchin, Molanna' by Shohachi
Fukuda in the *Spenser Encylopedia.*

69  For a reading of the fountain in exclusively theological terms – as a symbol
of baptismal regeneration, see Fowler, 'Image of Mortality.' He also discusses the association of Faunus with concupiscence throughout the Renaissance and, specifically, in emblems (101).

70  Spenser, *The Ruines of Time,* l. 56.

71  Davies often uses this word to describe Old English settlers; see *True Causes,*
73, 75, and 144.

72  Spenser, *View,* ed. Renwick, 24, 86, and 22.

73  Spenser, *View,* ed. Renwick, 84 and 86.

74  The words 'reare' and 'reard' appear repeatedly in this episode; see
2.1.45.1; 2.1.46.3; 2.1.61.5; and 2.2.40.6.

75  Spenser, *View,* ed. Renwick, 38–9.

76  Spenser, *View,* ed. Renwick, 48.

77  For a discussion of Guyon's status as an 'avenger of blood,' see Hugh
MacLachlan 'The "carelesse heauens": A Study of Revenge and Atonement in
*The Faerie Queene,'Spenser Studies* 1 (1980): 135–61, esp. 143. MacLachlan substantiates my reading of Guyon's paternal surrogacy insofar as he notes that
the burial scene establishes Guyon as 'a kind of godfather' to Ruddymane,
since it witnesses the 'blood covenant' he makes on the child's behalf (143).

78  See Bryskett, *Discourse of Civill Life*, fols. 189, 182, 196, and 201.

79  The voice-over for Spenser reads: 'For sure I am, that it is not unknowne vnto you, that I have already vndertaken a work [tending] to the same effect, which is in heroical verse, under the title of a Faerie Queene, to represent all the moral virtues, assigning to euery vertue, a Knight to be the patron and defender of the same: in whose actions and feates of armes and chiualry, the operations of that vertue, whereof he is the protector, are to be expressed, and the vices & vnruly appetites that oppose themselues against the same, to be beate downe & ouercome' (Bryskett, *Discourse of Civill Life*, 26–7).

80  Bryskett, *Discourse of Civill Life*, 74–5.

81  For an excellent collection of essays on this topic, see Christopher Ivic and Grant Williams, eds., *Forgetting in Early Modern English Literature and Culture: Lethe's Legacies* (London: Routledge, 2004).

82  Moryson, *Shakespeare's Europe*, 220.

83  Davies, *True Causes*, 185.

84  For the significance of the transference of armour from father to son in burial rites, see Peter Stallybrass and Ann Rosalind Jones, 'Of ghosts and garments: the materiality of memory on the Renaissance Stage,' in *Renaissance Clothing and the Materials of Memory* (Cambridge: Cambridge UP, 2000), 245–68.

85  *Supplication*, 33–4 and 19.

86  See Brady, *Chief Governors*, 25. For further details, see Brendan Bradshaw, *The Irish Constitutional Revolution of the Sixteenth Century* (Cambridge: Cambridge UP, 1979), 195.

87  Brady, *Chief Governors*, 72.

88  See Sir Henry Sidney, *A Viceroy's Vindication?: Henry Sidney's Memoir of Service in Ireland, 1556–1578*, ed. Ciaran Brady (Cork, Ireland: Cork UP, 2002), 54, 87.

89  The early modern word *erased* often appears in contracted form as *razed* or *rased* in early modern texts; see, for instance, William Camden's discussion of the city of Verlame, which he notes 'was rased and destroyed by the Britains' during the reign of Boadicea (*Britain or A Chorographical Description of the Most flourishing Kingdomes, England, Scotland, and Ireland* ..., trans. Philemon Holland [London, 1610], 408–9). Spenser, too, plays on the pun, using it, in effect, to emphasize his claim that races are hardly indelible inscriptions. He does this famously with reference to Verdant of Canto XII, when he describes how 'his braue shield, full of old moniments, / Was fowly ra'st, that none the signes might see' (2.12.80.3–4). Elsewhere, in his poem *The Ruines of Time*, the spirit of Verlame wonders why she grieves 'that my

remembrance quite is raced' (240, l. 177). If the noble markings of race can be so readily 'ra'st,' Spenser suggests, they may be an overvalued form of cultural currency.

90  Sidney, *Viceroy's Vindication?*, 121 (emphasis added). For Grey's words, see McCabe, *Spenser's Monstrous Regiment*, 29.

91  See Moryson, *Shakespeare's Europe*, 204, 212, and 196. McCabe argues that this tendency was popularized by the 'New English partisan John Hooker in his contributions to Holinshed' (*Spenser's Monstrous Regiment*, 35) and suggests that it was a frequent practice both for Sidney and Grey.

92  See Davies, *True Causes*, 156.

93  The quote is from Harry Berger Jr, 'The Chronicles: Temperance in History and Myth,' in *Allegorical Temper: Vision and Reality in Book II of Spenser's* Faerie Queene (New Haven, CT: Yale UP, 1957; rpt. 1967), chap. 4, esp. 110.

94  Berger, 'Chronicles,' 105.

95  Berger, 'Chronicles,' 103.

96  Spenser, *View*, ed. Renwick, 3.

97  For a reading of this canto as translating the theme of distemperance to the political realm, see Joan Warchol Rossi, '"Britons moniments": Spenser's Definition of Temperance in History,' *English Literary Renaissance* 15 (1985): 42–58.

98  Davies, *True Causes*, 172 (emphasis added). Davies's language makes explicit that to be 'raced' in the early modern period was to be 'marked' with noble inscriptions, and that to lack such markings was the condition of abjection.

99  This is how Hamilton glosses the line at 2.10.37.1–2.

100  See the detailed analysis of source materials for this history in Carrie Anna Harper, 'The Sources of the British Chronicle History in Spenser's *Faerie Queene*' (PhD diss., Bryn Mawr College, 1910). She observes, 'Spenser also adds details, such as the gathering of the princes to choose Dunwallo, and Dunwallo's title, the 'Numa of great Britany' (94).

101  Spenser, *View*, ed. Renwick, 87.

102  Moryson, *Shakespeare's Europe*, 222; and Davies, *True Causes*, 184.

103  Spenser, *View*, ed. Renwick, 84.

104  Davies, *True Causes*, 151 and 154.

105  Moryson, *Shakespeare's Europe*, 228 and 196–7. In his word 'yoke,' we might hear some of the earliest soundings of the critique of the 'Norman yoke' that would spur the English Civil War. It is fascinating to consider how the colonization of Ireland – and the racial upheaval that it produced – set the stage for this subsequent phase of English history.

106  Beacon, *Solon His Follie, or, A politique discourse touching the reformation of*

*commonweales conquered, declined or corrupted*, ed. Clare Carroll and Vincent Carey (Binghamton, NY: Medieval and Renaissance Texts, 1996), 100.

107  See Spenser, *View*, ed. Renwick, 18.

108  Moryson, *Shakespeare's Europe*, 198.

109  Spenser, *View*, ed. Renwick, 40.

110  Shuger, 'Irishmen,' 515; Sidney, *Viceroy's Vindication?*, 99.

111  Moryson, *Shakespeare's Europe*, 196.

112  Shuger, 'Irishmen,' 520, n. 105.

113  See Hamilton's gloss to Proem to Book 2, 5.8.

114  See the entry for *faeries* by Hamilton et al. in the *Spenser Encyclopedia*.

115  Bryskett, *Discourse of Civill Life*, 7 and 12.

116  Spenser, *Tears of the Muses*, 273, l. 94; and 'Colin Clouts Come Home Again,' 546, l. 538. For a discussion of Spenser's poetry in relation to these presumed familial connections, see Judson, 1–7.

## 2. Uncouth Milk and the Irish Wet Nurse

1  See 'The Historie of England,' in Raphael Holinshed, *The Chronicles of England, Scotland, and Ireland*, 2d ed., 6 vols. (1587; rpt. London: J. Johnson, 1807–8), 1:500. This episode is discussed by Jodi Mikalachki in *The Legacy of Boadicea: Gender and Nation in Early Modern England* (London and New York: Routledge, 1998), particularly in her chapter 'The Savage Breast,' 129–39. Here she situates 'this graphic historical account of breast mutilation in the context of conflicted early modern attitudes to maternal nature and nurture,' specifically fears about 'non-nurturing mothers' (135) and female rule. I aim to situate it in the context of colonization, and the anxieties about bloodlines that transplantation occasioned.

2  See Holinshed, *Chronicles*, 3:20 and 34; the passage was inserted by Abraham Fleming in the 1587 edition. For a comprehensive discussion of this incident as it relates to Shakespeare's Henriad and the emasculating of the Welsh, see Jean E. Howard and Phyllis Rackin, *Engendering a Nation: A Feminist Account of Shakespeare's English Histories* (London and New York: Routledge, 1997), chap. 11, esp. 168–72. While Phyllis Rackin performed an invaluable early reading of this passage, if not *the* earliest reading, in her *Stages of History: Shakespeare's English Chronicles* ([Ithaca, NY: Cornell UP, 1990], 170–4), endless reiterations of this textual moment, too numerous to cite here, have appeared in criticism ever since, demonstrating the extent to which this moment speaks to our own contemporary paradigms, which conceive of conquest and its reversals almost exclusively through reference to the male body, as phallic penetration or castration.

3 The classic study of gender and conquest is Louis Montrose, 'The Work of Gender in the Discourse of Discovery,' *Representations* 33 (1992): 1–41. See also the work of Anne McClintock, *Imperial Leather: Race, Gender and Sexuality in the Colonial Contest* (New York and London: Routledge, 1995).

4 For the relation between representations of ancient Britain and colonial initiatives, see Andrew Hadfield, 'Bruited abroad: John White and Thomas Harriot's colonial representations of ancient Britain,' in *British Identities and English Renaissance Literature*, ed. Willy Maley and David J. Baker (Cambridge: Cambridge UP, 2002), 159–77; see also his 'Briton and Scythian: Tudor Representations of Irish Origins,' *Irish Historical Studies* 28 (1993): 390–408.

5 For discussion of the humoral body's compellingly porous boundaries, see Gail Kern Paster, *The Body Embarrassed: Drama and the Disciplines of Shame in Early Modern England* (Ithaca, NY: Cornell UP, 1993), and her *Humoring the Body: Emotions and the Shakespearean Stage* (Chicago: U of Chicago P, 2004); Mary Floyd-Wilson and Garrett A. Sullivan Jr, eds., *Environment and Embodiment in Early Modern England* (New York and Houndmills, UK: Palgrave Macmillan, 2007), and 'Embodiment and Environment in Early Modern Drama and Performance,' a special issue of *Renaissance Drama* 35 (2006); and Mary Floyd-Wilson, *English Ethnicity and Race in Early Modern Drama* (Cambridge: Cambridge UP, 2003).

6 See, for instance, Glenn Hooper, 'Unsound Plots: Culture and Politics in Spenser's *View of the Present State of Ireland*,' *Eire-Ireland* 32 (1997): 117–36. He discusses 'the trope of the unnatural mother' in New English tracts on Ireland (130–2). So, too, Christopher Highley has noted that 'The body of the Gaelic woman with its nourishing and corrupting powers was a special site of English anxieties'; see his *Shakespeare, Spenser, and the Crisis in Ireland* (Cambridge: Cambridge UP, 1997), 102.

7 'The Description of Scotland,' in Holinshed, *Chronicles*, 5:24. William Harrison here translates into English the Scottish translation by John Bellenden of the original Latin by Hector Boetius. Bellenden's translation says 'thay held that thair barnis war degenerat fra thair nature and kynd, gif thay war nurist with uncouth mylk'; for a complete transcription of this passage and for analysis of how Harrison's translation alters its source, see A.R. Braunmuller's introduction to the New Cambridge Shakespeare edition of *Macbeth* (Cambridge: Cambridge UP, 1997), 38. For a discussion of the masculine force still legible in this act of breastfeeding, see Phyllis Rackin, 'Dating Shakespeare's Women,' *Shakespeare Jahrbuch* 134 (1998): 29–43. See also her *Shakespeare and Women* (Oxford: Oxford UP, 2005).

8 R.V. Schnucker quotes William Gouge as saying that wet-nursing was the

norm in 19 out of 20 instances in the seventeenth century; see 'The English
Puritans and Pregnancy, Delivery and Breast Feeding,' *History of Childhood Quarterly* 1 (1973–4): 637–58, esp. 637–8. For common aristocratic
use of wet nurses, see Dorothy McLaren, 'Marital Fertility and Lactation,
1570–1720,' in *Women in English Society, 1500–1800*, ed. Mary Prior (London:
Methuen, 1985), 22–53, esp. 27–8. See also the discussion in Paster, *Body
Embarrassed*, 199–208.

9 Jacques Guillemeau, *The Nursing of Children* (London, 1612), sig. Ii4ᵛ.

10 See Valerie Fildes, *Breasts, Bottles, and Babies: A History of Infant Feeding* (Edinburgh: Edinburgh UP, 1986), 169. See also her *Wet Nursing: A History from
Antiquity to the Present* (Oxford: Blackwell, 1988).

11 See Fildes's chapter 'Wet Nursing: The Ideal Wet Nurse: Medical Ideas and
Opinions' in her *Breasts*. See also Guillemeau's chapter 'Of a Nurse, and
what election, and choice ought to be made of her' and the section on this
same topic in *The birth of mankinde, otherwise named The Womans Booke* (London, 1598).

12 See Sir Thomas Elyot, *The Book Named the Governor*, ed. S.E. Lehmberg (London: J.M. Dent, 1962), 15. See also Rebecca Bushnell, *A Culture of Teaching:
Early Modern Humanism in Theory and Practice* (Ithaca, NY: Cornell UP, 1996),
esp. chap. 3.

13 Lodowick Bryskett, *Discourse of Civill Life: Containing the Ethike part of Morall
Philosophie. Fit for the instructing of a Gentleman in the course of a virtuous life*
(London, 1606), 91 and 51. Bryskett's connections to Spenser were extensive, as he was secretary to the Council of Munster and employed Spenser as
his deputy. If the text is complicit in actively encouraging a kind of upward
mobility on the part of 'mean' gentlemen, by suggesting they can achieve
the 'same virtues' as the nobility, it does not extend these privileges to all.
Compellingly, an 'apothecary' – the one merchant present for the first discussion of virtue – does not return to the discussion on the second day. We
are told his absence is due to the fact that the discussion of virtue does not
provide 'profit to his shop' (92).

14 Bryskett, *Discourse of Civill Life*, 52–3 and 50.

15 For Erasmus's extreme views on wet-nursing, as compared with many other
humanists, see Fildes, *Wet Nursing*, 68.

16 Erasmus, 'The New Mother' (1526), in *The Colloquies of Erasmus*, trans. Craig
R. Thompson (Chicago: U of Chicago P, 1965), 267–85, esp. 273 and 280.

17 Laurent Joubert, *Popular Errors* (c. 1578), trans. and anno. Gregory David de
Rocher (Tuscaloosa: U of Alabama P, 1989), 192–4.

18 For a discussion of this fantasy, and the considerable obstacles that it faced,
see Valeria Finucci's introduction to the collection of essays *Generation and*

*Degeneration: Tropes of Reproduction in Literature and History from Antiquity to Early Modern Europe*, ed. Valeria Finucci and Kevin Brownlee (Durham, NC: Duke UP, 2001), 1–16.

19 For a discussion of the social body in these Bakhtinian terms, see Peter Stallybrass and Allon White, *The Politics and Poetics of Transgression* (Ithaca, NY: Cornell UP, 1986). See also Mikhail Bakhtin, *Rabelais and His World*, trans. Helene Iswolsky (Bloomington: Indiana UP, 1984).

20 For the various stages of blood's concoction, see Paster's chapter 'Laudable Blood: Bleeding, Difference, and Humoral Embarrassment' in *Body Embarrassed*, 64–112, esp. 71; and for breast milk as concocted uterine blood, see 194. See also Paster's discussion of the class-anxieties associated with wet-nursing in her chapter 'Quarreling with the Dug, or I am Glad you Did Not Nurse Him' from the same book, 215–80.

21 Guillemeau, *Nursing of Children*, sig. Ii2.

22 Guillemeau, *Nursing of Children*, sig. Ii4.

23 Joubert, *Popular Errors*, 193.

24 Braunmuller, introduction to *Macbeth*, 38. Rachel Trubowitz makes a similar point in her article '"But Blood Whitened": Nursing Mothers and Others in Early Modern Britain,' in *Maternal Measures: Figuring Caregiving in the Early Modern Period*, ed. Naomi J. Miller and Naomi Yavneh (Aldershot, UK, and Burlington, VT: Ashgate, 2000), 82–101; here she argues that 'the affective ties between nurse and child thus had the potential to generate strangeness and strangers, to interrupt the genealogical transmission of identity, and so to tarnish a family's good name and disrupt the hereditary transmission of properties and titles' (85). She also suggests that the 'pollution of blood-lines' was another potential side effect of wet-nursing, reading discussions of 'complexions' in these accounts as indicative of an emergent dichotomy between the 'white' and 'dark' breast. I, too, wish to emphasize the physical connections produced by the child's act of suckling what is, in effect, a stranger's blood. But I also would like to stress the humoral resonance to the term 'complexion,' a term not easily reducible to subsequent racial polarities of white and black. In giving her milk to a suckling child, the wet nurse is thought to convey through it her humoral complexion – the precise balance of humoral fluids characteristic of her own body; she thereby 'conceives' the child anew in her own image and undoes the physical inheritance passed from the parents to the child. By emphasizing the 'humoral' referent to the term 'complexion,' I wish to retrieve the complexity of this earlier embodied discourse without too hastily collapsing it into an emergent racial discourse grounded in skin colour. The early modern moment records a less rigid account of difference, emphasizing the body's internal

temperature and degree of liquidity alongside external coloration as indicators of its ruling 'complexion' and recognizing a fundamental fungibility of such complexions.

25 Fildes, *Breasts*, 189.

26 M. Steeven Guazzo, *Civile Conversation*, trans. George Pettie and Bartholomew Young, 2 vols. (New York: AMS Press, 1967), 1.47–8. Willy Maley's documentation of a meeting of New English leaders to hear a reading of Lodowick Bryskett's translation of Cinthio's *Tre dialoghi della vita civile* suggests that literature on civil life by authors like Guazzo might have been the cornerstone for New English conceptions of civility and barbarity; see Maley, *Salvaging Spenser: Colonialism, Culture and Identity* (London: Macmillan, 1997), 68–72.

27 The radical potential of wet-nursing to figure a breach of bloodlines is indicated by Queen Anne's condemnation of the practice: 'Will I let my child, the child of a king, suck the milk of a subject and mingle the royal blood with the blood of a servant?'; quoted in Marilyn Yalom, *A History of the Breast* (New York: Ballantine Books, 1997), 85.

28 For an analysis of the threatening power of Irish wombs in the context of a discussion of *Edward III*, see Patricia A. Cahill, 'Nation Formation and the English History Plays,' in *A Companion to Shakespeare's Works: The Histories*, ed. Richard Dutton and Jean E. Howard (Oxford: Blackwell, 2003), 70–93, esp. 77–83.

29 The best treatments of the gendering of Ireland include Ann Rosalind Jones and Peter Stallybrass, 'Dismantling Irena: The Sexualizing of Ireland in Early Modern England,' in *Nationalisms and Sexualities*, ed. Andrew Parker et al. (New York and London: Routledge, 1992), 157–71; Clare Carroll, *Circe's Cup: Cultural Transformations in Early Modern Ireland* (Notre Dame, IL: U of Notre Dame P, 2001), esp. chaps. 2 and 3; and Sheila T. Cavanagh, '"The fatal destiny of that land": Elizabethan Views of Ireland,' in *Representing Ireland: Literature and the Origins of Conflict, 1534–1660*, ed. Brendan Bradshaw, Andrew Hadfield, and Willy Maley (Cambridge: Cambridge UP, 1993), 116–31.

30 For this formulation, see Norbert Elias, *The History of Manners* (1939), vol. 1 of *The Civilizing Process*, trans. Edmund Jephcott (New York: Pantheon, 1978).

31 Fynes Moryson, *An Itinerary*, 4 vols. (Glasgow: James MacLehose and Sons, 1907), 4:196, 201.

32 Gail Kern Paster provides an interesting context for viewing English consternation at the freedom Irish women enjoyed during delivery in arguing that for English women the birthing period involved various conscriptions of freedom, presumably designed to protect her excessively 'open' (because

pregnant) body from external 'invasions'; see her chapter 'Complying with the Dug: Narratives of Birth and the Reproduction of Shame' in her *Body Embarrassed*, 163–214.

33 Moryson, 'The Irish Sections of Fynes Moryson's Unpublished *Itinerary*,' ed. Graham Kew, *Analecta Hibernica* 37 (1998): 1–137, esp. 108. David Dickson argues in his article 'No Scythians Here: Women and Marriage in Seventeenth-Century Ireland,' in *Women in Early Modern Ireland*, ed. Margaret MacCurtain and Mary O'Dowd (Edinburgh: Edinburgh UP, 1991), 223–35, that although much of what the New English wrote on the Irish was derivative of medieval ethnography, as from Giraldus Cambrensis, the details pertaining to the reproductive facility and fecundity of Irish women first appears in Camden, Spenser, and Moryson.

In analysing the appropriation of women's reproductive power for the colonialist project in the context of the West Indies in her chapter '"Some Could Suckle Over Their Shoulder": Male Travelers, Female Bodies, and the Gendering of Racial Ideology,' Jennifer L. Morgan convincingly argues that 'indigenous women bore an enormous symbolic burden as writers from Walter Ralegh [*sic*] to Edward Long employed them to mark metaphorically the symbiotic boundaries of European national identities and white supremacy' (*Labouring Women: Reproduction and Gender in New World Slavery* [Philadelphia: U of Pennsylvania P, 2004], 14). I differ with Morgan only in that I find anachronistic her assertion of 'white supremacy' at a time when the categories of 'white' and 'black' were anything but stabilized into a binary opposition. By framing her analysis in terms rooted in skin colour, she excludes the Irish from participation in the category of 'indigenous women,' narrowing the possible meaning of that phrase to women of colour. However, the discourse she traces with regard to the West Indies, which describes the African female as barbaric by virtue of her reproductive excess, similarly describes the discourse occurring simultaneously in Ireland, where skin colour was clearly not the operative difference. See her note 52 for a description of childbirth in Guinea that parallels almost exactly the account Moryson here gives.

34 As quoted in Cavanagh in '"The fatal destiny of that land,"' 123.

35 See Moryson, 'Irish Sections,' esp. 111. For the construction of women generally as open and 'leaky,' see Gail Kern Paster's chapter 'Leaky Vessels: The Incontinent Women of City Comedy' in her *Body Embarrassed*. For early modern investments in enclosing the grotesque/open female body, see also Peter Stallybrass, 'Patriarchal Territories: The Body Enclosed,' in *Rewriting the Renaissance: The Discourses of Sexual Difference in Early Modern Europe*, ed. Margaret W. Ferguson, Maureen Quilligan, and Nancy J. Vickers (Chicago: U of Chicago P, 1986), 123–42.

36 See Bakhtin, *Rabelais and His World*, 26.

37 Nicholas P. Canny, *The Elizabethan Conquest of Ireland: A Pattern Established, 1565–76* (Hassocks: Harvester Press, 1976), 136.

38 Edmund Spenser, *A View of the Present State of Ireland*, ed. W.L. Renwick (London: Eric Partridge Ltd. At the Scholartis P, 1934), 88. Andrew Murphy provides the only published account to my knowledge of how this passage constructs the Irish as physically, as well as culturally, at a remove from the English. As he observes, 'in the case of the child suckled by a native Irish wetnurse, a significant component of the 'Temperature of the bodye' is native Irish and, as such, physically contributes an Irish component to the composition of the child's mind' (75); see his *'But the Irish Sea Betwixt Us': Ireland, Colonialism, and Renaissance Literature* (Lexington: UP of Kentucky, 1999). My own reading, while independent of Murphy's, will build on this observation. For an analysis of how this passage relates to linguistic contamination, see Jacqueline T. Miller's excellent article 'Mother Tongues: Language and Lactation in Early Modern Literature,' *English Literary Renaissance* 27, no. 2 (1997): 177–96.

39 I emphasize the word *complexion* to point up its early and, at the time of Spenser's writing, still very much operational meaning in humoral theory to denote the body's inner disposition or temperament. Although related to the external colouration of the body, it is not reducible to such colouration in the early modern period.

40 The phrase 'cultural degeneration' recurs in Richard McCabe's otherwise excellent book *Spenser's Monstrous Regiment: Elizabethan Ireland and the Poetics of Difference* (Oxford: Oxford UP, 2002), esp. 4 and 35. The problem with this formulation is that it seems to posit a firm divide between 'culture' and 'nature' for the early modern period, in part as a function of the form of these modern concepts. By contrast, I demonstrate throughout that what makes early modern 'race-thinking' so different from its modern versions is its emphasis on the interpenetration of these two concepts, which has the effect of granting that racial identity can be undone and remade through processes that we no longer perceive to have any relation to 'physical' or 'biological' or 'racial' identity.

41 Richard Beacon, *Solon His Follie, or, A politique discourse touching the reformation of common-weales conquered, declined or corrupted*, ed. Clare Carroll and Vincent Carey (Binghamton, NY: Medieval and Renaissance Texts, 1996), 102.

42 Fynes Moryson uses this word to describe those who have fallen under the power of great Old English overlords; see *Shakespeare's Europe: A Survey of the Condition of Europe at the End of the 16th Century. Being unpublished chapters of Fynes Moryson's* Itinerary *(1617)*, ed. Charles Hughes, 2nd ed. (New York: Benjamin Blom, 1967), 198 and 227.

43 Compellingly, David Baker discusses the image of Irish women draining, by sucking, the bosoms of Englishmen in the anonymous tract *Supplication of the Blood of the English*. The passage reads 'Shee that at night suckes from yo*re* bosome what soever the store house of yo*re* harte containeth, laboreth in the morninge (as if she were w*th* childe) until she have delivered it' (as quoted in '"Men to Monsters": Civility, Barbarism, and "Race" in Early Modern Ireland,' in *Writing Race Across the Atlantic World: Medieval to Modern*, ed. Phillip A. Beidler and Gary Taylor [New York and Houndmills, UK: Palgrave Macmillan, 2005], 153–69, esp. 161).

44 Moryson, 'Irish Sections,' 108.

45 Moryson, *Shakespeare's Europe*, 196.

46 Fynes Moryson, 'Manners and Customs of Ireland,' excerpted in *Illustrations of Irish History and Topography, Mainly of the Seventeenth Century*, ed. C. Litton Falkiner (London and New York: Longmans, Green, and Co., 1904), 310–25, esp. 318–19.

47 Davies, *True Causes*, 166 and 170.

48 Davies, *True Causes*, 166.

49 Moryson, *Shakespeare's Europe*, 200.

50 Spenser, *View*, ed. Renwick, 150–2. See Debora Shuger's excellent study of Spenser's disdain for the 'overmighty subject' in 'Irishmen, Aristocrats, and Other White Barbarians,' *Renaissance Quarterly* 50 (1997): 494–525.

51 Spenser, *View*, ed. Renwick, 148. Davies, *True Causes*, discusses the royal bloods of Ireland in detail on 126–7.

52 Spenser, *View*, ed. Renwick, 149.

53 Spenser, *View*, ed. Renwick, 151.

54 Moryson, *Shakespeare's Europe*, 238.

55 Spenser, *View*, ed. Renwick, 161.

56 See Edmund Spenser, 'Letter of the Authors,' *The Faerie Queene*, ed. A.C. Hamilton, text ed. Hiroshi Yamashita and Toshiyuki Suzuki (Edinburgh and London: Longman, 2001), 714. All future quotations are to this edition and will appear parenthetically in the text with reference to book, canto, stanza, and line number.

57 See Fildes, *Breasts*, esp. her chapter 'Wet Nursing: Wet Nursing as a Social Institution'; see also her *Wet Nursing*. And see Lawrence Stone, *The Family, Sex, and Marriage in England 1500–1800* (New York: Harper and Row, 1977), 106–8.

58 Stone, *Family*, 108.

59 Spenser specifically describes them as having '*sucked vp* their dying mothers bloud' (1.1.25.8, emphasis added), linking this moment quite specifically to the act of suckling. For a fuller discussion of Error and her 'cannibalis-

tic progeny,' see Maureen Quilligan, *Milton's Spenser: The Politics of Reading* (Ithaca, NY: Cornell UP, 1983), 80–5, esp. 82. Interestingly, Milton's Sin may well be indebted to Spenser's cannibalistic image, since she, too, breeds 'Monsters' who 'Gnaw / [her] Bowels' (*Paradise Lost*, II.795, 799–800, ed. Scott Elledge [New York: Norton, 1993]). Trubowitz associates Sin with Milton's 'critique of Stuart kingship as foreign tyranny and imperial conquest' (45), further delineating the association I am here making between perverse maternity and the foreign (Irish).

60  Spenser, *View*, ed. Renwick, 81.

61  Spenser, *View*, ed. Renwick, 135. The Moryson quote appears in Norah Carlin, 'Ireland and Natural Man in 1649,' in *Europe and Its Others*, 2 vols., ed. Francis Barker et al., *Proceedings of the Essex Conference on the Sociology of Literature* (Essex: U of Essex P, 1984), 2:91–111, esp. 100.

62  Spenser, *View*, ed. Renwick, 89. The language of 'fashioning' in association with the Irish wet nurse indicates her status as the poet's chief rival. In this passage, Spenser suggests that her ability to imprint the child far exceeds his own literary attempts to fashion gentlemen.

63  As quoted in John P. Harrington, 'A Tudor Writer's Tracts on Ireland, His Rhetoric,' *Eire-Ireland* 17 (1982): 92–103, esp. 99.

64  Note the similarity of this description to Columbus's description of the breast-like earthly paradise in the journal of his explorations to the New World; see 'Third Voyage of Columbus,' in *Four Voyages to the New World: Letters and Selected Documents*, trans. and ed. R.H. Major (New York: Corinth Books, 1961). The land he describes as the 'highest and nearest the sky' has powers consonant with its analogous anatomical part of the female breast: it forces the sea into a 'great turmoil' and makes water run 'with great impetuosity towards the east.' Columbus reveals the extent of its aggressive powers in choosing to name its derivative water sources 'Serpent's Mouth' and 'Dragon's Mouth' (130 and 135).

65  As Hamilton explains in his note to Stanza 78, 'Since the Bower is described in terms of earth and air, and Acrasia is linked with fire and water, all four elements oppose Guyon's temperance.'

66  See Stephen Greenblatt, 'To Fashion a Gentleman: Spenser and the Destruction of the Bower of Bliss,' *Renaissance Self-Fashioning: From More to Shakespeare* (Chicago: U of Chicago P, 1980), 157–92.

67  Rachel Trubowitz argues for the 'implicit analogy between the reformed maternal breast and the public fountain' in her article '"Nourish-Milke": Breast-Feeding and the Crisis of Englishness, 1600–1660,' *JEGP* 99 (2000): 29–49, esp. 41. Apparently James Harrington modelled his ideal system of irrigation in *Oceana* on the flow of breast milk.

68 Patricia Parker discusses the net as an image of the poet's 'fine "spell of words"' that alone has the power to save the castrated male 'from a "dumb" and paralyzing "charm" and, perhaps, from an enchantress'; see her '"Suspended Instruments": Lyric and the Power of the Bower of Bliss,' in *Cannibals, Witches, and Divorce: Estranging the Renaissance*, ed. Marjorie Garber (Baltimore: Johns Hopkins UP, 1987), 21–39, esp. 34 and 36. Parker reads Verdant through the dynamics of a 'Lacanian family romance,' perceiving his infantilization in observing how the grown man inhabits 'the posture of the speechless *infans* caught within a spellbinding female space' (34). She does not, however, read this posture as anticipating a contamination of a future heir.

69 As quoted in Nicholas Canny, *The Upstart Earl: A Study of the Social and Mental World of Richard Boyle, First Earl of Cork, 1566–1643* (Cambridge: Cambridge UP, 1982), 97.

70 Guillemeau, *Nursing of Children*, sig. Ii4$^v$.

71 Spenser, *View*, ed. Renwick, 84.

72 Joubert, *Popular Errors*, 194. This trope of the nursling rejecting its proper mother recurs in texts on the topic of wet-nursing, as when William Gouge argues in his *Of Domesticall Duties*, STC 12119 (London, 1622) that those 'who haue sucked others milke ... loue those nurses all the daies of their life' (512).

### 3. *Cymbeline* and Virginia's British Climate

1 See, in particular, Valerie Forman, *Tragicomic Redemptions: Global Economics and the Early Modern English Stage* (Philadelphia: U of Pennsylvania P, 2008); and Zachary Lesser, 'Tragical-Comical-Pastoral-Colonial: Economic Sovereignty, Globalization, and the Form of Tragicomedy,' *ELH* 74 (2007): 881–908.

2 Throughout this chapter, as in the book at large, I use the word *race* in its early modern meanings to denote a 'group of persons ... connected by common descent or origin' (*Oxford English Dictionary*, sb. I), including 'a set of ... descendants' (1a), 'a family, kindred' (2a), a 'tribe, nation, or people, regarded as of common stock' (2b), or 'a group of several tribes or peoples' (2c).

3 All citations of *Cymbeline* are to the *Norton Shakespeare*, ed. Stephen Greenblatt et al. (New York: Norton, 1997), and will be cited parenthetically in the text.

4 For a fuller discussion of the play's various anachronisms, see Patricia Parker, 'Romance and Empire: Anachronistic *Cymbeline*,' in *Unfolded Tales: Essays*

*on Renaissance Romance,* ed. George M. Logan and Gordon Teskey (Ithaca, NY: Cornell UP, 1989), 189–207.

5 Jean Bodin, *Method for the Easy Comprehension of History* (New York: Columbia UP, 1945), 146.

6 Bodin's *Six Books of the Commonwealth,* originally published in 1576, was translated into English in 1606, and Botero's *Relations, of the most famous kingdoms and common-weales through the world* went through six English editions between 1608 and 1630. Although Bodin's *Method for the Easy Comprehension of History* did not get 'Englished' until the nineteenth century (it first appeared in a Latin edition in 1566), L.F. Dean has argued that it was read 'by most serious English students of history from 1580 to 1625'; see 'Bodin and his *Methodus* in England before 1625,' *Studies in Philology* (1942): 160–6.

7 For an overview of European editions of these classical texts and their infiltration of the grammar school curriculum, see Joyce Chaplin, *Subject Matter: Technology, the Body, and Science on the Anglo-American Frontier, 1500–1676* (Cambridge, MA: Harvard UP, 2001), chap. 3, esp. 93–4. Chaplin notes, for instance, that 'the first half of the seventeenth century saw more European editions of Tacitus than of any other Greek or Roman historian' (93).

8 For a fuller discussion of these rival plays, see John E. Curran Jr, 'Royalty Unlearned, Honor Untaught: British Savages and Historiographical Change in *Cymbeline,*' *Comparative Drama* 31, no. 2 (1997): 277–303. Performances of *Cymbeline* at the Globe are recorded in Simon Forman's *Diary* prior to his death in September 1611; subsequent records indicate that it was performed at the Court of Charles I in 1634. For an overview, see The *Riverside Shakespeare,* ed. Blakemore Evans (Boston: Houghton Mifflin, 1974), 1517.

9 Christopher Wortham, 'Shakespeare, James I and the Matter of Britain,' *English* 45 (1996): 97–122.

10 See, for instance, Karen Ordahl Kupperman's analysis of Tacitus's popularity among English colonists in 'Angells in America,' in *Writing Race across the Atlantic World, 1492–1763,* ed. Philip Beidler and Gary Taylor (Houndmills, UK, and New York: Palgrave Macmillan, 2005), 27–50. For a discussion of Spenser's connections to the antiquarian movement, see Bart Van Es, 'Discourses of Conquest: *The Faerie Queene,* the Society of Antiquaries, and *A View of the Present State of Ireland,*' *English Literary Renaissance* 32, no. 1 (2002): 118–51.

11 For an overview of the environmental theories of classical texts, see Clarence J. Glacken, *Traces on the Rhodian Shore: Nature and Culture in Western Thought from Ancient Times to the End of the Eighteenth Century* (Berkeley: U of California P, 1967), 134–56.

12 Tacitus, *Agricola* and *Germany,* trans. Anthony R. Birley (Oxford: Oxford UP, 1999), 10.

13 For the connections between physiology and environment, see Nancy
Siraisi, *Medieval and Early Renaissance Medicine: An Introduction to Knowledge
and Practice* (Chicago: U of Chicago P, 1990); see also Mary Floyd-Wilson,
*English Ethnicity and Race in Early Modern Drama* (Cambridge: Cambridge UP,
2003).

14 For elaboration of humoralism, see Gail Kern Paster, *The Body Embarrassed:
Drama and the Disciplines of Shame in Early Modern England* (Ithaca, NY: Cornell UP, 1994). Humoralism defines the body as composed of various qualities (hot, cold, wet, and dry), which in turn characterize bodily fluids called
humours. One's disposition was considered a function of the dominance
of certain humours. The phlegmatic person was ruled by the cold and wet
humour called phlegm; the melancholic by the cold and dry humour called
black bile; the choleric by the hot and dry humour of yellow bile; and the
sanguine by the hot and wet humour of blood.

15 Aristotle, *The Problems*, trans. W.S. Hett, Loeb Classical Library, 2 vols. (Cambridge, MA: Harvard UP, 1936), 'Problem XIV,' 1:319–21.

16 *The Politics of Aristotle*, trans. Ernest Barker. (Oxford: Clarendon Press, 1961),
VII.vii.1. The passage continues by observing: 'The peoples of Asia are
endowed with skill and intelligence, but are deficient in spirit; and this is
why they continue to be peoples of subjects and slaves. The Greek stock,
intermediate in geographical position, unites the qualities of both sets of
peoples. It possesses both spirit and intelligence: the one quality makes it
continue free; the other enables it to attain the highest political development, and to show the capacity for governing every other people – if only it
could once achieve political unity.'

17 Bodin, *Method*, 97.

18 Botero, *The Reason of State & The Greatness of Cities* (1606; trans. Robert
Peterson), trans. P.J. and D.P. Waley (New Haven, CT: Yale UP, 1956), 40.

19 Botero, *Reason of State & The Greatness of Cities*, 38.

20 Floyd-Wilson in *English Ethnicity* provides an excellent overview of how
climate implicates humours, a phenomenon she calls 'geohumoralism.' She
uncovers an extensive early modern archive that associates different regions
and climates with the production of unique physical traits, but she does not
track how this model informs and is affected by widespread efforts at transplantation. Moreover, my own interest is to show how this 'geohumoral'
model challenges long-standing notions of race-as-genealogy.

21 Bodin, *Method*, 87.

22 On the obstacles to travel posed by these physiological theories, see Jim
Egan's analysis in *Authorizing Experience: Refigurations of the Body Politic in
Seventeenth-Century New England Writing* (Princeton, NJ: Princeton UP, 1999).

23  The second definition of *race* in the *Oxford English Dictionary* defines it as 'A limited group of persons descended from a common ancestor; a house, family, kindred' (sb.; 2a).

24  For a collection of essays discussing the imbrication of subjects in objects in the early modern period, see Margreta de Grazia, Maureen Quilligan, and Peter Stallybrass, eds., *Subject and Object in Renaissance Culture* (Cambridge: Cambridge UP, 1996).

25  William Camden, *Britain or A Chorographical Description of the Most flourishing Kingdomes, England, Scotland, and Ireland*, trans. Philemon Holland (London, 1610). John Speed, *The History of Great Britaine Under the Conquests of ye Romans, Saxons, Danes, and Normans* (London, 1614).

26  Speed, *History of Great Britaine*, 181.

27  Camden, *Britain*, 26 and 20.

28  Camden, *Britain*, 115.

29  For a fascinating discussion of physical 'imprints,' see Margreta de Grazia, 'Imprints: Shakespeare, Gutenburg and Descartes,' in *Alternative Shakespeares Volume II*, ed. Terence Hawkes (London: Routledge, 1996), 63–94.

30  Speed, *History of Great Britaine*, 182.

31  Definition 6 of the verb 'derogate' is defined in the *Oxford English Dictionary* as 'To do something derogatory to one's rank or position; to fall away in character or conduct from; to degenerate.' For a wide-ranging discussion of the mobility of genealogical lines, see Valeria Finucci and Kevin Brownlee, eds., *Generation and Degeneration: Tropes of Reproduction in Literature and History* (Durham, NC: Duke UP, 2001).

32  For a fuller discussion of Italy's role in the play, see Thomas G. Olsen, '"Drug-Damn'd Italy" and the Problem of British National Character in *Cymbeline*,' *Shakespeare Yearbook* 10 (1999): 269–316.

33  It is interesting to recall that their absent mother is remembered in the play only as the maker of their swaddling clothes ('a most curious mantle, wrought by th' hand / Of his queen mother [5.6.362–3]); indeed, her role in their reproduction is very much repressed, and is in fact coopted at the play's end by their father, who imagines himself in the moment of reunion as giving birth to the three children ('O, what am I / A mother to the birth of three?' [5.6.369–70]).

34  Janet Adelman, *Suffocating Mothers: Fantasies of Maternal Origin in Shakespeare's Plays*, Hamlet *to* The Tempest (New York: Routledge, 1992), chap. 8, esp. 204–5.

35  Raphael Holinshed, *The Chronicles of England, Scotland, and Ireland*, 2nd ed., 6 vols. (1587; London: J. Johnson, 1807–8). For discussions of Holinshed as a source text for Shakespeare's play, see Joan Warchol Rossi, 'Cymbeline's

Debt to Holinshed: The Richness of III.i,' in *Shakespeare's Romances Reconsidered*, ed. Carol McGinnis Kay and Henry E. Jacobs (Lincoln: U of Nebraska P, 1978), 104–12.

36 Holinshed, *Chronicles*, 1.73–4.

37 Holinshed, *Chronicles*, 1.193.

38 Holinshed, *Chronicles*, 1.279.

39 Holinshed, *Chronicles*, 5.2.

40 Holinshed, *Chronicles*, 5.3.

41 For a complementary argument in relation to New World tobacco, see Jeffrey Knapp's chapter 'Divine Tobacco' in his *An Empire No Where: England, America, and Literature from* Utopia *to* The Tempest (Berkeley: U of California P, 1992), which suggests evidence of a fear that 'tobacco will turn the English body into a torrid zone,' literally recolouring its inner parts black (163).

42 For Boetius's quotes on the Lowlanders, see Holinshed, *Chronicles*, 5.22, 5.2, 5.23, 5.2, 5.26–7, and 5.25.

43 See, for intance, Curran's article 'Royalty Unlearned, Honor Untaught,' which outlines the various breaks from Geoffrey of Monmouth that Camden's new historiography performs.

44 Camden, *Britain*, 115.

45 Camden, *Britain*, 659.

46 Camden, *Britain*, 665, 667.

47 See Kupperman's 'Angells in America,' which establishes the widespread consultation of Tacitus during the early seventeenth centuries and argues for the text as containing models for early English colonial efforts in Virginia. She notes Henry Savile's translation into English of Tacitus's *Life of Julius Agricola* in 1591 as part of *The Ende of Nero and the Beginning of Galba,* and its subsequent publication with Richard Greneway's translation of the *Germania* in 1598. Moreover, she observes the widespread interest and consultation of Tacitus's works by the likes of Camden, Francis Bacon, William Cecil, and members of the Earl of Essex's circle. See also Peter Stallybrass, 'The World Turned Upside Down: Inversion, Gender and the State,' in *The Matter of Difference: Materialist Feminist Criticism of Shakespeare*, ed. Valerie Wayne (Ithaca, NY: Cornell UP, 1991), 210–20, esp. 209–10. Stallybrass argues for the central role of Tacitus in republican ideology, but points up the extent to which such ideology is profoundly masculinist, resting on a rejection of the feminine.

48 For a fuller discussion of the union in the context of Shakespeare's play, see Constance Jordan, *Shakespeare's Monarchies: Ruler and Subject in the Romances* (Ithaca, NY: Cornell UP, 1997), esp. chap. 3. See also Leah S. Marcus, '*Cymbeline* and the Unease of Topicality,' in *The Historical Renaissance*, ed. Heather Dubrow and Richard Strier (Chicago: U of Chicago P, 1988), 134–68.

49  Sir Francis Bacon, 'Of the True Greatness of the Kingdom of Britain,' *Letters and the Life of Francis Bacon,* ed. James Spedding, 7 vols. (London: Longman, 1861), 7:47–64, esp. 7:58. See also Constance Jordan's excellent discussion of this text in her *Shakespeare's Monarchies.*

50  Bacon, 'Of the True Greatness,' 7.58.

51  Bacon, 'Speech for General Naturalization,' 10:307–25.

52  Bacon, 'Speech for General Naturalization,' 10.324–5.

53  Bacon, 'Speech for General Naturalization,' 10.315, 10.325.

54  Stephen Gosson, *The School of Abuse* (London, 1579).

55  Gosson, *School of Abuse*, sigs. B8ᵛ–C.

56  Camden, *Britain*, 29.

57  Camden, *Britain*, 57 and 29–30.

58  Camden, *Britain*, 15.

59  Bodin, *Method*, 95.

60  Camden, *Britain*, 15–16.

61  Holinshed, *Chronicles*, 1.450.

62  Holinshed, *Chronicles*, 1.193.

63  Bodin, *Method*, 111 and 102.

64  For a discussion of the signifiance of Milford Haven in relation to Henry Tudor, see Emrys Jones, 'Stuart *Cymbeline,*' *Essays in Criticism* 11, no. 1 (1961): 84–99.

65  Camden, *Britain*, 123.

66  Holinshed, *Chronicles*, 1.192.

67  Bodin, *Method*, 102.

68  Camden, *Britain*, 659.

69  Camden, *Britain*, 51.

70  Interestingly, in this respect, the play mirrors notions that King James I himself espouses in *Basilikon Doron*, where he advises his son: 'ye must be of no surname nor kinne, but equall to all honest men'; as quoted in Arthur H. Williamson, 'Scots, Indians, and Empire: The Scottish Politics of Civilization 1519–1609,' *Past and Present* 150 (1996): 46–83.

71  Camden, *Britain*, 45.

72  Speed, *History of Great Britaine*, 179.

73  Many critics, including Leah Marcus and Constance Jordan, have attended to the play's engagement with the unification of Britain, but few have considered its relevance to other 'imperial' pursuits.

74  Robert Johnson, *Nova Britannia: Offring Most Excellent fruites by Planting in Virginia* (London, 1609), fol. E2ᵛ.

75  In departing to 'North Virginia' in 1603, Martin Pringe records that 'We set saile from Milford Hauen'; see 'A Voyage Set Out from the Citie of Bristoll,' 1603, in *The English New England Voyages, 1602–1608*, ed. David B.

Quinn and Alison M. Quinn (London: Hakluyt Society, 1983), 216. See also David B. Quinn, *The new found land; the English contribution to the discovery of North America. An address delivered at the annual meeting of the Associates of the John Carter Brown Library, May 14, 1964* (Providence: Associates of the John Carter Brown Library, 1965). The Pembrokeshire context of the play also carries many affinities with the conquest of Ireland. In providing an account of this region of Wales, for instance, Camden describes Pembroke as the intermediary site enabling the eventual winning of 'the walles of Ireland' (652). He also describes the Welsh region of Cardigan as producing Robert Fitz-Stephens, who 'set foote in Ireland, and by his valour made way for the English to follow, and second him for subduing Ireland under the crowne of England' (657).

76 For discussions analogizing the Old World to a hive, an image that resonates with that of Imogen's 'nest,' in the context of sermons about Virginia, see Thomas Scanlan, *Colonial Writing and the New World: 1583–1671, Allegories of Desire* (Cambridge: Cambridge UP, 1999), chap. 4.

77 Patricia Parker observes as much when she notes that 'Imogen is also linked, as an object to be 'voyaged upon,' to the other imperial history of mercantile ventures upon new worlds' ('Romance and Empire,' 201, n. 16).

78 Shakespeare's connections to the Virginia enterprise are indeed material as well as theoretical. William Herbert, third Earl of Pembroke, was one of two brothers to whom Heminge and Condell dedicated Shakespeare's First Folio in 1623. In their dedicatory epistle, they make mention of Pembroke's interest in Shakespeare and his plays. In 1609, Shakespeare's sonnets were published following a dedication to an elusively named 'Mr. W.H.' Some have connected this person to William Herbert, although others have disputed this assignment on the grounds that the Earl would not have been addressed by means of the title 'Mr.' Leeds Barroll connects Pembroke to Shakespeare's company, the King's Men, seeing him as an even more interested patron of the arts than Shakespeare's other patron, Southampton. He describes Pembroke as a participant in the 'center of intellectual activity at the court'; see Barroll, *Politics, Plague, and Shakespeare's Theater: The Stuart Years* (Ithaca, NY: Cornell UP, 1991), 38–9.

Pembroke's connections to an emergent English colonialism include his decision to invest 'financially in all of the major colonizing ventures of his time, including the Virginia and Bermuda Companies, the Council for New England, and the East India Company; see Richard L. Greaves and Robert Zaller, eds., *Biographical Dictionary of British Radicals in the Seventeenth Century* (London: Harvester P, 1983). More centrally, he was appointed to the Council of Virginia in 1609 – a body that then consisted of 50 men representing roughly 650 investors. The Earl of Southampton and Francis Bacon were also elected to this Council. For Southampton and Bacon, see Wesley Frank Craven, *The Virginia Company of London, 1606–1624* (Williamsburg, VA: Virginia 350th Anniversary Celebration Corp., 1957), 18. For Pembroke's relation to the Council, see Susan Myra Kingsbury, ed., *The Records of the Virginia Company*, 4 vols. (Washington, DC: United States Government Printing Office, 1933), 3:29, 68.

79 Jonson, Marston, and Chapman's *Eastward Ho*, in *The Revels Plays*, ed. R.W. Van Fossen (Manchester: Manchester UP, 1999), for instance, associates the land with death and beggary and urges transplanting Scots there as a solution to the problem of peopling its vast expanse ('we should find ten times more comfort of them there than we do here' [3.3.51–2]).

80 Johnson, *Nova Britannia*, sig. B2.

81 William Crashaw, *A Sermon Preached Before The Lord Lawarre, Lord Governour of Virginea* (London, 1610), sig. F2.

82 Alexander Whitaker, *Good Newes from Virginia Sent to the Counsell and Company of Virginia* (London, 1613), sig. A4.

83 Robert Johnson, *The New Life of Virginea: Declaring the former successe and present estate of that plantation, being the second part of Nova Britannia* (London, 1612), epistle.

84 One might read a good deal of success into this propaganda machine, as Craven does, in observing that in 1609 and 1610, they succeeded in attracting at least ten thousand pounds in funding and successfully shipped fourteen hundred colonists aboard twenty-two vessels to Virginia (23–4).

85 As compared with Shakespeare's play, which seems to value the ancient Briton as against later foreign conquerors like the Saxons, many of these sermons define 'forefathers' with reference to 'English,' which is to say 'Saxon' forebears. Consider, for instance, William Symonds' *A Sermon Preached at White-Chapel in the Presence of many the Aduenturers, and Planters for Virginia* (London, 1609), which urges collective rallying around 'Noble Saxons Blood' (fol. 15), the father that 'first brought him in his lynes [i.e., loins] from forreigne parts into this happie Isle' (fol. 15).

86 Crashaw, *Sermon Preached Before Lord Lawarre*, sigs. E4 and F1$^v$.

87 Crashaw, *Sermon Preached Before Lord Lawarre*, sigs. G$^v$, G3, F4$^{r-v}$.

88 Crashaw, *Sermon Preached Before Lord Lawarre*, sig. F4.

89 Crashaw, *Sermon Preached Before Lord Lawarre*, sig. F4$^v$.

90 For reference to Bodin in these tracts, see, for instance, Robert Gray, *Good Speed to Virginia* (London, 1609), sig. B2.

91 Gray, *Good Speed*, sig. C3.

92 Crashaw, *Sermon Preached Before Lord Lawarre*, sig. F4$^v$.

93  Johnson, *New Life*, sigs. G and G1ᵛ.
94  Crashaw, *Sermon Preached Before Lord Lawarre*, sig. F1.
95  Crashaw, *Sermon Preached Before Lord Lawarre*, sig. E4ᵛ.
96  Johnson, *New Life*, sig. G2.
97  Symonds, *Sermon Preached at White-Chapel*, 15.
98  Symonds, *Sermon Preached at White-Chapel*, 32.
99  Joyce Chaplin, 'Natural Philosophy and an Early Racial Idiom in North America: Comparing English and Indian Bodies,' *William and Mary Quarterly* 54 (1997): 229–52, esp. 242. See also her *Subject Matter*, cited above in n. 7. Chaplin shares many of my observations about the experience of radical embodied flux articulated in and through the English colonization of America. I find, however, that her emphasis is more forward-looking than my own, given her desire to trace a teleology of 'essential difference' as expressed in the consolidation of racist attitudes to Native Americans. I am more interested in the transitional nature of the early modern period, the shift from a dominant notion of race to emergent notions.
100  Crashaw, *Sermon Preached Before Lord Lawarre*, sigs. E and E2.
101  See Edward Hayes, 'A Treatise, conteining important inducements for the planting in these parts' in John Brereton, *A Briefe and true Relation of the Discoverie of the North part of Virginia, 1602*, in *The English New England Voyages*, ed. Quinn and Quinn, 168.
102  Peter Heylyn, *Cosmographie in four bookes, containing the chorographie & historie of the whole world: and all the principal kingdoms, provinces, seas, and isles thereof* (London, 1657), fol. 121.
103  Bodin, *Method*, 89.
104  See Karen Ordahl Kupperman, 'Fear of Hot Climates in the Anglo-American Colonial Experience,' *William and Mary Quarterly* 41 (1984): 213–40.
105  Bodin, *Method*, 95.
106  Edward Arber, ed., *The first Three English books on America. Being chiefly Translations, Compilations, &c. by Richard Eden, from the Writings, Maps, &c. of Pietro Martire, Sebastian Munster, and Sebastian Cabot* (Birmingham: Kraus Reprint Co., 1971), 104.
107  Michel de Montaigne, 'An Apology for Raymond Sebond,' in *Essays*, trans. Florio (1603), ed. George Saintsbury, 2 vols. (New York: AMS Press, 1967), 2:297–8. In light of these observations linking human complexion to climate, I find very convincing Karen Ordahl Kupperman's observation that early English emphasis on the 'perfect constitution of body' observable in the Indians should be seen as in part demonstrating 'the holsomnesse and temperature of this Climate' – that is, as a response to anxieties of self-alteration on the part of the English; see her *Indians and English: Facing off*

*in Early America* (Ithaca, NY: Cornell UP, 2000), esp. 9. I also see this sort of defensive recuperation at work in English insistence on the 'whiteness' of native skin colour; by emphasizing the extent to which Native Americans have been altered in colour through the application of dyes and oils, rather than by exposure to Virginia's climate, the English appeased their own fears that they would be remade in an unfamiliar climate. For a discussion of native skin colour, see, for instance, William Strachey, *The Historie of Travell into Virginia Britania*, ed. Louis B. Wright and Virginia Freund, The Hakluyt Society (London: Maclehose, 1953), 71 and 113; see also Karen Ordahl Kupperman, *Settling with the Indians: The Meeting of English and Indian Cultures in America, 1580–1640* (Totowa, NJ: Rowman and Littlefield, 1980), 35–7. In his *New Englands Prospect* (London, 1634), by contrast, William Wood preys on these fears. He argues that New England's climate is ideal for 'English bodies' (7) by contending that Virginia is too hot to be 'suiteable to an ordinary English constitution,' since the heat alters the natural English complexion by '[drying] up much English blood ... changing their complexion not into swarthinesse, but into Palenesse.' By contrast, he observes that the New England climate maintains their 'naturall complexions,' which he describes not as 'white' but as 'ruddy,' denoting a sanguine (i.e., hot and wet) temperament characteristic of northern nations (9–10). He, therefore, defines the English as a red race.

108  Johnson, *Nova Britannia*, sig. B4.

109  Whitaker, *Good Newes from Virginia*, sig. I2.

110  Whitaker, *Good Newes from Virginia*, sig. E$^v$.

111  See Crashaw, *Sermon Preached Before Lord Lawarre*, sig. E2.

112  For an excellent discussion of how this ambivalence, this 'dynamic of dread and regeneration,' characterized settlement in the New World, see Michael Zuckerman, 'Identity in British America: Unease in Eden,' in *Colonial Identity in the Atlantic World, 1500–1800*, ed. Nicholas Canny and Anthony Pagden (Princeton, NJ: Princeton UP, 1987), 115–57, 120. Zuckerman quotes John Lawson's observation of 1709 regarding 'how apt human nature is to degenerate' (137). For an excellent discussion of the alien nature of America for early English settlers and fears of its transformative powers, see also John Canup, *Out of the Wilderness: The Emergence of an American Identity in Colonial New England* (Middletown, CT: Wesleyan UP, 1990). For the perception that America produced her English 'offspring' as degenerative still later in the eighteenth century, see Kariann Yokota, '"To pursue the stream to its fountain": Race, Inequality, and the Post-Colonial Exchange of Knowledge across the Atlantic,' *Explorations in Early American Culture* 5 (2001): 173–229.

## 4. Passion and Degeneracy in Tragicomic Island Plays

1 In the early modern period, 'hot waters' and 'hot drinks' refer to spiritous liquors. *OED*, 'hot water,' sb. 2

2 Sir Henry Colt, 'The Voyage of Sir Henry Colt,' in *Colonising Expeditions to the West Indies and Guiana, 1623–1667*, ed. V.T. Harlow (London: Hakluyt Society, 1925), 54–102, esp. 66.

3 English plantation in Barbados began in 1627, alongside planting efforts in St Christopher, Nevis, Antigua, and Montserrat, all of the Lesser Antilles; according to Richard S. Dunn, these were 'the only successful English settlements between 1604 and 1640'; see his *Sugar and Slaves: The Rise of the Planter Class in the English West Indies, 1624–1713* (Chapel Hill: U of North Carolina P, 1972; rev. ed. 2000), 17. Dunn estimates that as many as thirty thousand people from the British Isles 'went to the Caribbean to colonize during the reigns of James I and Charles I' (16). For a discussion of the 'Barbados distemper' and the diseases associated with the hot climate, see his chapter 'Death in the Tropics' (300–34, esp. 303).

4 Colt, 'Voyage of Sir Henry Colt,' 66.

5 Colt, 'Voyage of Sir Henry Colt,' 73.

6 Samuel Purchas, *Hakluytus Posthumus: or Purchas His Pilgrimes: Contayning a History of the World in Sea Voyages and Lande Travells by Englishmen and others*, 20 vols. (Glasgow: James Maclehose and Sons, 1905–7), 19:222, as quoted in Gordon McMullan, *The Politics of Unease in the Plays of John Fletcher* (Amherst: U of Massachusetts P, 1994), 212.

7 Early Americanists have been attentive to the discourse of degeneracy in the context of colonization for some time: see, for instance, John Canup, 'Cotton Mather and "Criolian Degeneracy,"' *Early American Literature* 24 (1989): 20–34, and *Out of the Wilderness: The Emergence of an American Identity in Colonial New England* (Middletown, CT: Wesleyan UP, 1990); and Jim Egan, *Authorizing Experience: Refigurations of the Body Politic in Seventeenth-Century New England Writing* (Princeton, NJ: Princeton UP, 1999), esp. chap. 1.

8 For comparative readings of these two plays, see McMullan, *Politics of Unease*, chap. 6; the introduction to *Three Renaissance Travel Plays*, ed. Anthony Parr (Manchester: Manchester UP, 1995), esp. 20–32; and Heidi Hunter, *Colonial Women: Race and Culture in Stuart Drama* (Oxford: Oxford UP, 2001), chap. 1. In addition to the broadly allusive Atlantic references that I find in the genre of romance at large, a range of dramatic productions of this period were precise in identifying an Atlantic context. Chapman's 1613 *Memorable Maske of the two Honorable Houses of Inns of Court; the Middle Temple, and Lyncolns Inne* was set in Virginia, for instance, and a now lost play on the

Virginia massacre, called *A Tragedy of the Plantation of Virginia*, was staged at the Curtain about the same time that Fletcher and Massinger's *Sea Voyage* was being performed; see McMullan, *Politics of Unease*, 242.

9  Influential arguments to this effect have been made in Paul Brown, '"This thing of darkness I acknowledge mine": *The Tempest* and the Discourse of Colonialism,' in *Political Shakespeare: New Essays in Cultural Materialism*, 2nd ed., ed. Jonathan Dollimore and Alan Sinfield (Ithaca, NY: Cornell UP, 1985), 48–71; Stephen Greenblatt, *Shakespearean Negotiations: The Circulation of Social Energy in Renaissance England* (Oxford: Clarendon P, 1988); and Meredith Skura, 'Discourse and the Individual: The Case of Colonisation and *The Tempest*,' *Shakespeare Quarterly* 40 (1989): 42–69.

10  For an overview of such approaches, see Peter Hulme and William H. Sherman, eds., *'The Tempest' and Its Travels* (Philadelphia: U of Pennsylvania P, 2000), especially the essays in part 2, 'European and Mediterranean Crossroads' (73–171). See also Richard Wilson, 'Voyage to Tunis: New History and the Old World of *The Tempest, ELH* 64 (1997): 333–57; and Jerry Brotton '"This Tunis, sir, was Carthage": Contesting Colonialism in *The Tempest*,' in *Post-colonial Shakespeares*, ed. Ania Loomba and Martin Orkin (London: Routledge, 1998), 23–42.

11  See, for instance, Barbara Fuchs, 'Conquering Islands: Contextualizing *The Tempest*,' *Shakespeare Quarterly* 48 (1997): 45–62; and Dympna Callaghan, 'Irish Memories in *The Tempest*,' in *Shakespeare Without Women: Representing Gender and Race on the Renaissance Stage* (London and New York: Routledge, 2000), 97–138.

12  Citations of *The Sea Voyage* are to the text edited by Parr in *Three Renaissance Travel Plays*. Citations will appear parenthetically in the text.

13  See McMullan, *Politics of Unease*, 245.

14  For this category, see Roland Greene, 'Island Logic' in Hulme and Sherman, eds. 138–48, esp. 141.

15  Brotton, 'Carthage and Tunis, *The Tempest* and Tapestries,' in Hulme and Sherman, *'The Tempest' and Its Travels*, 137.

16  Citations of *The Tempest* follow *The Norton Shakespeare*, ed. Stephen Greenblatt et al., 2nd ed. (New York: Norton, 1997) and will appear parenthetically in the text.

17  For these observations, I am very much indebted to McMullan, *Politics of Unease*, esp. chaps. 2 and 6.

18  As quoted from the excerpts of Fynes Moryson's *An Itinerary* (1616) included in *Illustrations of Irish History and Topography, Mainly of the Seventeenth Century*, ed. C. Litton Falkiner (London: Longmans, Green, & Co., 1904), 214–325, esp. 310.

19  The body of literature excavating these connections is impressive; see, for

instance, John Sutton, *Philosophy and Memory Traces: Descartes to Connectionism* (Cambridge: Cambridge UP, 1998), esp. chap. 2; Mary Floyd-Wilson, *English Ethnicity and Race in Early Modern Drama* (Cambridge: Cambridge UP, 2003); Roxann Wheeler, *The Complexion of Race: Categories of Difference in Eighteenth-Century British Culture* (Philadelphia: U of Pennsylvania P, 2000); Joyce E. Chaplin, *Subject Matter: Technology, the Body, and Science on the Anglo-American Frontier, 1500–1676* (Cambridge, MA: Harvard UP, 2001).

   Particular credit is due to Karen Ordahl Kupperman for opening this field of enquiry in two pioneering essays: 'Fear of Hot Climates in the Anglo-American Colonial Experience,' *William and Mary Quarterly* 41 (1984): 213–40, and 'The Puzzle of the American Climate in the Early Colonial Period,' *American Historical Review*, 87, no. 5 (1982), 1262–89. For a broad historical survey of how Western texts have seen culture as shaped by environment, see also Clarence J. Glacken, *Traces on the Rhodian Shore: Nature and Culture in Western Thought from Ancient Times to the End of the Eighteenth Century* (Berkeley: U of California P, 1967).

20 Gail Kern Paster, *The Body Embarrassed: Drama and the Disciplines of Shame in Early Modern England* (Ithaca, NY: Cornell UP, 1993), 9; Sutton, *Philosophy and Memory Traces*, 96.

21 Floyd-Wilson, *English Ethnicity*, esp. the introduction and chap. 1.

22 In fact, the *Oxford English Dictionary* reveals the extent to which 'base' behaviour was thought to be characteristic of the lower social ranks in that the term 'villain,' also spelled 'villein,' was in its earliest usage a term describing a low-born 'rustic' (sb. 1).

23 Sir Thomas Elyot, *The Book Named the Governor*, ed. S.E. Lehmberg (London: J.M. Dent, 1962), 29. *The Governor* went through eight editions between 1531 and 1580, while *The Castel of Helth* (London, 1537) went through some sixteen editions between 1537 and 1610.

24 For connections between the language of temperance and colonialism, see David Read, *Temperate Conquests: Spenser and the Spanish New World* (Detroit, MI: Wayne State UP, 2000). See also the discussion of the varied response of early modern writers to the Aristotelian ethic of moderation and temperance in Joshua Scodel, *Excess and the Mean in Early Modern English Literature* (Princeton, NJ: Princeton UP, 2002). For a reading of this virtue as embodied, see Michael C. Schoenfeldt, 'Fortifying inwardness: Spenser's castle of moral health,' in *Bodies and Selves in Early Modern England: Physiology and Inwardness in Spenser, Shakespeare, Herbert, and Milton* (Cambridge: Cambridge UP, 1999), 40–73.

25 The words are those of John Ferne, *The Blazon of Gentrie* (1586), as quoted

by Frank Whigham, *Ambition and Privilege: The Social Tropes of Elizabethan Courtesy Theory* (Berkeley: U of California P, 1984), 83. See also the connections that Lee Patterson makes between servitude and Cain's incontinence in '"No Man His Reson Herde": Peasant Consciousness, Chaucer's Miller, and the Structure of the *Canterbury Tales*,' in *Literary Practice and Social Change in Britain, 1380–1530*, ed. Lee Patterson (Berkeley: U of California P, 1990), 113–55.

26  Floyd-Wilson, chap. 2.

27  Colt, 'Voyage of Sir Henry Colt,' 66.

28  Colt, 'Voyage of Sir Henry Colt,' 65.

29  See, for instance, Floyd-Wilson's overview of how early modern writers understood climate's effect on the body's humours in *English Ethnicity*, chap. 1, esp. 35–6.

30  For a further discussion of the medical theories governing these choices, see Kupperman, 'Fear of Hot Climates,' 221–2.

31  Colt, 'Voyage of Sir Henry Colt,' 99–100 and 66.

32  Colt, 'Voyage of Sir Henry Colt,' 69.

33  Colt, 'Voyage of Sir Henry Colt,' 69 and 92.

34  We learn, famously from John Smith, of the presence in the colony of one woman who was the desperate victim of cannibalism at the hands of her husband during a period of famine: 'And amongst the rest, this was most lamentable, that one of our colony murdered his wife, ripped the child out of her womb and threw it in the river, and after chopped the mother in pieces and salted her for his food'; see Philip L. Barbour, *Pocahontas and Her World* (Boston: Houghton Mifflin, 1970), 65. Karen Ordahl Kupperman notes that the second colony sent to Roanoke in 1587 consisted of families, rather than young men, but this colony famously failed to take root; see her *Indians and English: Facing Off in Early America* (Ithaca, NY: Cornell UP, 2000), esp. 12. She describes the early Jamestown settlement as being 'a relatively small company of young men under military leadership' (12). She notes further that the Plymouth Colony of 1620 and the Massachusetts Bay Colony of 1630 'began with families' (13), indicating a shift in colonial ideology for this later period.

35  *A Declaration of the State of the Colony and Affaires in Virginia. With the names of the Adventurous, and Summes adventured in that Action* (London, 1620), fols. 10 and 17.

36  For the discovery of documents (the Ferrar papers) providing details of this subsequent shipment of women, see David R. Ransome, 'Wives for Virginia, 1621,' *William and Mary Quarterly* 48, no. 1 (1991): 3–18.

37 As quoted in Ransome, 'Wives for Virginia,' 7.

38 Ransome, 'Wives for Virginia,' 12.

39 *Declaration*, fols. 4 and 5.

40 For the Council's early attempts to frame transplantation to Virginia as physically restorative, see the discussion in chapter 3.

41 For this meaning of *subject*, see *OED*, v. 4, where it is defined as 'To place *under* something or in a lower position; to make subjacent *to*.' I am grateful to Peter Stallybrass for this observation.

42 For Restoration responses to this play and to the Fletcher canon at large, see Lawrence B. Wallis, *Fletcher, Beaumont and Company: Entertainers to the Jacobean Gentry* (Morningside Heights, NY: King's Crown P, 1947). Pepys, for one, described *The Sea Voyage* as a '"mean" piece compared to Shakespeare's *The Tempest*' (27).

43 Nicolas Coeffeteau, *A Table of Humane Passions. With their Causes and Effects*, trans. Edw. Grimeston (London, 1621), sig. A3–4.

44 For further detail on these sources, see Parr, *Three Renaissance Travel Plays*, introduction, 23–4.

45 For Fletcher's poem to the Countess of Huntingdon praising the estate at Ashby, see McMullan, *Politics of Unease*, 17–18.

46 For the Earl of Huntingdon's role in quelling the civil unrest provoked by acts of enclosure, see McMullan, *Politics of Unease*, esp. chap. 2. For an elaboration of James's policies at this time, see Leah S. Marcus, *The Politics of Mirth: Jonson, Herrick, Milton, Marvell, and the Defense of Old Holiday Pastimes* (Chicago: U of Chicago P, 1986), 19–20 and chap. 3.

47 For continuities of representation between Fletcher and Spenser, see James J. Yoch, 'The Renaissance Dramatization of Temperance: The Italian Revival of Tragicomedy and *The Faithful Shepherdess*,' in *Renaissance Tragicomedy: Explorations in Genre and Politics*, ed. Nancy Klein Maguire (NY: AMS P, 1987): 114–37.

48 Thomas D'Urfey, *A Commonwealth of Women. A Play as it is Acted at the Theatre Royal By their Majesties Servants* (1685), ed. Edmund Goldsmid (Edinburgh, 1886). Citations are to this edition and will appear parenthetically in the text and refer to page numbers.

49 For a compelling discussion of the ways in which Restoration theatre will rescript these associations, such that 'expertise in the passions diffuses from elite skill to something all subjects are expected to understand in themselves,' see Katherine Rowe, 'Humoral Knowledge and Liberal Cognition in Davenant's *Macbeth*,' in *Reading the Early Modern Passions: Essays in the Cultural History of Emotion*, ed. Gail Kern Paster, Katherine Rowe, and Mary Floyd-Wilson (Philadelphia: U of Pennsylvania P, 2004), 169–91, esp. 178.

## 5. High Spirits, Nature's Ranks, and Ligon's Indies

1 John Evelyn, *The Diary*, ed. William Bray, 2 vols. (Oxford: Clarendon P, 1955), 1:43. The passage in its entirety reads as follows:

> 'I saw the magnificent entry of the French Ambassador Colbert, received in the banqueting house. I had never seen a richer coach than that which he came in to Whitehall. Standing by his Majesty at dinner in the presence, there was of that rare fruit called the king-pine, growing in Barbadoes and the West Indies; the first of them I had ever seen. His Majesty having cut it up, was pleased to give me a piece off his own plate to taste of; but, in my opinion, it falls short of those ravishing varieties of deliciousness described in Capt. Ligon's history, and others; but possibly it might, or certainly was, much impaired in coming so far; it has yet a grateful acidity, but tastes more like the quince and melon than of any other fruit he mentions.'

2 Richard Ligon, *A True & Exact history of the Island of Barbados* (London, 1657), 11. All subsequent quotations of Ligon will be included parenthetically in the text with reference to this edition's pagination.

3 Keith A. Sandiford interprets Ligon's text in these terms, insofar as he argues for a reading of the text as inaugurating a Creolean struggle to 'win and secure cultural legitimacy' by 'colonizing the metropole with Creole desire and colonial ethics'; see his *Cultural Politics of Sugar: Caribbean Slavery and Narratives of Colonialism* (Cambridge: Cambridge UP, 2000), 16 and 29.

4 For an excellent discussion of how attitudes toward nature begin to split across the seventeenth century along royalist and republican lines, and how these political differences intersect with Cavalier and Metaphysical poetics of this era, see Robert Watson, *Back To Nature: The Green and the Real in the Late Renaissance* (Philadelphia: U of Pennsylvania P, 2006), esp. chap. 5, 'Metaphysical and Cavalier Styles of Consciousness.'

5 Bruno Latour, *We Have Never Been Modern*, trans. Catherine Porter (Cambridge, MA: Harvard UP, 1993). Latour observes: 'I am not claiming that the moderns are unaware of what they do, I am simply saying that what they do – innovate on a large scale in the production of hybrids – is possible only because they steadfastly hold to the absolute dichotomy between the order of Nature and that of Society' (40). He contrasts this tendency to instate a 'Great Divide' (39) between 'humans and nonhumans' (41) with 'the premoderns,' whom he describes as '[dwelling] endlessly and obsessively on those connections between nature and culture' (41).

6  See Karen Ordahl Kupperman, 'Ligon, Richard (c. 1585–1662),' in *Oxford Dictionary of National Biography* (Oxford: Oxford UP, 2004). See also Susan Dwyer Amussen, *Caribbean Exchanges: Slavery and the Transformation of English Society, 1640–1700* (Chapel Hill: U of North Carolina P, 2007).

7  According to Amussen, Thomas Modiford was a 'fellow Royalist from Exeter' and 'the son of a wealthy merchant and former mayor,' who offered Ligon 'a place on a ship to the West Indies' (*Caribbean Exchanges*, 46). Compellingly, in the early 1650s, Modiford would defect to the Parliamentarians and would later become an early governor of Jamaica (46, 32).

8  See Kupperman, *ODNB*.

9  In describing the period leading up to the Civil War, Lawrence Stone describes the tensions as deriving from 'a single society of two distinct cultures, cultures that were reflected in ideals, religion, art, literature'; see *The Causes of the English Revolution, 1529–1642*, 2nd ed. (London: Ark, 1986), 105–6, as quoted in Watson, *Back to Nature*, 143. David Underdown builds on this view in proposing that the body politic of the 1640s be seen as expressing 'two quite different constellations of social, political, and cultural force ... On the one side stood those who put their trust in the traditional conception of the harmonious, vertically-integrated society ... On the other stood those ... who ... [sought to] use their power to reform society according to their own principles of order and godliness'; see *Revel, Riot, and Rebellion: Popular Politics and Culture in England, 1603–1660* (Oxford: Clarendon P, 1985), 40–1, as quoted in Watson, *Back to Nature*, 143.

10  This point is made forcefully in Michael Craton, 'Reluctant Creoles: The Planters' World in the British West Indies,' in *Strangers within the Realm: Cultural Margins of the First British Empire*, ed. Bernard Bailyn and Philip D. Morgan (Chapel Hill: U of North Carolina P, 1991), 314–62, esp. 327. Indeed, as Craton argues, the plantations of the West Indies tended to perpetuate 'a native class of landed gentry even more tightly tied to the aristocratic system than were their English counterparts' and 'gravitated toward an aristocratic norm or ideal, derived from feudal culture, in their attitudes and behaviour' (329). Precisely because these principles were being so strongly challenged by the 'rising tide of bourgeois capitalism' expressed in the Civil Wars, these attitudes witnessed a powerful resurgence in the context of planter culture (327). Such attitudes, I suggest, are everywhere visible in Ligon's account of Barbados. Kim F. Hall observes them as well in a description of the plantation of Sir Modiford, friend of Ligon and eventual governor of the colony; she observes that 'his nostalgic lens turns the Barbadian landscape into a feudal estate where slave-trading sugar capitalists become benevolent lords of their own castles. His vision promises aspiring gentry "castles" which rep-

resent both wealth and paternalistic control over labourers'; see her 'Culinary Spaces, Colonial Spaces: The Gendering of Sugar in the Seventeenth Century,' in *Feminist Readings of Early Modern Culture: Emerging Subjects*, ed. Valerie Traub, M. Lindsay Kaplan, and Dympna Callaghan (Cambridge: Cambridge UP, 1996), 168–90, esp. 184.

11 This is the argument that Debora Shuger makes in her important essay 'Irishmen, Aristocrats, and Other White Barbarians,' *Renaissance Quarterly* 50 (1997): 494–525. She demonstrates the intimate connections between natural and social forms underpinning this text by observing how the cultivation of crops is viewed as analogous to the cultivation of people.

12 See, for instance, the edited collection by Gianna Pomata and Nancy G. Siraisi, eds., *Historia: Empiricism and Erudition in Early Modern Europe* (Cambridge, MA: MIT Press, 2005); and Barbara J. Shapiro, *Probability and Certainty in Seventeenth-Century England: A Study of the Relationships between Natural Science, Religion, History, Law, and Literature* (Princeton, NJ: Princeton UP, 1983).

13 See, for instance, Jennifer L. Morgan, *Laboring Women: Reproduction and Gender in New World Slavery* (Philadelphia: U of Pennsylvania P, 2004); Hall, 'Culinary Spaces.' Importantly, Amussen argues that the text is also embedded on a crossroads of sorts regarding conceptions of race, identifying the 'specific set of social relations in the Caribbean colonies' as paving the way for 'the emergence of what we now think of as "race"' (*Caribbean Exchanges*, 23). As such, she sees the text as actively remaking *race* rather than inheriting a race system that was already rooted in the oppositions of skin colour.

14 Amussen records that in 1644 – a few years before Ligon's arrival to the island – there were about eight hundred African slaves in Barbados, or less than 10 per cent of a population of ten thousand. But the purchase of slaves was rapidly on the rise and by 1660, approximately fifteen years later, the number of enslaved Africans on the island is estimated at forty thousand (*Caribbean Exchanges*, 29–30).

15 Amussen, *Caribbean Exchanges*, 10 and 42.

16 As quoted in Wrightson, 'The social order of early modern England,' 192.

17 For this argument, see Ezra Tawil, *The Making of Racial Sentiment: Slavery and the Birth of the Frontier Romance* (Cambridge: Cambridge UP, 2006).

18 In this respect Ligon embodies a way of perceiving nature that is characteristically royalist, one that Watson suggests typifies Cavalier poetry of the same period. He suggests that Cavalier poetry and Metaphysical poetry split along the tension of 'whether the manifest world is an arbitrary mental and verbal construction or a stable material hierarchy,' with royalists clearly favouring the latter view (*Back to Nature*, 34). Royalists, Watson explains,

remained 'closely in touch with nature along established hierarchical terms' (137–8).

19 That the terms *race* and *kind* function as synonyms for Ligon is made explicit when he discusses the island's flies. An advocate of spontaneous generation, Ligon urges 'there is not only a race of all these kinds, that go in a generation, but upon new occasions, new kinds' (63). Here, Ligon understands *race,* even in the context of this family of flies, to designate a common lineage, describing creatures linked in kinship or 'kind,' a dominant usage that I have tracked throughout this book.

20 See, for instance, Mary Floyd-Wilson and Garrett A. Sullivan Jr, eds., *Environment and Embodiment in Early Modern England* (New York and Houndmills, UK: Palgrave Macmillan, 2007). See also 'Embodiment and Environment in Early Modern Drama and Performance,' special issue of *Renaissance Drama* 35 (2006), devoted to the same topic, for which Floyd-Wilson and Sullivan Jr served as guest editors.

21 John Sutton describes early modern bodies as 'semipermeable irrigated containers, moist sponges filled with interchangeable fluids'; see his *Philosophy and Memory Traces: Descartes to Connectionism* (Cambridge: Cambridge UP, 1998), esp. 42.

22 Gail Kern Paster describes her work as challenging notions of an autonomous early modern subject in her essay 'The Tragic Subject and Its Passions,' in *The Cambridge Companion to Shakespearean Tragedy,* ed. Claire McEachern (Cambridge: Cambridge UP, 2002), 142–59, esp. 153.

23 For a more extensive critique of the use of ecological models in early modern literary criticism, see Julian Yates, 'Humanist Habitats; Or, "Eating Well" with Thomas More's *Utopia,'* in *Environment and Embodiment in Early Modern England,* ed. Mary Floyd-Wilson and Garrett A. Sullivan Jr (Houndmills, UK, and New York: Palgrave Macmillan, 2007), 187–209.

24 This is the direction that the introduction to Floyd-Wilson and Sullivan's *Environment and Embodiment* moves in deconstructing the oppositions that seem to inform the collection's title and the collection's emphasis more at large.

25 In defence of this claim, see Raymond Williams's well-known account of culture, prior to the eighteenth century, as a process, as something that is *done* to animals or plants, as in 'cultivation.' He observes: 'Culture as an independent noun, an abstract process or the product of such process, is not important before lC18 and is not common before mC19'; see *Keywords: A Vocabulary of Culture and Society* (New York: Oxford UP, 1983), 88. See also Lorraine Daston, 'The Nature of Nature in Early Modern Europe,' *Configurations* 6, no. 2 (1998): 149–72, esp. 154. Daston argues that where moderns set 'nature' in opposition to 'culture,' early moderns positioned it in rela-

tion to a set of terms such as 'supernatural,' 'preternatural,' 'artificial,' and 'unnatural.'

26  See Bruno Latour, *Pandora's Hope: Essays on the Reality of Science Studies* (Cambridge, MA: Harvard UP, 1999), 16.

27  Compare Ligon's concern to emphasize the elite attributes of Barbadian nature with Spenser's concern that English culture – styles of dress, language, gendered relations – not be disrupted in Ireland.

28  This seems to be Sandiford's understanding of the tract's genre insofar as he attempts to deconstruct the title's 'pretensions to truth' in what he describes as a 'historical narrative of Barbados'; see 'The Pretexts and Pretenses of Hybridity in Ligon's *True and Exact History*,' *Journal of Commonwealth and Postcolonial Studies* 9, no. 2 (2002): 1–23, esp. 1.

29  José de Acosta, *The naturall and moral historie of the East and West Indies.: intreating of the remarkeable things of heaven, of the elements* ... (London, 1604).

30  Barbara J. Shapiro, 'History and Natural History in Sixteenth- and Seventeenth-Century England: An Essay on the Relationship between Humanism and Science,' in *English Scientific Virtuosi in the 16th and 17th Centuries: Papers read at a Clark Library Seminar 5 February 1977* (Los Angeles: William Andrews Clark Memorial Library at UCLA, 1979), 3–55, esp. 13. See also the more extended treatment of these arguments in her book *Probability and Certainty in Seventeenth-Century England*.

31  Shapiro, 'History and Natural History,' 3 and 4.

32  See Pomata and Siraisi, *Historia*, 2 and 5. For a discussion of the term *history* in the context of drama, specifically how 'histories' were not yet generically distinct from 'tragedies' and not yet yoked to 'historical materials,' see Margreta de Grazia, Hamlet *without Hamlet* (Cambridge: Cambridge UP, 2007), esp. 51–2. De Grazia indicates that '"History" was applied as loosely and broadly to playtexts as to other kinds of texts to signify a narrative or story' (51). She argues for the lability of early modern notions of 'history,' explicating how 'history' was not yet severed from poetical discourse, much in the way that Pomata and Siraisi suggest it did not yet express a kind of representation exclusively dedicated to human affairs and temporality.

33  Brian W. Ogilvie, 'Natural History, Ethics, and Physico-Theology,' in Pomata and Siraisi, *Historia*, 75–103, esp. 98. See also his *The Science of Describing: Natural History in Renaissance Europe* (Chicago: U of Chicago P, 2006).

34  Amussen, *Caribbean Exchanges*, 45. See also her discussion of an intermediary text between those of Ligon and Sloane by John Taylor; although his 'Multum in Parvo' remained unpublished, it conveys the knowledge of Jamaica he gleaned after a visit to the island in 1686.

35  See, for instance, Jorge Cañizares-Esguerra, *Nature, Empire, and Nation: Explo-*

*rations of the History of Science in the Iberian World* (Stanford, CA: Stanford UP, 2006), esp. chap. 2.

36 Paula Findlen, 'Courting Nature,' in *Cultures of Natural History*, ed. N. Jardine, J.A. Secord, and E.C. Spary (Cambridge: Cambridge UP, 1996), 57–74, esp. 72.

37 See Sir Francis Bacon, *Sylva Sylvarum: Or, A Natural History, in Ten Centuries*, in *The Works of Francis Bacon*, ed. Basil Montagu, 16 vols. (London: William Pickering, 1825–34), 4:280. Subsequent editions of this text would appear in 1629, 1631, 1635, 1639, 1651, 1658, 1664, and 1670.

38 Bacon indicates that he has read Spanish writers like Acosta in his *Great Instauration*. In this text he drums up interest in new accounts of nature by urging: 'we must absolutely insist and often recall that men's attention in the research and compilation of natural history has to be completely different from now on, and transformed to the opposite of the current practices'; see his *Novum Organon*, ed. Lisa Jardine and Michael Silverthorne (Cambridge: Cambridge UP, 2000), 169 and 146.

39 See Kupperman's entry 'Ligon, Richard (c. 1585–1662),' in the *ODNB*, which establishes these patronage connections. For the widespread opposition to the draining of the fens, see *Sir William Killigrew His Answer to the Fenne Mens Objections Against the Earle of Lindsey his Drayning in Lincolnshire* (London, 1649).

40 See Robert J. Mayhew, '"Geography is twinned with divinity": The Laudian Geography of Peter Heylyn,' in *Enlightenment Geography: The Political Languages of British Geography, 1650–1850* (New York: St Martin's P, 2000), 49–65.

41 See, for instance, Daniel Carey, 'Compiling Nature's History: Travellers and Travel Narratives in the Early Royal Society,' *Annals of Science* 54 (1997): 269–92.

42 See Hall, 'Culinary Spaces,' esp. 180 and 184.

43 The story becomes popularized in the eighteenth century by Richard Steele in *The Spectator* (Tuesday, 13 March 1711). Here the relatively minor episode in Ligon's text begins to accrue a sentimental emphasis, insofar as the author indicates that after hearing this tale, he 'was so touch'd with this Story ... that [he] left the Room with Tears in [his] Eyes' (3). Compellingly, the narrative is introduced by a woman, Arietta, as defence against the railings of men 'done to her Sex.' She appeals to Ligon's history as a narrative shorn of embellishments, one that expresses the 'Facts' that come 'from plain People, and from such as have not either Ambition or Capacity to embellish their Narrations with any Beauties of Imagination' (2). Her reference to Ligon as an 'honest Traveller' presumably concerned only with the facts of nature, severed from culture, already testifies to the epistemic

shift this chapter seeks to identify. In his own moment, Ligon's 'facts' were culturally and politically charged events, not the 'plain' factual discourse that natural history of the eighteenth century will aspire to be.

44 The use of 'romance' to denote the trappings of poetical or literary writing is characteristic of both Thomas Sprat, *The History of the Royal Society* (London, 1667), and René Descartes, *Discourse on Method* (London, 1649).

45 For the connections of these tropes to romance at large, see Patricia A. Parker, *Inescapable Romance: Studies in the Poetics of a Mode* (Princeton, NJ: Princeton UP, 1979).

46 Amussen substantiates this view in observing that 'Ligon had a strong sense of rank. He distinguished between "gentlemen," "passengers," and "women"'; his views – both of labouring women and people of African ancestry – were 'shaped by expectations of the social hierarchy; in this case, class trumped national or racial identity.' She also suggests a necessary tension between his view of the world and those dominant for the Portuguese planters in noting that 'the social distinctions that mattered so much to Ligon were invisible to the Cape Verdeans, while the Cape Verdeans' conception of collective honor was alien to the English' (*Caribbean Exchanges*, 48).

47 Today this island, the largest within the Cape Verdean archipelago, is called 'Santiago,' or 'Santiagu' in Cape Verdean creole, although in English it has been rendered in different forms across time. During Darwin's day, it was referred to as 'St Jago.' Throughout this chapter, I follow Ligon's usage in referring to the island as 'St Iago.'

48 In Spanish the title of the text is *Espejo de príncipes y caballeros, en el cual se cuentan los immortals hechos del Caballero del Febo y de su hermano Rosicler, hijos del grande Emperador Trabacio* (1555), and it was authored by Diego Ortúñez de Calahorra. The heroic protagonist – Caballero del Febo – was translated alternately as 'Knight of the Sun' and 'Knight of the Dawn.'

49 See also Keith Sandiford's account of this moment in 'The Pretext and Pretenses of Hybridity in Ligon's *True and Exact History*,' 6.

50 See, for instance, Amussen, *Caribbean Exchanges*, 63. Although Amussen sees this moment as a muted version of the 'pornographic' attitude that Ligon displays toward African slave women in Barbados, she also allows that it expresses 'muddled language' and 'confusion' on Ligon's part in terms of socially locating an elite woman of African ancestry, in that he addresses her with 'courtly compliment' at the same time that he seeks to confirm whether she has the white teeth that many attribute to Africans (47–8). Although I differ somewhat with Amussen's reading of this moment, her account of Ligon's optic more generally captures Ligon's ambivalence in the face of African difference, and the text's dependence on early modern

social forms. She tracks continuities with modern racialism without collapsing the difference of two quite distinct epistemologies, arguing that 'Ligon's account demonstrates that the construction of racial identities for both the English and those they enslaved, was a process – that it did not happen all at once ... The views of slavery and race held by English men in the Caribbean changed as the social structure of plantation economies became more settled. The very categories through which these men understood the world shifted' (67). For a reading that understands Ligon's ideology as contiguous with modern racialism, see Morgan's chapter '"Some Could Suckle over Their Shoulder": Male Travelers, Female Bodies, and the Gendering of Racial Ideology,' in *Laboring Women*; Morgan sees Ligon's description of the Padre's black mistress as expressing his sense of 'the deceptive beauty and ultimate savagery of blackness' (14). Given Ligon's emphasis on the majestic demeanour and graceful comportment of the Mistress, I see the claim that he associates her African identity with 'savagery' as moving too quickly to flatten the power dynamics of this highly transitional historical moment. I suggest, by contrast, that Ligon's emphasis on her rank – her queenly status – here impedes his ability to denigrate her because she has dark skin. He expresses, that is, what is fast becoming a residual racial system – valuing the ontological charge carried by blood – rather than an emergent one – emphasizing the ontological charge of skin colour.

51  Kim Hall emphasizes the courtly emphasis in this allegory of Barbados as a Queen by observing the extent to which it refigures long-standing representations of foreign lands as '"open," innocent, and nude.' This queen, by contrast, is 'dressed in tapestry and embroidery' ('Culinary Spaces,' 180).

52  A critic like Jennifer Morgan who reads Ligon for his emphasis on African monstrosity cannot account for the presence of this comparison to Queen Anne. She says that this comparison 'must have surprised his English readers' for dignifying a black woman (*Laboring Women*, 13). Perhaps surprise at this description expresses less the assumptions of an early modern readership than a modern one, insofar as we are unaccustomed to the ways that a person's rank – in this case an African person – could trump physiognomic differences that modern racial ideologies encourage us to perceive as the more important register of difference. Aphra Behn's royal African king, Oroonoko, suggests a similar emphasis; see her *Oroonoko: Or, the Royal Slave*, in *Oroonoko, The Rover, and Other Writings*, ed. Janet Todd (New York: Penguin, 1992).

53  See the concluding passage in Sir Walter Raleigh, *The discoverie of the large, rich, and bewtiful Empyre of Guiana*, ed. Neil L. Whitehead (Norman: U of Oklahoma P, 1997), 196. See also the now-famous discussion of this trope

in Louis A. Montrose, 'The Work of Gender in the Discourse of Discovery,' *Representations* 33 (1991): 1–41.

54 For the centrality of clothing as a marker of social identity for this period, see Ann Rosalind Jones and Peter Stallybrass, *Renaissance Clothing and the Materials of Memory* (Cambridge: Cambridge UP, 2000).

55 Analysing the 'art of Cookery' that consumes much of Ligon's interest while in Barbados, Kim Hall notes that 'Ligon's emphasis … is on the duplication of already known (aristocratic) dishes. His overwhelming concern is whether the delicacies found on the English table can be replicated in Barbados' ('Culinary Spaces,' 181).

56 Ligon is very aware of his tendency to digress and often blames those he perceives to embody a form of degeneracy for encouraging this tendency in him. An early example is when he says 'But I am misled into this digression by this wicked *Portugal*, whose unlucky Countenance before we came to the *Island*, gave me the occasion to say somewhat of him, and his miscarriage in the *Island*, before I came at it' (8).

57 There is a long-standing debate among historians about precisely this question. For those who argue that a racialist ideology preceded the institution of slavery, see Jordan Winthrop, *White Over Black: American attitudes toward the Negro, 1550–1812* (Chapel Hill: U of North Carolina P, 1968). For those who have argued that racial ideology gets produced as an effect of the economic institution of slavery, see Eric Eustace Williams, *Capitalism & Slavery* (Chapel Hill: U of North Carolina P, 1944); David Brion Davis, *The Problem of Slavery in Western Culture* (Ithaca, NY: Cornell UP, 1966); and Barbara Jeanne Fields, *Slavery and Freedom on the Middle Ground: Maryland during the Nineteenth Century* (New Haven, CT: Yale UP, 1985). Susan Amussen has expressed support for this latter view in her *Caribbean Exchanges*, arguing that 'slaveholding … pushed the English to move toward systematic racial thinking,' observing as well that 'race based on skin colour coexisted with other methods of defining difference' (*Caribbean Exchanges*, 12).

58 See, for instance, his description of a slave who died in a fire at the ingenio as 'an excellent servant' (93) and his use of the phrase 'poor Negres and Christian servants' (107) which links the two groups under the rubric of a servant class. Elsewhere he urges that 'servants, both Christians, and slaves, labour and travel ten hours in a day' (27). Conversely, he seems to place servants in the same category as slaves in being regarded as 'tradeable objects' when he observes: 'The Commodities these Ships bring to this Island, are, *servants* and *slaves*, both men and women' (40). Elsewhere he describes how newly arriving servants are scrutinized and then 'bought' by planters before stepping foot on the island (44).

59 For a detailed analysis of the system of service that prevailed in England, see 'Shakespeare and the Bonds of Service,' Michael Neill, in *The Shakespearean International Yearbook*, ed. Graham Bradshaw, Tom Bishop, Robin Headlam Wells, 5 (2005): 1–144, and Neill, '"His Master's Ass": Slavery, Service, and Subordination in *Othello*,' in *Shakespeare and the Mediterranean*, ed. Tom Clayton, Susan Brock, and Vincente Forès (Newark: U of Delaware P, 2004), 215–29. See also Peter Laslett, *The World We Have Lost* (New York: Scribner, 1966).

60 The work of historian Hilary McD. Beckles gives credence to Ligon's claim that the island's population of indentured servants lived in deplorable conditions comparable to those of the island's slave population during the first two decades after the introduction of sugar; see *White Servitude and Black Slavery in Barbados, 1627–1715* (Knoxville: U of Tennessee P, 1989).

61 In support of the view that white servants and black slaves were merged in early planter economies into something akin to a homogenized underclass, Keith Wrightson argues that 'Relations between masters and servants were highly exploitative. A servant was '"a thing, a commodity with a price," to be bought and sold, or even gambled for … subject to a degree of bondage which as John Rolfe observed, would be "held in England a thing most intolerable."' In speaking specifically of conditions in Virginia, he argues further that: 'they were not slaves. They had hopes of freedom and even of advancement if they survived the conditions of their servitude … But the distinction between their situation and that of the small numbers of African slaves introduced into Virginia from Barbadoes at this time was not necessarily apparent to them. White servants and black slaves sometimes joined in conspiracy or ran away together – a fact which has led some historians to speculate that in early Virginia, as in those Caribbean plantation economies which initially combined servitude and slavery, "class rather than race may have been the bond that united workers"' ('Class,' 140).

62 Bacon discusses these substances in many of his works, but see especially his *Novum Organon*, 173.

63 For a discussion of how this concept changed during the Renaissance, see Katharine Park, 'The Organic Soul,' in *The Cambridge History of Renaissance Philosophy*, ed. Quentin Skinner and Eckhard Kessler (Cambridge: Cambridge UP, 1988), 464–84.

64 Sir Thomas Elyot, *Castel of Helth* (London, 1541), 11; and Marsilio Ficino, *The Book of Life*, ed. and trans. Charles Boer (Texas: Spring Publications, 1980), 94.

65 Bacon, *Sylva Sylvarum*, 4:280.

66 Bacon, *Novum Organon*, 107–8.

67 As quoted in Sutton, *Philosophy and Memory Traces*, 96.

68 For this phrase, see, for instance, his reference to the construction of enclosures for the hogs as a form of 'good ordering' (34); his praise for the planters' ability to '[order] every thing so well' as regards their political disputes (57); and his observation that 'with good ordering' the poisonous cassava root can assume the restorative form of bread (68).

69 Amussen, *Caribbean Exchanges*, 63–4.

70 For an elaboration of this point, see Amussen, *Caribbean Exchanges*, 62–4.

71 Nicholas Foster, *A Briefe Relation of the Late Horrid Rebellion Acted in the Island Barbadas, in the West-Indies. Wherein is contained Their Inhumane Acts and Actions, in Fining and Banishing the Well-affected to the Parliament of England; (both men and women) without the least cause given them so to doe: Dispossessing all such as any way opposed these their mischievous actions. Acted by the Waldronds and their Abettors* (London, 1650), 16–17. All references are to this edition and appear parenthetically in the text.

72 Griffith Hughes, *The Natural History of Barbados* (London, 1750), 9–11. See also an overview of English perceptions of Barbadians in the seventeenth and eighteenth centuries in Jack P. Greene, 'Changing Identity in the British Caribbean: Barbados as a Case Study,' in *Colonial Identity in the Atlantic World*, ed. Nicholas Canny and Anthony Pagden (Princeton, NJ: Princeton UP, 1987), 213–66.

73 Ligon's moralistic condemnation of the levelling energies of withs, explored above, stands in contradistinction to Hughes's treatment of nature as beyond the purview of moral and social censure.

74 Hughes, *Natural History of Barbados*, preface, ii, iii, v.

## Coda: Beyond the Renaissance

1 See Hilary McD. Beckles, 'A "riotous and unruly lot": Irish indentured servants and freemen in the English West Indies, 1644–1713,' *William and Mary Quarterly* 47, no. 4 (1990): 503–22, esp. 506 and 517. See also his 'The concept of "white slavery" in the English Caribbean during the early seventeenth century,' in *Early Modern Conceptions of Property*, ed. John Brewer and Susan Staves (London and New York: Routledge, 1995), 572–84. Here Beckles refers to a major shift from a 'white to a black labor régime between 1645 and 1680' in the English West Indies (572–3) and describes the institution of indentured servitude that emerged in the context of these plantations as resembling 'chattel slavery more than the traditional English servitude' (575). He links it to a 'wider system of property and possessory relations in human beings developed in the colonies' (578).

2 For a discussion of servant insurrections of 1634 and 1647, see Beckles, 'The concept of "white slavery,"' 580.

3 Aphra Behn, *Oroonoko: Or, the Royal Slave*, in *Oroonoko, The Rover, and Other Writings*, ed. Janet Todd (New York: Penguin, 1992), 133–4. For further discussion of this text and its use of an Irish villain, see Elliott Visconsi, 'A Degenerate Race: English Barbarism in Aphra Behn's *Oroonoko* and *The Widow Ranter*,' *ELH* 69 (2002): 673–701, esp. 686–7.

4 Henry Neville, *The Isle of Pines*, in *Three Early Modern Utopias*, ed. Susan Bruce (Oxford: Oxford UP, 1999), 187–212. All references are to this edition and appear parenthetically in the text.

# Bibliography

Acosta, José de. *The naturall and moral historie of the East and West Indies.: intreating of the remarkeable things of heaven, of the elements* ... London, 1604.

Adelman, Janet. *Suffocating Mothers: Fantasies of Maternal Origin in Shakespeare's Plays*, Hamlet *to* The Tempest. New York: Routledge, 1992.

Alexander, Catherine M.S., and Stanley Wells, eds. *Shakespeare and Race*. Cambridge: Cambridge UP, 2000.

Amussen, Susan Dwyer. *Caribbean Exchanges: Slavery and the Transformation of English Society, 1640–1700*. Chapel Hill: U of North Carolina P, 2007.

Anderson, Perry. *Lineages of the Absolutist State*. London and New York: Verso, 1974.

Arber, Edward, ed. *The first Three English books on America. Being chiefly Translations, Compilations, &c. by Richard Eden, from the Writings, Maps, &c. of Pietro Martire, Sebastian Munster, and Sebastian Cabot*. Birmingham: Kraus Reprint Co., 1971.

Aristotle. *The Complete Works*, edited by Jonathan Barnes. 2 vols. Princeton, NJ: Princeton UP, 1984.

– *The Politics of Aristotle*, translated by Ernest Barker. Oxford: Clarendon Press, 1961.

– *The Problems*, edited by W.S. Hett. 2 vols. Loeb Classical Library. Cambridge, MA: Harvard UP, 1936.

Armitage, David, and Michael J. Braddick. *The British Atlantic World, 1500–1800*. Houndmills, UK, and New York: Palgrave Macmillan, 2002.

Avery, Bruce. 'Mapping the Irish Other: Spenser's *A View of the Present State of Ireland.*' *English Literary History* 57 (1990): 263–79.

Bacon, Francis, Sir. *Novum Organon*, edited by Lisa Jardine and Michael Silverthorne. Cambridge: Cambridge UP, 2000.

– 'Of the True Greatness of the Kingdom of Britain.' *The letters and the life of*

*Francis Bacon including all his occasional works: namely letters, speeches, tracts, state papers, memorials, devices, and all authentic writings not already printed among his philosophical, literary or professional works,* edited by James Spedding. 7 vols. London: Longman, 1861. 7:47–64.

– 'Speech for General Naturalization.' *The works of Francis Bacon,* edited by James Spedding, Robert Leslie Ellis, and Douglas Denon Heath. 15 vols. Stuttgart-Bad Cannstatt: F. Frommann Verl. G. Holzboog, 1963. 10:307–25.

– *Sylva Sylvarum: Or, A Natural History. In Ten Centuries.* In *The Works of Francis Bacon,* edited by Basil Montagu. 16 vols. London: William Pickering, 1825–34. Volume 4.

Baker, David. *Between Nations: Shakespeare, Marvell, and the Question of Britain.* Stanford, CA: Stanford UP, 1997.

– '"Men to Monsters": Civility, Barbarism, and "Race" in Early Modern Ireland.' In *Writing Race Across the Atlantic World: Medieval to Modern,* edited by Philip Beidler and Gary Taylor, 153–69. New York and Houndmills, UK: Palgrave Macmillan, 2005.

– '"*Wildehirissheman*": Colonialist Representation in Shakespeare's *Henry V.*' *English Literary Renaissance* 22 (1992): 37–61.

Bakhtin, Mikhail. *Rabelais and His World,* translated by Helene Iswolsky. Bloomington: Indiana UP, 1984.

Balibar, Etienne, and Immanuel Wallerstein. *Race, Nation, Class: Ambiguous Identities,* translated by Chris Turner. London and New York: Verso, 1991.

Banton, Michael. 'The Idiom of Race.' In *Theories of Race and Racism: A Reader,* edited by Les Back and John Solomos, 51–63. New York and London: Routledge, 2000.

Barbour, Philip L. *Pocahontas and Her World.* Boston: Houghton Mifflin, 1970.

Barroll, Leeds. *Politics, Plague, and Shakespeare's Theater: The Stuart Years.* Ithaca, NY: Cornell UP, 1991.

Bartels, Emily C. 'Making More of the Moor: Aaron, Othello, and Renaissance Refashionings of Race,' *Shakespeare Quarterly* 41, no. 4 (1990): 433–54,

– '*Othello* and Africa: Postcolonialism Reconsidered.' *William and Mary Quarterly* 54, no. 1 (1997): 109–59.

– *Speaking of the Moor: From* Alcazar *to* Othello. Philadelphia: U of Pennsylvania P, 2008.

Barthes, Roland. 'Myth Today.' In *Mythologies,* translated by Annette Lavers, 109–59. New York: Hill and Wang, 1972.

Bartlett, Robert. *The Making of Europe.* Princeton, NJ: Princeton UP, 1993.

Beacon, Richard. *Solon His Follie, or, A politique discourse touching the reformation of common-weales conquered, declined or corrupted,* edited by Clare Carroll and Vincent Carey. Binghamton, NY: Medieval and Renaissance Texts, 1996.

Beckles, Hilary McD. 'The concept of "white slavery" in the English Caribbean during the early seventeenth century.' In *Early Modern Conceptions of Property*, edited by John Brewer and Susan Staves, 572–84. London and New York: Routledge, 1995.

– 'A "riotous and unruly lot": Irish indentured servants and freemen in the English West Indies, 1644–1713.' *William and Mary Quarterly* 47, no. 4 (1990): 503–22.

– *White Servitude and Black Slavery in Barbados, 1627–1715*. Knoxville: U of Tennessee P, 1989.

Behn, Aphra. *Oroonoko: Or, the Royal Slave*, in *Oroonoko, The Rover, and Other Writings*, edited by Janet Todd, 75–141. New York: Penguin, 1992.

Berger, Harry, Jr. *The Allegorical Temper: Vision and Reality in Book II of Spenser's Faerie Queene*. New Haven, CT: Yale UP, 1957.

Bhabha, Homi. 'The Other Question: Difference, Discrimination and the Discourse of Colonialism. In *Out There: Marginalization and Contemporary Cuture*, edited by Russell Ferguson et al., 71–88. New York: New Museum of Contemporary Art; Cambridge, MA: MIT Press, 1990.

Bodin, Jean. *Method for the Easy Comprehension of History*, edited by Beatrice Reynolds. New York: Columbia UP, 1945.

– *Six books of the commonwealth*, edited by M. J. Tooley. New York: Macmillan, 1955.

Boesky, Amy. *Founding Fictions: Utopias in Early Modern England*. Athens': U of Georgia P, 1996.

Boose, Lynda E. '"The Getting of a Lawful Race": Racial discourse in early modern England and the unrepresentable black woman.' In *Women, 'Race,' and Writing in the Early Modern Period*, edited by Margo Hendricks and Patricia Parker, 35–54. London and New York: Routledge, 1994.

Botero, Giovanni. *The Reason of State & The Greatness of Cities*, translated by Robert Peterson (1606), translated by P.J. and D.P. Waley. New Haven, CT: Yale UP, 1956.

– *Relations of the most famous kingdoms and commonweales thorough the world …* London, 1608.

Bovilsky, Lara. *Barbarous Play: Race on the English Renaissance Stage*. Minneapolis: U of Minnesota P, 2008.

Braddick, Michael J. 'Civility and Authority.' In *The British Atlantic World, 1500–1800*, edited by David Armitage and Michael J. Braddick, 93–112. Houndmills, UK, and New York: Palgrave Macmillan, 2002.

Braddick, Michael J., and John Walter. 'Introduction. Grids of power: order, hierarchy and subordination in early modern society.' In *Negotiating Power in Early Modern Society*, edited by Michael J. Braddick and John Walter, 1-42. Cambridge: Cambridge UP, 2001.

Bradshaw, Brendan. *The Irish Constitutional Revolution of the Sixteenth Century*. Cambridge: Cambridge UP, 1979.

238    Bibliography

Bradshaw, Brendan, Andrew Hadfield, and Willy Maley, eds. *Representing Ireland: Literature and the Origins of Conflict, 1534–1660*. Cambridge: Cambridge UP, 1993.

Brady, Ciaran. *The Chief Governors: The Rise and Fall of Reform Government in Tudor Ireland, 1536–1588*. Cambridge: Cambridge UP, 1994.

Braude, Benjamin. 'The Sons of Noah and the Construction of Ethnic and Geographical Identities in the Medieval and Early Modern Periods.' *William and Mary Quarterly* 54, no. 1 (1997): 103–42.

Braunmuller, A.R. Introduction to *Macbeth*, by William Shakespeare. Cambridge: Cambridge UP, 1997.

Brenner, Robert. *Merchants and Revolution: Commercial Change, Political Conflict, and London's Overseas Traders, 1550–1653*. Princeton, NJ: Princeton UP, 1993.

Brotton, Jerry. 'Carthage and Tunis, *The Tempest* and Tapestries.' In *'The Tempest' and Its Travels*, edited by Peter Hulme and William H. Sherman, 132–37. Philadelphia: U of Pennsylvania P, 2000.

– '"This Tunis, sir, was Carthage": Contesting Colonialism in *The Tempest*.' In *Post-colonial Shakespeares*, edited by Ania Loomba and Martin Orkin, 23–42. London: Routledge, 1998.

Brown, Paul. '"This thing of darkness I acknowledge mine": *The Tempest* and the Discourse of Colonialism.' In *Political Shakespeare: New Essays in Cultural Materialism*, 2nd ed., edited by Jonathan Dollimore and Alan Sinfield, 48–71. Ithaca, NY: Cornell UP, 1985.

Bryksett, Lodowick. *Discourse of Civill Life: Containing the Ethike part of Morall Philosophie. Fit for the instructing of a Gentleman in the course of a virtuous life*. London, 1606.

Bryson, Anna. *From Courtesy to Civility: Changing Codes of Conduct in Early Modern England*. Oxford: Clarendon P, 1982.

Burns, Kathryn. 'Unfixing race.' Unpublished essay.

Bushnell, Rebecca W. *A Culture of Teaching: Early Modern Humanism in Theory and Practice*. Ithaca, NY: Cornell UP, 1996.

Cahill, Patricia Ann. 'Nation Formation and the English History Plays.' In *A Companion to Shakespeare's Works: The Histories*, edited by Richard Dutton and Jean E. Howard, 70–93. Oxford: Blackwell, 2003.

– *Unto the Breach: Martial Formations, Historical Trauma, and the Early Modern Stage*. Oxford: Oxford UP, 2008.

Callaghan, Dympna. *Shakespeare Without Women: Representing Gender and Race on the Renaissance Stage*. London and New York: Routledge, 2000.

Cambrensis, Giraldus. 'The Irish Historie,' translated by John Hooker. *The Chronicles of England, Scotlande, and Irelande*. 1580. 6 vols. New York: AMS Press, 1976. Vol. 6.

Camden, William. *Britain or A Chorographical Description of the Most flourishing Kingdomes, England, Scotland, and Ireland* ... translated by Philemon Holland. London, 1610.

Campion, Edmund. *The Historie of Ireland.* London, 1571.

Cañizares-Esguerra, Jorge. *Nature, Empire, and Nation: Explorations of the History of Science in the Iberian World.* Stanford, CA: Stanford UP, 2006.

Canny, Nicholas P. 'Edmund Spenser and the Development of an Anglo-Irish Identity.' *The Yearbook of English Studies* 13 (1983): 1–19.

– *The Elizabethan Conquest of Ireland: A Pattern Established, 1565–76.* Hassocks: Harvester Press, 1976.

– *Making Ireland British, 1580–1650.* Oxford and New York: Oxford UP, 2001.

– 'The Permissive Frontier: The Problems of Social Control in English Settlements in Ireland and Virginia 1550–1650.' In *The Westward Enterprise: English Activities in Ireland, the Atlantic, and America 1480–1650*, edited by K.R. Andrews, N.P. Canny, and P.E.H. Hair, 17–44. Detroit: Wayne State UP, 1979.

– *The Upstart Earl: A Study of the Social and Mental World of Richard Boyle, First Earl of Cork, 1566–1643.* Cambridge: Cambridge UP, 1982.

Canup, John. 'Cotton Mather and "Criolian Degeneracy."' *Early American Literature* 24 (1989): 20–34.

– *Out of the Wilderness: The Emergence of an American Identity in Colonial New England.* Middletown, CT: Wesleyan UP, 1990.

Carey, Daniel. 'Compiling Nature's History: Travellers and Travel Narratives in the Early Royal Society.' *Annals of Science* 54 (1997): 269–92

Carey, Vincent P. 'John Derricke's *Image of Irelande*, Sir Henry Sidney, and the massacre at Mullaghmast, 1578.' *Irish Historical Studies* 31 (1999): 305–27.

Carlin, Norah. 'Ireland and Natural Man in 1649.' *Europe and Its Others*, edited by Francis Barker, Peter Hulme, Margaret Iverson, and Diana Loxley, 2:91–111. 2 vols. Proceedings of the Essex Conference on the Sociology of Literature. Essex: U of Essex P, 1984.

Carroll, Clare. *Circe's Cup: Cultural Transformations in Early Modern Ireland.* Notre Dame, IL: U of Notre Dame P, 2001.

– 'The Construction of Gender and the Cultural and Political Other in *The Faerie Queene* 5 and *A View of the Present State of Ireland*: The Critics, the Context, and the Case of Radigund.' *Criticism* 32 (1990): 163–93.

Cavanagh, Sheila T. '"The fatal destiny of that land": Elizabethan Views of Ireland.' *Representing Ireland: Literature and the Origins of Conflict, 1534–1660*, edited by Brendan Bradshaw, Andrew Hadfield, and Willy Maley, 116–31. Cambridge: Cambridge UP, 1993.

Chaplin, Joyce. 'Natural Philosophy and an Early Racial Idiom in North America:

Comparing English and Indian Bodies. *William and Mary Quarterly* 54 (1997): 229–52.

– *Subject Matter: Technology, the Body, and Science on the Anglo-American Frontier, 1500–1676*. Cambridge, MA: Harvard UP, 2001.

*Chronicon a monacho sancti albani*, Vol. I: A.D. 1271–1381, edited by Henry Thomas Riley. London, 1863.

Coeffeteau, Nicolas. *A Table of Humane Passions. With their Causes and Effects*, translated by Edw. Grimeston. London, 1621.

Colt, Henry, Sir. 'The Voyage of Sir Henry Colt.' In *Colonising Expeditions to the West Indies and Guiana, 1623–1667*, edited by V.T. Harlow, 54–102. London: Hakluyt Society, 1925.

Columbus, Christopher. 'Third Voyage of Columbus.' *Four Voyages to the New World: Letters and Selected Documents*, translated and edited by R.H. Major. New York: Corinth Books, 1961.

*Comprehensive Concordance to the Faerie Queene 1590*, edited by Hiroshi Yamashita, Masatsugu Matsuo, Toshiyuki Suzuki, and Harua Sato. Tokyo: Kenyusha, 1990.

Corfield, Penlope J., ed. *Language, History and Class*. Oxford: Basil Blackwell, 1991.

Covarrubias Horozco, Sebastián de. *Tesoro de la lengua castellano o española*. Barcelona: S.A. Horta, 1943.

Crashaw, William. *A Sermon Preached Before the Lord Lawarre, Lord Governour of Virginea*. London, 1610.

Craton, Michael. 'Reluctant Creoles: The Planters' World in the British West Indies.' In *Strangers within the Realm: Cultural Margins of the First British Empire*, edited by Bernard Bailyn and Philip D. Morgan, 314–62. Chapel Hill: U of North Carolina P, 1991.

Craven, Wesley Frank. *The Virginia Company of London, 1606–1624*. Williamsburg, VA: Virginia 350th Anniversary Celebration Corp., 1957.

Crenshaw, Kimberle Williams. 'Mapping the Margins: Intersectionality, Identity Politics, and Violence Against Women of Color.' *Critical Race Theory: The Key Writings that Formed the Movement*, edited by Kimberle Crenshaw, Neil Gotanda, Gary Peller, and Kendall Thomas, 357–83. New York: New Press, 1995.

Curran, John E. Jr. 'Royalty Unlearned, honour Untaught: British Savages and Historiographical Change in *Cymbeline*.' *Comparative Drama* 31, no. 2 (1997): 277–303.

Daston, Lorraine. 'The Nature of Nature in Early Modern Europe.' *Configurations* 6, no. 2 (1998): 149–72.

Davies, John. *A Discovery of the True Causes Why Ireland Was Never Entirely Subdued, nor brought under Obedience of the Crowne of England, until the Beginning of his*

*Majesties happie Raigne,* edited by James P. Myers Jr. Washington, DC: Catholic U of America P, 1988.

Davis, David Brion. *The Problem of Slavery in Western Culture.* Ithaca, NY: Cornell UP, 1966.

Dean, L.F. 'Bodin and his *Methodus* in England before 1625.' *Studies in Philology* (1942): 160–6.

*A Declaration of the State of the Colony and Affaires in Virginia. With the names of the Adventurous, and Summes adventured in that Action.* London, 1620.

Degenhardt, Jane Hwang. *Islamic Conversion and Christian Resistance on the Early Modern Stage.* Edinburgh: Edinburgh UP, 2010.

De Grazia, Margreta. Hamlet *without Hamlet.* Cambridge: Cambridge UP, 2007.

– 'Imprints: Shakespeare, Gutenburg, and Descartes.' *Alternative Shakespeares Volume 2,* edited by Terence Hawkes, 63–94. London and New York: Routledge, 1996.

De Grazia, Margreta, Maureen Quilligan, and Peter Stallybrass, eds. *Subject and Object in Renaissance Culture.* Cambridge: Cambridge UP, 1996.

Derricke, John. *Image of Ireland.* London, 1581.

Descartes, René. *Discourse on Method.* London, 1649.

Dickson, David. 'No Scythians Here: Women and Marriage in Seventeenth-Century Ireland.' *Women in Early Moden Ireland,* edited by Margaret MacCurtain and Mary O'Dowd, 223–35. Edinburgh: Edinburgh UP, 1991.

D'Urfey, Thomas. *A Commonwealth of Women. A Play as it is Acted at the Theatre Royal By their Majesties Servants,* edited by Edmund Goldsmid. Edinburgh, 1886.

Durling, Richard J. 'A Chronological Census of Renaissance Editions and Translations of Galen.' *Journal of the Warburg and Courtauld Institutes* 24 (1962): 230–45.

Dunn, Richard S. *Sugar and Slaves: the rise of the planter class in the English West Indies, 1624–1713.* Chapel Hill: U of North Carolina P, 1972; rev. ed. 2000.

Egan, James. *Authorizing Experience: Refigurations of the Body Politic in Seventeenth-Century New England Writing.* Princeton, NJ: Princeton UP, 1999.

Elias, Norbert. *The History of Manners* (1939). Vol. I of *The Civilizing Process,* translated by Edmund Jephcott. New York: Pantheon, 1978.

Elyot, Thomas, Sir. *The Book Named the Governor,* edited by S.E. Lehmberg. London: J.M. Dent, 1962.

– *The Castel of Helth.* London, 1537.

Erasmus, Desiderius. 'The New Mother.' 1526. In *The Colloquies of Erasmus,* translated by Craig R. Thompson, 267–85. Chicago and London: U of Chicago P, 1965.

Evelyn, John. *The Diary,* edited by William Bray. 2 vols. Oxford: Clarendon P, 1955.

Falls, Cyril. *Elizabeth's Irish Wars*. London: Methuen, 1970.

Feerick, Jean. 'Botanical Shakespeares: The Racial Logic of Plant Life in *Titus Andronicus.*' Special issue: 'Shakespeare and Science,' edited by Carla Mazzio. *South Central Review* 26, no. 1 (2009): 82–102.

– 'Spenser, Race, and Ire-land.' *English Literary Renaissance* 32, no. 1 (2002): 85–117.

Ferne, John. *The Blazon of Gentrie*. London, 1586.

Ficino, Marsilio. *The Book of Life*, edited and translated by Charles Boer. Texas: Spring Publications, 1980.

Fields, Barbara Jane. *Slavery and Freedom on the Middle Ground: Maryland during the Nineteenth Century*. New Haven, CT: Yale UP, 1985.

Fildes, Valerie. *Breasts, Bottles, and Babies: A History of Infant Feeding*. Edinburgh: Edinburgh UP, 1986.

– *Wet Nursing: A History from Antiquity to the Present*. Oxford: Blackwell, 1988.

Findlen, Paula. 'Courting Nature.' In *Cultures of Natural History*, edited by N. Jardine, N.A. Secord, and E.C. Spary, 57–74. Cambridge: Cambridge UP, 1996.

Finucci, Valeria, and Kevin Brownlee, eds. *Generation and Degeneration: Tropes of Reproduction in Literature and History from Antiquity to Early Modern Europe*. Durham, NC: Duke UP, 2001.

Fletcher, John, and Philip Massinger. *The Sea Voyage*. In *Three Renaissance Travel Plays*, edited by Anthony Parr, 135–216. Manchester: Manchester UP, 1995.

Florio, John. *A Worlde of Wordes, or Most Copious and Exact Dictionarie in Italian and English*. London, 1598.

Floyd-Wilson, Mary. *English Ethnicity and Race in Early Modern Drama*. Cambridge: Cambridge UP, 2003.

– 'Temperature, Temperance, and Racial Difference in Ben Jonson's *The Masque of Blackness.*' *English Literary Renaissance* 28 (1998): 183–209.

– 'Transmigrations: Crossing Regional and Gender Boundaries in *Antony and Cleopatra.*' In *Enacting Gender on the Renaissance Stage*, edited by Viviana Comensoli and Anne Russell, 73–96. Urbana: U of Illinois P, 1999.

Floyd-Wilson, Mary, and Garrett A. Sullivan Jr., eds. 'Embodiment and Environment in Early Modern Drama and Performance.' Special issue of *Renaissance Drama* 35 (2006).

– *Environment and Embodiment in Early Modern England*. Houndmills, UK, and New York: Palgrave Macmillan, 2007.

Forman, Valerie. *Tragicomic Redemptions: Global Economics and the Early Modern English Stage*. Philadelphia: U of Pennsylvania P, 2008.

Foster, Nicholas. *A Briefe Relation of the Late Horrid Rebellion Acted in the Island Barbadas, in the West Indies* ... London, 1650.

Foucault, Michel. *The History of Sexuality: An Introduction*, translated by Robert Hurley. London: Penguin, 1978.

– 'Nietzsche, Genealogy, History.' In *Language, Counter-memory, Practice: Selected Essays and Interviews*, Edited by Donald F. Bouchard, 139–64. Ithaca, NY: Cornell UP, 1977.

Fowler, A.D.S. 'The Image of Mortality: *The Faerie Queene*, II.i–ii.' *The Huntington Library Quarterly* 24, no. 2 (1961): 91–110.

Fredrickson, George M. *Racism: A Short History*. Princeton, NJ: Princeton UP, 2002.

Freedman, Paul. *Images of the Medieval Peasant*. Stanford, CA: Stanford UP, 1999.

Fuchs, Barbara. 'Conquering Islands: Contextualizing *The Tempest*.' *Shakespeare Quarterly* 48 (1997): 45–62.

Fumerton, Patricia. *Cultural Aesthetics: Renaissance Literature and the Practice of Social Ornament*. Chicago: U of Chicago P, 1991.

Gardnyer, George. *A Description of the New World. Of America Islands and Continent*. London, 1651.

Gillies, John. *Shakespeare and the Geography of Difference*. Cambridge: Cambridge UP, 1994.

Giraldi, Giovanni Battista Cinthio. *De gli Hecatommithi*. Vinegia, 1566.

Glacken, Clarence J. *Traces on the Rhodian Shore: Nature and Culture in Western Thought from Ancient Times to the End of the Eighteenth Century*. Berkeley: U of California P, 1967.

Goldberg, Jonathan. 'The Print of Goodness.' In *The Culture of Capital: Property, Cities, and Knowledge in Early Modern England*, edited by Henry S. Turner, 231–54. New York: Routledge, 2002.

Goldenberg, David M. *The Curse of Ham: Race and Slavery in Early Judaism, Christianity, and Islam*. Princeton, NJ: Princeton UP, 2003.

Gosson, Stephen. *The School of Abuse*. London, 1579.

Gouge, William. *Of Domesticall Duties*. London, 1622.

Gray, Robert. *A Good Speed to Virginia*. London, 1609.

Greaves, Richard L., and Robert Zaller, eds. *Biographical Dictionary of British Radicals in the Seventeenth Century*. London: Harvester Press, 1983.

Greenblatt, Stephen. *Renaissance Self-Fashioning: From More to Shakespeare*. Chicago: U of Chicago P, 1980.

– *Shakespearean Negotiations: The Circulation of Social Energy in Renaissance England*. Oxford: Clarendon P, 1988.

Greene, Jack P. 'Changing Identity in the British Caribbean: Barbados as a Case Study.' In *Colonial Identity in the Atlantic World*, edited by Nicholas Canny and Anthony Pagden, 213–66. Princeton, NJ: Princeton UP, 1987.

Greene, Roland. 'Island Logic.' In *'The Tempest' and Its Travels*, edited by Peter Hulme and William H. Sherman, 138–48. Philadelphia: U of Pennsylvania P, 2000.

Grennan, Eamon. 'Language and Politics: A Note on Some Metaphors in

Spenser's *A View of the Present State of Ireland.*' *Spenser Studies* 3 (1982): 99–110.

Guazzo, M. Steeven. *Civile Conversation,* translated by George Pettie and Bartholomew Young. 2 vols. New York: AMS Press, 1967.

Guillemeau, Jacques. *The birth of mankinde, otherwyse named The Womans Booke.* London, 1598.

– *The Nursing of Children.* London, 1612.

Guillim, John. *A Display of Heraldrie.* London, 1611.

Gosson, Stephen. *The School of Abuse.* London, 1579.

Hadfield, Andrew. 'Briton and Scythian: Tudor Representations of Irish Origins.' *Irish Historical Studies* 28 (1993): 390–408.

– 'Bruited abroad: John White and Thomas Harriot's colonial representations of ancient Britain.' In *British Identities and English Renaissance Literature,* edited by Willy Maley and David J. Baker, 159–77. Cambridge: Cambridge UP, 2002.

– *Edmund Spenser's Irish Experience: Wilde Fruit and Salvage Soyl.* Oxford: Clarendon P, 1997.

Hall, Kim F. 'Culinary Spaces, Colonial Spaces: The Gendering of Sugar in the Seventeeth Century.' In *Feminist Readings of Early Modern Culture: Emerging Subjects,* edited by Dympna Callaghan, Lindsay M. Kaplan, and Valerie Traub, 168–90. Cambridge: Cambridge UP, 1996.

– 'Guess Who's Coming to Dinner? Colonization and Miscegenation in *The Merchant of Venice.*' *Renaissance Drama* 23 (1992): 87–111.

– 'Sexual Politics and Cultural Identity in the *Masque of Blackness.*' In *The Performance of Power: Theatrical Discourse and Politics,* edited by Sue-Ellen Case and Janelle Reinelt, 3–18. Iowa City: U of Iowa P, 1991.

– *Things of Darkness: Economies of Race and Gender in Early Modern England.* Ithaca, NY: Cornell UP, 1995.

Hamer, Mary. 'Putting Ireland on the Map.' *Textual Practice* 3 (1989): 184–201.

Hannaford, Ivan. *Race: The History of an Idea in the West.* Baltimore and London: Johns Hopkins UP, 1996.

Harper, Carrie Anna. 'The Sources of the British Chronicle History in Spenser's *Faerie Queene.*' PhD diss., Bryn Mawr College, 1910.

Harrington, John P. 'A Tudor Writer's Tracts on Ireland, His Rhetoric.' *Eire-Ireland* 17 (1982): 92–103.

Harriot, Thomas. *A briefe and true report of the new found land of Virginia …* London, 1590.

Harrison, William. 'The Description of Britain.' In *The Chronicles of England, Scotlande, and Irelande.* 6 vols. London: AMS Press, 1976.

– *The Description of England,* edited by Georges Edelen. Ithaca, NY: Cornell UP, 1968.

Hayes, Edward. 'A Treatise, conteining important inducements for the planting in these parts.' In John Brereton, *A Briefe and true Relation of the Discoverie of the North part of Virginia, 1602.* In *The English New England Voyages, 1602–1608,* edited by David B. Quinn and Alison M. Quinn, 167–80. London: Hakluyt Society, 1983.

Heffner, Ray. 'Spenser's Acquisition of Kilcolman.' *Modern Language Notes* 8 (1931): 493–8.

Helgerson, Richard. *Forms of Nationhood: The Elizabethan Writing of England.* Chicago: U of Chicago UP, 1992.

– 'Tasso on Spenser: The Politics of Chivalric Romance.' In *Critical Essays on Edmund Spenser,* edited by Mihoko Suzuki, 221–36. New York: G.K. Hall, 1996.

Hendricks, Margo. 'Surveying "race" in Shakespeare.' *Shakespeare and Race,* edited by Catherine M.S. Alexander and Stanley Wells, 1–22. Cambridge: Cambridge UP, 2000.

Hendricks, Margo, and Patricia Parker, eds. *Women, 'Race,' and Writing in the Early Modern Period.* London and New York: Routledge, 1994.

Heng, Geraldine. *Empire of Magic: Medieval Romance and the Politics of Cultural Fantasy.* New York: Columbia UP, 2003.

Herbert, William, Sir. *Croftus, Sive, De Hibernia Liber,* edited and translated by Arthur Keaveny and John A. Madden. Dublin: Irish Manuscripts Commission, 1992.

Heylyn, Peter. *Cosmographie in four bookes, containing the chorographie & historie of the whole world: and all the principal kingdoms, provinces, seas, and isles thereof.* London, 1657.

Highley, Christopher. *Shakespeare, Spenser, and the Crisis in Ireland.* Cambridge: Cambridge UP, 1997.

Hill, George. *An Historical Account of the MacDonnells of Antrim.* Belfast: Archer & Sons, 1873.

Hippocrates. 'Airs, Waters, and Places.' In *The Medical Works of Hippocrates,* edited by G.E.R. Lloyd and translated by John Chadwick and W.N. Mann, 90–111. Oxford: Blackwell, 1950.

Holinshed, Raphael. *The Chronicles of England, Scotland, and Ireland.* 1587. 2nd ed. 6 vols. London: J. Johnson, 1807–8.

Hooker, John. 'The Irish Historie.' In *Chronicles of England, Scotland, and Ireland.* 6 vols. London: J. Johnson, 1808. 6:99–232.

Hooper, Glenn. 'Unsound Plots: Culture and Politics in Spenser's *A View of the Present State of Ireland.*' *Eire-Ireland* 32 (1997): 117–36.

Howard, Jean E., and Phyllis Rackin. *Engendering a Nation: A Feminist Account of Shakespeare's English Histories.* London and New York: Routledge, 1997.

Howard, Jean E. 'Shakespeare, Geography, and the Work of Genre on the Early Modern Stage.' *Modern Language Quarterly* 64, no. 3 (2003): 299–322.

Huarte, Juan. *The Examination of Men's Wits,* translated by Richard Carew (1594), edited by Carmen Rogers. Gainesville, FL: Scholar's Facsimiles & Reprints, 1959.

Hughes, Griffith. *The Natural History of Barbados.* London, 1750.

Hulme, Peter, and William H. Sherman, eds. *'The Tempest' and Its Travels.* Philadelphia: U of Pennsylvania P, 2000.

Hunter, Heidi. *Colonial Women: Race and Culture in Stuart Drama.* Oxford: Oxford UP, 2001.

Isaac, Benjamin. *The Invention of Racism in Classical Antiquity.* Princeton, NJ: Princeton UP, 2004.

Ivic, Christopher. 'Spenser and the Bounds of Race.' *Genre: Forms of Discourse and Culture* 32, no. 3 (1999): 142–73.

Ivic, Christopher, and Grant Williams, eds. *Forgetting in Early Modern English Literature and Culture: Lethe's Legacies.* London: Routledge, 2004.

Iyengar, Sujata. *Shades of Difference: Mythologies of Skin Color in Early Modern England.* Philadelphia: U of Pennsylvania P, 2005.

James, Mervyn. 'English Politics and the Concept of Honour 1485–1642.' *Past & Present Society* (1978): 1–92.

Jarcho, Saul. 'Galen's Six Non-Naturals.' *Bulletin of the History of Medicine* 44 (1970): 372–7.

Jenkins, Raymond. 'Spenser: The Uncertain Years 1584–1589.' *PMLA* 53 (1938): 350–62.

Johnson, Robert. *The New Life of Virginea: Declaring the former successe and present estate of that plantation, being the second part of Nova Britannia.* London, 1612.

– *Nova Britannia: Offring Most Excellent fruites by Planting in Virginia.* London, 1609.

Jones, Ann Rosalind, and Peter Stallybrass. 'Dismantling Irena: The Sexualiz-ing of Ireland in Early Modern England.' In *Nationalism & Sexualities,* edited by Andrew Parker et al., 157–71. New York and London: Routledge, 1992.

– 'Fetishisms and Renaissances.' In *Historicism, Pscyhoanalysis, and Early Modern Culture,* edited by Carla Mazzio and Douglas Trevor, 20–35. New York: Routledge, 2000.

– *Renaissance Clothing and the Materials of Memory.* Cambridge: Cambridge UP, 2000.

Jones, Emrys. 'Stuart *Cymbeline.' Essays in Criticism* 11, no. 1 (1961): 84–99.

Jonson, Ben, John Marston, and George Chapman. *Eastward Ho,* edited by R.W. Van Fossen. Manchester: Manchester UP, 1999.

Jordan, Constance. *Shakespeare's Monarchies: Ruler and Subject in the Romances.* Ithaca, NY: Cornell UP, 1997.

Joubert, Laurent. *Popular Errors.* 1578. Translated and annotated by Gregory David de Rocher. Tuscaloosa: U of Alabama P, 1989.

Judson, Alexander C. *The Life of Edmund Spenser*. Baltimore: Johns Hopkins UP, 1945.

Kidd, Colin. *British Identities before Nationalism: Ethnicity and Nationhood in the Atlantic World, 1600–1800*. Cambridge: Cambridge UP, 1999.

– *The Forging of Races: Race and Scripture in the Protestant Atlantic World, 1600–2000*. Cambridge: Cambridge UP, 2006.

Killigrew, William, Sir. *Sir William Killigrew His Answer to the Fenne Mens Objections Against the Earle of Lindsey his Drayning in Lincolnshire*. London, 1649.

Kingsbury, Susan Myra, ed. *The Records of the Virginia Company*. 4 vols. Washington, DC: United States Government Printing Office, 1933.

Knapp, Jeffrey. *An Empire No Where: England, America, and Literature from* Utopia *to* The Tempest. Berkeley: U of California P, 1992.

Kupperman, Karen Ordahl. 'Angells in America.' In *Writing Race across the Atlantic World, 1492–1763*, edited by Philip Beidler and Gary Taylor, 27–50. New York and Houndmills, UK: Palgrave Macmillan, 2002.

– 'Climate and Mastery of the Wilderness in Seventeenth-Century New England.' In *Seventeenth-Century New England: A Conference*, edited by David G. Allen and David D. Hall, 3–37. Colonial Society of Massachusetts. Boston: The Society, 1984.

– 'Fear of Hot Climates in the Anglo-American Colonial Experience.' *William and Mary Quarterly* 41 (1984): 213–40.

– *Indians and English: Facing off in Early America*. Ithaca, NY: Cornell UP, 2000.

– 'Ligon, Richard (c. 1585–1662).' In *Oxford Dictionary of National Biography*. Oxford: Oxford UP, 2004.

– 'The Puzzle of the American Climate in the Early Colonial Period.' *American Historical Review* 87, no. 5 (1982): 1262–89.

– *Settling with the Indians: The Meeting of English and Indian Cultures in America, 1580–1640*. Totowa, NJ: Rowman and Littlefield, 1980.

Laslett, Peter. *The World We Have Lost*. New York: Scribner, 1966.

Latour, Bruno. *Pandora's Hope: Essays on the Reality of Science Studies*. Cambridge, MA: Harvard UP, 1999.

– *We Have Never Been Modern*, translated by Catherine Porter. Cambridge, MA: Harvard UP, 1993.

Laurence, Anne. 'The Cradle to the Grave: English Observations of Irish Social Customs in the Seventeenth Century.' *The Seventeenth Century* 3, no. 1 (1988): 63–84.

Lawson, William. *A New Orchard and Garden*. London, 1618.

Lennon, Colm. *Sixteenth-Century Ireland: The Incomplete Conquest*. New York: St Martin's Press, 1995.

Lesser, Zachary. 'Tragical-Comical-Pastoral-Colonial: Economic Sovereignty, Globalization, and the Form of Tragicomedy.' *ELH* 74 (2007): 881–908.

Ligon, Richard. *A True and Exact History of the Island of Barbados.* London, 1657.

Linke, Uli. *Blood and Nation: The European Aesthetics of Race.* Philadelphia: U of Pennsylvania P, 1999.

Loomba, Ania. *Gender, Race, Renaissance Drama.* Manchester: Manchester UP, 1989.

– *Shakespeare, Race, and Colonialism.* Oxford: Oxford UP, 2002.

Loomba, Ania, and Jonathan Burton, eds. *Race in Early Modern England: A Documentary Companion.* Houndmills, UK, and New York: Palgrave Macmillan, 2007.

Lupton, Julia Reinhard. 'Home-Making in Ireland: Virgil's Eclogue I and Book VI of *The Faerie Queene.' Spenser Studies* 8 (1990): 119–45.

– 'Mapping Mutability: or, Spenser's Irish plot.' In *Representing Ireland: Literature and the Origins of Conflict, 1534–1660,* edited by Brendan Bradshaw, Andrew Hadfield, and Willy Maley, 93–115. Cambridge: Cambridge UP, 1993.

*Lust's Dominion: or, The Lascivious Queen,* edited by J. Le Gay Brereton. Louvain: Librairie Universitaire, 1931.

MacCaffrey, Wallace T. *Elizabeth I: War and Politics, 1588–1603.* Princeton, NJ: Princeton UP, 1992.

MacDonald, Joyce Green, ed. *Race, Ethnicity, and Power in the Renaissance.* Madison, NJ: Fairleigh Dickinson UP, 1997.

MacLachlan, Hugh. 'The "carelesse heauens": A Study of Revenge and Atonement in *The Faerie Queene.' Spenser Studies* 1 (1980): 135–61.

McCabe, Richard. 'Edmund Spenser, Poet of Exile.' In *Proceedings of the British Academy: 1991 Lectures and Memoirs.* Oxford: Oxford UP, 1993. 73–103.

– *Spenser's Monstrous Regiment: Elizabethan Ireland and the Poetics of Difference.* Oxford: Oxford UP, 2002.

McClintock, Anne. *Imperial Leather: Race, Gender and Sexuality in the Colonial Context.* New York and London: Routledge, 1995.

McCoy, Richard. *Rites of Knighthood: The Literature and Politics of Elizabethan Chivalry.* Berkeley: U of California P, 1989.

McLaren, Dorothy. 'Marital Fertility and Lactation, 1570–1720.' In *Women in English Society, 1500–1800,* edited by Mary Prior, 22–53. London: Methuen, 1985.

McMullan, Gordon. *The Politics of Unease in the Plays of John Fletcher.* Amherst: U of Massachusetts P, 1994.

Machiavelli, Niccolò. *Discourses,* translated by Leslie J. Walker. London and New York: Routledge, 1991.

Maley, Willy. *Nation, State, and Empire in English Renaissance Literature: Shakespeare to Milton.* New York: Palgrave Macmillan, 2003.

– *Salvaging Spenser: Colonialism, Culture and Identity.* London: Macmillan, 1997; and New York: St Martin's Press, 1997.

Marcus, Leah S. '*Cymbeline* and the Unease of Topicality.' In *The Historical Renaissance,* edited by Heather Dubrow and Richard Strier, 134–68. Chicago: U of Chicago P, 1988.

– *The Politics of Mirth: Jonson, Herrick, Milton, Marvell, and the Defense of Old Holiday Pastimes.* Chicago: U of Chicago P, 1986.

Marx, Karl. *The Ethnological Notebooks of Karl Marx,* edited by Lawrence Krader. Assen: Van Gorcum, 1972.

Mayhew, Robert J. *Enlightenment Geography: The Political Languages of British Geography, 1650–1850.* New York: St Martin's Press, 2000.

Mikalachki, Jodi. *The Legacy of Boadicea: Gender and Nation in Early Modern England.* London and New York: Routledge, 1998.

Miller, Jacqueline T. 'Mother Tongues: Language and Lactation in Early Modern Literature.' *English Literary Renaissance* 27, no. 2 (1997): 177–96.

Miller, Shannon. *Invested with Meaning: The Raleigh Circle in the New World.* Philadelphia: U of Pennsylvania P, 1998.

Milton, John. *Paradise Lost,* edited by Scott Elledge. New York: Norton, 1993.

Monardes, Nicolás. *Joyfull newes out of the newe founde worlde,* translated by John Frampton. London, 1577.

Montaigne, Michel de. 'An Apology for Ramond Sebond.' In *Complete Essays of Montaigne,* translated by Donald M. Frame, 318–45. Stanford, CA: Stanford UP, 1958.

– 'An Apology for Raymond Sebond.' In *Essays,* translated by John Florio. 1603, edited by George Saintsbury, 2:127–332. 3 vols. New York: AMS Press, 1967.

Montrose, Louis. 'The Work of Gender in the Discourse of Discovery.' *Representations* 33 (1992): 1–41.

Moretti, Franco. '"A Huge Eclipse": Tragic Form and the Deconsecration of Tragedy.' In *The Power of Forms in the English Renaissance,* edited by Stephen J. Greenblatt, 7–40. Norman, OK: Pilgrim, 1982.

Morgan, Hiram. *Tyrone's Rebellion: The Outbreak of the Nine Years' War in Tudor Ireland.* London: Royal Historical Society, 1993.

– 'Writing Up Early Modern Ireland.' *Historical Journal* 31 (1988): 701–11.

Morgan, Jennifer L. *Labouring Women: Reproduction and Gender in New World Slavery.* Philadelphia: U of Pennsylvania P, 2004.

Moryson, Fynes. 'Description of Ireland.' In *Illustrations of Irish History and Topography, Mainly of the Seventeenth Century,* edited by C. Litton Falkiner, 214–32. London: Longmans, Green, and Co., 1904.

– 'The Irish Sections of Fyne Moryson's Unpublished Itinerary,' edited by Graham Kew. *Analecta Hibernica* 37 (1998): 1–137.

– *An Itinerary.* 4 vols. Glasgow: J. MacLehose, 1907.

– 'Manners and Customs of Ireland.' In *Illustrations of Irish History,* edited by C. Litton Falkiner, 310–25.

– *Shakespeare's Europe: A Survey of the Condition of Europe at the End of the 16th Century. Being unpublished chapters of Fynes Morsyon's Itinerary,* edited by Charles Hughes, 2nd ed. New York: Benjamin Blom, 1967.

Muldoon, James. *Identity on the Medieval Irish Frontier: Degenerate Englishmen, Wild Irishmen, Middle Nations.* Gainesville: UP of Florida, 2003.

– 'The Indian as Irishman.' *Essex Institute Historical Collections* 111 (1975): 267–89.

Murphy, Andrew. *'But the Irish Sea Betwixt Us': Ireland, Colonialism, and Renaissance Literature.* Lexington: UP of Kentucky, 1999.

Murray, J.A.H. *The Oxford English Dictionary: Being a Corrected Re-Issue with an Introduction, Supplement, and Bibliography of a New English Dictionary on Historical Principles.* Oxford: Clarendon P, 1933.

Neill, Michael. 'Broken English and Broken Irish: Nation, Language, and the Optic of Power in Shakespeare's Histories.' *Shakespeare Quarterly* 45 (1994): 1–32.

– '"His Master's Ass": Slavery, Service, and Subordination in *Othello*.' In *Shakespeare and the Mediterranean*, edited by Tom Clayton, Susan Brock, and Vincente Forès, 215–29. Newark: U of Delaware P, 2004.

– *Putting History to the Question: Power, Politics, and Society in English Renaissance Drama.* New York: Columbia UP, 2000.

– 'Shakespeare and the Bonds of Service.' *The Shakespearean International Yearbook*, edited by Graham Bradshaw, Tom Bishop, and Robin Headlam Wells. 5 (2005): 1–144.

Neville, Henry. *The Isle of Pines.* In *Three Early Modern Utopias*, edited by Susan Bruce, 187–212. Oxford: Oxford UP, 1999.

Ogilvie, Brian W. 'Natural History, Ethics, and Physico-Theology.' In *Historia: Empiricism and Erudition in Early Modern Europe*, edited by Gianna Pomata and Nancy G. Siraisi, 75–103. Cambridge, MA: MIT P, 2005.

– *The Science of Describing: Natural History in Renaissance Europe.* Chicago: U of Chicago P, 2006.

Olsen, Thomas G. 'Circe's Court: Italy and Cultural Politics in English Writing, 1530–1615.' PhD diss., Ohio State U, 1998.

– '"Drug-Damn'd Italy" and the Problem of British National Character in *Cymbeline*.' *Shakespeare Yearbook* 10 (1999): 269–316.

Ortúñez de Calahorra, Diego. Espejo de príncipes y caballeros, en el cual se cuentan los immortals hechos del Caballero del Febo y de su hermano Rosicler, hijos del grande Emperador Trabacio. Caragoça, 1555.

Ottoson, Per-Gunnar, *Scholastic Medicine and Philosophy. A Study of Commentaries on Galen's Tegni.* Naples: Bibliopolis, 1984.

Palmer, William. 'Gender, Violence and Rebellion in Tudor and Early Stuart Ireland.' *Sixteenth Century Journal* 23, no. 4 (1992): 699–712.

Park, Katharine. 'The Organic Soul.' In *The Cambridge History of Renaissance Philosophy*, edited by Quentin Skinner and Eckhard Kessler, 464–84. Cambridge: Cambridge UP, 1988.

Parker, Patricia A. *Inescapable Romance: Studies in the Poetics of a Mode.* Princeton, NJ: Princeton UP, 1979.

– 'Romance and Empire: Anachronistic *Cymbeline.*' In *Unfolded Tales: Essays on Renaissance Romance,* edited by George M. Logan and Gordon Teskey, 189–207. Ithaca, NY: Cornell UP, 1989.

– '"Suspended Instruments": Lyric and the Power of the Bower of Bliss.' In *Cannibals, Witches, and Divorce: Estranging the Renaissance,* edited by Marjorie Garber, 21–39. Baltimore: Johns Hopkins UP, 1987.

Parr, Anthony, ed. *Three Renaissance Travel Plays.* Manchester: Manchester UP, 1995.

Paster, Gail Kern. *The Body Embarrassed: Drama and the Disciplines of Shame in Early Modern England.* Ithaca, NY: Cornell UP, 1993.

– *Humoring the Body: Emotions and the Shakespearean Stage.* Chicago: U of Chicago P, 2005.

– 'The Tragic Subject and Its Passions.' In *The Cambridge Companion to Shakespearean Tragedy,* edited by Claire McEachern, 142–59. Cambridge: Cambridge UP, 2002.

Patterson, Lee. '"No Man His Reson Herde": Peasant Consciousness, Chaucer's Miller, and the Structure of the *Canterbury Tales.*' In *Literary Practice and Social Change in Britain, 1380–1530,* edited by Lee Patterson, 113–55. Berkeley: U of California P, 1990.

Peck, Linda Levy. 'The Mentality of a Jacobean Grandee.' In *The Mental World of the Jacobean Court,* edited by Linda Levy Peck, 148–68. Cambridge: Cambridge UP, 1991.

Perkin, Harold. *The Origins of Modern English Society.* 2nd ed. London and New York: Routledge, 2002.

Perrott, Sir James. *The Chronicle of Ireland, 1584–1608,* edited by Herbert Wood. Dublin: Stationery Office, 1933.

Pliny the Elder. *The historie of the world: commonly called, the naturall historie of C. Plinius Sedundus,* translated by Philemon Holland. London, 1601.

Pomata, Gianna, and Nancy G. Siraisi, eds. *Historia: Empricism and Erudition in Early Modern Europe.* Cambridge, MA: MIT P, 2005.

Pringe, Martin. 'A Voyage Set Out from the Citie of Bristoll.' 1603. In *The English New England Voyages, 1602–1608,* edited by David B. Quinn and Alison M. Quinn, 214–28. London: Hakluyt Society, 1983.

Purchas, Samuel. *Hakluytus Posthumus: or Purchas His Pilgrimes: Contayning a History of the World in Sea Voyages and Lande Travells by Englishmen and others.* 20 vols. Glasgow: James Maclehose and Sons, 1905–7.

Quilligan, Maureen. *Milton's Spenser: The Politics of Reading.* Ithaca, NY: Cornell UP, 1983.

Quinn, David Beers. *The Elizabethans and the Irish*. Ithaca, NY: Cornell UP, 1966.

– *The new found land; the English contribution to the discovery of North America. An address delivered at the annual meeting of the Associates of the John Carter Brown Library, May 14, 1964*. Providence, RI: Associates of the John Carter Brown Library, 1965.

– 'Sir Thomas Smith (1513–1577) and the Beginnings of English Colonial Theory.' *Proceedings of the American Philosophical Society* 89 (1945): 543–60.

Quinn, David B., and Alison M., eds. *The English New England Voyages, 1602–1608*. London: Hakluyt Society, 1983.

Rackin, Phyllis. 'Dating Shakespeare's Women.' *Shakespeare Jahrbuch* 134 (1998): 29–43.

– *Shakespeare and Women*. Oxford: Oxford UP, 2005.

– *Stages of History: Shakespeare's English Chronicles*. Ithaca, NY: Cornell UP, 1990.

Raleigh, Sir Walter. *The discoverie of the large, rich, and bewtiful Empyre of Guiana*, edited by Neil L. Whitehead. Norman: U of Oklahoma P, 1997.

Ransome, David R. 'Wives for Virginia, 1621.' *William and Mary Quarterly* 48, no. 1 (1991): 3–18.

Rather, L. J. 'The "Six Things Non-Natural."' *Clio Medica* 3 (1968): 337–47.

Read, David. *Temperate Conquests: Spenser and the Spanish New World*. Detroit, MI: Wayne State UP, 2000.

Rich, Barnabe. *A New Description of Ireland*. London, 1610.

Rivlin, Elizabeth J. 'Service, Imitation, and Social Identity in Renaissance Drama and Prose Fiction.' PhD diss., U of Wisconsin-Madison, 2004.

Rossi, Joan Warchol. ' *"Britons moniments"*: Spenser's Definition of Temperance in History.' *English Literary Renaissance* 15 (1985): 42–58.

– '*Cymbeline*'s Debt to Holinshed: The Richness of III.i.' In *Shakespeare's Romances Reconsidered*, edited by Carol McGinnis Kay and Henry E. Jacobs, 104–12. Lincoln: U of Nebraska P, 1978.

Rowe, Katherine. 'Humoral Knowledge and Liberal Cognition in Davenant's *Macbeth*.' In *Reading the Early Modern Passions: Essays in the Cultural History of Emotion*, edited by Gail Kern Paster, Katherine Rowe, and Mary Floyd-Wilson, 169–91. Philadelphia: U of Pennsylvania P, 2004.

Said, Edward W. *Culture and Imperialism*. London: Knopf, 1993.

Sandiford, Keith A. *Cultural Politics of Sugar: Caribbean Slavery and Narratives of Colonialism*. Cambridge: Cambridge UP, 2000.

– 'The Pretexts and Pretenses of Hybridity in Ligon's *True and Exact History*.' *Journal of Commonwealth and Postcolonial Studies* 9, no. 2 (2002): 1–23.

Scanlan, Thomas. *Colonial Writing and the New World: 1583–1671, Allegories of Desire*. Cambridge: Cambridge UP, 1999.

Schiebinger, Londa. *Nature's Body: Gender in the Making of Modern Science.* Boston: Beacon Press, 1993.

Schiesari, Juliana. 'The Face of Domestication: Physiognomy, gender politics, and humanism's others.' In *Women, 'Race,' and Writing in the Early Modern Period,* edited by Margo Hendricks and Patricia Parker, 55–70. London and New York: Routledge, 1994.

Schnucker, R.V. 'The English Puritans and Pregnancy, Delivery and Breast Feeding.' *History of Childhood Quarterly* 2 (1973–4): 637–58.

Schoenfeldt, Michael C. 'Fortifying inwardness: Spenser's castle of moral health,' In *Bodies and Selves in Early Modern England: Physiology and Inwardness in Spenser, Shakespeare, Herbert, and Milton,* 40–73.Cambridge: Cambridge UP, 1999.

Scodel, Joshua. *Excess and the Mean in Early Modern English Literature.* Princeton, NJ: Princeton UP, 2002.

Shakespeare, William. *The Norton Shakespeare,* edited by Stephen Greenblatt et al. New York: Norton, 1997.

– *Macbeth,* edited by A.R. Braunmuller. New Cambridge Shakespeare. Cambridge: Cambridge UP, 1997.

– *The Riverside Shakespeare,* edited by G. Blakemore Evans et al. Boston: Houghton, 1994.

Shapiro, Barbara J. 'History and Natural History in Sixteenth- and Seventeenth-Century England: An Essay on the Relationship between Humanism and Science.' In *English Scientific Virtuosi in the 16th and 17th Centuries: Papers read at a Clark Library Seminar 5 February 1977,* 3–55. Los Angeles: William Andrews Clark Memorial Library at UCLA, 1979.

– *Probability and Certainty in Seventeenth-Century England: A Study of the Relationships between Natural Science, Religion, History, Law, and Literature.* Princeton, NJ: Princeton UP, 1983.

Shuger, Debora K. 'Irishmen, Aristocrats, and Other White Barbarians.' *Renaissance Quarterly* 50, no. 2 (1997): 494–525.

Sidney, Henry, Sir. *A Viceroy's Vindication? Henry Sidney's Memoir of Service in Ireland, 1556–1578,* edited by Ciaran Brady. Cork, Ireland: Cork UP, 2002.

Simms, Katherine. *From Kings to Warlords: The Changing Political Structures of Gaelic Ireland in the Later Middle Ages.* Dover, NH: Boydell Press, 1987.

Siraisi, Nancy. *Medieval and Early Renaissance Medicine: An Introduction to Knowledge and Practice.* Chicago: Chicago UP, 1990.

Skura, Meredith. 'Discourse and the Individual: The Case of Colonisation and *The Tempest.*' *Shakespeare Quarterly* 40 (1989): 42–69.

Sloane, Henry, Sir. *A Voyage to the Islands of Madeira, Barbados, Nieves, St. Christophers, and Jamaica …* London, 1707–25.

Smith, Thomas, Sir. 'Tract by Sir Thomas Smith on the Colonisation of Ards in County of Down.' In *An Historical Account of the MacDonnells of Antrim*, by George Hill, 405–15. Belfast: The Glens of Antrim Historical Society, 1873.

Speed, John. *The History of Great Britaine Under the Conquests of ye Romans, Saxons, Danes, and Normans*. London, 1614.

– *The Theatre of the Empire of Great Britaine*. London, 1611.

Spenser, Edmund. 'Colin Clouts Come Home Again.' In *Yale Edition of the Shorter Poems of Edmund Spenser*, edited by William A. Oram, 530–2. New Haven, CT: Yale UP, 1989.

– *The Faerie Queene*, edited by A.C. Hamilton, text edited by Hiroshi Yamashita and Toshiyuki Suzuki. Edinburgh and London: Longman, 2001.

– *The Ruines of Time*. In *Yale Edition*, edited by William A. Oram, 232–61.

– *The Tears of the Muses*. In *Yale Edition*, edited by William A. Oram, 263–91.

– *A View of the Present State of Ireland*, edited by W.L. Renwick. London: Eric Partridge Ltd at the Scholartis Press, 1934.

– *A View of the Present State of Ireland*, edited by Willy Maley and Andrew Hadfield. Oxford: Oxford UP, 1997.

*Spenser Encyclopedia, The*, edited by A.C. Hamilton, Donald Cheney, and W.F. Blissett. Toronto: U of Toronto P, 1990.

Sprat, Thomas. *The History of the Royal Society*. London, 1667.

Stallybrass, Peter. 'Dismemberments and Re-memberments: Rewriting the *Decameron*, 4.1, in the English Renaissance.' *Studi Sul Boccaccio* 20 (1991–2): 299–324.

– 'Patriarchal Territories: The Body Enclosed.' In *Rewriting the Renaissance: The Discourses of Sexual Difference in Early Modern Europe*, edited by Margaret W. Ferguson, Maureen Quilligan, and Nancy J. Vickers, 123–42. Chicago: U of Chicago P, 1986.

– 'The World Turned Upside Down: Inversion, Gender and the State.' In *The Matter of Difference: Materialist Feminist Criticism of Shakespeare*, edited by Valerie Wayne, 210–20. Ithaca, NY: Cornell UP, 1991.

Stallybrass, Peter, and Allon White. *The Politics and Poetics of Transgression*. Ithaca, NY: Cornell UP, 1986.

Stallybrass, Peter, and Ann Rosalind Jones. *Renaissance Clothing and the Materials of Memory*. Cambridge: Cambridge UP, 2000.

Stanyhurst, Richard. 'Description of Ireland.' *Chronicles of England, Scotlande, and Irelande*. 6 vols. New York: AMS Press, 1976. Vol. 6.

Steele, Richard. *The Spectator*. 13 March 1711.

Steinberg, Clarence. 'Atin, Pyrochles, Cymochles: On Irish Emblems *in The Faerie Queene*.' *Neuphilologische Mitteilungen* 72 (1971): 749–61.

Steiner, Emily. 'Commonalty and Literary Form in the 1370s and 80s.' In *New Medieval Literatures*, edited by David Lawton, Rita Copeland, and Wendy Scase, 199–222. Vol. 6. Oxford: Oxford UP, 2005.

Stoler, Ann Laura. '"In Cold Blood": Hierarchies of Credibility and the Politics of Colonial Narratives.' *Representations* 37 (1992): 151–89.

– *Race and the Education of Desire: Foucault's History of Sexuality and the Colonial Order of Things.* Durham, NC: Duke UP, 1995.

Stone, Lawrence. *The Causes of the English Revolution, 1529–1642.* 2nd ed. London: Ark, 1986.

– *The Crisis of the Aristocracy, 1558–1641.* Oxford: Oxford UP, 1967.

– *The Family, Sex, and Marriage in England 1500–1800.* New York: Harper and Row, 1977.

Strachey, William. *The Historie of Travell into Virginia Britania,* edited by Louis B. Wright and Virginia Freund. The Hakluyt Society. London: MacLehose, 1953.

*Supplication of the Blood of the English,* edited by Willy Maley and Andrew Hadfield. *Analecta Hibernica* 36 (1995): 3–78.

Sutton, John. *Philosophy and Memory Traces: Descartes to Connectionism.* Cambridge: Cambridge UP, 1998.

Swann, Marjorie. '"Procreate Like Trees": Generation and Society in Thomas Browne's *Religio Medici.*' In *Engaging with Nature: Essays on the Natural World in Medieval and Early Modern Europe,* edited Barbara Hanawalt and Lisa Kiser, 137–54. Notre Dame, IL: Notre Dame UP, 2008.

Symonds, William. *A Sermon Preached at White-Chapel in the Presence of many the Aduenturers, and Planters for Virginia.* London, 1609.

Tacitus. *Agricola* and *Germany,* translated by Anthony R. Birley. Oxford: Oxford UP, 1999.

– *Germania,* translated by H. Mattingly and S.A. Handford. Middlesex: Penguin, 1970.

Tawil, Ezra. *The Making of Racial Sentiment: Slavery and the Birth of the Frontier Romance.* Cambridge: Cambridge UP, 2006.

Tennenhouse, Leonard. *Power on Display: The Politics of Shakespeare's Genres.* New York and London: Methuen, 1986.

Trubowitz, Rachel. '"Nourish-Milke": Breast-Feeding and the Crisis of Englishness, 1600–1660.' *JEGP* 99 (2000): 29–49.

– '"But Blood Whitened": Nursing Mothers and Others in Early Modern Britain.' *Maternal Measures: Figuring Caregiving in the Early Modern Period,* edited by Naomi J. Miller and Naomi Yavneh, 82–101. Aldershoot and Burlington: Ashgate, 2000.

Underdown, David *Revel, Riot, and Rebellion: Popular Politics and Culture in England, 1603–1660.* Oxford: Clarendon Press, 1985.

Van Es, Bart. 'Discourses of Conquest: *The Faerie Queene,* the Society of Antiquaries, and *A View of the Present State of Ireland.*' *English Literary Renaissance* 32, no. 1 (2002): 118–51.

Vaughan, Virginia Mason. *Performing Blackness on English Stages, 1500–1800.* Cambridge: Cambridge UP, 2005.

Visconsi, Elliott. 'A Degenerate Race: English Barbarism in Aphra Behn's *Oroonoko* and *The Widow Ranter.*' *ELH* 69 (2002): 673–701.

Vitkus, Daniel. *Turning Turk: English Theater and the Multicultural Mediterranean, 1570–1630.* New York: Palgrave Macmillan, 2003.

Wallis, Lawrence B. *Fletcher, Beaumont and Company: Entertainers to the Jacobean Gentry.* Morningside Heights, NY: King's Crown Press, 1947.

Watson, Robert N. *Back to Nature: The Green and the Real in the Late Renaissance.* Philadelphia: U of Pennsylvania P, 2006.

Wheeler, Roxann. *The Complexion of Race: Categories of Difference in Eighteenth-Century British Culture.* Philadelphia: U of Pennsylvania P, 2000.

Whigham, Frank. *Ambition and Privilege: The Social Tropes of Elizabethan Courtesy Theory.* Berkeley: U of California P, 1984.

Whitaker, Alexander. *Good Newes from Virginia Sent to the Counsell and Company of Virginia.* London, 1613.

White, Hayden. 'The Forms of Wildness: Archaeology of an Idea.' In *Tropics of Discourse: Essays in Cultural Criticism.* 150–82. Baltimore: Johns Hopkins UP, 1978.

Williams, Eric Eustace. *Capitalism & Slavery.* Chapel Hill: U of North Carolina P, 1944.

Williams, Raymond. *Keywords: A Vocabulary of Culture and Society.* New York: Oxford UP, 1983.

– *Marxism and Literature.* Oxford and New York: Oxford UP, 1977.

Williamson, Arthur H. 'Scots, Indians, and Empire: The Scottish Politics of Civilization 1519–1609.' *Past and Present* 150 (1996): 46–83.

Wilson, Richard. 'Voyage to Tunis: New History and the Old World of *The Tempest.*' *ELH* 64 (1997): 333–57.

Winthrop, Jordan. *White Over Black: American Attitudes toward the Negro, 1550–1812.* Chapel Hill: U of North Carolina P, 1968.

Wither, George. 'Hyman X. For a Gentleman.' *Halelviah or, Britans second remembrancer.* London, 1641.

Wood, William. *New Englands Prospect.* London, 1634.

Wortham, Christopher. 'Shakespeare, James I and the Matter of Britain.' *English* 45 (1996): 97–122.

Wright, Thomas. *The Passions of the Mind in General,* edited by William Webster Newbold. 1601. New York and London: Garland Publishing, 1986.

Wrightson, Keith. 'Class.' In *The British Atlantic World, 1500–1800,* edited by David Armitage and Michael J. Braddick, 133–53. Houndmills, UK, and New York: Palgrave Macmillan, 2002.

– *English Society, 1580–1660*. New Brunswick, NJ; Rutgers UP, 1982.
– 'Estates, Degrees, and Sorts: Changing Perceptions of Society in Tudor and Stuart England.' In *Language, History and Class*, edited by Penelope J. Corfield, 32–44. Oxford: Basil Blackwell, 1991).
– 'The social order of early modern England: three approaches.' In *The World We Have Gained: Histories of Population and Social Structure: Essays Presented to Peter Laslett on His Seventieth Birthday*, edited by Lloyd Bonfield, Richard M. Smith, and Keith Wrightson, 177–202. Oxford: Basil Blackwell, 1986.
Yalom, Marilyn. *A History of the Breast*. New York: Ballantine Books, 1997.
Yates, Julian. 'Humanist Habitats: Or, "Eating Well" with Thomas More's *Utopia*.' In *Environment and Embodiment in Early Modern England*, edited by Mary Floyd-Wilson and Garrett A. Sullivan Jr, 187–209. Houndmills, UK, and New York: Palgrave Macmillan, 2007.
Yoch, James J. 'The Renaissance Dramatization of Temperance: The Italian Revival of Tragicomedy and *The Faithful Shepherdess*.' In *Renaissance Tragicomedy: Explorations in Genre and Politics*, edited by Nancy Klein Maguire, 114–37. New York: AMS P, 1987.
Yokota, Kariann. 'To pursue the stream to its fountain': Race, Inequality, and the Post-Colonial Exchange of Knowledge Across the Atlantic.' *Explorations in Early American Culture* 5 (2001): 173–229.
Zuckerman, Michael. 'Identity in British America: Unease in Eden.' *Colonial Identity in the Atlantic World, 1500–1800*, edited by Nicholas Canny and Anthony Pagden, 115–57. Princeton, NJ: Princeton UP, 1987.

# Index

*Page numbers for illustrations and captions are given in italic type.*